THE
PROTECTOR

A NOVEL OF RICHARD III

KATHLEEN M. KELLEY

PAGE PUBLISHING, INC.
New York, NY

First originally published by Page Publishing, Inc. 2017

ISBN 978-1-63568-895-5 (Paperback)
ISBN 978-1-63568-896-2 (Digital)

Printed in the United States of America

CAST OF CHARACTERS

HOUSE OF YORK

Richard, Duke of York* (1411–1460)—married to Cecily Neville (see Neville); father of Edward IV, George, Duke of Clarence, and Richard, Duke of Gloucester; slain in the Battle of Wakefield

Edward IV, King of England (b. 1442, ruled from 1461)—eldest son of Richard, Duke of York, and Cecily Neville; married to Elizabeth Woodville (see Woodville)

George, Duke of Clarence* (1449–1478)—son of Richard, Duke of York, and Cecily Neville; brother to Edward IV; married to Isabelle Neville (see Neville); executed for treason

Richard, Duke of Gloucester (b. 1452)—youngest son of Richard, Duke of York, and Cecily Neville; brother to Edward IV; married to Anne Neville (see Neville); named Protector by Edward IV in his will; becomes Richard III

Elizabeth, Princess of England (b. 1466)—eldest daughter of Edward IV and Elizabeth Woodville, also known as Elizabeth of York

Edward, Prince of Wales (b. 1470)—elder son of Edward IV and Elizabeth Woodville, becomes Edward V

Richard, Prince of England (b. 1473)—younger son of Edward IV and Elizabeth Woodville, also known as Duke of York

Edward of Middleham (b. ca. 1473?)—only son of Richard, Duke of Gloucester, and Anne Neville

THE NEVILLES

Cecily Neville, Dowager Duchess of York (b. 1415)—widow of Richard, Duke of York; mother of Edward IV, George, Duke of Clarence, and Richard, Duke of Gloucester

Richard Neville, Earl of Warwick* (1428–1471)—known as the Kingmaker, nephew of Cecily Neville, father of Isabelle and Anne, slain in the Battle of Barnet

Isabelle Neville, Duchess of Clarence* (1451–1476)—elder daughter of Richard Neville, Earl of Warwick; married to George, Duke of Clarence; died from natural causes

Anne Neville, Duchess of Gloucester (b. 1456)—younger daughter of Richard Neville, Earl of Warwick; wife of Richard, Duke of Gloucester; previously married to Edward of Lancaster, Prince of Wales (see Lancaster); becomes queen on Richard's ascension to the throne

THE WOODVILLES

Elizabeth Woodville, Queen of England (b. ca. 1437)—wife and then widow of Edward IV, formerly married to John Grey of Groby

Thomas Grey, Marquis of Dorset (b. ca. 1453)—elder son of Elizabeth Woodville by her first husband

Richard Grey (b. ca. 1457)—younger son of Elizabeth by her first husband

Anthony Woodville, Earl Rivers (b. ca. 1438)—eldest brother of Elizabeth Woodville, governor of the Prince of Wales

Lionel Woodville (b. 1446)—bishop of Salisbury, brother of Elizabeth

Katherine Woodville, Duchess of Buckingham (b. ca. 1450?)—sister of Elizabeth Woodville; wife of Henry Stafford, Duke of Buckingham (see Stafford)

Richard Woodville (b. 1453)—brother of Elizabeth Woodville

Sir Edward Woodville (b. ca. 1454)—brother of Elizabeth Woodville

THE STAFFORDS

Henry Stafford, Duke of Buckingham (b. 1454)—married to Katherine Woodville

Henry "Harry" Stafford (b. ca. 1471)—son of the Duke of Buckingham and Katherine Woodville

Anne Stafford (b. ca. 1473)—daughter of the Duke of Buckingham and Katherine Woodville

COURT OF KING EDWARD IV

William Hastings (b. ca. 1430)—chief baron, lord chamberlain to Edward IV

John Howard (b. ca. 1425)—baron allied with Hastings, becomes Duke of Norfolk under Richard III

Thomas Stanley (b. 1435)—baron allied with Hastings, married to Margaret Beaufort (see Lancaster), and stepfather of Henry Tudor

Jane Shore (b. ca. 1445)—mistress to Edward IV and becomes mistress to Thomas Grey, Marquis of Dorset, and then to William Lord Hastings

THE BISHOPS

Thomas Bourchier (b. ca. 1404)—archbishop of Canterbury and a cardinal of the church

Thomas Rotherham (b. 1423)—archbishop of York and lord chancellor under Edward IV

Robert Stillington (b. 1420)—bishop of Bath and Wells

John Russell (b. ca. 1425)—bishop of Lincoln, becomes lord chancellor under Richard as protector and as king

John Morton (b. 1420)—bishop of Ely

John Alcock (b. ca. 1430)—bishop of Worcester and tutor to the Prince of Wales

Thomas Kempe (b. ca. 1403)—bishop of London

HOUSE OF LANCASTER

Henry VI, King of England* (1421–1471)—probably slain by Edward IV

Margaret of Anjou, Queen of England* (1430–1482)—wife of Henry VI

Edward of Lancaster, Prince of Wales* (1453–1471)—son of Henry VI and Margaret of Anjou, married to Anne Neville, slain in battle at Tewkesbury

Margaret Beaufort, Lady Stanley (b. 1443)—also known as Countess of Richmond; married to Thomas, Lord Stanley; previously married to Edmund Tutor (deceased) and to Henry Stafford (also deceased), an uncle of the Duke of Buckingham

Henry Tudor (b. 1457)—son of Margaret Beaufort by her first husband, Edmund Tudor, Lancastrian pretender to the throne of England; later became Henry VII

Jasper Tudor (b. 1431)—uncle to Henry Tudor

HOUSEHOLD OF RICHARD, DUKE OF GLOUCESTER

Ralph Assheton (b. ca. 1421)—knight, becomes vice-constable of England under Richard III

Robert Brackenbury (b. ca. 1430?)—knight, becomes constable of the Tower of London under Richard III

Francis Lovell (b. ca. 1454)—knight, becomes Viscount Lovell and lord chamberlain to Richard III

Anna Lovell—wife of Francis Lovell and lady-in-waiting to Anne Neville

Robert Percy (b. ca. 1453?)—knight

Margaret Percy—wife of Robert Percy and lady-in-waiting to Anne Neville

Richard Ratcliffe (b. ca. 1445?)—knight

James Tyrell (b. ca. 1445)—knight

Dame Joan**—nurse and governess of Edward of Middleham

Master Wilde** (b. ca. 1425)—physician

John Kendall (b. ca. 1435?)—secretary
Tom Lynom (b. ca. 1453?)—solicitor

OTHER CHARACTERS (IN ORDER OF APPEARANCE)

John Argentine (b. ca. 1433)—royal physician
William Catesby (b. ca. 1455)—solicitor attendant on Lord Hastings
Sir William Percival** (b. ca. 1443)—knight attendant of Henry Stafford, Duke of Buckingham
Sir Thomas Vaughan (b. ca. 1410)—chamberlain in the household of the Prince of Wales
Robin Vaughan** (b. ca. 1457)—son of a Welsh chieftain, distant cousin of Sir Thomas Vaughan
Thomas Woode (b. ca. 1443?)—goldsmith and alderman of London
Piers Curteys—master of the royal wardrobe
Reginald Bray (b. ca. 1440)—steward to Margaret Beaufort, Lady Stanley
Friar Ralph Shaw (b. ca. 1443?)—noted preacher, brother of the lord mayor of London
Morgan Owen** (b. ca. 1466)—servant in the household of the Duke of Buckingham
John Rush—London merchant, advisor to the Duke of Buckingham
Sir William Knyvet—knight, advisor to the Duke of Buckingham
Thomas Nandick—astrologer, advisor to the Duke of Buckingham
Walter Devereux (b. 1431)—Lord Ferrers of Weobley, baron living in the Welsh Marches
Ralph Bannister—tenant of the Duke of Buckingham at his manor of Wem
Emma Bannister**—wife of Ralph Bannister
Master Ralph Mitton**—sheriff in Shropshire

*Denotes that the character is deceased prior to April 9, 1483.
**Denotes fictional character

Author's Note

This is a work of fiction and should not be construed as a history of the period. Both real and fictional characters are based on the author's imagination and act in ways dictated by that imagination. While some persons, incidents, and events may have a basis in history, they have been used here for dramatic effect.

BOOK I

The Child

April 9 to May 4, 1483

Chapter 1

THE KING WAS dying.

Within the royal bedchamber of Westminster Palace, King Edward IV of England, the Sun in Splendor and the fair White Rose of York, was struggling to take his final breaths. When the great oak doors swung open to admit some black-robed physician, cleric, or solicitor, Hastings caught a brief glimpse of the dimly lit room beyond. However, the form in the large canopied bed was hidden from sight by the army of leeches who swarmed around it, revealing by their frantic activity as much as anything else the extent of their desperation.

For the king was dying, and no one knew how to save him.

William, Lord Hastings—member of the Privy Council, lord chamberlain of England, and boon companion of the king's idle hours—had been roused from his bed in the middle of the night and, after being informed that Edward's death was imminent, had been rushed to the palace. Until that moment, he had not fully realized the gravity of the king's condition. Of course, he had known that Edward was ailing of a cold and a cough; he even had better reason than most to know the cause of the malady.

Two weeks ago, when he had been bored with his ministers and high flown with wine, the king had suggested a cruise down the Thames to his palace at Sheen. It had been early in the season for such a venture; ice had vanished from the river only a week or so before. But that particular evening had been balmy for late March with the promise of spring in its breezes. With scarcely a murmur of dissent, Hastings had bowed to the royal will, placing his black-and-silver pleasure barge at Edward's disposal.

At first, it had been a fine night with drink and song and the merry laughter of Jane Shore, the king's favorite mistress. But then while attempting to execute the intricate maneuvers of a galliard on the narrow deck, Edward had tripped over a loose plank and plunged headlong into the black river. Although he had been quickly fished out by the oarsmen and dragged back onto the barge, he had caught a chill that evening that he had been unable to shake off.

It had seemed such a trifling thing at first and he such a giant of a man. Monumental was the only word that suited him. He was well over six feet tall and almost as broad. He was in the prime of life too, having not yet reached his forty-first birthday. It was almost impossible to imagine how so small a chill could have taken such a hold on the once-magnificent body, but so it had, settling in his lungs, from where it launched the virulent assault that now threatened his very being. Edward had battled many foes in his life, but he was no match for this one. He breathed with a heavy, choking wheeze and coughed up great quantities of phlegm. And now in the next room, he was dying—drowning, the leeches said, in his own fluids.

With the rest of Edward's councilors who had also been roused from their beds, Hastings endured the interminable waiting. Too sad, too stunned, and too weary for speech, they sat along the walls of the antechamber, newly alert each time the massive doors opened, newly disappointed each time they shut behind a scurrying yeoman of the bedchamber, his arms full of soiled linen. Through the broad mullioned windows that looked out over the river, dawn came sputtering in a shower of rain, and still they were not summoned.

Hastings turned at the sound of a light footfall on the marble stairs that led up from the hall below. His heart beat suddenly with unexpected pleasure, for Jane Shore had come to share their waiting. The small white face beneath the flaming whorls of hair showed her distress; the quick eyes darted around the crowded room, searching. With some difficulty, Hastings stood, feeling the stiffness in his joints from the long hours of sitting. He started to go to her, but another man, younger and more agile than he, moved before he did. She caught at his hand in a gesture of unconscious familiarity. Her questioning voice was low. Hastings guessed at her words, at the other's murmured reply. Her eyes, her lovely brown eyes, filled with tears before she buried her face against the man's padded velvet shoulder and began to weep. Hastings permitted himself an audible sigh. It seemed that the Marquis of Dorset would be her comforter today.

Although Jane Shore had been the dying king's companion for several years, Hastings had nonetheless ardently admired her from the distance that propriety and common sense decreed. Now it seemed that she was a prize for the Woodvilles' enjoyment. The queen's eldest son was obviously anxious to bed her after his stepfather's demise.

And why should there be any surprise in that? Hastings asked himself bitterly. What had the queen's greedy kin failed to take for themselves in the way of honors, titles, power, and prizes during all the years of Edward's reign? Now there would not even be the occasional frown of his displeasure to curb them, only a weak and willing boy king who was by blood half a Woodville and by training completely so. The queen had seen to that. With Edward gone, the whole of England would be a field ripe for their harvest.

Hastings tasted bitter bile rising in his throat, and he tore away his gaze away from the couple now seated close together on a cushioned bench. With difficulty, he reminded himself that he too had received a full share of the royal bounty. Captain of Calais, Edward had named him, a rare plum plucked from under the very nose of Anthony Woodville, the queen's eldest brother. There was also the important post of lord chamberlain, which required a high degree of intimacy with the king. And there had been other posts as well, too numerous to count, lofty positions that had vastly enhanced both his wealth and his status.

Yet all that was in the past. Edward, his great and good friend, was dying, and the future was a blank or else so thickly populated with Woodvilles that he did not care to contemplate it.

At last, the great doors opened. This time, they framed no hurrying yeoman or page but the impressive figure of John Argentine, the royal physician. His topaz eyes swept the assembly; his hands, trailing the fox fur that edged his full sleeves, were held up for attention, a rather unnecessary gesture since every eye in the room was already turned on him. Argentine, who had recently come from Ludlow, where he had been attendant on the Prince of Wales, was not a man one could easily ignore in any case.

"The king's grace has asked that you be allowed to come into his presence," he announced in a deep, resonant voice. "I ask you to remember the delicacy of his condition. Please do not tire him unnecessarily. He is very weak. I've argued against so many of you being allowed to see him at one time. I thought perhaps that a single representative would have sufficed." His eyes fell on Dorset as if he considered him a likely candidate for that honor. He stroked the white beard that bristled from his cheek and chin and went on, "My arguments were to no avail. He wants to see you—all of you. He hasn't much time left. Come quickly please."

Dorset was the first to move. He was on his feet and halfway to the door when Hastings recognized the opportunity that was suddenly open to him. Jane Shore remained seated, weeping noiselessly into a handkerchief. Quickly he crossed the emptying room and placed a hand beneath her chin.

"Dry your eyes, lady," he said gently. "Edward won't want to see his merriest mistress with tears on her cheeks."

Jane's reddened eyes looked up at him. Even in disarray, she was incomparably lovely. Her hair hadn't seen a comb that morning, and the cream satin and peacock brocade gown was obviously left over from last night's banqueting. A small gravy stain marred the bodice, but Hastings had eyes only for the firm white flesh that swelled over its low neck.

"I'm afraid that today Edward must lose his merry mistress," she replied.

Hastings nodded solemnly. "So it would seem, but don't think that because he is gone, you will lack for friends."

Her eyes strayed questioningly from Hastings to Dorset, who had stopped at the door and was regarding Hastings with glowering disapproval. "You are most kind, my lord," she murmured, but her gaze was fixed on Dorset.

"Come, come, Hastings," Dorset called. "What's all this? Will you allow my father's life to expire while you amuse yourself with his doxy?"

"Stepfather," Hastings muttered beneath his breath. "Stepfather, not father."

Jane's cheeks flushed hot pink, but Hastings marked the black look in Dorset's eyes for what it was—part of an old rivalry. There was no doubt that the marquis had certain advantages. In addition to being only about half Hastings's age, he was also one of the most handsome men at court. Only an arrogant, mocking expression distorted the perfection of his modeled features.

"The lady seems to need some sympathy, Dorset," Hastings said aloud. "Oh, I know you've not hesitated to give her yours, but as an old friend, I claim the privilege as well."

"You swoop upon her like a vulture before the king's flesh is even cold. I would have thought you had done enough already."

Hastings flinched under this well-aimed reproof. He would never be able to exonerate himself from blame for Edward's illness. If only he had checked his barge after the long winter to make sure it was in good repair. If only he had not bowed so easily to the king's whim. If only . . . Why, he should have taken hammer and nail to that loose plank himself if there were no one else to do it!

Nevertheless, these futile recriminations would not serve to revive Edward, nor was Hastings one to nurse such melancholy. With a half bow to Jane, he joined Dorset and entered the royal bedchamber.

The room was very dark. Heavy curtains of mulberry damask were drawn against the gray morning. Two tapers, tall candles of white beeswax, had been lit, one on either side of the bed. There were also pannikins of burning myrtle and ambergris scattered about, but they gave only a smoky half light and did not begin to mask the sickly sweet stench of decay that permeated the chamber. A number of councilors choked on the odor, and one of the younger Woodvilles had turned away to vomit.

"Hastings . . . Dorset . . ." came a weak but querulous call from the bed. "Where are you?"

"Here, sire," Hastings replied as he hurriedly stationed himself on one side of the royal bed, while Dorset took his place on the other. He was shocked as he looked down at Edward. Beneath the embroidered coverlet lay a bloated, shapeless mound that might once have been a human body but gave little evidence now of its original form. The skin of the face was as waxy white as the tapers and so swollen that the eyes were almost swallowed up in folds of flesh. Yet they were still acute as they took in the heightened color on Hastings's cheeks and on Dorset's.

"Quarrelling again," the king muttered. "By the mass, couldn't you have left off this one day?"

"I tried to tell him that, Your Grace," said Dorset.

Edward lifted a feeble hand for silence. "Spare me, please . . ." He stopped, gasping for breath. "I don't want to hear . . . who started it . . . what it was about. It's an old story by now and not a very pretty one. They've been going on far too long—these battles of yours. No wonder I've come to such an early end—" He fell into a fit of coughing.

Argentine came to the bedside, tilted back the king's head, and trickled a potion down his throat. The deep, hooded eyes closed, and for a time, it seemed that he slept. But when they fluttered open again, he seemed a little stronger, his breathing more regular.

"Maybe I could bear your bickering," Edward went on, "because I know that both of you love me. But my son . . . he cannot. He is so young, my Ned, so very young, his mettle untested. I fear for him if you persist in these rivalries. And I fear for England . . ." He stopped, shaken once more by coughing. Argentine was there with a towel to wipe away the spume.

"He's a good lad, sire, bright and quick," the physician offered. "I came to know him well at Ludlow."

"Bright, quick," Edward repeated. "These are worthy virtues, but my boy is only twelve. Can he overcome a court that is so divided? Come, gentlemen, my lords all, will you not be friends?"

Hastings was touched by the simple appeal of Edward's words and not a little ashamed of his own past conduct. "Your Grace needn't worry any longer about that," he said slowly. "I am most sorry for my part in these rivalries and would offer my lord of Dorset the hand of friendship, if he will but take it."

The marquis looked at him from across the bed, the light of the tapers flickering uncertainly in his narrowed hazel eyes. Plainly he had misgivings about this new turn of events, but he could hardly afford to be less magnanimous than Hastings. There was after all the governance of Edward's heir to be considered.

"Well, Dorset?" The king's voice still held the prerogative of royal command. Hastings was very much aware that his hand, stretched forward in conciliation, remained empty.

At last, the marquis took it. "I too, milord . . . repent any wrongs I or those close to me by blood or marriage may have done you. We shall no doubt have threats enough from Lancaster without quarreling among ourselves."

Edward smiled and sank back against his pillows. "Now I can die in peace, and I thank God for it. We have nothing to fear from Lancaster or the Tudor if you will stand by one another."

Hastings was aware that behind him, his friend and ally Thomas, Lord Stanley, was shifting his weight from one foot to the other and back again. He had reason to be uneasy. Not only had he once sworn allegiance to Lancaster, but he was also closely connected to Henry Tudor by his marriage to Lady Margaret Beaufort, the young pretender's mother. Hastings knew that he was very sensitive to the ambiguity of his position.

"Your Grace?"

The heavy eyelids fluttered open. "Yes, Dorset?"

"Shouldn't you name someone to be . . . ah . . . a governor to your son, to attend him and guide him in his minority?"

Along the other side of the bed, the Woodvilles and their supporters pressed closer to hear the answer. Undoubtedly, they believed that Anthony Woodville, the Earl Rivers, eldest of the queen's brothers and currently governor to the Prince of Wales, would be named to the position that would make him, during the boy's minority, the most powerful noble in the land.

"Yes, Dorset, my lords all" came the rasp. "Indeed, that is the main reason I have called you all together. There is only one man I would trust with the governance of my son and my kingdom, one man who will be . . . protector of the king and the realm. My entirely right well-beloved brother . . . Richard, Duke of Gloucester."

Dorset's face paled with shock and disbelief. A chorus of muttered protests erupted from the Woodville side of the bed.

Edward, fully alert now, tried to raise himself up on his elbows. "I would have you give him the honor which is his due," he said sharply.

"B-but Anthony . . ." one of the Woodvilles objected. It was Lionel, bishop of Salisbury and another of the queen's brothers.

"Anthony . . . will be a trusted advisor to my son as he has been to me," Edward whispered, sinking down again onto the pillows, his brief show of strength spent. "But he . . . and all of you . . . must bend a knee to Gloucester. Come now, how could I have chosen one of you? Too much strife . . . always too much . . ."

Hastings made no effort to conceal his relief. Richard of Gloucester was a trusted ally, as fair and just as any man who walked the earth. "A wise and proper choice, sire," he said as he knelt to kiss Edward's bloated hand. "He shall, of course, command my complete loyalty."

"And you, Dorset, Lionel? What about you?"

Once again, they were trapped. They must have known that Edward held his younger brother in high esteem, but Richard lived in the north, far from the capital, and he visited it but seldom. They had not considered him a force to be reckoned with.

"Well, my lords?"

Lionel of Salisbury, at a rare but temporary loss for words, seemed bent to argue the point. "It only seemed that Anthony . . . ah . . . the Earl Rivers has been the prince's constant companion from the cradle. It seems more fitting that he—"

"Do you intend to beat down a dying man, Lionel? Or for all that you're my brother-in-law and a prince of the church to boot, I shall—"

"No, no, Your Grace misunderstands—"

"Sire," Dorset interrupted, "we shall, of course, swear allegiance to Gloucester, each one of us. My uncle Salisbury only expresses the surprise we all feel at your choice. The duke has scarcely been prominent at court of late."

"All's the better!" said Edward. "He's been serving me . . . in the north, a real tyrant against the Scots, a very whelp of the devil, my little brother. If only he were here now . . ." Edward's voice trailed off as though it were coming to them from further and further away.

Master Hobbes, another of the royal physicians, produced an iron-tipped lancet. "He needs to be bled."

Argentine nodded agreement. He shooed them away with his hands. "That's quite enough, all of you. You've overtired him just as I feared. Now leave him in peace."

"Is . . . is the Mistress Shore outside?" Edward's lips barely moved.

Hastings and Dorset exchanged a quick glance and even more quickly looked away. "She awaits Your Grace's pleasure," Dorset said.

"Send her in then," said Edward, "and afterwards . . . you had best find my priest. I have a good deal to confess before I go to God."

Hastings blinked hard. Tears blinded him as he stumbled from the room. While Dorset led in Jane Shore, he went for the priest. By the time the sun reached its zenith on that ninth day of April, anno Domini 1483, Edward the king was dead, and a new Edward was king.

Chapter 2

IT WAS RAINING. Beyond the leaded casements of the Painted Chamber, Hastings could see the mists still clinging to the chimney tops of the bishops' mansions along the Strand. A low layer of fog shrouded the Thames and blurred the ramparts of Lambeth Palace on the far bank. It was a thoroughly miserable day; nonetheless, it was an appropriately somber one for the event that marked it: the first meeting of the Privy Council since the king's death.

In his passing, Edward had achieved a reconciliation between the opposing factions of his court that had eluded him in life. Numbed or at least subdued by grief, Hastings's party and the Woodvilles had knelt side by side in Westminster Abbey, had partaken of the body and blood of Christ, heard requiems sung for the dead king's soul, told their beads and lighted candles to speed him from purgatory to paradise. But beneath the façade of harmony, old enmities still smoldered that could flare at a glance. Two nights before and quite by accident, Hastings and Dorset had arrived in the abbey at the same time to do homage at the dead king's bier. Despite signals of outward civility, their reverential keeping of the watch had quickly devolved into a wordless but excruciating contest to see which of the two rivals could stay on his knees for the longer time. With a groan and a grimace, Hastings had at last been forced to concede victory to the younger man.

But it was here in the council chamber that Edward's tenuous truce would face its greatest challenge. Hastings was suddenly aware of how much he missed the king's booming presence in the Painted Chamber, of how empty the gilded throne seemed beneath its mulberry canopy. The unaccustomed void at the center of the room made manifest the truth his heart had not yet fully grasped: Edward was gone and was never coming back.

He sighed audibly and shifted in his chair. The black wool serge mourning garments he wore to honor that same Edward were wet from the ride to Westminster and stuck to his skin in uncomfortable, itching bunches. A stubborn fire, coaxed reluctantly from green yew logs on the hearth, did little to dry them or to drive the damp chill from the room. It gave off only a smoky resin that smarted in his eyes and made him cough.

"You would think that they might have found some dry logs for this occasion," he grumbled to John Howard, who sat next to him at the long table.

"It seems that even in the royal Palace of Westminster, properly cured wood is in short supply at this time of the year," Howard replied then added with a knowing smile, "One more discomfort among many."

Recently arrived in London from his estates in East Anglia, John, Lord Howard, had the plain, homely countenance of a country squire and the equally plain and sturdy loyalty that Hastings valued highly in his subordinates. Here was a man he could trust, whatever happened, one whose humble origins guaranteed that he would never seek to rise too high. He was less certain about Tom Stanley, who sat on his other side. Stanley's face was too dour, his expression too secretive behind the forked auburn beard. Hastings imagined he could see the figure of Henry Tudor, Stanley's banished stepson, lingering in the shadows behind him and waiting for an opportunity—any opportunity—to seize the crown for Lancaster. A boy king and a divided court could provide the opening wedge he needed.

The sound of a large party approaching from the broad marble-floored corridor that led to the royal apartments reminded him that there were more pressing matters requiring his attention. The Woodvilles were coming, punctual to the hour and in force. That was to be expected. What he had not expected was the one who marched at their head. Could it be that the queen, bold as he knew her to be, would commit this unthinkable violence to all tradition and take a seat on the council? Surprise quickly turned to astonishment. Clearly, she meant not only to take a seat but also to take Edward's seat, the gilded throne at the table's head. Only if she had been named regent for her son would this outrage have been permissible, and she had surely not been named regent!

She stood before them, regal and erect despite her base blood, slender as a willow wand despite her advancing years and the ten children born of her body. By wordless authority, she commanded the obeisance due a reigning sovereign. Reluctantly, his body heavy as lead, Hastings pushed back his chair and stood, bowing his head ever so slightly in her direction. Beside him, Howard and Stanley struggled to their feet as well. She acknowledged them with a barely perceptible tilt of her head.

Elizabeth Woodville was a formidable person, a woman of quicksilver and ice. Even now, Hastings had to admit her beauty. Framed by the white barb and wimple of recent widowhood, her face, with its striking violet eyes, tapered in a smooth oval from high cheekbones to a small, determined chin. Her forehead, with hairline and eyebrows fashionably plucked for height, was remarkably unlined beneath her gold coronet. The jeweled hands folded before her were long fingered and smooth as alabaster.

On a September morning twenty years before, she had appeared much the same when, then as now newly widowed, she had waylaid the fledgling King Edward as he went out to hunt. She had stepped out rather suddenly from the dense shade of an oak in Whittlebury Forest, clutching two small boys by their hands. Hastings recalled that meeting now with a sense of destiny that the intervening years had given it.

She had come to throw herself on the king's mercy, she had explained in a low whisper of a voice, to plead for her two young sons, who were now penniless orphans. Her husband, Sir John Grey of Groby, had been slain at the second battle of St. Albans, fighting on the Lancastrian side, and all his goods and estates had been forfeited to the crown. Would not His Grace, King Edward, to whom God had given so much, take pity on her plight?

Edward had obviously been entranced. With difficulty, he tore his eyes away from the mother to look upon the children—solemn, awed, innocent as choir boys. "It hardly seems fitting that the sins of the fathers should be visited on the children," he had agreed.

Elizabeth's plot had succeeded beyond her wildest hopes. Edward had been unable to rid himself of the memory of her, of that first start of surprise as she stepped out from the oak's shadow, of the morning sun striking blindingly from pale gilt hair, of the limpid pools of pleading eyes, of the imagined sensuousness of the body beneath the black mourning robes. He had returned often to hunt at her parents' manor of Grafton Regis. At first, Hastings had accompanied him on these ventures, but later he did not. The king had set his sights on other game than deer.

In that pursuit, he was constantly frustrated.

"So the quarry has once more eluded the net?" Hastings had asked when Edward returned to Westminster after one such journey.

"A pox on all virtuous women!" Edward had cried, red-faced. "God's teeth, Will, but she will have none of me. Have you ever heard the like?" He was a young man then and sure of his amorous prowess. He stretched his long legs before him while his squires struggled to remove his tawny deerskin riding boots. "Do you know what she says to me? Shall I tell you? She says that she knows she is not nearly good enough to be my queen, but that she is far too good to be my mistress. Can you believe such virtue?"

Virtue? Privately, Hastings had another less charitable name for it, but wisely he held his tongue. In a few months, the chaste Elizabeth had come to Westminster Palace and to Edward's bed as England's queen. At the same time, she had ignited a firestorm of protest that rocked the kingdom and sent the mighty Earl of Warwick scuttling to his war chest in rebellion. Not only was the new queen a commoner and of Lancastrian sympathies but she also came from a very large family, all of whose members had to be accommodated in some way.

So far had she come that today Elizabeth Woodville Grey, Queen of England, by the grace of God and her own virtue, dared to take the high seat. Lackeys scurried to hold it for her while she settled her slender body on its cushions.

As for the two boys who had stood beside her on that fateful morning, they were now grown men and stood by her still, one on either hand: Thomas Grey, Marquis of Dorset, and Lord Richard Grey. The elder brother, Hastings knew only too well, but the younger was more of a mystery to him. Lord Richard Grey had only lately returned from Ludlow Castle on the Welsh Marches, where he had been in attendance on his half brother the Prince of Wales, now King Edward V.

Anthony Woodville, the Earl Rivers, had remained behind with his charge until the council ordered him brought to London. Strangely, since he bore Rivers no love, Hastings regretted his absence from the council. They had been major combatants on the lists of court too long and too often in Edward's time, and he still carried the scars of those encounters white on his memory. Nevertheless, he was forced to admit that Anthony Woodville was probably the only man in England who might exercise any degree of restraint on his family's headlong rush to power.

Certainly the queen's remaining brothers would not. He flicked an uneasy look at Richard, handsome and arrogant, secretary to Edward and known to have his ear on many matters, and at Lionel, suave and elegant in the purple mantle of Salisbury's bishop. He was learned too, men said, though without a shred of self-control to temper ambition.

Edward, the queen's youngest brother, also took a seat at the table. He was a noted wastrel, and all of his sister's considerable influence had been able to procure for him only a knighthood and the honorary post of a royal admiral. Yet today he wore a look strange for him—complacency perhaps or even self-importance. His beard was freshly shaven, his sandy hair neatly trimmed, his black doublet clean and carefully pressed. But just as Hastings was contemplating what wonder could have wrought these changes, his thoughts were interrupted by a new group of arrivals.

The bishops, late for the meeting, had probably come from their own council elsewhere. Certainly they would have much to discuss and not all of it for unconsecrated ears. They were a curious lot and far less uniform in their attitudes and alliances than their nearly identical attire would suggest. Hastings wondered, if it came to a fight, which of the five men now entering the room could be expected to side with his party and which with the Woodvilles?

First among them was Thomas Cardinal Bourchier, archbishop of Canterbury, wearing the scarlet of his rank. He was of mature years, an able and a just man, if somewhat inscrutable. He was deliberately neutral on secular affairs, and Hastings did not think he could be counted on by either party though he might well cast the deciding vote.

Thomas Rotherham, archbishop of York and lord chancellor, was another matter, for he had been favored by the queen and was notably loyal to her. He had visibly aged of late and seemed to be slipping into an early dotage, but he was still formidable because of his high office.

Robert Stillington, bishop of Bath and Wells, was certainly not a member of the queen's party. As timid now as one of the mice in his episcopal palace, he had once known greater influence than he currently enjoyed and had in fact risen to the post of lord chancellor before being hounded from office by the queen herself. Five years later, the reasons behind her enmity were still not clear.

John Russell, bishop of Lincoln, came next. He was a learned scholar with a keen, insightful mind and an iron-clad sense of right and wrong. Hastings counted on him to be in his camp although he knew that the good bishop could flash independence when he felt it warranted.

Lastly, there came the prelate, who generated the most speculation in Hastings. John Morton, bishop of Ely, was a man of deprecating charm and wily cleverness. Originally aligned with Lancaster, he had somehow managed to survive every political reversal unscathed, his head still attached to his shoulders and his reputation unimpeached. As master of the rolls, he had served Henry VI, the last Lancastrian king, with distinction and, to no one's particular surprise, had continued that office under Edward of York. Hastings had heard rumors that the Woodvilles were courting him assiduously.

Elizabeth Woodville waited for the bishops to settle themselves then gestured to Rotherham to begin. As soon as he had given a few short raps of his gavel and called them to order in a wavering treble, the queen took the floor. Hastings was no longer surprised at her daring.

"My lords and bishops all," she began in the same low voice that had once captivated a king, "we have come together at a time of great sorrow for us all. Some of us who dearly loved England's king have suffered a deep personal loss."

Howard nudged Hastings and leaned over to whisper in his ear. "Have you noticed how her eyes are red from weeping?" In fact, they were not. The whites of Elizabeth's eyes were as clear as milk.

"Do witches weep?" Hastings whispered in reply. There was gossip that Dame Woodville Grey had used sorcery as well as chastity to inflame Edward's lust.

The object of their scrutiny went on. "There are those of you who looked with surprise and, dare I say it, even astonishment to see our presence here today. To that, we can only reply that we stand in the place of our husband, who is no more, and of our son, who is not yet among us. Yes, my lords, I—a woman, poor and unworthy—stand here in the stead of our uncrowned king."

How smoothly she slid into the imperial plural, Hastings noted, and how easily she slid out of it when she wished to make her point. If she had been a man, she might have made a venerable leader, a worthy foe.

"You will no doubt agree that this is hardly an ideal situation," the smooth voice continued. "You will no doubt agree that this leaves us extremely vulnerable. You will no doubt agree that in all wisdom, we must bring Edward, our new sovereign lord, up to London with all possible haste and that we must prepare immediately for his coronation."

"No!" Hastings cried out. He knew as well as she what an early coronation could mean: the end of the protectorate, the ceasing of Richard of Gloucester's authority before it began. Once he was crowned, the king might claim the power to choose his own advisers. Could any man doubt who those advisers would be?

Beneath her glowering gaze, Hastings cleared his throat, attempting to regain composure. "We haven't even buried the fourth Edward yet," he said. "Must we be in such a rush to crown the fifth?"

Again, Howard's teasing murmur came in his ear. "It's a matter of economy. We'll be able to celebrate the funeral feast and the coronation banquet together."

"If you have anything to say, my Lord Howard, please speak up so that we may all partake of your wisdom."

Howard's eyes fell as his face reddened, like some mischievous schoolboy caught passing notes in class. "I have nothing to add, except that I agree right well with my Lord Hastings. This indecent haste—"

"Indecent haste?" the queen echoed incredulously. "You would counsel us to . . . to wait?" Her voice dropped, became silky, almost cajoling. "You have, I believe, some experience in battle, do you not? I am only a woman and unschooled in such matters, so tell me what would you do, my lord, if in the heat of battle you saw that the captain of your enemies had suddenly fallen? Wouldn't you find new heart, new strength to see him lying dead on the ground? Wouldn't you go among his forces, flailing at them with your sword, putting them to rout?

"I ask all of you, my lords, how do you think Louis of France— that ever-scheming, ever-patient spider—looks across the channel today? What thoughts pass through Henry Tudor's mind as he dreams his treasonous dreams?" She flicked a quick, deft look at Stanley. "And you, my Lord Stanley, what say you? Do we or do we not hasten to crown our king?"

"Yes, madam, we'll crown him. We'll crown him when Richard of Gloucester arrives in London and not a moment before."

Hastings could have applauded. He felt a surge of new respect for his old friend who had both extricated himself from the queen's trap and also brought up the name no one else had dared.

"Gloucester?" The queen sniffed as if a midden had opened at her feet. "What has he to do with this?"

"He has everything to do with it, Your Grace," said Hastings. "You were not present at your late lord's deathbed when he called his last council together, but I cannot believe that you are ignorant of his will. Gloucester is just the man we need in these troubled times— against the French, against Lancaster. With all due respect to our young sovereign, it must be admitted that a coronation in itself will not add one jot to his stature nor more than a few hours to his years. We need a man of proven valor, one who will truly give pause to our enemies. We need Richard of Gloucester."

There was a moment's quiet in the council chamber during which the only sound was the crackling of the logs on the hearth.

"Nor should we plan for a coronation or a government until we have Gloucester's advice on these matters," Russell added.

Dorset spoke up for the first time. "But as you see, my lords, the . . . uh . . . protector is not here, and the issues facing us are critical ones that will not await his arrival. We cannot afford to dawdle about while Gloucester makes his way from the north. We must act now on these things."

"He has, of course, been informed of his brother's death and of his own appointment?" Hastings asked blandly.

Dorset gave him a quickly concealed little smirk. "Why, of course. But then, as you are aware, the roads from London to the north are in bad repair and never more so than at this time of the year. I grant it's most unfortunate, but one must be realistic. It may take some time for our messenger to reach Middleham."

"I don't doubt that anyway," Howard muttered, this time aloud.

"What's that, my lord?" asked Dorset. "Surely we're not going to slip back so quickly into our old habits."

He was answered with silence. Silence was at the moment the only bond that united Hastings's party and the Woodvilles. It was an uneasy truce since it rested entirely on the fact that Hastings wished to avoid all discussion of a coronation while the Woodvilles were equally anxious to ignore Gloucester. Someday, and soon, both topics would have to be dealt with fully and openly, but not today.

"I thought we were to discuss the French," Rotherham prompted, looking to the queen as a child looks for approval to an adult.

"You are right, good father," she replied, favoring him with a smile. "You do well to remind us."

The French were an indisputable problem and one on which all true Englishmen of whatever political persuasion could agree. On learning of the death of his archenemy, King Louis had wasted no time in making the Narrow Sea perilous to English shipping.

"What a thorny knot of troubles we have here, my lords." Elizabeth gave an exasperated little sigh. "Cordes, the one they call lord but who is in reality little more than a pirate, has already seized three of our ships. The merchants of the staple are howling that they will soon be cut off—both from Calais and from their markets in Bruges. A most devastating prospect, Hastings, would you not agree?"

Hastings did agree, and fervently. The captaincy of Calais was one of the brightest gems in his own crown of wealth and influence. Calais was the shrunken remnant of a once-mighty empire, the last bit of England on French soil. But more importantly for Hastings, Calais was also the seat of the wool staple. By law, all wool, the chief export of England, must pass through its harbor to be taxed. It went without saying that a generous portion of that tax found its way into the captain's purse.

Dorset regarded him from under straight black brows. "Then you would also agree that swift action must be taken to avert such a catastrophe?"

Hastings eyes narrowed. He knew that he was being baited like a bear in the pits. "I see a need to act, yes," he replied hesitantly.

"Ah, but first we must have a plan, a scheme to dash that shifty varlet Cordes and deal with his master, Louis, as well. Fortunately, my esteemed uncle Sir Edward has only this morning hit upon such a scheme."

Sir Edward! Although the queen's youngest brother was a champion of many jousts, Hastings doubted he had ever been called upon to develop any strategies for a real war. No wonder he suddenly looked so pompous. Nor was his plan, if indeed it was his plan, in any way remarkable: the outfitting and equipping of a navy and, since the crown boasted few suitable ships, the seizure of certain merchant vessels, both foreign and domestic, from London harbor. Their crews would be impressed to fight the French.

"Where will the funds come from to finance this undertaking?" Hastings asked. The raising of revenue by taxation was a slow and arduous business and necessitated the gathering of Parliament.

"Why, Hastings"—Morton blinked in surprise—"didn't you know? King Edward has left us a veritable fortune in the Tower vaults." He did not add, indeed he did not need to add, that a sizable part of that fortune had been raised by his own cunning.

"Do we have a right to touch that?"

"Who has a better right?" Morton retorted. "Certainly our late beloved king would have no quarrel with its appropriation or its use. And this will hardly touch it. The clerks of the Exchequer have been busy tallying it for days. A substantial sum."

Hastings could argue no more, lost to Morton's irrefutable logic.

Dorset said, "Now that we are apparently all in agreement on that point, I would suggest that the one who developed this plan should be responsible for its execution. I propose that we make Sir Edward Woodville captain of the fleet."

"But why Sir Edward?" Hastings protested. "With all due respect, Dorset, he has but little naval experience. Indeed, there is only one present today who can boast some knowledge of ships and their uses."

"You are speaking of Lord Howard?"

"Of course. Who else?"

"And with all due respect to Lord Howard, my dear Hastings, my uncle Woodville was made an admiral of the fleet by the late king early in his reign. Or have you conveniently forgotten that?"

"An honorary title, Dorset, as I'm sure you are aware." Privately, he considered that if Sir Edward had ever captained any craft more seaworthy than a river scow, he himself would swim from Dover to Calais.

"All right then, but you must admit that a few naval skirmishes against the Scots hardly make Howard lord high admiral." This reference was a mistake, and Dorset must have realized it as soon as the words had left his lips. Richard of Gloucester was lord high admiral.

He hastened to correct himself. "Not that . . . er . . . even he . . . in these days has had much occasion to battle on the sea. I submit, Hastings, that none of us is truly suited to the task. That being the case, it would appear that Sir Edward is no less equipped for it than anyone else. It's his plan. Let him implement it."

"A poor enough showing we made today," Hastings said to Howard as they left the Painted Chamber.

"The Woodvilles do seem to sweep all before them," said Howard.

"And the gall, the absolute absurdity of appointing Edward Woodville to head a navy when you yourself, Howard, are eminently more qualified!"

Howard shook his head slowly, smiling a little. "You are only kicking against the pricks, my friend. Don't you see? It isn't a matter of who is qualified and who is not. It's a matter of who is a Woodville and who is not. I warrant the queen and her pretty son have reasons for wanting one of their own in charge of the fleet. We can only pray for the early arrival of Richard of Gloucester."

"Yes, we can pray, but our prayers will go unanswered if Dorset has his way. A long way to Middleham, indeed! And longer still if no courier has yet set foot upon the road."

"Come," Howard said, "we ought not to speak of it here. The very walls of the palace may have ears. Why don't you stop by the Greyhound with me, where we can discuss it more privately over a pint?"

Hastings shook his head. "No, John. I have other matters to attend to. If Dorset and the queen have neglected their duty to Richard of Gloucester, I mean to amend it—and quickly."

Chapter 3

THREE DAYS LATER, under a fitful afternoon sun, William Catesby clattered across the drawbridge of Middleham Castle and crashed to a sudden halt amid a flock of ducks, chickens, and geese. The ancient servant who tended them clucked disapproval as outraged fowl and feathers scattered about the courtyard together. He still held a handful of corn from a sack draped across his shoulders.

"Have a care, mon, have a care," he cautioned, "or ye'll be tramplin' the laird's supper next!"

Catesby dismounted and gave the man what he hoped was a disarming smile. "My apologies for that, good father, but I've come in haste from London and must see His Grace of Gloucester at once."

"Fra' London, is it?" the servant asked, staring at him with a rheumy eye. "Well, be it so, it excuses naught."

Catesby shook his head in exasperation. He had indeed ridden from London, two hundred miles to the south, and ridden hard, stopping only to grab a meal and a few hours' sleep in a wayside inn or to change horses as he winded them. Despite the poor roads and occasional showers, he had made excellent time and was justly proud of himself, all the more so because he was no mere courier but a solicitor schooled under Hastings's patronage at the Inns of Court and highly placed in his lord's household. He had been chosen for this mission because of its extreme urgency and secrecy, and he was proud of that too.

He drew himself up to his full, rather modest height. "I will offer my regrets directly to the duke. I pray thee, sirrah, I'm Lord Hastings's man and my business is pressing. Please take me to your lord at once."

The gaffer's withered face split into a smile that revealed pink toothless gums. "Fra' Laird Hastings, is it now?" he asked, bending closer to inspect Catesby's once-rich livery. The sable and argent of Hastings's arms were torn, spattered with mud and barely discernable on his sleeve. The weak eyes squinted in vain.

Finally, he shook his head. "An' ye be t'angel Gabriel coom down from heav'n, I canna take ye to him. They be out there." He waved his hand at the castle gate and the greening valley of Wensleydale beyond. "Gan' a'hawkin' they be, me laird and lady and the bairn as well. Yet," he added, seeing Catesby's crestfallen look, "it nay be so bad as all that. Only yestereve the laird came back from the border, so ye ha' some luck about ye after all."

That seemed to be small consolation at the moment. Catesby slumped against the horse's flank, feeling suddenly drained and tired, but the animal's side, wet and heaving against his back, reminded him that the mare was worse off than he. And he had promised the innkeeper at York that he would return her in good shape.

"Can you find oats for my mount and a groom to rub her down?"

"Aye." The servant nodded. "It can be done. Here, Jamie lad, to stable wi' this nag."

For the first time, Catesby noticed a ring of faces, servants' faces, watching him curiously from the perimeter of the outer bailey. Also for the first time, he had a chance to examine the castle itself. It was of Norman vintage, a grim and mighty fortress left behind from ancient days, a retreat in times of siege, formidable behind its ditches and moat, its curtain wall and high-toothed battlements, its inner and outer bailey wards. Catesby had no doubt that such defenses were still quite useful so near the troubled Scottish border.

Yet some attempts had been made recently to modernize it. Remodeling had enlarged most of the window slits into tall lancets, and there was even an oriel protruding anomalously from what

Catesby assumed to be the great hall. The tall square keep remained much the same as the Norman masons had left it, but there was a new round dovecote and a falcon mew, whitewashed and gleaming in the sun, next to the stables. And the stables themselves—along with the cookhouse, buttery, and brewery—appeared to have been either newly built or recently enlarged.

Nowhere was there any sign of mourning: no black wreath over the gate, no black bunting draped from the windows, no black armbands on the servants. The only banners in the yard displayed the white boar cognizance of the Duke of Gloucester. It was then as Hastings had feared. It would be up to Catesby to break the painful news and to inform Richard Plantagenet both of his beloved brother's death and of his own new role in the governance of the realm.

"You've had no other messenger from London in the past few days?" he asked against hope.

The old man scratched his head. "N-nay," he said slowly, "nor for a fortnight afore that. Should we ha' had then?"

"No," Catesby replied, "I suppose not," but his voice was swallowed by a trumpet call from beyond the ramparts.

"Be like that be they now, me laird and lady," the gaffer told him, tugging at his sleeve with a corded hand.

From the gateward came an answering call, and Catesby turned to see the Duke and Duchess of Gloucester as they rode over the drawbridge, their young son, a boy of about nine, between them and their knights and henchmen, an array of buff and black, behind. His heart was beating in his throat as they neared him, faces flushed from wind and exercise, eyes narrowing in puzzlement at the sight of the stranger.

It was the child who asked the question, whining a little as if he resented the intrusion. "Who's that man, Father? What's he doing here?"

A weak-looking child, Catesby thought. He was swathed in furs against the mild chill of April. A stiff wind might blow him away. Yet he had to allow him a certain pride in the way he sat his pony and held the small sparrow-hawk in imitation of his father's great peregrine.

The duke replied, "I don't know, Ned, who he is or what his business is with us, but we ought to make him welcome."

Welcome indeed, Catesby thought. *The plague would be more welcome.* But he noted and was grateful for the kindness in Gloucester's eyes. It was not a face in which one would ordinarily have looked for kindness. Beneath hair that was an indeterminate shade of brown, the features were sharp and angular with a prominent nose, long jaw, and high cheekbones. The mouth was a thin drawn line. The eyes, though, softened it. They were a deep blue flecked with gold, the color of the sky on a summer's evening just after the sun had set.

Catesby watched as Gloucester handed his hooded hawk to the falconer and alighted easily from the white stallion. He went then to his duchess and, placing a hand on either side of her slender waist, gently lifted her from her gray mare with no more trouble than he might have lifted a child. In fact, she might have been a child, this Anne Neville, Duchess of Gloucester. Her body was petite and thin in her green velvet riding habit. Her eyes, two dark pools too large for her small heart-shaped face, regarded Catesby with deep mistrust.

Gloucester, though, did not know, did not even guess. His squint of puzzlement changed to recognition, even to pleasure, as he approached his uninvited guest.

"Will Catesby, isn't it?" His smile transformed his face and revealed even white teeth. "For the sake of your lord, sir, you are most welcome to Middleham."

Off his mount, Gloucester too was small, no taller than Catesby himself, and his right shoulder was somewhat higher than his left, a defect that he took pains to disguise with both his dress and his bearing. Somehow he had always loomed larger in London, or was it just that at this moment he seemed so peculiarly vulnerable?

Catesby managed an awkward bow. "Y-your Grace."

"Well, what brings you so far from home?" Richard asked. "And in such obvious haste as well?"

Catesby made a belated effort to brush some of the dried mud from his livery. Richard was amused, nothing more. Still he had no inkling.

"M-my lord, I-I don't know how to t-tell you this," he stammered. "I-I wish I didn't have to tell you."

"Come, come, man! Out with it! Have the French invaded? Has Henry Tudor turned up in Wales? Does King Edward have need of my immediate services? Surely it can't be as bad as all that."

"It is, I'm afraid, and worse. It . . . it's the king. I regret to s-say he is dead."

Richard reeled as if he had been struck. Behind him, there was a woman's strangled gasp. "Edward . . . dead?"

"Yes, Your Gace."

"But there must be some mistake. When I last saw him, barely three months ago, he seemed as hale as you or I. What accident? What illness? Speak, sir, and be quick about it!"

"It-it was only a catarrh at first, caught from a spill he took while boating. But it passed into his lungs, and I am no leech, but they tell me that gout and dropsy made it much worse. He-he was not the man he once was, King Edward."

Richard's eyes flashed with sudden ire. "He was a good man and a great king except that some men—and your lord not least among them—indulged his appetites and weakened his body with intemperate living. Speak no ill of him to me!"

"Please, forgive me. I meant no disrespect."

"No," said Richard, his brief flare of anger spent. "No, of course, you didn't. And it's I who should ask your pardon for barking at you like that as well as your lord's, who is very dear to me. Didn't I see with my own eyes how the king deteriorated in body each time I went up to London? At the Christmas revels last year, it took three strong men to lift him from the table after he had gorged himself. Perhaps he was his own ruin. Still, I remember him as he once was, a young bull to my child's eye and as powerful as any knight who ever rode into battle. In my mind, he will always be so. But stay! I wander. and your business is pressing. When did he die?"

"Last Wednesday, my lord."

"Last Wednesday! But this is Tuesday. Almost a week. Are the roads from London so poor that no one could bring me word before this?"

Catesby shrugged. "Poor enough, but passable if one has the will. This may explain it." And he gave Richard the letter drafted by Lord Hastings.

Richard's hand trembled as he broke the seal and untied the intricately wound string. The parchment shook a little as he read.

"There will be an answer?" Catesby asked when he was done.

"Ah, yes," Richard replied thoughtfully. "I will give you an answer to take back with you."

"I think Lord Hastings had hoped that you and your knights would do me the honor of riding with me."

"As urgent as that, is it?"

"My lord thinks so."

Richard put a hand to his face. It was small and blunt fingered but well trimmed with jewels. "Yes, I suppose you're right. I'll have to go soon. But you see, I've only just gotten back from the border last night, and there are matters here that need my attention. It may be some time before I return again." Richard gave him a faint, rueful smile. "To lose a brother and a home all in the same day . . . it isn't easy, Catesby."

"I-I can well understand that. I grieve for your loss."

"I can see that, and I'm grateful that if I had to learn this news, it was from your lips." Richard clapped a hand to Catesby's shoulder briefly then let it drop. "I seem to be forgetting my duties as a host. You've ridden hard from London and with little thought for food and rest, I warrant. My steward shall see to your refreshment and to a fresh suit of clothes, and then we'll discuss this matter further."

Catesby bowed as Richard turned away. He saw Anne Neville, her face still wearing its stricken look, lay a tentative hand on her husband's sleeve.

"Go in, Anne," he told her, not unkindly. "I'll come to you when I can, but there's no time now for grief or pity. Lord Hastings informs me that I have been named protector of the king and of the realm."

Catesby heard the sharp intake of her breath as the impact of that title hit home, but Richard apparently did not, for he turned and went off with his knights, leaving her standing there in the yard clutching their son tightly by the hand.

The day had turned colder. The sun had fallen behind the edge of a fast-moving cloud bank, and a freshening wind blew off the moor. Anne moved involuntarily to smooth back the folds of her headdress, which flapped about her face like a gull's wings, but her eyes watched Richard. The familiar curve of his back, which he was usually at such pains to straighten, now seemed slumped and weary, and she marveled at how slack his long purposeful stride had become. On the steps of the hall, he stumbled, and she caught her breath. Francis Lovell put out a quick hand to steady him. She was amazed at that. Richard never stumbled.

And then he was gone.

There was enough of the woman in her to feel a swift stab of jealousy even in the midst of grief. She wished fervently that he had turned first to her, that just this one time he had sought solace from her in their private apartments rather than from his knights in the hall. But she knew that if she, petulant, were to question this in her woman's way, he would have given her a tender, indulgent smile and explained very patiently that while the news of Edward's death brought with it a private grief, it also brought a public charge. She of all people, a daughter of the kingmaker, Earl of Warwick, should know that. It was both natural and right that he should consider that latter aspect at this moment.

The rest of the world might well believe that the private grief had been swallowed up in the public charge, but then the rest of the world did not know Richard as she did. For Richard had been devoted to Edward with every fiber of his being.

Devotion? she asked herself, rejecting the word like a bauble and choosing another. *No, it was more like dedication, constant and unswerving.*

It had been evident from Richard's childhood during the long years of struggle that had brought Edward to the throne and through the continuing challenges, including one from her own father, that had allowed him ultimately to keep it. It stood out stark and brave in the words of his motto: "Loyaltie me lie." Loyalty bound Richard's every act. He never questioned his duty to family, to friends, to the York city fathers who were always beseeching his aid in one cause or another, to the peasants who came in increasing numbers to Middleham to beg some boon. But first and foremost, his loyalty had been to Edward as steady as the needle of a compass pointing out the north.

Only once had she seen it waver, and that had been over Clarence.

She thought of it now, that cold February day five years before, and even now she shivered not only because of the chill April wind gusting through the outer bailey. It had been the coldest day of the winter. A snowstorm had blanketed London the night before, and though the sun shone blindingly that morning, it gave no warmth. Men-at-arms huddled about the great hearth fires at Westminster Palace, and hurrying pages blew on chilblained fingers to keep away frostbite. In the presence chamber, Edward had sat massive and uncomfortable in robes of ermine and sable, trying to avoid Richard's accusing gaze, while beside him his queen was as stiff and cold as one of the icicles that glittered from the palace roof.

Richard's breathing came in labored little puffs of vapor, for he had rushed headlong and unannounced into Edward's presence chamber from another part of the palace. Only a few moments before, Lord Hastings had delivered the stunning news that the king had finally signed the death warrant for George, Duke of Clarence. Though golden in appearance and demeanor, the duke was a notorious malcontent, and none could argue, least of all Richard, that he had not deserved his fate several times over. But he was also brother to both Edward and Richard, the middle brother in age between them. Shocked and titillated court gossip reported that the execution had been carried out straightaway, very privately, in the Tower and that he had been drowned at his own request in a butt of his favorite malmsey wine.

"Is it true then, what I've heard?" Richard had asked.

Edward had not even nodded, only bowed his head.

"You have killed him, killed your own brother? I didn't believe it. I couldn't believe that you of all people could be guilty of such monstrous wrong. The primal sin, Ned—the curse of Cain! And you, my brother as well, how could you do it?

Edward had withdrawn his hands from the sheltering warmth of his robes and spread them in a little placating gesture. Even then the fingers were so swollen that the rings bit into his flesh. "It was Parliament that attainted him—you know that—and Parliament that found him guilty of high treason."

"Yes, but it was you, and only you, who accused him. It was your hand that signed the death writ."

Edward stared for a moment at the offending hand and thrust it back into his robe. "Ah, Dickon, do you think I'd have done it if there had been any help for it? I tell you it had to be done."

"Had to be done? But why? Why now? Oh, I grant he's been guilty of much—a rogue and a renegade if ever there was one, his mind a fertile breeding ground for every new treason. I had as much cause to hate him as anyone. Do you remember how he schemed to keep Anne and her fortune from me, how he hid her in a scullery? He had Isabelle and would have kept the whole Neville inheritance for himself. Anne—he had marked for a nunnery. But even then, despite all that, I would not have done what you've done. You've always forgiven him before. Why not now?"

Edward flinched under Richard's words; his hand shook visibly as he poured some wine from a flagon on the table beside him. Richard watched as he took a great swallow of the malmsey, anger rising sharp in his face. He brushed the cup from the royal lips as he might swat away a fly. It clattered loudly to the tiles, staining the king's ermine and the queen's white brocade with a crimson brand.

"Don't try to hide from my questions behind a wine cup . . . or do you but drink to his memory?"

He turned then and stalked from the chamber. Edward's raised hand trembled after him from its scalloped sleeve. "Dickon, please . . ."

But before she turned to follow, Anne had seen the restraining hand Elizabeth Woodville had placed on her husband's knee and had caught something else as well: the look on her demurely lowered face. Her eyes, a smoky violet beneath their thick fringe of lashes, held unmistakable triumph, and the smile that played around the corners of her rosebud mouth was very like a smirk.

Anne had known then what Richard himself had only half-guessed, known that the rumormongers spoke true. The Woodvilles had actively and relentlessly sought the death of Clarence; the queen herself had whined and pleaded and cajoled for it with all of a wife's secret wiles. And at last she had it on some trumped-up charge that did not even bear close scrutiny. Like Salome, she might have had his head served up on a platter had she desired it.

Five years had passed, but Anne still remembered only too well how Richard's rage leapt into sudden flame again when she told him what she had seen and what the ladies of the court were whispering behind their orange pomanders and lavender-scented handkerchiefs. "Mark you, Anne, I'll have my vengeance over that pack of wolves someday. They'll be brought as low as they've brought Clarence."

"But Edward," she had reminded him, "what of Edward?"

"Ah, yes. Well, I have no doubt that he was led to it by that witch of a queen. God's blood, but how I wish he had never set eyes on that woman! And I'm sure that he regrets his rashness now. Did you see how he flinched?" His voice softened, even grew a little defensive when he spoke of his beloved elder brother. "While Edward lives, there's not a great deal I can do. My loyalty is sworn. But I'll have my vengeance someday, if it takes me till the day I die."

Anne shuddered, remembering those words, for she realized with a sinking heart that Edward's death released Richard from his vow of fidelity. There was nothing now to prevent him from carrying out his threat. She shivered again, drawing the folds of her cloak more tightly about her, and then she realized that she was shivering from cold as well as from fear. The sky was dark with storm clouds, and the wind that swept through the barred portcullis and swirled the dust of the courtyard carried the first drops of rain in its teeth.

She stood alone. Even the animals had sought shelter—the dogs to their kennels, the fowl to their roosts. Yet she was not quite alone, for Ned was still beside her. Ned! All at once, she was fully conscious of the limp, dry hand in hers and the hoarse cough that came from her son.

"Please, Maman, can't we go in now? I don't feel very well." Even though he still wore his fur wrappings, his teeth chattered like the leaves of last autumn.

She stooped to look at him. "Ah, Ned. Yes, poppet. Forgive your foolish mother. Are you ill again?"

His only answer was another wracking cough. Anne put a hand to his forehead and found it hot and dry, like kindling that would flame at a touch. "Ar't warm, Ned?"

"Aye, warm and cold, all at once. Please, Maman . . ."

She bent and gathered him to her, a light weight in her arms though she was by no means strong. Though he was convalescing from a cold, Richard had insisted on the day's outing as a kind of cel-ebration, arguing the healing and strengthening properties of a fresh wind on the moors. Once a sickly child himself grown to a healthy, virile manhood, he disdained coddling in the rearing of his son and heir.

But he had been wrong today. It had been too soon, Anne told herself as she made for the castle keep. Now Ned had taken a fever or worse, and she herself was as much to blame as Richard for lingering too long in the yard.

The rain was slashing down in earnest as she entered the keep and climbed the stair to the nursery.

On the face of it, there was only one decision Richard could make. He studied Hastings's letter until the words squirmed before his eyes like black snakes and listened to the excited counsel of his men until his ears rang. Both told him what must be done. He must leave for London at once.

Why then did he feel this heavy reluctance? Not one of his knights shared it. Even Assheton and Brackenbury, the eldest and normally the most cautious, urged him to take action. The others—and particularly the young hotheads, Ratcliffe, Tyrell, Percy—even suggested a show of force might be necessary, perhaps an army to counter whatever measures the Woodvilles had taken since Edward's death.

"By the rood, this talk of delay is folly, Your Grace!" Rob Percy blurted out. He blushed as red as his carrot-colored hair at this impertinence but then plunged wildly on. "The Woodvilles are your sworn enemies. Everyone knows that. Everyone knows too how you swore vengeance on them for Clarence. Now the game is yours. You can rout them from England forever."

"Is that what Edward intended when he named me protector, do you think? Are you going to argue that I now have his royal permission to set aside his widow and all her kin? Ah yes, Edward would be well pleased with me for that bit of work, wouldn't he, Percy? Wouldn't he? Well, answer me, any one of you. I can't believe that you've all been struck dumb when your tongues wagged so freely a moment ago."

None of them could even meet his eyes, let alone give him an answer, and Richard, knowing that to a man they sought his own best interests, softened somewhat his fierce look. "I know you mean well," he said. "The Woodvilles have done me a grave wrong, and I might still seek revenge if the memory of Edward or grief at his passing—I don't know which—didn't lay on me so heavily. This much I do know: I haven't the stomach for it now. And I want you to understand that when we leave for London tomorrow, there is to be no suggestion of offense—not to the queen, not to Rivers, not to any of the Woodvilles. Is that understood?"

"Yes, my lord," said a shamed and repentant Percy.

"Yes, my lord," echoed the others.

"But . . . what if they give us offense?" argued the bull-necked James Tyrell. "Certainly you don't expect us to sit idly by and do nothing to stop them."

"I didn't say that," Richard replied, "nor will I know until the time comes, if it comes. Pray God that it does not."

"Yes, pray God," said Ratcliffe between clenched teeth. "Much good may it do."

None of them had heard the approach of Dame Joan, the old nurse who tended Richard's son, but suddenly she was there, biting anxiously at her lower lip, fearing to interrupt yet knowing she must. "Master, master, ye must come. My lady is nigh distracted."

Richard would have reprimanded her for the intrusion, but something in her wrinkled red apple of a face stopped him short. "Well, dame, what is it? Is my duchess ill?"

"Nay, nay," she replied with a vigorous shake of her gray head. "'Tis not my lady. 'Tis he, the poor wee bairn. Taken of a fever and dreadful ill, he be. My lady, she do take on so. Ye must come."

"Ned? But how can that be? He was well enough an hour ago."

The only answer to this was another impatient head-shake. Her hand plucked at his sleeve as if she would have dragged him bodily after her, but he needed no more urgings. He bounded up the narrow nursery stair two steps at a time.

The boy was indeed ill, tossing about on his bed, coughing wetly and babbling incoherently. Anne was bent over him, still in her riding habit, but her brown hair with its gleaming copper lights streamed unbound over her shoulders. She lifted a tearstained face to him with a look that was oddly accusing.

"When did this happen?" he asked.

"Directly after we got back, after you left with your knights. Oh, Dickon, didn't I tell you that we shouldn't have taken him out today? It was too soon. He wasn't well yet."

"He looked well enough," Richard replied, somewhat sharply. "He looked quite well. I wouldn't keep my son locked in a cage, madam, like your pet thrush. He gets overmuch of mothering as it is."

"Mayhap it's needed if his father hasn't the time to concern himself . . . ." She stopped suddenly, for Richard had picked up the clothing they had removed from Ned moments before.

"Wet!" he exclaimed. "Soaked with rain!" He held out the offending bundle to her. "Why is that, lady? It wasn't raining when we returned. Did you keep him out in the storm?"

Her hands flew to her face. "I didn't mean to . . . I didn't realize . . . the shock of Edward's death. I'm sorry, so very sorry." She wiped her eyes on her green velvet sleeve.

Timidly he reached for her hand. Their quarrels were so rare that he could hardly recall the last one, but he knew it had concerned this very issue, the rearing of the son they both loved almost to distraction. He would be their only one. Anne was too delicate to bear another.

He felt her hand relax in his, and she gave him a look that contained only a loving sorrow. "I'm sorry too, Dickon, if I've displeased you. It wasn't the time with Edward newly dead, and now this to be speaking of blame."

"Nay, Nan," he murmured as he drew her to him, but there was a thickness in his throat, and no more words would come. Why couldn't he say them, the words of apology, of forgiveness, of love? Why were they dammed up in him like some deep and secret lake? Insanely, he wished he were back in the hall, safely surrounded by his knights.

She hushed his thoughts with a small clear voice. "There was blood, blood on the handkerchief when he coughed."

He took the folded linen square from her and slowly opened it. There it was, a little spot of red drying now to brown, a very little spot against the white sea of the handkerchief.

"Aye, 'tis the wasting sickness," said Dame Joan with utter assurance. "Poor bairn! Poor wee bairn. Me sister in Cumberland, she died of it only this twelvemonth past."

"My sister too," Anne whispered sadly. "Isabelle. Isabeau . . ."

"No!" Richard cried so loudly that both women jumped. "It can't be as severe as that. The lad has a cold. He probably had a nosebleed. It's not uncommon in children, you know. He'll be mended soon. Look! Even now he sleeps."

Anne did not contradict him. She too seemed to draw some comfort from the fact that Ned had slipped into a more quiet slumber, though the small face turned toward them on the pillow had the translucence of a wax image.

"I wonder what's keeping the leech," she said. "It must be half an hour since he was sent for." But Master Wilde, the physician who had attended the Nevilles since the old earl's time, could not immediately be found. Richard momentarily cursed the generosity with which he allowed his own physician to attend to the peasants of the village. No doubt one of them suffered from some minor complaint while his son and heir wasted away from lack of attention. It seemed a lifetime later when the leech finally appeared, his black robe sodden with rain.

"What kept you, Master Wilde?" Richard asked shortly.

"A birth and a death, my lord," the doctor answered wearily. "John Easebourne has a fine new son but no wife now to warm his bed. The babe came breech."

Anne murmured her regrets while Richard repented his earlier impatience. John Easebourne was his gamekeeper and a man he both liked and respected. His wife had been a mere slip of a girl, barely rising sixteen.

"And now, what have we here?" Wilde asked.

"My son in a fever. My lady here fears the lung sickness."

Wilde looked at the telltale linen square and shook his grizzled head in disbelief. "What?" he cried. "This tiny spot? If Your Graces would know what death looks like, you may behold it here on the front of my gown. Mistress Easebourne hemorrhaged out her life's blood before she passed."

Richard saw that much of the wetness he had taken for rain was in fact the viscous texture of blood drying into stiffness.

"For our patient here," Wilde went on, pressing a thumb to Ned's pulse, "a bleeding is what is needed. As can be seen in the blood he coughed up, his body is trying to rid itself of some vile humor. Aye, a letting and a compress of pig's urine to bring down the fever and he should be right enough in a few days' time."

It wasn't until a cup of the boy's blood sat in a pewter basin and the stench of pig's urine permeated the bedchamber that Richard broached to Anne the subject of his departure for London.

"On no, Dickon!" she cried. "You can't go, not now."

"But I must. You should understand that."

Anne shuddered. "But what of Ned?"

"What of him? He'll be all right. Master Wilde said so."

"I heard what Master Wilde said as clearly as you did, but I'm afraid. I'm very much afraid."

Richard might have protested this as foolishness, but he had lived with Anne long enough to know that her fears were seldom groundless. Besides, it was quite possible that Hastings, with distrust of the Woodvilles deeply engrained in his heart, might have exaggerated the urgency of the situation in London. Surely it could do no harm for him to bide a while longer in the north, to await the arrival of a more official missive from the Privy Council. In the meantime, he could do some writing of his own and make the necessary preparations for an extended absence from Middleham. Yes, now that he considered this alternative, it made a great deal more sense than a headlong rush to London. He gave Anne a kiss on the forehead.

"Very well," he said indulgently, "I'll stay here for a few more days, but only until the lad mends."

Anne smiled, the first time she had smiled since earlier that afternoon when her peregrine had snared a grouse in flight on the moor. With her, all seemed almost right again.

Will Catesby, on the other hand, greeted Richard's decision with a swift shake of the head. "Do you think that's wise, Your Grace?" he asked, grown suddenly bold. "My lord asked me to impress upon you the need for haste if his letter did not suffice."

"It sufficed," Richard replied curtly. "Just tell him that I recognize the greater wisdom of staying at my son's bedside. Tell him I'll come as soon as possible, but that I need time yet to prepare, to comfort and, aye, to mourn."

Catesby bowed his head. "As you will, my lord."

"I shall give you two letters to take back with you. One of them will be to your good lord, of course, who has been so thoughtful as to send me word of my brother's passing."

"And the other?"

"The other will be to the queen and will be one of commiseration for her loss and a pledge of allegiance to her son."

Catesby's eyes bulged from his head. "You would write to the queen, my lord?"

"Why should I not?" Richard regarded him with a twinkling eye. "Isn't she my brother's widow, my good sister, and the mother of our sovereign lord? Do you find these words surprising, Catesby? Ah,

I daresay you have heard that in the past I sometimes called her other names much less pleasing. The past is dead, and I hope it will remain so. Nevertheless, I think it best to remind her that nothing should be done that is contrary to her late husband's will. Do you think that would be wise?"

"Most wise."

"And I think I shall write also to her brother, Lord Rivers, to seek a union of our two parties as we ride for London. Yes, it would be well for the people to see us joined together in the service of King Edward V."

Catesby swallowed hard, but there was little more he could offer in the way of argument or protest. Who could fathom the ways of princes? He had expected a lion to come roaring down out of the north; he had found instead a housecat that might preen itself on a lady's lap. But there was nothing more that he could do. As Richard retired with his secretary to an inner chamber, Catesby could think only of the wet, dismal ride back to London and of Lord Hastings's keen disappointment when he arrived there—alone.

Chapter 4

ON THE BATTLEGROUND that was the Painted Chamber, Hastings feared that he was fighting a war already lost. The Woodvilles aimed at dominance by any and all means possible. To be sure, they had made no more mention of an early coronation, though what secret activities they engaged in to that end Hastings could only guess. Nor were the rights and prerogatives of the still-absent Gloucester given any consideration. The Woodvilles ignored his very existence.

"They aren't doing anything more than is necessary for the continuance of government," Morton intoned to Hastings's muttered disapproval after one council session. "The appointment of judges, the collection of taxes . . . would you have these matters await my lord of Gloucester's pleasure?"

"But they are doing these things in their own names. 'Uterine brother to the king,' 'uterine uncle to the king.' Christ, how the blood boils at that!"

"Whose name should they be using then? Someone's who has nothing to do with these matters, who has as yet been conspicuous by his absence?"

Morton's benign smile scarcely had the soothing effect he intended. Richard's prolonged delay increasingly rankled Hastings. He might have added that although Lord Rivers also remained among the missing, his name was prominently displayed as "Avunculus Uterine Regis."

"You yourself have fared well enough if I may say so," Morton went on. "The appointment to head no less than . . . how many was it, seven of the tax commissions? Don't tell me you won't come out all right there, eh?" Morton's eye gave a tiny wink.

Hastings sniffed. "A bone that the queen might throw to a dog."

"A suitable distraction perhaps while Sir Edward prepares to set sail for Calais," Howard added.

"You are overly suspicious, my lord," Morton said.

"I wouldn't be too certain of that," said a voice behind them. The speaker was Thomas Bourchier. With his thick salt-and-pepper brows knit across the top of his long rapier of a nose, he would have made an imposing figure even without the cardinal's scarlet. As archbishop of Canterbury, he was Morton's spiritual superior. Hastings's heart leapt with the hope that he might prove an ally.

"I must agree with Lord Hastings on this," the archbishop continued. "Whether or not, as they insist, they but carry on the business of governance, the queen and her party go too far. They are flouting both the law and Edward's will. I for one will not tolerate it."

"Hear, hear!" Hastings cried while Morton, unable to rebuff a prince of the church, looked down at his piously folded hands.

"Your Eminence may speak a piece of the truth," he admitted.

"More than a piece of it, Morton," Hastings replied jubilantly. "A battle is brewing, and sides must be chosen. It must come to a field, it must come to a field."

But even with Bourchier's support and that of another wavering cleric, John Russell, bishop of Lincoln, Hastings still found himself hopelessly outnumbered. At the next meeting, the Woodvilles appeared more openly confident than ever before. The queen was poised and gracious, but every muscle in her slender body seemed tense as a cat's about to spring. And Thomas Dorset, standing by his mother's right hand, was equally bold. As Rotherham pounded his gavel for order, Hastings knew too well that the battle so narrowly averted several days before was about to be joined.

Dorset quickly seized the floor. "My lords," he began without preamble, "we are faced—England is faced—with a problem of the most serious implications. My lady mother has several times declared to this council the nature and probable consequences of this problem, yet we dally like sheep afraid to act. Can we call ourselves men when we can be so easily shamed by a woman?"

Hastings and Howard exchanged warning glances; Bourchier leaned forward, eyes narrowed under his craggy brows. Dorset paced the tiled floor behind his mother's gilded chair, eyes lighting on no one.

"You all know, or ought to know, of what I am speaking. Why then do we delay? Is it because we truly are sheep without a shepherd to guide us? In truth, that is exactly what our enemies will think. The spider Louis across the Narrow Sea marks our sloth and no doubt thinks us a fine fly to trap in his web. In his eyes, England has no king."

There was a loud murmur of shock, surprise, disbelief, and from Morton, who doubtless had been informed, even a shout of approval.

"How say you, sir?" Rotherham asked. "Certainly we all claim allegiance to Edward V."

"Claim, claim," Dorset mocked, albeit gently, for he knew the archbishop of York to be one of his own party. "Yes, we claim, but our sovereign lord remains a figurehead without power. He does not yet wear England's crown. Therefore, I propose we arrange for his coronation with all due haste. I suggest that Sunday fortnight would not be too soon."

"B-but, my lord!" exclaimed Russell. "Have you any knowledge of all that's required for a coronation? Surely you jest."

"No, my good bishop, I do not jest. I consider this a matter of the utmost seriousness and of primary import to the safety and security of the realm. What's more, I believe it can be done. You have some experience with coronations, Eminence," he added, turning to Bourchier. "What is your opinion on this matter?"

The cardinal let out a great sigh, but he knew on this that he must prove an unwilling ally to Dorset. Historically, coronations had been arranged with almost indecent haste, particularly if the king's claim was uncertain or the succession in doubt. An anointed and crowned king could hope to quiet rumors of dissent.

"Yes, it can be done," he answered slowly, "but should it be done? No one questions the succession. There is no need then for undue haste. And we must ask ourselves once more if we should move without the counsel of him whom our most dear lord, God rest him, named protector?"

"Please, if I may have a word . . ." The speaker was Stillington, bishop of Bath and Wells, and since his voice was seldom heard in the council chamber, all eyes turned toward him in mild surprise. Hastings noted that his face was twisted as if in pain. "I-I have something to say here . . ."

"What could you possibly have to say that would interest us, old man," Dorset said ruthlessly, "when you have kept your silence all these years? As for Gloucester, I don't think we need to fear him. Even without him, we have enough power in ourselves to make and enforce these decisions." His hands rested firmly on the back of his mother's chair.

"There are those who might say that what we do here does not have the power of law behind it," said Hastings.

"And you, my lord, not the least of those." Dorset shot him a knowing look.

"You well know where I stand on the matter."

"Of course. And the rest of us are traitors."

"I didn't call you that."

"But you thought it. Ah, my dear Hastings, you were always an open book where one might read . . . many things. Not least of all, perhaps, envy over a certain issue that has little to do with affairs of state."

Hastings opened his mouth to protest, but Dorset held up a restraining hand. "Ah, but we were discussing the prerogatives of my lord of Gloucester, were we not? Yes, the good duke who unfortunately has not yet taken his rightful place as the head of our council. Isn't that so?"

"Edward meant him to be more than that, more than a mere head of council. 'Protector of the king and of the realm'—those were his words."

"Perhaps. Yet whatever his words, our late sovereign failed to instruct us on how we were to obtain the advice or, aye, the commands, if you will, Hastings, of one who has yet to put in an appearance even though Edward drew his last breath ten days ago. Maybe we should have a steady stream of couriers running between London and the north to learn His Grace's will—an impractical arrangement though some, I understand, have tried it."

Hastings felt his skin growing warm under Dorset's steady gaze. The marquis had his spies everywhere.

"My lords, a word if I may." Elizabeth Woodville's honeyed voice cut across the debate. Cool, conciliatory, indulgent, she had sat in silence while the tide of discussion had flowed around her. Now she turned her vivid gaze on Hastings while her lips curved into a gracious smile. "Our debate grows fruitless, and we are straying far afield. Suffice it to say that my late lord, whom God assoil, never intended to invest his worthy brother with near-regal powers. You know as well as I that the wine of power is a heady brew that a king alone should partake of. No regent ever gave it up voluntarily once he possessed it. Rather, most of them have become drunk with it, much to the sorrow of both king and country. Let Gloucester be the first person of our council but no more than that, I pray you."

"A most moving speech." Howard's acid whisper was low in Hastings's ear. "Would you cast your lot with a thief who would steal a child's throne?"

But elsewhere there was general agreement with the queen, even among the bishops who had earlier spoken out in support of Hastings and the protectorate. She had raised the ugly specter of usurpation, that most dreaded of all political upheavals. As Morton gave another long speech in favor of Elizabeth Woodville's proposal, only Stillington, apart from Hastings's own party, voted for the protectorate, croaking out his "Yea."

"And now for the coronation, my lords." The queen was still relentless in pursuit of her primary objective. "If there is no opposition, we will write this very day to our son and sovereign and to our brother Rivers and instruct them to leave Ludlow with all possible haste."

Hastings was suddenly alert. He might yet be able to manage things to his liking and to perform a master stroke for Richard from here. "I am sure, madam, that there could be no objections to such a suggestion," he said smoothly. "All of us would welcome His Grace's presence among us."

"We are grateful for your support," the queen purred, "especially since it comes unlooked for."

"You will not find me a disloyal subject, lady, to your royal son." He heard his own voice like a gentle stroking on fur and saw Elizabeth Woodville visibly relax in her chair. She thought she had won all while he still held the ace, the trump card, in his hand. "Of course, we must decide on a suitable escort for the king."

She waved an airy hand. "No need for concern there. I have already instructed my brother Rivers . . ." Too late she saw the trap.

"Instructed him, madam?" Hastings's eyes widened in mock surprise. "When you were to write to him only today?"

"It's a question of some urgency. There is so little time."

"Time? But surely unless Your Grace intends to raise an army . . ."

Red stained Elizabeth's orris-powdered cheeks. Her fingers strayed nervously to the pearl reliquary that hung between her breasts. "An escort to do the king honor, my lord. And a force to withstand any emergency that might arise along the way."

"How large a force?"

Her eyes stared at him with the look of a hunted animal while, around the table, those of the clerics she had courted so relentlessly were turned on her with renewed suspicion. Her tongue flicked over cochineal-reddened lips. "Five thousand men," she whispered.

"What?" Russell bellowed. "Are we at war that so large a force is required? An army in fact if not in name?"

Bourchier shook his head and pushed back his chair so that it scraped loudly on the tiles. "If you proceed in this, madam, you must look for other hands than mine to crown your son. I'll have no part in a rule by armed might."

"Nor I," Hastings echoed, rising as well. "I'll retire to Calais before I live to see the king of this land with an army to . . . uh . . . protect him from his loyal subjects."

Elizabeth exchanged anxious glances with the marquis and with Morton. Hastings's threat to retire to Calais made the situation desperate, the more so because he had a number of retainers of his own who could be raised at a whim and also because from Calais he could play havoc with Edward Woodville's fledging navy and the trade of the Cinque Ports.

"Peace, my lords, peace," Dorset called after them.

Russell and Bourchier, Hastings and Howard were already nearing the door while Stanley looked after them as if deciding whether his own best interests dictated that he too should bolt. They heeded Dorset no more than if he were an empty bladder of wind.

"Hastings, my lord of Canterbury!" It was Morton who spoke now, Morton who had somehow kept his wits about him even in the face of imminent disaster. "Come, come, there's no cause to split the council. Maybe we can reach a compromise of some sort. Are we children to leave the game when the play goes against us?"

Bourchier hesitated then turned back, and Hastings followed soon after. Morton's voice held a note of genuine distress, and in this case, Hastings reflected, to compromise might well be to win all. Feigning affronted dignity, he resumed his seat while Morton cajoled and prodded first one side and then the other. He was a past master of diplomacy, and no doubt each one believed when it was over that he or she had the better of it.

For her part, the queen agreed, albeit reluctantly, to limit the king's retinue to two thousand men, scarcely a paltry number but one that Hastings hoped Gloucester could exceed in his muster of men from the north. Nor was he willing to leave it to chance. He would send another courier to Richard that very day with these new instructions. Gloucester could waylay the king along the route to London.

For their part, Hastings and his party gave ground on the coronation date, which was accordingly fixed for the fourth day of May. However, this was no longer a major cause for concern. If the king were not in Gloucester's control well before then, it would matter little when he was crowned. But he would be; Hastings had no doubt now that he would be, or he did not know Richard of Gloucester.

He was therefore in remarkably jovial spirits when he left the Painted Chamber and found himself matching steps with Bishop Stillington.

"I'm most grateful for your support today, m'lord bishop," he said, throwing an arm about the smaller man's shoulders.

Stillington shook his head. "For all the good it did. I would have said more, but . . ."

"But that blasted coxcomb Dorset cut you off. Damned unchivalrous about it he was too. Tell me, what was it you were going to say?"

Stillington stopped, one hand gripping his chest. He was panting hard, and his lean face glistened with sweat.

"Come, man," Hastings said, "it can't be worth all of that."

"No, of course, it wasn't." He gave Hastings a long look and then broke into a dry chuckle. "Mother of God, do you know I've quite forgotten what I was going to say? How silly of me!"

"Well, it couldn't have been terribly important then," Hastings replied. He regarded the timid little bishop with something like contempt.

"No, I'm sure. It-it wasn't important at all."

Chapter 5

ONE WEEK AFTER he had learned of Edward's death, Richard sat alone at the high table in Middleham's great hall and pondered what he should do. A second messenger had arrived from Lord Hastings only an hour before and, after devouring the midday meal as if he had not eaten the whole long way from London, had retired to an upper chamber where Richard surmised he slept like the dead.

Richard himself had lingered at the board longer than was his wont, a fact that had not gone unnoticed among the servants. They cleared away the dinner plates in unusual quiet with many an anxious glance toward the dais. He paid them no mind, only sipped his sugared Bordeaux and thought about the latest events in London— or rather, the latest that he knew for this news was already three days old.

There was a note of urgency in this last message more pronounced even than had been in the one before it. Obviously, events were turning against him in London. The Woodvilles were in power and threatening to remain there unless some desperate act dislodged them. But Hastings's blatant demand that Richard raise an army and seize the king bodily was as repugnant to him now as it had ever been.

A page brought him word that yet another courier waited in the yard.

"The road to the north groans with heavy traffic," Richard said wryly. "Who does this one proclaim as his master? Not Lord Hastings again, surely?"

"No, milord. This one says he comes from Brecknock Castle in Wales. He wears the badge of the Duke of Buckingham."

Richard's brow creased in a frown. "Buckingham? What can he want? Well, show him in, lad, show him in."

Richard scratched absently as the ears of his favorite deerhound who, having finished gnawing at the last of the venison bones under the table, now thrust his great muzzle into his master's lap for his customary petting. However, that petting was merely perfunctory today, and the beast's small whimpers attested to its lack of satisfaction. It was the only sound in the hall now that the trestles had been stashed along the walls and the servants had gone. On the black-draped gallery, the musicians had put away the lute, viol, and rebec with which they had entertained the duke at dinner, and they too had gone. Only Richard still sat and pondered.

Why Buckingham? he asked himself. Why Buckingham now?

Although Henry Stafford was a cousin (his grandmother a sister to Richard's own mother), they had never been close. In fact, the whole court was a skein of tangled and complex family relationships. What mattered most was not so much kinship, for blood brothers could be the fiercest of rivals. No, what counted above all else was political persuasion, and that of the dukes of Buckingham had always been devoutly Lancastrian. The present duke had lost a father and a grandfather to York and had scant cause himself to love it.

Yet, Richard recalled, he might have sufficient cause to hate the Woodvilles. As a child and a pawn in the shifting fortunes of Lancaster and York, he had been granted by King Edward as a ward to his Woodville queen. It had been a grave miscalculation. Elizabeth, with no more thought than it took to clap her pretty hands together, had joined him in marriage to Katherine, one of her younger sisters. Like all of the Woodvilles, she had been fair, though a few years senior to her boy-husband, but the duke's displeasure had been wondrous to behold. Richard could still recall the scowl that had marred his handsome face as he beheld his bride at the nuptial altar, could hear the clipped and forced replies to the marriage vows. And how had the sweet-faced Katherine offended? In nothing else but that he considered her blood not the proper tincture of blue to be mated with his own. Great offense indeed for that proud stripling of a duke!

It was said that for some time after he was capable of the nuptial act, he had refused to bed her. Later, strict reason must have told him that if he hoped for a legitimate heir to his fine title, he had no other recourse than to beget a son on the body of his lawful wife, no matter how unworthy he deemed her. He had in fact fathered several children on her and had retired, still with a trace of a sulk, to his ancestral estates at Brecon in Wales, as far from Woodville-infested London as he could go. There for the most part he had remained, taking little interest in the happenings at court—until today.

Richard looked up as the man approached him, striding easily and confidently the length of the great hall. He noted the plum-velvet livery with its richly embroidered Stafford knots and the flaming-wheel badge on the sleeve that proclaimed its wearer to be high in the service of his master. The messenger doffed his velvet cap and touched finger to forelock in the prescribed manner.

"Your Grace, I greet you on behalf of my noble lord, the Duke of Buckingham. I am Sir William Percival at your service."

The words too were the prescribed greeting. Everything was correct. Yet Richard felt a sense of unease as he studied the man's visage. Perhaps it was the eyes—yellow green, proud, and wary as a cat's and strikingly pale in the tanned leather of his face. Perhaps it was the long livid-white line of a scar, the relic of some ancient battle, that cleft his face into two distinctly unequal halves, missing the left eye only by the breadth of an eyelash then cutting in close to the curved lips to shape them into a perpetual one-sided sneer. It was not an ugly face by any means and might once have been handsome before a sword point had done its hideous work, but it was a distinctly unpleasant face, one that would not have shamed the devil himself.

Richard forced a smile, but his voice was cool as he made his reply. "Welcome, sir, to Middleham. And what, may I ask, brings you here?"

"I bear a message from my lord, which I had hoped to be at leisure to convey to Your Grace over a plate of victuals and a mug of ale." The mouth curved into a one-sided smile.

Richard sensed impudence in the voice even as he realized that as host he should already have offered hospitality. "Our dinner hour is passed, though no doubt we can find something for you to nibble on."

"For that, you'll find me most grateful. It's a hungry ride and a thirsty one from Brecon." Again, there was that slow twist of a smile.

"I daresay," Richard said, signaling to the page to provide the necessary refreshments.

While Percival feasted hungrily but daintily, leopard-like, on a platter of cold meats and creamy Wensleydale cheese, Richard examined the parchment he had produced from his pouch. It was covered all over in a bold, careless script, the duke's own Percival hastened to assure him.

Henry Stafford, second Duke of Buckingham, greeted his cousin the protector well. Richard smiled at that. Apparently, the news of his appointment had spread more swiftly to Wales than to Yorkshire. Or had Buckingham, while eschewing the capital, not completely divorced himself from its events? Richard noted further that the duke had not failed to claim the kinship between them.

There was a flourish in the very words as Richard continued to read. In the new world that was a-making, Henry Stafford placed himself, life and limb, at the protector's disposal and declared himself to be his man. His noble cousin of Gloucester had only to bid him do a thing, and it would be done. For a beginning, he was ready to march to the protector's aid with a thousand armed men. He was now in Wales. Let him make the short march to Ludlow, and the king would be safely in his hands.

Richard shuddered and dropped the letter on the table. "Just like Hastings," he muttered. "Won't anyone counsel me to take a more cautious course?"

Percival looked up from his plate. "Your Grace?"

"Do you know what is written here?" Richard asked.

"Why, in faith, I do. Or most of it. My lord keeps little hidden from me."

Richard gave him a questioning look. "As close to him as that, are you?"

Percival shrugged, a languid, careless gesture. "I have been of service to the duke for a number of years and have been rewarded with his confidence . . . in all matters."

"Then you must know that what he is suggesting to me here smacks of treason?"

"Treason?" Percival's eyes widened. "Nay, I heard naught of treason."

"Seizure of the king is no treason?"

"'Sblood!" Percival spat onto the rushes. "'Tis the Woodvilles who commit treason. They have the king in their power at this very moment. They make the laws and order everything to their liking. While Your Grace, the lawful and duly appointed protector—"

"Hold your tongue, man," Richard snapped, for he was afraid that in the next breath, he would hear himself called coward. "I would have peace in England," he went on, more quietly. "I would not anger them."

"And yet the foxes must be routed from their holes, and rightly so, when they despoil the countryside."

Richard sighed. The problem was like a nettle wherever he picked at it, and there seemed to be no one who could help him. Ned's illness had seemed at the time like divine intervention to keep him at Middleham a little longer, but Ned mended now, and the problem grew ever thornier. There had been nothing but an ominous, worrisome silence from the Privy Council, an indication if any were needed that Hastings spoke the truth. Why then did he linger here? Had he turned coward? Was it craven to hope for peace between the factions as a tribute to Edward's memory?

Richard said, "I will not meet my sovereign with an army at my back, nor will I find him prisoner in the camp of another. Do you take my meaning?"

Again there was that indolent shrug, the face a mask of consummate indifference. "As you wish, though our enemies may have an army even if we do not."

"Enemies? Enemies? Must we always speak of enemies? We are all loyal subjects of King Edward V. Who then is an enemy, except perhaps the French?"

Percival's thin lips wore a decided smirk before he wiped it away with his napkin. "Loyal subjects all, my lord, to the king's grace. But that is hardly the issue. It is not the rights of the king that stand questioned but those of the protector."

There was a heavy silence in the hall. Beneath the table, the deerhound whimpered and snorted in his sleep then lay still. Richard looked at Percival, disliking the man to the very root of his soul yet knowing he spoke the truth, knowing it yet even then refusing to admit it.

When he spoke again, he was on his feet, and his voice was cold. The decision had been made.

"You may take this message back to noble Buckingham. You may tell him that I thank him for his loyalty and accept with gratitude his offer of assistance. I would welcome his company on the London road if he sees fit to join me at Northampton in one week's time. Further, you shall tell him that he is not to venture near Ludlow nor to offer any threat to the king and that he is to limit his retinue to three hundred unarmed men. My own shall be twice that number and will be dressed in black out of reverence for my late brother. Thus, when the new king comes with his two thousand men to Northampton, where I am proposing to Lord Rivers that we meet, there will be no suggestion of an opposing army. From there, our several retinues will journey together peaceably the last miles to London. Is that clear?"

"Perfectly so, my lord." Percival bowed. His face was impassive, his manner correct.

"Then I don't need to repeat myself?"

"No. All shall be arranged according to Your Grace's pleasure."

"I myself shall leave Middleham in two or three days' time, but I shall not travel with any great haste. It is not the time for great haste."

"No, my lord, though I've fair-winded several horses in coming here."

Richard sighed in exasperation. "Go to the stables. My grooms will give you a fresh mount."

"You are most gracious, my lord."

As Richard watched the proud, retreating back, he thought that he would gladly be rid of half his stable to see Percival safely gone from Middleham.

Chapter 6

THE SACRED DIMNESS of St. Mary Magdalene's Chapel at Ludlow was starred with candles and perfumed with incense. Kneeling before the high altar on a cushion of purple velvet, Anthony Woodville, Earl Rivers, prayed for divine guidance as he had seldom prayed for anything in his forty-four years. His lips moved soundlessly as the beads of rare crystal clicked through his fingers. Somehow God would tell him what was to be done—God or his own St. Anthony, patron saint of travelers.

But no. Too soon he heard the priest's blessing, the choir soaring into a "Te Deum" of rejoicing he was far from sharing. The mass was over. He had received the body and the blood of Christ, but the Eucharist had brought no lightening to his heart, no wisdom to his mind. His limbs were heavy and stiff as he genuflected and stood like one in a dream.

Beside him, Edward's face was radiant, not so much with joy as with impatience. "How long, Uncle?" he asked. "How long before we march?"

"Not long, Your Grace. Time enough though for you to have breakfast first."

The boy's face fell in a scowl. "How can I eat, how am I supposed to swallow when this morning we leave for London?"

The earl's eyes took in the long slender face, the slim young body—too slim, some might say, for the boy lacked appetite and the ache in his jaw constantly pained him. "Nevertheless, you must try. Bishop Alcock will see to it, won't you, my lord?"

The boy's tutor smiled his gentle smile. "Yes, of course. Come along, Your Grace."

"And you, Nuncle, won't you join us?"

"No, I'm . . . not hungry." He did not add that he thought it best to fast on this day of departure as propitiation to God for a swift journey and a safe arrival.

He went instead to the outer ward, where the red light of a rising sun smote his eyes and the sound of a great commotion struck his ears. So stout were the walls of the round chapel, built fast by Norman conquerors, that there had been no hint of it inside. Yet he should have expected it. Baggage carts and sumpter mules were laden almost to the ground, and milling men and horses were everywhere—a considerable number of men, two thousand to be exact. Sir Thomas Vaughan, the chamberlain of Edward's household, had seen to it that the quota was filled to the limit, moaning all the while that there were not enough, not nearly enough.

"The lady queen must know that we cannot manage with so few," he had lamented. "If anything happens along the way . . ."

"What exactly do you expect to happen?" Anthony had asked.

Vaughan had shaken his gray head ominously as if he feared some dire but nameless catastrophe. Anthony did not tell him that he himself had misgivings about their journey, vague anxieties that he could neither name nor express. Perhaps they came from the letters he had recently received from his royal sister and her impudent whelp of a son, the marquis.

Haste, haste, they commanded. *Make haste to London at all cost.*

The name of Gloucester leapt out from these missives penned in the swift, harsh strokes of fear and hatred. Under no circumstances was he to allow Gloucester access to the king.

In contrast to this had come Gloucester's own message—courteous, conciliating, and proposing a meeting at Northampton. It had seemed a reasonable enough request, and Rivers had granted it. He and Gloucester had been through much together in the struggle with Warwick and Lancaster. They had shared war, exile, victory, and a binding loyalty to that Edward who was now dead. Despite the enmity between their parties, they had become friends of a kind. Anthony thought the duke honest and honorable and had to admire those qualities in any man. Why then the misgivings? He did not know.

He walked now among the baggage wagons. There were so many, all covered with canvas tarps. He would not have believed the household possessed so many movables. Puzzled, he found Vaughan, a tally roll in his hand, marking off each wagon as he passed it with a piece of charcoal.

"Is everything all right?" he asked.

"Why, yes, my lord. We are almost ready."

"There are so many wagons. I had not thought . . ."

Vaughan pressed prim lips together. "Why, yes, of course. We must move all the household goods, you know—furnishings, kitchen utensils, bedding, provisions for the journey. One does not realize—"

Suddenly he stopped, for Anthony had flipped back one of the tarps where a strap was loose. He let out a low whistle of surprise. "And arms, Thomas? Must we take arms with us as well? Curious kitchen pots, these!"

Sallets and gorgets, brigantines and cuirasses, swords, shields, and pikes greeted his eye. Vaughan faltered, his wrinkled face gray in the dawn light. "Better to have them and not need them," he began then added boldly, "but if I may speak plainly, my lord, if you persist in this . . . this madness of meeting with Gloucester, we may very well have need of them."

Anthony shook his head, but he did not know what answer to give.

"They are here by the queen's command," Vaughan persisted.

"I heard nothing of it."

"No," came the reply. "Her Grace feared you would not permit it."

"Nor would I. But let it pass now that they're here. If they ease your sleep at night, it may be worth the nuisance, and I guess they can't do too much harm in the wagons."

A half hour later, as he sat on his horse, awaiting the signal to depart, Anthony viewed the final preparations with a detached, almost cynical eye. He suddenly felt that none of this activity had anything to do with him; he no longer controlled it, nor could he be affected by it.

Within the confines of the Castle Green, it seemed that there were even more than two thousand men. They were not all men-at-arms by any means. Tutors, confessors, almoners, and apothecaries swelled the train. But the vast majority had some military training. That was apparent from the way they fell into line. They looked too much like an army.

One fact about this "army" he found curious, even dangerous, was that almost to a man, it was Welsh. Perhaps it was understandable that Vaughan, being of that nationality himself, should put so much faith in the prowess of his countrymen, but Anthony could not share his trust. His own experience in the Marches had taught him that every true Welshman drank in a hatred of all things English with his mother's milk. Most of them would give their lives, and gladly, to throw off the yoke of foreign rule. However, it was doubtful that any one of them would risk so much as a cut finger in the defense of an English king. If old Sir Thomas expected trouble along the London road, he had certainly devised an odd method of meeting it.

Not that Vaughan's loyalty itself was suspect. The Woodvilles had long ago bought him with power and preferment. But it became clear to Anthony just how much of an oddity the chamberlain was as he looked about him now. At the head of the line, his eye caught that of one of the younger Welshmen, a man whom he recognized as Robin Vaughan, son of one of the tribal chieftains, the uchelwyrs, who still exercised considerable influence over their people. This particular Vaughan—of only distant kinship to Sir Thomas—had come to Ludlow several times with his father to pay reluctant homage to the Prince of Wales or to seek redress for some wrong. Where did he hail from now? Ah yes, it was Breconshire, was it not? The hatred of the Vaughan tribe for the Duke of Buckingham, who ruled there, was notorious, and Anthony had little reason to believe that Robin Vaughan thought better of anything else that was English. Nevertheless, he was a well-made man with an inborn pride that radiated from every pore of his body. He would not have been out of place in the household of a prince.

Anthony raised his riding crop in greeting. "Robin, isn't it? I must say I didn't expect to see you here today," he said.

Young Vaughan did not return his smile. Something moved in his blue-gray eyes, as slaty as the hills from which he came. "This is a journey I have long desired to make," he replied icily.

Anthony flushed scarlet and turned away. The hair-shirt he habitually wore for penance beneath his silk sarcenet doublet chafed at this neck. In his mind, he finished the Welshman's thought, *Aye, to rid Wales of her bastard prince, I would go far indeed.*

In fact, the hope of securing Wales had led the late King Edward to establish his three-year-old son as its prince, with his own court, at Ludlow. That had been nine years ago now, but Welshmen still dreamed of having one of their own in his place. Their bards foretold the coming of a liberator, one who would strike off the yoke of English oppression. He would be a second Arthur, a second Owen Glendower, and some were bold enough to declare that this true Prince of Wales was none other than Henry Tudor, now a penniless exile living in Brittany at the whim of Duke Francis. True, the blood of Welsh nobility from his father's side did flow in his veins, but so did, though slightly adulterated, the blood of Lancaster from his mother's. This was a dangerous attribute to harbor in a land ruled by Yorkists.

"Ho, Uncle! We march!" Edward's voice, high-pitched and shrill, called him back from his unquiet wanderings. Dutifully, he spurred his horse forward. Behind him, he heard the clomping of other hooves, the stamp of marching feet, and the grinding roll of heavy wagons. They passed by bleak Mortimer's Tower, through the castle's iron gates, and down the precipitous slope that led to the River Teme. The Yorkist town of Ludlow, straggling along their path, still bore some scars from the sacking it had received from Queen Margaret's Lancastrian forces in 1459. Usually, Anthony averted his eyes from this ugliness, from the charred timbers that had once been houses and shops but whose occupants had fled long ago. Today he noticed that wild gorse flowered yellow among the ruins and that ivy twined thickly around blackened beams. Twenty-four years was a long time, after all. He himself had been fighting for Lancaster then, and Bessie, his pretty older sister, was only plain Dame Grey and not the Queen of England. Then fortune's wheel had turned. And perhaps still turns, he reminded himself.

They crossed Denan Bridge, and Anthony turned back for a last look at the castle, his home for the past nine years, perched high on its cliff. A dark pile of masonry, the Norman keep soared beyond the curtain wall, the saw-toothed edge of its battlements jagged against a pale April sky. Forbidding it looked; forbidding it was. In winter, the north wind found its way through every chink and crack in the stonework. In summer, the heat could be oppressive. The land and the castle were as inhospitable, even at times as hostile, as the Welsh themselves. He should be glad to be leaving it behind in favor of the comforts, the luxuries of London. He too should be rejoicing with the bells of St. Mary Magdalene and the parish church of St. Lawrence that peeled their homage after the departing sovereign. Why then did they sound in his ears like the passing bells lately rung for King Edward?

By the time they reached Northampton early on the afternoon of April 28, Anthony found that his melancholy had vanished completely. The journey had been remarkably swift, thanks mainly to the urgings of Thomas Vaughan, who roused them early each morning and so got all of the king's retinue on the road at a reasonable—or as Rivers often thought, an unreasonable—hour. The earl was not blind to old Vaughan's maneuverings for haste, nor was he insensitive as to the reason for them, but apart from uttering one or two half-jesting protests at the way the chamberlain drove them on, he made no real objections. Richard of Gloucester had set their rendezvous for the twenty-ninth, and if Vaughan had to cool his heels for an extra day or two in Northampton, it would do him no harm.

Even the weather had smiled on them along the way. The notorious English spring, which could be as fickle as a Southwark whore, gave them skies of pale robin's egg blue and only a few drops of rain to remind them of her powers. Through gentle hills cloaked with green they rode, past thickets of willow, beech and alder, swelling at their tips with new life, and meadows spangled with the yellow of buttercups, kings-cup and daisies. Near towns and manors, villeins were busy with teams of oxen plowing the fields for spring planting. The rich, dusky smell of new-turned earth was as pungent in Anthony's nostrils as the perfume of a woman.

Everywhere in the towns and villages of Shropshire and Warwickshire, it was the same. Edward was greeted with a curious mixture of reverence and acclamation. Anthony's heart was warmed as though it were he himself who received the bows and curtsies, the loud hurrahs. He was inordinately proud of Edward, and he could not have loved him more if he had in fact been his own son.

The lad was beautiful; there could be no question about that, taller than most boys his age and graced with the winsome fairness of both his parents and, when he chose, his father's easy charm. His thick golden hair, touched with copper lights, curled gently about his shoulders, and his eyes, a deep greenish blue, looked out with quick intelligence from a face that had not yet lost all its childish softness. Even so, the black mourning robes invested him with a dignity beyond his years, and he carried himself with the poise and command of a born monarch. Yes, Anthony reflected, he had reason for both love and pride.

Of course, if he were to be honest, he must admit there were other things about his nephew that gave him cause for concern. His health had always been delicate, though this had not prevented him from hunting and hawking and tilting at the quintain in company with other youths of his age. It had, however, resulted in a rather undue prominence for Argentine, the royal physician who, until he had been called to London to treat the late king's final illness, had been in almost constant attendance on the prince. Anthony was grateful that Edward's health seemed unimpaired by the rigors of the journey and that Argentine had remained in London.

The boy's youth was another concern, but one that could scarcely be altered now. Anthony could only hope that the years diminished somewhat the querulous set to the mouth and the stubborn out-thrust chin. Edward could be most formidable when roused. Anthony had never himself felt the lash of the royal temper, but he had witnessed it on occasion, most recently when a page, new and somewhat clumsy, had tripped and spilled a tureen of soup onto the prince's lap. Edward was set to have the boy whipped before his uncle had intervened and convinced him that there was more to be gained from mercy than from vengeance. He was certain, even now, that he could in time have softened Edward's occasional bursts of hauteur, but time had run out for them at Ludlow. Edward was his province no longer. He was the king now and bound for London.

At Northampton, they were welcomed with the same enthusiasm that had greeted them in all the towns and villages along the way. The narrow streets were hung with banners, and the townspeople thronged to catch a glimpse of Edward and to pelt him with offerings of spring flowers. The boy received their homage graciously; he never seemed to tire of the honors done to his royal person, yet it was he who spotted the familiar figure, standing square in the center of the street, blocking their path, and refusing to give way to the heralds.

"Look, Uncle! It's our brother Grey come up from London to greet us!"

Indeed, it was Lord Richard who stood there, feet planted well apart, head cocked at a provocative angle, hands planted firmly on narrow hips. Anthony noticed that he had purchased a new suit of clothing in London: black samite doublet, very rich, banded with ermine and trimmed with gold satin under a mantle of black velvet lined with miniver. It was all very appropriate to his new rank as half brother to the king. As Edward approached, he doffed his new hat, a tower of black beaver graced with a long white ostrich plume, and swept a deep bow.

Edward's eyes were lit with unexpected pleasure while Anthony could only stare in troubled curiosity. "Greetings, nephew," he saluted from his horse. "What's ado? I hadn't thought to see you again till London."

"Greetings yourself, Uncle," came the somewhat peremptory reply. "I've come on urgent business. There are matters we must discuss—privately."

"Oh, very well," Anthony said as he dismounted. "Thomas, you might begin the business of settling in. We're to spend the night here."

Vaughan opened his mouth to protest, for it was only early afternoon, but Grey spoke more quickly. "Nay, Uncle, none of that. Wait until you've heard me out."

Anthony shrugged, but he felt his gorge rise. What right had this young dandy to order his men about? The look of smug satisfaction Vaughan gave him from his horse did little to improve his temper. Nevertheless, he determined to remain calm, particularly as he perceived that Grey's outward swagger was only a front for inward agitation.

At Anthony's suggestion, they adjourned to a nearby inn where he and the king were to spend the night. The landlord directed them to a private parlor that had obviously been cleaned to a polish in honor of their visit. Fresh rushes strewn with thyme covered the floor and a newly laid fire burned on the grate against the chill of a damp afternoon. Anthony loosened his boots and stretched his legs toward the fire, giving evidence that he was preparing for a long stay.

"Ar't thirsty, Dick?" he asked casually. "I could do with a mug myself."

Grey shrugged as his uncle ordered two tankards of ale brought in, but Anthony noted, not without some satisfaction, that he was having difficulty controlling his impatience. He failed even to pay proper attention to the barmaid, a buxom country lass who flushed prettily with downcast eyes as she served them.

"A right toothsome wench, that," he said, gesturing after her with his mug.

"Was she?" Grey asked tartly. "I hardly noticed."

"So I see, and I marvel," Anthony replied. He regarded his nephew coolly over the rim of the tankard, savoring the steaming nut-brown sweetness of the ale on his palate.

"Fie, Uncle!" Grey ejaculated. "This is no time to play with doxies, nor did I think you so inclined to the sport."

Anthony sighed and relented. Grey had apparently been entrusted with his first mission of any real importance, and it wasn't fair to toy with him so. "Very well, Dick. What is it?"

"You should know the answer to that. God's teeth! Why, against all advice to the contrary, against my mother's specific instructions, did you arrange to meet Gloucester here?"

"Why?" he echoed with a faint half smile. "Why? Because he asked, of course. And why not? It's his right."

"Do you think it wise?"

"I think any other course would be most foolish. He is after all protector of the king and of the realm." He said these last words slowly and emphatically, as if by reiteration he might make them more palatable.

"'Swounds, Uncle!" Grey pounded the table with such emphasis he almost knocked over his own untouched mug. His handsome features were twisted with rage and a ball of white spittle edged one corner of his mouth. "Protector of the realm," he mimicked. "What, may I ask, is that? Mere words, and the words of a dead man to boot! My stepfather must have been out of his head when he spoke them." Grey dropped his voice and leaned across the table toward Anthony. "And yet those words could spell doom for all of us. Don't you realize how diligently my mother and brother have worked for us in London?"

"Yes, Dick," Anthony answered with a sigh, "to be sure, I know."

"Then have you forgotten that Gloucester hates us and that he has in fact sworn vengeance on us for the death of Clarence?"

"That was a long time ago. I don't think the hatred burns so hot in him now. His letter was most courteous."

"Aye," Grey said grimly. "I too have read his courteous letters. Most fair they sound, and yet who knows what villainy lurks in the man's heart? If you misjudge him, then we are all lost, and yourself not least of all."

Anthony quaffed the last of his ale, disgruntled to find it now flat, lukewarm, and tasteless on his tongue. He stood up, no longer smiling. "Come, Dick. Enough of this twaddle. You tell me nothing that I have not already thought of while the king's grace sits his horse in the street. I don't have time to listen further."

"Wait, Uncle, for I believe I do have one piece of information that you haven't considered. Indeed, could not have considered."

Despite himself, Anthony felt his pulse quicken. Unconsciously, he tugged at the neck of his doublet. "Very well, then. Let's have it."

"What would you say if I told you that the Duke of Buckingham also joins Gloucester here tomorrow and with a goodly number of men?"

"Buckingham?" Anthony questioned. This was stunning news indeed.

"Yes, Buckingham. The very one who has pronounced himself the scourge of all our tribe. The same one who feels himself tainted by marriage to the queen's sister—*your* sister, Uncle. The news reached London only yesterday."

Anthony dropped heavily into his chair while his mind chewed on this latest revelation. He felt as if he had been unhorsed in a joust, as if all of the wind had suddenly been knocked from his lungs.

"This puts . . . a different face on things, although their intentions may still be honorable—"

"*May* be honorable? *May*? Do you really wish to take that chance?"

Anthony hesitated only a moment. "No," he said, his voice very low. "We must take the necessary precautions."

"Good!" Grey replied, hitching his chair closer to the table and leaning forward so that his nose was only inches away from his uncle's. Anthony could smell the cloves he habitually chewed to sweeten his breath. "Here is what we must do."

Chapter 7

WHEN RICHARD APPROACHED Northampton late on that Tuesday afternoon, the town seemed to sleep under a pall of gray cloud as peacefully as if nothing had ever disturbed it. Once he was inside the tawny brick walls, it seemed much the same. Banners of leopards and lilies dangled limp in the lowering fog; the high street was littered with crushed and wilted gilly flowers and piles of horse dung, where flies swarmed. There was no other sign of the king or his retinue.

"This is Northampton, is it not?" Richard asked with a puzzled squint at Francis Lovell. "And isn't it Tuesday, the twenty-ninth day of April? Or am I mistaken?"

"No, my lord. You are correct on both counts."

"Then something else is amiss, or this small country town hides two thousand men with greater ease than even London could."

At the Sign of the Tabor, where they were to spend the night, the landlord greeted them with profuse courtesy.

"Where lies His Grace, the king?" Richard asked him without preliminary.

"Not in Northampton, milord, that I know."

"But wasn't that his plan?"

The innkeeper shrugged, but his face grew suddenly solemn above his curling black beard. "The king and his party did pass through yesterday afternoon, and we gave them a grand welcome. They were supposed to stay the night here. Heralds had been sent ahead to all of the innkeepers, telling us to prepare a goodly number of rooms for the king and his meinie. And then, without a by-your-leave to any of us, suddenly they all took off again down the London road. I canna tell you how much custom was lost in Nor'ampton last night. It was a grave disappointment to us all, I can tell you that much."

"Hmmm . . . yes, I'm sure it was. Did anyone happen to mention where they were going?"

"Well, an' it please Your Grace, I did hear someone say Stony Stratford."

"When was this?"

"Yesterday, just after midday."

Richard toyed thoughtfully with the dagger in his belt. "I thank you for your information, though it was hardly what I wished to hear."

The innkeeper looked at him as if he was afraid that this client too would turn tail and vanish. With some difficulty, Richard smiled. "Now could you busy yourself with finding a bit of ale for my men and me? We have ridden far today, and the dust lies thick on our palates."

The ale, when it came, was surpassingly good, foaming thick white froth over the lip of the tankard. Richard took a moment to reflect on that even as his mind churned on other much less pleasant concerns. He heard the mutterings of his men, and the look on Rob Percy's expressive face revealed he was losing the struggle to stay silent.

"No, Rob," Richard cautioned, "don't say it. I will not press on to Stony Stratford, not tonight. It's too far. And we have another appointment to keep. The Duke of Buckingham is to meet us here."

"Perhaps that's the duke now," Lovell said. They heard the sound of hooves on the flagstones of the courtyard and the cries of men shouting for ostlers.

"It'd better be," growled Tyrell, "for I think we do ill to tarry here when Lord Anthony and the king elude us like foxes wi' the hounds after 'em."

"And yet," Richard said as the newcomers burst through the door of the public room, "if I'm not much mistaken, Jamie, the foxes even now are seeking the hounds." Rising with a bound, relief lighting his eyes and welcome on his lips, Richard hastened to offer his hand to Anthony Woodville, the Earl Rivers.

For several moments, he did not even realize that Rivers had not brought the king with him. The earl's smile held genuine warmth, and Richard mentally chided himself for his doubts. Anthony Woodville was far different from the rest of his grasping, insatiable clan. He was learned, erudite, and urbane in a way that few men could boast, yet he wore his many accomplishments with a self-deprecating humor that was immediately endearing. How could Richard ever have thought that Anthony would deceive him? True, it did not appear that the king was with him, but surely that would be satisfactorily explained in due course.

"Have you dined yet, Anthony?" Richard asked. "I was about to call for supper."

"Why, no, Your Grace, I have not and would deem it a privilege to share the board with you."

It was a meal that Richard would not soon forget. They spoke of many things: old battles lost and won, the perils of keeping peace along the marches, the relative merits of the Scotsman and the Welshman as opponents, the hazards of springtime travel, and also of Anthony's newly published book, *The Dictes of the Philosophers*. The earl even produced a copy as a gift for Richard, printed on Mr. Caxton's marvelous new printing press in London.

The fire that blazed on the hearth also gleamed on the polished oak paneling of the inn's best parlor, glowed warmly on the pewter mugs and plates, glittered on the diamond panes of the mullioned windows. Night had come early, and a thick fog wrapped the town in muffled peace. It was a fine evening to be indoors and resting after the rigorous days spent in the saddle, to be dining on fresh bread and country cheese and on thick slabs of roast venison and goose pasty washed down with more of the landlord's excellent ale and a lively Rhenish. It was a fine evening to reminisce with an old friend too seldom seen and to listen to a passing minstrel strum out a song or two on a well-tuned lute.

"Alas, my love, you do me wrong to treat me so discourteously," sang the rich tenor voice. The words reverberated in Richard's brain like a sudden warning. They had sat together at the table for several hours, and not once had Rivers mentioned the king.

"I had hoped," Richard paused, cleared his throat, and went on, "nay, I had expected to greet the king's grace here tonight, Anthony. Where is he? I hope he's not ill."

Rivers hesitated fractionally, his knife poised in midair as he was about to hack off a slice of bread from one of the loaves. The knife blade wavered in the firelight.

"No, he's not ill. It was simply feared there would not be enough lodging in Northampton to accommodate both the king's retinue and Your Grace's as well." The words came out smoothly, as if they were rehearsed, but Anthony's eyes were on the knife blade, not on his dinner companion.

Richard started to point out that the county town of Northampton was far larger than the tiny borough of Stony Stratford and thus better equipped to deal with a great number of men, the majority of whom were, after all, in the king's train. However, he checked himself and let Anthony go on with his increasingly improbable explanation.

"It was decided that it would be better for us, seeing that we arrived so early, to push on down the road a bit. I-I hope you weren't alarmed."

"Alarmed?" Richard asked. "Why, no. Merely, shall we say, disappointed. It's been a long time since I've seen my brother's son."

"I-I shall convey your . . . uh . . . greetings to Edward and tell him of your disappointment. It's most strange. I had not thought before how many of us there would be. Too many, really, to hope for beds enough in one small town, especially with Buckingham joining you here . . ."

"Yes?" Richard breathed, instantly alert. He watched the flush creep up in Rivers's cheeks. There was a little beading of perspiration along his upper lip.

"Cotsbody, but 'tis warm in here! That fire . . . too great a blaze for such a small chamber." Rivers tugged at the throat of his doublet with agitated fingers then downed a gulp of wine.

So he knew of Buckingham then. How, Richard wondered, had he learned? Obviously, he had not intended to mention it though he had. It explained much.

"Yes, it is overwarm," Richard agreed. "It's the dampness, I think, that makes the air so heavy. My dear Anthony, you look somewhat pinched. Are you sure you're well?"

The earl pressed his fingers to his temples. "It's only a headache. They do trouble me from time to time. A pity though that I had to suffer one tonight."

He would make his escape at any moment now. His eyes already shifted around the room, seeking to collect his men. He pushed back his chair, half rising. But he was not quite quick enough. From the courtyard came the noise of another commotion, snapping the leash of tension, and Anthony was forced to stay on a while longer. It would be unthinkable that he not pay his respects to the Duke of Buckingham.

Henry Stafford, second Duke of Buckingham, stood for an instant in the doorframe, his full mouth screwed up in obvious doubt. His eyes swept over the scene before him, clouding as they came to rest on Rivers sitting next to Richard at the high table.

What are you doing here? they seemed to ask. *I didn't expect to find you two together.* Swiftly, he appeared to recover himself. His eyes cleared, and he broke into a wide engaging grin. A stride of his long legs brought him to Richard's chair.

Clarence! Richard thought. *He is like Clarence risen from the grave—handsome, golden, ebullient Clarence as he looked and acted in his last days on earth.*

"My lord protector," said the duke, bowing deeply. "I greet you well. I cannot tell you what joy I have in this meeting."

"Nor I, dear cousin. Though it grieves me that we must be brought together under such sad circumstances."

"Ah, yes, your kingly brother. I mourn for him."

Rivers had once more risen from his chair and, with a flourish, offered it to the newcomer. "I much regret, my lord duke, that I was about to seek my bed. However, in doing so, it seems I vacate my seat to one better suited to fill it."

Buckingham did not quibble with this generosity. As he handed his cloak to an attendant and took the chair, Richard noted with wry amusement that the cloak bore on its right shoulder the four ermine slashes of his rank, which properly belonged only on a robe of state.

"Must you leave us so soon, Rivers?" Buckingham drawled from Rivers's chair. "I vow that though we're almost neighbors, it's been a long time since we last met."

"That it has, Your Grace. Too long, in fact. And how does my sister, your duchess?"

The duke's mask of cool civility crumbled at a breath. "Well enough, Rivers, I daresay. Well enough. But then that seems to be one of the outstanding characteristics of all your tribe. You always seem to do well for yourselves. You might try engraving it as a motto. It would go well on your coat of arms." He laughed then, a deep full-throated laugh that belied the hostility of his words. Rivers visibly eased, while Richard, giving his cousin a sharper look, wondered how the enforced marriage should still rankle him like a burr after all these years.

Rivers's reply was gentle. "I suppose there might be worse traits for a family to possess."

"Come, Anthony," Richard interrupted. "My cousin Buckingham is right about one thing, I think. It is far too early to end the evening. In fact, we would both consider it a grave breech of courtesy if you were to desert us now. Come, sit down. I heard the landlord say he was about to break out a hogshead of his best Bordeaux."

Rivers sat. The wine was served with a plate of almond cakes, and Buckingham and his retinue were brought the remains of the feast as the landlord stumbled all over himself at the privilege of waiting upon two dukes and an earl. The talk returned to lighter levels, effervescent, far above the dark valleys of doubt and suspicion.

Finally, when the wine was drunk and the plates emptied, Rivers stifled a polite yawn behind his hand and pushed back his chair. "The hour grows late, my lords, and I must be up betimes tomorrow. I think I had best find my own lodgings."

"We will be seeing you in the morning then, won't we?" asked Buckingham.

The earl hesitated. "I-I doubt it. I've promised Edward that I would join him at sunrise so that we might start for London."

"Join him?" questioned Buckingham, looking up from his plate. "Isn't the king with you then?"

"Why, no, my lord. He lies at Stony Stratford tonight."

Buckingham's knife clattered to the table. He opened his mouth to reply but was checked by a swift kick under the table from Richard's riding boot. And Rivers, obviously intending no more delay, slipped into the mantle held for him by one of his attendants. With a sweeping bow to the two dukes and a polite "God give Your Graces good rest," he was gone. The mist-wrapped night received him.

"And now," cried Buckingham, turning to Richard, "in the name of all that is holy, what is going on here?"

"I wish I knew, Harry."

Buckingham took the last almond cake from the plate and nibbled at it absently. Around them, the room had grown suddenly quiet. All chatter had ceased. Expectant faces turned to the dukes' table: Lovell, Tyrell, Ratcliffe, Assheton, Percy, Brackenbury, and the new arrival in their midst, William Percival.

"Why is the king at Stony Stratford," Buckingham asked, "when we are here?"

Richard shrugged. His fingers twirled the stem of an empty wine goblet. "Northampton, it seems, is too small to accommodate both us and the king."

Buckingham spat into the rushes. "Aye, and I'm sure if it were up to Rivers, England herself would be too small."

"Yes," Richard agreed, "I've thought the same thing."

"God's head!" Buckingham swore, suddenly incensed. "How these upstarts do tamper with the old blood royal of this realm! Do they take us for fools and japes?" That Buckingham considered himself part of "the old blood royal," he made no effort to conceal. The lining and sash of his black doublet were both royal purple; the badge worn on his sleeve carried the arms of his ancestor Thomas of Woodstock, youngest son of Edward III, quartered proudly with his own. He had requested this right of the late King Edward, and it had been granted. Yet for all of his pretensions, Richard warmed to him. He was in some ways like a spoiled wanton boy who could still be utterly charming at need.

"I don't think Rivers is entirely to blame," Richard said. "He seemed almost embarrassed. No, I think he acted in haste and on specific orders from London."

Buckingham laughed at that, a rich, husky bellow. "So even Rivers performs hugger-mugger at the queen's command. Still it's hardly to be wondered at. Have you heard what's going on in London?"

"I've heard some things from Hastings."

"Then I'll wager you have not heard all. The Woodvilles are aiming to get him in their pocket."

Now it was Richard's turn to laugh. "What rot! It can't be done. Hastings despises the sight of 'em. He would have me storm London with an army to be rid of them."

"Would he indeed? But surely I heard they had named him to head seven of their tax commissions."

"You are suggesting he can be bought?"

"No, no," Buckingham replied. "Why should I speak ill of him? To be frank, I hardly know the man. I only say that the Woodvilles are everywhere, that their power and influence are spreading to places as yet unguessed at. Only yesterday, I heard rumors that they are nibbling at the royal coffers like mice at a cheese. And there is no doubt that they are issuing decrees in the name of the 'queen regent,' and . . . ah yes, 'uterine brother' and 'uterine uncle' of the king."

"The 'uterine uncle'—that would, of course, be Rivers?"

"Of course. He may have been far from London, but they've obviously kept him well informed of what transpires there."

"I would have sworn an oath he was honest."

"Yet the king lies at Stony Stratford tonight, fourteen miles nearer to London."

"And moves still nearer at first light."

"Tell me, my lord, though you've been named protector of the king, do you think they mean to let you near enough to lay one finger on their sacred whelp? Do you think they would hesitate to slay you if you tried?"

"It-it would appear not."

The words were uttered with a creeping sense of finality. Gone for good was the mellow bubble of intimacy, blown of the wine and ale, with which Richard had entertained Rivers. Gone as well was the hope for a peaceful settlement with the Woodvilles. They were revealed as they had always been, the foul murderers of Clarence and his own sworn enemies. And Rivers, with whom he had broken bread and shared a cup, was a liar, albeit he lied most charmingly, albeit he lied almost innocently. He stood among them; indeed, he stood in their front ranks.

They had murdered Clarence, murdered him for reasons that were shrouded in mystery and were still unguessed at. Would they scruple to murder Gloucester, who was now a direct obstacle in their path to power? It could not be. He must not let it happen.

"They must be stopped," Richard muttered aloud. "We must stop them."

Chapter 8

IN THE DARKNESS well before dawn, Richard knew some regrets. He had slept badly, risen early, and was now being dressed and shaven with unaccustomed haste. He would have liked also to hear mass, but there was no time for that. Buckingham, straining and eager as a racehorse at the gate, had urged him to hurry. And Richard Ratcliffe had burst into his chambers shortly thereafter to announce that the Earl Rivers had risen and wished to depart for Stony Stratford.

"Does he now?" Richard asked as he tore the barber's cloth from his neck and wiped away the last flecks of lather from his chin. "What answer did you give him, Rich?"

"Why, none, except that Your Grace begged leave to have a word with him before he left."

"Good man!" Richard said, laying a hand briefly on Ratcliffe's buff liveried shoulder. Painful as it might be, he felt it was his personal duty to break the news to Rivers that he would be riding nowhere that day.

He had not looked forward to this meeting, and as he and Buckingham clattered beneath the arch of the Golden Bull, he felt positively wretched. His men were everywhere; the yard was bright with torch flame shining haloed through the mist. Anthony Woodville stepped out from the center of them, for once ruffled and indignant as a turkey cock.

"My lord protector," he called, "what's the meaning of this . . . this outrage? Your men here are keeping me from joining the king. Surely there must be some mistake."

"No, Rivers, there's no mistake. I think you know well enough what it means. When you play a game for high stakes, you must be prepared to lose everything on a roll of the dice."

An uneasy laugh rumbled in Rivers's throat. "But Your Grace knows that I'm not a gambling man. I know nothing of this game of which you speak."

"Don't you, Anthony?" Richard asked softly. "Don't you really?"

Rivers stood silent as the gray dawn crept over the courtyard. The bells of St. Andrew's Abbey tolled for lauds, distant and piercing sweet. Nearer by a rooster crowed, then a thrush chirped from a thicket. All around them, the nesting birds took up their morning chants.

"I meant you no harm—you must believe that." Rivers's voice was barely audible over the chorus of birdsong.

"If keeping me from what is mine by right is not doing me harm, then I might agree with you," Richard said, more harshly than he had intended.

Anthony Woodville shook his head. His face was drawn and tired, and he looked every one of his forty-four years. "I did what seemed best to me at the time."

"Though it doesn't seem so wise now, does it, Rivers?" Buckingham asked, triumphant. When the earl ignored him, he looked to the torches paling in the growing light. "The hour grows late," he reminded Richard. "We must be off to Stony Stratford."

Rivers stepped nearer at that and laid a gloved hand on the bridle of Richard's horse. "One thing only I ask of you, my lord. One boon, if you will. The king expects me today. I know him. I know how distressed he will be that I am . . . uh . . . detained. Please be gentle with him. I would not have him alarmed for the world."

"I have no intention of alarming him, Rivers," Richard replied, more shaken than he cared to admit by the pleading look in the earl's gray eyes. More sharply, he added, "He is my nephew, you may recall, as well as your own."

They turned then toward the street, the horses weary of waiting, neighing and anxious for the ride. Behind Richard and Buckingham rode their nine hundred men, save for those who were left behind to guard the earl. They were nine hundred men riding to meet two thousand—a great black congregation, a congregation of crows flying swiftly into the dawn.

The narrow high street of Stony Stratford bristled with men and wagons. At first, Richard was glad simply for the sight of them; he had feared that, sensing danger in the earl's delay, one of his subordinates might have already given the order to march. Obviously, the king's train had been packed and ready to leave for some time. Mules and baggage wagons were piled high. A number of attendants, grown bored with the wait, diced on the cobbles or lounged in the doorframes of inns, sharing a parting cup.

Richard advanced toward them under the protective covering of the fog. A few of the men looked up from their gaming with curious, sullen stares as he passed. Welsh they were by the look of them, with sooty hair and eyes. Paid mercenaries, no doubt, pressed hastily into service. So much the better. Buckingham's finger pointed out the gleam of cold metal between the leather strappings.

"Weapons, my lord, and harness. All stamped with the Woodville arms. Didn't I warn you that their business was bloody?"

"Let's hope they have no opportunity to use them," Richard replied. "We shall show them no cause—yet."

Carefully, they threaded their way down the narrow street, under the protruding gables of the houses that lined it. At the head of the procession, his eyes straining back up the Northampton Road, sat the boy king, mounted on his pony and richly clad in marten and velvet.

"There he is!" Richard heard the shrill, boyish cry through the mist. "There is our uncle now."

"He's right about that, at any rate," Buckingham muttered beneath his breath. "Here are two uncles for His Grace—though not, I warrant, the one he hoped to see."

Richard's eyes swept over the scene. He could discern the banners of Lord Richard Grey and Sir Thomas Vaughan next to the king's and, a little further removed, that of Sir Richard Haute, a Woodville cousin. He searched for a friendly face in all that company, and his eyes lighted only on John Alcock, bishop of Worcester. Only one friend he could trust among so many foes!

The look of disappointment on Edward's face as Richard dismounted and stepped toward him cut deep. "My uncle of Gloucester . . . and of Buckingham! What are you doing here? We did not expect to see you today."

Richard had fixed in his mind during the long ride south how he would greet Edward and what he would say. Now as he fell to his knees on the damp cobbles and kissed the furred hem of the king's gown, the well-rehearsed speech of homage and fealty, of consolation and service, sounded stiff and hollow even to his own ears. And Edward, it seemed, was not listening at all.

"Yes, yes, of course," the boy replied with an airy wave of his hand. "Only tell us, Uncle, you rode from Northampton, did you not? Did you see our Uncle Rivers on the road? He went there yesterday to meet you."

Richard drew a heavy breath. "Yes, sire. We have seen him. He remains behind."

"But . . . I don't understand. He was to join us here before prime so that we could start for London."

"Aye," said Buckingham, "with much undue haste, if I may say so."

Edward's voice cracked with fear. "What are you talking about? I cannot abide riddles. Speak plainly."

"I deeply regret, sire, that my news is so painful," said Richard. "Your Uncle Rivers is under arrest."

"Arrest?" Edward cried. "But why? For what crime?"

"Because he has conspired to keep the governance of the realm from its lawful ruler."

"But I am the lawful ruler!" Edward protested. "I am the king."

"So you are, sire," Alcock said, placing a soothing hand on the boy's shoulder. "None will dispute that, least of all these two good dukes. Listen to them now, and let them explain. Haven't I taught you that things are not always as they seem?"

Edward turned to Alcock and seemed to find some reassurance in the tutor's kindly, familiar face. Around him, his Woodville kin pressed closer as if to shield him from Gloucester and his black-gowned men of the north.

"Speak, Uncle, for we are most anxious to hear," Edward commanded, slightly imperious now.

"My liege, it is certain that you are your father's undoubted heir. Had he lived to see you grown to manhood, none of this would have been necessary. I regret that . . ." Richard's voice grew thick, halted, went on. "I regret it more than I can tell you. Nevertheless, on his deathbed, your father in his wisdom felt it necessary to appoint me as your protector to guard you and guide you until you are old enough to govern for yourself."

Edward's mouth gaped open.

Buckingham asked, "Has no one told Your Grace of this?"

He shook his head, slowly and disbelievingly, and looked at Grey and Vaughan, who lowered their eyes and would not meet his gaze. "Nay, no one. But what of it? I shall soon have leave to choose my own advisors."

"Or so, madam, your mother had hoped," Buckingham said. "She and her son the marquis have conspired in every way possible to thwart your father's will. They rule in their own names. They have illegally appropriated your father's treasury and portion it out among themselves. They have completely disregarded the will of your protector. In all these things, they wrong your fair realm of England."

Two large tears slid down the boy's cheeks to be awkwardly wiped away on his sleeve. "What my mother and my brother the marquis have done, I cannot say, but I know that my Uncle Rivers is innocent of these charges."

"Naturally," said Buckingham, "for he has kept his dealings in these matters far from Your Grace."

"Peace, cousin," Richard said, seeing the growing anxiety in Edward's pinched face. "There is no need to speak so harshly." He took the king's hand in both his own and felt it as cold and flaccid between his palms as a lily petal. "Your Grace, I know that it's most painful to hear those who nurtured you from the cradle branded thieves and traitors. I know, for it happened to me when I was only a little older than you are now. Earl Warwick, whom I loved as a father, turned treacherous and rose in armed rebellion against my brother Edward. In truth, I thought my heart would split in two and half go to each. It could not be, of course. I had to choose between them just as you must choose now.

"You must think first of the stability and security of your kingdom, and try to understand what would happen if your mother's family managed everything to their liking. They have always wielded too much power, even in your father's time, seeking to distract him by revelry and riotous living. In that, they succeeded only too well. Now they grasp at opportunities undreamt of and think to play hoodman's blind with the rightful rulers of this land. I tell you that by the blood of our blessed Lord, it shall not be!"

He had intended to speak gently, soothingly, but righteous indignation, festering for years, had poured out of him in a veritable torrent, unbidden and unchecked. Helpless, he watched the swift recoil in Edward's eyes, watched as he withdrew his hand in distaste and wiped it on the fur of his cloak.

The boy's voice came sharp as ice. "We would not have you speak ill of our father nor of those he placed near us for our guidance even if you were twenty times our uncle. In all things, we trust our Uncle Rivers, our brothers Dorset and Grey and our mother, the queen, who it is fitting should be regent during our minority."

"But . . . a woman, sire?" Buckingham questioned, anger flaring. "A woman to rule? Certainly they have no place in the councils of the great, these flighty creatures God made only for adornment and child-bearing. No woman shall rule this land, not while Harry Buckingham draws a breath and certainly not that black-biled sorceress besotted Edward saw fit to make his queen!"

"Speak no ill of the queen!" Sir Thomas Vaughan stepped forward with dangerous suddenness from the ranks of the Woodvilles, fire flashing in his eyes and a sword brandishing in his hand. "Speak no ill of our sovereign lady, or I'll cut your vitals from you here where you stand. Come, men! Are you going to stand there like dumb show puppets and listen to these insults? After them, I say. Have at these dukes!"

Later, Richard would wonder how a pitched, open battle had been avoided that day and why the gutters of Stony Stratford had not run red with blood. He would recall the dark mutterings in the Woodville ranks, the ominous rattlings and scrapings among them as men reached for dagger and sword. Yet all the while, the vast majority stood in apparent indecision, eyes shifting from Richard to Sir Thomas and back again. These were the Welsh, the hired men, men who did not care enough for the Woodvilles to fight for them or who perhaps would not have fought at all in the absence of a strong leader. Anthony Woodville, gallant soldier and champion of many jousts, might have commanded them with sheer personal magnetism; Thomas Vaughan, graybeard that he was, could not.

Richard's eyes flashed on a Welshman in the front rank, a slender reed of a man with strength in his wiry body and intense black-fringed eyes. His hand still rested on his scabbard.

"You there," Richard called, his voice ringing a challenge. "Will you also lift your sword against the rightful protector of the realm?

The man stepped forward slowly with every eye on him.

"What is your name?" Richard asked him. "And where are you from?"

"I am Robin Vaughan from Breconshire."

Beside him, Buckingham gave an audible gasp. Richard held up a restraining hand to forestall any further outburst, but his eyes never left the younger man's face.

"Are you by any chance kin to Sir Roger Vaughan?"

"He is my father."

Richard's face relaxed in a half smile. "I remember him well from my days as governor of the marches. A most valiant knight. How does he?"

"Still alive though the hardships of many winters sit ill on him."

"I'm sorry to hear it. He did me good service once. God grant he has more cause for rejoicing from now on."

"So I hope too," the younger man replied, "though I see scant hope of it when men who are alien to Wales gobble up lands we have held for centuries." He turned on Buckingham a look of withering hatred.

The duke's hand itched toward his sword hilt. "Cotsbody! Why do we stand here and parley with this hill ruffian? It's time and past to settle the matter."

"For once, His Grace of Buckingham speaks true," came old Sir Thomas's crackling reply. He lunged at Richard, sword hand outstretched, naked point menacingly near. Behind him, Richard Grey and Richard Haute plunged into the breach along with a few, a very few, others. It was soon over. Old Vaughan was unarmed by Francis Lovell who, ignoring his years, embraced him with a firm grip. His sword clattered uselessly to the cobbles. Robert Percy had taken Grey with a stranglehold around the neck and held him panting and sweating like a young stag at bay. Haute and the others—aware of the looming presence of Ralph Assheton, Robert Brackenbury, and James Tyrell—came to an abrupt, unhappy halt. Even the king's household knights looked fearfully askance at the black-robed host that stood at the protector's back.

And the Welsh—the unfathomable, unpredictable Welsh—turned quickly away from the small scuffle as if it meant nothing at all. They still awaited the outcome of young Vaughan's encounter with Richard. The pale sun of morning, breaking through clouds for the first time that day, shot a beam of light that irradiated the two men.

Richard's voice was low and steady. "I have no quarrel with you nor with any man here except those who would keep from me what is mine by law and right."

Still Vaughan hesitated, his eyes flicking back and forth from Richard to Buckingham as if measuring dawning respect for the one against his long-held hostility toward the other. The moment was delicate. The man was a natural leader, and the Welsh might well follow him if he chose to offer battle.

"Come, sir," Richard said. "Won't you believe me?"

The hand fell from the scabbard. "You need not 'sir' me. I am no knight."

"Then perhaps you should be. You have about you the look of one."

The slate-gray eyes caught Richard's and held, flickering with a grim amusement. "Isn't it strange then that a moment ago I was a hill ruffian?"

"My cousin spoke in anger. You are more than that, I think. Far more."

"Perhaps." He gave him a brittle laugh. "You may keep your knighthood. I don't want it while my country lies in subjection. My father had his in happier times, but I think that even he is sorry for it now. Although others who bear our name may think it high honor . . . and shame the clan of Vaughan." A volley of curses erupted from Sir Thomas and split the air between them, but the younger Vaughan made no response.

"I've never been one to fight battles I don't believe in nor to stand in the way of justice when it is clear," he went on. "If you wish to take custody of yon puling lad, Robin Vaughan will not stand in your way."

Rising higher than Sir Thomas's cries of "Traitor!" and "Felon!" came a general sigh of relief, both from the ranks of Welshmen, who like their young leader had neither the heart nor the will to fight for an English cause on English soil, and from Richard's attendants, who knew themselves hopelessly outnumbered had the Welsh pressed their case.

Richard watched Robin Vaughan's retreating figure with unfeigned admiration. "A pity. I could have used him in my household. Such men are rare."

"Aye, but not rare enough," Buckingham muttered. "A pox take him! Last spring, I found three score sheep and twenty cattle dead on Brecknock lands with Vaughan arrows protruding from them. But it wasn't for that I would have taken him to task today but because he showed no deference to Your Grace. Did you not think him overbold? He's little better than a savage. You're better off to see the back of that one, my lord."

"Still, I wonder . . . He has given us the day in any case, and for that, we should all be grateful. And now it's high time to see to the king."

Except for Bishop Alcock, the King of England sat on his pony quite alone. Thomas Vaughan, Grey, and Haute were all in custody, and the other members of the royal household had been dispersed lest they too prove belatedly treacherous. Edward's face was hard as stone without even the softening presence of tears. His blue-green eyes, like marbles, fell coldly on Richard. Here was a much more difficult battle to be won.

"Edward . . ." he began, "sire . . ." He lifted a hand toward the boy's shoulder then let it drop. "Don't think that this action threatens you . . . or your crown. We move only against the enemies of that crown."

"We never thought them our enemies, Uncle. If you have made them yours, we are right sorry for it."

"It was not I who made them so, Your Grace. Look at the wagons that accompanied your escort. What do you think they contain?"

Edward shrugged. "My household goods, I deem. We kept a great estate at Ludlow."

"That's what they told you, but what they did not tell you was that many of these wagons are crammed with weapons and harness to be used against me."

Edward's eyes pierced him through. "Then isn't it strange that they failed to use them?"

Richard would have answered that it was only because Anthony Woodville had not chosen his men carefully enough for their treasonable task that they had not been used, then thought better of it. Bishop Alcock's face was unusually solemn and creased with a frown.

"His Grace is under a great deal of strain," the bishop said, "and I believe it would be best to leave this place where so much—" He stopped abruptly, turning bright pink. "Do we ride for London today?"

Richard considered this thoughtfully. He had not really prepared for what would happen after the king was in his custody. "No," he said finally. "No, I don't think so. We'll return to Northampton, where His Highness can be more comfortably lodged than here. I think it best to await news of how these events have settled on the capital."

"Won't we be in London before Sunday?" Edward whined. "It was to be my coronation day."

Richard shook his head sadly. "No, sire, not this Sunday. But it will be soon, very soon. I promise you that."

Edward sniffed into his sleeve and turned away, even as Alcock threw a sheltering arm around him. Grooms brought the two dukes their horses: Richard's White Surrey and Buckingham's huge black destrier Saladin, richly trapped with gold. They mounted and took Watling Street northwest out of Stony Stratford, away from London. The king, on his bay pony, was a small and most unhappy figure between them.

Chapter 9

ELIZABETH WOODVILLE WAS not ordinarily given to hysteria. Few men had ever seen her either scream or weep. Yet in the first hours after one of the king's loyal knights had brought her news of the day's events from Stony Stratford, she had felt herself walking a dangerous knife edge between reason and insanity.

She had been in her bedchamber at Westminster Palace, clad only in a nightshift, as a tiring woman brushed out the long gilt hair that shimmered like a waterfall to her slender thighs. Without warning, the tall doors had burst open, and a young man she did not recognize was on his knees before her. Words of harsh reproach died on her lips.

"Highness, Highness!" he had cried. "Treachery, most foul treachery!" His tale was enough to chill the blood: Anthony taken and young Dick—brother and son in the protector's clutches—and, worst of all, most deadly of all, Edward.

The palace had rocked with instant pandemonium. Pages, squires, and yeomen men-at-arms had sprung from the woodwork and been pressed hastily into service. Dorset too had come, finally, nostrils flaring in irritation at having been torn untimely from the embraces of Mistress Shore. Irritation turned swiftly to indignation as she explained the situation.

"Cock's muddy bones!" he exploded. "Didn't we tell that mulish lot of a council that this would happen? Those treasonous Welsh! Cursed be the day that we listened to council or to your brother, madam. We should have sent armies of our own and men who knew how to fight."

"No doubt Anthony has cause to regret his leniency now, Thomas. But enough of recriminations. What are we to do?"

Apparently, there was little they could do. Thomas dressed quickly and carelessly—his hose bagged at the knee, an imperfection unheard of in him—and left the palace. When he returned less than an hour later, just as the great clock in the tower boomed eleven, his shoulders also sagged, and his face told of a singular lack of success at rallying support to their cause.

By that time, the queen was already establishing herself in sanctuary in the abbot's palace across the Strand. She had roused her younger children from their beds and cossetted them as long as she dared. Their sleepy eyes spoke their confusion. Only Bess, who was seventeen and the eldest of her five daughters, could remember another night like this one when the last King Edward had fled before Warwick's onslaught and the queen, heavy with child, had taken to sanctuary. There she had given birth to England's heir, who was now himself King Edward and who had himself been captured.

Fortune's wheel turns heavily, she thought. *I have been a long time on top, but now comes my fall.*

She felt a certain weariness calm the rising tide of panic. What use to run, what use to fight? Why not stay and await her ultimate fate? But the thought of her black-visaged brother-in-law of Gloucester ended any such considerations. Beneath the outward courtesies that marked their infrequent correspondence, she well knew that he had just cause to hate her. And her other brother-in-law of Buckingham, he too hated her, more violently though with less cause. No, she could never allow herself and Edward's remaining heirs to fall into the hands of these vengeful dukes.

It was difficult to explain this to Bess, whose heart was as gentle as her beauty. "But why, madam, why must we flee like felons?" she questioned, gesturing to the growing turmoil about her. Gentlemen ushers and men-at-arms had suddenly become sumpters, clattering down the palace stairs, their backs straining under trunks and chests and coffers. One tore his rich mulberry livery on a doornail and emitted a violent curse, heedless of the queen and princess. Across the street, a giant hole gaped in the masonry of Abbot Eastney's great hall, where battering rams had been used to speed the transfer of the queen's property.

Elizabeth was caught off guard by the simplicity of the question. She looked strangely at her daughter, at the pale oval face with its high Plantagenet cheekbones, at the wide-spaced eyes the clear blue of cornflowers, at the fall of bright hair that was closer to Edward's gold than to her own extraordinary gilt. Yes, there was more of her husband in this eldest daughter than of herself.

"Why?" she parroted. "You ask me why?"

"Yes, madam. I know my uncle of Gloucester well, and he's not at all a bad sort—certainly not a man from whom to flee."

"Are you that naive, Bess? Ah, yes, you probably recall a kindly uncle who used to dandle you on his knee and listen to your childish prattle. The case is far different now, I assure you."

"My father loved him," Bess said, obstinate.

"No doubt, as one loves a cur which can still snap and bite. It doesn't matter now in any case. Your father is in his grave, and your mother bears Gloucester little love, nor he her. There's bad blood between us, Bess. Does it mean nothing to you that he has taken your own brother prisoner? Do you think he'll scruple over the rest of us?"

"Edward, prisoner?" The girl's eyes widened. "I heard it not so."

"Enough!" Elizabeth exclaimed, a shrill edge of imperious wrath creeping into her voice. "It's enough that I tell you so. Don't question me further."

Bess fled then, blinking back anguished tears. The rest of the children accepted their mother's wisdom without question, only being grateful, once carried across the street, to find their beds again. But one she kept with her: little Dickon, Duke of York, her only other son by Edward and now England's heir. Some instinct, political as well as maternal, told her to shield him closely.

Sleep was far from her in the abbot's palace of Westminster as that long, desperate night wore on. At last, she sank down in a corner of the hall on one of the many chests that had been stashed there and where her youngest son dozed. There was some satisfaction in looking down on the downy, drowsy head that now lay in her lap, more satisfaction in watching the porters unload their heavy burdens—trunks heavy with plate, chests bulging with gold and jewels, and coffers full of coin.

It was small compensation, however, for what she had been forced to abandon. She might still have many of her children with her and riches enough to keep her in a state of luxury for the rest of her days, but power she had lost. Of that, she had been most grievously cheated and robbed. She kicked a silken toe at the fetid rushes at her feet. What good were riches to one who now, even if by her own choice, was little more than a prisoner?

She had no supporters. Even Abbot Eastney, forced by the laws of the church to grant sanctuary to any felon or vagabond who entered his enclosure, had barely managed to conceal his outrage at the damage done to his fine wall. He openly resented her intrusion and had stomped off to bed, muttering dark curses. He would not have dared to treat her thus if she were still truly the queen and not some discredited dowager.

Oh, it would go ill for them all, her and her family. They would be universally despised now that they had no more favors to grant. And she, Queen of England, would finish out her days in this cramped pigsty, living on the reluctant sufferance of a church she had once almost controlled. God's curses on Gloucester! She balled her fists tightly at her sides as unaccustomed tears of anger and self-pity slid down her cheeks unchecked.

"Pray, lady, do not weep."

She looked up into the lined, weathered countenance of Thomas Rotherham, into milky-blue eyes that stared at her in anguished disbelief. The archbishop of York had come to her in her extremity. He sank stiffly to the rushes as she held out her hand for his kiss.

"I would not weep, Your Excellency, but the cause is grievous." Then she said more softly, "I am grateful you have come. My other comforters have fled, it seems."

Rotherham blinked hard. Tiny lines crinkled like a mesh around his eyes. "Fled, Your Highness?"

"Aye, like birds in winter, they seek a warmer clime—no doubt in Gloucester's presence."

"Then they are turncoats—treacherous, most treacherous! There should have been an army to defend you."

"That was what I sought. Don't you remember? But the council . . . Lord Hastings's faction voted it down. Even Morton did not think it necessary. Where is he now, I wonder?"

Rotherham shook his craggy head. The light of a taper flickered on his bald pate. "That I cannot say. It was Lord Hastings's man who came to me tonight. He told me that all would soon be well."

The queen laughed at that—a cold, bitter laugh. "And so it will, for him and his ilk. He has always been an enemy to me and my blood. I don't doubt he is in league with the dukes and has been all the while. What will happen now to me and mine?"

Rotherham was silent for a time, apparently trying to fashion words of hope or comfort. His gaze fell on the sleeping prince, and his look brightened. "But you must be of good cheer, lady, for if they crown any king other than your son, whom they have with them, we shall on the morrow crown his brother, whom you have with you here."

Elizabeth smiled tolerantly at this foolishness though it once again raised the terrible specter of usurpation. "I hope that will not be necessary, my lord."

"Yes, of course, madam. I didn't mean that we take the crown from our fair young sovereign, may God preserve and strengthen him in this ordeal. But it is well to remember that we have something left of value despite these dukes."

Elizabeth hugged the sleeping body closer to her breast. "The same thought has occurred to me."

Rotherham's voice dropped to a confidential tone. "And, my lady, I have here another thing of value, an' it please Your Grace." So saying, he dropped into her hand the great seal of England.

This was divine foolishness indeed! She started to say, "But I can't use this here. What decrees with my name on them will be obeyed now though gilded with fifty great seals?" Then as she looked once more into the archbishop's face, where the frost of many winters was warmed by a smile, the words would not come. He stood before her like a faithful dog that had performed a new trick for its mistress and expected praise in return. Another thought came to her as well: wouldn't the disappearance of the seal cause Gloucester some minor inconvenience at the least?

"My dear lord," she said at last, "I am speechless." Gently, she took his veined age-spotted hand into her own and kissed the emerald of his arch-episcopal ring. It was a mark of deference Rotherham had seldom known from her, and he left her presence well content, still smiling his foolish smile.

Some time later, she shifted the sleeping burden from her lap and went to the window. Pale gray was beginning to streak the sky. The Thames flowed by, the color of lead in the early light, and on its waves rode many small boats. Although it was still too dark to see clearly, she wondered whose flags they flew and what they were doing there. Could they be Gloucester's ships sent to guard her sanctuary and, at the same time, prevent her brother Edward from returning upriver to attack London? They had grown strong in a short time, her enemies, and they would show her no mercy. Yet she felt less totally bereft than she had before.

Old, doddering and ineffectual as he might be, Rotherham had still had the courage to seek her here. Others would come; she was certain of it. Others would follow where he had led.

She clutched the great seal of England tightly in her hand.

She had only to wait.

Chapter 10

Hastings had been dreaming of Jane Shore. He awoke, stretching his arms toward the empty side of the bed, toward her imagined warmth and softness. A delicious fire flickered in his loins, leaving him weak but unfulfilled. He rolled over with a groan and opened his eyes to see Catesby's face peering between the bed curtains.

"My lord, it's gone eight, and there's much to be done today."

Hastings stretched, yawned, and sat up in the bed. The softness of feather mattresses surrounded him, but the tiny fire was momentarily doused. Yes, he remembered now. How could he have forgotten? Last night, very late, Sir Richard Ratcliffe had come pounding on his door with glorious news. The whole city of London had throbbed with it. Bonfires burned in the streets, and crowds of cheering citizens roamed about, heedless of the night watchmen.

He opened his eyes in earnest now, throwing his naked legs over the edge of the bed. "What news this morning? Where are the Woodvilles?"

"Fled like rats to their holes, as I heard it. The queen has gone into sanctuary at Westminster, she and her younger children . . . and the marquis as well."

Hastings's tongue flicked quickly over his lips. "The marquis, you say? Dorset in sanctuary? It's more than I could have hoped."

"Yes, though it's said he attempted to raise an army and met with scant success. The tide has turned against them this time."

Hastings stood while two attendants helped him into an apricot dressing gown. The whisper of silk was soft against his skin.

"And Jane Shore? What of her?"

Catesby frowned slightly. "The Mistress Shore? Why I have heard naught of her. If she went with Dorset into sanctuary, none spoke of it."

Hastings rubbed his plump, bejeweled hands together in satisfaction. "Ah, Catesby, you bring me good tidings indeed, very good. It's the first of May, isn't it?" Moted sunlight danced through mullioned windows. On Moorfields, outside the city, there would be a maypole, and the young would be dancing and gathering flowers for wreaths, making vows and breaking them. "I may be too old for such sport," he said aloud, "but I'll have my turn at wooing before the day is over."

"If I may remind you, my lord, the day is far from over. Half London awaits you below. I took the liberty of telling them that you would speak to them shortly about yesterday's events in Stony Stratford."

"Have they come for an explanation, do you think?"

Catesby nodded. "For explanation or to show support for Gloucester. Though none would dare not show it today."

Catesby watched with visible impatience as ushers and pages came into the bedchamber, bearing basins and ewers of hot scented water and piles of linen towels. He saw with disbelief that they were setting up the bathing tent, on today of all days.

"The first of the month, you will recall," Hastings said, smiling at his discomfiture. "It is a ritual with me and one I don't wish to dispense with today. Besides, it will give me a chance to clear the cobwebs from my brain. You will allow me that, Will, won't you?" He dipped his big toe into the tub, stirring the water with his foot.

"Why, yes, my lord, of course," Catesby replied as the scents of rosewater, lavender, and balsam mingled with the steam that filled the bedchamber.

"So . . . half London, you say?" Hasting asked from behind the curtains. A page, a pretty pouting boy of twelve, poured a stream of water down his back.

"Yes," Catesby answered. "Beginning with the lord mayor himself."

"Master Shaw?"

"In the flesh, and his brother—"

"Friar Ralph? Excellent, most excellent!" Hastings clapped his hands together in delight.

"A goodly representation of aldermen as well."

"The Woodvilles were roundly hated. I knew it!"

"Some surprises too, I might add. Lord Lisle for one."

"The queen's own brother-in-law? Go to, man, go to!"

"No, it's true. I swear it on a finger bone of St. Jude. And itching to be of service to his noble grace of Gloucester."

"Aye, and no doubt itching to save his pretty skin as well."

"No doubt. And then there is Morton."

"Morton?" Hastings sat up so suddenly that a wave of water lapped over the sides of the wooden tub, soaking into the fine Turkey carpet. Another page scurried to clean it up. "Tell me, Catesby, what did he have to say for himself?"

"Very little, actually. He turned up on the doorstep quite early this morning, though not so early as to be conspicuous. He acted as though he had always belonged there."

"The scoundrel!" Hastings said, though not without a grudging affection. "Still, you have to admire him for all that. He seldom gets so deeply embroiled in the plots of one party that he cannot leap to the other at need. No fly in treacle is our Morton!"

"No," Catesby agreed, "though he may have had some difficulty this time deciding which way to jump. There was many a light burning at Ely Place last night."

"Oh, yes," Hastings said, resting once more complacently against the sponges that lined the tub. "What of your midnight venture? What of Rotherham? Is he among our guests today?"

Catesby hesitated before answering. He had been sent last night on what seemed an easy mission—to soothe the lord chancellor's fears and win him to their cause. Rotherham would be old, soft, and malleable, would he not? He would crumble at a touch, like rose petals falling apart. He had found petals of steel that would not open, let alone crumble.

"Well?" Hastings asked.

"He was not overjoyed at the change in leadership," Catesby said at last.

"And didn't you try to placate him, make him listen to reason?"

"Yes, my lord, I did, but he will have none of Gloucester, and that's the fact of it. He is so old and feeble. I doubt his opinion counts for much in any case."

"Maybe not, but he is still the lord chancellor, and I'd rather he were for us than against us. I would have him . . . gently led. Ah well, perhaps in time. And meanwhile, we are triumphant. All things are ours!"

Catesby watched, a little embarrassed, as his benefactor was toweled, shaven, pomaded, and dressed in a doublet of black brocade with royal-blue facings. When it was done, Hastings surveyed himself in the gilt-edged mirror with a critical eye, but Catesby knew it was not concern for the nobles and commons downstairs that furrowed his brow. Hastings ran a hand through his thinning brown hair threaded with silver, noted the puffiness under his eyes, the thickened girth of his waist.

"Do you think I look old, Catesby? I am fifty-three, you know. Somehow, it never seemed to matter before this."

"Old, my lord? I would not say so," he answered. "You have many good years left, years to enjoy health, power, riches—"

"And love. Don't forget that. It's all no good without that. Though if I may say so, the old hammer still rings sweetly in the forge. Sweeter yet may it ring tonight." His eyes strayed wistfully to the disheveled bed as if he already imagined her there.

"The people await you, my lord."

"Ah, yes, the people. Good citizens of London. I mustn't keep them waiting too long." He gave a little lovelorn sigh and went out.

"Edward's treasure has vanished from the Tower." Howard's voice came to Hastings from a long way off. He watched as the steward ladled pungent galantine over a trencher of fresh bread, but his thoughts were elsewhere, far removed from his own hall, where he played reluctant host to those of the great and noble classes who had chosen to stay through the dinner hour.

It had gone quite well that morning. With Ratcliffe beside him, he had spoken with an eloquence he had not known he possessed. He had even drawn laughter and applause when, holding up his little finger for the crowd's inspection, he announced that Richard of Gloucester had achieved his ends without spilling as much blood as would flow from a cut finger—this to stifle mutterings that perhaps the arrest of Rivers had not been entirely necessary.

He knew who the mutterers were: Lord Lisle, who sat at a lower table (having indulged himself on Hastings's hospitality, he now wiped daintily at his mouth with a linen napkin); Sir Thomas St. Leger, who sat next to him, husband to Richard's eldest sister, Anne, Dowager Duchess of Exeter (low and mean of appearance, he tended to comport himself like the duke he was not); and lastly, Bishop Russell, although he had not muttered his doubts but spoken them aloud.

He spoke again now, answering Howard, "Are you certain?"

"As certain as can be. I stopped at the Tower this morning before coming here. Sir Edward Woodville, we know—or strongly suspect—took some of it with him when he sailed, but now a mouse could find no refuge in the treasury storeroom."

"But that's outright thievery!" Russell cried.

Hastings could not resist a gentle jibe. "What do you think now, Russell, of your fine Woodville friends?"

Unflinching, Russell returned Hastings's look with a steady gaze. "They are no friends of mine, my lord, as you should well know. I didn't mean to defend them. Neither do I wish to see my friend Gloucester commit an illegal act in search of his just goals. The words I said had to be spoken—if not by me, by someone less friendly to his cause. Would you have preferred that?"

"N-no. You speak, and spoke, rightly as always. But we stray from the issue. What is to be done? Where do we look now for what has been taken, and how do we recover it?"

Morton stroked his chin thoughtfully. "As to your first question, William, I believe that I may provide some clue. Though if what I suspect is true, there may well be no answer to the second. You have probably noted Rotherham's absence from the assembly today."

"That's scarcely surprising," said Stanley. "A Woodville diehard to the last. The queen bought him long ago. But surely you don't mean to imply . . ."

"No, of course not," Morton replied. "Not directly, at any rate, for though he has access, he lacks the cunning. No, he is not our thief though, unwittingly, I believe he has seen the treasure—seen it only last night or rather very early this morning."

"What are you talking about, Morton?" Russell demanded.

Morton wiped a piece of lark pasty from his nether lip for effect; his small gimlet eyes held them all. "He has called upon the queen in sanctuary, or so he said when I visited him this morning."

"Indeed?" Hastings asked, newly alarmed. "By the saints!" His eyes sought Catesby, who sat at one of the lower tables. Had his mission gone completely awry then?

"Oh, dear me," Morton said, misunderstanding or pretending to. "Surely I did not mean to implicate myself in any such . . . unwarranted acts as poor Rotherham may be guilty of. I assure you that my visit was intended merely to win him over to the protector's cause."

"Aye," Howard said beneath his breath so that only Hastings could hear. "Now that cause is won."

"I needn't tell you that I had no success," Morton continued. "In truth, he railed at me, called me a traitor and a turncoat and a few less savory names before he gave me the boot. Very glad I was to leave too. Terribly stuffy place, York House. Cockroaches in the rushes fat as eunuchs." Morton gave a repulsed shudder before he continued. "But where was I? Oh yes. He told me he went to the queen as soon as he learned the news. A very great bustle, he described too. The abbot's palace won't be the same for some time, I fear. A queen has many belongings, no doubt, but what, may I ask, was she so anxious to have stowed safely away that she effected a few unneeded alterations to expedite her ends? The answer to that question is obvious, I believe."

"God's nails!" cried Hastings, bringing a fist down on the table. "So both she and it are beyond our grasp. And both right here in London under our very noses."

"But a fact, nonetheless," Russell said. "You were not considering a breach of sanctuary were you, my lord?"

Hastings's mouth twitched in impotent rage. "No, my good bishop, I honor the laws of holy Mother Church. And I suppose that we can't be absolutely certain that all those coffers really did contain the treasure." He looked hopefully at Morton. "Rotherham didn't actually see what was in them, did he?"

"No, he was more intent on other matters, or . . . uh . . . rather one other matter in which I fear he erred most grievously. But I believe from the weight of all those trunks, they contained something other than ball gowns, which in any case the queen and her daughters will now have scant use for."

Russell said, "You keep alluding to some infraction on the part of Rotherham. Perhaps it would be appropriate for all of us to know just what it is."

"Yes, of course. I had meant to tell you sooner. He has given the great seal into the queen's hands for her keeping."

"Merciful mother of God!" Hastings swore, thinking only that if he had it to do again, he would surely keep Catesby at home. "That the old addlepate would . . ."

"That was most irresponsibly done, Morton," said Russell with a rebuking glance in Hastings's direction. He did not like to hear a primate of the church called by such a name even though he could not argue that it didn't fit. "The seal may be relinquished only to the reigning sovereign."

Morton spread his hands in a helpless gesture. "So I am afraid he considers Her Grace."

"We must get it back."

"Yes, of course. So I advised him, and I think he concurs now. Even 'the old addlepate' can see the foolishness of his act. He will send for it today."

"If she will give it up," Hastings said.

Morton turned a bland eye upon him. "What else can she do? And when it is returned, it must be entrusted to someone other than Rotherham, the well-intentioned fool. It must go to one with the discretion to use it wisely, rationally."

Something in Morton's voice betrayed him: a shiver, a tremor of expectancy, of desire. Suddenly, as clearly as if it were carved in the stone of the wall, Hastings read that the bishop of Ely regarded himself as the most qualified candidate for both the seal and the high office that went with it. No wonder he had jumped so swiftly into the protector's camp!

Across the table, John Russell gave his fellow prelate a knowing look. "You are correct in that, I daresay, but shouldn't a discussion of these matters wait upon Gloucester's arrival in London? The choice will be his, after all."

The two men's gazes locked for some little time until the tension at the table became rather uncomfortable. Hastings was thoughtful as he sugared his wine. He did not want the battle for the chancellery to begin at his own high table. He cleared his throat and changed the subject. "I suppose despite these temporary setbacks, it is safe to advise the duke that he may bring the king up to London?"

"It would seem so," Stanley drawled, "though one might question if we should not refer to 'dukes' in the plural rather than the singular." There was a bit of acid on Stanley's tongue. Like Howard, he had spoken little during the long meal and had sat brooding into his plate.

"You mean by that Buckingham, I take it?" asked Hastings.

"Who else? It does appear that he played a rather prominent role in the events at Northampton and Stony Stratford."

"You may be right," Morton acknowledged. "Ratcliffe certainly gave him fulsome praise. He seems to have come from nowhere and propelled himself into a position of some importance."

"Scarcely from nowhere," Stanley corrected. "He is cousin to Gloucester and nephew by marriage to my lady wife. My word on it, I know the Staffords well. He is not without ambition, my lords, and it appears that he has not hesitated to hitch his cart to the protector's rising star."

"He will bear watching," Morton agreed. "I know him but little, and yet I believe that the Plantagenet lust for power burns as brightly in him as it ever did in any of our kings. And he has already overstepped the bounds of the council by going directly to the protector with his aid."

"Aid that was sorely needed," Howard retorted. "Or have you forgotten that? Maybe some of us should have been as quick about it as he was instead of remaining safely and comfortably at home. In fact, without his aid, we might now be the ones in hiding or in sanctuary." He threw an accusing look at Morton as if to imply that he belonged there in any case. The bishop, who was at that moment deeply absorbed in sponging a speck of gravy from his cassock, paid him no heed.

"Well said, John," Hastings agreed. "Buckingham may well have been vital to our hopes. In this, at least, he has proven himself to be our friend as well as Richard's."

Stanley's fingers played with the points of his forked beard. "I still don't trust him."

Hastings shrugged. "You will see for yourself, Thomas, when they come to London. He will be one of us. What else could he be? I'll even wager ten guineas that he returns to Brecon immediately after the coronation."

"You may keep your money and your bets. I would not so easily rob you." But Tom Stanley gave him a rare smile, his teeth flashing white and even in the deep auburn of his beard.

It made a rather jovial ending to a meal that had been fraught with its share of doubt, disappointment, and tension as well as celebration. When Hastings stood to signal it was time for his guests to depart, no one lingered.

While the servers cleared away the tables and stashed the long trestles against the walls, he retired to his private chambers to write to Richard and inform him of the latest events in the capital. He no longer felt the morning's ebullience, but his heart was far from heavy as he wrote. There was one final triumph left him that colored all his thoughts and that nothing could sour, though he made no mention of this private hope to the protector.

Chapter 11

FOR JANE SHORE, the day had been one of painful loss and almost interminable waiting. What she was waiting for, she did not know. However, she did know that she could not long remain in this silence and emptiness with the house around her echoing her every move. It was her own dwelling in West Chepe that she had retreated to, the one Edward had purchased for her several years before. It was small but comfortable with a charming little garden in the back, overgrown now and running to seed. She had spent little time lately in either the house or the garden; she had been almost continuously at Westminster. Her servants had been dismissed long ago. The house itself had been kept locked, and only when some skirmish at court had made necessary a temporary absence had she sought refuge here.

She sought it now but found no solace. She had left the house with its hollow, ringing emptiness for the lush, overgrown emptiness of the garden. On any other afternoon, she might have found comfort in the riotous rows of bluebells stretching unchecked along the wall, in the tall purple iris bobbing in the sun, in the gay yellow primrose twining out of control among them, the fragrant tansy, the tiny bright clusters of speedwell. On any other afternoon . . . But then, on any other afternoon, she would not have known the bitter pain of having her entire world collapse around her ears and that for the second time in hardly as many weeks.

There was a stone bench beneath the cherry tree, half-hidden by its perfumed pink blossoms, and there she sat so still that a flock of tits alighted near her and began to peck for insects in the high grass, oblivious to her presence. Her eyes watched their busy little black bodies bobbing to and fro without seeing them.

She had only one thought: *What is to become of me now?*

Dorset was gone. That was the pain that bit deeper than all other pains. He had fled into sanctuary with scarcely a thought for her.

"Can't I go with you?" she had pleaded, she who was used to begging nothing of anyone, she who was accustomed only to receiving in bountiful measure whatever she desired.

He had tossed his head back and laughed richly at that one. "Yes, I'm sure my lady mother would much appreciate the company of one who warmed my royal stepfather's bed. And the old abbot, who counts himself so pious and worthy, would no doubt relish the thought of sharing his palace with . . ." His voice trailed off and stopped. Perhaps he had seen the hurt standing sharp in her eyes. He stroked her cheek lightly and spoke more softly. "Ah, puss, you cannot come—don't you see it?—though my nights shall be long and my bed cold without you. Besides, I am not of a mind to stay long in sanctuary, and where I go after that, you cannot follow. There will be small time for bed sport, small time indeed."

He had turned away from her then but had seen to it that one of the palace guards escorted her to her doorstep. It was his final consideration, and small as it was, she had little else to cherish.

How different it had been earlier that evening when he had bedded her, all hot and lusty and panting with desire! She had teased him mercilessly, telling him that she thought it better to keep to her own apartment that night, that the morrow would be May Day and time enough then for love. It inflamed him, this teasing of hers. She had even gone so far as to indulge in a little innocent flirtation at supper with the effeminate Lord Lisle, who was seated next to her. Dorset had glared at them from the high table, his face the color of raw meat, as Lisle broke off a piece of the marchpane and dropped it playfully into the low-slashed bosom of her gown.

"Would he have all your sweets?" Dorset demanded when they were alone as he tore at the laces of her bodice. He had ruined more than one gown in his haste. He bent down and bit with sharp teeth at Lisle's sticky morsel. From past experience, Jane knew there would be a purpling bruise there now. The marquis was not a tender lover.

Despite that, she had never in her life known such bliss as the weeks since Edward's death had afforded her. As fond as she was of the king, she had no longer anticipated with delight those nights when he summoned her to his bed. In fact, he had grown so grossly fat in the months before his death that he was no longer able to manage the act of love in the normal fashion. To pleasure him, Jane was forced to resort to other methods at which she was well-skilled but that brought her little joy. Often he seemed only to desire her company, to hear her sing and strum the lute or to be entertained with amusing jests and anecdotes.

There was none of this with Dorset. Though his absences from the palace during the day were frequent and unexplained, at night he was always there to bed her—randy as a goat, she had teased him, lusty as a young buck. With delight and wonder, she felt her own passions kindled as well, heights of ecstasy undreamt of, depths of desire unknown. They burned together, she and Dorset, the hot fire melding them into one. And how gloriously sweet was that conflagration!

She recalled with a trembling thrill that went through her like water and left her babe-weak how, incensed almost to madness by the marchpane incident, he had pushed her back on the bed and proceeded with a vigorous assault of her yielding body.

"Just so," she murmured in his ear one last, teasing time, "just so does my lord Lisle."

He had torn her petticoat right up the middle. "Oh? Does Lisle do this to you then—or this?"

They were both far gone, moaning and rolling about on the bed, when the knock—small, timorous, and fatal—came at the door. She wondered how they had even heard it or why, having heard it, they paid it any heed. Timid it had been but insistent as the steady drip of water, and finally, it had penetrated their fogged senses. Dorset groaned and pulled away from her, sweating wildly and still unsatisfied.

"By the Virgin!" he cried.

Jane suppressed a smile at the inappropriate oath even as her body clamored for the release a moment's longer endurance would have brought. Her lover folded a tunic about his engorged nakedness and went to the door.

"Can't a man sleep in peace in Westminster Palace without this constant, infernal racket?" he cried. "Can the king's own brother be afforded no rest? Well, answer me!"

There was silence. Jane could see nothing beyond Dorset's naked shoulders framed in the doorway.

"Cat got your tongue, guttersnipe?" Dorset's arm shot out and pulled the intruder into the room, a small boy of perhaps eight or nine clad in the blue-and-murrey livery of York. The other arm reached out and cuffed the lad's ear—not heavily, but enough to bring a whimper to his lips.

"If your message is so damned important it can't wait till morning, I'd certainly like to hear it. Or mayhap it will be I, not the cat, who shall have your tongue."

Jane drew the sheet up over her bare breasts and regarded the intruder with sympathy. "Please, Tom," she said. "It's only Simkin. He's from the queen's household."

"Oh, yes, of course." Dorset brushed a hand across his face as if to wipe away a mist. "Come, lad. I didn't mean my harsh words. Tell me, please, why you were sent."

"It's-it's the queen, m'lord. S-she wishes to see you . . . at-at once."

"Can't it wait until morning?"

"N-no, m'lord. It-it's urgent that you come n-now," the page stammered.

Dorset sighed. "Oh, very well. Tell Her Grace that I will come when I've dressed. I trust she would not have me parading through the halls of Westminster in nothing but the skin in which she bore me."

"I-I know n-naught o' that, m'lord, to be sure." Making a hurried bow, he sped away at a fast sprint toward the queen's apartments.

"Poor urchin!" said Jane, watching her lover don his recently discarded garments in a none-too-careful fashion.

"'Poor urchin!'" he mocked. "And what of me? Am I forever to be at the beck and call of that woman at all hours of the day and night? It's a rutting shame when a grown man must dance like a puppet to his mother's tune and all because she bore him."

"Her womb also bore a king," Jane reminded him. "Don't forget that."

He laid a hand on Jane's rounded belly, rosy now with the glow of their love. "Ah, ma mère, ma mère, I had a mind for other meat tonight."

"Go to, go to!" Jane cried. "It wouldn't do to keep Her Grace waiting and certainly not on my account. Remember that the sooner you go, the sooner you may return."

But in fact, he had not returned for some time, and when he did, his mood was completely altered. His face was stormy, and he did not look at her. Unceremoniously, he tossed her a shift as if she were only an inmate of a Southwark stew and he had had his fill.

"You had best put this on," he said, "and whatever else you need to go out into the street."

"Into the street? But why? What's the matter? Are we in danger? Is there a fire? A mob? What's wrong?"

"It's worse, far worse than any of those, my pet," he replied, reaching into the wardrobe for his cloak. "The news has just come from Stony Stratford. The Duke of Gloucester has taken the king."

Jane wondered how those few words could change the whole world. The palace had been thrown into an uproar as Woodville adherents dashed about in panic. The sounds of their turmoil echoed down the long halls. Dorset went out and returned almost an hour later, looking even more grim than before. It was then that he had sent her home. She had caught one glimpse of Elizabeth, pale and cold as a marble statue, standing firm amid the chaos and issuing orders as one who was born to it. Jane envied her sangfroid. Her own blood was racing. If Richard of Gloucester was no friend to the queen, he certainly was no friend to her either.

Already the thought was in her mind. *What will become of me now?*

In the past five years, she had become so completely a creature of the court that she did not know if she could survive without it. She had drifted through its amours and intrigues, its banquets and balls like a beautiful butterfly in a summer's meadow, flitting from flower to flower. When winter comes, the flowers die, the leaves drop and the snow falls, what then becomes of the butterfly? She had a little money of her own, of course, for Edward had not been ungenerous. However, it was hardly enough to maintain her in royal estate, and she had grown all too accustomed to royal estate. Without the glamor of court life by day and, yes, the excitement of Dorset's arms around her at night, she doubted her life would even be worth living.

She remembered Lord Hastings and his many kindnesses that she suspected hid a thinly veiled passion. Here would be a buttress against the protector indeed against all ill fortune. But even as the lord chamberlain's image flashed on her mind, blue eyes softening at the sight of her, lips twitching with laughter at some jest, she felt a wave of hot shame. She was not so blind to all but Dorset's attentions that she didn't realize Hastings had wished to claim her for his own when Edward died. Even when Edward was alive, she had danced attention on him for the sole purpose of arousing Dorset's jealousy. No, she could not turn to Hastings for protection. Now he would most likely toss her back into the street from whence she had come. Jane had not seen him since they had met at Edward's deathbed. She knew nothing of his present feelings for her, nor could she risk the humiliation of rejection.

The afternoon lengthened, and shadows crept over the garden wall. The flock of tits flew off in a great fit of chirping, and the air grew chill. She wrapped her arms tightly across her chest for warmth and saw they were prickled with gooseflesh. In the haste of the night before, she had thrown on a gossamer gown with low neck and sheer sleeves, scarcely suited to the cool spring evening. Her stomach rumbled with neglect; she had eaten nothing since the previous night's supper, though then she had eaten rather overmuch. Cold and hungry but without either food in her larder or a servant to light the fire and prepare it, she realized she could no longer delay the living of her life no matter how altered she found it.

The knocking broke loud upon her silence. It had a command-
ing ring, almost like a summons. Jane started from her seat like a
wild thing. Had the protector's men already come to arrest her? She
had hoped at least he would let her live in peace, exiled from the
court. Perhaps he hated her even more than she knew. Perhaps, as
it was whispered at court, he held her personally accountable for his
brother's destruction.

For a moment, she wavered, not knowing whether to turn and
bolt or to gather her courage and answer. Again the knock came,
louder now, more insistent. The garden wall blocked her. There was
no place she could go. With quaking knees, she walked through the
empty house. Her hand trembled on the bolt as she drew it back.

"Yes?" she asked, her voice little more than a whisper.

To her great relief, she saw in the fading light not, as she had
feared, the dour face of the protector glaring at her with dark, hostile eyes nor even a contingent of the royal guard come to arrest her.
Instead, there was a young knight who regarded her with a rakish
grin and doffed his velvet cap in a courtly bow. Even more to the
point, he wore the black belled sleeve on silver, the gallant cognizance
of the Lord Hastings. Irresistibly, she smiled.

"Good evening to you, mistress," he said pleasantly. "My lord
has sent me to request that you give him the pleasure of your company at supper tonight." He did not add that Hastings had also given
him strict instructions not to return without her, hence the urgency
of his knock. Jane did not know any of this. She only knew that she
was being politely asked rather than bidden, that this was a request
and not a summons.

She gave him a pretty laugh. "But of course, I shall be most
happy to join your master for supper." She looked up at him coyly
through the thick fringe of her lashes. "My own servants are . . .
indisposed. I'd be most grateful if you would wait for me but one
moment—I'll not be long—and do me the honor of accompanying
me to your lord's house."

Chapter 12

Richard had slept badly on the Tabor's second-best bed, having vacated the best, where he had spent the previous night, in favor of the king. To one who had spent too many days in the saddle, the mattress was as hard and lumpy as an old alewife, and he tossed about, wondering why the landlord could provide them with only one good bed. God grant that Edward at least slept well and that his humor improved with the night's rest.

It was not yet time for rising. The moon, a fattening crescent, had set sometime before, sliding past the western window and lighting the chamber with pale phosphorescence. Now in the darkness, Richard could dimly discern the shapes of Francis Lovell and Rob Percy curled tightly in their bedrolls on the floor, like caterpillars in their cocoons. He envied them their soft snoring. Sleep, long sought, eluded him.

"Our green bud has a frost on it." Buckingham's words haunted him now, adding to his unrest. It was true. The chill of premature winter hung on Edward. Although both dukes had actively courted him after their return to Northampton, they had been met by a wall of cold hostility. The king had spent the greater part of the previous day sulking in his chambers and had returned his dinner tray untouched. Richard had gone to him to no avail. Buckingham was next. Jovial, witty Buckingham, trying diligently to make amends for his harsh words at Stony Stratford, had been dismissed within a quarter of an hour.

Supper had brought the hopeful sign of a thaw, for Edward had deigned to partake of the meal with them in the inn's best parlor. Thinking of that supper now, so hopefully begun, Richard cringed, but he forced himself to relive it on the chance that he might find where he had erred in dealing with the king. Had it been in the mention of Rivers? He heard his own voice once more. So hollow it sounded in his ears, so stilted.

"Your Grace must believe me when I tell you I bear no ill will to your Uncle Rivers." He had been deliberately casual, lifting a morsel of roast veal to his lips while his eyes sought Edward's. But Edward would not meet them. He merely shrugged his shoulders but made no reply.

"In truth, sire," Buckingham boomed on the other side of him, "this very night past, we supped together in great amity and harmony here in this very room."

"Yet today he is a prisoner," the youth replied icily.

"Let's just say that he is being detained for a time," Richard said, "until our affairs are settled. This does not mean that he is being treated like a prisoner—nor is your brother Grey or old Vaughan. All of them are being treated with the deference due their ranks."

Edward opened his mouth as if to reply then snapped it shut again. His eyes were fixed rigidly on his untouched plate.

"Isn't the veal to your liking, sire?" Buckingham asked, solicitous. "Then pray try some of the sturgeon. It seems to be fresh caught, and the sauce is excellently spiced. Won't you taste it?"

"I'm afraid that I haven't much appetite."

"A pity to waste such a kingly dish."

Richard had a sudden inspiration. "Then maybe we can find another use for it. Do you think your Uncle Rivers would enjoy such a dish?"

"I don't know."

"I daresay he might. Ho, landlord!" He beckoned to the innkeeper who, as usual, hovered near their table. "Bear this tureen to the Earl Rivers, with the king's compliments as well as my own. Tell him to . . . uh . . . be of good cheer. All shall soon be well."

The landlord made them a deep, obsequious bow and balanced the tureen so precariously that Richard wondered if he would manage to deliver it all in one piece. When he returned some time later, Edward looked up with a flicker of interest.

"What news of my uncle?" he asked.

"My lords, he thanks Your Graces all for your kindness to him . . ."

"Then he enjoyed the dish?" Richard asked.

"Why, no . . . not exactly though to be sure he would have if he had laid a knife to it. It is my specialty, so to speak, from a recipe passed down from father to son through many generations. It is a princely dish, if I may say so."

"Yes, yes," Richard said, "go on."

"Well, I bore the sturgeon to the earl as Your Graces bade me, and he gave me a goodly greeting. He said that if he had a mind to feed his belly, he would doubtless enjoy it, but this night he lacked appetite. He would have me bear it to Lord Grey for—how did he say it now? Oh, aye—for the comfort of his table. Lord Grey, says he, being less accustomed to adversity—those were his words, beggin' Your Lordships' pardons—would have greater need of the gift."

The boy permitted himself a small fond smile. "That was always my uncle's way. He was ever wont to consider others before himself." He pushed back his chair from the table without having touched a morsel on his plate. "God give you good rest, my lords," he said and was gone with Bishop Alcock trotting along behind.

"That tomfool of a landlord!" growled Buckingham. "Why did he have to go and repeat the earl's very words?"

"It's I who was the fool," Richard said. "I thought to make a generous conciliatory gesture, and now it's all gone awry. No doubt Rivers stands higher in the boy's esteem than ever. Why didn't I send Lovell?" He glanced across the room at his faithful henchman, who he knew would have brought back a far-less-favorable report of the earl, omitting all implications of resigned martyrdom. Too late now, though, for regrets. The harm had already been done.

Outside it was growing light. There was another gray dawn, but this one gave promise of a fair day to follow, the first one of May. From the street below came a girl's laugh, high-pitched, excited, almost a squeal. Hard upon it was another laugh, deeper, masculine, raucous. His interest aroused, Richard threw back the bedcovers and crept to the window.

The couple stood in a doorway, hung with ivy and hawthorn on post and lintel. She wore a gown of white gauze, disarrayed as if she had been running, and a straggling wreath of flowers: moon daisies, clover, kingcups. He was green suited and brawny, a prentice smith perhaps or a mason. With strong arms, he barred her way. They both panted, out of breath. The laughter stopped; they talked together earnestly, words that Richard could not catch. Then suddenly, coyly, she darted under one of her lover's arms and vanished in a trail of white gauze while he, heavy booted, stumbled after. Out to take her maidenhead, Richard guessed, and she to give it.

The maying ceremonies were a mere excuse to indulge fleshly lusts and, at the same time, do homage to a pagan god. He did not normally observe them, yet as he thought of that couple, so fortunate in their innocence, he felt a pang that was almost jealousy.

"You're up and about early, my lord," said Lovell behind him. "Have you a mind to go maying?"

Richard shook his head. "Heavens, no! Yet I think of how it used to be at Middleham. Do you recall when we were children?"

A shadow crossed Lovell's fine-boned face. "Yea, my lord, I do indeed. And the time when the Lady Anne wore the white dress and bade you follow her, but you would not."

"So you went instead," Richard finished, strangely smarting from that old wound.

Belatedly, he had donned the green suit and gone after them, finding the pair at last in a greening copse surrounded by myrtle and arbutus and pussy willow. Anne had been weeping into Lovell's hand-kerchief—she would not have been more than thirteen—though Francis had sworn by all the saints in the church calendar that he had not harmed her. Later, though, when Anne had let Richard touch her budding breasts, he wondered if she had allowed Francis the same liberties. By the next May, she was a stranger to them both, a pawn in the intrigues of her father Warwick, and destined to wed another man.

The memory was bitter. He shut his mind to it.

"Where is that wantwit simpleton of a landlord?" he asked irritably. "A man could die of thirst in this place if the lumps in the mattress didn't break his back first."

"Say no more, m'lord," said Ralph Assheton, pushing his big frame through the door. "There is somewhat here to heal your thirst if naught for your back."

Behind him came the innkeeper, grinning broadly through the curls of his beard and carrying a tray laden with four steaming mugs of breakfast ale. Rob Percy stirred from his bed on the floor and brushed a shock of red hair from heavy-lidded eyes. The day had begun.

From Edward's bedchamber, there was a full view of the May Day festivities taking place on the greensward. The youth stood at a lectern, Alcock beside him and an open book before him, but it was plain as Richard and Buckingham entered that the pretense of a lesson had been given up long ago. Edward's eyes were fastened on the scene below, his lips curved in a wistful smile.

"We had a maypole at Ludlow," he said with the air of an old man recalling the happier days of his youth. "Look, would you, at Robin Hood, bishop! He seems not much older than I." Then, turning swiftly to Richard, remembering neither greeting nor hauteur, "Oh, may I, Uncle, please . . . ?' His voice and eyes pleaded the question he was afraid to ask.

"May you what, sire?"

"May I go down below? May I join the dance?"

The question caught Richard off guard. He too looked down on the familiar festival, on the tall maypole where youths and maidens wove cloth streamers in and out in a bright blur of red and green and gold, on the slightly older youths who shot at the butts in competition for a fat pig squealing in a nearby poke, on the lad dressed as Robin Hood in a green as deep as Sherwood Forest, on another lad perhaps a bit younger than Edward who played a simpering Maid Marian in golden wig and long skirt, and on the menacing sheriff of Nottingham, who, padded out with pillows, took a shaft from Robin's bow square in his ample stomach yet lived to flaunt a rope in the outlaw's face.

Slowly Richard shook his head. He sighed and glanced at Alcock. "No, Your Grace. These are pagan revelries as I'm certain the good bishop of Worcester will agree."

Alcock cleared his throat nervously. A hand flew up to his tight collar. "Well, my lord, it is true that they are . . . are . . . ah . . . hardly Christian in origin, being instituted as they were to do homage to the Green Man of the forest . . ."

"That's not what you said at Ludlow," Edward snapped. "You agreed with my Uncle Rivers that they were only harmless games."

Alcock flushed and looked down at his locked hands.

"No, bishop," Edward went on, "you needn't reply, nor would it do any good. I see that my Uncle Gloucester has determined I shall not go down. Like Rivers, I am to be held a prisoner though doubtless I shall be treated—how did you put it, Uncle?—with the deference due my rank."

Richard's mind was torn. It seemed to be such a simple request on the surface, so easy, so harmless. The granting of it might go a long way toward winning Edward. Yet the crowd on the green was large, and he feared that there might be Woodville adherents among them waiting for just such a lapse in judgment. Who knew, for example, if the juggler were not a messenger sent from the queen? Or perhaps the jester, with his particolored red-and-gold doublet and hose and his belled cap, was a servant of Lord Rivers? And the ragged troubadour—did his eyes not stray to the king's window with more than idle curiosity?

"To be a king has its restrictions as well as its privileges," Richard said at last. "Even though you are young, you are still bound by them. You will learn that sometimes a humble cotter has more freedom than you do. Although I would not be your jailor, I think it well to remind you that you had better spend your time in more kingly pursuits than attending village festivals. Then, too, you are still in mourning for your father."

It was this last argument that quieted Edward. He was nothing if not conscious of filial obligation. He slumped forward sadly at the lectern. "You're right about that, Uncle. I'm sorry."

Richard smiled. "No need for apology, sire. These days of waiting are tiresome for us all, and you are young and have little with which to occupy yourself. I'm sure they are most wearying for you."

"Well, to be sure, I would like to know what are these kingly pursuits of which you speak."

Richard looked dubious. "As to that, sire, I must confess I have little knowledge, having never been a king."

"And you, my uncle of Buckingham, what would you suggest?"

Buckingham was thoughtful for a moment, elaborately stroking his cleft chin. Then he gave a snap of his jeweled fingers. "Ah yes, I think I've hit on it! It's a rather simple thing, yet it seems to me, sire, that a good deal of kingship is tied to the signing of one's name. Here on letters patent and proclamations of state, there on royal grants and decrees. Ah, yes, I'm certain that signing the royal signature with a proper flourish must be a matter of some importance."

"The signing of my name? But surely . . ."

"Not just your name, sire." Buckingham bent close so that his fair head was next to Edward's. "But Edwardus. Edwardus Quintus. Edwardus Quintus Rex."

A light leapt in the boy's blue eyes. "Yes, my title. A goodly title, is it not?"

"Right goodly, sire. Have you practiced it yet?"

"N-no."

"That's an oversight that can soon be remedied," Richard said. To a page, he added, "Go fetch my secretary, Master Kendall. Bid him bring pen and parchment, ink pot, and sand shaker, for our sovereign lord would set his hand to them. Go to, boy, go to!"

From the green came the piping of a flute and the rhythmic tapping of sticks of the morris dance. Youth and maid, dressed in white tunics with red sashes across their breasts, lined up opposite one another and stamped their feet in gay, careless abandon. Edward paid them no heed. For a long time, the only sound in the room was the scratch of his pen on parchment. The piece was soon covered with scratched-out words and ink blots, and another was procured to replace it.

At last the words blazed forth in solitary splendor, written in Edward's careful, deliberate, though somewhat-awkward script: "Edwardus Quintus." Edward himself regarded them with a faint frown of puzzlement.

"Is it not to Your Grace's liking?" asked Buckingham.

The boy shrugged. "Yes . . . no. It seems so alone, the page so blank except for my letters."

"A king's state is solitary," Buckingham expounded. "A lofty eminence . . ."

"And he but a boy, Harry?" Richard argued. "It shouldn't be so. Even a king must have friends and counselors." With that, he took the pen and wrote beneath Edward's signature in his own bold hand, "Loyaltie me lie." It was his raison, and always, through many dark and perilous times, he had held fast to it. Never had the challenge been greater than at this moment. Loyalty bound him still to the son as to the father. The way would not be easy—when had it ever been easy?—though just now, gazing down at Edward's upturned face, he felt more hope than he had before. "Loyaltie me lie" and beneath it "Ricardus Gloucestere."

Buckingham was not to be outdone by this chivalry. Seizing the pen with a flourish, he scribbled in his own distinctive scrawl, "Souvente me souvene." Remember me often.

Richard inspected the motto with a curious interest. The words were ambiguous. A pledge of fealty or a plea for recognition? A promise or a warning? It was difficult to tell which. Did the duke even now threaten to bully the king?

But there was no hint of guile in Buckingham's face as he set down the quill, only a smile of self-satisfaction. As the devisor of this most cunning entertainment, he held a claim on the protector's gratitude. Edward, however, still was not satisfied.

"It doesn't say anything," he told them.

"But surely it says a great deal," Richard objected. "My motto declares my fealty—"

"Nay, Uncle, I know what the words mean. I am no want-wit schoolboy. But shouldn't a parchment . . . declare something? Shouldn't there be a grant or a writ or a pronouncement? I take it kings do not go about putting their names to blank paper only for the novelty of it—though overwrought uncles may employ such strategies to amuse troublesome children."

The boy was clever—Richard had not quite owned just how clever—nor had Buckingham, who stood beside him now, mouth agape and crimsoning to the roots of his golden hair.

"Yes," Richard replied, "I think I see what you mean. Though I don't know . . ."

"Oh, Uncle, it doesn't need to be any grand pronouncement, anything of great import. But if I truly am to practice this matter of kingship as you bade me, surely there must be something I can set my hand to, don't you think?"

Richard looked for aid first to Buckingham, who was still regaining his composure, then to Alcock. "What do you think, bishop? You must know of some matter that requires our sovereign lord's attention."

Alcock too looked thoughtful. He had a mild, kindly face, turning pinkly rotund in his middle years, a round bald pate, and extraordinarily large, wide-spaced gray eyes. It was not the ascetic face of a scholar by any means, for though Alcock was not lacking in wisdom, he had been selected as Edward's tutor more for his skill and enthusiasm as a teacher than for his knowledge of philosophy. It had worked out well for them both, for Edward had developed a true love of learning while Alcock had established himself close to the heart of his royal pupil. He was overshadowed in the boy's affections only by Rivers and the physician Argentine. The bishop would know how to please the king.

"Ah, yes," he said at last with a slow, dawning smile. "I believe I know of something. You remember, Edward, Master Jeffrey at Ludlow?"

"My chaplain? Yes, of course. What of him?"

"I fear his duties will be rather light now that Your Grace goes up to London. He confided in me that he would much like a parish church of his own now that he has fulfilled his obligations to you. Such a grant lies in the king's power, does it not?"

"Do you know of such a parish, bishop?" Edward asked.

"Why, yes," Alcock replied, smiling broadly. "It happens that the parish priest of Pembrigge in Your Grace's own earldom of March was taken suddenly ill and died last month. Do you think that Master Jeffrey would find it a suitable appointment?"

"Most suitable, I should think," replied Edward. "Marry, I think it would please him most excessively!"

"Then so be it," said Richard. "The stroke of your pen on parchment will accomplish all. Master Kendall, come, draw up the grant and in your best hand, if you please, for your words will go above the seal of the king."

John Kendall, a quiet, unimposing man of about thirty, took a seat at the writing desk, dipped his quill in the pewter inkpot, and quickly set down the necessary terms. When he was done, the parchment covered with the uniform black strokes of his fine hand and the sand shaken over it and brushed away, Edward picked it up, examined it with an eye to minute detail and, apparently finding no fault, set his "Edwardus Quintus" on the bottom line.

"Le roi le voit," Richard said, expansively placing an arm around the boy's thin shoulders. "Your first royal command is given."

"Ah, isn't it a grand thing to be a king?" Buckingham asked, draping his arm about the royal waist. "Isn't it glorious to say 'come' and they come or 'go' and they go or to say 'so I will it' and have none to gainsay you? 'I have a mind to dispose of a parish in March today. To whom shall the honor be given? Ah, to whom but he who has served me so well, to my old friend, Master Jeffrey.' And so, with a flick of the royal wrist, it is accomplished and Master Jeffrey made the new rector of Pembrigge."

Edward spun about so quickly that both dukes found their arms embraced only empty air. There was a fire in his eyes and a snarl on his lips.

"Oh, yes, for certain it's a fine thing to be a king. And were I king in fact as well as in name, mayhap I would applaud your words, Uncle Buckingham. But just look at this scrap of paper!" It was impossible not to, for Edward waved it in their faces. "An honor has been given, a gift bestowed, but it wasn't Master Jeffrey who was the recipient, was it? No, it was me. Like a puppet master, you sought to pull my strings, to make me dance to the music you set out. This much power I might have but no more. This far I might go but no further. Many a boon I might grant but only so long as they agree with your wishes. The one nearest my heart, the only one that matters to me, I might not grant. I think you both know what it is."

"Yes, sire," Richard said heavily. "I know."

"Then may I not, Uncle? I pray thee, may I not? May I not sign the paper that will free the earl and my brother Grey and Haute and Vaughan? He's a harmless old graybeard really, without the strength to harm a flea. Come, Uncle, the king pleads before you." So saying, he dropped to his knees on the rushes, the same beseeching look in his eyes that he had worn earlier when he had begged leave to go to the May fair. Only now he was plainly desperate.

Deeply moved, Richard could only shake his head slowly. "Please rise, Your Grace," he said sadly. "A king should not kneel before his subject."

"Not even if that subject fancies himself mightier than the king?" Edward taunted, but he stood, brushing bits of straw and saffron from his knees as he did so. His mood had changed again without warning, shifting before their very eyes like quicksilver. His eyes baited them as hounds bait a bear in the pits, challenging the dukes to lift a hand against him.

"Name of God, Edward!" Richard cried. "Stop this foolishness before I lose all patience. Rivers and the others have committed serious crimes. Do you think they should go unpunished?"

"They have committed no crimes against me that I know of. What would you charge them with? Answer me that."

It was Buckingham who spoke, cool and dangerously low. "What think you of high treason?"

"Treason is a crime against the king."

"Or his lawfully appointed protector."

Edward's face blanched with sudden fear. "You have no right—"

"Haven't we then? Don't push us beyond the limits of our endurance, or you may learn to your sorrow—"

"Peace, Harry!" Richard broke in. "You go too far. It isn't necessary to threaten . . ."

But the damage had already been done. Edward regarded them both indiscriminately, wide-eyed with horror. The black of his pupils had swallowed up all the lovely blue of his irises. He began to weep. Richard, who would have comforted him, could not. It was Alcock who was there with the enveloping arm, murmuring words of healing like a mother soothing a distraught babe.

He turned on Buckingham with a look that would have withered green grass. "I think His Grace needs to be left alone."

"In faith," the youth said, "I feel unwell—perhaps a fever."

"You had better take to your bed, sire," Richard said. "I'll have the landlord send up a posset, wine and honey in warm milk."

"Argentine. I must have Argentine."

"Argentine?"

"The king's physician," Alcock explained. "He is in London."

"He shall be sent for. Is there anything else?"

Alcock shook his head. "No, there's been too much already for one day."

Richard sighed. He heard in the ensuing silence the sounds of merrymaking from below. There was a sharp burst of laughter from a puppet show on the green. With a pang, he recalled Edward's scathing indictment of him: puppet master. The last thing he saw before closing the door was Edward's pale face, sulking at him from behind the bishop's purple cowl.

Chapter 13

ARGENTINE ARRIVED THE following evening in the company of Sir Richard Ratcliffe and in time to partake of a Friday supper of trout and eel pasty. There was no sturgeon served that night; Richard had recently lost his taste for sturgeon.

"You have come quickly," Richard said as Argentine stood before the high table to pay his respects. He took in the hawk-like face shadowed into razor sharpness by the rushlights and the mane of hair and beard that glistened white and cold as snow over the black gown.

The leech gave him the curtest of nods. "Aye, and would go much further if His Grace have need of me."

"Most commendable of you. I would start for London tomorrow and therefore would have you examine the king tonight to determine if he is strong enough to undertake such a journey."

Another curt nod. "I will do my best to see that he is." He then took a seat at a lower table where he ate quickly and sparingly, after which he was led away to the king.

Argentine was closeted with Edward for some time, long enough for Richard to complete his own meal and return to his chamber in a fit of increasing agitation. He was very anxious that the examination prove Edward whole not only because it would speak well for his care of the king but also because he was growing impatient to embark for the capital. Ratcliffe had brought back good news and letters—for the most part, very encouraging letters—from Lord Hastings. His own name, Richard was told, had been cheered "like to shake the very rafters" in Hastings's great hall. The powerful and noble persons gathered there to pay him homage had been almost too numerous to count. Riding a wave of such popularity, he could surely march triumphantly into London if he acted soon. Richard was painfully aware of how abruptly the tide of public opinion could change.

Hastings's letters had been just as ebullient as Ratcliffe's oral account, although there did appear to be some rather thorny problems to be dealt with: empty coffers in the treasury, a rebellious and possibly senile lord chancellor, and potentially most alarming of all, a well-provisioned Woodville navy patrolling the English coast. These facts only sharpened his urgency to be on the London road. They were issues that required his immediate attention. More importantly, they were problems that could in some measure be dealt with; they were amenable to solution, unlike the increasingly difficult situation with Edward.

Richard paced up and down before the hearth in his bedchamber. Only a small fire had been laid since the evening was very pleasant with a pink sunset glowing through the mullioned windows. But at the thought of Edward, a chill rippled down his spine and along his arms. He had not visited the king since the fiasco of the day before, nor had Edward seen fit to leave his own chambers. Lack of any contact undoubtedly magnified the breach, yet Richard could not ignore the wretched feeling that everything had gone awry between them, that he and Buckingham were in fact prime targets of the royal displeasure.

He had, perhaps in frustration, taken his fellow duke sharply to task for his role in the unhappy little episode, but his anger had quickly melted at the sight of Buckingham's own distress.

"Yes, yes, I know I spoke out of turn," Buckingham had rapidly agreed, "but didn't you see how sweetly he led us, how he played us like fools with the signing of his name and the writing of the writ, and all the while the words he was going to say sliding towards his tongue like quince jelly? All the while, it was Rivers on his mind, Rivers and his cohorts. And when he saw there was no hope for their freedom, he made me turn on him and say the words that should never have been spoken, the words I repent I should ever say to my sovereign lord."

The duke's eyes were downcast; his very jowls seemed to sag about his chin. Richard laid a comforting hand on his shoulder. "Don't blame yourself too much, cousin," he said. "I also felt the pull of his teeth as he baited us. He is crafty and sly beyond his years, and I have little doubt how he came by it."

Buckingham's hand came up to cover his own, and Richard was suddenly very glad to have this companion in his misery, although it did little to alleviate the basic problem: what was to be done about Edward?

As if in answer to his thoughts, a page knocked at his chamber door and announced the arrival of Argentine. The physician's face was stern and composed. Try as he might, Richard could read nothing there.

"How does the king?"

The answer was equally noncommittal. "Well enough, I should say, well enough."

"And the journey . . . will he be fit for it? Watling Street is an easy way. If it proves necessary, we could arrange for a horse litter."

The effect of this suggestion on Argentine was immediate and pronounced. "A horse litter?" he scoffed. "What sort of a king needs a horse litter? Do you want a weak and sickly sovereign unable to show himself to his people? Bah! I tell you, it's no good, no good at all. Nay, His Grace will travel tomorrow, and he will ride a horse."

Richard nodded. "I am most happy to hear it."

Argentine did not reply, though his amber eyes raked Richard's face as if questioning his sincerity.

"You find him improved then?" Richard asked to break the silence.

"Improved? I don't know quite what you mean by that. I find him well in body, though perhaps a little underfed and suffering still from the old ache in his jaw. But I also find him gloomy in spirit, and that disturbs me greatly."

"He has perhaps an overabundance of the black bile?"

Argentine shrugged. "If Your Lordship wishes to call it that. Only I think it has another cause."

"Yes, I can guess it."

"The prisoners—he has heard . . . rumors that they have been . . . uh . . . moved to the north."

"And so they have. They are—" Richard stopped short, realizing how nearly he had revealed their destinations to this leech who wore his Woodville sympathies as prominently as the Aesculapian symbol that hung about his neck. "They are perfectly safe, as I have assured His Grace many times over."

"You must forgive him then. He is, after all, little more than a babe, and he is sometimes given to fond and foolish fancies. For example, he appears overly concerned about how safe these prisoners will be in your northern dungeons."

Richard returned this mock innocence with an angry glare. "I don't believe I should have to justify myself to you, leech, as well as to my sovereign lord. However, you and he may rest content that they are not riding to dungeons. They are to be treated with courtesy more befitting honored guests than prisoners. They will be free to ride forth—though, of course, under guard. They will dine at the high table and sleep on feather beds. Does that sound like a prisoner's life to you?"

Argentine bowed. "Well, as to that, I wouldn't know, having only my small skill in leechcraft to occupy my time. Politics, I confess, is a foreign matter to me, so I don't know what you would call a guest and what a prisoner. I had always thought in my ignorance that a guest had the freedom to take his leave at his own choosing while a prisoner did not. But since you are gracious enough to enlighten me otherwise, I will naturally inform His Grace that Rivers and Grey only partake of your kind hospitality."

"Have a care, sirrah," said Richard between clenched teeth. "You go too far."

"Do I, my lord?" Argentine asked with sudden mildness. "Then I am most sorry for it. Do I have your leave to seek my bed? The journey to and from London is long, and I no longer young."

"You have it, leech. In fact, I grant it most willingly."

"Very well. Good night, my lord."

They departed Northampton early the next morning before the mists had lifted from the dimpled vales, before the sun had poked its way through the low-hanging clouds. It had rained a little in the night, a gentle sprinkle of rain. It was enough to lay the dust on the roads and to wash the landscape a shade of green that rivaled the emerald in Richard's cap. It was a countryside at peace through which they rode.

Within the royal retinue, there was also peace of a kind. Edward had resumed his mask of disinterested courtesy toward both dukes, and Argentine had similarly curbed the barbs on his venomous tongue. For most of the way, the king rode between Alcock and Argentine or, as Buckingham had dubbed them in private conversation, the dove and the hawk. Alcock, with his pinkly bland face and gentle gray eyes, and Argentine, with his fierce beak of a nose and sharp feline stare, clearly had little in common except for the one thing that mattered most—their intense, protective loyalty to their young sovereign.

They spent the night at St. Albans and rose quite early the following day. Now they were only about fourteen miles northwest of London, and a different excitement charged the whole company. Not least of all did it affect Edward, who came to breakfast bright of eye and pink of cheek. Suddenly, he seemed to have become a boy again instead of a prematurely wizened old man.

When they took to their horses that morning, he spurned both hawk and dove to ride between his two late-despised uncles. Less than an hour after they set out, their road took them through the tiny hamlet of Barnet then dipped abruptly to the Middlesex plain. Twelve years before, one of the fiercest battles between York and Lancaster had been fought on the slopes of that plateau.

Edward's eyes widened as the company lingered for a while on the top of the bluff. "This is where my father vanquished the traitor Warwick, is it not?" he asked, turning to Richard.

"Yes, Your Grace."

"It was a very great battle, wasn't it? And a great victory for York. I wish I could have been here then."

"You were in swaddling clouts, sire," said Richard, amused.

"Yes, with my mother in sanctuary, awaiting the outcome." For an instant, the boy's face screwed up in distaste, and Richard feared that the inevitable comparison of his mother's plight today to that Easter morning so long ago would plunge the king into another fit of recrimination or, worse, melancholy. But Edward smiled almost sweetly and continued, "You were here that day, Uncle. Won't you tell us about it? Where was mighty Warwick when he met his end? And whence came our father when he slew the foe? We would hear it all. Spare no detail, no matter how trivial—every trumpet call, every sword's thrust."

It was no niggling order, for the battle had involved more than twenty thousand men. Richard told it as he remembered it and with as much relish as he could bring to the task, for his own enthusiasm was considerably less than Edward's. He recalled a morning of darkness and thick mists and overwhelming confusion where no man knew who was friend and who was foe. Lancaster had fought Lancaster and York had fought York, being unable to tell the difference in the fog. The rayed-star banner of the Lancastrian Earl of Oxford had been fatally mistaken for the blazing sun of King Edward, and panic had pushed seasoned Lancastrian warriors into a rout. Yes, it had been a morning of triumph for York, though the fortuitous mists had perhaps as much to do with the victory as prowess and strategy.

On that morning, he had found the body of Richard Neville, Earl of Warwick, his old friend and the mentor of his boyhood lately turned traitor. The visor of his dented sallet had been thrust open, and he had bled out his life's blood from a great gash in his throat. A thin trickle of red oozed from his parted lips while yet more blood, or that of his enemies, stained the tawny bear and ragged staff of his jupon. Thus had mighty Warwick perished on the day of Resurrection. Richard found it difficult then not to weep at the sight of him. He would have spared the earl, treacherous though he was.

"Aye," he whispered sadly, forgetting Edward's presence, "like a father he was to me once."

"It appears, Uncle," Edward responded, "that you still mourn the traitor, and we are puzzled. Certainly he met his just end. He was a rebel against his king and therefore deserved to die."

"'Deserved,' sire? Yes, I daresay he did. So do many who walk the earth whole, if God is our judge. There is such a thing as mercy."

"Oh, yes, mercy," Edward's voice piped, high and thin as a flute. "Mercy for such as Warwick, for doubtless it would have found you favor in the eyes of his daughter. Mercy for Warwick, but none for Rivers. Most strange, is it not? But come! We do but dally here, and I want to see the steeples of London before tierce." He nipped a spur into his pony's flank. "Let's move on."

They did not see the steeples of London before tierce. At Hornsby, still several miles outside the city walls, they were faced with another delay but one that could neither be helped nor regretted. There they were met by a sizable delegation of London's leading citizens led by the lord mayor himself, William Shaw, on a huge dappled-gray mount ornately trapped with gold. Beside him rode all his sheriffs and aldermen in deep scarlet furred with ermine and budge and, behind them, five hundred of the city fathers in mulberry velvet. They shimmered against a backdrop of brilliant green like jewels of color in a stained-glass window. Edward rode toward them in greeting, resplendent himself in bright-blue velvet threaded with gold, the morning sun pouring down benediction like the oil of unction on his head.

Richard watched with swelling pride, forgetting for the moment Edward's cutting remark of a short time before. He was young yet and a victim of forces he did not understand. Nevertheless, his very youth augured well for Richard. He was still malleable; in time, he would be weaned away from his mother's troublesome kin. Eventually, he would accept Richard as his protector. What else could he do?

Their first sight of London came at late morning. How lovely she was from a distance by her broad bend of the Thames, her many-gabled, red-tiled roofs gleaming in the sun! On her eastern wall stood the tall White Tower, a formidable bulwark from Norman days; on her western, the soaring spire of St. Paul's with its gilded weathercock dwarfing a hundred lesser steeples. And each steeple clanged with a peal of bells that day; the clamor came to them on the breeze, a great paean of joy and praise.

Reality struck Richard a sudden blow. At Bishopsgate, they did not so much enter the city as they were sucked into its roiling, teeming maw. Richard felt himself stiffen and hold back as if he were passing beyond some boundary from which he could never return. The din was harsh in his ears—not only the cacophony of the bells but also the howls of welcome from ten thousand open mouths reverberating along the narrow, tightly jammed streets. In some places, people and banners were so thick he wondered how there would be room to pass, but pass they did, inch by perilous, suffocating inch.

Edward was enjoying it all. He was beaming; there was no other word for it. His lap and the pony's mane and tail bore the floral tributes of his subjects—yellow jonquils and primroses, pale buttercups, and blue harebells. Beneath banners of white roses and triple suns, he passed, beneath gold leopards of England and silver lilies of France. And he was his father Edward all over again come fresh from Towton's bloody field to claim the crown.

Buckingham too looked to be in fine form. He smiled and waved almost as if it were he himself the crowds cheered, basking in the reflected glory of his place at Edward's left hand. The black of his mourning weeds made a fine counterpoint to the king's magnificence. They both possessed in full measure the one thing Richard knew he lacked: the golden beauty of the Plantagenets. There was no sign now that Buckingham regretted the necessity for his plain black garments, though earlier that morning he had appeared in Richard's chamber most sumptuously clad with mantle and hose of apple green, doublet of brilliant lapis velvet, over all a vermilion surcoat with his emblem of the flaming wheel blazoned in gold and topaz thread.

Richard had stared at him in astonishment then slowly shaken his head. "You look . . . quite splendid, Harry, but I hardly think this is the day for it."

"What better day for it? Today we enter London and amidst great rejoicing if what Hastings says is true. Surely a cause for celebration . . ."

"True enough, but I don't need to remind you that our late king's month-mind has not yet been kept."

Buckingham had stood in the center of the room, looking slightly ridiculous, like one who came dressed for a ball and found himself commandeered to wait tables. "No, you need not remind me, but what of the king? He arrays himself in all manner of splendor, mourning or no. Only a moment ago, I saw him preening in a mirror like a maid expecting a suitor."

"So he does, after a fashion. That is the way I've ordered him to be dressed, for it's his day after all and not ours. It is he who is to be presented to his people and not us who exist only to do him reverence. Therefore, I intend to wear my mourning black and have instructed my men to do likewise. So I wish you to do, if you will."

Richard had stopped just short of a direct command. He was already growing accustomed to the volatile quickness of Buckingham's moods, nor did he wish to insult the man who in a few brief days had become a party to his every thought. But the quiet authority in his voice had carried its own weight. Pouting but complying, Buckingham had retired to his chamber to divest himself of the offending finery.

It struck Richard now that he hardly needed such finery being handsome enough in himself to make richness of dress almost an offense against nature. Even the somber black, which made Richard appear more drab than usual, served as a foil for Buckingham's golden fairness. Richard saw heads turn and eyes swivel to follow him as they passed and heard from some of the women lewd little giggles of appreciation. A bawd's voice, overloud, cried out, "God's arse, but I should welcome that one's slippers 'neath me bed!"

The woman's bawdry repelled him—such vulgarities always repelled him—but it also made him feel, as he had not felt for a long time, the smallness of his own stature, the imperfections of his posture, the plainness of his features. He was a changeling among the fair Plantagenets, as his own father had been, a sparrow born into a nest of eagles. As a child, he had loved and envied that great golden brood of brothers and sisters, always striving to be like them but never quite succeeding. Once again, his eye lighted on Buckingham. How much he was like Clarence, how very like! Clarence whom he had loved as a boy and envied most of all when Edward, ten years older and off fighting a man's war, was like the distant figure of a dream.

They had passed through the city now and out into the countryside again. They approached Fulham Palace, the ancient and venerable residence of London's bishop, where Edward was to be temporarily lodged. There stood his host, old Thomas Kempe, whose eyes were still lucid and alert in his wrinkled face though he neared eighty years of age. Next to him was the Lord Chancellor Thomas Rotherham, archbishop of York. Though younger by a score of years, he bore those years much more heavily. He quaked now like an aspen leaf in a gale as if he expected a reprimand on the spot, and Richard wondered what amount of bribery or bullying it had taken to make him appear today at all. Standing with him were Bourchier and Russell and John Morton, bland and imperturbable as always, and in a separate group, there were John Howard and Thomas Stanley with his brother Sir William. Along with the other nobles and knights, they fell to their knees as Edward's pony neared them.

But for Richard, there was only one face he sought in all that crowd, and his eyes quickly picked it out. Soon after he had dismounted, Hastings was beside him with laughter in his eyes and a kiss of greeting on his lips, and all the fears and troubles that had plagued them both over the past weeks were flown like geese in autumn.

"God's greetings to Your Grace," said Hastings. "We are well met on this happiest of days."

"Well met indeed, Will," Richard replied, clutching his friend's arm. "As God is my witness, your face has never looked so good to me."

"I fear the past weeks have aged me," Hastings demurred. "The king looks well."

"With Edward's blood in him, how could he not? But tell me, Will, was it difficult for you here?"

"For a while, yes," Hastings admitted, "but I'm sure the dangers I faced were as nothing compared to yours. I'm most anxious to hear it all—and from your own lips."

"Then you shall," said Richard, "though I must warn you that in payment I shall expect to receive your own account."

Edward had already been helped from his mount by a number of hovering aides and had received, as one who has grown accustomed to obeisance, the homage of his lords temporal and spiritual. Surrounded still and giving gracious ear to the welcoming phrases of his host, he walked up the marble stair to the bishop's palace. Behind him, Richard and Hastings followed, chatting amiably, arms linked in the old comradeship that came so easily to them. Suddenly, Richard sensed the presence of another close by, falling like a shadow between them. He turned, and there was Buckingham walking alone. His full lower lip trembled very slightly.

"Why, Harry," Richard said, checking himself abruptly. "You are, of course, acquainted with my Lord Hastings?"

"I have had that honor though it has been a long time now," the duke replied.

"Then please join us, Your Grace," Hastings said amicably, "for surely you too have much to tell of our great victory."

Buckingham was only too eager to oblige. He stepped adroitly between them, placing a hand on the shoulder of each. It was his hearty baritone that filled the courtyard as they entered the bishop's palace.

BOOK II

𝕿𝖍𝖊 𝕮𝖚𝖕

May 6 to June 13, 1483

Chapter 14

RICHARD WAS WELL pleased with his London mansion of Crosby Place. Built less than twenty years before, it raised walls of creamy stone and soaring gabled roofs over the busy district of Bishopsgate. Inside, the house was as imposing as it was outside. The great hall was spacious and well provided with windows; the tall oriel, rising to its own small vault fretted with gold starts, was Richard's particular favorite. The hall ceiling—beamed, painted, and gilded—arched loftily above a floor of unpolished Purbeck marble that swept away like a calm sea. In contrast to Middleham, which despite alternations still retained the unmistakable air of a border fortress, Crosby Place was a princely dwelling, fully worthy of sheltering any of the great and noble. It amused Richard not a little to think that all this magnificence had been commissioned and paid for by a mere commoner, a wealthy tailor and alderman; indeed, he himself only leased it from John Crosby's widow.

He did, however, make worthy use of it and was doing so that very evening. Around the table with him were those men on whom he had called for counsel in the past and those whom he would call upon in the future. They made a goodly gathering. Flushed with wine and excellent food, the men were in an amiable mood. There was much toasting in vintage claret brought up from the well-stocked cellars, much talk (all of it optimistic), and much laughter. Hastings looked particularly content, roaring wholeheartedly as he leaned forward to catch some witticism from Buckingham. Even the usually somber Howard and Stanley were engaged in animated conversations with Percy and Assheton, reliving the siege of Berwick. And Richard himself had seldom felt more cause for thanksgiving. He had that very day, the second since his arrival in London, been unanimously acclaimed protector by a full session of the council.

If possible, he would have ignored the two empty seats at the table. Archbishop Rotherham, who had been removed from the lord chancellor's office that same day, had sent a message saying he was sick with a belly gripe and could not attend. Richard was piqued. Under the circumstances, he felt he had been exceptionally generous with Rotherham and had even allowed him to keep his seat on the council. Pity perhaps or the memory of the archbishop's long service to the realm had stayed his hand. That the former chancellor could find anything to resent in the reprimand after his extraordinary conduct with the seal still rankled Richard.

John Morton had also excused himself from the gathering. It seemed that both the abbot of Croyland and the prior of Ely were expected in London that very evening to discuss a dispute over revenues in the diocese. "The Bishop of Ely very deeply regretted . . . an urgent matter that would brook no delay . . . Surely the Protector would understand."

The protector understood only too well. He remembered the brief flash of resentment in Morton's eyes as the gold collar of the chancellery had been lowered over the head of John Russell. There had been no question of a contest in the naming of Rotherham's successor. In Richard's opinion, Russell surpassed every other candidate for the office, including Morton, as a cathedral outranks a parish church.

"My word on it, he had ten women to his bed that night." A ripple of laughter from one end of the table, led by Buckingham's loud guffaw, broke upon Richard's thoughts. From the sheepish grin that creased Lord Hastings's round face, Richard guessed that Edward's former boon companion had been regaling them with one of his ribald stories, though he himself had not been listening. He found Hastings's anecdotes less than amusing, concerning as they so often did the vast appetites (sexual and otherwise) of the late king and the depravities of his court.

He looked sharply at the lord chamberlain, but then his eyes softened. Hastings had meant no disrespect; he was nothing if not loyal. Richard recalled the expression on the chief baron's face that very morning in the dim vastness of St. Paul's Cathedral when Hastings, along with the other lords temporal and spiritual, had sworn fealty to Edward's son. The face that could so easily break into laughter had been solemn, even rapt, as the baron extended his hands between the boy king's and vowed to be his liege man of life and limb.

Yet the words on his lips now were far from sacred. "After the king was finished with her, we tossed for her, Dorset and I. When I won her for the night, the marquis was fit to be tied. True Spaniard she was, with great black snapping eyes and breasts like clotted cream. Give a man the rise just to look at her. Dorset wanted her, wanted her bad. I wouldn't have been long for this world if he had known the dice were loaded in my favor."

"You had better not speak of it now then," Buckingham said casually, nibbling on a piece of marchpane.

Hastings gave him a puzzled look. "Whyever not? He's safely out of the way in sanctuary, I daresay."

"Do you now?" Buckingham cocked one eyebrow. "Well, perhaps there's been some mistake then. I understood he had fled Westminster."

Hastings choked on his wine. Beside him, Howard pounded his back. "Precious blood of our Lord! Escaped? But how?"

"We don't know the answer to that," Richard said, "though we wish we did. I wouldn't have it generally known as yet, but we are all friends here. I see no harm in your knowing."

"You-you've searched for him, I take it?" Hastings voice was barely audible.

"Yes, of course. The whole town of Westminster and the surrounding countryside as well. He seems to have vanished without a trace. We could find no sign of him."

"Nor are we likely to," Buckingham added. "He's probably joined his uncle Edward Woodville at sea. An easy task to bribe a boatman on the Thames then a small ship from Gravesend. By any reckoning, he has most of the coin of the realm to do it with. Why, he might even have taken a lady along, Spaniard or otherwise, to soften somewhat the rigors of exile. Aye, he's safe on the Narrow Sea now or soon will be."

Hastings's face was drained of color. He suddenly looked old and rather unwell. It was Howard who spoke. "That certainly bodes ill for us. Sir Edward alone is little to fear, even with his navy. A mere coxcomb . . ."

"While Dorset might lead his men," Richard said. "Is that what you're thinking?"

"Yes. We should not delay long in dealing with the Woodville navy. If I might commend myself to Your Grace, I do have some small experience in these matters."

Richard smiled at this singular understatement. "And do you also have a plan?"

"Why, now that you mention it, m'lord, I believe I do," Howard replied, breaking into a wide, slow grin.

"Then let's hear it."

Howard leaned toward Richard, ignoring Hastings, who sat between them, toying with the silver-gilt salt cellar. "Edward Woodville has his navy, we all know that, and it's surely a larger one than we could hope to muster in a matter of days."

"Particularly since he has seen fit to commandeer every galleon of any size in London harbor," Stanley interjected with a trace of a sneer.

"Precisely my point. He has his galleons, but they are clumsy vessels, not built for speed. And his crew is little better, Italian merchant seamen—Venetians, Sicilians, Florentines. Hardly the sort of crew you'd choose for an *English* navy, would you say, my lord?"

Richard shook his head thoughtfully. "No. Go on."

"If we could get some ships, any ships, but preferably small ones, lighter and more maneuverable than Sir Edward's heavy carracks . . ."

"You may have to take fishing trawlers then," Buckingham said, "for there is little else."

"Very well then fishing trawlers—a perfect choice!"

"Do you mean to say that you are going to wage a naval battle with . . . fishing boats?" Buckingham asked, incredulous.

"There will be no battle, not if my plan works. All I intend is to get close enough to Sir Edward's ships to do a little preaching like any good friar."

"And what will be the text of this sermon?" asked Richard.

"Mutiny, Your Grace. What else? I mean to tell those sailors that there is a new regime in London, that the days of the Woodvilles are over. Sir Edward and his pretty nephew the marquis are nothing but fugitives with a price on their heads, and so shall any man be who chooses to remain with them. But to those who find it provident to change their minds and hoist their sails for London, the protector will grant a full and free pardon."

"I wasn't aware that I had grown so generous," Richard said, but he was smiling both from amusement and from sheer delight at the audacity of Howard's plan.

"It's too risky," Buckingham protested. "It can't work. Sir Edward does have some warships and gunpowder as well. What if he fires on our poor, hapless little vessels?"

"I didn't say my idea was without risk. Most surely it is not. But I do have men who are willing to attempt it."

"Not yourself, John," Richard said quickly. "I couldn't allow that. I have too much need of you here."

Howard's face fell. "I-I had thought to go, Your Grace. There is something to salt spray in a man's face and gulls crying overhead and sails bellying in the wind like a woman nigh her time."

"I won't deny it," replied Richard. "The sea is a siren, but you must not listen to her song this time. Do you have others you could send as captains?"

"If it pleases Your Lordship, I do. You are perhaps familiar with Tom Fulford and Ned Brampton?"

Richard's brow furrowed ever so slightly. "Yes, I believe. Brampton—isn't he the Portuguese Jew who hung around Edward's court like a gadfly? As for the other, Fulford, I don't immediately place him. Did he serve under you 'gainst the Scots?"

"Yes, both men did. Fulford captained the western fleet . . ."

"Ah yes, I remember now," Richard said abruptly. "He acquitted himself well enough there, but as I recall, he was not always so loyal. He once served Queen Margaret."

"Years ago, my lord, in the foolishness of his youth."

"Do we dare trust him now?"

"Emphatically, yes. He is much changed."

"I don't know," Richard argued, shaking his head doubtfully. The very breath of the word Lancaster was anathema to him. "The situation is delicate."

Howard's brown eyes looked full into Richard's. "Do you trust my loyalty, my lord?" It was more than a question; it was a pledge of allegiance to the protector and his cause.

"With all my heart," Richard replied, suddenly moved.

"Then no less do I trust his."

"Why, then we shall have him!" Richard cried. "Here, steward, refill our cups. Let us drink a toast to Lord Howard and his great venture—and to his stalwart seamen as well."

"Hear, hear!" It was Buckingham who led the cheer, while Howard sat back in his seat, beaming his pride.

Suddenly, Hastings rose, his chair clattering noisily on the marble floor. He held his hand palm down over the rim of his hanap. "No, steward, none for me. I-I must be going."

"So soon, Will?" Richard asked. "It's still early. Never in all the years I've known you have you been the first to leave a gathering."

Hastings stared down at his empty cup. "That's the problem, I'm afraid. Too many years, too many gatherings. The day has been a long and a tiring one, and my old bones ache for their bed. My apologies, Your Grace, for my bones. You must not take their impatience as a slur on your hospitality, which has, as always, been superb."

Richard stood, still puzzled. He noted that the candied tangerines, which were Hastings's favorite sweetmeat, lay on his plate, untouched. "You're not ill, I hope?"

"What? Ill? Oh no, no, nothing of the sort. I'll be quite myself after a night's rest."

"So be it then." Richard clapped a hand to his friend's shoulder. "Far be it from me to keep an old man from his bed."

Stanley too was on his feet, ready to follow the one who had always been his patron, but Howard reluctantly, awkwardly, held back, fumbling at the arms of his chair. He too was Hastings's man. By precedent and tacit agreement, he did not go where the lord chamberlain was not invited, nor did he linger at a feast after Hastings had gone. However, tonight it was clear that he wished to stay.

"My lord Howard?" It was Hastings at the door, inquiring from long habit. Howard rose finally and made his good nights and good evens, but the long backward glance he gave Richard revealed that Hastings's man had almost become the protector's man that night by quiet declaration.

"Splendor of God!" Richard exclaimed in agitation. "Hastings and that Shore creature? I wouldn't have believed it. Are you certain?"

Buckingham gave him a languid shrug from the depths of a pile of cushions. The firelight leapt high on his face and on the amber liquid in his glass. They had retired to the solar after Richard's other guests had departed, but an occasional bellow or shout from the hall below told them that Richard's household knights, unwilling to retreat so early to their beds, still played at the dice.

"It's the common report," Buckingham drawled. He took a sip of the hippocras. "Didn't you notice how he started at the news of Dorset's escape, as if he had a great treasure and had just learned that a master thief was on the loose?"

"Not Hastings, please not Hastings." Richard shook his head in disbelief. "And she as worthy as any in London to wear the rayed hood and be whipped at the cart's tail! Oh God, not Hastings!"

"He does have worthy predecessors, my lord. Don't forget who once loved her."

"You needn't remind me of that!" Richard snapped. The face of Shore's wife, as he still thought of her, was etched indelibly on his memory—sensual and mocking beneath those flaming whorls of hair that could never have come from nature. No one was born with hair of that color. Then there were the pouting, slightly parted lips, the coy umber eyes beneath their fringe of darkened lashes, promising anything, everything . . . And there was the round white body with its melon breasts, insinuating delights that a man might dare the fires of hell to enjoy.

She was evil dressed in a guise of beauty, but still evil. Richard felt himself stained by the mere thought of her. That Edward should have taken her to his bed was injury enough, but Edward had been a king, and kings would have their way. Hastings was no king, and he was also well past the age to be simpering like a schoolboy over a new mistress.

"I will speak to him about it," Richard said. "He must see that she is . . . uh . . . unsuitable and no fit companion for one of my chief councilors, however much my late brother indulged himself with her. I-I cannot allow this . . . this wickedness to flourish like some rank poison weed in my garden."

Buckingham looked faintly surprised, as if failing to perceive how this tidbit of gossip had so provoked Richard's wrath. "I meant the man no harm," said the duke by way of apology. "I don't wish to play the tattler. You must understand that."

"Of course, I understand. You could not have known how much this particular liaison would disturb me. Yet I thank you, cousin, for your information."

Buckingham regarded Richard with cool blue eyes. "Your Grace should always be . . . well informed. But perhaps you are troubled unnecessarily. By now, Dorset may have gotten rid of the wench for us."

Richard laughed but without mirth. "If God is good, may he so will it."

It took Hastings a long time to get home.

He was annoyed beyond words when his retinue was halted by a night watchman who held a gleaming pike across their path and cried out in a voice with the harsh twang of the west in it, "Thou mayn't pass!"

It was an irritation that he did not normally experience. The mere sight of his badge was generally enough to make the staunchest guard uncover in respect to his lowliest henchman. But this one was young, little more than a boy from the look of him, inordinately proud of his livery and determined to fulfill every jot of his duties. Moreover, he was an outlander newly arrived from Devon or Cornwall, and he recognized neither the lord chamberlain's face nor his cognizance.

It was not until a sergeant of the watch threatened to have him publicly flogged that the red-faced youth offered apology, tugging anxiously at his forelock. By this time, the nagging doubt in Hastings's mind had turned to painful certainty. All Hallows Barking was tolling eleven. He had stayed much too long at Crosby Place.

He should have left as soon as he heard of Dorset's escape. There had been no merriment for him after Buckingham, all unknowing, had dealt him that crippling blow to the stomach. The talk that had flowed around him after that was as unintelligible as the buzzing of so many bees. Necessity born of long habit had forced him to stay, but it had not been quite enough to permit normal behavior. Richard had been puzzled by his abruptness; Richard had not been pleased at all. They had been in the midst of offering a toast to Howard, though what Howard had done to merit this esteem Hastings could not recall. He only knew that suddenly he could not bear the uncertainty any longer. By then, the pain had become a searing fire in his vitals. He really was ill then, or near it.

Poor Howard, though. He had been snatched away at a very inopportune moment, or so it seemed now. No wonder he had looked annoyed as they had said their good nights. But at least he had been easily enough detached, unlike Stanley who had hovered about him like a persistent mosquito, burning to discuss the day's events. He had even had the temerity to suggest a foray into Southwark for a pint of ale in a tavern there and perhaps even a tilt with some of the bishop of Winchester's geese. Hastings had ignored the lewd wink. He was not of a mind to chase skirts this evening, not with Jane waiting—if indeed she was waiting.

Hours later, it seemed, they rode into the courtyard of his riverside mansion. The house loomed dark, the yard deserted. Nevertheless, a sleepy ostler slipped from the shadows to take his horse.

"Any news?" Hastings asked sharply.

The lad was dim-witted. His head rolled heavily to one side on a scrawny neck. "News, milord?" he slurred. "What news should be?" A dab of spittle trickled down his chin.

Hastings turned away in disgust that a man of his importance should be so ill served! He forgot that he himself had taken in poor Jack in a fit of pity because the boy had a way with horses. Like as not, his mind was no better than theirs.

His hand trembled on the latchkey; he did not even wait for the porter. He took the stairs two at a time, though he had to stop for a moment, panting, at the top. Jane's room was deserted, the bed unmussed, though her bower still showed signs of feminine habitation: the neat rows of unguents and powders and perfumes on the dressing table, a tiny bouquet of violets fresh from the garden, a wisp of petticoat trailing over the linen chest. Strangely, he took no comfort from these signs. They were things she probably would not have taken with her when she fled. Without her, their presence only mocked him.

Robbed! He had been robbed! The mounting dread rose to his lips in a great groaning cry. He buried his face in the silken hangings of her bed and wept.

"My lord?" The voice was low, gentle, thrilling. He turned to see her face, soft with concern and blurred with his tears, in the light of the taper she was carrying.

"Jane! Where were you?" He was at once both relieved and angry. "Don't you know I've been worried half to death about you?"

"Worried?" Her wide eyes blinked. "Why worried? I know of nothing—"

"Dorset-Dorset is free."

"Ah," she said softly, dipping her taper to the candelabra on the mantle. "And you thought that I . . . ?" She left the question unfinished. He could not see her face. Her hair shimmered with a flame of its own in the lightening room.

"I . . . yes," he replied, ashamed now. "I thought, nay feared, that you had gone with him."

"You doubt my fidelity then?" she asked, cocking her head, laughing at him with her eyes. His own eyes traveled downward.

Through the thin lawn of her nightshift, he could see the tips of her breasts, rose petal pink; below her navel was the little mound of her belly and the bright patch of hair at the top of her legs.

"Cock's arse, Jane, do you think I can forget you were his before you were mine? I heard he was loose, and then when I came back, your bed was empty."

"Only because I was waiting for you in yours."

"In . . . in mine?"

She nodded. "Do you think me a shameless hussy for confessing it?" She slipped her arms around his neck. He could feel the ripe softness of her body pressing against him, the warmth of her breath on his cheek.

"What a simpleton I've been!" he cried, laughing with sudden delight into the sandalwood fragrance of her hair. "What a tomfool of a simpleton! Can you forgive me, Jane? Can you ever forgive me?"

"Well," she considered, "I will admit the offense is great. You must, of course, do strict penance to the goddess of love—a night of hard labor between the sheets . . ."

He caught her to him and kissed her hungrily, his fingers slipping through the silken masses of her hair. Strangely, he recalled the scrawny braid that his wife, Katherine, habitually wore to bed—mouse brown, flecked with gray now, and as tightly plaited as her screwed-up face itself. She had once had some beauty to recommend her, along with an ample share of the Neville inheritance, but never, not even in his lusty youth, had it been for him as this was, not with Kate, not with any of the women who had taken their turn in his bed.

"Jane, dearest Jane," he murmured against the nape of her neck. "I hope you are not jesting with me, for by the mass, I do love thee sore."

Chapter 15

AT MEALTIMES, THE great hall of Baynard's Castle took on many of the aspects of an abbey refectory. There was no music, no sweet strains of lute or viol or dulcimer drifting down from the gallery. Nor was there the constant hum of conversation, the voices of almost one hundred servants and retainers discussing the day's events as they tore at great hunks of beef and venison. Instead there was silence broken only by the clicking of utensils and the steady drone of a black-gowned monk reading in Latin from the lector's pulpit. The Dowager Duchess of York spent much time at the abbey at Syon, and each time she returned to London, she managed to bring back more of the monastic life with her.

Richard was there almost by accident. He had, of course, stopped by on his first day in London to pay his filial respects to his mother, but he had planned to spend no more time than that in her household. It had been a simple matter of convenience that had made him decide to call the morning's council meeting for Baynard's instead of Crosby Place. He favored its location on Thames bank at the point where the city's west wall touched the river, midway between the Tower and Westminster and so easily accessible to both. Or had it been merely a matter of location? Baynard's was a venerable pile of gray stone, reeking of history and invulnerability. In Richard's boyhood, it had been the London residence of his father, the Duke of York, a man who in the opinion of many should have been king. If Baynard's Castle served to remind the council that Richard, as sole surviving son of this great sire, was also heir to much of his power, surely that knowledge could not work against him.

But it did not, at that moment, appear to have worked in his favor either. The morning meeting had not gone well. Moreover, it had left him here at the noon meal, something he did not relish but could not escape since his mother had summoned him to share her table. Yes, *summoned* was the only word for it. The Dowager Duchess of York was no more to be refused than a crowned queen.

He supposed there was some matter she wished to discuss with him but knew he would learn nothing of it here, where she kept her vow of silence. She had acknowledged his presence with only a nod as he had taken his seat beside her, along with a little frown of disapproval because he was late. The galling thing was that he could not even apologize, not then at any rate, nor explain that he had been closeted with Hastings after the adjournment of the council. Much good that had done him as well!

After the initial nod, Cecily of York had turned back to her simple repast: a bowl of broth flavored with leeks, a bit of white goat's milk cheese, some coarse dark bread, a hanap of watered Rhenish. She sipped daintily at the soup and only nibbled sporadically at the cheese, her attention rapt on the sonorous voice of the monk. Richard had been served somewhat more elaborate fare than that provided his mother, but he too only touched briefly on the milk-poached carp and beef pasty. He supposed that the morning's disappointments had stolen his appetite.

Everything had gone awry with the first mention of Rivers and his cohorts. It was not a topic Richard would have broached for discussion though he suspected that sooner or later one of the council would: Morton perhaps or Rotherham, surely one of the Woodville sympathizers. He had been shocked and annoyed when Russell had raised the question—Russell, his own hand-picked and newly installed chancellor.

"What are we to do with them?" Richard had echoed foolishly. He himself was perfectly content to let things remain as they were for the present.

"Yes," Russell replied. His broad, intelligent face was quite composed. "We cannot keep them locked away in the north forever. There are no charges against them. What crimes have they committed?"

Buckingham had drawn himself up smartly in his new black samite doublet. "Why, my Lord Chancellor, can it be that you have not heard a full account of the events at Northampton and Stony Stratford? Certainly if you had, you could not doubt that they stand guilty of no less an infraction than treason."

Russell's jaw had jutted outward like the prow of a battleship. "Treason, is it? And does my lord protector concur in this assessment?"

"Why, I . . ." Richard faltered, looking from Russell to Buckingham and back again. In truth, he did not know what he thought. A charge of treason against Rivers and Grey had been no part of his original intent, yet his thinking had shifted subtly over the past few days. Or had it been Buckingham, breathing softly in his ear the word he now brandished like a sword, who had wrought this change? "I-I don't know," he finally admitted lamely.

Russell nodded his satisfaction. "That is well. We must remember that treason is a crime only against the king."

"Or against his lawfully appointed protector," Buckingham argued.

"Ah, yes, my lord duke, you speak correctly. But the protector was not the protector until confirmed in that office by this council—after his arrival in London."

Buckingham had lost then though he fought on with fierce intensity. Russell had marshaled his case well without spite or malice but with a clear eye to the legalistic niceties of the situation. And when Buckingham thundered against the arms and harness found in the king's baggage wagons, Alcock, his loyalties plainly divided, was called upon to testify that Rivers had never intended that they be used.

"In faith, he would not have had them there at all," the bishop of Worcester added. "He was that afraid they might lead to trouble."

And why had he shipped the king off to Stony Stratford when they were to meet the protector at Northampton, Buckingham had demanded, if he were not a party to the queen's duplicity?

Here Alcock shook his head. He did not know. It had been his understanding that they were to await Gloucester at Northampton. He had been as surprised as any when the order was given—by Rivers—to press on.

"Aha!" Buckingham pounced on that. "Rivers gave the order. He was actively seeking to prevent Gloucester's access to the king."

"Perhaps," Russell admitted, "but at most it appears he was guilty of an error in judgment, not of high treason."

There had been a long moment of silence. Far below, through the unglazed window slits, they heard the gentle lapping of the Thames against the castle wall, the occasional cry of a boatman on the river. Howard would be down there somewhere, readying his small fleet. Richard sorely missed his sturdy, rock-strong presence in council that day and idly wondered if his support might have made a difference in the outcome. Hastings's presence certainly had not. He had failed to open his mouth even once during the debate and now looked dreamily through the window toward the bright sky of May. Once, Richard had even caught him nodding.

Buckingham had carried the burden of the argument, and though at the end he slumped defeated in his chair and stared deject-edly into his lap, Richard felt a swift rush of affection for him. He had been wrong, and they had lost, but that did not alter the strength of his loyalty.

"And now, my lords all," Russell said, "I ask you once more, what is to be done with Lord Rivers and his companions?"

"Perhaps, Russell," Morton ventured, "if they are as blameless as you suggest, they should be allowed to go free."

"No!" Richard said sharply. "Though neither would I have them beheaded for treason. My Lord Chancellor, I most humbly thank you for pointing out the law on these matters and for setting my feet on the proper path. I would not begin my reign in a bloodbath—." A chorus of audible gasps cut him off. Richard felt the warm rush of blood to his face as he stammered awkwardly for words. "I mean . . . er . . . of course, my protectorate. I would not . . . uh . . . begin my protectorate in a bloodbath. Let Rivers and his cohorts stay where they are a while longer. They are comfortable enough, I assure you.

And though I don't like the situation any better than you do, I feel our circumstances are still too volatile to permit their release."

"Of course, Your Grace." Russell inclined his head briefly, raising it to give Richard a beatific smile. His teeth were as square as his face and the pale yellow of aged ivory. "I pray your forgiveness if I seemed to play the devil's advocate. No more would I have you begin your . . . uh . . . protectorate under a cloud. Just be on notice that the present situation cannot continue indefinitely."

They had adjourned shortly thereafter, but then Richard had been faced with a confrontation even more unpleasant than the one in council. He had decided to speak to Hastings that very morning concerning the Mistress Shore.

It had begun easily enough. Hastings had been in a genial, expansive mood and had already guessed at the topic Richard wished to discuss. He had run a plump hand over his thinning hair. "Do you know then?" he asked.

"Yes, I've heard, though I did not wish to believe it."

"Oh, Dickon, you must understand. Jane has been much maligned, much. But her heart is warm and loving. She is a woman that any man must gladly cherish."

"Not any man, Will." Richard's voice sounded shrill, even to his own ears. "I do not cherish her."

Hastings chuckled, a bit nervously. "You've been more fortunate on the lists of marriage than have I. The Lady Anne is a prize beyond rubies. Your fondness for her and hers for you are legend. I am not so blessed. The Lady Katherine, for all that she is your first cousin, is a shrew. Her main virtue is that she chooses to remain at Ashby and let me follow my own pursuits here in London. Would you have me foreswear all feminine companionship?"

Richard shook his head. Beyond the window, a gull wheeled above a fishing trawler, and the sun glanced a white flash off its wing. The rising tide brought the brackish smell of the sea.

"No," he said, "I would not. Though I've scarcely applauded your liaisons, I would not have meddled in them. They were none of my affair. Oh, come, Will, I'm hardly a saint to be prating to you of virtue. I've never taken a vow of chastity, and I have my bastards—

though they were fathered in the green days of my youth, not in the ripe years of maturity. What of it? It isn't that which concerns me."

"What then?" Hastings stood stiffly against the rough stone of the wall.

Richard shook his head. "She has always been . . . particularly repugnant to me. I don't know why."

Hastings saw the weakness and pressed. "Jane—repugnant? Why, she is in every detail the very opposite. Sweet, lovesome, bedsome . . . You don't know her. Come home with me and see for yourself—"

Richard cut him off. "I know her only too well, and I don't wish to further the acquaintance. There is a danger in her. I don't know. I can't explain."

Hastings shook his head, incredulous. His round cheeks glowed red as he stepped into the sunlight. "Dickon . . ."

"You won't give her up then?"

"By the mass, how should I? You may ask of me anything else you wish. My right arm? I would cut it off and lay it at your feet. Goods, houses, lands—all at your disposal. I'd even part with my own children before I'd harm a hair on my dearling's head."

"You're besotted," Richard breathed.

"Aye, besotted. Have it so. I'll not argue that. But what of it, Dickon? I am most gloriously besotted, and the town crier may shout it in the marketplace for all that it matters to me."

Richard turned away. His fingers massaged at a growing pain behind his temples.

"Ah, but I do run on," Hastings was saying, still jovial. "It's hard on the dinner hour, and my table is laid as fine as it ever was. Come home with me today, and I'll give you a welcome you won't soon forget. You may speak to the lady yourself and so ease your mind, for by all the saints, I don't want you troubled on account of this. It would tear me apart to see the two that I love best in all the world at each other's throats like bull mastiffs on a feast day. Please, Dickon, won't you come?"

Richard shook his head sadly. "No, I can't come today. Proud Cis has summoned me to her table. But you may share it with me if you would. It will be frugal enough, I daresay, but I would be glad for your company."

Hastings had shifted uncomfortably on his feet. His tongue flicked restlessly over his full lips as he framed an answer, and his eyes strayed involuntarily to the door.

"No," Richard answered for him. "I see that your heart is straining at its leash and even now she tugs at you like a mighty pulley. Go to, man, go to. I'll keep my solitary state none the worse for it."

Hastings had rewarded him with a grateful smile. Bowing swiftly, he had raised the hem of Richard's houppelande to his lips and had vanished in a trice, not even pausing to collect the coterie of hovering attendants that awaited him outside the door.

Moonstruck as a young calf, Richard thought now. He might not even have spoken to Hastings at all, for the lord chamberlain was deaf to all but words of praise for his mistress. And Richard hadn't the faintest idea what to do about it.

At last, the droning from the lector's pulpit ceased. The duchess signed herself, wiped her mouth carefully with her linen napkin and, folding it neatly into a square, stood as the steward hastened to hold her chair. Her hand rested lightly on Richard's shoulder. Her eyes conveyed the unmistakable message: "Attend me in my chambers." One glance from her could still command him, grown man that he was. He rose to his feet to honor her departure. She swept from the room, black skirts rustling about her, like a ship in full sail. And like a small attendant vessel, he followed in her wake.

The duchess's apartments smelled of must and seclusion. At first, Richard could make out little in the dimness colored mulberry by the heavy ancient draperies. Only one curtain was open to the day, and there stood a large tapestry frame where Cecily was embroidering an Annunciation scene. The bright skeins of thread—rose, blue, green, and gold—were vivid in the unaccustomed swath of sunlight. Something else shared the sunbeam as well, a child on a three-legged stool, her glowing blonde head bent over a smaller frame.

"Grand-mère!" the girl cried, looking up. "*S'il vous plaît.* I need help with this stitch."

"Hmmm . . . let me see it, Meg." Cecily took the linen square and studied it as she might once have reviewed an important document of state. It was a picture of two swans—a black and a white—and, to Richard's untutored eye, very prettily done. "Ah, yes, I think you are using the wrong stitch here on the lily. Tear it out and try *peut-être*, a true lover's knot."

"*Merci, Grand-mère.*"

"Have you no word for your uncle, child?" Cecily asked, who had herself not yet acknowledged Richard.

Meg looked up, and Richard saw her face for the first time. So this was Clarence's daughter, Margaret. She was growing up, but then she would be almost ten by now. There was a rather fey beauty about her; she was like a fairy child with her cap of gold ringlets and those huge dark eyes, gray-black like Cecily's, peering at him uncertainly through her pale lashes.

"*Bonjour, ma oncle,*" she said, dipping in a polite curtsy.

"*Bonjour, mademoiselle.*"

"Margaret is studying French," Cecily said by way of explanation.

"I wish to go to the French court," Meg informed him, and Richard felt a swift stab of pity for the girl who, because of her father's attainder, would have small place in the English one.

"*Bien tôt,*" said Cecily, and reaching into the ample pockets of her black gown, she drew forth some sugared violets. "Would you like some, *ma petite?*" she asked.

"*Oui! Merci. Merci bien!*" came the excited reply.

"And these are for your brother. Why don't you take them to him?"

Sweeping another curtsy, the girl was gone, her quick footsteps tapping away in the corridor.

"She's growing up," Richard said. "I didn't realize . . . we shall soon have to find a husband for her. But, Maman, the violets! I hadn't thought—" His eyes swept the sparsely furnished chamber, which was almost barren of all luxuries. On the far wall, an ivory Christ writhed on a crucifix above an oaken prie-dieu.

"You hadn't thought them appropriate to my way of life?" she asked. "Nor are they, at least not now. But once, long ago in Rouen, before your brother Edward was born, there were violets like these growing in a wood. Your father and I rode out one day alone and saw them there, and he plucked a bouquet for me. We were like lovers then, Dickon, though I know it may be difficult for you to believe that. And there was I, as big as a barn with our child, and he, the tenderest knight that ever came courting. You will think me wanton if I speak more of that bed of violets and of the glide of the stream going by us and the warble of a thrush from a thicket . . ."

Her whole face was changed, softened, transformed with a sort of radiance as she had related the tale. Between the stiff white barb and the wimple, her skin was smooth once more like a young woman's. Her lips curved in a gentle smile. Her eyes—those sharp, piercing, gray-black eyes—misted over with memories. Never before had Richard seen her like this. She had always seemed so stern and proud even in his infancy, and she had borne from his earliest memory the scars of many sorrows. Of the thirteen children she had carried, most had already been laid to earth. And she had suffered as well the ultimate horror of seeing her dead husband's head piked on a lance tip and crowned with a paper crown, staring sightlessly from York's Micklegate Bar. It was the price he had paid for daring to think himself rightful King of England.

Black was her color now, for she was in perpetual mourning—black and starkest white, stiff with arrowroot. Only now for the first time could he imagine her in something else: rose perhaps or rich saffron or deep sapphire blue. Only now could he conceive why she had once been called the Rose of Raby.

Cecily released a barely audible sigh and took her seat before the tapestry frame. For a time, she did not speak, only worked steadily while the warm flush gradually died from her cheeks.

Whom does she remind me of? Richard wondered, suddenly struck by some similarity in her manner to another. Who else had looked on him with that same dazzled look while hymning praises of love? And then he knew. It had been Hastings that very morning while speaking of the Shore creature. But the cases were not alike. How could they be? Surely the holy, sanctified union between his mother and father was far from Hastings's lecherous itch for his whore.

"No!" he said aloud. "It can't be."

"What can't be, Dickon?" Cecily asked, raising her head from the tapestry. Her large blue-veined hand held the needle poised for the next stitch.

He shook his head, shamed by the thought. "Nothing," he told her. "It's nothing."

"Is it?" she asked, stabbing her needle through the angel's wing. "I wonder. Don't try to play hoodman's blind with me. Remember, I gave you birth. I know something is troubling you—that's why I've asked you here. I know how the thunderclouds gather on your brow when you're thwarted even as they used to gather on your father's, and I know, as I used to know with him, when a storm is coming. So tell me now—what's wrong?"

Richard swallowed a rebuke. He wanted to tell her that it was none of her affair. Outside of the usual filial obligations, he had never been particularly close to his mother. Proud and strong and distant she was and always had been—strong, but coldly strong like the stone walls of a fortress. In his childhood, she had been more concerned with his father and elder brothers than with him; in his manhood, with her own religious devotions and world-weariness. Once he might have welcomed her interest; now it came almost as an intrusion. But she held him pierced on the point of a pin with her eyes.

"I was thinking of Hastings . . . of Hastings and the Mistress Shore."

Cecily nodded, almost with satisfaction. "So it's true then. For your sake, I'd rather hoped that it wasn't."

"I don't like it either," Richard agreed, "yet I can't say why precisely."

Cecily drew the thread through her strong, even teeth and bit down. It was a point of some pride with her that she still had all her own teeth in good condition and not the rotted, decaying stumps of most older women or, worse, the gleaming and ill-fitting porcelain substitutes affected by the well-to-do.

"She is in league with the queen."

"The queen? But that, madam, is preposterous."

"No," Cecily said, drawing a strand of rose thread through her needle, "it's not. While Edward lived, his queen and her brothers and her sons and God alone knows how many more distant kin reigned. I knew it and shunned the court like the plague. Why do you think I mewed myself up here so tightly? Why, Jacquetta of Bedford in her day would hardly deign to treat me as an equal—me, mother to the king, and she, mere dam to the queen!" Cecily's eyes snapped with outrage at the memory of those old slights. "She used to patronize me with the most charming condescension. 'Ah, my dear Cecily, which seat would you like for the feast? Perhaps we can squeeze you in somewhere at the high table.'"

"Yes, yes," Richard said, holding up a hand to stem the verbal flood. "All this I know only too well, but what does it have to do with Jane Shore?"

"Ah, well. I am coming to that. They employed her to distract Edward, to keep him amused, to hoodwink him, if you will. She was all part and parcel of Elizabeth Woodville's grand scheme. And Edward was biddable. He was too easy, too wanton, especially in his later years. It's evil to speak ill of the dead, yet I must say it, I who loved him better than any, because now it is you who are threatened. I would not have the Woodville lovers around you. By St. Ninian, your role will be difficult enough."

Richard had taken the seat his niece Margaret had vacated on the little three-legged stool. He reached out and took his mother's hand, feeling the pulse leap rapidly beneath his fingers. "You shouldn't distress yourself so, Maman," he told her. "It's not good for your heart."

"Bah! My heart is strong enough. I shall probably outlive all my children." She bit her lip and turned quickly away. "Perhaps I have lived too long already."

"It's all right," Richard said, trying to soothe her. "I can live with the thought of the Shore creature though I don't like it. Hastings was probably right about that. It may be my own prejudices that make me detest her so. As for the Woodvilles, well, sooner or later, I must come to terms with them. I began by thinking I could make peace with them, but I've botched that, I'm afraid. Only this morning, I considered executing Rivers and his cohorts. Buckingham thought that was the solution. Now I'm not so sure."

"God forbid that you should keep any counsel but your own, yet I don't know that I would advise you differently." Her eyes grew hard, like two black pebbles.

"No," he replied, shaking his head. "That's not the way, though it may be easy, convenient. Russell refuses to believe them guilty of treason, and I'm forced to agree. I haven't the right. And even if I did, what should I say, how could I ever explain to Edward?"

"Ah, yes," Cecily said softly. "I had almost forgotten the boy."

"I wish I could forget him!" Richard cried with some vehemence. "It has all become so complicated I don't know where to turn."

"Within, Dickon, to yourself and without, to God."

He laughed a little hollowly. "So easily said."

"Have you a chaplain?"

"No, not here. In Middleham."

"You may have the services of one of mine."

"That is most kind of you, Maman." He patted her hand and rose from his cramped seat. "Just don't let it be the one who spoke today at dinner. I fear the good brother would put me to sleep with his droning."

"Even so, you have need of such, I think. The way will not be easy, even harder than if you yourself were king. Much more difficult always to rule in the stead of another. Your father learned that lesson with poor, mad Harry VI and to his sorrow. And your enemies are particularly vicious, Dickon, though they may seem powerless now. Like baying hounds, they can tear you to shreds before you're well aware they are on you. They have already had a taste of our blood."

He stared at her, uncomprehending. Her eyes looked fully into his. "Have you so quickly forgotten your brother Clarence?"

"No," he answered, "I haven't forgotten. There is scarcely a day that goes by that I don't think of him and ask myself the reason why."

Cecily flushed, the blood beating crimson into her cheeks. Too quickly, she turned away.

"And you know the answer!" he said wonderingly. "You know why they killed him, don't you? Tell me!" He seized her wrist and pressed hard. He felt her bones, old and brittle, in his grasp and the throbbing of her heartbeat like a wild thing's, surprised. "*Nom de Dieu!*" he shouted. "Tell me!"

She shook her head and wrenched away her hand, rubbing at the white marks his fingertips had left on her skin. "I can't tell you that. Never seek to know. I've already lost two sons to their cunning. Don't ask me to risk a third."

"Maman, forgive me," he said, suddenly contrite. "The riddle torments me."

"There are some things that, by the grace of God, it is best not to know." She stood then in dismissal. Topping him by inches as she once had his father, she bent her check for his filial kiss. "God keep thee, Dickon. God ever keep thee."

Chapter 16

"Sire, I have some documents here that require your signature."

Richard had seldom visited Edward at Bishop Kempe's palace in the days since their arrival in London. It seemed as if something always prevented him. Now he was only too aware that the look of sullen resentment Edward had cast toward him as he entered was well justified. He had neglected the king of late. As John Kendall unfurled his papers on the small table, Richard cleared his throat and began again.

"Your Grace will see that plans for your coronation are progressing nicely. We may be able to set the ceremony for as early as the Nativity of St. John. That would be the fourth Sunday in June."

"Ah . . . indeed," Edward said listlessly, but there was a small spark of interest in his eyes, quickly doused. "Set it for when you will, Uncle. It's all the same to me."

He sat down at the table and began to scrawl his "Edwardus Rex" in a careless, cursory fashion. Richard thought with a pang of the boy at Northampton who had once written his name with such pride.

"Your Grace does not wish to read these papers?" he asked.

"Why, no. We trust you, Uncle, do we not?" Edward asked. The irony in his tone was unmistakable.

"Edward . . ." Richard began, looking for an opening, any opening with the boy, "you . . . you are not happy here?"

Edward tossed down the quill and, at the same time, knocked the parcel gilt sand shaker onto the floor. As Kendall hastened to retrieve it, the king cried out, "Happy? Look around you! Are you as blind as my good host? How should I be happy here?"

The room breathed of dust and the old leather bindings of many books. The few once-rich tapestries were now frayed and mildewed. Heavy curtains draped most of the windows. Though more sumptuously furnished, it reminded Richard very much of his mother's apartments at Baynard's Castle, even to the heavy prie-dieu in a recessed alcove of the wall. It might once have been a fit refuge for saintly, witless Harry VI; however, it was hardly an appropriate environment for a twelve-year-old boy.

"Has Bishop Kempe treated you well?"

"Yes, of course," Edward answered impatiently. "He's been the soul of cordiality, but he's so old, and his servants are old. There is no one of my own age to talk to—*no one*—and little to do except watch the weathercock on top of the cathedral yonder turn in the wind. I wish I were the lowest gutter urchin. Do you know I look on them with envy, naked little jackanapes rolling in filth? I'd trade places with them if I could."

"Hush, Edward," Richard cautioned, "you must not talk that way. It's a sin against nature, wishing to be less than you are." But watching the boy, lower lip thrust out, fists balled in defiance at his sides, Richard felt sympathy for him.

Kempe was old, and though his mind was still alert, it was probable he had long ago forgotten the entertainments of youth, probable as well that he did not even see the dingy, dust-moted decay of his mansion. And yet Richard could think of no other residence among the bishops' palaces that would be more suitable except perhaps John Morton's Ely Place at Holburn. He did not trust Morton enough to commit the king to his keeping, and to turn Edward over to one of the secular barons would be an act of rank favoritism, reducing him to little more than a pawn in the hands of some powerful magnate. One remaining possibility—to have him as a guest at Crosby Place— was equally unthinkable to Richard and for reasons that he did not wish to examine too closely.

"I'll bring the matter to the attention of the council," Richard said at last. "There must be some solution."

Edward cast him a calculating, sideways look from the tail of his eye. "If I could perhaps have my brother and sisters about me . . . They have done nothing to offend you, I hope?"

"No, and I wish they could be with you. Believe me, I most fervently wish it. But you must know that it's not possible at the present time." He wondered if he should remind Edward of the queen's intransigence. Elizabeth Woodville had refused even to negotiate with any of the spokesmen he had sent to her for that purpose, this despite the fact that his terms had been most generous: the title of Queen Dowager, an ample pension, and access, under watch, to her son. But Elizabeth did not wish to be merely a ceremonial figure. She had been much more than that for far too long. Now with the coronation plans being set, the situation was growing more urgent. It was unthinkable that the heir to the throne, whom she kept close as a baby chick under her protective wing, should not participate in his brother's coronation.

"Sire, if I may say so . . ." he began, but the words were only half out when the porter announced a new arrival. William, Lord Hastings, had come to call upon the king.

From the moment that Hastings strode into the room, wearing a warm smile of greeting, Richard ceased to exist for Edward. It was obvious from the quick look of gladness in the boy's eyes that this was not the first time the lord chamberlain had visited the king. And today, he brought something with him, a great gyrfalcon perched on his gauntleted wrist and trailing a tangle of leather jesses.

"Is she yours, my lord?" Edward asked wonderingly, touching the bird's feathers with his forefinger.

The hawk started in a flurry of feathers and bells, beating broad wings at the touch. "Gently, sire, gently," Hastings cautioned, "or she'll bate. She's a young bird and used to no hand other than my own and the falconer's. If you must, stroke her thusly." He ran a teasing finger lightly down her breast.

"She is so beautiful," Edward breathed. "How proud you must be!" He stared at the hawk in the light from the window. The iridescence of her feathers rivaled the jewels in her plumed hood. And there was power in her as well as beauty, in the wings that had beaten so passionately, in the curve of her cruel beak, in the sharp, clinging talons.

"I would be proud if she were mine," Hastings said, "but she's not. She is yours, sire."

"Mine?" Edward asked in disbelief.

Hastings nodded. "Your very own. I've raised her from a hatchling on the finest meat. Better even than some served at my own table." This was said with a smile and a wink at Richard. "I hope she will give you good sport."

"Oh, yes, I can see she will. I've never known her like. At Ludlow, my Uncle Rivers allowed me a peregrine once early this spring but, before that, only a mere kestrel. He said that the larger hawks were too dangerous."

"Dangerous?" Hastings repeated. "Yes, I daresay they are. You must handle them carefully as you have seen. You must never startle them either with a loud noise or a rough touch. You must keep them hooded all the time when they aren't in flight, and most important of all, you must always wear a gauntlet when handling them. These claws could scratch the life's blood from your unprotected hand. But the rewards are just as great as the perils. I shall teach you all you need to know. This is a gyrfalcon, sire—the king's falcon, if you will. None is considered worthy to handle her save *le roi*."

Edward brushed his fingertip lightly down her speckled breast. The falcon stiffened but did not panic. "I wish I could hold her," he said.

"There will be time for that later, Your Grace."

"Yes, but when? Why, there isn't even a mew here where I might keep her."

Hastings bowed. "If you will permit me to have the custody of her until you are permanently established here in London . . ."

Edward nodded. "Yes, we could allow that. But . . . we are kept close in hand here. When will we be able to take her out to watch her fly?"

Richard heard the sharp intake of his own breath. Edward was permitted to go abroad on occasion, but only under guard. There were too many supporters of the queen about yet to give him complete freedom.

"I'm certain your Uncle Gloucester would allow an expedition, say, into the woods beyond Holburn. Surely there could be no harm in that—no Woodvilles obscured in thickets or hiding behind tree trunks, eh, Dickon?" Hastings gave him a disarming smile.

"N-no," Richard stammered, weakening under the pleading gazes of boy and man. "No, I suppose there would be no harm in it."

"Good then!" Hastings exclaimed with a clap of his hands. "Let's say then, sire, within the next fortnight, after your father's month-mind, we'll take your hawk out and try her wings. Even I have not yet flown her without the jesses."

Edward looked suddenly stricken. "But suppose . . . suppose she doesn't come back to the lure? Suppose she keeps flying on and gains her freedom?" This was not like a sparrow hawk, his eyes were saying, this great, wild, magnificent creature. A half hour before, he had not known she existed; now he was bereft at the thought of losing her.

Hastings shook his head. "It may happen, it could happen. She will return to you only if she chooses, but you must permit her that choice. Oh, we'll do what we can beforehand. You will try her with the jesses and train her to come to your hand by offering her meat. But if when she is freed, the skies take her anyway, then you must let her go. It's the way of all things living."

Richard felt suddenly as if Hastings, in some oblique manner, were addressing him. *You cannot keep jesses on the heart of a man—is that what he is saying? You cannot keep Edward forever under guard. Oh, nonsense! It is only a bird he is speaking of, nothing more.*

"Come, Will," he said. "Are you attending council? I'll ride with you to the Tower."

"I am, of course, my lord, but first I must stop at home to attend to the king's gyrfalcon."

Aye, and to pleasure yourself with the Mistress Shore, no doubt, Richard thought unkindly. There was no reason Hastings should prove prompt for this particular meeting when he had been late for all the others this week. Richard subdued his thoughts as unworthy and tried to concentrate instead on the great joy Hastings had given Edward with his gift. A fine piece of hawk flesh—there could be no mistaking that. Richard himself could not boast her like in his own mew. Was that perhaps why the gift rankled in him so? Or was it because Hastings, and not he himself, had been the giver?

For Hastings, there was only one topic of any significance in the council meeting that day. He yawned politely behind his hand through a discussion about turning the protectorate into a regency after the coronation (Richard and Russell were, as ever, at odds about the precise details); he drummed his fingers on the table through yet another tirade on Edward Woodville's navy, last seen off the coast of Sandwich. That subject had not possessed any real interest for him since the night of Dorset's escape, and all he knew of John Howard's fleet was that it had sailed several days before, a scrappy though hardly seaworthy little band.

For Hastings, the question of primary importance, indeed the only question of any importance, was the changing of Edward's lodgings. He had remained behind at Fulham Palace long after Richard had left it; in fact, he had stayed on too long and was in consequence very tardy for the meeting. He had incurred Richard's knotted little frown of disapproval as he hastily took his chair, and though he would not have minded so much on his own account, he felt a trifle embarrassed for poor Catesby, who, this day for the very first time, had been granted a seat on the council. Richard had been impressed with the young solicitor from the day of his arrival in Middleham, and Catesby was understandably eager to continue in the protector's goodwill. He had dressed in his best brown fustian, neatly brushed in honor of the occasion, and his face visibly fell when Richard's frown greeted their entrance as if he himself were somehow responsible.

He was not, of course. And neither was Jane Shore, whatever Richard's glowering look implied. No less a personage than the king himself had kept Hastings past the appointed time. Edward was unhappy. That idea was somehow unthinkable, but there it was. Even the gift of the hawk had saddened him.

"But then I don't have to worry about losing her," Edward had said, gesturing to the door where Richard had just left. "He'll never let me take her out. I know he won't, whatever he says. I'm a prisoner here like my Uncle Rivers." The boy had bitten his lower lip as if afraid to say more, but Hastings, casting a look around him, did not need to question the cause of Edward's despondency.

After a conference with Argentine, he had taken the falcon, whom Edward had christened Griselda—"Maybe she'll teach me patience to bear my heavy lot"—back to his falconry. He had fed her a gobbet of raw venison from his own fingers, carefully avoided the tearing beak. She was indeed a royal bird, the finest he had ever seen. Even now, with his head filled with other thoughts, he felt a swift, keen admiration for her. He had bought her very early in the spring and intended her as a gift for that Edward who was now dead. Three sleepless days and nights had gone into her taming, and she was now a fit gift for a king, though not for the one originally intended. Nor did it appear that she was the gift most needed. Another residence— that was what Edward required.

"The king must be removed from Kempe's palace." Hastings was hardly aware that he had spoken his thoughts aloud until he felt fourteen pairs of eyes turn on him in mild surprise.

"What did you say?" asked Buckingham, cocking one eyebrow. "Isn't the bishop's palace luxurious enough for His Grace?"

"No," Hastings replied, warming to the debate, "it is not, though it's hardly a question of luxury. It's more an issue of suitability."

"Henry VI stayed there, and none thought it unsuitable."

"Precisely my point. Indeed, I could not have phrased it any better."

"Nor do you need to try," Richard said. Richard was coming to his aid. What luck! "The only question I would pose is, where should we install him?"

Here plainly was the stumbling block, for no ready answer presented itself. Morton fingered his pectoral cross, his face as expressionless as an egg. Russell stroked his square chin and Stanley the clipped forks of his auburn beard. Rotherham, who had been dozing in a stray sunbeam, came to life suddenly and stared wide-eyed around the room.

There were suggestions. The palace of the Knights Hospitaller, crammed with material comforts brought back from the Crusades, won Hastings's personal nod but was quickly vetoed by Russell.

"As it stands now, the king's grace is the guest of the church. If we move him to the Hospitallers' palace, he is still a guest, this time of a holy order. I ask you, my lords, what sort of a country is it that has no place in its capital to properly house its own king?"

"Well then," Stanley ventured, his hazel eyes blazing with either innocence or impertinence, "what of Westminster? It is the royal palace, is it not?"

Richard slammed his fist down on the table. "No!" he cried. "I'm amazed at you, Tom, for even suggesting it. I never took you for a Woodville lover. One short walk across the street into the arms of his waiting mother, and all of our efforts go for naught."

"There is . . . another palace in London, my lords," suggested Buckingham. "I marvel that none of you have thought of it."

"Another?" asked Russell.

"Yes. Just look around you."

"You can't mean the Tower!" Hastings cried, appalled.

Buckingham regarded him with detached amusement. "Do you know of another, my lord? If so, we should most like to hear of it."

Hastings shook his head. Of course, there was no other. Sheen, downriver, and Windsor, upriver, were both too far from London to serve. Hastings looked about the room they were in. Perhaps it was handsome enough in an austere way. The knights' pennons, swinging high from the oak-beamed ceiling in their scarlet and azure, emerald and gold added color. And the armor from long-forgotten battles that lined the far wall might be of interest to a child, though it was a bit rusty and tarnished. But the windows were tall and thin like arrow slits, the ceiling too high, the room as a whole too narrow. Its walls pressed in on one after a time. The Tower was the most ancient of all the royal abodes, but its use in recent years had become largely ceremonial.

The fourth Edward had always preferred the spacious luxury of Westminster, as well he might. Privately, he had confided to Hastings that he did not like to sleep the night in the Tower for fear of encountering old King Harry's ghost. He spoke in jest, but Hastings knew he had good reason to fear.

"Well, my lords, what do you say?" Buckingham questioned.

"I say . . . no!" said Alcock with effort to Hastings's silent applause. He was amiable by nature and usually tried to be amenable to suggestions, but now he looked unusually stubborn. "It's too vast a place and, at the same time, too enclosed—too much of a fortress for one so young." Hastings's eyes traveled outward to the crenulated curtain walls beyond. "I might have almost said a prison," Alcock continued, "for that's the way I've come to think of the place in recent years."

"It was a palace before it became a prison," Richard reminded him. "For many years, it was the sovereign's principal dwelling."

"Men cared less for comfort then than they do now." Hastings still entertained visions of the Hospitallers' palace. "In those days, they were concerned only with safety."

"Are we so far removed from danger that we can neglect safety?" Richard asked softly. "I hadn't thought so."

"But what of the dampness here?" Alcock argued, persistent as a yapping terrier. "It can't be beneficial for his health."

"My lord bishop, I find it most admirable in you to be so concerned for the king's welfare," said Buckingham in his warm-honey voice. "Indeed, I would that all His Grace's subjects would show him such love. And yet it must be said that this is summer, not winter, and that this move is temporary, not permanent. And I might add that if dampness disagrees with the king's health, I fail to understand how he survived nine years at Ludlow. Now there's the very devil for dampness. Those winds sweeping down the Teme Valley, freighted with rain and sleet and snow, whistling like demons through every chink in the masonry, and finding their way to a man's bare skin no matter how many furs he wraps it in. I tell you, my lords, it makes my skin prickle with gooseflesh at the mere thought of it." He pulled his maroon velvet cape tightly about him and shuddered.

Alcock smiled at the memories he evoked, and Hastings knew him lost. "Ah, you have hit on it, you have it to the letter. There is no other place like Ludlow on God's earth."

"For which God be thanked," Buckingham replied, the flash of his smile a white wound in his bronzed face. "Even the Tower cannot compare then."

"No, not even the Tower."

"But it is still a prison," Hastings insisted, pleading now as for his own life. "Not all of you have seen Edward of late. He is in a fearful state of melancholy. Argentine tells me that he suspects *l'accidie*. *L'accidie*, my lords, the monks' disease, the disease suffered by those who take up a solitary life. This, I ask you, in a twelve-year-old child? Are we to tolerate it, even to aggravate it by locking him away in the Tower?"

Hastings looked about him for support but found none. Buckingham was openly mocking. Stanley stared stonily at the far wall. Morton was impassive, his thick lids blinking toad-like over his small colorless eyes. And Catesby . . . even Catesby looked skeptical.

"You're not suggesting, I hope, that we would make the king our prisoner?" Richard asked coldly, his hand clenched on the hilt of his dagger. "By the rood, I would take it most ill . . ."

Hastings spread his hands in a pleading gesture. The opal on his little finger threw out ruby-and-emerald shards where the sun struck it. "No, of course not. Splendor of God, Dickon, do you know me so little as to think I would ever accuse you of any such thing?"

Richard's face softened; he shook his head. "Very well then, but as you yourself were the first to remind us, it is a matter of some urgency that we find a place to house the king. Why do you continue to quibble?"

"Quibble? I . . ." he stammered, swallowed, and was almost relieved to feel Catesby's tentative hand on his sleeve

"My lord, it's not so terrible a place. There is a greensward, even a garden where the king may take his exercise."

"And the royal apartments are quite comfortable, Will," Richard reminded him. "You know that. Listen to your man there. He speaks the truth."

Hastings sighed his unhappiness, but he managed a weak smile. "Well, I suppose it is still the custom for the king to lodge in the Tower prior to his coronation, isn't it? I was never one to flout custom."

Mingled in somewhere with Richard's relief and Buckingham's open rejoicing, he detected in that moment of stinging defeat an enigmatic glance from the silent purple bulk that was Morton. Strange! Was it sympathy or a signal of some sort that the bishop of Ely beamed to him from across the table?

Hastings could not have said later how long the session went on after that, dragging its tail behind like some weary, ponderous serpent. The interminable sounds of discussion and debate flowed around him like waves around a rock, but he took no more part in them, nor could he have said if that fact was noted by his fellow councilors.

He thought it would never end, yet end it did though not in the usual way. He perhaps heard it first, the distant shout that seemed to come from the riverfront, but whether it was born of terror or exultation, he could not tell. It did, however, penetrate his fogbound mind as none of the rattle of the debate had been able to do. Soon he heard other cries, other voices nearer now, raised in a current of excitement, and the trampling of feet far below in the courtyard. Footsteps in the corridor pounded on the flagstones, growing ever closer. Then the mighty door thrust open, and Howard was framed in it, his homely, weathered face beaming like a beacon.

"My lord of Gloucester!" He ran to Richard, half falling, half stumbling on the lozenge tiles. "Oh, my lord! News, great news! The fleet, the fleet is in. And with it, the greater part of Sir Edward's navy."

Richard, cut off in midsentence, rose to his feet. "Your plan, John . . . it has been successful?"

"Oh, yes, my lord. Almost beyond hope. Will you not come and look?"

Richard made for the nearest window; the rest of the council were in close pursuit, cramming the narrow window slits for a view of this latest wonder. Hastings, wedged in between Lovell and Morton, could barely make it out at first, but then they came into view, riding on the rising tide: the small ships of Howard's navy, the caravels and trawlers, and behind them, lordly and mighty, the car-racks of Genoa, broad bowed, high decked, sails bellying in the east wind, and on their masts, fluttering gold and red, silver and blue, the leopards and lilies of England.

"How did you manage it, John?" Richard asked, gripping Howard's shoulder in a bear hug. "Never have so few taken so many. By the mass, even seeing it I can hardly believe it."

Howard turned now to the two men who had followed him into the council chamber—one Hastings knew by his small stature and swarthy complexion to be Sir Edward Brampton, the Portuguese Jew who had several years ago converted to Christendom, and the other, a man of mature years and uneasy stance, he assumed to be Fulford.

"I cannot claim full credit, my lord," said Howard, "nor would I rob these two of their share in the victory. Brampton, would you be so good as to inform our lord protector of these events?" This, it appeared, Brampton was only too eager to do. Despite his conver-sion, despite his knighthood, he was still something of an outcast at court. Though small of stature and undeniably homely of face, as he spoke, he commanded their respect.

"We cannot fight them, no? So we preach to them of the par-don. On the largest of these vessels, there are sailors of Italy growing homesick, very homesick. When they learn their Woodville lead-ers are rebels and traitors, they get them drunk on their fine wine. And when these guards are high flown with drink, when they can no more even stagger about the deck, the Italians chain them in the holds, hoist the flag of King Edward, and straightaway set sail for Thamesmouth."

"And Sir Edward himself," Richard asked eagerly, "what of him? Is he too in chains?"

The two sailors exchanged awkward glances. Their downcast eyes told Richard the answer. Howard cleared his throat. "Regretfully, no, my lord, he is not. I . . . I fear he and one or two small ves-sels slipped through our nets and made for France. It could not be helped."

Richard's face darkened; his hand closed and unclosed on the jeweled hilt of his dagger. "Holy Jesu, will all our enemies flee to France?" he asked bitterly. "Must we always live in fear of a south wind? First the Tudor and now Sir Edward. Was Dorset with him?"

Howard shrugged. Fulford answered, "We do not know, Your Grace, if the marquis was with his uncle or no."

"But the booty was, I take it, or at least Sir Edward's share of it. Ah, yes, our enemies are well provisioned. The king's kin have riches to spare while we must finance his coronation with ha'pennies." He pounded an impotent fist on the windowsill even as the carracks drew into harbor at Tower Wharf and longboats rowed out to greet them.

The lines of Howard's face were once more deeply scored. He looked stricken. "I . . . I am most sorry the victory is not as complete as we all might have wished. I would have laid Sir Edward's stolen treasure at your feet, my lord, as well as the varlet himself, if it had been in my power."

"Aye, John," Richard replied, "but it was not, and I should have known it. I should not have permitted myself to hope for a miracle."

Buckingham asked, "And Lord Cordes, the French pirate, what of him?"

Howard eyed the duke sternly. "It was no part of our plot to deal with him as you must realize. Sir Edward and his fleet were our sole concern."

"Then he still threatens our trade on the Narrow Sea?"

"Yes."

Richard turned on Buckingham a reproving frown. "Don't be so hard on Lord Howard, cousin. He has done well, surpassingly well. No fault of his if our enemies persist. I have half a mind to appoint him lord high admiral for the service he has rendered us today." Howard's gasp of surprise and pleasure interrupted him; Richard smiled and went on. "In fact, if by some miracle as yet unknown and undreamt of he should rid us of the menace of both Sir Edward and Lord Cordes, I wouldn't stint at granting him a duchy."

Hastings enjoyed almost obscenely the sight of Buckingham's face, purple and engorged, as he chewed on the implications of this remark. It was no secret that he regarded Howard far beneath himself, which by birth he was. The son of an East Anglian squire, he had noble blood on his mother's side but precious little else to recommend him for a dukedom.

Buckingham chuckled harshly in his throat while John Howard, still only plain Lord John, found his voice and made some pretty disclaimer to the effect that the opportunity to serve his king and protector was all the reward he needed or aspired to. He too was laughing.

So it was only a jest, Hastings thought, and he found that he, like Buckingham, was breathing a heavy sigh of relief. Strangely, as he looked about for confirmation that it was indeed only a jest, he caught a glimpse of Morton, plump hands folded piously across his ample waist, watching him again with that queer, covert little smile.

Chapter 17

HASTINGS AND STANLEY left the rank darkness of the falcon mew and stepped out into the sun-washed brilliance of the garden. It was mid-May, and after several days of drizzle and blowing rain, the skies had cleared to a perfect, flawless blue. Hastings closed his sun-dazzled eyes for a moment and turned his face heavenward, savoring the unfamiliar warmth. His thoughts were as buoyant as the weather. Edward had spent most of the day with him, working with Griselda and taking instruction in the rudiments of falconry. He had been overjoyed when the hawk, still bound to him by the creance, had flown away as far as its reach, then returned voluntarily to his outstretched wrist to take meat from his hand. In a few days would come the real test when the bird, with no restraints upon her, would have her first taste of open flight, but Hastings believed there would be no problems then either. He recognized the beginning of a bond between the boy and the hawk that was tantamount to success, and he rejoiced in it. Edward himself had been openly jubilant when he had returned to the Tower a short time before.

"How does His Grace like the Tower?" Stanley asked, echoing his thought. Hastings blinked his eyes open abruptly and looked at his companion. He had almost forgotten Stanley and indeed had been none too pleased to see him arrive just as Edward was leaving. He had already made other plans for the afternoon, and they did not include listening to a recital of Tom Stanley's grievances.

"It's somewhat too soon to tell, isn't it?" Hastings said. "They only took him there yesterday."

"He won't like it, you may be sure of that. Westminster—now there's a palace fit for the blood royal. But you might have thought I'd suggested tossing him into his mother's lair, the way Gloucester jumped on me. Woodville lover indeed!" He spat contemptuously onto the ground.

"So you're still moaning over that, are you, Tom? Cock's arse, it's been almost a week now."

"I don't easily forget an insult," Stanley retorted. "Why, the two of us risked our necks for Gloucester while he dallied in the north, and little's the thanks we got for it. First it's insults, then he shoves us aside and leans on his fine new friend for all the world like he's a one-legged man and Buckingham's a crutch."

Hastings checked a smile. Try as he might, he could recall no instance where Tom Stanley had risked his neck in the protector's cause or, for that matter, even committed himself to it. And this business of being shoved aside, well, to be sure, Richard and Buckingham had been living in one another's pockets of late, but Hastings felt no particular discontent. Or was it the sight of Jane, waving to him from an upper-story casement window that choked off such unpleasant thoughts? God, but how her hair shone red gold as fire in the sunlight! How proud her full white breasts pushed over the laced bodice of her gown! Damn Stanley and his gloom anyway. A quick send-off for him, and there'd be time yet for a romp with that intoxicating wench before supper. Already he felt the blood pulsing in his groin.

"Aren't you exaggerating, Tom?" he asked. "Perhaps by the minutest fraction?"

"Exaggerating, am I? Tom retorted. "Exaggerating, when there's talk of splitting the council? Talk of putting me—aye, and you too—on an inferior council while he packs his own with his precious duke and his northern cronies? You tell me if that too is exaggeration."

Hastings frowned as he stooped to twist off the dead blossom of a daffodil. Most had finished their blooming some days ago and stood a forlorn patch of brown in the midst of fragrant pink-fringed gilly flowers and white marguerites and the purple bells of iris. He would have to speak to his gardener, have him tend to the daffodils. He could not abide their blot on his beauty, their sad reminder of a past glory.

"As you say, Tom, it is merely talk. Now I thought that next year, I would enlarge the herb garden here, perhaps let Jane plant some of her simples. Better, she says, than seeking a leech every time you have a headache or a belly gripe. I've no doubt she's right."

"It is not idle talk," Stanley pressed, obdurate. "I have it from one who should best know what is in the protector's mind—from no less than the Duke of Buckingham himself."

Hastings plucked a branch of thyme and raised it to his nostrils. Clean and pungent, the odor came. He would have coney roasted with thyme for supper tonight. And afterward, he would have Jane.

"Are you listening to me?" Stanley hissed between his teeth. "Won't you pay me any heed? I tell you there's going to be trouble. Won't you step out of your muddle-headed dream and see what's going on around you?"

Hastings turned mild eyes on his friend. "I hear you, Tom, I hear you. And I see as well as you do, though I see nothing amiss. Richard wishes to split the council? Very well, let him do it. It would certainly be more efficient if one committee dealt with one case and another with something else. I don't know how you feel, but my arse aches of late from so much sitting. I have been spending entirely too much time in council in recent days, and I'm more than willing to relinquish some of it."

Stanley shook his head. "Ah, you will see, Will, and to your sorrow."

"My lord, oh, my lord!" The call reached them down the flagged garden path. Catesby ran toward them, flushed and eager as a bridegroom, dressed once more in his best brown fustian, a new gold chain of office around his neck, a parchment scroll in his hand.

"Holy blessed martyrs, what's this then?" Hastings murmured.

"God give you good day, my lords," Catesby said, breathless. "I . . . I've just come from Baynard's Castle. Won't you look?" He unfurled the scroll with a flourish and pushed it toward them. In the red wax at the bottom was the unmistakable imprint of the privy seal.

Hastings looked up, puzzled. "But Catesby, what's this?"

"Be it known, my lords, that you are addressing the new chancellor of the earldom of March."

"Is it true?" Hastings asked as he studied the document with greater care. "Why, Catesby, this is good news indeed! And a fair post, one that carries with it the king's ear, for he is also Earl of March."

"I am . . . very pleased," Catesby admitted, rather unnecessarily. "I did not expect it."

"Perhaps not, but you are worthy of it as Richard of Gloucester must know, as I have always known." He beamed with undisguised warmth on his protégé who had been in his household from boyhood; who had been fed, clothed, and educated at his expense; who was in truth more son to him than servant.

"The lord protector must have been in a generous mood today," Stanley drawled. "Were there other such grants?"

Catesby hesitated because Stanley's voice had an edge to it as sharp as cut glass. "Why . . . yes, my lord, there were . . . others."

"How, for example, fared His Grace of Buckingham?"

Catesby shrugged. "He fared well enough."

"How well is 'well enough,' Catesby?"

"He . . . he has been given the power of supervision and array in the western counties."

Stanley nodded. "The western counties. And Wales, what of Wales?"

"I . . . I do not recall exactly. I think he was made chief justice—chamberlain too, I believe—for north and south Wales."

"Was that all?"

"N-no," Catesby replied, looking suddenly quite wretched. "He is also supervisor and governor of all the king's subjects in Wales."

Stanley whistled through his teeth and lifted his auburn brows heavenward. "Did I not tell you that the protector was in a generous mood today? He has just given away Wales."

"My lord!" Catesby said hotly. "I must protest your implication that these awards were not justly given."

"Ah but look, Will," Stanley said, turning back to Hastings. "Your lamb here has become a roaring lion."

"And none too soon," Hastings replied. "You, my lord, will find yourself most unwelcome here if you persist in the present vein of this conversation. I, for one, applaud Richard's judgment. A strong hand is needed in Wales now that our sovereign lord no longer abides there as its prince. Would you have every tribal chieftain and marcher baron ravishing the countryside?"

"It was not only my lord of Buckingham who fared well at the protector's hand today," Catesby said. "Lord Howard has been appointed steward of the duchy of Lancaster south of Trent. Earl Arundel is now master of the game of the royal forests of Trent. And Lord Dynham, your own deputy of Calais, has been granted the stewardship of the duchy of Cornwall."

Hastings nodded his head. He should have applauded each of these appointments. All these men were known to him; indeed, all were his friends, yet he stood there unable to speak.

It was Stanley whose acid voice replied, "Oh, yes, the protector has been most lavish with his bounty. None neglected, none omitted. To each his just reward."

Catesby spread his hands pleadingly. "I . . . I know, my lords, you must feel you have been . . . uh . . . overlooked—very well, neglected—in the grants today. But I beg you, don't think of it like that. Before I left Baynard's, His Grace took me aside and very kindly assured me of his high regard for both of you. He asked me to tell you that you shall both keep your present offices which, I needn't remind you, are among the highest, the richest in the land."

"But no others are to be forthcoming," Stanley said. "That's what he meant, wasn't it?"

"Peace!" Hastings cried, holding up his hand. "Tom, he's telling the truth, and you know it. We are both full and gorged with honors. Why I don't know if I could even name by rote all the posts I hold, and I have a guinea in my pocket that says you couldn't do it either. Buckingham's new prominence in Wales is natural and right, and if you are about to mutter that he and the Welsh deserve each other, mayhap I won't argue with you too much there. As for the others, they are our friends, men for whom we have the highest respect and regard. It's Richard's way of showing his love for us that he is so generous to our friends."

"Aye," Stanley growled, "though it puts not a groat in your purse nor in mine neither."

"My purse is quite well lined already, thank you. And I don't hear the wind whistling empty through yours."

Stanley opened his mouth as if to speak then snapped it tightly shut.

"Enough talk of politics," Hastings said lightly. "It does bore me after a while. And now, gentlemen, if you will excuse me, I have plans for the afternoon that unfortunately cannot be changed." He winked at them and nodded toward the house. "I wouldn't be so unchivalrous as to keep a lady waiting."

But once they were gone, he made no move toward the house, nor indeed did he even look for Jane at the window. Instead he ambled as slowly as an old man in the opposite direction, down the flagstone walk between the tall yew trees and clipped boxwood hedges, down the terraced slopes that flanked the river.

It was there exactly as he had left it, moored at the end of his dock: the great gilded pleasure barge. Once it had been his chief pride and delight. There had been sultry summer days spent on the river, rowing to Sheen or Windsor, and warm summer nights with the moon a fat melon hanging low on the horizon and lanterns flickering ruby through the raised chalice of a wine glass. There had been music, the strumming of a lute, the stroking of viol and cintern, and there had been laughter, Jane's laughter low and rippling as the river, along with the admonishing giggle of some palace strumpet and Edward's hearty guffaw.

Edward. Here the memory grew painful, like a brand burned into his heart. He looked up from the barge to the river beyond, heavy with its freight of commerce. Ferries threaded a treacherous path across the current; petermen trailed fishing nets behind. Boats for hire that rented by the day rowed in a steady stream from Tower Wharf to Westminster. High-piled cargo barges, ugly and cumbersome, rode the waves between them. All these were moths, moths to his butterfly, to the bright and delicate creature that rose and fell gently on their wake.

He would never use her again. Rain would rot the tent of striped black and silver and mildew the damask upholstered seat. The proud banners would hang sun-bleached and limp, and the eight pairs of matched oars would rust in their oarlocks before the boatmen took them up once more.

Here Edward had caught his last, his fatal illness.

Hastings stood for some time looking on his empty, forgotten fantasy, the fairy boat his pride had created long dreams ago. Then he turned to gaze again on her homely sisters who plied with much skill, though with little grace, the great river. With a sort of wonder, he knew that whatever else might be said of them, they at least fulfilled their purpose; they were useful, and they were used. They moved with the current or across it or against it, but they moved.

It came to him then that a man must also move in some direction or else be totally, hopelessly lost. He feared himself lost, for all his paternal pride in Catesby, for all his brave rebukes to Stanley. No new offices had been granted him; no new honors had come his way. The old he might keep: captaincy of Calais, sinecure of the mastership of the mint and exchange, the post of lord high chamberlain. But that was neither motion nor direction. That was stagnation, standing idle on the bank. That was to be stranded in a backwater, unable to break free, while far out in the channel the current raced by, taking others with it but leaving him behind, lapped only by the small brown wavelets that found their way to shore.

Chapter 18

IF IT WERE up to him, William Catesby would have avoided the narrow streets of London during the busy midmorning hour. The crowds that gave way grudgingly to cries of "Way, way for Lord Hastings," pressing back into gutters still filthy with last night's refuse, were not always willing to grant his retinue the same courtesy. Catesby was jostled on one side by a butcher and a shop boy, a side of beef slung between them, and on the other by a mercer's prentice struggling under a bolt of cloth. But far worse than the crowd was the mingled stench of unwashed bodies and of urine and ordure, both horse and human, that assailed his nostrils.

Catesby scowled a little at Hastings's back as the baron rode ahead on his larger mount. A fool's errand—that was what he secretly called their venture.

Didn't my lord have other matters to attend to? Must he give every waking thought over to that strumpet? He had not, of course, uttered these sentiments aloud. Even he was not so well placed that he could with impunity malign the Mistress Shore. But he had only thinly veiled his exasperation when Hastings had declared that he must perforce buy her a gift that very day.

"But . . . but, my lord, surely she has already been gifted most royally."

"True enough," Hastings had agreed, "but I have wronged her, Catesby. I must set it right."

"Wronged her? I fail to see how. And you know that the protector wishes to consult with you this morning on the new knighthoods."

"Bah! With the coronation more than a month away, the knighthoods can wait. The protector can wait. Tell him I am indisposed. Tell him whatever you wish." Laughter rumbled in his throat as he leaned toward Catesby with a confidential air. "She doubts my love, Will. Can you conceive it? This morning, she came to me dressed as a penitent, all in black, and said that since I no longer wished to take my pleasure with her, she would leave my house very quietly, without fuss. She asked only my aid in finding a suitable convent where she might live out her days. And do you know why she doubts my love? Because I did not seek her bed last night. Ah, Jane, my poor, lovesome little wench, how I do adore thee! Can you imagine it, those breasts, those thighs hidden beneath a nun's habit? That glorious hair, cropped? God protect us, what a loss that would be for mankind! And since I cannot be responsible for such a crime, I must find her a gift. Women set great store by baubles and trinkets."

Catesby had not argued the point further. He was glad to see this lightening in his lord's spirits, which had been unusually gloomy since the afternoon before. But he regretted that it must be Shore who brought it about. If only he did not dote on her so. If only he could have been persuaded to attend on Gloucester that morning! Catesby sensed that the protector was ill pleased with Hastings's latest liaison and would be most wroth if he learned the reason for the lord chamberlain's absence.

But all these thoughts he kept to himself. A not-quite-willing accomplice, he nonetheless jogged along behind Hastings through congested byways to West Chepe, the domain of the goldsmiths.

Thomas Woode, sheriff of London and master goldsmith, was justly and exultantly proud of both his rank and his skill. In a street of towering mansions, any one of which could have been mistaken for a baron's, his was the grandest. Four stories above the street, its gabled roofs were pitched, rivaling for height and splendor on the London skyline the protector's own residence of Crosby Place. The facade of his shop, on the ground floor of his mansion, was unmistakable, an advertisement of his formidable skill even though he had resorted to baser metals in its construction. Surrounding his coat of arms, he had depicted a bas relief of woodmen, a pun on his name, riding fantastical beasts through a great forest. The whole had been cast in lead and painted with gilt so that it gave the appearance of being wrought from pure gold.

Master Woode stretched his hands across his expansive stomach and smiled to himself. He had reason for content, for he had only just completed one of the most elaborate commissions of his career after staying up all night to do it. He yawned, thinking that soon he would go above stairs to the great tester bed that he shared with his pretty young wife. His life was full of such satisfactions. Beneath the cloth-of-gold stomacher, his belly was as fat as a Christmas goose. He ate well, slept well, loved well, and was revered both by his guild and the city at large.

The shop bell tinkled. No matter. A clerk could take care of that—unless, of course, it happened to be the favored customer for whom he had cast his latest prize. He peeked out into the shop and then almost fell over his own feet, pushing his scurrying clerk out of the way. For though it was not the expected customer, it was another to be treated with equal courtesy. No less a patron than the great Lord Hastings himself and with a fine retinue. St. Dunstan be praised! What good fortune it was to be honored by two great men in a single day. Mayhap Hastings too would commission him to create a piece of exquisite beauty and extravagance.

"Good morrow, my lord," Woode said eagerly. He bent a trifle at the waist, a necessary obeisance despite the fact that it was no longer an easy one for him to make. "What a privilege to see you here! How might I be of service to Your Gracious Lordship?"

Hastings gave him a conspiratorial smile and a wink. "Tell me, Master Woode, have you a pretty jewel that might enhance a lady's frock?"

So that was it—a trinket for a wench! Well, one would have expected a more worthy, not to mention a more lucrative, objective than that. Somewhat less eagerly, Woode motioned the loitering clerk to fetch a tray of brooches from their case.

"Perhaps one of these will do a fair lady proud," he murmured.

"Ah, yes, I daresay I might find something here." Hastings fingered the collection with great care while Woode, struggling to conceal his impatience, hovered beside him. The goldsmith considered the entire tray to be of inferior craftsmanship, all of it the work of his less-skilled apprentices. He offered its contents for sale only because common men could seldom tell the difference and many had a taste for such trifles. Besides that, it was a profitable sideline while he created his own more worthwhile works of art.

"Here," Hastings said at last. "I think this one will complement her coloring." He held up a pretty brooch of filigree fashioned like a cluster of golden flowers and studded with beryl, turquoise, and tiny seed pearls.

"An excellent choice," Woode said, "and only twelve guineas."

"Twelve guineas? I fear you rob me, my good friend, but I'm not in a mood to haggle. Please pay the man, Catesby."

Catesby was drawing the gold sovereigns from his leather pouch when the bell jangled once more at the entrance and another retinue, almost as large as Lord Hastings's own, entered the shop.

"Ah, my Lord Howard!" Woode cried, grinning broadly. In a trice, he had gestured for the clerk to finish waiting on Hastings and had turned his full attention to the newcomer. This time, he made the effort to bow quite deeply. "Your cup is ready, my lord, and a magnificent piece it is, if I do say so myself. You'll not find its like in England, nay, nor on the continent either."

Hastings, standing off to one side and half-forgotten, acknowledged Howard's greeting with a nod, but there was no opportunity for conversation. An apprentice bore to the counter a chalice so rich, so beautifully wrought that all eyes turned instantly to it. In that shop crammed with golden wonders—plate and saltcellars, hanaps and collars, rings and brooches—it shone like a moon among the stars.

"Sixty-five ounces of beaten gold," Woode announced proudly, "and with a cover to match. I designed it myself and stayed up most of the night to finish it. My 'prentices are good lads all, mind you, but I'd not trust them with something like this. Not for His Grace the protector."

Howard turned to smile at Hastings. "Do you think it will please him?"

"Why, man, how could it not? Truly a masterpiece! His Grace has always had an eye for craft and beauty. Marry, you could have chosen no better gift!"

"Aye, so I hope," Howard replied. "I ordered it last week and would not so have hurried our good friend here were it not for the grant given to me yesterday. I wish to present it to him this evening when we dine at Crosby Place."

"Are you dining with His Grace tonight then?"

Woode thought Hastings's question sounded deliberately casual.

"Why, y-yes." Howard turned red as a maid. "Aren't you?"

"No. I fear I've received no such invitation."

In the silence that followed, Woode turned discreetly away to wrap Howard's purchase in sheepskin, though not so far that he couldn't hear what was happening behind him. What talk this would make at the next guild meeting! "My lord Howard rises high in the protector's favor, I trow, while my lord Hastings . . ." He would let his voice trail off into innuendo, shaking his head sadly and clicking his wooden teeth.

Howard's embarrassment must have deepened, for it was Hastings who spoke next. "Why, John, think nothing of it. It doesn't matter, not in the least. Perhaps some oversight on the part of Master Kendall . . . or mayhap someone in my own household has forgotten to tell me. And even if it isn't that, well, there's no law that says I must be invited to dine whenever you are."

Howard shrugged sheepishly. He looked like a small boy guilty of some infraction.

"I congratulate you on your appointment to the stewardship of Lancaster," Hastings added kindly. "A right lucrative post, that."

"I . . . I shall need it if I'm to afford these gold cups," Howard replied, attempting a weak smile.

"I daresay, though I'm certain that Master Woode here has given you the best possible price. I wish His Grace much joy in the gift. You must give him my warmest regards."

They parted with a handshake, much to the disappointment of Woode, who had hoped for an open breach between them to report to his cronies' ears. "They quarreled hotly, right there in my shop, because Gloucester has shown preference to Howard!" He had already begun to frame the story in his mind when he saw both men were gone. He knew then that he had no story, only a frail tissue of suspicion that could be blown away at a breath tomorrow when someone saw Hastings and Howard entering Crosby Place arm in arm. He shrugged wearily and turned toward the stairs.

Jane shut the tooled leather book cover with a snap and wondered why the familiar tale of Troilus and his false Creseyde should cause such a swift, unaccustomed stab of guilt. She was not Creseyde, nor had anyone, except perhaps her long-forgotten husband, ever asked fidelity of her or expected it. Edward, Dorset, Hastings—they had known her for what she was and enjoyed her for it. Dorset. Her mind lingered on him lovingly for a moment as it always did, on the oddly tilted green eyes, the sensuous full lips, the thick dark hair that curled so beguilingly about the nape of his neck. In her own way, she was faithful, faithful in mind if not in body, though Dorset would have been as amazed to know it as Troilus had been to learn of Creseyde's wantonness. Was it for Hastings then, that small bothersome stab of guilt?

That Hastings adored her, she knew only too well. That his adoration might prove useful, she was beginning to guess. He might serve a turn in the great game of chess being played out between the protector and the Woodvilles. He was already chafing under some injury or another, though she had not been able to pry it from him that morning even by employing the strongest of her wiles. She had accused him of love lack, a preposterous charge but one certain to bring a response. It had, though not the response she sought. He did love her; oh, most tenderly he loved her. She was his own, his darling girl and must never even consider leaving him.

"Then, my lord, what is the matter?"

"As for that, Jane girl, I wouldn't have you troubled. Some trifling matter of no consequence."

Jane opened the book once more and focused on the strong black strokes, the prettily illumined capitals. The words had no meaning; they shifted before her eyes. The book was only a prop anyway, she reminded herself. She had planned precisely how he would find her when he returned home: sitting on a stone bench in a garden bower, framed by foaming white apple blossoms and fragrant purple lilac, her gown the shade of April violets with a white diapered border, its neck cut low enough to show her white shoulders and just a suggestion of cleavage at the bosom. Alluring yet demure, as befitted one who only that morning had suggested retiring to a nunnery.

"Ah, Jane, so you are out here."

She looked up to see him walking toward her down the garden path. His face was a mask, expressionless.

"Why, yes, my lord. I was waiting for you."

He sat down heavily on the bench beside her. His skin was ashen gray.

"Will . . ." She rested a hand on his momentarily. It felt as cold as the stone of the bench.

"Here," he said, "this is for you." Without ceremony, he dropped the brooch into her lap. No play this time, no hiding it in a bowl of blossoms or setting it under her plate at breakfast or making her guess which of his hands held it.

"Oh, Will, it's lovely! Thank you!" She pinned it at the neck of her dress.

He shook his head. "It's not the color for that dress. I should have bought amethysts."

"I think, my lord, if you're as distraught as you seem, you should not have bought it at all."

He smiled for the first time, a weary, wintry smile. "Aye, you're right about that, sweeting. God alone knows how right."

"Won't you tell me what's wrong?"

Hastings nodded. "Yes, for I'm afraid I shall go mad if I don't tell someone. Howard . . . I met Howard today in Master Woode's shop. And shall I say it, Jane? He courts Richard's favor like a servile cur. You should have seen it, the gift he plans to bestow on the protector. He must have half-beggared himself to do it. A golden cup, so high and weighing over four pounds. Can you believe it?"

Jane dutifully shook her head, but he did not acknowledge it. He continued, his voice rising. "Me, he used to gift like that. Oh, never so richly, of course, but richly enough. Silver chafing dishes, pipes of Bordeaux, and tips for my butler, cook, and steward when he dined with me. And he often dined with me in those days when he sought my favor. He called me friend then. Now he dines with Richard when I receive no invitation. Don't you see, Jane? I've lost Howard." And in a lower voice, he muttered, "And I fear I'm losing Richard as well."

Jane placed a finger over her mouth and gestured to the daffodil beds nearby where a gardener pruned away the dried blossoms. "Hush, my lord. These things should be heard by no ears except mine." She stood and took his hand. "Come with me where we will have some privacy. Perhaps I can offer you some comfort."

He smiled at her again, that pale, wintry smile. "How, Jane? It isn't even noon yet. Would you make a wanton out of me in the middle of the day?"

"That's not what I intended, Will," she said softly. "There may be other comforts I can offer that you know nothing of yet."

In his great canopied bed, they sat on the ermine counterpane, the curtains drawn against the light of day. A small luncheon of cold capon stuffed with herbs, fresh bread with honey, and pale-white wine was spread between them. Though he had little appetite for it, she coaxed him to take a few morsels as he spilled out the rest of his story: other slights from Richard (real or imagined), the absence of his name from the rolls of yesterday's grants, his defeat in council over the removal of Edward to the Tower—small matters in themselves, each one, yet in accumulation, the seeds of discord richly sown.

"It seems he no longer looks on you with favor, this Richard of yours," she said at last, nibbling on a leg of the capon.

"But why? He's always been my friend till now. Why suddenly in two short weeks should I be outside the pale of his grace?"

She shook her head sadly. "Who knows the answer to that, Will, except perhaps Richard himself? You have been too trusting of him, I think, believing too much in his goodness. He was never a friend to me, that much I can tell you. How he used to rail at Edward about the lechery and debauchery of the court! And all the while his bony finger was pointed right at me as if he held me personally responsible. We . . . uh . . . ladies of the court used to laugh at him behind his back and mimic him too. He was always a good sort to mock."

Suddenly, her mood changed, and the mischievous mirth that was never far below the surface peeked out from the widened brown eyes. "It went something like this." She was up with a bounce that almost upset the wine flagon, tossing aside the bed curtains and stomping about the room with Richard's characteristic stride. Her face was puckered in a frown, her hands fidgeted nervously with her finger rings, and one shoulder was even raised higher than the other.

Hastings looked doubtful for a moment, then he lay back on the pillows and roared, all the pent-up anxiety of the last few days finding an outlet in free laughter. "That's him, Jane. In very faith, that's him to the life. How do you manage it?"

"I've always had a talent for mimicry. Edward loved it. When we were alone, he would have me mimic his courtiers—though not, of course, his noble brother of Gloucester. Then we would collapse into fits of laughter. Do you remember what he used to call me?"

"Yes. You were his 'merriest harlot,' I well remember."

Her face softened at the memory, reaching back into the happy years with Edward. "It's a pity he isn't with us now, for what couldn't I do with his most noble grace of Buckingham!"

"Buckingham!" Hastings exclaimed. "Yes, he is ripe for it."

She laid a cautionary finger over his lips. "Ah, but take care how you speak of him. Our lord protector loves him well. Some would say only too well."

"Surely, Jane, you don't mean to suggest . . . but that was never Richard's way."

"Well, I don't know it to be true, of course," she admitted, "but you will allow that Gloucester has never been one to chase a skirt. Even the Lady Anne, it's said, he wedded more for the love of her purse and lands than of her fair self. Don't you recall the row he had with Clarence over her inheritance? Then too while his duchess remains behind in the north, I'm told that he has sought no solace from women here in London though Buckingham is constantly in his company, strutting about, proud as a popinjay."

And now she was Buckingham with the bold strut of his walk, the high tilt of his aristocratic nose, and the noble, slightly bored, slightly petulant expression he took pains to affect. Once again, Hastings fell into a fit of laughter, a laughter that had more of true mirth in it than before since it cost him no struggle of conscience to poke fun at Buckingham.

"Name of God, but they do make a pretty pair, don't they?" He blinked back tears of laughter. "A pity, Jane, that you can't be both at once."

"Oh, but I can try," she said. With apparent ease, she shifted back and forth between them, playing first the one and then the other, mocking Richard's upcast eyes as he gazed on his favorite and called him "Hinny" and Buckingham's lowered ones as he looked down from his great height with devoted, nay slavish, adoration.

"Swounds, it's too much!" Hastings cried between gusts of laughter, holding his shaking sides. "No more, no more, I pray thee, or I shall fall into apoplexy!"

Suddenly, Jane grew serious. She sat down beside him on the bed and took his hands in hers. "It's unfortunate that there is in truth so little real humor in your situation. These men have the power, and you must find the means either to placate them . . . or remove them."

Hastings's jaw dropped open. "Remove them? But it was I who worked so hard to set Richard in his place and at no small risk to my own person."

"Yes, so you did." She tucked her legs up beneath her skirts and leaned toward him so he could see down the neck of her gown. "But you were misguided in that, I think, and so I thought then. There are those who say that Richard grasps at more power than befits a mere protector. Some imply he would even remove his nephew and be king in his own right with Buckingham as his chief lieutenant."

"Those who say that are liars!" Hastings said hotly. "Richard will be loyal to the son as he was the father. I know the man."

"Do you, Will?" she asked softly. "Do you really know him? He has shut young Edward in the Tower, poor lad. Does he keep him there as king or as prisoner? Tell me that."

Her words hit home, but still Hastings struggled with their implication. "I . . . I can't believe he would harm Edward's boy."

She straightened and flashed fire from her eyes. "Would you wait until the boar strikes before you run for cover, when perhaps there is no cover to be found, crying all the while, 'I would not have believed it of him'? Oh, Will, there is help for you yet if you would but seek it. Richard knows very well that you would never countenance his usurpation, that your first loyalty will always be to Edward and Edward's heir. He will have to be rid of you before he acts. That is why he has removed his favor, why he toadies to the likes of Buckingham and Howard. And that is why you will need assistance in this matter. I promised you comfort. This was the comfort I meant—the presence of an army at your back, my lord, and no less."

Hastings was astounded by this outburst. He scratched his head and wondered vaguely how a little dissatisfaction at some misplaced grants had suddenly mushroomed into armed rebellion. And for Jane, sweet little Jane, of all people to have suggested it! "Just how, sweeting, would you go about raising an army?" he asked somewhere between mockery and indulgence.

"Not I, my lord, but my friends."

"And who might these 'friends' be?"

"None other than the queen and her kin."

"Saints preserve us!" Hastings threw back his head and roared. "The queen? Didn't I tell you that I'd had enough laughter for one day?"

"I did not speak in jest and would not have you take it so."

"But we are enemies of old."

"As you and Gloucester are friends of old, but far that seems to have gotten you now. You and the queen's kin have a common enemy, and the survival of you both depends on your joining together." She leaned close to him and laid her head sweetly on his shoulder.

"Sweetheart," he said gently, stroking her hair beneath its veil. "I'm not yet brought so low that I must consort with the Woodvilles. The words you speak could easily be construed as treason if they were uttered outside these walls and might mean death for us both. Please, Jane, concern yourself only with love and music and laughter, the lighter parts of life, and stay well clear of politics. It was never the place for a woman."

She pouted into the black sarcenet of his doublet. "I don't agree, but I shan't argue the point now. All I ask is that you not forget what I've told you. At some future time, you may have need of it."

"Oh, very well, though I find it difficult to believe that you, of all people, should have the queen's ear."

Jane smiled a secret smile. "We're not such enemies as you might think. At least, if I offered her help, I doubt she would refuse it."

"Don't offer it yet, Jane. God help me if I should ever come to that pass, though it does make me happy that you should be so distressed by my troubles as to think of a remedy." He pulled her tightly to him, his nose nuzzled at her temple, and his hand cupped over her breast. "Now tell me, love, what are we doing here on this fine feather bed talking of politics? Kings and queens be damned, aye, and dukes and protectors too. We have some time to make up for, do we not? A whole night lost to love."

He undressed her slowly. She felt his hands on her body, but her mind soared far away, a peregrine in flight. She shut her eyes to the lined old man's face, and it was Dorset who lay beside her, murmuring endearments; Dorset whose trembling fingers unlaced her bodice; Dorset who removed the golden cauls, freeing her bright masses of hair. Though Dorset would never be so gentle . . .

No matter. Soon it would be Dorset, she had no doubt of that. The seeds planted today would sprout into glorious blossom. Her beloved would be restored to his rightful place beside the king and in her arms.

Chapter 19

THE BELLS OF All Hallows Barking tolled for tierce as Hastings stepped from his rented barge onto the sturdy planking of Galley Quay. Smiling to himself, he squeezed past a group of Venetian sailors who, gibbering like articulate monkeys in their alien tongue, unloaded a tall galley of her precious cargo—rolled Cyprian carpets threaded with gold, packets of damask and velvet glowing in deep-hued tones, barrels of spices, their mingled aromas of clove and cardamom, saffron and cinnamon wafting above the tidal reek of the river. On the Wool Quay nearby, a less exotic cargo awaited transport to Calais. Hastings's smile broadened as he looked on those bales of fine cream-tufted English wool, each of which was destined to add its share to his personal fortune.

His spirits soared as high today as the silver-webbed cranes of the Steelyard beyond the bridge, reaching for a sky of cloudless blue. He even bowed and tipped his cap to a gaggle of London house-wives lined up, baskets in hand, on Marlowe's Quay while the water bailiff finished his inspection of an eel ship anchored in the river. They tolerated this ritual of waiting with varying degrees of impatience and watched anxiously as red and undersized eels were tossed over the side of the vessel into the Thames. They were wondering if there would be enough for all when he was done. Hastings's gesture momentarily diverted them. The raucous, shrewish cries ceased and were replaced by whispers and tittering. They might not have known his name, but they could tell by his dress and manner that he was a man of some importance.

Hastings's sense of well-being stayed with him as he walked toward the Tower. A surge of his old complacency puffed out his chest beneath the black velvet surcoat. He wanted to laugh at the foolish whim of a week ago that had sunk him into such despondency. Richard was still his cherished friend – why had he ever thought otherwise? – though to be frank he had paid him more court in the past few days than he had ever intended. He had been forced of necessity to spend more evenings out of Jane's company than he would have liked—Richard was still strangely adamant about Jane—but if it had restored himself to the protector's favor, to the easy intimacies of their old relationship, then he counted it well worth the cost. Better that by far than to take the absurdly dangerous path Jane had suddenly opened at his feet. Even contending with Buckingham, that troublesome gadfly, was preferable to alienation and rebellion.

The outer walls of the Tower bailey reared above him, feet thick and battlement crowned. Inadvertently, his steps slowed as he crossed the drawbridge, and the gates swung open to admit him. The Tower—and another long, hair-splitting session with the unholy trinity, as he secretly referred to Stanley, Morton, and Rotherham— awaited him. Inwardly, he thought that there must be some more rewarding pursuit on a balmy spring day than listening to their interminable, half-mumbled grievances against Richard.

In point of fact, the four of them were responsible for planning the coronation, but Stanley (wary and sullen), Morton (impenetrable and bland), and Rotherham (senile and vaguely resentful) showed little enthusiasm for the coronation or anything else pertaining to the governance of the realm. Only by persistent and dogged determination had Hastings been able to eke out any progress to report to Richard. And he missed more than he cared to admit participation in the protector's larger council, though Catesby assured him that he was only foregoing some of His Grace of Buckingham's longer and more eloquent tirades.

The Tower green flashed before him, an emerald in a stone setting. Beyond a margin of lime trees, their branches hung with pale-yellow flowers, rose the bulwark of the royal apartments. It was as if a shadow blotted out the sun for a moment. Edward was immured somewhere within those walls. No, he must not think of it like that. Edward had provoked Richard's wrath to the point where even a sainted martyr would have lost patience.

Still, he is only a child, another part of him replied sadly. And it had been only a boyish prank he was guilty of, albeit an uncommonly dangerous one.

Hastings stopped and looked from the turreted White Tower gleaming like a chalk cliff in the sun to the royal apartments and back again. He could perhaps be a little late for the council, a charity to the unholy trinity who could therefore be more outspoken in their complaints against Richard. And Edward would probably welcome his company: a brief visit, a few moments only, to see how His Grace fared.

At the porch, a lowered pike barred his way. "What are you doing here?" questioned a thin, arrogant voice. "Have you the dukes' permission to seek an audience with the king?"

Gooseflesh prickled on Hastings's arms as he looked into the pale, feline eyes of Sir William Percival. For a moment, he trembled before the maroon apparition, clad in Buckingham's livery. The badge of the golden cartwheel blazed like fire on his sleeve, and on his cheek, the disfiguring scar pulsed livid white.

Behind his back, Hastings made the sign against evil. "As lord chamberlain to the king, I neither need permission to attend him, nor do I seek it."

"My orders are specific." Percival brandished the pike menacingly. "No one except the dukes."

"A tin groat for your orders, sirrah. Or do you wish me to report this insolence to the protector when I dine with him tonight? You have received no orders barring me, I daresay."

The flickering yellow light wavered in Percival's eyes. Hastings pressed. "Your duke is not yet supreme in this land, and I have the protector's ear as well as the next man."

There was a flash of something coldly dangerous in Percival's gaze before he turned sharply away and swung the pike aside.

Hastings pushed open the heavy studded doors and stepped into the vast, empty hall. In the dim silence his heart pounded with the tabor's wild beat, but he was in. From the open windows on the other side of the hall, there came sounds of men's shouts and laughter as well as the outraged squawks of two roosters. Some of Edward's guards apparently were not above amusing themselves with a cockfight though they had best take care not to let their master know of this diversion. Something told Hastings that Sir William Percival would never stomach such a blatant neglect of duty.

He did not hear Argentine's approach. When he turned, the physician was simply there like an apparition in his long black robes. His hand rested on his breast over the jacinth stone he wore for protection from the plague. Strangely, he smiled.

"My lord chamberlain! This is a surprise."

"I don't doubt that," Hastings grunted. "I was almost refused admission by your watchdog out there."

"Ah, yes. Cerberus, the guardian of the underworld. He does tend to be a bit overzealous."

"But then I suppose he has an obligation to preserve the king's safety."

"*Of course, the king's safety,*" Argentine repeated wryly.

"How does the king?"

The physician shrugged. "I believe you had better see for yourself, my lord."

He led Hastings under a round Norman arch and up a flight of stone steps grooved from centuries of passing feet. Argentine's own sandals slapped softly on the stairs, and the black train of his gown whispered behind him.

Hastings had occasionally been in the royal bedchamber before, but he had never seen it so bleak. Drawn velvet still covered the windows and even the bed-curtains had been pushed back only far enough to admit Edward's breakfast tray. Poached pears and porridge sprinkled with saffron and nuts lay untouched on the bed beside him, as did a pot of fragrant thyme tea, no doubt provided by Argentine as a cure for melancholy.

Edward sat propped up with pillows beneath a coverlet that bore the royal arms. His face was pale and smudged with blue hollows beneath eyes, cheeks, and throat. One hand rubbed his jaw, and Hastings recalled that Argentine was treating him for an abscess as well as his persistent melancholy.

"Good day, sire," Hastings boomed in his most cheerful voice. He bent to kiss the limp hand. "How does Your Grace?"

It was the wrong question. Edward gave him a listless shrug. "The same as we always do here. We stay alive but no more than that."

"What a pity it is only to exist on such a day as this!" Hastings thrust back the curtains with a sweep and opened the windows. "I don't think there's been another like it since the dawning of creation. The first flush of summer lies on London. Won't you come out with me and walk in the constable's garden?"

Edward's eyes narrowed at the sudden brightness. "Why exchange one set of walls for another?" he asked.

"Sire," Hastings said gently, "it is your own fault that you are forbidden to leave the confines of the Tower. After what happened last time . . ." Hastings did not like to think about the hawking expedition, which had ended in near disaster.

Edward's fingers plucked at the golden threads of the coverlet. "I didn't mean any harm. I wouldn't have stayed. I only wanted to see them for a little while, my mother and brother and sisters. Where was the harm in that? I would have come back."

Nevertheless, he had frightened ten years off Hastings's life. It had been almost a week ago now, a fine day like this one but perhaps a trifle cooler. They had taken Griselda out to the fields beyond Holburn for her first hunt. Edward had ridden proudly on his new roan gelding, a gift from his uncle Gloucester, who had declared that if the king was old enough to have his own gyrfalcon, he was obviously too old for a mere pony.

The hounds had quickly flushed out game from a bramble thicket, and Edward, as he had been taught, untied the leather jesses from the hawk's legs and then, very carefully, removed the jeweled hood. She had stayed only for a moment on his gauntleted wrist, blinking in the unaccustomed sunlight, her tiny cruel eyes taking in the scene about her. Then the boy, raising his arm, had shaken her free. Her pounding wings shone like jet as she rose slowly, endlessly in a lazy spiral toward the blue vault of heaven. Hastings had shielded his eyes, watching her intently as she became a black speck, reached her pitch, and was lost in the sun.

Below her, two pheasants fluttered in green-gold agitation at the baying dogs. They had stayed close to the nest, guarding their hatchlings, vainly attempting to chase away the hounds with their beating wings. They did not see the angel of death swoop down on them from the skies. Hastings cried in delight as Griselda made her strike, her talons curling in the speckled back of the male pheasant. For a moment, his long train trailed on the ground; then both hawk and pheasant fell into the thicket.

"A royal kill, Edward!" Hastings cried. "Those tail feathers will look well on your bonnet. Edward? Edward!" For when he turned, Edward was nowhere to be seen. "Catesby . . . the king! Have you seen the king?"

Catesby looked abashed. "No, milord. I was watching the kill."

So were we all, Hastings thought. *All of us but Edward.*

At first, he cursed the boy's cunning, then he pitied the desperation that had spawned it. There could be no doubt of Edward's love for the hawk. That he could so easily turn his back on her first kill was a measure of his deep unhappiness.

He had not stopped to consider that then. Leaving Catesby and his other attendants to bring the falcon back to the lure, Hastings had spurred his horse sharply over the hummocks, hollows, and tufted furze of the meadow, trying only to avoid the rabbit holes that pitted it. A lamed horse could have meant all was lost. Not for one moment did he question Edward's destination. He had caught him at the abbey's postern gate, already dismounted and about to ring the bell.

"Edward, what's the meaning of this? That was poorly done, lad, very poorly done."

The boy had been near tears, though whether of shame or frustration, Hastings could not tell. He looked down into the dust at his feet, where the toe of his kid boot scored a rough circle. "It was the only way, the only way I could see them." And he was to repeat over and over again to Gloucester's disbelieving ears, "I would not have stayed. I only wanted to visit them."

Richard had been livid, of course. "Edward, are you so naive as to believe your mother would willingly let you go once she had you in her clutches?" There had been those tight white lines bracketing his mouth, and his stormy eyes flashed fire. It had been Edward who had taken the brunt of his anger and not the obviously shaken Hastings, who had been accorded a hero's welcome by both dukes for his prompt retrieval of their wayward charge. But Hastings had suffered more that day than if he had been racked. Edward had been confined to the Tower then in earnest with the odious Percival and his handpicked henchmen standing guard.

"You mustn't be like my uncles," Edward was saying now. "You mustn't think me wicked because of what happened that day. Do you, my lord?"

Hastings shook his head and smiled a little. "Wicked, Your Grace? Nay, the thought never entered my head. And I'm sure that your uncles don't think it of you either. You must understand that their position is delicate. They are trying to do not only what is best for you but what is best for England . . . your England, my liege."

Edward wagged his head in swift denial. "No, not *my* England, *their* England! Me, they keep captive here while they wield the power. My Uncle Gloucester . . . perhaps he aims to do what he thinks best, I don't know. Perhaps if it were he alone without the other one—"

"Speak softly, Edward. There are those about just waiting to carry a tale."

"You don't need to remind me of that. His lackey Percival is never far away. He brought me my breakfast tray this morning, and straightaway I lost all appetite for it. How I do loathe the man! Even his smiles are like poison. Thank heaven he smiles so seldom. He is stern, like my Uncle Gloucester, and keeps much to himself, but I think I'd trust Gloucester well before I'd trust him."

Hastings smiled to see the color rise in the thin, beardless cheeks. "He doesn't mean any harm," he said with more conviction than he felt. "The protector would not let him near you if he thought there was danger in him. Besides, it will be different after your coronation. You will have more freedom to choose those you would keep by you."

"I don't know if there will be a coronation," Edward said, sullen again. "I don't know if they will allow me so near my mother's sanctuary for fear I'll bolt and run during the ceremony. Oh, you needn't worry. I've thought about it, all right, but I wouldn't do it," he added to Hastings's look of alarm.

"That is well, Your Grace."

"Even so, I don't think they want me crowned."

Hastings bridled at that. "You wrong your Uncle Gloucester even to suggest such a thing! Why, he has worked diligently for your crowning. In fact, I'm afraid you know him but little to think of him as you do."

"Perhaps," Edward replied stubbornly, plucking at the coverlet again. He had succeeded in unraveling a thread of the royal arms, and it lay on the deep-blue velvet like a thick golden hair. "Oh, Hastings, if only I had some freedom to move about. Then I would feel differently about everything. And I promise on my father's tomb I wouldn't try to escape. I'd behave myself admirably, you'd see."

"You know it is forbidden."

"I shall waste away to nothing if I stay here. I shan't eat nor sleep. I shall become the very wraith of a king. A pretty sight I'll make at my coronation, don't you think?" He sucked in his cheeks so that the bony effect was even more pronounced than before.

Hastings sighed. "Edward, it's pointless to talk . . ."

"Oh, very well," the boy interrupted, turning peevish. "I can see that you don't love me either." He looked up at Hastings through demurely lowered lashes. "And you, the only one I can turn to, the only one who could convince them that it's safe."

"I don't think even I could convince them of that. And if I tried, they would say I had been seduced by your blandishments."

"And you, my lord," said Edward, innocent as a maid, "do you think you're being seduced?"

"No."

"Well then?"

"Perhaps a private outing might be arranged," Hastings said, visibly wavering. His mind was leapfrogging ahead, meeting the obstacles, calculating the risks. "Yes, it just might work. We shall need the assistance of Argentine, of course. He can say you are ill or asleep and not to be disturbed. And I would think we might be able to find a page's doublet and hose to fit you. If Your Grace finds the mantle of state a bit heavy on your shoulders, perhaps you won't mind shedding it for a few hours."

Edward's eyes shone vivid blue green with excitement. "Oh no, not at all. It's a burden I will most gladly relinquish . . . for a little while. But when, dear Hastings, when can we go?"

Hastings looked toward the open window, to the Tower walls and beyond where the gables and pinnacles of London, the tall chimneys and steeples sparkled in the morning light. He thought of the council meeting and just as quickly dismissed it. What was one council meeting, more or less? "Well, and why not?" he said aloud. "What's to stop us from going this very day? It's a fine day for both of us to play truant from school."

It was in truth a nearly perfect day. They slipped quietly through the kitchens while Edward's would-be guardians still gambled with their roosters. Plainly dressed, they appeared to be ordinary citizens of the city, a tradesman perhaps with his son. No one paid them any particular attention as they left the Tower and were swallowed up in the vast, churning stomach that was London.

Through a maze of animal, foot, and vehicle traffic, they picked their way, stepping carefully over piles of droppings left by passing horses or ducking to avoid the spray of a poorly aimed chamber pot. Occasionally, they were pushed back against the house and shop fronts to make way for heavily laden trains of sumpter mules or an aggressive carter or the retinue of some noble or prosperous merchant.

They knew an anxious moment when a herald called out, "Way, way! Make way for the Duke of Buckingham!" And the duke himself passed by them, within an inch of their noses it seemed, heading down Thames Street toward the Tower, formidable in his pomp and as aloof as an Olympian god. Edward shrank back, pressing his face into Hastings surcoat, while Hastings himself trembled, whey-faced, as he waited for the duke's party to pass. But pass it did, finally. Fortunately, Buckingham had not even deigned to glance at the commons his retinue had so rudely displaced.

"God's bones, but that was close," Edward said, exhaling his relief. "I thought he had us sure."

"But he didn't," Hastings reminded him. "He didn't even look our way."

Edward peered down Thames Street to where the duke had disappeared. "Suppose . . . suppose he goes to the Tower?" he asked uncertainly.

"We shall have to trust Argentine. He'll keep our secret—never fear. Meanwhile, since you ate no breakfast, what would you say to a bit of luncheon?"

They dined simply but abundantly on spicy hot sausages and meat pasties purchased from a cook boy. Edward savored the pasty, its crust brown and crisp from a nearby oven and inside a rich, steaming gravy with great gobbets of beef and venison. Hastings rejoiced to see him eat and thought then that their adventure had been worth any risk.

They toured the London shops, admiring absurdly the display of pewter and plate in one craftsman's shop, the array of rich Genoan damasks in another and the sturdy English woolens in yet another. Tailors and scriveners, cordwainers and haberdashers, they visited them all. A cook shop yielded up a loaf of freshly baked bread for a ha'penny, and Edward gnawed at it hungrily, washing it down with a tankard of ale in a taproom. Yes, it was balm beyond blessing for Hastings to see the color rise in the boy's sallow cheeks, to hear the merry shriek of his laughter while viewing a puppet show or the tricks of an organ grinder's monkey.

Then Hastings tempted the very fates. He consented to a boat ride upriver to Westminster after Edward, pleading, had clutched his sleeve. "I won't try to see my mother," he said, "only to see where she stays and to look on my royal palace of Westminster."

Hastings hesitated. "Have you forgotten that for these few hours you are no longer king?"

The boy drew himself up to his full height. The look he gave Hastings was nothing short of imperious. "We are always the king," he said loudly. "Do *you* forget yourself, my lord?"

And Hastings, who had been only "Hastings" or "my dear Hastings" or even on occasion that day "sweet Will," had laid a restraining finger to his lips. "I haven't forgotten, but must you proclaim it to the entire world?" A one-eyed beggar was giving them a wondering stare from a nearby doorway, and two housewives, one of whom Hastings thought he recognized from the riverfront that morning, had paused in their conversation to gawk at them openmouthed. Hastings took his young charge by the hand and fled toward the quays.

For the rest of the day, Edward acquitted himself with distinction. Under Hastings's watchful eye, he made no move to bolt, only gazed with rapt interest at the huge abbey with its soaring vault, jeweled stained-glass windows, and coronation chair; at the abbot's palace next to it; and at the vastly larger and far more sumptuous royal palace across the street. And he showed keen enthusiasm at the shop of William Caxton, where, beneath the sign of the red pale, two sweating apprentices worked the very first printing press in all of England.

"My Uncle Rivers brought Master Caxton to Westminster," Edward said proudly. "And his *Dictes* was the first book to be printed here. I have one of the very first copies."

"Indeed?" Hastings felt decidedly uncomfortable. The name of Rivers aroused an assortment of unpleasant emotions and even a little guilt.

"How I miss him now!" Edward was saying. "The book is all I have left of him. Sweet Will, do you think you could whisper a word in the protector's ear? I will vouch for my uncle's loyalty, and it would gladden my heart to have him with me here."

Once again there was that pleading look in those vulnerable sea-blue eyes. Well, perhaps Rivers had been penalized enough. Even Gloucester should consider himself secure enough now to allow the earl his freedom. After all, Richard had never been enthusiastic about arresting Anthony Woodville in the first place until Buckingham had blundered his way into their affairs. "I-I will see what I can do, Your Grace."

Edward was content. Nevertheless, Hastings had breathed a grateful sigh when they were seated in the stern of a wherry bound downriver and the dangerous precincts of Westminster faded behind them. Edward hung over the side of the boat as they shot the bridge at falling tide and gasped with delight as the boatman took them into the churning wash beneath one of the nineteen narrow arches. He reached out with his hand, almost touching one of the wooden piers and might easily have tumbled into the river if the boatman had been less skilled, but Hastings did not scold him. For Edward, such treats were all too rare. Let him enjoy them to their fullest while he could.

Only when they reached the Tower wharf did Edward's mood change. He dragged himself so reluctantly from the wherry that Hastings feared the boatman might charge them another fare. He too felt the heavy chill of foreboding overtake him as the walls of the outer bailey loomed from the late-afternoon shadows.

"I wish I didn't have to go back," Edward said. "I wish I could stay with you and that we could do every day the things we did today."

"I wish it also, Edward," Hastings replied sadly. "Indeed, I most fervently wish it."

They met no resistance. The gatekeeper admitted them with hardly a glance and clanged the gate shut behind them with a resounding finality. They crossed the green, empty and silent at this hour though the sun still shone on the topmost ramparts and turrets of the White Tower, washing them with rose. The kitchen entrance was deserted.

Where are the guards now? Hastings wondered. *Off pursuing some new diversion?* He mentally blessed the laxness that had given their venture success.

He held fast to that illusion almost until they reached Edward's private apartments. Argentine, stepping noiselessly from a side chamber, gave them their first clue of disaster. He had lost his customary presence and looked only old and very frightened. "My lords, I am sorry. I could not stop them. They burst in."

"They?" Hastings asked.

"The dukes."

"Did you tell them anything?"

"No. They knew you were missing from the council. I think they assumed that Edward was with you."

"Then we should have nothing to fear," said Hastings. He pushed past him to the door of the king's privy chamber. Edward's hand, held fast in his own, had begun to sweat.

Percival greeted them with a deep mock bow. "I am most happy, sire, to see you safely returned. You have caused Their Graces not a little concern."

"There was no need for concern," Edward replied somewhat loftily. "I have been out among my people. What harm in that?"

Percival regarded him with his pale eyes so unnerving in the deeply tanned face. "Nonetheless, your escapade has cost your guards dearly, I'm afraid. For neglecting their duty, they have all had their right hands struck off at the wrist."

Edward blanched, and Hastings felt his own stomach give way inside him. Percival smirked. "Ah, but let's not speak of that now. I wouldn't delay another moment giving Their Graces the pleasure of seeing you."

With a lithe, cat-like motion, he threw open the heavy oaken door. Hastings felt Edward's hand clutch his mindlessly like a vise and, despite his own faltering stomach, tried to return a reassuring pressure.

"After you, my lords."

They entered. The lowering sun shot brightly through the western casement. Richard was pacing the floor near the window, and the sun turned his lank hair dusky red, his black mourning weeds a dingy shade of brown. Beyond him, Buckingham rested comfortably on a window seat, resplendent in a green brocade doublet and cloth-of-gold hose. His high-piked shoes were chained to just below the knees. He wore an expression that contained more of satisfaction than of worry.

Richard turned sharply at the opening of the door and, seeing Edward, ran toward him. He looked genuinely relieved. Strangely, it was not at all what Hastings had expected. "Edward! Thank God you are safe. I cannot tell you what a panic I was in."

"We are quite all right, Uncle," Edward replied, adopting a haughty air when he saw that retribution was not to be immediately forthcoming. "You need not have troubled yourself on our account. We have spent a passing fine day in our capital."

"Weren't you aware that you are forbidden to leave the Tower?" asked Buckingham from his perch by the window.

"There was no danger," Edward said.

"Indeed, Dickon, I can vouch for that," Hastings added.

"You?" Richard turned on him a look of withering scorn. "You're a fine one to vouch for anything! Who knows better than you what happened the last time you took Edward on an outing?"

"The lad gave me his word that he would not try to escape," Hastings argued. "Nor did he."

"The *lad* is hardly trustworthy," Richard said. "No thanks to you, he is not at this very moment hiding behind his mother's skirts in sanctuary."

"And yet he is not."

"No, not now," Buckingham broke in, "but what of the next time or the time after that? Oh, he is cunning, make no mistake. What if his brother Dorset happened to be strolling the streets of London on the very same day you chose to go adventuring? Do you think you would be able to hold him then?" The duke's voice dropped. "Would you even try?"

"If you are accusing me of disloyalty—"

"You have no doubt heard of what happened to those we appointed to guard the king. Is your crime any less than theirs?"

Hastings felt the blood leave his face. Beside him, Edward trembled violently, the tears about to come. "You have no right to blame my lord Hastings," he cried shrilly, "no right at all. He has only done my bidding and has therefore proven more loyal to me than others I could name. By the holy rood, I wish I were with my mother in sanctuary or with my brother Dorset. Then at least I would be with those who love me."

Richard shut his eyes tightly; his hands sought his temples in a little massaging motion. When he spoke, his voice was low and dangerously controlled. "Don't talk to me about love, Edward. You don't know what you are saying. Your mother's kin do not love you so much as they seek to use you as a weapon against me, against England, to milk her of her riches. Power. Power is what they seek, not love. As for me, sire, why I would love you quite well if you gave me but one sign, one gesture that my efforts on your behalf have called forth one particle of gratitude from you."

Edward dropped his eyes, and tears seeped out from beneath his lowered lashes, but once again, Hastings could not tell whether they were born of shame or frustration. Richard extended a hand toward him, let it hover briefly in midair, and then let it drop. It curled into a fist at his side.

"Send for the leech," Richard told Buckingham. "His Grace is obviously tired and distraught. I would not have him upset further."

When Edward had gone, Hastings stood alone and faced the dukes. Richard's anger seemed to have spent itself. He looked weary now and sad though he continued to pace the lozenged tiles with a heavy step. Buckingham resumed his place on the window seat for all the world as if he were enjoying a friendly chat over port.

"I am grieved, William," Richard said at last. "I would not have expected this of you."

Hastings spread his hands in a deprecating gesture. "I . . . I am sorry, Dickon, if I've caused you anguish, yet I fail to see what harm has been done. Why, this day has been better for Edward than all of the potions Argentine has in his arsenal. I tell you, if you could have seen him an hour ago—"

"Fortunate for you that I did not, or I don't know that I would have been responsible for my actions. Edward must know that he cannot be cosseted forever. He must learn that there are duties and obligations that go with kingship as well as privileges. He is not an ordinary boy and cannot behave like one. We will not tolerate any more such lapses. I will be brief. I think it best that you not be allowed access to the king for a time. You seem to arouse, perhaps through no fault of your own, a spirit of rebellion in him. We do well to vanquish it here and now."

Hastings staggered like a drunken man. He stared uncomprehending at Richard, mouth agape. Through moted shafts of sunlight, Richard returned him stare for bitter stare. "Not . . . not see Edward? But why, how? I don't understand . . . I can't conceive . . . Not see Edward?" Then his eyes fell on Buckingham, twisting his hand up to the sun so that its dying light glanced liquid sparks off his jeweled fingers. Complacent, unconcerned Buckingham.

"It's he who has done this to you, isn't it?" Hastings said, turning back to Richard. "He who's been filling your ears with poison against Edward, against me, against God alone knows how many of your other loyal friends. Oh, yes, he would be glad to have me banished from Edward's presence, to have everyone banished. There is one who would wield more power than Dame Woodville Grey ever dreamt of!"

"William!" Richard cried. "Be reasonable, for God's sake. This is not a harsh punishment. By your own admission, you have merited far worse. Because I love you, I have been gentle with you, but don't presume too far on my love, I pray you."

Hastings brushed a hand across his eyes. Some instinct more potent than outrage told him to keep silent, to dissemble. *Speak no further word against Buckingham; argue not with Gloucester. Accept your punishment with a grateful hand and go. Some remedy may yet be found, some means to redress these grievances. Ah, yes, a remedy.*

"I am sorry, my lord," he said in a voice not his own. "You are right. I have wronged you, and I have subjected the king to grave danger without even realizing . . . I pray in time I might earn your forgiveness, your trust."

Richard gave him a sad, sweet smile. He was like a father forced to discipline a favorite child. "I'm glad to hear it, Will, very glad indeed. I think even Harry here might be prevailed upon to forgive your unkind words if you show such penitence."

Buckingham stood, smiling also, his white teeth flashing like sentinel stones. He accepted Hastings's outstretched hand. "Forgive? Why, I have already forgotten. Words alone never caused an injury, and surely I would never wish to offer or to take offense against you, my dear lord."

The streets of London were almost deserted as he left the Tower gate. Hastings walked the whole distance in the gathering dusk, scarcely knowing where he went, dumb as a horse who feels only the pull of the stable. Bow bell tolled for curfew—nine sweet, piercing strokes—as he entered his own courtyard. He climbed the stairs in the hall without acknowledging the greetings of any of his servants. In fact, he did not even hear them. At the entrance to Jane's room, he pushed open the door without knocking and stood on the threshold. Jane looked up from a fan of cards spread in her long fingers. Three women of the household were with her.

"My lord, you are home early," she said. At a signal from her, the women vanished, leaving their cards where they were. "You are unwell?" she asked, puzzled by his silence. "Will, what is it? Tell me. Please, love, do not look that way."

At her touch, he crumbled. For the second time since he had known her, he wept openly and unashamedly. "Jane, oh Jane," he choked against her breast.

Her fingers smoothed his hair. "It's all right," she crooned. "It's all right. Cry it out, Will, then tell me. Tell me all of it."

Elizabeth Woodville was fast wearying of sanctuary life. She was wearying of the four walls—narrow, close, and shabby—that constantly confined her. She was wearying of the monks' interminable plainsong chant that echoed in a mournful, muted undertone from the nearby abbey. The sound of it was a fever in her brain morning, noon, and night. And she was wearying of the food. Not that she and her household were expected to partake of monastic fare—far from it. The law specifically forbade the feeding of criminals in sanctuary, and Abbot Eastney observed every jot of the law. No, she must depend on the charity of her friends, and friends there days were few and short of memory. Rotherham occasionally sent her a dish from his kitchens when he remembered to do so and Morton as well when he thought it safe, but these hardly sufficed to fill the bellies of her own children, let alone the rest of her household. She had been forced to sell her jewelry and pawn her plate with alarming frequency. Of course, she still possessed a large share of the royal treasure, but for this, she had other plans.

Most of all, she wearied of the loneliness and boredom, the endless weeks with the same faces about her day after day and night after night till she feared she would go mad. She would scold poor little Dickon or snap at Bess over some trivial matter; then she would see the hurt expression, the sliding tear and embrace them in a rush of endearments. And all the while, she wondered what was happening out there in the street, in the real world where men walked in light, not in shadow, and listened to music and laughter, not to the dim and distant orisons of monks. Most of all, she wondered about Edward. News of him, like everything else in sanctuary, was scarce.

And then one day there came a visitor. Her eyebrows arched at that. Visitors were few. A nun, the page told her, tugging at her sleeve, a nun who said it was most urgent that she speak to the queen at once. The lad had a new penny in his pocket to prove it.

Elizabeth followed though privately she thought that if she saw one more tonsured male or habited female, she would pull her own gilt hair out by its roots. The woman stood with her back to Elizabeth, staring out the window. It was raining and the streets were wet. Her habit had been splashed with mud by a passing cart and was torn at the hem. A hood covered her hair.

"What do you want with me?" Elizabeth asked coldly.

The woman turned. Beneath the hood was a face no nun every possessed. She flushed with joy or discomfort and then fell to her knees, kissing Elizabeth's extended hand. "My blessed lady and my queen," she murmured.

Despite herself, Elizabeth was moved. "That is an extravagant greeting for these times," she said.

"But no less true for all that," Jane replied.

"And what, may I ask, brings you here? I understood you had no need of sanctuary."

Jane bit anxiously at her lip. "No, madam, I do not."

"Well, what then? It seems passing strange to me that my husband's harlot seeks an audience for my favor."

"I seek nothing, my lady. Instead I've come to offer aid."

Elizabeth gestured to a chair while she herself took the one opposite, a gilded throne-like seat with the arms carved in the shape of leopards couchant.

"Why, this is an even greater wonder, that you should offer me aid." Her voice still gently mocked, but she looked at Jane with new interest. "Very well then, what is this assistance you have brought?"

Jane's brown eyes regarded her without blinking. "My lord Hastings and some of the other lords of the council are growing disenchanted with the protector's rule."

"Hastings?" Elizabeth asked, incredulous. "Not the same Hastings, surely, who only a week ago prevented my son from joining me here, who waylaid him on my very doorstep and delivered him back safely to the protector's hand? Ah, yes, I heard of it, so you will perhaps pardon my amazement."

"Much has changed since then."

"I would sooner believe that a carp could grow wings and fly like an eagle or that a snake could get off its belly and walk like a man than that your Lord Hastings would throw in his lot with me and mine."

"And yet I tell you it is so."

Elizabeth fingered her pearl reliquary and considered this turn of events. To herself, she wondered how Jane had led her latest bedfellow to this most remarkable of decisions. Aloud, she said with an air of finality, "I cannot believe you. It sounds too much like a trap set by the protector to discredit me."

Almost instantly, Jane was on her knees in the rushes, her hand clutching desperately at the queen's. "Madam, you must believe me. You must! It is the only solution for all of us."

"Does it mean so much to you then?"

Jane's nod was barely perceptible. The hood had fallen away, and her hair tumbled free in all its red-gold glory.

"Does Hastings know that you love my son?"

A pink flush crept along Jane's cheekbones. "N-no, of course not. But if I do, what's the harm in that?"

"No harm, perhaps, though I think Hastings would be loath to see you restored to Dorset's arms. 'Tis said he loves you well."

"I am not hurting him, my lady. He is in truth most unhappy with the governance of the protector and especially with the lot of the king. He would do anything to have Gloucester out of the way, and if I reap my own rewards from what I do, that's neither here nor there."

Jane rose from her knees and took her seat once more. In the silence between them, the distant plainsong swelled and died. Elizabeth watched her visitor coolly, speculatively, darting her little pointed tongue over her lips. There was no doubt that the girl was acting out of her own wanton lust, but what of that? She could still do her service, had already done her service if she had in fact converted Hastings to the cause.

She did well to remind me of the king too, Elizabeth thought. Edward was the key to it all; she must stop at nothing to get him into her custody once more.

"I will write this very morning to your . . . ah . . . would-be paramour and inform him of this latest development. With news of the defection of so great and powerful a baron, I'm sure he and my brother Sir Edward will have little difficulty raising an army. Hastings's support comes late and unlooked for, but I will not refuse it. By the blessed Virgin, if only a month ago . . ." She stopped and smiled. "But I should not chide you for that, dear Jane. You have done your part and admirably too."

Jane knelt and kissed the queen's hand with moist lips. "I thank you, my lady. I shall return in several days to bring you any news there may be."

"In your nun's habit, my dear? How well it becomes you."

When Jane was gone, Elizabeth sat and thought, her hands coiling and uncoiling over the leopards' heads of her chair. Not only Dorset would hear of this new hope, she decided, but Rivers and Grey as well in their northern prisons. Gloucester was reputedly an easy jailor, and Middleham and Sheriff Hutton were fortresses that could be easily breached by trickery. Yes, she would have her eldest brother and her second son as well to aid her in the coming battle.

Her hand reached out and tugged at the tapestry bellpull.

Chapter 20

BISHOP STILLINGTON'S UNEXPECTED arrival shattered the peace of the Sabbath afternoon. It was the eighth day of June; the coronation was only two weeks away, the gathering of Parliament only a few days beyond that. Richard's writing desk spilled over with stacks of important documents. So much to be done, so little time to prepare. And then there was the red-and-white liveried page hovering at his elbow.

"Stillington, you say?" Richard asked, faintly puzzled. "What the devil can he want?"

"My lord, I don't know. He wouldn't say."

Across the room, Anne looked up from her embroidery to reproach him with her eyes. It had been like this ever since she had arrived in London several days before. The long days with their endless round of councils and conferences and diplomatic sessions merged into equally long nights of rushlights flickering on parchment, the scratch of John Kendall's busy quill, the rasp of the sand shaker over some document. Even on this day of rest, he was not to be spared.

Anne had brought with her from the north a letter from William Wrangwysh, prominent citizen of York and one of Richard's closest friends, complaining that a certain monastery upstream from the city had once again set up illegal fishgarths in the River Ouse to the great harm of the fishermen of York. It seemed at first a laughably trivial issue with which to concern the protector of the realm, yet Richard knew the economic hardships these fishgarths caused and, as York's good lord, was determined to do what he could to remove them. He had at that moment been composing a remonstrative letter to the abbey prior. And now there was Stillington to be dealt with as well.

"Oh very well," he said. "Show him in."

The boy looked anxiously about him. "The bishop has requested a private audience with Your Grace."

Whatever else the solar of Crosby Place may have been that afternoon, it certainly was not private. With Anne were two of her ladies: Anna, her cousin who was married to Francis Lovell, and Margaret, Rob Percy's plump little heiress of a wife. Francis himself sat on a cushion at their feet, reading in his elegant French from *La Roman de la Rose*, while Tom Lynom, Richard's young solicitor, squatted nearby on the rushes, listening to the tale almost as raptly as the ladies. Rob Percy, who was vaguely scornful of love visions, rolled about noisily on the unlit hearth with two deerhounds. He was like a huge overgrown puppy himself, innocent and perfectly content.

"The bishop awaits you in your privy chamber, my lord," said the page, oddly insistent.

"Yes, yes, of course," said Richard as he rose and made for the door. He noted that Anne stabbed her needle into the linen with peculiar vehemence as he walked out.

"Well, Stillington, what is it then?"

The bishop of Bath and Wells acknowledged the greeting with a rather stiff bow. His nose twitched like a frightened rabbit's, and Richard had the distinct impression he would rather have been any-where else at that moment than where he was.

"Won't you be seated?" Richard asked, more kindly.

Stillington lowered himself into an X chair, arranging the purple folds of his cassock about him with great deliberation. Richard was suddenly aware of how much he had aged. The fur-like fringe of hair that fell from beneath his biretta was almost completely gray.

"First of all, let me beg Your Grace's pardon for this intrusion," he said at last. "I know how busy you must be, especially at this particular time. It was not my intent to . . . ah . . . infringe upon your Sabbath."

"Yes, yes, go on."

"On the other hand, there is something I think you should know, something I must tell you. I won't deny it costs me much to say it. I've spent many hours in prayer for divine guidance, wondering if our Lord would have me speak at all. Yet in the end, it seems I must."

Richard's eyes narrowed. For his life, he could not conceive what sort of guilty secret this mild, ineffectual little man could be privy to. Perhaps some minor infraction of ecclesiastical law, some episcopal irregularity in his diocese, but then he should go to Bourchier.

"Very well," he said. "Let's have it out. You may dispense with the preliminaries."

"As you will, my lord." Stillington nodded. "The truth is simple enough after all. Your royal brother King Edward was never the wedded husband of Elizabeth Woodville."

"What did you say?" Richard barked. "But how so? There was a priest, a marriage ceremony, witnesses. Edward himself told me of it."

Stillington held up a blue-veined hand for silence. "Yes, or so I've been given to believe, yet hear me out, my lord. The truth is that Edward was not at that time free to marry. He was in fact trothplight to another. I myself united them."

"And this . . . this other?"

"The Lady Eleanor Butler, daughter of Lord Talbot, Earl of Shrewsbury."

Richard sank heavily into a chair. He toyed with the ring on his little finger as if it were a talisman against chaos. "Can this be true?"

"Only too true, I'm afraid. In the eyes of the church, Dame Elizabeth Grey was never Edward's lawful wife. She was in reality no more to him than the Shore creature—a royal mistress, nothing more."

Richard did not answer. Stillington leaned forward in his chair, warming to the subject. "You are aware of course that the king, whom God assoil, was something—ah, shall we say—free in his attentions to the female sex. His eye roamed far and liked whatever it looked upon. Before he ever met Dame Grey in the chase at Grafton Regis, his gaze fell on the Lady Eleanor. However, she being a pious widow and possessing virtue as well as beauty, would have none of him, not until he vowed before God to take her to wife. Very secret it was, for the lady's family were devout Lancastrians and the king feared Warwick's wrath. Most secret. No one was to know."

Still silent, Richard considered the possibility of truth in Stillington's revelation. How well the tale, preposterous as it might sound at first hearing, fit his brother's character. Edward had always possessed a fatal penchant for beautiful widows. If they were a few years older than he and of Lancastrian sympathies into the bargain, then so much the better. Perhaps like a naughty child, he loved to taunt his mentor Warwick by flirting with the enemy. Surely he had done something very similar with Elizabeth Woodville. Warwick, who had already arranged a very advantageous French marriage for the young king, had his nose tweaked in earnest.

One thing was certain: when Edward desired a woman, he became like a man possessed, losing appetite, losing sleep, unable to concentrate on even the simplest exercises of statecraft until he hit on a strategy to make her yield. Small wonder then if twice that strategy had included marriage or the nearest thing to it.

"No one was to know," repeated Stillington, "so Edward cautioned me. The lady herself, England's rightful queen, kept the secret to her grave, though she was understandably heartsick over his abandonment. She entered the Carmelite monastery at Norwich and died there some years ago.

"But I . . . I, to my shame, let it slip to your brother Clarence. Somehow, perhaps from your lady mother, he had caught wind of the fact that there was something irregular in Edward's marriage. Somehow he learned also that I was linked to it. He would not rest until he knew all."

"Ah, Clarence!" Richard exclaimed, seeing for the first time the pieces of an old puzzle fall into place.

"Yes, Clarence," the bishop echoed sadly. "I'm afraid that knowledge was his undoing."

Swiftly, Richard's mind leapt back over the intervening years to the cold winter day that had marked Clarence's execution. "They hunted him down like a pack of wild dogs, the Woodvilles. Oh, I don't argue that he didn't deserve his fate several times over, but Edward would have pardoned him, I thought, as he had so many times before, out of sheer brotherly love and kindness. I could not conceive of the deed, the taking of a brother's life. Edward had always been kind, quick to smile, easy to forgive. How could he sign the death writ? How could he consign his own brother to the executioner? And yet he did. That time, his forgiveness had run out."

Richard felt the waves of old bitterness wash over him with a violence the years had not diminished, felt too the old sorrow for Georgie, the youngest of his three older brothers, the one who had been closest to him in age, and the playfellow of his childhood. He pictured the golden, ebullient Duke of Clarence ebullient no more, his golden hair floating like lank seaweed on a butt of sweet malmsey.

"But now you see why Edward had him slain, do you not?" Stillington asked. "And why I too was jailed, as I believe was stated in the indictment, for 'uttering words prejudicial to the king and state.' And why I must step forward now." He blinked his bright rabbit eyes. "The matter of the succession . . ."

"Yes, the succession!" Richard cried, clapping a hand to his forehead.

"Just so, my lord. Edward V is not the rightful King of England. Neither he nor his brother York is entitled to inherit the crown. They are royal bastards, nothing more."

Richard heard the sharp intake of his own breath. "My lord bishop, you know that Clarence's son is still a child and lies under his father's attainder. Also, he is not quite right in his head." Richard had seen the eight-year-old Earl of Warwick only recently in his mother's household, a sweet-tempered lad but with vague, watery eyes and a drooling lip. "In the normal course of things, he would come next in the line of succession, but if we set him aside as unfit . . ."

Stillington touched his pectoral cross and nodded. "Just so, Your Grace."

Was it true? Could he believe it? He knew suddenly that Stillington had given tongue to all the unbidden, unspoken desires of his heart—to be a king, to rule in his own right! How much simpler, how infinitely preferable was that to being a protector, even a regent, for an openly hostile boy with a pack of scheming relatives? But no, he was forgetting. The boy was Edward's son true enough, legitimate heir by his father's will and in the sight of the English people. He was also Richard's blood nephew whom he had sworn before God to preserve and protect, sworn to serve. Such a one was not to be set aside lightly.

Stillington sat quietly, respectfully, hands folded in his lap, waiting with a patience born of long years. Richard wondered as he looked at the man's careworn face why he could not have taken his awful knowledge to the grave. Why did he bring it forth now to trumpet it in Richard's face, to torment him with a dream that could never be? The fourth son of a duke, the youngest brother of a king—no, it was not intended that such glory should ever be his. And yet . . .

"You will, of course, keep your secret a while longer, my lord bishop. I and only I will decide when and even if the council is to be told." It came to him that he need tell no one. Richard too could have the truth buried with him and be none the worse for it.

Stillington nodded. "Yes, Your Grace. With but one lapse, I have kept it nigh on these twenty years. Yet if I may remind you, the coronation is only a fortnight away. If we don't act quickly, we will come perilously close to anointing one who has no claim to that unction. We shall crown a bastard."

"I shall be the judge of that," Richard snapped. "Edward is my brother's son. No one is disputing that, I hope."

"None, my lord."

"Though I have often thought that the queen—or Dame Grey as you will—had but little help with his conception. There seems to be more of Woodville about him than of Plantagenet."

"That thought has occurred to me as well," Stillington agreed. "In fact, if I may say so—"

He was interrupted by the sound of raised voices from the antechamber.

"I tell you, I must see the protector immediately. My business is urgent." That would be Buckingham. His unmistakable baritone soared above all others.

"And I tell you that he is in conference with the bishop of Bath and Wells and not to be disturbed," a lower voice replied, straining against temper. That would be Tom Lynom.

"Stillington? That moth-eaten woolsack of a cleric? What can he be discussing that requires such privacy? Your lord will thank me for the interruption, I assure you."

With that, the door burst open, and Buckingham sailed triumphantly through it, followed closely by an exasperated Tom Lynom and less closely by Sir William Percival.

"My lord, I apologize," Lynom said to Richard. "I couldn't hold him. He would see you whether or not you would be seen."

"It's all right, Tom," Richard said wryly. "It seems I am to play host today to all sorts of uninvited guests."

Buckingham acknowledged Stillington's presence with a lordly tilt of his head. "How do you do, bishop?"

"Quite well, thank you, for a moth-eaten woolsack of a cleric."

Buckingham had the grace to look embarrassed. "I . . . er . . . I regret that remark. It was born of my impatience to see the protector. I hope you took no offense from it."

"Offense? Why, no, my lord. If my skin were as thin as all that, I would never venture from my own lodgings. Wool has some resiliency, you know."

"What? Oh, yes, quite. And now, Stillington, if you will excuse us, there is an issue of some importance for the protector's ears alone."

Stillington stood, not quite managing to conceal an air of injured dignity. Richard was kind in dismissal. "We were just about finished with our chat anyway, were we not? You know that I will give your matter my deepest consideration."

"Matter? Consideration?" Buckingham asked, eyes swiveling from Richard to the bishop, who bowed and padded softly toward the door. "What possible matter could he have for your consideration?"

Richard hesitated. Should he tell Buckingham? Should he take his counsel on this issue? No, he had better wait. "A trivial problem," he said, "of no great consequence."

Buckingham nodded toward Lynom with some satisfaction. "Did I not tell you, Tom? You would have me cool my heels in an antechamber while Stillington babbled of trivialities, though Percival and I bear the most alarming news you shall hear in many a day." Turning back to Richard, he announced, "The Woodvilles are raising an army and a navy. They mean to fight us over custody of the king."

Percival, it soon became apparent, had been quite busy in the fortnight that had elapsed since he had been removed from Edward's guard. Richard had accomplished his banishment with not a little satisfaction. Openly, he reasoned that if Percival's hand-selected men had been lax in their vigil, then Percival himself rightly ought to share some of the blame. Privately, he deeply mistrusted the man and was eager for any excuse to remove him from Edward's presence.

In an attempt to redeem himself, Percival had taken ship for Brittany where he had spied on the activities of their enemies. His efforts had proven most fruitful. As he unfurled a map of France, there was no mistaking the gleam of triumph in his eyes.

"A goodly amount of English coin has suddenly appeared in the court of Duke Francis," Percival was saying. "Indeed, the gold fairly drips from the pockets of some of his courtiers."

"The royal treasury of England," Richard said. It was not a question.

"Aye," Percival continued, "and what does it buy? Ships, my lord, and men. Oh, they are secret enough about it, you may be sure. Sir Edward Woodville acts the aggrieved exile in public. Only two days ago, I spotted him in a tavern in Nantes, moaning into a tankard of English ale and in the company of none other than Henry Tudor, that self-styled Earl of Richmond. Of his nephew, the marquis, I saw nothing, only heard of his presence from a laundry maid who warmed his bed for a night. She apparently found my gold as good as his and hastened to boast her tale.

"But there can be little doubt of their more illicit activities. All along here"—he pointed to a strip of Breton coast that jutted close to England—"and particularly here, at St. Malo, there are warships arming quietly and without publicity. Gold, it seems, also buys silence. In yet another tavern, I found a man of arms willing enough to brag of the booty that would be his on his lord's latest conquest. He would not name his lord, nor would he reveal the place of invasion, though I plied him with much of their sour wine. Perhaps he suspected me. My Breton is hardly a native's, but it did serve me well enough, I think. There can be no denying that we must prepare for an invasion."

Richard looked down at the map, at the Narrow Sea, and at the long, unprotected line of beaches along England's southern coast. "Yes," he agreed. "But how? And with what?"

"The funds must be raised," Buckingham said. "We meet with the council in the morning."

"It will take more than the council. It will take parliament to levy taxes, and we don't have time to wait."

"Your late brother used benevolences," Buckingham suggested.

"Bah!" Richard spat. "Another name for robbery. I wouldn't stoop so low." He cut himself off immediately, regretting the disloyalty. "Edward had a certain finesse for extracting funds, which I lack."

"Then it is council who must act and parliament approve, after the fact."

"Yes," Richard agreed, "so it would seem."

He looked up to see Lynom's head wagging in disapproval. "You must forgive me, my lord. Legally it should not be done."

"And what would you have me do, Tom? Wait until Dorset knocks on the door of Crosby Place? I don't like it any better than you do. Still, there is an emergency. I should have guessed something was afoot yesterday. A messenger from my nephew Lincoln at Sheriff Hutton brought me word that Rivers was apprehended while trying to escape. They found on him a letter from his queenly sister bidding him to be of good courage and to flee my prison as quick as may be. Further word would come."

"A letter, my lord?" Buckingham asked. "How did it find its way to Sheriff Hutton?"

"A traveling minstrel, Lincoln said, who sang most sweetly, sang to shame a lark and who, it now seems, sang a special siren song for Anthony Woodville's ears alone. He won't sing again. His tongue has been ripped from his mouth, and he molders now in the keep's dungeon, where no doubt I should have clapped Rivers in the first place."

Buckingham delicately cleared his throat. "Aye, no doubt. Or worse. Didn't I warn you? If it hadn't been for that mule-headed Russell . . . Ah, but that's in the past now. We do better to consider the present and the future. And I think we do best of all to consider what allies these traitors have right here in London."

Richard frowned. "What do you mean by that, Harry?"

"Well, it's obvious that they must have supporters. How else could the queen know of these plots, sanctuary bound as she is?"

"Speak plainly, cousin."

"I don't think you need look too far to find her allies. Haven't you noticed how close a certain foursome on your council has grown lately, how often they meet outside the council chamber, how frequently they dine at one another's houses?"

Richard smiled in relief. "I assume you are speaking of Hastings and his party. Yes, of course, I am aware of their gatherings. Hastings is attempting to reconcile them to my appointment as regent after the coronation and with some success. As you know, Morton had his nose knocked askew when he was denied the chancellery, Rotherham when he lost it, and Stanley . . . well, Stanley seems given to general discontent. But none of them is dangerous. What—old Rotherham, a conspirator? It makes me laugh to think about it. *Nom de Dieu*, Harry, don't I have enough real foes in Brittany that you must look for bogeys on my council?"

Buckingham appeared skeptical. "All the same, I think it would be wise for you to meet with them. Even Hastings has some cause for resentment, you know."

"Over the affair of Edward? Perhaps, but he has certainly shown none to me. And he's no dissembler to feign love where he feels none. Him, at least, I know well. But if it will ease your mind, I will speak to the four of them perhaps sometime this week."

Buckingham nodded. "Very well, my lord. There is . . . ah . . . one other matter I think you should know about. One of the sanctuary guards swears he has seen a woman who looks very like Jane Shore entering and leaving the postern gate of the abbot's palace."

Richard's raised hand faltered. "Shore is seeing the queen?"

"Or one who bears her some resemblance."

"You are not certain that it was she?"

"I . . . no, I am not," Buckingham admitted. "I did not see her myself. The guard said she wore the habit of a nun, deeply cowled. He caught only a glimpse of her face, but of her famed hair, unfortunately, he saw nary a strand."

"It couldn't be Jane Shore," Lynom said. "There would be no mistaking that face, that body beneath any nun's robe ever made. Nor could such loveliness be guilty of the evil you imply, my lord duke. The face is a mirror to the soul."

Richard shot his solicitor a long, appraising look. "I'm not so sure of that, Tom," he said, shaking his head. "Not in this instance anyway. Still there does seem to be precious little evidence in all your innuendoes, Harry. I prefer in this case to think your information false."

Buckingham's full lower lip trembled slightly. "You are thinking perhaps that I'm being overzealous? Mayhap you're right. But if so, it is only because I would have nothing of hurt touch nigh you. If I could, I would make all your pathways smooth."

Richard felt a tide of surging warmth rush over him. Something in him leapt high at Buckingham's words, at the husky tone in his voice. He drew a deep breath. For a moment, there were only the two of them in the room. Lynom and Percival had vanished, forgotten. In that moment, it seemed that Buckingham's future and his own were inextricably linked. Here was a man who was utterly his, one whom he could trust with the glorious possibilities that awaited him as with his dying breath.

Percival was gathering the map from the table; Lynom stood already at the door, his hand pressing the trefoil-etched latchkey. Buckingham too turned to go. Richard laid a hand on his arm, detaining him. "Please, cousin," he said softly, "stay awhile. There's something I want to discuss with you, alone."

Chapter 21

John Morton kept a goodly estate at Ely Place in Holburn, so Hastings was forced to admit as he gazed about the luxuriously furnished solar with its numerous arras tapestries and its profuse display of plate. The oriel window itself was a masterpiece. Recently installed, its fan-vaulted bow commanded a sweeping view of the garden below and of its famed strawberry beds. The window's clear glazed diamond panes were enriched with jeweled medallions of stained glass depicting scenes from the fen country, where Morton had his diocese of Ely. It was an uncharacteristically cozy touch. Morton did not often disturb the Benedictine prior who tended the episcopate in his absence. It had probably been months since he had stood beneath the octagonal lantern that was the hallmark of his cathedral church. When Hastings had asked him about the window, Morton had smiled his deprecating little smile and suggested that a shepherd should never forget his sheep, busy though he might be with wolves or, he had added almost sweetly, with boars.

Watching Morton now, languidly dipping a plump strawberry into a pile of rare white sugar, Hastings found it difficult to imagine him being busy with anything at all. He had partaken as heartily as any of them of the saddle of lamb, the roast swan and pheasant, the venison frumenty, and rather more than Stanley, who always ate sparingly, or Rotherham, who still chewed carefully on the pheasant, or for that matter, Catesby, who had taken only enough for courtesy though he had drunk more than was absolutely necessary of the bishop's fine Burgundian wine. But then Catesby had experienced a bit of a shock that evening and still showed the effects of it. If Morton had his way, Catesby might not have been included at all in their little gathering, but Hastings was convinced he could only add to the success of their venture. His very youth was an asset. Who else among them was young?

Nonetheless, Hastings was forced to admit that Catesby did appear to be under some strain – or was it only that the saffron chamlet of his new short gown accentuated his sallow complexion and made his mouth look tighter than usual? Will Catesby had never been handsome. Now he looked like a stuffed doll with his own narrow shoulders padded to outrageous proportions. Stiff as a doll too, Hastings thought, despite all the claret that had found its way down his gullet. He still wore a vaguely stunned expression, like a sleepwalker awakening in a strange place. Hastings knew that he himself must have worn much the same expression several weeks ago, the first time he joined ranks with this small band of conspirators in plotting against his old friend. And yet there had seemed no other choice left to him, then or now.

He popped one of the luscious ripe berries into his mouth and belched contentedly into a surnap. He had eaten too much as usual, but then Morton had always kept a fine table. Tomorrow he would have his tailor ease the seams of his doublet; tonight, he could only surreptitiously loosen the laces that snugged at his waist.

A page offered a basin of scented water. Gratefully, Hastings laved his sticky fingers while the butler and sewer cleared away the plates. On a cooler evening, the bishop and his guests might have adjourned to the hearth, but the twelfth of June had been a hot, sultry day, and the temperature hadn't dropped yet. The sun still hung low in the western sky like a bloated orange.

A servant lit the candles of the chandelier that hung over the table. The light flickered fitfully over their faces. It was Stanley who broke the silence. "Why do you think Gloucester called this council for tomorrow?" he asked, fixing Morton with his wary gaze.

Smiling, Morton shrugged. "How should I know, Thomas? I've never been privy to the boar's private thoughts. Maybe he means to make another attempt at raising an army."

Stanley snorted. Hastings shifted his bulk uncomfortably in his chair. The memory of the Monday morning session three days before was still painful. Gloucester had brought before them tales of Woodville treachery and had pled with them for the authority to raise an army. In this, he had failed despite his obvious sincerity and Buckingham's ever-ready eloquence. Largely because of Morton's talent for innuendo, he had left the council chamber empty-handed. With a few choice words, the bishop of Ely had cast suspicion on the protector's entire case. Hastings could still hear him.

"My lord," he had said to Richard in his bland voice, "are these reports . . . reliable?"

"I believe they are, Morton."

"You . . . ah . . . believe?"

"They are reliable," Buckingham had declared. "You have my word on it. My own man Percival returned from Brittany only yesterday."

Percival! Hastings almost choked aloud. He was becoming widely known and just as widely mistrusted.

"Then it is . . . your man Percival who makes these reports?"

"Why, yes, Morton." Buckingham's famed choler already reddened his cheeks. "Just what are you insinuating?"

Morton's eyes widened with wounded innocence. "Why, nothing that I know of, m'lord, except that it could be a disastrous and costly error on our part to act on such . . . ah . . . information then learn it is, shall we say, inaccurate."

Buckingham had argued on, of course, badgering them with dark, obscure threats. "You don't know what is at stake," he cried at one point, only to be stopped cold by Richard's glare. "I mean . . . if we lose custody of the king, it could go ill for all of us."

Though not half so ill if you do not, Hastings thought to himself. Torn by his own complicity in the plot and by the knowledge that Richard looked to him for support, he had said very little. When questioned directly, he had only mumbled a tepid endorsement.

"Surely if there is danger, then we ought to respond to it." But his tongue had hung too heavily on the *if.*

He had turned away from Richard's look of keen disappointment then as he turned away now from the tapestry on the opposite wall: Judas Iscariot kissing Christ in the Garden of Gethsemane. "Surely," he rasped to Morton, "he won't bring up that subject again."

"The thought distresses you, William? And well it might. You should have given him the support he sought."

"But I? How could I?" Hastings demanded. "What was I to do? Let him raise an army and destroy us completely?"

"What you were to do, what you *are* to do, is to play the devoted friend, the loyal comrade in arms, the unquestioned ally. What you are not to do, under any circumstances, is to arouse the boar's suspicions. His tusks are sharp. The fury of hell burns in him.

"And as for the army," Morton added more softly, "there was little danger of that thanks to the archbishop of Canterbury and his own handpicked lord chancellor." Hastings noted how Morton spat out the last words. "They played into our hands precisely as I knew they would. They serve us well though they don't know it. Perhaps we should have invited the bishop of Lincoln to join our cause. He has after all contributed most admirably to it."

Hastings shook his head. "He would never do it. I know the bishop. He is Richard's man despite the fact that he often confronts him in council. And he is loyal." His voice echoed on a dying fall.

"Ah, yes, so he is," Morton replied. "And because you are not, you cannot afford to confront him."

Hastings hung his head, feeling a familiar pain gnaw at his vitals. Stanley said, "Enough of this, Morton. We don't have time for the pot to cast names at the kettle." Then slowly, with effect, he added, "I doubt that Richard will bring up the subject of an army again since he has already made some preparations along that line."

Morton's eyes widened in unaccustomed surprise. "What did you say?"

"Yesterday he sent Sir Richard Ratcliffe riding posthaste to the north with a call to arms."

"The north?" Rotherham echoed, suddenly alert.

"York, Excellency, the seat of your arch-episcopal see," Stanley replied, "and, it must be noted, where men are under Gloucester's spell. He has them in the palm of his hand up there, or so I'm told."

"I . . . I should have spent more time in York," Rotherham said with a vague wave of his hand in that direction. "Hap I might have won them to me."

"Hap you might have, father. Only it's somewhat late to bemoan the fact now."

"Where . . . how did you learn of this?" Morton questioned. He did not seem to be so concerned by the news itself as by the failure of his own sources to turn up the same information.

Stanley's teeth flashed white in his auburn beard. "I've been no laggard, Morton. You will recall that my lady wife was wed to Buckingham's uncle for many years. No doubt that's a fact my lord duke would choose to forget if he could, but family ties persist despite him. As it happens, Margaret's steward, Reginald Bray, gained access to Buckingham's manor where it took no great skill to learn that the duke had dispatched Percival to Wales to raise a force there. Parenthetically, Bray also learned of Ratcliffe's flight to York, though judging from Buckingham's lack of a following in Wales, I'd say it's from the north our greatest danger comes."

"Ah yes." Morton regarded them thoughtfully over his steepled fingers. "From the north. I would agree with you there, Tom. Gentlemen, we must act more quickly than I had thought. In fact, there is no time for delay."

Hastings raised his head. "But surely we can't move yet. The Woodvilles aren't ready. It will take another week at least, perhaps two. We will have no support."

"True, true, and true," Morton admitted, "but if we go according to our original schedule, we may well find ourselves in rebellion against more than a mere protector."

Stanley gave him a puzzled look. "What are you saying, my lord bishop?"

Morton smiled at him with some satisfaction. "I haven't been napping either, Thomas. And it has come to my ears from quite reliable sources that Richard of Gloucester has recently been informed of an old and highly dangerous secret."

"Pray, go on," Stanley urged.

"As much as I would like to, there is one among us who can tell the tale far better than I. Catesby, you know what it is, don't you?"

Catesby turned beet red. "Y-yes, m'lord, I believe so."

Hastings was suddenly on alert. "Then let's hear it, Will, by all means."

Catesby nodded and took another swallow of wine. Then in halting terms, he stammered out the most astounding story that Hastings had heard in many a day. Through a daze, he heard Rotherham's quick response. "It's a lie! A filthy execrable lie fabricated by those who hate our gracious queen. Foul blackguards all! May they rot in hell for this work!"

"Peace, Excellency," Morton said soothingly, palm upraised. "Rest assured that none of us wishes to give it credence."

"Nor shall we," Stanley added.

"I wonder, I wonder," Hastings murmured, half to himself. To Catesby, he added reprovingly, "If you knew, why didn't you tell me before this?"

"My lord, I learned of it only today. There has been no opportunity to tell you."

"He's telling the truth, Hastings," Morton said. "The protector revealed it only this afternoon to Catesby and a few of his other . . . ah . . . intimates."

"But, Morton, I take it you knew beforehand?"

"Let us say I had strong suspicions. It's an old tale, really, and I'm quite surprised you hadn't picked up rumors of it at least although, quite naturally, Edward made every effort to stifle them."

"Then how did you know?" Stanley asked.

Morton gave them an enigmatic shrug. He closed his eyes as if considering what answer to give. "I heard rumors, shall we say, years ago when I fought for Edward's foes. It was a lady of Lancaster he took after all, and so it was—as you would say, Stanley—not difficult. I have always made it my business to know what is going on around me. In this particular instance, after I knew the cause of

Lancaster lost and was myself happily reconciled to the Sun of York, I deemed it to be in the best interests of the crown and of England herself to keep my silence. Not to mention, of course, that it was also in my own best interest." He drew a finger across his throat, smiling at his own grim jest. "Clarence, poor Clarence, was quite undone by it—the king's eldest brother. Imagine the possibilities opened to him if the king's marriage were invalid, the king's sons illegitimate."

"The selfsame possibilities it opens to Gloucester," Stanley said.

"Precisely."

"But if it is true," Hastings said softly, "then Richard is king—by law, by right, by just inheritance."

Morton fixed him with a cold stare; his tiny eyes were the tips of icicles. "Its truth or untruth does not concern us in the slightest, William. Don't forget that for a moment. The only thing that does concern us is its effect on the boar."

"A very pretty pretext for usurpation," Stanley said.

"Do y'think Gloucester means to be king then?" Rotherham's milky eyes widened as if for the first time, he realized the story's implications.

"I have no doubt of it," Morton said, "though he would hardly call it usurpation. He had a rather lengthy conversation with Stillington last Sunday afternoon. Now, Stillington is involved in all of this somehow. You will no doubt recall that at the time of Clarence's troubles, he too was imprisoned. And the queen's family has always loathed the man with a fury that would hardly be credible if they did not also greatly fear him. We can assume that Stillington knows something. He may well hold the proof that Richard needs in his . . . manipulations."

Hastings turned to Catesby. "Did he say anything to you of his plans?"

"No, my lord. He only laid out before us the facts as he saw them. H-he did not embellish them with references to their implications."

"But he was sounding you out, was he not?" Morton asked.

"H-he wished our opinion on the matter, yes."

"And what was your reply?"

"I said nothing, my lord, or very little. The shock was great as you can perhaps imagine. All of us were dumbstruck."

"His own men—Lovell, Assheton, Tyrrell—what did they say? Didn't they urge him to it?"

"Why, yes, finally. When they had regained the use of their tongues."

"But you did not?"

"No, bishop. I told him the matter required further study and n-needed some sort of proof. I could not answer to it."

Morton smiled, visibly relaxing. "Good lad, very good. I will confess I had some doubts about you at first, but now I see you are truly one of us."

"Of course, he is," Hastings snapped. "He is my man entire. Did I not tell you?"

"Yes, yes, of course. And if we had all night, I would be happy enough to sit here and listen to you extol his virtues. But unfortunately, we don't have much time and a great deal still to be decided. Which brings us back to Tom Stanley's original question: what of the council tomorrow?"

"Do you think Richard suspects us?" Hastings asked, a cold knot of fear twisting in his stomach.

"No, nothing as desperate as that. Though, indeed, it is only too obvious that he means to treat us as a group since there will be only ourselves, Buckingham, and Howard in attendance. No, if he suspected we were in league against him, we would all now be rotting in the Tower or worse." Morton went smoothly over the sound of Catesby's strangled cough. "On the other hand, I believe that some of us, and myself not least of all, have been a little too open in our discontent—you, Tom, with your sullen air, your perpetually long face, and you, my lord archbishop, with your bitterness over the seal—"

"But it was mine! He took it from me."

"Not before you gave it away. As for you, Hastings, well, we have already commented sufficiently on that, I think. Minor infractions all and certainly not indicative of treason. But more dissension than he wishes on his council if he is to grab at the crown. He will treat us most kindly, I think. Woo our support. Try to win us to his cause. I'd take an oath that his purpose in meeting with us on the morrow is innocent. It is we who must be, shall we say, somewhat less than innocent."

"Tomorrow!" They gasped in unison as Morton's meaning caught. The morning was so near.

"What shall we do with him?" Stanley asked.

"That, my friends, is something that bears discussion. We have two alternatives, have we not? We could arrest both of the dukes, for don't doubt for a moment that we must deal with that coxcomb Buckingham the same as Gloucester. Or we could . . . ah . . . dispatch them forthwith. Frankly, I favor the second alternative as being a somewhat cleaner cut and far easier to accomplish as well. Either way, our end is clear: to gain possession of the king while he is still the king."

Hastings shuddered. "I don't care what you do with Buckingham. But Richard . . . Richard was my friend. Let's not slay him."

Morton gave him an eloquent shrug. "As you will. It comes to the same thing in the end. The people will not allow a usurper to live."

"And how, Morton, by all that is holy, do we go about this?" Stanley asked.

"Dear Thomas," Morton chuckled, "as skeptical as the apostle whose name you bear. I've been thinking about it, never fear. And I believe I have a plan that might work."

Looking at Morton then, Hastings felt a swift revulsion. Plainly, the bishop of Ely was in his mettle, like a three-year-old child with a new toy. His eyes glowed eagerly; the corners of his full lips twisted upward as he leaned closer and lowered his voice in a conspiratorial whisper. "Once we are all seated in the council chamber, that will be the time to act. There will be guards outside, of course, but very few of those—two or three at the most. We must find some means to get our own men into the Tower. Although we cannot arrive with a large contingent of armed retainers, we could arrange for some to be nearby, waiting. It should be easy enough, I think, as long as the dukes suspect nothing."

"Ah, yes, I see it," said Stanley. "We must have a signal arranged, some way to let our men know that all is settled and ready."

"And I think I have just such a pretext," Morton said. "Gloucester has always been fond of fresh strawberries, and as you have seen tonight, they are ripe in the gardens of Ely Place right now. In years past, he has sometimes asked me for a mess of them. I will offer to send for some at the beginning of our gathering."

"But it'll be more than strawberries that he'll get," Stanley drawled. "Oh excellent, Morton! Perfect! You are a genius."

The bishop acknowledged this praise with a modest bow. "All talent comes from God, Thomas. It would be a sin to hide mine beneath a bushel.

"Hastings, since you have seen fit to accumulate a goodly number of retainers, the men will be your responsibility, yours and young Catesby's here, who can manage things from the outside. They must be waiting to come into the Tower, armed and ready, as soon as the signal is given. The Tower guards are used to seeing men in your livery coming and going about the place. I doubt they'll even raise a question at the entrance of, say, half a dozen or so. And even if they do, your men have only to say that you've been stricken with an illness and they've come to collect you. It should be like child's play, really. There will only be the seven of us from the council, with no one except Buckingham and Howard to stand by Richard, and those two like fighting cocks, each itching to get at the other's throat."

Hastings sighed heavily. "Yes, it sounds easy enough. Can you arrange for the men, Catesby?"

"Yes, my lord, of course."

"Then there is nothing more to be said, is there?" Morton remarked, dismissing them. "We meet in the Tower at tierce."

Hastings rose stiffly for the chair had almost grown into his buttocks. "There is one more matter I would bring to your notice, Morton," he said. "We have chosen a most unlucky day for our enterprise—the thirteenth day of the month and a Friday to boot."

"Have you grown superstitious, Hastings?"

"What—I? No. That is, I don't think so. And yet—"

"Then think no more of it. We ourselves will manage our fate . . . er . . . with heaven's help, of course."

"'Twill be ill omened enough for the hog tomorrow, make no mistake," Rotherham cackled in his ear. Hastings could feel the old man's fetid breath on his cheek. He turned sharply away.

Daylight still lingered in the sky, a long, thin line of crimson on the western horizon though the hour neared eleven. It would be a short night and a long day tomorrow. The conspirators had parted amicably enough. Stanley had left them bound for Ludgate; Rotherham's coach had clattered noisily away toward the Strand. Hastings and Catesby rode together, each lost in his own thoughts, past the sleeping mansions and the darkened gardens of the wealthy and the well-to-do. Their horses' hoofs clopped loudly in the stillness. Behind them, their retinue followed at a discreet distance.

Catesby's eyes were fixed on the sunset. "How bloody the sky is tonight," he muttered, "how terrible and bloody."

Hastings shot him a worried look. "Is something amiss, Catesby?"

"No, milord. Perhaps I took too much of the bishop's claret. Nothing more."

"A good night's sleep should fix that," Hastings said.

"Yes. I shall be glad to find my own bed."

Hastings drew in his reins. "Would you rather that I spoke to the men tonight?" he asked. "That would spare you."

"No! I mean that won't be necessary. Already the night air has soothed my aching head. And you, my lord, I know you have . . . other plans. There's little enough I can do to repay your kindness to me. Let me do this much."

Hastings smiled at the thought of Jane waiting for him. It was true that he wanted no further delays to keep him from her. He nudged his horse forward. "As you will, Catesby," he said. "As you will."

Jane awoke as Hastings drew apart the curtains and crawled into bed beside her. She yawned sleepily. "My lord was abroad late tonight. What time is it?"

"A little before midnight," he replied. He drew her against him and lay quietly for a while, staring up at the shadows beneath the vast canopy. She could hear the gurgling of his stomach and feel beneath her hand the tenseness of his body.

"Listen, Will," she said, raising her head and regarding him quizzically. "I'll show you my skill as a teller of fortunes with the aid of neither palm nor tarot cards. The bishop of Ely dined you well tonight, I think, yet something happened that has unsettled you. Isn't it true?"

He gave her a wry smile. "Aren't even my digestion and private thoughts safe from your scrutiny?"

She shook her head. "No, nor should they be. Between two who love, there should be no secrets."

He drew her head down again on his naked chest and stroked her hair awkwardly, almost without thought. "We move against the protector tomorrow."

"So soon?" She raised herself up once more and looked at him in wide-eyed alarm. "But how can you? You can't have any support yet from . . . from the queen's party."

"We shall have to manage without it. There's no time now to wait. Richard . . . Gloucester intends to seize the throne, or so we have reason to believe. We must act now."

"Ah, didn't I tell you that he would do it? You wouldn't listen to me then, and now . . ."

"Now I must destroy him."

"You don't seem overjoyed at the prospect."

"I'm not. All of a sudden, my stomach fails me. I look back over the years and remember Dickon when he was only a lad, weak, sickly, and much afflicted by the changing fortunes of York. I comforted him in those days, dried his tears, wiped his runny nose. Edward's little brother, small but with a spark of greatness in him even then. And I remember that later, much later, Edward himself chose him to lead the government in his will. And now it appears even as though he may well have a legitimate claim to the crown. It's a difficult matter to set aside."

"I don't think your stomach fails you so much as your heart," Jane replied, not unkindly. "There is too much of softness in you. You must not think that you thrust Richard aside. It is he who is in the wrong if he thrusts aside Edward's will and robs the crown from Edward's heir. Do you honestly think that whatever claim Richard advances now, Edward would stand by and watch his brother usurp his son's throne?"

"No."

"Then look at it this way. In setting Richard aside, you are acting in Edward's stead, doing what he would have done. Can't you see that?"

He smiled up at her then, a warm dawning smile of appreciation. "Yes, when you put it like that," he told her. "Ah, sweeting, you are a rare woman indeed to be able to lay such phantoms to rest. I half-believe that behind your lovely face, there lurks the mind of a man."

"So! The mind of a man, you say?" Jane sat bolt upright and cried in mock outrage. Pulling off the flimsy silken nightshift, she cupped her hands beneath her full, rose-tipped breasts. "Do these also belong to a man? Or this?" she asked pointing to the fiery triangle at the top of her thighs. "I see no prick growing there."

"No," Hastings answered, laughing, "there you are completely a woman, lovesome and bedsome." He lunged for her in the bed and pulled her down still uttering shrill protests on top of him. He kissed her hungrily, probing deeply the velvet wetness of her mouth, exploring the familiar yet exciting hills and valleys of her body. A lifetime would not have been long enough to know them all. Beneath his mouth and hands, her protests gradually ceased. Her arms came around his neck.

"Ah Jane, I do love thee," he murmured in her ear. "Whatever happens tomorrow, you must remember that."

When she opened them, her brown eyes were softer than he had ever seen them. "Hush, foolish man," she whispered. "What's this silly prattle? Nothing is going to go wrong. And the next time you come to my bed, it will be as the greatest man in all England!"

Chapter 22

RICHARD WAS LATE for the meeting. Beneath the lofty hammer beam roof of the council chamber, the six men who awaited him huddled like dwarves around the huge, oak slab table. There were many vacant chairs, not least among them the one at the table's head.

The Duke of Buckingham had taken his seat, by now his completely accustomed seat, at the protector's right hand and had already engaged Morton in a lively discussion of who should receive which honors in the upcoming coronation procession. If either of them knew that he was beating a dead horse, he did not betray it to the other by even the flicker of an eyelid.

Seated next to Hastings, as he had for so many past meetings, John Howard was quiet and withdrawn, not bothering to feign interest in the debate. The two old friends had exchanged the usual pleasantries that morning, pleasantries that did nothing to bridge the deep and widening gulf between them. Now Howard squinted at the window, his eyes fixed on the western horizon, where dark clouds towered ominously beyond the chimneys and steeples of London. In the east, the sun still shone, throwing the city into brilliant relief like a vision of heaven untimely caught.

Across the table, Rotherham slouched uneasily in his chair. He had tried several times to engage Howard and Stanley in conversation, only to be brushed off unceremoniously as each was lost in his own thoughts. Hastings could see a vein pulse rapidly in his throat.

The old fool was in a state of nervous frenzy. Surely the protector would have only to look at him to read the guilt written in his face. God grant that he did not give them all away.

And Stanley—Stanley was even worse. He looked both gloomy and tense. His eyes traveled ceaselessly to the open door and back again to the protector's empty seat. If he had his way, Stanley would not have been there at all. A dream had troubled him, a silly, childish dream! Hastings had almost laughed aloud as Stanley confided his fears on the boat ride to the Tower.

"A dream? But, Tom, didn't you hear the good bishop last night berating me for my superstitions?"

"Yes, but this is not the same thing. I tell you, Hastings, it was so real I'm still shaking from it. I swear I saw the boar and he charged us both, slashing at our heads with his tusks until our blood flowed red down our faces."

"I've never known you to give cognizance to dreams."

"No, nor have I. But this was no illusion. This was a sign from God. We ought not go to the Tower today."

"And let our enterprise topple?"

"Better that than our lives . . ." Stanley did not finish. The boatman had turned to cast them a long, curious look from beneath the jutting brim of his cap. He was very young, perhaps only sixteen or seventeen, but who knew where Richard and Buckingham placed their spies? Conversation became dangerous; a misspoken word could prove fatal. Stanley had clenched his teeth and was silent.

Their craft had rocked pleasantly on the wake of a huge carvel bound upriver to dock. Still unconcerned, Hastings smiled to himself as he trailed his fingers over the side of the wherry, dabbling them in the water's coolness. Far from sharing Stanley's alarm, he found himself merely amused at the change in both of them since the previous night. He who had trembled at the deed now perceived it as a necessity, a means to remedy wrongs greater than itself, while Stanley, who had openly championed the act at Holburn, quailed in the face of it at the Tower. But then, Stanley did not have Jane to cheer him on.

Incomparable wench! Hastings saw her again as she had been earlier that morning, sprawled on the bed. The cover had been kicked askew and tangled at her feet, for the night had been warm. Her white body had smelled of musk and glistened through a fine sheen of sweat; her hair was dampened into ringlets that half-covered one breast. He had stooped and kissed her forehead very lightly so as not to wake her and listened for a moment to the sound of her breathing coming heavy and regular from between parted lips. Then he had tiptoed softly from the bedchamber.

Her words came to him now in the council chamber, a cheering comfort for the dark hours ahead. "The next time you come to my bed . . ."

At last, Richard joined them. For a moment, as they rose and faced him, the tension increased to an almost intolerable pitch then faded rapidly as he smiled and took his seat, murmuring apologies for his tardiness. His looks were mild; his laughter almost merry.

Bloody dreams and portents indeed, Hastings thought with a triumphant glance in Stanley's direction. Richard was in as good a humor as he had ever seen him. Was it the promise of the crown that lured him from his customary solemnity?

They had taken their chairs, and Richard had just opened his mouth to speak when he was interrupted by a cry of alarm from Morton.

"Oh dear me!" Morton clapped a hand to his forehead. "How could I have forgotten? I had them picked at dawn this morning, all washed and packed in a hamper, ready to bring."

"What are you talking about, my good bishop?" Richard asked, perplexed but obviously amused.

"Why, the strawberries, of course! I know how much they please Your Grace, and I had planned to bring you a mess of them today."

"I appreciate that, Morton, and the thought no less than the gift, but surely later—"

"Ah, no, no, I'm afraid not. They are now at the very peak of flavor and freshness. Another day, even a few more hours, will leave them overripe. My page is outside. You must allow me to send for them."

Richard frowned. "But Holburn is some distance away, and it looks as though it's going to rain. I wouldn't cause you such inconvenience."

Morton's face took on an aggrieved expression. "For Your Gracious Lordship, no inconvenience is too great."

"Oh very well," Richard said, yielding. "Send for them then since I see we shall have no peace until you do." The smile left his face to be replaced by a puzzled squint as he watched Morton bustle to the door. The bishop was almost ludicrous in a tight purple cassock that bulged a bit at the waist. Hastings thought that it fit well the image of the good-natured buffoon, the addle-pated bumpkin that Morton was at pains to convey. And yet Richard was well enough acquainted with Ely's bishop to know him neither bumpkin nor buffoon. Hastings's own eyes narrowed as the bishop, his purpose achieved, resumed his seat with an air of exaggerated diffidence. To go from stubborn opposition to fawning servility was a leap that not even the master strategist could make with ease.

Richard was speaking now, but Hastings hardly heard him. He caught words here and there, snatches of phrases: "divided council," "opposing parties," "not my wish that one group on council should be elevated at the expense of another." Gradually, he became aware that Richard was indeed treating with them, making an effort at reconciliation as Morton had predicted. "Certain dissatisfactions," Richard was saying, "have reached my ears."

Across the table, Buckingham was engaged in scraping some dirt from under his fingernails with the point of his dagger. His expression was impassive, almost too impassive, as if he had deliberately voided his face of all emotion. Hastings needed no oracle to tell who had preached their dissatisfactions so loudly in the protector's ear. Rotherham's clenched hands were pasty white; their brown liver spots stood out like pock marks on a whore. Morton's fingers clasped and unclasped his pectoral cross.

"Such dissatisfactions can grow to rage like a canker through the body politic," Richard continued, "if they aren't excised at first discovery. Stanley, Morton, Rotherham . . . Hastings, if there is anything that displeases you, let us hear it now. How say you, my lords?"

Someone's stomach, probably Rotherham's, growled loudly in the silence. Far beyond the Tower walls, there echoed the low rumble of thunder. Hastings dared only the briefest of glances at Richard, who was smiling a little even now, looking from one to the other with an air of patient expectancy, even of tolerance.

How can we speak? Hastings thought. *What should we answer? Dissatisfactions—hadn't it passed beyond that and long since?*

Morton purposefully cleared his throat. *Aye,* Hastings thought, *let him speak, Morton of the nimble tongue, he who possesses the quick wit and the slipperiness of a weasel. Let him offer his innocuous lies until our swords speak the truth.*

But the words never left his mouth. Suddenly, there was a knocking, loud and insistent, at the door. Hastings and Morton shared surreptitious glances. Certainly it was too soon yet to expect their men.

"By the mass!" Richard did not bother to conceal his annoyance, but he called out permission to enter. A member of the Tower guard stood in the doorframe. "Beggin' your pardon, my lord. There's a gentleman without beseeches a word with thee."

"Can't it wait until we adjourn?"

"He . . . he says not, m'lord. He says 'tis most urgent that he must speak to you at once."

"So be it," Richard said, exasperated. "Let's see what it is that's so pressing that it can't even bide a meeting of the king's council. I crave Your Lordships' pardons. I shan't be long."

In that, he lied. He was gone for an eternity. And in the strained silence he left behind, Hastings shot Morton a questioning look. He was even more alarmed to see that the normally implacable prelate also seemed uneasy and knew that this time it was no jest. Morton's face had gone fish belly white; sweat lapped his jowls like dew and prickled his domed forehead.

"It's uncommonly warm today, isn't it?" he asked, pulling a huge linen square from the folds of his tunic and mopping it ineffectually across his face.

"The heat will break soon, I think," Howard replied. "There's a storm building up in the west. If I were at sea, I'd say we're apt to get quite a blow out of it."

"Indeed?" Morton said weakly, for once at a loss for words.

There was silence once more, broken only by the boom and rumble of the approaching storm. Buckingham twisted restlessly in his chair like a small boy denied the use of the privy. His eyes strayed, as did all their eyes, to the heavy door studded and framed in lead through which Richard had vanished uncounted ages ago. Through which Hastings' men might burst at any moment to find that their quarry had eluded them.

Better not to think of that. Hastings could only pray that they did not come too soon. How much time had passed? He had no way of knowing. He only knew that the room was growing steadily darker as a huge phalanx of clouds blotted out the sun. His eyes peered anxiously around the chamber, moving upward to the beamed ceiling lost in shadow, traveling down the dangling pennons of the knights of the Garter that hung from it. He picked out Richard's boar, white on azure, and next to it his own familiar cognizance, the black belled sleeve on silver.

The sight of their banners so close together stirred long-dead memories: he and Richard, little more than a boy, keeping vigil together on the eve of their induction into the Order of the Garter; he and Richard in the heat of battle hacking away at their enemies; he and Richard fighting together for Edward at Barnet and Tewkesbury, their banners dripping blood that was both their enemies' and their own.

Edward's armor, worn at both of those great battles, still dominated the far wall of the council chamber. Hacked and dented by many a mace and many a sword's thrust, it stood proud and invincible as Edward himself had been, six feet four inches tall and almost as broad. But the grieves were thick now around formless calves, the hauberk swelled over an invisible chest, and the helm, high and plume topped, closed on empty air. Edward with Richard and Hastings beside him, his two chief captains, what had happened that they were brought now to this—one dead and the other two plotting against each other?

A flash of lightning hit near, flickering blue fire over motionless faces. The crack that followed struck like doom.

"The storm grows close," said Howard.

"Aye, too close," agreed Morton, shifting his bulk.

"I'll go and see what's keeping the protector," said Buckingham, leaping to his feet. The sound of the door slamming behind him was swallowed up in thunder.

"For the love of God," Richard cried, "what's going on here?" He could not see the man's face, only the darkness of his presence making a deeper shadow beneath the heavy Norman arch. "Do you have business with me? Come, sirrah. Out with it! I have affairs of state to attend to."

His harsh look faded as the intruder stepped out of the shadows. "Ah, Catesby! So it's you. But I don't understand. The guard seemed to think it was urgent."

"S-so it is, Your Grace. Most regrettably urgent. "It . . . it concerns . . . m-my lord Hastings."

"Hastings? But I only left him a moment ago. I don't see how—"

"Hear me out, please," said Catesby, palm uplifted, "then you may judge." The tale came out finally in halting, stumbling phrases that were often hardly intelligible though their meaning was plain enough at the end.

"Ah, but you must be mistaken, Catesby," Richard said, shaking his head. "This is preposterous. Do you know what you're saying? It's treason, man, no less."

"No less," Catesby echoed.

Richard shook his head again emphatically. He even smiled a little as if to deny Catesby's bleak, heavy look. The darkness had deepened around them, though now and again lightning shivered silver bright through the unglazed window slit.

"Hastings is my friend," Richard argued. "He would never betray me. God's teeth, man, I've known him from my cradle! The others now—Morton, Stanley, Rotherham—I wouldn't give you a groat for the lot of 'em. Let them all be trussed up together and cast into the Thames for all I care. They're as bad a bunch of scheming malcontents as ever plagued any ruler. But God take me for a fool if I can number Hastings among them."

"He's changed of late," Catesby said quietly. "Haven't you noticed how he keeps his own counsel or that of the three you mentioned?"

"Well, to be sure, I've known he was . . . discontented." Richard recalled with a start the reason he had summoned them to today's meeting in the first place. "But mere discontent is no crime, and it's a long way from treason." He regarded Catesby with sudden suspicion. "Have you grown ambitious perhaps? Are you playing Judas to your lord, hoping I might reward you with some of his holdings?"

Catesby turned paler still. "No, I swear not, by the holy blessed Virgin."

They stood in an old guardroom with only one narrow window slit that looked out toward the river. Richard could see a curtain of gray water rushing toward them, the storm breaking at last in a drumroll of thunder.

Catesby fell to his knees. "What can I do to make you believe me? It may well mean your life. Ah, I have it! The strawberries . . . Morton has sent for strawberries, has he not?"

"Why . . . yes."

"That was the signal that all was ready. I was to have brought Hastings's retainers to waylay you and the Duke of Buckingham in the council chamber. Won't you believe me now?"

"I—but Hastings!"

"It was the harlot, I think, who drove him to it. He dotes on her almost to distraction."

Richard's voice echoed hollowly. "Ah, the strumpet Shore, ever mine enemy."

"And she has made Hastings your enemy as well. My lord, I pray you, won't you believe me now?"

The rain came, slopping wet through the unglazed window, splashing the front of Richard's houppelande with fat drops. He neither moved nor spoke.

"My lord?"

Something cold and hard as a steel blade was in Richard's eyes when at last he turned. "Yes," he hissed, "I believe you. Before God, I believe you. Hastings is false, and no man living is true. Are you satisfied now?"

Catesby flinched before the intensity of that gaze and lowered his face from its onslaught. He was on his knees still, quaking because his feet would not hold him. "No man living is true." The words struck home with the force of a thunderbolt. He began to protest, felt his throat thicken with his own guilty betrayal, and managed to utter only an unintelligible groan.

It did not matter. When he raised his head, Richard was already gone. He was alone, and the windblown rain was beating in upon him. He buried his face in his hands and wept.

Richard burned with mindless intent as he hurried back to the council chamber. His only thought was that he must confront the man who, only a few moments before, he had numbered among his most intimate friends. What would happen after that confrontation he did not know, nor did he particularly care. The betrayal was vast. He could not comprehend it.

Heavy footfalls echoing in the corridor before him brought him back to reality. Alert to a new danger, he stopped and slipped into a niche in the wall. The rough stones pressed into the flesh of his back; he hardly dared to breathe.

It was Buckingham who came. For a moment, he regarded the duke with hostile suspicion. Was even he not to be trusted?

"My lord, what's ado?" Buckingham asked, solicitous as always. The specter of his falseness at least immediately collapsed.

"Treason, cousin. Most foul treason."

"Ah . . ." Buckingham's voice held just a hint of satisfaction. "Treason within?" he asked, cocking his head down the long corridor toward the council chamber.

"Yes, of course. Hastings!"—he spat the word—"Stanley, Morton, even old Rotherham."

Richard started to walk toward the chamber, but Buckingham seized his arm. "Surely you don't mean to go back to them as you are now, unarmed."

Richard looked down at the vulnerability of his pleated black houppelande and the pitiful inadequacy of one small dagger stuck in his belt more for adornment than defense. "No, I suppose not."

"Then come, we must find arms. I've known this was coming. I tried to tell you . . ."

"But Hastings . . . Hastings! I still can't take it in," Richard argued. "He loved me. I would have sworn on Edward's tomb that he loved me."

Buckingham shook his head sadly but did not break stride.

"He'll die for it," Richard said suddenly. "Now. Here. This very day."

"That would be wise. Such a villain should not live."

They found arms, such as they were, in an old storeroom stocked with gear from days long past. Doubtless the guard rooms would have provided richer offerings, but they were more distant, and there was little time to lose. As Richard buckled on a rusty, ill-fitting brigandine too large for his slight frame, Buckingham was already alerting a guard to the coming danger and bidding him to gather together a corps of his fellows to await their signal outside the chamber.

Richard's hand shook as he thrust a sword into its scabbard. It too was rusty and antiquated, but it would serve the purpose. Over all, both dukes donned long black capes to conceal their preparations. Then they were ready.

"You must lead them sweetly," Buckingham exhorted him as they neared the door. "Toy with them as a cat toys with a mouse. And then the pounce!"

Richard was not listening. His hand pressed hard on the latch.

The rain was still driving down when the dukes at last returned. Hastings needed only one glance at Richard to know that trouble was upon them in earnest, though he could not conceive how or why. The protector's face wore the ghastly look of a death's head; its skin stretched white over sharp cheekbones, its eyes burning in their sockets like two live coals. Only a thin veneer of control kept his rage within bounds. His words came out slowly and distinctly, each one the knell of a hammer.

"I have just learned of a plot," Richard began, pacing back and forth at the table's head, "a plot to seize the government of this kingdom by force and to do away with the old blood royal of the realm. Now as might be expected, the queen and her kin are in the thick of it. That should come as no surprise to any of us here. Elizabeth Woodville will stop at nothing to retrieve what she has lost. No!" he shouted. "This is the surprise. It appears that the Woodvilles have found new allies to aid them in their vile schemes. Unlikely allies, I would say, for isn't it unheard of that a widow would consort with her late husband's harlot?"

Hastings's stomach heaved within him. The unmistakable reference to Jane dashed any hope that his own complicity had escaped notice. He had only one hope now: to hold out until his retainers arrived. Body and blood, but they should have been here by now!

"Will Shore's errant wife and the Queen of England," Richard was saying. "I wouldn't have believed it, but there it is. Your opinion, my lords, if you please. What should we do with them? Hastings?"

Hastings flinched involuntarily. Swallowing down a wave of nausea, he tried to find his voice. "Why, I . . . er . . . certainly, Your Grace, if this report is true, and if they have done these wrongs, then they ought to be punished."

"'If,' Hastings? 'If'? Do you serve me with ands and ifs? I tell you they have done them and worse besides. As who should know better than yourself? It was your body that led you astray, and on your body shall the punishment be laid."

Hastings hung his head. Thoughts were flying through it so thick and fast he could hardly sort them out. Richard turned his attention to the other conspirators, but his voice had lost much of its passion. "You, Stanley, Morton, Rotherham, you were all with him in this, were you not?" They nodded bleakly. Rotherham began to whimper. "Then you must be punished as well."

Out of the tail of his eye, Hastings saw Stanley's hand inch toward his sword hilt. Before he was well aware of it, they were all standing, brandishing their weapons. Stanley was lunging for Richard's throat as Richard cried out "Treason!" and brought his fist down hard on the board. Suddenly, the room was filled with armed men; they flooded around Hastings like a tidal wave of steel. But they were not his men. No hoped-for black-and-silver livery shone among them. These wore the blue-and-scarlet uniforms of the Tower Guard.

It was over almost before it had begun. Hastings felt himself apprehended by a rough grip; his arms were pinioned behind him, and his sword clattered uselessly to the floor. He looked back over his shoulder to see John Howard's blunt, homely face grown strangely grim. It was Howard who had restrained him.

Hastings managed an ironic smile. "What's this, my good lord? You were my man once and proud of it. Once you would have followed me anywhere."

"Not so far as this," Howard answered between clenched teeth.

They had been brought to bay without even much of a scuffle. Stanley was the only one who had sustained a wound. Blood oozed from a gash on his temple, trickled around his right ear, and soaked into his beard. He looked dazed, but then that was to be expected. Hastings knew he must wear the same expression although he was physically whole.

There was one thing he still did not understand. Why had his men not come? What had kept them? The answer struck him with such sickening force that he staggered and might have fallen if Howard had not held him in an iron grip. They were never going to come. They had never even been summoned. Catesby! It was Catesby who had called Richard out.

"Oh, God," he groaned, "let this cup pass from me."

"Take them into custody!" Richard bawled at the guards. "And as for this one," he added, pointing to Hastings, "for this one, find a priest and a headsman, for I will not go to the enjoyment of my dinner while he yet lives."

Two of the guards took him roughly from Howard's grip; a third hastened to obey the protector's command. Hastings stood numb as a statue, disbelieving. His life was forfeit, but all he could think of now was Catesby, who was like a son to him—Catesby, who had betrayed him.

He looked into Richard's taut, tight-lipped face and was amazed to see in the depths of the other's eyes a mirror to his own hurts. To be sure, there was anger there—hot, molten anger—but something else as well—pain, sorrow, despair—lurked there, struggling for release. In that moment, a dreadful sympathy linked them; the betrayed and the traitor, who had himself been betrayed, gave each other stare for anguished stare. When Hastings tried to raise a hand toward him, he was not certain whether he pleaded mutely for his life or offered Richard comfort for his woes. Richard probably had not even seen the gesture. Twitching his mantle over one shoulder, he turned and was gone.

The other prisoners were led quietly away. Rotherham wept openly, his tears sliding unchecked down sunken cheeks. Stanley, still dazed, pressed a cloth to his temple to staunch the flow of blood from his wound. Morton limped along behind, lifeless and quiescent as an old flour sack.

The priest came, dragged forth unwillingly from his devotions in the Chapel of St. John. He was a sad, frightened little man in a dirty habit stinking of sweat. He looked at Hastings with blank horror as if his head had already been struck from his shoulders. Hastings gave a brief confession, realizing as he did so that if he had it to do over again, he would change nothing. He had done what he thought he had to do, and whatever transpired from that was the fate he had chosen for himself. He knelt to be shriven and, when it was done, gave the priest a gentle smile and a shilling for his troubles.

"Don't look so aghast, sir priest," Hastings told him. "I wouldn't cheat death even if I could. The cup must be drunk down to the dregs."

The priest muttered a Latin benediction, shook his head, and went out, dabbing at his eyes with his surplice.

The rain had stopped, and the sun had broken through in splendor on the green. Newly washed, the air smelled like fresh linen.

Hastings blinked at the unaccustomed brightness and looked around him as if he were beholding the sight for the first time. The green shone like a forest of lance tips spearing dew. Each blade of grass was etched clear and distinct from its fellows. Sunlight burnished the iridescent wings of the ravens as they tugged at fat worms brought out by the rain. Silently, Hastings blessed these birds of good omen. Legend had it that the Tower—and England—would stand as long as there were ravens on the Tower green. He was glad for their promise even if he would share in it no more.

His eyes caught the figure of Buckingham in an upper-story window, standing with others of lesser rank who had thronged to watch him die. In an insane gesture, he gave the duke a cavalier salute as if to say, "You can't hurt me now. I shall soon be beyond all hurts." Buckingham did not return the greeting. He wore an expression of aloof satisfaction as if gratified by this triumph of justice. Richard was not with him, nor for that matter was Catesby. He was not surprised, knowing somewhere in his heart that neither of the two architects of his doom would care to witness his execution.

The flutter of a curtain in the royal apartments warned him that there might be another spectator, one for whom he would give much to spare this ordeal. He briefly saw a boy's face, pinched and pale and struggling against tears, before an older man, whom he recognized as Argentine, drew the youth back from the casement and closed the curtain securely over it. Hastings breathed a quick prayer of thanks to St. Anthony for that.

"Come, you!" one of the guards shouted, taking his arm. "You'll be keeping the protector from his dinner next."

Hastings went willingly enough. "I wouldn't cause His Grace any inconvenience," he said sweetly.

"Humph!" the guard muttered. "Nor shall have the chance."

There had been no time to erect a scaffold, of course. There was only a large log, left over from some repair work being done to the walls of the White Tower, and the executioner had selected it as the best spot for Hastings's death. He stood by it now, black garbed and black hooded, a figure of death incarnate. Hastings thrust a shilling into his palm as another of the guards—not the surly one—bound his eyes with a handkerchief. He accepted this offering with gratitude, then knelt on the wet grass and groped his way into position. The log felt mossy damp beneath his naked neck and bore the richly pungent odor of the earth itself, the earth to which his body would so soon return.

He thought fleetingly of his wife, Katherine, at his manor of Ashby-de-la-Zouch. *How will the news come to her?* he wondered. *And how will she take it?* He imagined her, thin lipped and sour, muttering pieties about the wages of sin. There was no consolation for him there, nor ever had been.

His last thought was of Jane. Sadly, he wondered what would become of her now. He made another prayer, hastily whispered, then lifted his hand to signal his readiness. He heard a swoosh as the axe fell. Night came on him of a sudden; he knew no more.

Richard, Howard, and Catesby waited in a side chamber. Richard slumped in a chair. His face had lost completely the fire of righteous anger; he now looked only stern and solemn and sad. He sat very still except for the hand that fingered the jeweled hilt of the dagger in his belt. John Howard stood at a window that looked out toward London. As always, his eyes were watchful. Catesby had taken a chair opposite Richard and, like him, sat motionless and mute. It seemed almost that the nightmare lay heaviest on him. He looked years older than his actual twenty-seven.

Suddenly, there was a sound of stamping feet in the corridor outside, and Buckingham burst in on their vigil. "He's been dispatched!" the duke cried. "You should have seen it! A veritable fountain spurted from the traitor's neck."

Catesby gave a groan and ran from the room, his hand clapped over his mouth. Richard seemed not to have heard. Buckingham, belatedly sensing the mood of those in the room, somewhat subdued his voice and manner. "The executioner wants to know what should be done with the body. Shouldn't the head at least be piked on London Bridge?"

"No," Richard replied without looking up. "It's enough that he is dead. I wouldn't have him made into carrion for crows. No, say he is to be buried in St. George's Chapel at Windsor in the chantry next to Edward's. Him at least he served well."

Buckingham gave him a quizzical lift of one gold eyebrow. "And well shortened his life in the process. I wouldn't have thought him worthy of such honor."

"It was what Edward wished. He had Hastings's tomb prepared with his own."

"But—"

"Don't give me any more buts," Richard said hotly. "The man is dead now and can do no further harm. Go and do as I say, or must I find others who are not so swift to question my will?"

Buckingham swallowed hard. His eyes, so animated a moment before, grew suddenly cold. "No, my lord. It shall be as you wish." Bobbing a bow in Richard's direction, he went out.

Howard beckoned from the window. "I think we need to publish a proclamation, Your Grace. A crowd is gathering outside the Tower gate, and I don't like the look of it. Hastings was a man . . . much loved by the people. They will be slow to understand how he could be convicted and executed without a trial. I'm afraid it could turn ugly."

Even as he spoke, a bell began to peal from the belfry of All Hallows Barking, the parish church nearest the Tower. And the first sharp strokes were quickly echoed and amplified by other, more distant bells until the whole of London seemed to join in the cacophony. They were passing bells for Hastings.

"You're right," Richard said. "I hadn't thought about that. We must let them know what has happened, tell them of the man's falseness, tell them . . . that a man's most fair-seeming outside can hide a heart that is rotten through."

He turned sharply away so that Howard could not see his face. "My lord, are you ill?"

"No, no. I'm all right. Don't fear for me. Send for Master Kendall. Tell him we have no time to lose. And the mayor . . . it would be well to have him nearby. He can calm the rabble if anyone can. And . . ."

"Yes, my lord?"

"I think . . . I think it would be wise if some men were sent to apprehend Jane Shore."

BOOK III

The Crown

June 16 to August 4, 1483

Chapter 23

JOHN HOWARD STEPPED easily from the stair of the Tower's water gate onto the waiting barge and was rewarded when the river craft gave a slight roll beneath his feet.

Rather like being on the deck of a ship again, he thought, *and wouldn't this be the day for it, though, with a rising tide bringing the smell of the sea and a freshening breeze shredding the morning mist?* A gull wheeling above gave a yelping screech. For a moment, he could almost taste the salt of blown spume in his mouth.

He watched as Richard stepped down, somewhat less steadily. He moved like a sleepwalker, and there were heavy marks beneath his eyes. Rumor had it that he had not slept the past several nights.

Just behind him, Buckingham and Thomas Bourchier, cardinal archbishop of Canterbury, walked out together from beneath the barred portcullis of the water gate. Suddenly, Bourchier gave an audible gasp as his eye moved downriver past the waiting barge. His hand, gnarled and knotted with age and rheumatism, clutched the breast of his scarlet mantle. Howard did not need to follow his gaze to know what had alarmed the good archbishop. Behind the state barge, with its cushions and striped awning and fluttering pennon bearing the English arms, were eight wherries hired only that morning by Howard himself and filled almost to the waterline with retainers wearing his silver-lion badge.

Bourchier's eyes sought Buckingham's accusingly. "I thought we had agreed there was to be no force. The queen's sanctuary is inviolate."

"Why so it is, Your Eminence." Buckingham's voice was mild with agreement. "And no force will be used if you are successful in your mission. We offer no threat to the queen's grace, but the little princeling she shields so fiercely rightly belongs here with his brother. The king is wasting away for want of a playfellow."

"It was decided," Bourchier snapped. "Haven't we argued the point long enough? I'm not yet so senile as to forget what we have debated these two hours past. And yet . . ." Warily, he scanned the boatloads of armed men fading back into the mist. Howard was aware that his imagination might find more in the obscuring fog than were actually there. "I've changed my mind. You won't have my stamp of approval on this day's work. I will not go."

Richard looked up from his seat beneath the canopy. "Have you known me so long, Eminence, and still don't trust me? You were my guardian, my tutor when I was a boy, younger than the one we are retrieving now. Surely you have more faith than that in your pupil."

Bourchier wavered visibly, his thin lips compressed, the white brows drawn tight over the long rapier's thrust of his nose.

"Come, the coronation is Sunday. It would hardly be fitting if the heir presumptive were absent."

"No," Bourchier admitted, "and yet I had not expected to see this . . ." He gestured a weak hand at the waiting boats.

"They won't be used," Richard said. "You have my word on it. No sanctuary will be violated."

Bourchier stepped forward, hesitated. His knees appeared to fail him. Quickly Buckingham was there with a steadying hand on his elbow. "Allow me to assist you, Your Eminence."

The archbishop turned as if to read the duke's face. *What did he expect to find there?* Howard wondered. *Smug triumph? The condescension of victory?* There was none there, or else the duke masked it well. Buckingham smiled patiently as if he dealt with an aging parent and propelled him forward, just as patiently, down the water stair and onto the waiting barge. Richard signaled the boatmen with an upraised hand. The oars cut rhythmically, deeply into the current bound for Westminster.

How much more would Bourchier have protested if he could have been privy to our discussions of recent days? Howard asked himself. He feared a violation of sanctuary. Did anything in his past experience whisper of usurpation? But then, it would not. His trust might be misplaced, but he did trust Richard of Gloucester implicitly.

At the moment, Richard appeared to be entirely worthy of that trust, the very soul of piety and propriety in his black frieze mourning weeds. Mother of God, thought Howard, Edward had been dead these two months past and more. Would Richard never cease this futile mourning? Or—unlikely thought—was it now Hastings whom he mourned?

Howard skimmed uncomfortably over Hastings's execution, a sore spot on his conscience that he had no desire to chafe. He admitted a flicker of guilt. Hastings had given him signs that he might betray Richard; Howard, reading them, had said nothing and had allowed his former great and good friend to pursue his demented course. Now he knew regret, but it was a strange sort of regret, rimed with contempt like ice fringing a winter pool. There was no denying, not even to himself, that Hastings's fall had removed an inconvenient obstacle from his path while throwing into vivid relief his own unquestioned loyalty. He had never encouraged Hastings's defection; he was not guilty of so great a sin as that. But he had permitted it to happen and all to gain favor with the man he one day hoped to call king.

John Howard was not without ambition. Oh, it was not the ostentatious greed for power that Buckingham displayed at times or at best managed to keep only thinly veiled. He was not by need or temperament as flamboyant in his desires as Buckingham. In his quiet, unassuming way, he had done well enough for himself, well enough indeed: from plain Squire John of Suffolk to Sir John to Lord John. Not badly done for one descended from honest but hardly noble East Anglian farmers.

His eye caught and held Buckingham's Plantagenet profile, sleek and golden as a new minted coin, save where the lower lip drooped a little. His mantle, with the four ermine bars of his dukedom proudly displayed, draped carelessly from one shoulder. Here was your noble stock. Here was blood that coursed as blue as any in England. Well, he would show Harry Buckingham a trick or two before he was done. He would show them all that the son of a Suffolk farmer was nothing to be despised. Buckingham might possess all the effervescence of a comet streaking fire across the sky; Howard preferred to be the North Star, steady and serene, burning long after the comet had dimmed and vanished.

True, it was difficult if not impossible to imagine Richard without Buckingham at his side as near and inevitable as some grotesque shadow, but John Howard had never been faint of heart. He possessed a patience born of the ages, a farmer's steady endurance of rain and drought, of dying ewes and stillborn lambs, of flooded fields and failing crops. He might almost starve one year, but always there was the next year and the one after that. He did not believe that Buckingham would remain a force to be reckoned with as long as that. The Plantagenet doom of power lust was stamped all too clearly upon him.

Already he had misstepped and over such a silly thing—the matter of Jane Shore.

She had been arrested on the very day of Hastings's execution by a party that included both Buckingham and Tom Lynom. It was an odd combination, Howard had thought at the time, and growing odder still, for Lynom had become her self-appointed champion, while Buckingham . . . but then it was difficult to determine exactly what Buckingham had become to her.

She had been tossed into Ludgate Prison that night and, the next day, had been sentenced to do penance for harlotry by the court of the bishop of London. It was a comparatively mild sentence in view of what might have been done to her. The talk around London was that she'd hang at Tyburn before the week was out. But here, at least, Richard seemed inclined to mercy. Perhaps he had listened to the pleas of his solicitor on Jane's behalf; perhaps he'd had enough of killing. At any rate, she had gotten off lightly enough: sentenced to walk in the bishops' procession in nothing but her shift from Bishopsgate to St. Paul's.

It was a sight that Howard, like most of the London populace, would have traveled far to see. He bore her no real malice. For all of her obvious transgressions, he considered her little more than a wanton, wayward child. No, it was more curiosity than triumph that had taken him to Crosby Place in Bishopsgate that Sunday morning. Here was a woman who had been loved by a king, who had influenced policy, who had risked all and, as it now appeared, lost all, destroying her latest lover in the process.

He had arrived early, but as he was good-naturedly jockeying for position at the window with Richard's knights, in had burst Buckingham in as distracted a mood as Howard had ever seen him. His clothes were askew, his hair mussed, and he bore four noticeable scratch marks down the left side of his face. Without so much as a "Good day" or a "God rest you" or even a by your leave, he helped himself to a cup of claret, pouring it full to the brim, downed it at a gulp, and poured himself another with a shaking hand.

"Why, cousin, what's the matter?" Richard had asked, looking up from his never-ending pile of state documents. Buckingham, waving his cup about as if in answer, splashed wine down the front of his cloth-of-gold doublet and on the ruffles and pleats of his paltock but scarcely heeded the stain.

"Are you ill?" Richard had asked, looking more concerned this time.

Buckingham's reply was barely audible. "Aye, but not as you conceive it. A malady not of the body but the soul."

Richard shook his head, not knowing what to make of it and almost afraid to ask. "Won't you . . . won't you tell me?"

Buckingham had looked over at the others, at Howard and his companions by the window as if seeing them for the first time. He gave them a queer searching glance and then, apparently not finding what he sought, turned back to Richard. "Very well . . . I'll tell you. But not here—in some private place."

When they had left, Mistress Shore's fabled walk seemed almost an afterthought. She came barefoot, all in white, her face demurely downcast, her eyes on the lighted taper she carried before her. More angel than devil she appeared with the luxuriant fox's brush of her hair concealing the ripe delights of her body.

"They should'a shaved her head," Tyrell muttered, shaking his own head in disappointment. "I was itching for a glance o' them pretty mammets. Nay, 'twas not the lass's hair I wished to see today."

"Nor I," Rob Percy agreed, "though I think even shaven there'd be something about her of comeliness. Ye mun guess why Edward, with a whole kingdom to choose from, loved her."

The crowd that had lined the street was strangely hushed, even awed. An old woman called out a blessing, a young child tossed a rose onto the cobbles at her feet. On the fringe of the crowd, they spotted a familiar figure on horseback.

"Look!" Lovell exclaimed, a chuckle in his throat. "Our Tom rides with her. I wondered where he was off to at cockcrow this morning."

They shared a laugh over that, but after Jane had passed and the bishops behind her, Tom Lynom stormed into the room, demanding to know where Richard was. His temper had not noticeably improved when he was informed that the protector was closeted with the Duke of Buckingham and not to be disturbed. He banged his fist hard against the linenfold paneling of the wall.

"He'll be filling his head with lies, no doubt," Lynom had said to no one in particular. "All lies."

Howard had shrugged and turned to engage Assheton in a game of chess. In a few moments, his interest aroused by the conflict, he had almost forgotten Lynom's presence. Assheton was a worthy opponent, with more patience for the strategies of the game than the younger bucks Richard kept about him, but Howard was winning. He held his hand poised, ready to unfrock Assheton's bishop when Richard and Buckingham reappeared. Howard looked up, hesitated, and the edge of his sleeve scattered ivory and ebony pieces together in a litter across the board.

Buckingham's mood had changed completely. He was smiling broadly as he strolled across the room to Tom Lynom, extending a hand in greeting. "Why, Tom! I hoped you would be here. I wanted very much to see you."

Lynom regarded him icily from the bench where he sat. "I can't imagine why."

Buckingham's smile shrank a little; the proffered hand went limp. "I wished to apologize to you for . . . for my unfortunate behavior at Ludgate . . . and to set right any false impression you may be harboring of my . . . ah . . . attentions to the Mistress Shore."

"False impression?" Tom spat. "I don't think so. My lord," he added, turning now to Richard, "I don't know what lies he has told you, but I'll tell you what I saw with my own eyes when I went with the bishops to Ludgate this morning. The turnkey expected us but would not let us into Jane's . . . the Mistress Shore's cell. 'Orders,' he said. He had orders she was not to be disturbed. 'Orders?' I asked. 'Whose orders, for we knew nothing of this.' 'As to that,' he told us, 'I canna say. Only come back in a little while.' The bishops, tired old sheep, would have obeyed. But at that moment, I heard a scream, muffled somewhat by the stone of the wall but clear enough to know who gave it. I wrested the key from the jailor's hand and opened the door myself. My lord, it shames me to tell you what I saw there. Rape! Rape *and* sodomy, no less!"

Buckingham's skin paled. He spread his hands placatingly and opened his mouth to speak when a sharp voice that was not his cut across the silence.

"Tom!" Richard cried. "You are forgetting yourself. I never expected to see a member of my household show such disrespect for any kin of mine."

"The disrespect has nothing to do with you, my lord. If you had only seen the things I saw . . ."

"I didn't need to see. My dear cousin Buckingham has explained everything to me. Women like Jane Shore cannot be raped. What, rape a whore? But they are skilled in the arts of seduction, as you should know yourself, and can inflame lust where none existed before. That is what happened to the duke. He was sorely tempted and perhaps he sinned, but that is not for you to judge. 'Look first to the beam that is in thine own eye.'"

Tom flinched and dropped his eyes under Richard's steady, accusing gaze. "It's not the same thing," he muttered, "not the same thing at all."

"I won't argue with you there. But if you wish to keep your place in my household and in my favor, let me hear you apologize to His Grace of Buckingham."

Howard had looked away, embarrassed for the youth and for his predicament. His fingers toyed idly with one of the chess pieces. It was the queen, the ebony queen, and the set of her face and body reminded him a little of Jane Shore. Now there was a queen for you, a true black queen who could move men in whatever direction she wished: Buckingham to lust and lechery, Lynom to adoration and protection, and Hastings – Hastings to perdition itself.

But when he had looked up again, it was Richard's face that intrigued him most. To be sure, he looked stern and angry as only Richard could, but like Tom, he also appeared strangely protective as if something he loved were being threatened. Buckingham then? Aye, who else but Buckingham? And what constituted the threat? Tom's accusations or Richard's own nagging disbelief at the cock-and-bull story the duke had given him? Even knowing little of the circumstances, Howard thought that Richard defended the duke's innocence with a trifle too much zeal. It would be hopeless and worse than futile to cross him now.

Lynom must have realized it too. All at once, he seemed to wither. He wiped his sweating palms on the maroon silk of his hose and offered Buckingham a tardy hand. "It . . . it is possible that I . . . I did misunderstand," he mumbled, half-choking on the words. "I most humbly crave Your Lordship's pardon."

"And I most gladly give it . . . with all my heart," replied the duke. He enveloped Lynom in a great bear hug to which the young solicitor submitted with a pained expression as if he knew there were no other way. Half-sickened, Howard had watched, wondering how soon it would also fall to him to kiss the dust at Buckingham's well-shod feet.

And then, hard upon that unpleasant speculation, there came a brighter, more comforting thought. How long before Buckingham himself lay in that selfsame dust? Richard would not always be at such odds with his own good sense, nor was he the sort of man to allow another mastery over him, no matter how intense his current infatuation. Buckingham would fall. There could be no doubt of it. Though as Richard, smiling and well pleased, had embraced Lynom in turn, it would have been difficult for a casual eye to detect any loss in the duke's stature.

Later, it had proven even more difficult. Word buzzed through the halls of Crosby Place that Buckingham had profited well from the morning's audience. Assheton whispered to Howard that Henry Stafford had been given permission to take all of Hastings's armed retainers into his household, no mean force to add to his own. In addition, he had been favored with the custody of Bishop Morton who had languished these two days past in a Tower cell.

"Morton!" Howard exclaimed. "What does he want with that old scoundrel?"

Assheton had shrugged. "I was told that he is taking him as a favor to my lord the protector with a promise to remove him far from London . . . and to keep him out of mischief."

"To Brecknock, do y'think?" Howard asked. "Aye, why not? We can only hope the duke means to depart for Wales himself—and soon."

Assheton had nodded agreement, and they had fallen into laughter like two conspirators.

The dark bulk of the Palace of Westminster loomed through the insubstantial mists. Beside it, the abbey precincts crouched like a kitten next to a mother cat. As the boatmen guided their craft through the low arch of the landing, Howard realized that he might have employed his time on the river to better advantage; he might have plotted what arguments he would use to woo little York away from the queen. Now that opportunity was gone.

Westminster was the seat of justice for the entire realm and therefore a very busy place. He had forgotten just how busy it was, for the presence of the queen's sanctuary had tainted it for all of Richard's followers and made it a place to be avoided. He was almost surprised to see that the normal round of activities continued here. Lawyers in their long gowns of ray bustled about the entrance to Westminster Hall along with the king's sergeants in their silken hoods. Hawkers proliferated in the broad street, adding their raucous din to the subdued chatter of solicitors and their clients. Pins and girdles and fine felt hats were for sale, as well as a new marvel—pieces of glass that would improve a man's vision.

Howard shook his head in skeptical amusement, almost forgetting his purpose in coming here, when he felt someone fall into step beside him.

"If you do well for me today," said a voice low in his ear, "you'll have no cause to regret it."

Howard turned to face Richard. "Your Grace need have no fear on that score. I vow to deliver little York to you within the hour by one means or another." He nodded toward the ranks of his men, the blue-and-silver legions that were falling into place around the abbot's palace.

Richard shook his head. "No, not that way. Bourchier is right there. It would damage my case with the churchmen. You know there may be more at stake here than readily appears."

Howard knew, though not from frequent iteration. As far as he was aware, Richard's mind still hung in indecision over the succession, to Buckingham's great and obvious dismay.

"I will do what I can," he said.

"I know you will do well," Richard replied, smiling at him from beneath the brim of his black velvet cap. "That's why I've chosen you for the job. Buckingham would rather it had been him, of course, but he lacks, shall we say, a certain finesse in such matters. No, you are the proper man for this mission. And while you are about it, you might consider that Norfolk's duchy goes begging."

He turned and walked away, giving Howard time for only a brief, confused bow.

The huge clock in the tower by Westminster Hall had tolled eleven times. Lying in her thickly curtained bed, Elizabeth Woodville heard its muffled strokes but made no move to rise. It was shamefully late to be lying abed and doing nothing except listen to the clock toll one's life away, she thought bitterly. Yet there seemed to be little purpose in rising. The latest failure of her efforts had robbed her life of all meaning, and if she had nothing more to greet her than a dull sanctuary day, she would just as soon stay in bed. This she had told her women when they had come to attend her that morning, sending them away with a furious lashing of her tongue.

And now, at the dying knell of the hour, came another knock on the door of her bedchamber.

"Go away!" she cried. "I told you once I will not rise today."

"Maman, it's Bess. Please let me in."

"Oh, very well." Elizabeth sat up and thrust back the bed hangings with an impatient hand. As Bess entered, she noted that the pale oval of her eldest daughter's face was lit with excitement.

"Well then?" she asked imperiously .

"A delegation from the protector"—Bess blanched at Elizabeth's sharp look of reproof at the forbidden title—"from my Uncle Gloucester waits outside. They seek an audience with Your Grace."

Bess's eyes, the same cornflower shade as her father's, were eager with the news. Elizabeth guessed at what she was thinking: an end to sanctuary life, a return to court. Doubtless the silly girl already visualized herself as the Princess Royal, marching coroneted and ermine robed in her brother's coronation procession. For herself, Elizabeth feared that this unexpected visit might indeed mean an end to sanctuary, but she saw no such honors following upon it. Bess knew little or nothing of her mother's plots. Given the girl's inconvenient and unreasoning attachment to her Uncle Gloucester, Elizabeth had carefully kept them from her.

She rose from the bed with an air of resignation, but her heart was pounding wildly in her throat. She must be calm and not panic. She couldn't let Bess know that she had anything to fear from Gloucester. She dressed quickly in a simple black houppelande. No time now to play the queen. Beneath the starched and pleated widow's coif, her face in the mirror looked every one of its forty-six years. She had aged in the past weeks, aged dramatically. Bess's face beside hers, flushed and glowing, only accentuated the difference with painful counterpoint. But what sort of madness was it to mourn the marks of passing years when one's own life hung in the balance? Slowly, and with practiced dignity, she made her way to the small room that served her infrequent need for a presence chamber.

Bourchier and Howard looked distinctly ill at ease as she entered. Howard had obviously been satisfying his curiosity as to her present status. His seeking eyes had taken in the meanness of the chamber and the huge chests and coffers that still crammed it, and his nose wrinkled in distaste at the moldy smell that suffused it. His bow, following the cardinal's, was awkward and belated as if he were not certain it was necessary.

"We give you God's greeting, my lady," Bourchier said rather stiffly. She acknowledged him with a nod of her veiled head and took her place behind a gilded chair as though it were a bulwark of defense. Her hands gripped its back like ivory claws. Behind her shoulder stood Bess; the girl's rapid breathing was a bellows in her ear.

"Well, my lords," she said coolly, "allow us to express some surprise. Might we inquire what brings you here?"

"We shall not mince words with you, madam," Bourchier replied. "It has been decided that the Duke of York, whom you are holding here, rightly belongs with his brother the king."

"Ah!" Elizabeth exhaled sharply. Relief that Bourchier's presence did not signal a church-sanctioned arrest was followed hard by alertness to a possible new danger. "And who has decided this?" she asked. "No, you needn't answer that, for I know who wishes to have him in custody."

"Whatever you are thinking, lady, you may put the thought away," Howard cautioned. "It is unworthy."

"Is it indeed?" She permitted herself a small smile. "I wonder."

"The issue was decided this morning at a full meeting of the council," Bourchier said. "No . . .no one person ordained it more than any other. The king's coronation is set for Sunday next. Surely that ceremony would be seriously maimed without the presence of the heir presumptive."

"Your Eminence need not remind me that he is next nearest the throne. Nor, unfortunately, am I the only one who recognizes that fact."

"Madam, what are you implying?" Howard bawled, losing patience. "Do you believe that the protector intends to harm your son? If so, let's hear it out."

"I . . .I don't know," she said. She was not smiling now. Behind her, the sound of Bess's breathing had stopped.

"You don't *know?*" Bourchier questioned. "Why, there is no one in the realm more honorable to his word than great Gloucester."

"Mother!" Bess was tugging insistently at her sleeve. "Are you forgetting that Uncle Richard stood godfather for Dickon at his christening?"

No, she had not forgotten. She recalled Dickon's baptism only too well. She had risen from childbed to watch the ceremony through the latticed screen of the chapel gallery, forbidden by custom and the church to attend or take part. She saw again her brother-in-law's face, young and stern, softening as he took the royal infant in his arms; heard again little Dickon's lusty howl as the holy water touched his brow. She recalled her own secret satisfaction that, in her middle age, she had borne England another prince and so had consolidated her own power.

But neither had she forgotten that Stillington and his perilous secret still walked abroad. Why in God's name hadn't Edward done him in when he had the chance, at the same time Clarence was executed? Richard stood now in the same position Clarence had then, with only her two small boys between him and the throne. Two small boys that the royal astrologer, shaking his head as he said it, had predicted would die violently and young. He had, of course, been banished from the court straightaway, but the fear, nagging and uncontrollable, remained.

"Well, madam," Howard said, "what do you say? While we babble here, your other son, the king, languishes for want of a playfellow."

"Is . . . is he lonely then, my Ned?"

"Aye, of course. There is no one of his own age of fit rank to keep him company. You may be sure he will be delighted to have his brother with him."

"If only I could be with him!" she cried, forgetting for a moment her circumstances and who was with her.

"But you could, Mother!" Bess exclaimed. "Oh, won't you see it?"

"That you could," Howard assured her. "If you would only throw yourself on the protector's mercy and seek the forgiveness he freely offers."

She shook her head. She doubted that there would ever be forgiveness for her now. Rivers and Grey, her brother and son, had been caught while attempting escape in the latest of her plots. Men spoke confidently of their pending executions. More than anything else, she feared the slicing of the axe blade on her own slender neck. There was little she wouldn't do to spare herself such an end.

"The lad is sickly," she said but without much conviction. "And he is little more than a babe. He needs a mother's care."

"The physician Argentine attends the king's grace," Bourchier countered. "Can the abbey infirmarian boast such skill? I doubt it. And your youngest son is something more than a babe. It's been nine years since I baptized him into Holy Mother Church. Your son Edward was far younger when you let him go to Ludlow."

"It was necessary. He was Prince of Wales, and Wales required its prince in residence, even if he was only a three-year-old child. My husband promised I could keep this son with me. It was a compensation, you see, for losing the other." Her voice faltered and died. She had spoken out of turn, spoken as a cotter's wife might speak, not as a queen. From beneath her lashes, she surveyed the effect of her candor on the two men. Bourchier's craggy face softened with sympathy. He turned tentatively to Howard as if to ask whether they might even now abandon their mission. However, Howard's eyes beneath his pea-green chaperon were set like forged steel.

"Madam, I for one have had enough of your arguments. If you refuse to relinquish your charge voluntarily into the protector's keeping, then look out your window. There you may see something that will make you change your mind."

Slowly, as if drawn against her will, she moved to the window. Through the tattered mists of the morning, she spied men, liveried men, all around. One across the way watched her most impudently. There was another at the corner of the building, two more directly beneath her. Her breath caught sharp as ice in her throat.

"You mean to arrest me, to violate my sanctuary!" She turned venomously on Bourchier. "Holy Father, I would not have believed this of you!"

Bourchier was obviously distressed. He reached out a hand to her from beneath his scarlet mantle. "The men are not to be used. Gloucester gave me his word on it."

"Unless they are needed," Howard said. "Now it seems that they may be. We both know this woman's crimes. It would be unthinkable to allow England's heir to remain in her possession. Even here, she plots and plots. She has forfeited her claim to sanctuary. And unless she gives up willingly the thing we seek . . ." The unspoken words dangled their threat upon the air, a naked sword.

Elizabeth bowed her head. Her hands clutched at the narrow wrists beneath the pleated sleeves of her gown. The silence in the room was deafening, as felt as the menace outside in the mist, watching, waiting for but a word to pounce.

She raised frightened eyes to Bess and saw with some pity that the girl's full lower lip trembled with disappointment and confusion. She did not know—how could she know?—what was at stake here. A place at court, a new gown—these were all she sought, and she was to be denied even these.

Elizabeth made her voice firm with command. "Fetch the boy," she said.

Chapter 24

RICHARD SURVEYED THE Star Chamber in Westminster Palace with new eyes: the thick Belgian carpet, the rich Bruges tapestries, the ceiling with its lierne-ribbed star vault. Before this, he had looked on these wonders as a guest; now his gaze was almost proprietary.

His finger absently traced the intertwined *Es* above the hearth: Edward and Elizabeth, king and queen. Their presence was everywhere—not only in the marble mantle sculpted with twisted branches and birds, but also in the maroon velvet draperies embroidered with the white rose of York, in the tapestries, in the canopy that hung over the twin thrones on the dais, blazoned in gold beneath the image of the crown. Edward and Elizabeth, living witness to a lie.

Richard drew his finger away from the mantle, frowning at the sooty streak left on it.

"The servants have grown lax now that they are without a master," said a voice behind his shoulder. "Look how the candlesticks are beginning to tarnish." Buckingham's gaze traveled meaningfully from the candelabra to the empty throne. "They need a king to serve again. Westminster needs a king. England—"

"They have a king," Richard said with more force than he felt. "It is no easy matter to remove him."

"They have a false king. All this is yours by right," Buckingham said with a sweep of his hand. "Just think about that a while."

"I have thought about it," Richard replied. "Indeed, I can think of little else."

"Ah, yes, of course. Thinking is well enough, I suppose, but unless you act soon, it may be too late."

Buckingham's tone implied that it might already be too late. The duke was clearly baffled by Richard's failure to move long before this. He had applauded such gestures as Richard had made toward a consolidation of power: the call for aid from Yorkshire, the execution of Hastings, the seizure of the Duke of York, if that in fact could be achieved. But all this had fallen far short of Buckingham's expectations, Richard knew. And Buckingham did not know how much some of these concessions had cost him in peace of mind, of how far they had violated his very nature.

"Don't press me, cousin. By my life—"

"My lords, may I present to you His Grace, the Duke of York!" They both turned on the instant, and Richard at least immediately forgot their conversation. For there was John Howard, proud as if he presented the prize goose for the Christmas feast, and before him stood the diminutive form of England's heir.

He was a most attractive child; Richard had forgotten just how attractive. For a moment, he only stood there, taffy hair springing in ringlets about his round face, hands planted firmly on his narrow hips in imitation of his elders. Then he was across the room, flinging himself headlong into his uncle's outstretched arms.

It had been no part of Richard's plan to be so exuberant in his own welcome. He had intended to be courteous but formal and correct. A simple handshake, a manly "How does Your Grace?" would have sufficed. Given the fact that he might in due course be responsible for the boy's disinheritance, he could hardly afford to show an excess of emotion.

Yet as he rose from the youngster's hearty embrace, he found himself wiping at his eyes with a corner of his sleeve.

"My uncle of Gloucester! How happy I am to see you again!"

"And I to see you, my sweet lord. I bid you welcome with all my heart."

He meant it. God help him, but he spoke the truth. He was vaguely aware of the amused, indulgent smiles on the faces of Buckingham and Howard; he heard Bourchier's long sigh of relief. But his eyes remained fixed on his godson and namesake, who had from his cradle been a personal and special favorite. If only his own son, almost the same age as this cousin, possessed the same robust vitality!

As if reading his thoughts, Howard said, "The queen told us he has been sickly, but by the saints, I can see no sign of it."

"Is it true, Dickon? Have you been ill?" Richard questioned.

The boy shook his head. "Nay, and I wouldn't have wished to be there. If I had, they"—he nodded his head in the direction of the abbot's palace—"would probably have kissed and cossetted me half to death." He grimaced and went on, "I'm glad to be free of that place, Uncle, let me tell you that. Too many women about, and the men, the monks, so funny and quiet. They wouldn't let me go outdoors even to play with my spaniel, and I couldn't make any noise in the halls. It was always 'Hush, Dickon' or 'Pray be quiet, Your Grace' all day long. I hated it. I won't have to go back there, will I, Uncle?"

"No, to be sure. You are going to be staying with Ned."

The blue eyes widened. "Is it true? Maman said something like that."

"Indeed, it is. Ned is the king now. Did you know that? And you are next nearest the throne." Richard's throat thickened. With effort, he forced the last words out. "That's a very important position."

The boy shook his head slowly, stirring the fringe of pale gold that hung over his forehead. "Ned is king as Papa was king?"

"Yes."

"B-but Ned is only a boy, the same as me. How can he be king? Why aren't you king, Uncle?"

Out of the mouths of babes. Has infant cunning seen into the falseness of my heart? Richard wondered. But no, the look was innocent enough in its questioning. "That . . . that's a long story, Your Grace, and someday I'll explain it to you. Now come and meet another uncle, one who loves you too—though, I confess, not half as much as I do."

"It's my Uncle Buckingham, is it not?" the boy asked, cocking his head at the duke. "I remember you though I haven't seen you very much."

Buckingham swept the prince a deep bow. "An oversight I hope will be soon remedied," he said solemnly. To Richard, he whispered, "A pretty weapon we have stolen from the queen's arsenal, is it not?"

Richard was not listening. He reached for his nephew's hand and felt it slide, warm and confident, into his own. *Such childlike trust,* he thought to himself. *Wherever did I lose it along the way?* Perhaps he had never really possessed it. Even his childhood had been torn by sickness and war and constant uncertainty.

He squeezed the small hand. "Come, Dickon. We go on the turning of the tide to find the king."

Edward did not at first acknowledge Richard. He was shooting at a butt that had been set up on the Tower green. Quite alone, he stood, one foot placed firmly in front of the other, eyes squinting at the target. The string snapped, the arrow flew, nipping the straw of the butt before it sailed to earth beyond it. Frowning, Edward carefully selected another arrow, and this time took even greater pains, holding his left hand firm on the bow, drawing with his right, pressing the slender weight of his body against the horns of the bow. This time, the arrow hit true, quivering satisfactorily near the bull's-eye.

"Bravo, sire!" Richard cried, applauding. "Your marksmanship is improving."

Edward turned cold eyes on his uncle. "Not from overmuch practice," he said. "It's lonely work here."

"Ah, so Your Grace would like a playfellow!" Richard took in the scene with a sweep of his hand. In a corner of the yard, knights of the body pursued their own diversions; there was laughter and the click of dice. On a stone bench, by a wall of rosy brick, Argentine dozed in the fitful sun, but Richard caught a watchful yellow glint from beneath his lowered lids. The hawk did not sleep.

"And who would you suggest, Uncle?" Edward asked. "I don't see anyone here of my own age, and those of more advanced years who befriend me seem to meet with untimely ends."

Richard swallowed hard. He had known that, sooner or later, he would have to discuss Hastings with the king. To his credit, he had sought an audience the very afternoon of the baron's execution three days before. He had been turned back roundly by Argentine, who informed him that Edward slept, drugged with poppy juice, so that he might forget the terrible sights he had witnessed. Richard had scarcely regretted the delay. And now he hoped to sweeten Edward's disposition with the gift he offered.

"I have one in mind, sire, that I think will be most suitable. Harry, will you bring in my lord of York?"

Bring was perhaps not the proper word. Freed from bondage like some wild bird, Young Dickon almost flew to his brother with happy shouts of "Ned, Ned!" that echoed from the Tower masonry. In an instant, Edward's face was transformed from sullen irritability to a mixture of joy and wonder that irradiated his widened blue-green eyes. His laughter flowed over the greensward like wine on a feast day.

"This will be a tonic for the king more potent than any I might have devised," said Argentine at Richard's shoulder. "Better than all the sage and rosemary and poppy on earth."

"So I hope," said Richard.

But if he had also hoped for a sudden thaw in his relationship with Edward, he was quickly disappointed. Looking up from his brother's embrace, the king addressed him still in the old formal manner. "We thank you most heartily for bringing us our entirely well-beloved brother of York. We would be pleased at this time to discuss the matter with you further, if you will."

"I'm at Your Grace's disposal," Richard replied with growing apprehension.

"Argentine, take our brother to the royal apartments and show him about the place. I shall come to you soon."

Distressed at this abrupt dismissal, the younger boy flung himself across the lawn, back to Richard's side. "Are you leaving so soon, Uncle?" The small face was contorted with dismay.

Richard knelt in the damp grass before him. "I'm afraid I must, Dickon, after I talk with Ned."

The child's lower lip trembled. "But why? I have only just seen you, and now already you leave me again. I thought we would all be together for a while."

"I wish we could, but I . . . I have other matters to attend to, I'm afraid. The coronation—" His voice cracked unexpectedly. He broke off and looked away to where a swift soared in the mottled sky above the chimney tops. "It isn't always possible for us to do as we might wish, Dickon. You must understand that."

"No, I do not!" cried the prince, stamping his foot. "I've been told that over and over again, but I still don't understand."

The dew-spangled grass was wet beneath Richard's hose; the dampness seemed to go through him. Suddenly, he drew the boy against him. "I'll come to see you tomorrow if I can."

"No, you won't," Dickon said stubbornly, his body straining back. "You're only telling me that to quiet me. You won't come back." Tears swam in the harebell eyes, the eyes of his own dead brother staring back at him in the face of his son.

"If you love me, you must believe me," Richard said. "I wouldn't lie to you." The words were out before he was even aware they had left his mouth.

Dickon hugged him then, and the storm passed like an April shower. "Very well, Uncle. I believe you because I know you love me. And I shall see you on the morrow."

Then he was gone, sprinting across the lawn and the border of white-starred chamomile, Argentine trailing after in his long black robes. Sighing, Richard rose from the grass, brushing bits of it from his hose in a methodical little gesture while Edward watched him with narrowed eyes.

"An affecting little scene," he said acidly. "Very moving. How fortunate for you that one of your nephews at least shows you proper affection."

"Dickon and I have been friends from his cradle days," Richard explained, "as I might have been your friend if we had the chance to know one another better."

They walked on a flagstone path that bordered the park, beneath a margin of lime trees, in full leaf now that midsummer's day approached. Edward said, "Children are like dogs. They love anyone who pets them. They don't stop to consider why they are petted or how it fits the purpose of one who does the petting."

"Speak plainly, sire."

"Very well, I will." Edward turned to him. His face was motley, dappled by light and shadow as the sun slanted down through the moving leaves. "Why did you bring my brother here from Westminster?"

"Well, beyond the obvious benefit of having the heir presumptive participate in the coronation, I did it for you, to ease your melancholy, to give you a companion as I have told you."

"Out of concern for me? Then I should perhaps be grateful. Why is it then that I have so many misgivings? Did you have no purpose of your own in this?"

Richard sighed. He had in fact almost forgotten his original intent in the genuine delight of seeing his younger nephew once more. Now it hovered in the background, dark, sinister, and best forgotten. "Yes, Edward, I did, and I must confess it. I'm not at all sure how to go about it seeing that I'm a proud man and pleading doesn't come easily to me."

"Pleading, Uncle? Pleading?" Edward echoed shrilly. "The mighty Duke of Gloucester, protector of all the realm, comes pleading to his lowly and erstwhile forgotten nephew? We are most amused."

A look from Richard silenced the peel of taunting laughter. Shamed, Edward plucked a large cordate leaf from one of the limes and began to shred it into tiny pieces. "All right then," he said low. "What is it you wish?"

"Nothing more or less than that you should look on me with some favor . . . that, if possible, you should love me."

"Indeed? You've never asked for such a boon before. And the last time the word *love* was mentioned between us, you told me not to speak of it again."

"I spoke in the white heat of anger and frustration, Edward. You must realize that. And as for asking for such a boon, it is not a thing a man ordinarily goes about pleading for. It's a gift he hopes will be given freely or that he will at least be able to earn. Perhaps I am not worthy of it. I know I have taken . . . several actions lately that appear to have been directed against you. I tell you now, they were not. Everything I've done has been for one purpose only: to present you with a peaceful and a united kingdom when you come of age so that you will not have to fight another Barnet or Tewkesbury."

"A moving speech, Uncle. You impress us greatly with your . . . diligence on our behalf. You must know that you already have our love. Why, you have only to pick up one of our proclamations to read above the signature, 'By the advice of our dearest and entirely well-beloved Uncle Richard, Duke of Gloucester.' What more endearing terms could you possibly wish?"

"Edward! Enough of this sarcasm! Surely you are aware that it is affection of a more personal nature that I seek. I know my shortcomings. I haven't been blessed with the vitality of your father or with the charm of your Uncle Rivers. I am a plain man and possess neither beauty of face nor eloquence of speech. Is that the reason you cannot love me?"

"No," Edward said, tiring of the game. The mask seemed to slip from his features. High above them in the tree branches a raven croaked. "Perhaps I don't even know why myself. Perhaps it's because that when I recall all the hurts of the past weeks, rightly or wrongly, you stand at the center of each one. This much I do know: I cannot change the way I feel."

Richard drew himself up, stiffening his back. Somehow the honest intensity of the boy's gaze struck deeper than the mockery of a few moments before. "I only did what was necessary," he replied, "and hurt myself not a little in the bargain. But all that is behind us now. Tell me, Edward, are we to go on like this, an armed truce between us every day of our lives until you reach your majority?"

"I see little else."

"It's a heavy sentence. I might almost have preferred death."

Through the moving shadows, Richard could see a change in the boy's features, a slow light dawning cold as a winter sunrise. "Ah, so that's it! Why didn't I guess it before? That's why you come currying my favor, begging my love. You're afraid of what I'll do when I come of age. All power will be mine then, in fact as well as in name, and you fear that, don't you? You are afraid of me! You are thinking, no doubt, that other royal regents have not always fared so well at the hands of ingrate monarchs. Oh, yes, I've studied my history. Many a king's uncle has met with the blade of an axe. Well, I wouldn't concern myself too greatly with that if I were you. It's a long time off yet and will probably be even longer if you have your way. Maybe by that time, I shall have forgotten that my Uncle Rivers and my brother Grey rot in your northern dungeons, that my mother and sisters, for fear of you, keep to their sanctuary like common criminals. Maybe by that time, I shall have forgotten that I myself, though rightful king, am kept mewed up here as if I too were a prisoner. Maybe by that time, I shall have forgotten Hastings."

The silence on the green was complete. Richard looked up to where the walls and windows of the Chapel of St. Peter ad Vincilla shimmered in the sun. "Have you had your say, sire?" he asked coldly.

"Yes."

"Then you can have no objection if I take my leave of you. There's only one thing I would add in parting. History teaches us to be wary, and what man could refrain from thinking of it? But I did not come here today because of that. I loved your father well and served him loyally all the days of his life. And though you probably don't believe me, I would have loved and served you in the same way. But you have raised barriers between us, walls that cannot be breached. And yes, I'll confess I've added my bricks to your own and mortared them fast, though not intentionally perhaps. But no matter—they are up, and there can be no tearing them down now. And since there can be no love between us, you might consider anything that happens now to be but the fruit of your own hate."

With a curt, ironic bow, Richard turned and stalked away. Edward stood for a moment, watching him with a thoughtful stare. A battle of sorts raged in his mind. Perhaps it had not been wise to offend the duke. Argentine would be displeased, would lecture him strenuously on the need for dissembling when truth became a danger, of baiting his uncle only so far and no further. His words had been most incautious and spoken out of turn. Even now he could run after Richard, retract, apologize, humble himself.

Humble himself? No, it should not, must not be. "I am the king!" he shouted to his uncle's retreating back. "Do you hear me? I am the king, and there is nothing you can do to change that. Nothing!"

Richard did not turn, did not even acknowledge that he had heard. From far above Edward's head, there came in reply only the harsh and bitter croak of a raven.

Chapter 25

CONTRARY TO HIS usual good fortune, Buckingham had slept badly that night, the first after the removal of little York to the Tower. He awakened at first light, tossed off the coverlet and walked to the wide bow of the eastern casement. Rain had fallen in the night, softly, quietly, a misting sort of rain he had not heard even in his sleeplessness, and now the sky glowed pale gray and opalescent like the inside of a pearl. It was a mild morning and gave promise of becoming a fair enough day if, he thought bitterly, that was all there was to it. The air was scented with the gillyflowers, pungent and clove perfumed, that grew in the pleasance beneath the open window. Beyond the flower beds, a peacock split the stillness with a raucous bray as it waddled past, dragging its tail in the mud behind it. A moment's distaste troubled him.

They were beautiful, these birds he kept to adorn his gardens, or so he had once thought. Why then had God, as if in jest, given them a voice that would shame a donkey? As if to each creature this much of beauty was to be allotted and no more. Was there no perfection to be found anywhere in the world?

"You're up and about early this morning, my lord."

"And you, Percival, had best learn to announce your coming," Buckingham replied testily, "or at least to make more noise about it. You're as stealthy as a cat."

"I'm sorry if I startled you," said Percival though his voice gave little evidence of contrition. "I thought that if you were restless, I might provide you with a remedy." His eyes stared pointedly to the open front of the duke's plum silk dressing gown.

Buckingham shook his head, pulling the lappets closed with his hands. "If it were that simple, do you think I would have banished you from my bed last night?"

"I should hope not. The pallet in your antechamber leaves much to be desired. It's neither so soft, nor does it offer the enticements of Your Grace's bed. Come, cast off this melancholy humor. I'll make you forget whatever it is that's troubling you. Yesterday I found a Persian boy in Southwark who taught me some pleasing new tricks . . ."

"No!" Buckingham exclaimed. "Didn't I tell you I wanted none of that now?" Percival's pale eyes looked his surprise. "I'm not in the mood for it. Later perhaps . . ." he added, but he did not think so. Nor could he tell Percival how disgusted he was now at the thought of all of those well-practiced and well-executed tricks, at the memory of all the exquisite nuances of pleasure and pain that the older man had, at one time or another, coaxed from his all-too-willing body.

"If you're ill, I could summon the leech."

Buckingham shook his head vehemently. "I'm not ill. I need nothing . . . no one!" And then to Percival's expression of sullen hurt, he added, "Though if you wish to stay with me, to listen to me if I should speak, you may do that."

Percival's face was smoothly impassive again as he made his graceful, assenting bow. The hurt was probably not genuine anyway, Buckingham reasoned. A cold, emotionless sort was Percival. No wonder Richard was so uncomfortable when he was about. Cold and emotionless, save in his unswerving devotion to Henry Stafford, and there he had many uses, both in and out of the huge curtained bed.

Buckingham had to confess some envy for his impassiveness. Certainly it seemed preferable now to being as he was himself, stripped bare of all protecting skin as if he had been flayed alive and every naked nerve exposed to the tormenter's art. With a word, Richard had annihilated him. And what had he done to deserve this ill treatment, to call forth the venting of Richard's spleen? Only urge him to take what was lawfully and rightfully his. To the day he died, he would not forget the way Richard had turned on him the afternoon before.

"Don't presume to tell me what I must or must not do!" he had said between clenched teeth. "Don't presume to tell me anything. Are you so hot after your own ambitions that you cannot conceive my dilemma? To disinherit Edward is one thing, but little York . . . Ah, don't look at me so innocently. I know you have ambitions. How do you see yourself, my dear cousin of Buckingham, a potentate in Wales with a sovereign state of your own? Or do you, like mighty Warwick, think to play kingmaker, holding tight to the reins of power in England? Is that why you follow me?"

"Your Grace knows I do not . . ."

"My grace knows nothing, damn you, except the way you show yourself. And you!" Richard had cried, wheeling on Howard in a sudden fury. "Yes, you are ambitious too though you try to hide it. You follow me about like a pet dog, waiting to lap up the crumbs Buckingham leaves untouched. St. Jerome take witness! Was ever a prince so poorly served?"

Buckingham had gone out then with the bitter words ringing in his ears. Following as they had on the heels of his regrettable and near-disastrous encounter with the harlot, they had shaken him to his core. He tried to excuse Richard's harshness because he had just come from a long and particularly difficult session with Edward. Also, he could take some pleasure in the fact that the upstart Howard had at last been put in his place—pet dog indeed! But these did nothing to lessen the sting of Richard's indictment against himself, which had been all the more cutting because he had indeed been harboring such thoughts. Yet it was not for hope of these rewards that he followed Richard, not exclusively at any rate. At first perhaps, but no longer.

"Richard . . ."

"What of him?" Percival whispered. Buckingham looked up with a start. He had forgotten Percival was there. "What of Richard?" Percival repeated.

"Why, he doesn't want to be king," the duke replied after a bit too much thought. "I fear he'll refuse the crown."

"And that means ill for you?"

"It does me no good surely. I have not exactly endeared myself to the present king."

"Ah, yes, the king who is in fact no king."

"The same."

"Well then, if Gloucester refuses the crown, perhaps another might be found of untainted royal blood to step into the gap."

Buckingham gaped at him open-mouthed, then laughed hollowly. "It's too high a reach for me though my blood is not unworthy . . ." He was in reality descended from two sons of Edward III and so had a better claim than any man except Richard. The descent he favored, because it was clean and direct and of the male line, was through the third Edward's youngest son, Thomas of Woodstock. This was the ancestor whose arms he had taken to quarter with his own. But he was hardly averse to pointing out his descent from the third son, John of Gaunt, through the Beaufort line to his mother, flawed though it might be with the bend sinister of bastardy. Henry Tudor's entire claim sprang from that same line, and he unblushingly declared himself the Lancastrian pretender.

He chuckled again at the thought of it: himself Henry VII, by the grace of God, King of England and of France, Lord of Ireland, seated on the marble throne at Westminster, the crown of St. Edward on his brow, the orb and scepter in his hands, the ermine-collared mantle of state draped around his shoulders.

"No, Percival," he said, "it isn't that I seek, though perhaps if I ever wanted it . . ."

He did not finish. Too tantalizing for dismissal, the suggestion would not quite leave his mind, but he refused to nurse it. He was pledged to another to whom it belonged by right. There would be reward enough in serving him and an easier way to power than the one Percival had suggested.

Over the eastern horizon crept the sun, a flattened disk of burnished gold. Soon the house would stir around him, and the city would come alive within its walls. And Richard. Richard too would wake. He must go to him before the council meeting that morning; he must make it right between them once more.

"Send in my barber!" he snapped at Percival. "There's much to be done today. Why are we wasting time gawking at the sunrise?"

Richard felt high anticipation as he dressed for the council that morning. The black frieze morning weeds, his uniform for the past two months, lay in a heap in a corner of the bedroom. Today he was attired in rich raiment: cloth-of-gold hose, shirt of soft French cambric embroidered with silver, doublet of purple satin lined with plum silk and shot through with gold. Jewels sparkled on the chain that hung around his neck, glittered on his fingers and the brim of his plum velvet cap. Dismissing his body squires with a wave of his hand, he paused before the mirror and critically appraised his own reflection.

The face was the same one that had stared back at him for many years. It had never been handsome, and the passage of time had scarcely improved it. His brow was permanently furrowed now. Deep vertical lines scored the bridge of his nose and bracketed his mouth. On the other hand, the brown hair that fell to his shoulders was still untouched with gray. The body beneath the bright plumage was still hard and lean—perhaps, judging from the way the magnificent clothes hung on it, even a bit too lean. He noted with pleasure that there was a luster in the blue eyes that had not been there yesterday, and a faint flush of excitement had replaced the usual pallor of his cheeks.

It will do, he decided. *It will do well enough.*

The clothes were fine even if they had been put away for a long time and smelled faintly of camphor. And as for the one inside them, while he might have wished that he possessed the beauty and the bearing of an Edward or a Clarence, there was nothing he could do to achieve it. His people would have to accept him as he was.

Something moved in the mirror beside his own image. Something was in the empty room behind him that set the blood pulsing through his veins. Another face wavered in the glass, a golden face whose smile mocked him even as he looked. Clarence? Could it be Clarence come from the grave to claim the crown from him? His breath caught; he reeled about to face Buckingham, an oddly hesitant Buckingham, who still stood uncertainly on the threshold. Richard's hand shook as he extended it.

"Welcome, cousin. I didn't expect to see you until council."

"I couldn't wait for that. I had to see you early—and alone."

"And now that you see me, what do you think?"

The duke's eyes traveled over him lingeringly. They missed no detail. "My lord!" he cried. "Nay, not my lord, but my liege, my king! In truth, every inch of him a king." A few strides of his long legs brought Buckingham across the floor, and before Richard could speak, the duke was on his knees before him, his bared head with its aureole of gold ringlets bent in homage.

"No, Harry," Richard protested, stretching out a hand to lift him. "There's no need for this, no need." But Buckingham did not rise. Instead he seized the proffered hand and kissed it fervently, like a devout pilgrim kissing the relic of a saint.

For a timeless moment, Richard felt the moist lips hot against his palm, felt too a tide of warmth, dizzying and irresistible, sweep over him from someplace in his loins. Of its own volition, his other hand came up to stroke the kneeling man's cheek. Freshly shaven, it felt smooth and soft to his touch as fine velvet. The tousled ringlets slid through his fingers like silken threads.

"Holy Jesu!" he breathed and snatched the offending hands away. "What are we doing?"

There was no sound in the room except for Richard's pounding heart and Buckingham's long sigh. Slowly, the duke rose. His face was flushed and contorted as if with pain. "Your Grace must forgive me. I . . . I allowed my joy at the sight of you dressed in your royal estate to overcome my own judgment. I . . . I quite forgot myself. The blame is mine."

Richard shook his head. "No, Harry, not yours alone. Mine too, God help me, mine too."

They stood like shamed children, afraid to look each other in the eye, afraid to face the deep and terrible truth that lay between them. Richard said, "This must not happen again. You understand that, don't you? Nor must we ever speak of it. It would be sin and damnation to us both."

Buckingham nodded, but he was obviously at odds with himself. The words came as if they were torn from him. "But I love thee, Dickon. Is there sin in that?"

Richard's hands covered his face. "I don't know. How am I supposed to know? Oh God!" He wanted to scream and rage at the injustice of it all. Why should he be so tested on the brink of his greatest glory? Why was he being permitted this shameful but excruciatingly sweet agony? Was he, like St. Paul, to be tortured by a thorn in the flesh? Then suddenly the heat in him subsided. Christ too had been tempted. Silently, he prayed, "I thank thee, Lord, that I am worthy of this temptation."

Aloud he said, "Be my friend, Harry. Be my strength and comfort in the days ahead. Be my good right arm, for I have need of you. But be no more than that to me, I beg you."

Buckingham looked down to where Richard's hand clutched the lapis sarcenet of his sleeve. His gaze seemed at once to caress and shrivel it. "*Le roi le voit,*" he said softly, but Richard heard the irony.

Richard moved through the rest of that day, perhaps the most important in his life, like one in a trance. He never actually lost consciousness of Buckingham's presence beside him; indeed, at times he was almost too acutely aware of it, like the throbbing of a toothache. But he did strive constantly to forget what had happened between them, and here he achieved some success. After all, what *had* happened really? It was merely an affectionate touch, such as a man might bestow on a close friend. No harm there surely. And if Buckingham loved him, why, he too loved Buckingham in the way a man might, with honor, love a cousin and a friend. He had done no great wrong, not even so great a wrong as to require confession before he took mass the next morning. So he told himself, and before the day was over, he had almost come to believe it.

Certainly there was no lack of other matters to claim his attention. From the moment he entered the council chamber dressed like a king, the room buzzed with wonder and expectancy. He caught doubtful looks from three of the clergy—Bourchier, Russell and Alcock—who, unlike his own men, knew nothing as yet of

Stillington's revelation and were therefore deeply puzzled by this sudden abandonment of mourning black in favor of royal purple.

He did not keep them in suspense for long. Stillington himself related the story, peering out at them timidly from his rabbit-bright eyes. Since he was a churchman, one of their own, they could neither question his veracity nor doubt his sincerity. However, they could, and did, express their shock.

Russell stirred as if waking from a heavy sleep. "Is this . . . is it true?" he asked.

"I swear to you before God and all his saints, it is just as I have told you," Stillington replied solemnly.

"Then . . . it would appear that the Duke of Gloucester is king by lawful right."

"It would appear so, yes," Bourchier echoed disbelievingly as if he had just seen every natural law twisted from its order. His eyes on Richard were red as his cardinal's scarlet; red too was the tiny netting of veins that veiled his cheeks. Stillington's revelation weighed heaviest on him who, with his own hands, would crown Richard if it came to that.

"Do you find that so abhorrent, Eminence?" Buckingham asked. "Is there any man in the realm more fit to be our sovereign than Gloucester? Any more courageous in battle, more just in peace than this great and mighty prince?"

"I did not say there was," Bourchier replied, "and yet I had always hoped to see the mantle rest on the one who was born to it . . ." His voice trailed off as if he feared to give offense.

Richard offered reassurance. "You may speak your mind, father. That's the reason we are gathered here."

"I don't know what I should say . . . how to answer this thing. I have said you should be king, for so my brother of Bath and Wells, whose integrity is unblemished, has told us. But I would rather almost he had not spoken . . ." He jerked his head away, but not before Richard saw the tears forming in the shadowed hollows of his eyes. "Have I . . . may I have Your Grace's leave to go? My head bursts with this . . . this news."

"You know you have it," Richard said, "and anything else you may require."

"Nothing else," Bourchier said, rising. "No, nothing else. I think I have received quite enough already from Your Good Lordship's hand."

The door clicked softly behind him as Richard regarded the remaining two key bishops who were still in doubt: John Russell, who delighted in playing devil's advocate, and John Alcock, mentor and tutor to the king who would now be deposed. How would they answer now that the cardinal had fled?

Russell stood, his iron-hewn face screwed up in puzzlement, his hands grasping the gold chain of his office. For a moment, Richard thought he would remove it and bolt for the door after Bourchier. Then slowly and with immense dignity, he crossed the floor to Richard and went down on his knees before him. The purple silk of his cassock billowed about him like an ocean wave as he placed both hands in Richard's in the ancient gesture of fealty. "I, John Russell, vow to be your humble liege man of life and limb . . ." As the words of the sacred oath poured clear from the chancellor's lips, Richard looked up to see Alcock standing behind Russell, awaiting his turn.

Council could not make him king; only an act of Parliament could do that, but it boded well that council had accepted him without a dissenting vote. Richard thought that even Bourchier, who was old and set in his ways, would come around in time. Russell was sure enough of Richard's ultimate acceptance to declare that they must immediately tell Edward what was happening.

"We can hardly proceed with the coronation," he argued, "and so he must be told, and the sooner the better. Poor lad! No fault of his that he was born bastard and the fact was not recognized until today." He shot Stillington a look as if to ask why he could not have spoken up years ago and so have spared them this unpleasant necessity.

Richard himself tried to dredge up some sympathy for Edward as they made the short walk to the royal apartments, and failed. Impudent whelp! He deserved this and more. To be so coldly spurned, so callously refused was something Richard could not accept. Edward had left him no choice but to act on Stillington's information—no choice at all. His own safety and the future of England demanded it.

He felt somewhat differently when the two boys stood in front of him. To be sure, Edward regarded him as coldly and as imperiously as always, but young Dickon would have run to him in greeting if it had not been for the strange and august body of men who accompanied him and the solemn looks they gave him. He stopped in midstride and looked back at Edward. The question marks hung large in his eyes.

Nor did he immediately take in the implications of Bishop Stillington's speech, croaked out this time in a voice that was hardly more than a whisper. "What's a bastard, Ned?" he asked loudly. "I don't understand."

"Neither do I!" Edward gave a shrill, mirthless chuckle. "For it means, little brother, that we are not the sons of our father, and no one knows better than our Uncle Gloucester here that's a damned lie."

Dickon gave Richard a sideways look that contained the seeds of doubt. "A lie? But our uncle wouldn't . . ."

"No, Your Grace, of course, I wouldn't. It is more a question of . . . of . . ."

"Of which side of the blanket?" Edward finished. "You don't need to mince words with me. It's the dirtiest, most deceitful trick under heaven. And now you will be king, I suppose?"

There was in truth no answer to this but the obvious one. Edward's lips curled away from his teeth in a grin that was almost wolfish. "Ah, yes, who else would it be? So that's your game? Strange that I suspected you of everything else but never of that. I didn't think that even you would stoop that low."

Dickon tugged insistently at his brother's sleeve. "What are you talking about, Ned? I don't understand. You are the king. He told me so yesterday. And I am next nearest the throne. Isn't that so, Uncle? Wasn't that what you said?"

"It . . . it's what I said, yes, but . . ." Richard's voice trailed off into silence. How did one answer such a question?

He was spared from having to answer by the sound of a small noise. It might have been nothing, a mouse scrambling about in the wainscoting perhaps. Then it came again, an unmistakable sniffling sound, and this time, they pinpointed its direction—behind the arras tapestry that closed off an alcove. Head cocked, Buckingham moved stealthily across the room, flung back the concealing curtain and revealed the formidable presence of Argentine, black-palled and breathing with fire like an avenging fury. He stomped out of his hiding place as if glad to be free of it. Involuntarily, Richard and the others gave ground.

"You have heard?" Richard asked. "Yes, I daresay you have."

"Well enough," came the reply. "All and everything. The most devilish deceit since our mother Eve was tempted in the garden." The leech bore down upon him, white hair and beard bristling about his face, eyes burning their topaz indignation. The man was a wizard, Richard thought, or a warlock. He would not have been at all surprised to see lightning flare from the tip of his staff.

"You won't succeed in this plot," Argentine went on. "You will never succeed."

"Who are you to stop me?" Richard asked, standing his ground at last.

"I stop you?" Argentine threw back his head and emitted a gust of laughter. "No, not I. But you shall be stopped, make no mistake. Ah yes, you will have what you seek—for a time. You will wear England's crown. But do not hope for a long and peaceful reign, for you will not have it. Friends will desert you. The blackest villainies will be done in your name. Wars and rumors of wars will plague your kingdom, and you shall never know another moment's peace or rest easy in your bed. Your days will be short, but you will long for their end well before it comes. Your line will fail, and everything you love will be lost to you. Even your name will be slandered and reviled until it becomes the blackest name in the history of your people. Therefore, take the crown and wear it, but know that for you it is a wheel of fire that will sear its heat into your brain."

He stopped at last, panting a little, his eyes no longer focused on Richard but on some vague, undefined point somewhere in the terrible future. Richard's face had gone parchment white. Russell moved quickly to cross himself while Howard made the sign against the evil eye.

Mad, Richard thought, *the man must be mad.*

"Seize him!" he commanded, regaining the use of his tongue. "Take him to the Tower guard and let them find some ship to take him back to his own country, for by the mass, he shall no more darken the shores of mine!"

As Buckingham and Howard hastened to obey, Edward cried out a loud "No!" and ran to Richard, throwing himself at his feet. "Please, let him stay with me. He won't harm you. I'll see to that. Oh, please, Uncle, I beg you."

"Beg, Edward? Too late for that, I think. Yes, far too late. The man is a traitor and will be dealt with as all traitors must. Be thankful that I'm sparing his life. Others will not be so fortunate."

"My Uncle Rivers?" asked Edward with a quaking voice.

"Will meet the end he deserves."

Edward scrambled awkwardly to his feet, wiping at his eyes, and sought his brother, who also wept rather loudly. They clung together like two bits of flotsam in a vast sea, no longer royal, no longer even important—two expendable bits of driftwood.

No, they are still my brother's sons, Richard reminded himself. They would be treated well but could be dealt with later. Right now, it was Argentine who claimed his attention.

The leech, brought to bay, was still a force to be reckoned with. He had not gone down without a fight, but he stood now, quiescent at last, between Buckingham and Howard, taller, broader, and seemingly more powerful than either of his captors. His eyes openly mocked Richard and the chilling words of his curse—if curse it was—seemed to hang between them.

"Take him away," Richard commanded. "I cannot bear to look at him another moment."

Argentine pursed his lips and, in a farewell gesture of pure bravado, spat on the Aubusson carpet at Richard's feet, missing by only a single thread the toe of his boot. Richard drew back his foot as if it had touched fire.

Chapter 26

THE STEAM THAT rose from the bathwater was scented with gillyflower and cardamom. Supported by two of his yeomen of the body, Richard stepped over the high sides of the tub and sank blissfully into the warm water, feeling it lap over him up to his armpits. Almost instantly, the knotted muscles of his back and arms relaxed, the doubts and tensions of the past week seemed scrubbed away by the ministrations of Master Jacques, the most skilled of his yeomen.

Four days had passed since he had openly claimed the crown in council, four days of hectic, almost frantic activity, of meetings and discussions, of banqueting and feasting lasting from shortly after dawn to almost midnight. In this season of midsummer, that had left little time for rest. In fact, Richard had not felt much need for sleep during those feverish days. He was propelled by a will that would not spare him, a desire to see this one or that whose support remained in doubt; to confer with Mayor Will Shaw or his brother, the eloquent Friar Ralph, both of whom he hoped would prove useful to his quest; to ride through the streets of the capital dressed in splendid purple and attended by more than one hundred retainers so that the people might see that here indeed was one worthy to be their king.

In the evenings, he entertained lavishly. The doors of Crosby Place were thrown open to all the great and near-great of London and Westminster. Oxen were slaughtered in their tens, geese in their hundreds, hares in their thousands to find their succulent way to Gloucester's table. Music of viol and cittern and rebec drifted through open windows on lingering June twilights, occasionally disturbed by a loud burst of laughter, the stomping of dancing feet, or the shattering of a wineglass when one guest had carelessly drunk too much.

All this unwonted display created much grist for the rumor mills as Richard had known and even hoped it would. A sparrow does not plume itself like an eagle and expect no one to notice. But while he was aware of the many wondering and admiring eyes cast in his direction, he knew also that many other eyes turned anxiously toward the Tower, where King Edward V (he was still King Edward) and his brother the Duke of York kept their solitary estate. Edward had his rituals too. On each day that the weather permitted, and even on some days when it was in doubt, he took his stance before the archery butt on the Tower green, loosing one arrow after another in the general direction of the bull's-eye. Inevitably, a crowd gathered beyond the barred portcullis, for Edward made certain that he and his pretty younger brother were always in full view of the gates. He did not deign to notice them directly, of course, for the rabble were beneath his kingly dignity, but he did provide them with an indelible image of a youth both fresh and fair, destined from birth to wear England's crown.

Admiring and pitying, the crowd responded, if only in the lowest of whispers. Richard heard them sometimes as he entered and left the Tower. "Poor lambs! What will become of them now, I wonder." The speaker would break off, flustered and suddenly afraid, when he realized who rode past him.

What would become of them indeed? The question was one that Richard did not care to consider, and in the busy circle of his days, he generally managed to bar it from his consciousness. However, the nights, brief as they were, had become another matter entirely. When his head should have sunk on his pillow in thoughtless, exhausted sleep, the words of Argentine—prophecy, curse or lunatic's ravings—came back to him: "You shall never know another moment's peace or rest easy in your bed . . . ." And when at least he slept, there was the dream.

That other Edward, his kingly brother, appeared before him once again. He had a cold, reproachful look in his eyes and an arm clasped tightly around each of his sons. "I charged you to defend the rights of my boys, Dickon; named you protector; and trusted you to carry out the terms of my will. Now see what you've done!" Invariably, Edward's eyes would focus on the crown Richard wore, so large that it kept slipping down over one eyebrow, so heavy that he could neither lift his head nor set it right. Edward bellowed with laughter at this ludicrous spectacle. "It was made for a larger man than you, Dickon. Aye, a much larger man."

Sometimes Buckingham was with him, but far from offering Richard support, he had only joined in Edward's mockeries. "Why, I am a larger man, cousin. Allow me to try it on . . . for size if you will."

Richard awakened, streaming with sweat and paralyzed with fear, as Buckingham's hand had touched the golden circlet. Francis Lovell, who slept these nights in a truckle bed at the foot of Richard's own, was wiping his face with a linen towel.

"Harry?" Richard stammered weakly, straining to see by the light of the lone tallow dip that flickered in a nearby bowl.

"Harry Buckingham, my lord?" Lovell asked. "He is no doubt sleeping peacefully in his own bed as you should be in yours. It was only a dream that disturbed you, nothing more."

Now in full daylight, as the water of the bath laved about his neck and trickled down his spine, Richard could admit the dream's absurdities. Edward could not come from the tomb to reproach him; no more could Buckingham play him false. It was unthinkable. Buckingham had made himself as much a part of Richard's hopes as Richard was himself. In the main matter at hand, that of informing the populace of the changes that were about to take place, he was proving indispensable.

On the next morning, Sunday, June 22, and the feast of the Nativity of St. John, Friar Shaw was to make a great sermon at Paul's Cross in the cathedral churchyard. At the same time, other preachers in lesser churches all over London were to speak on the same topic: the illegality of Edward's marriage. By this means, all the parishioners of London, virtually the entire populace, were by indirection to become acquainted with Richard's claim. The idea, at once so brilliant and so simple in concept, was Buckingham's. The task of informing the preachers Richard had left to the duke and his appointed henchmen. Buckingham would know far better than he what to say and how to say it.

On Monday, Henry Stafford himself would speak at the Guildhall to the merchants and craftsmen of the city, enlarging on the same topic. On Tuesday, as the magnates and commons from the shires assembled for Parliament in the chapter house of Westminster Abbey, they too would be told. And on the following Wednesday, if all went according to plan, Buckingham would lead the lords and commons to the doorstep of Crosby Place, and Richard would be proclaimed king throughout the land.

If he was vaguely troubled by the prominence Buckingham had assumed in all these events, he could only be grateful in the next breath that he had such a firm rock on which to stand. He did not know what he would have done without him. The changes he planned were momentous; they could not be achieved without the support of the man who was, after himself, the premier noble in the land. And if that placed Buckingham in the role of kingmaker—a title that, after Edward's experience with the Earl of Warwick, he shunned to use—then so be it.

Yet he also knew he must broaden his base of support. He already counted Howard as a second prop worthy of his throne, but another noble, whose acquiescence was crucial, remained outside the pale of grace. The influence of the Stanleys in the country at large and particularly in the midlands and the northwest could not be minimized. How could he hope for their compliance, let alone their aid, when he kept their chief mewed up under house arrest? Thomas Stanley had many connections. His brother Sir William and his son Lord Strange each had thousands of men at their disposal, and his stepson, Henry Tudor, could become a dangerous rallying point for all discontent.

Perhaps, he reasoned, *the time has come for me to call on Tom Stanley.*

He closed his eyes and settled back against the sponge-lined tub. Only a few more moments, he thought, and then he must be up and about the business of wooing Tom Stanley. His body felt languid and content, heavy almost with sleep. Almost, he could drift away . . .

A mild disturbance at the door of the room brought him back. "But I tell you, my lord duke, that His Grace is in his bath and is not to be disturbed."

"He will see me." There was no mistaking that voice or the authority behind it. Buckingham's face seemed to float disembodied through the steamy vapors between the parted curtains of his bathing tent.

"Well, cousin!" Richard did not try to hide his annoyance. "You've chosen an inopportune moment, I must say."

"For which I beg Your Grace's pardon," the duke replied. "Only for a matter of supreme importance would I disturb your ablutions."

The attendants were already taking up basins, towels, and ewers, preparing to depart. Richard stopped them with an uplifted hand. "No, Jacques, stay," he said.

"Nay, my lord, dismiss them. What I have to tell you won't wait."

Again they gathered up the stray accoutrements of the bath. Again Richard would have countermanded him, but he was wondering now if something was seriously wrong. Perhaps a number of parish priests had balked at the subject matter for their Sunday sermons. If so, he surely did not want twenty of his yeomen to hear of it. He gave the gesture for dismissal.

"Now, Harry, what is this important matter?" he asked when they were alone.

"I think you know the answer to that as well as I do."

Anger choked Richard's throat as Buckingham's meaning caught. To bring up such a subject at such a time, when he was naked and defenseless in his bath! Only the look on his friend's face, so vulnerable and pain filled, kept his wrath from exploding in a torrent of words. "I thought," he said finally, "that we agreed never to speak of that again."

"You may be able to dismiss it from your mind as easily as that, but I cannot. Do you know what I suffer on your account? When I'm not with you, I ache to see you, and when I am with you, I ache . . .

ah, but what use to speak of it? You obviously think me a wanton foolish boy, if you think of me at all, which apparently you do not."

"There you are wrong, cousin," Richard said softly, "as wrong as this thing you would put between us."

Buckingham pouted like a schoolboy, full lower lip outthrust, gold-fringed eyes regarding him sullenly. "I don't understand. Why is it wrong? Who would be hurt?"

"My wife . . ." Richard said, aware that he had not thought of her for days. "Anne . . ."

"What of her?" Buckingham asked. "Would I be taking anything from her that is hers? She has a son from you, has she not? And by the look of things, she gives little promise for more. Can you lose yourself in her, Dickon? Can you forget yourself with her? I think not."

Richard shifted in the tub, rippling the tepid water. He said nothing, unwilling to reveal how near Buckingham was to hitting the mark. He could not forget himself with Anne. There could be no more sons of York born from her womb. The birthing of Ned had nearly killed her.

Sensing weakness, Buckingham pressed on. "It wouldn't be the same between us, you know, as between a man and a woman. You've read Plato. The coming together of two men is a noble thing, and the ancients, that noblest of races, practiced it often. They had a proper view of the sexes. Men are the superior creatures. Women are mere vessels for the habitation of our children, dross to our gold." He leaned closer; his face was only a few inches from Richard's. "It was man whom God created to have mastery over the earth. Why then should it be a sin for two men to love each other?"

Richard's voice was stiff. "I've always been taught that it was. You must remember, this is England, not Greece, and we are Christians, not pagans. Ah yes, I know it isn't unheard of . . . even in England . . . even among the kings of England. But I don't want the lecherous decay of those other courts festering in my own."

"Nor do I," Buckingham quickly agreed. "But there is a difference here. Don't you see it? What we do, we do from love, not from the body's appetite. Why do I go on so?" he asked, laughing suddenly and running a hand nervously through his hair. "I love thee, Dickon, almost to distraction. Don't you love me?"

Richard was more moved than he cared to admit by this simple appeal. He felt it again, the deep singing in his loins. "You know I do."

"Then God will forgive us, and who else will know?"

The bathwater had grown cold, and Richard shivered. He sat suspended, afraid to speak, afraid to rise. Buckingham smiled at his discomfiture.

"You'll shrivel away to nothing if you stay there much longer," he said. "I shall say no more. Reason tells me I have said too much already." He reached for a cruet of warmed oil, still wrapped in its towel, and looked about as if surprised by the absence of servants. "Your body yeomen seem to have deserted you, Dickon. Come, I'll perform that office for you."

"And no more than that?"

"You may stop me at any time you wish."

Richard rose, ignoring—or choosing to ignore—the quick light of appreciation in Buckingham's eyes. He was doing no wrong, he told himself. To be massaged with scented oils was an accepted part of his bathing ritual. What did it matter whose hands did it? But as he quickly learned, the hands of Buckingham were like no others, and almost at once, they kindled a sweet fire that consumed him, body and soul. For a long, breathless moment, time itself seemed to stand still as if it were suspended. Richard shut his eyes and said no more.

He awoke to a semidarkness that was ripe with the acrid odors of sweat and semen. In the scarlet dusk of the great bed, he could perceive Buckingham's still form sprawled beside him, his long golden lashes making a deeper shadow on high-boned cheeks, his full lips parted in a peculiar little smile.

Richard shuddered as he thrust aside the heavy mulberry velvet curtains and was amazed to see that full daylight flooded his bedchamber. He struggled to shaking feet and was rewarded by a sharp, jabbing pain somewhere between his buttocks. Vomit rose in his throat as the unspeakable knowledge hit home. Fighting the weakness in his limbs, he ran to the garderobe and retched out his shame into the stinking void.

His bathwater was icy cold by this time, but it sufficed. Meticulously, he washed away every outward mark of the morning's deed. Then over his nakedness, he pulled on a pair of tawny hose and a shirt of apple bloom cambric laid out in readiness hours before. From the slant of the sun, he judged it was still a little before noon. Time enough yet to wrest something from the day.

He turned to see Buckingham, head propped up on one hand, regarding him from the depths of the bed. "Why, Dickon," he drawled, "up and about so soon? I thought we had time yet for more such . . . amusements. The hour is still early, is it not?"

"Early enough, though quite late for lying abed," Richard replied tartly.

"What's the matter, Dickon?" The duke's eyes widened in hurt surprise. "Didn't I please you? I thought you were pitched high on love's horn."

Blood stained Richard's sallow cheeks. The memory of that one ecstatic moment of perfect pleasure glowed bright for an instant like the last coal of a dying fire, then it winked into eternal blackness. He ignored the questions that lingered on Buckingham's lips and in his eyes. "Come, Harry. We don't have time to dally. My men will wonder what is keeping me."

"Cock's arse, Dickon!" Buckingham's rich laughter rumbled in his throat. "Why should they wonder that you stay close-closeted with the nearest of your counselors? We have much to discuss, have we not?"

"At this moment, I can think of nothing."

Buckingham gave an extravagant sigh and rose from the bed. With practiced ease, he tied the points of his silver cloth-of-gold hose beneath the dagged hem of his satin doublet. Richard watched him with creeping disgust. While he himself had been as naked as the day he came from his mother's womb, Buckingham had removed little more clothing than he would have done to use the privy.

However, there was something more solemn in the duke's eyes as he raised them to Richard's. "If I have displeased you in some way, if I have taken too great a liberty . . . and yet I thought you wanted it as much as I did."

Richard shook his head. "No, I don't know what I wanted. I'm sorry . . ." His voice trailed off as he turned and made for the wardrobe, where he fumbled among the shimmering wealth of silks, velvets, and sarcenet. Pulling out a doublet of chartreuse damask lined with periwinkle blue satin, he dropped it over his head and tugged with awkward fingers at the lacings. He was not used to dressing himself. Twenty squires waited outside to do the job if they were summoned, but he was not of a mind to summon them now. His jewel box yielded a gold chain with a great emerald pendant dangling from it like a green fruit.

"You mean to go out now?" Buckingham asked, faintly puzzled.

Richard pulled stubbornly at his calf skin boots. They were new and a bit stiff. "Yes. I think I'll call on Tom Stanley."

"Call on him?" Buckingham's eyebrows shot heavenward. "Splendor of God, it would be a charity to hang the man."

"Aye, no doubt," Richard replied. His boots yielded at last to his tugging, and he stood, busying himself now by rummaging in his glove chest.

"Then why?"

"Well, I can hardly afford to hang him now, can I? His brother Sir William would be on me like a fiend while he still danced from the gibbet. And if he must live, you will allow that it would be better to have him for a friend than a foe. He's too powerful to ignore and too full of trickery to keep even closely guarded."

Richard selected gloves of supple fawn-colored leather and pulled them on over hands that had almost stopped their trembling. The black velvet cap with its turned-up brim was next. The jeweled pin winked at him as he surveyed his image in the glass. The chartreuse was wrong; he realized that at once. It made his skin look bilious, but it would have to do. And as for the rest of him, strangely he looked much the same as he always had.

Behind him, he caught a glimpse of Buckingham, a subdued and somewhat chastened Buckingham chewing thoughtfully on his lower lip.

"Come along, Harry," he said, not unkindly. "I believe you have some affairs of your own to attend to, don't you?"

"Affairs?" Buckingham gave him a blank, unseeing look. "Oh, aye, the preachers."

"I imagine that should take most of what remains of the day," Richard said as he buttoned a light mantle. "Best to get on with it. I can hardly manage it myself."

"No, and Your Grace has other matters to attend to," Buckingham said impassively. "Tom Stanley . . ."

"The auld eagle," Richard replied. "Best to get that over with as well."

"B-but you will still dine with me tomorrow, won't you? After the sermon at Paul's Cross?"

Richard shrugged. "Yes, I suppose so. I see no reason why not nor why this should . . . interfere with our friendship." He waved a vague hand toward the bed then turned sharply away, striding to the door. A nearby church bell began to toll for sext. "Are you coming, Harry?" he asked.

Chapter 27

MARGARET STANLEY SAT at the loom in her private apartments, watching the gray woolen fabric take shape before her without actually seeing it. She had spent many hours here in the past week since her husband had returned from the Tower and been placed under house arrest. Although it seemed that the protector's men swarmed all over their Ludgate mansion, turning it into a hive of restless bees, here at least they were absent. Also, the simplicity of the room suited her with the mindless activity of the loom, the clutter of devotional books, and the small writing table on which rested an unfinished letter to her exiled son.

By rights, she should be completing it now and sending it off to France with the usual admonition to be of good cheer and good courage, but the words would not come to her. Ever since Tom Stanley's fall from grace, she had begun to wonder whether heaven would ever again smile on her and hers. This was so uncharacteristic an emotion that it frightened her a little, but there it was. Tom Stanley, whom she had chosen for her third husband more out of regard for his position than for any other reason, had failed both her and her son by losing that position, risking all, as it now seemed, for nothing.

She sighed as the shuttle moved in her dexterous fingers, marrying the warp and woof in a perfect union. In contrast, the fabric of her own life seemed hopelessly rent. There was neither joy nor purpose left. Indeed, she felt only mild interest when Reginald Bray, her steward and most trusted man of affairs, burst in on her solitude without knocking.

He stumbled on the doorstep and fell forward into the room, still puffing hard from the stairs. "Now see here, Bray—" she began, meaning to reprimand him. This behavior was so unlike him.

"My lady, forgive—" he gasped, clutching his side. He was in his forties and, by any standards, no longer young. "Gloucester . . . the protector . . . downstairs."

"Gloucester—here?" She stiffened and dropped the shuttle, heedless of the tangling threads. "What's he doing here? How does one greet her husband's jailor, I wonder?"

"Ah . . . the protector has asked to speak to His Lordship alone."

"Alone? Yes, of course." She rose, smoothing the long gray skirt of her gown. Although Bray was by no means a tall man, she did not even reach his shoulder. "That is most interesting. And where is my husband entertaining his distinguished guest?"

"In the solar, I believe."

"Excellent choice," she said with a sudden mischievous smile. "I think it's time for me to make my devotions in the chapel."

She did not go to the chapel to pray for her husband's welfare in his ordeal, though for all she knew he might well have need of her prayers. Richard's arrival could well signal his end. She went there instead because the builders of their fine London townhouse had thoughtfully provided it with a squint, which gave an excellent view of the downstairs solar. Normally, the aperture was covered by a gilded statue of the Virgin, but this was easily moved aside. She did so now and stepped up on a small stool to peer down into the room below.

Yes, there was the hog in the flesh. Her eye took in every detail of his rich and colorful doublet. This was a change surely. What could it mean? And opposite him sat Stanley, wary as always and slightly bemused. An ugly red welt creased the hairline above his right ear. He pressed it unconsciously as he leaned forward to speak.

"Let me understand this then," he said. "You aren't going to hang me?"

"Hang you?" Richard laughed, a dry peculiar sound. "No, Thomas, I don't think so. Instead I mean to restore you, give you back your seat on the council, reinstate you as steward of the household, restore all your offices and estates . . ."

Stanley shook his head, disbelieving, and said something under his breath she couldn't catch. "I can't believe you would destroy Hastings, the friend and mentor of your youth, yet pardon me," he added more loudly.

Hush, foolish man! Margaret cautioned mentally. *Hush or you'll ruin everything.*

"Well, I can hardly pardon him now, can I?" Richard snapped. "If you like, you may think that I pardon you in his stead, but I will say this. The offense is greater where the betrayal is great. You at least were open in your discontent. You did not pretend to love me . . ."

"Neither did he. You wrong him there. He still loved you even at the end."

Richard rose and began to pace. His back was turned toward Margaret, and she barely caught his words. "How can you say so? He showed it most strangely."

"If our plot had succeeded, he would have spared you. The rest of us wished to give you the same short shrift you gave him."

Oh, most foolish man, to be so open! She was seized with a desire to fly down the stairs and pacify Richard. Didn't Tom realize what was at stake?

"And now," Stanley asked with a twist of a smile, "would you still pardon me, my lord?"

There was a long heavy silence, during which Margaret scarcely dared to breathe. Richard paced up and down, up and down, like some desperate caged beast, and Margaret at last saw her husband's game. He must be absolutely certain that Richard needed him as much as he needed Richard. He was insuring their future safety. At last, Richard turned and looked directly at Stanley. Behind him, a tapestry depicted Perseus holding aloft the head of Medusa writhing in a blend of orange and crimson and purple.

"Yes," he said simply. "I'll spare you. Even more, I want you beside me. I mean to be king, Thomas. You must have heard the rumors by now." (Margaret, who in her chosen seclusion had not, stifled a gasp.) "And I'll be plain. I need your support."

Stanley still eluded him. "I don't know what to say. It is hardly what I expected. I haven't exactly done you good service in the past."

"At Berwick, against the Scots," said Richard, turning, justifying. "Surely it's not so long ago now that you've forgotten. You served me well enough there. A long, difficult siege. You brought them to their knees."

"I served Edward."

"So I would have you serve me. Will you refuse? For by the rood, I'll—"

Stanley held up a restraining hand. Again, a little smile of amusement flickered in his beard. "Refuse you, Your Grace? By what right does a man refuse his lawful king?"

"Good then!" Suddenly, Richard relaxed, the tension gone from his eyes and shoulders. "You will see, Thomas, we'll get on well enough, I daresay. I'll be a good and generous lord to you, and I'm sure you'll give me no cause to regret it."

"And my wife, the Lady Margaret, what of her?"

"Well, what of her?" Richard asked as if dismissing her. (*I shall not be so easily dismissed as that, my lord*, thought Margaret.) "She'll be welcome at court if she chooses to show herself. For the rest, she is in your charge. 'The husband is the head of the wife even as Christ is head of the church.'"

Stanley moved his head slowly from side to side. "Then a thousand pities on Christ, my lord, for I'm afraid it goes most ill with his church. There is only one man who can control the Lady Margaret, and I am not he."

"Her son?"

"Aye, her Tudor whelp," Stanley regarded Richard over his own clasped hands. "This will change nothing with her."

Margaret was a little disturbed by the tenor of this conversation. It seemed almost that Tom was warning Richard that one day he might be forced to choose sides. She had no wish to remind him of that.

"Henry Tudor is an exile, an outcast. Let him show his face in England, and he will be clapped in irons and thrown into the darkest hold of the Tower keep. She must be made to understand that, Thomas. I trust you to see to it."

"Ah, I see. The price of my freedom is my wife's loyalty."

A very high price, Margaret decided, *and not one likely to be exacted. The hog might find my husband an easy mark, but my son and myself, we are another matter.*

"Call it what you will," Richard was saying. "Whatever service you find to hand, I expect you to do it."

Stanley dipped his head in an ironic little bow. "As Your Grace wills," he said. "And now, may I suggest a toast to our new venture?" He rang for a page, but Margaret decided on the instant that it would be no page who took their drinks to them. Stepping down from her stool, she fled the chapel and made for the stairs.

She swept into the room like a queen, but even as Richard watched Lady Margaret Beaufort Stanley deftly balance the porcelain tray on one hand, he wondered what it was that made her so regal. The self-styled Countess of Richmond possessed few of a queen's desirable attributes. At first glance, she appeared to be little more than a child though she had in fact celebrated her fortieth birthday three weeks before. She was very small, short as a dwarf, and with no hint of a woman's roundness beneath the gray habit-like gown. With a wimple covering her hair and a white barb surmounting to her chin, she reminded him of his own mother recently come from the nunnery. The face between barb and wimple was gray as putty and sharp as the blade of a hatchet. Yet there was a confident grace in all her movements as if she were always aware of her superior status.

She set her tray on a small table between the two men and swept Richard a low curtsy. "I must apologize for my delay in greeting Your Grace. I was in the midst of my prayers."

Richard looked into her eyes and found them oddly arresting: gray flecked with gold, solemnity relieved by a promise of humor, and behind them, a crafty, purposeful intelligence.

"Your piety is to be commended, madam," he said, noting the crystal rosary tucked into her girdle. "We would not have hindered your devotions. My business was with your husband and is now concluded to the satisfaction of us both, I think."

She looked thoughtfully from one to the other. Stanley poured the amber liquor into twin goblets. The sun struck them with pale flame as each lifted his glass in silent salute and drank.

"You look like two wool merchants who have arrived at a price," she said.

"Aye," replied Stanley, "and that after very little haggling."

"Might one be so bold as to ask what would be the commodity?"

"My freedom, Meg."

"Then I am most indebted to you, my lord," she said, turning to Richard with a smile. "He was growing troublesome in confinement. One day more of it, and I swear by the saints he would have driven us both to distraction. In freeing him, you have freed me as well."

"I am happy, madam, to be able to do you both such good service."

She moved away then, tiring of the game perhaps, and took a seat of her own. However, her eyes never left Richard's face, and he found himself growing increasingly uneasy under this silent scrutiny. He knew, or thought he knew, what was on her mind. How would this change affect her darling boy, her sweet Henry, watching and waiting for his chance from beyond the sundering seas?

He gulped the last of the sweet sack and stood and Stanley with him. Margaret too rose, all calm decorum. He took his leave of Stanley with a handshake.

"I've a mind to hear Friar Shaw's sermon tomorrow at Paul's Cross," he told him. "Will you join me there?"

Stanley nodded solemnly, aware that this was not a request but a command. Margaret stood, pale and translucent by the window, the sunlight gold in her gray eyes, her voice low. "God grant you success in all your endeavors, my lord." Once again, there was the deep curtsy of obeisance.

Feigned obeisance, Richard thought. *Liar! No doubt you go off to pray before the icon of your son!*

He wanted to smash the empty goblet to the floor, shattering it into a thousand fragments, wishing all the while it was the Tudor's head. But he did not do it; he did not even speak. From this time on, he could not afford to anger either of the Stanleys. They must be given place, given preferment. Honors must be heaped on top of honors until, surfeited at last, Margaret's devotion to her gray-eyed son waned and shriveled, matching any mother's reasonable expectations for her offspring—an earldom perhaps or a quiet place neither too near nor too far from the court for Henry Tudor.

And in the meantime, God help Tom Stanley!

Chapter 28

IT WAS TO have been Edward's coronation day, that sultry Sabbath morning, the twenty-second day of June. Instead, the sun beamed down from a milky sky on a knot of men who danced attendance on Richard, Duke of Gloucester, lord protector of the realm, a slight but magnificent figure clad in velvet of Tyrian purple embroidered all over with the Plantagenet arms in threads of pure gold. On the other side of the city, Edward, once Prince of Wales and now briefly king though soon to be reduced to the status of a royal bastard, sulked behind the thick walls of the Tower keep.

Richard did not think too much about Edward that day. He noted with pleasure and relief that Thomas Stanley awaited him on a chestnut mare at the entrance to St. Paul's churchyard. They did not speak, nor did they need to. Everything of importance had already been decided between them. Stanley was now his man entire and by his presence openly proclaimed his allegiance.

But if Stanley's presence was a comfort and a reassurance, Buckingham's was proving to be something of an embarrassment. As they met that morning, Richard had felt the quick racing of his pulse, and he had not been able to control completely the sudden rush of blood to his face. Buckingham had seen it and had sent him a knowing smile. Even after the abrupt dismissal of yesterday, perhaps all might yet be well? His lingering eyes asked volumes of questions that Richard could not answer. And so he had merely looked away.

The churchyard was crammed to the walls with London citizens; the crowd overflowed even to the cloisters of the cathedral itself. With certain knowledge that an event of major importance was about to take place, they had thronged in unprecedented numbers to hear Friar Ralph preach his Sunday sermon. As Richard and his party appeared, an expectant murmur rippled through the assembly. The moment was approaching. Like Moses walking dry-shod through the Red Sea, he moved through the parted ranks to the foot of the weather-beaten wooden cross.

From his pulpit, Friar Ralph looked down and smiled. A small breeze stirred the folds of his brown habit. He had the lean, taut face of the ascetic and a bony frame most unlike the well-padded corpulence of his brother, the lord mayor. Also unlike his brother, he possessed the fiery eyes of the demagogue. But they were one in spirit, these two Shaws, joined in the belief that Richard should be king—though for vastly different reasons. While the friar decried the illegitimacy of Edward's birth, the lord mayor considered only that it was better for the future prosperity of his city and the kingdom at large to be governed by a man instead of a boy.

From the squat tower near the cross, the great Jesus bell began to toll deafeningly, rolling over the yard in pounding waves. When the last echo died away, there was utter silence. A man could have heard a feather falling to earth in the hush. Only then did Friar Ralph begin to speak. He had carefully chosen his text from the Wisdom of Solomon, chapter 4, verse 3: "But the multiplying brood of the ungodly shall be of no profit, and with bastard slips they shall not strike deep root, nor shall they establish a sure hold." To Richard, the bass of his voice held the same authority as the toll of the great bell that had preceded it.

As the great secret, by now so familiar to him, was being skillfully unveiled, Richard stopped listening to the friar and began watching for signs of reaction in the assembled masses. There was little to be concluded. The faces he could see were astonished into blankness; he could read neither acceptance nor rejection. Around him, the stillness was absolute.

He began to feel ill. The stench of the crowd, of a thousand sweating, unwashed bodies, pressed in on him. Overhead, the mid-summer sun soared to its zenith in a cloudless sky. Sweat trickled down his sides under the velvet doublet. Anne had warned him that it would be too warm a day for it. He was certain to faint or worse. But he had insisted. Velvet, the most regal of fabrics, would proclaim him king as surely as Friar Shaw's words. Lulled by the sun, by the smell, by the voice that swelled over and around him, alternately shouting and whispering, pleading and cajoling, he stood almost in stupor, aware only of a throbbing in his temples and an urgent desire to be gone from this place. Then he was shocked into sudden consciousness.

"And here you have before you the very image, the undoubted son and heir by lawful right of the great Duke of York, whose passing we still mourn. I give you Richard Plantagenet, Duke of Gloucester! Look on the man. Is he not the very spit and image of the father that got him?"

A thousand pairs of eyes turned on him. He could feel the scrutiny of all that mighty mass. Some stood on tiptoe. Some were hoisted onto the shoulders of their neighbors for a better view. Some climbed the buttresses of the cathedral. He heard one woman weeping. Others, his own men among them, were smiling. Most of the rest looked merely curious or stunned or smugly satisfied as if to say, "Didn't I tell you it would come to this?"

Richard drew himself up into a semblance of kingly dignity and attempted to make his face impassive as if he had no interest in the day's events. But beneath the padded purple of his doublet, his heart was racing with an uneasy question. What did it mean, Friar Ralph's proclamation that he was "the undoubted son and heir by lawful right" of his father? There had been other sons. Shaw was ignoring completely his golden brother who had admittedly borne the Duke of York little resemblance. He was ignoring Edward.

No, not ignoring him but denouncing him! In the next breath, he was praising Richard's unflawed moral character in contrast to the intemperate living and wanton debaucheries of the late king. Richard's hand slid to the jeweled hilt of his dagger where it clasped and unclasped with tense fingers. The words echoed in his disbelieving ears. This had been no part of his plan. It was to have been only a simple announcement that Edward had never been legally wed to Elizabeth Woodville; a few moments' sympathetic evocation of England's true queen, Lady Eleanor Butler, dying childless in her nunnery; and a tantalizing suggestion of what that boded for the succession. Not, pray God, this portrait of a royal whoremaster driven by unslakable lust from whom no female flesh had been safe and not, pray God again, the dirty linen of York aired for the edification of the masses.

Beside him, Buckingham's profile was frozen. An absent smile touched his lips, and his eyes stared far away. If the duke had used this as a means of pricking him, as a sort of vengeance for the way things had ended between them yesterday . . . but no. Surely this must be the friar's own blatant invention. He was a notorious evangelical. The opportunity to lecture his flock on the evils of self-indulgence was perhaps too tempting not to be used. For Richard, it was on this particular day a most unfortunate choice of subject.

At last it was over. The crowd broke up and drifted away, down West Chepe, down Ludgate Hill in straggling twos and threes. The strange hush was still on them. They appeared to move in separate shells, devoid of sense like crabs scuttling back to their lairs.

Richard himself felt the same intense need for privacy. His comments to Shaw were brief and complimentary. He ached to get safely away. There was a pain behind his eyes, and the light of the noonday sun shivered in a thousand splintered fragments. He longed for his own darkened bedchamber, a cool compress on his brow, a cordial of lily of the valley in white wine, certain cure for headaches.

But as he took his leave of the lords in the churchyard and lifted his foot to White Surrey's stirrup, Buckingham hastened to him, stammering protests. Surely my lord had not forgotten that he was pledged to dine with the duke that afternoon. Was he not still pleased to grant the honor of his presence?

Richard had entirely forgotten that obligation. In reality, there was no place in London where he would have been less pleased to dine that day. He hesitated, his lips shaping an excuse, a denial, a postponement, until he saw the crestfallen hurt in Buckingham's eyes. His cooks had been busy for days, up since matins preparing for a very great banquet. All his lords and knights were to attend. How could he have forgotten?

Wearily, Richard turned away from West Chepe and Bishopsgate, the dear and familiar way home, and spurred his horse in the opposite direction, toward the Manor of the Rose in Suffolk Lane.

To give the duke his due, he surpassed even himself as a host that day. The boar, white on azure, was everywhere—draped from the high windows of the hall, from the lofty hammer beam ceiling, and from the minstrels' gallery, where a dozen musicians regaled them throughout the feast. On the board, a ferocious-looking wild boar, roasted whole, reigned supreme over lesser but still exotic fare, such as larks' tongues and roast quail; it was followed at last by a huge subtlety depicting a white boar doing battle with a dragon in imitation of St. George.

When the meal was finished, Richard sat back satiated in his chair, surveying the shambles before him with an ironic smile. "I don't know if we have honored the boar here today or massacred him," he said. The animal's ribs, still tattered with shreds of pink meat, jutted sharply from the huge platter, which was a mess of congealing lard. The subtlety had fared no better. It was a sticky ruin, unrecognizable as ever having possessed either form or substance.

"Why cousin, you might liken it to the Mass," said Harry of Buckingham, speech slightly slurred with his own vintage Bordeaux.

Richard blinked surprise. "To the Mass?"

"Aye, of course. Isn't the Mass the body of Christ, and by partaking of it, do we not become one with him? Since we have partaken of the boar today, we are all now his men entire."

"Hail to the white boar of England!" Rob Percy bellowed, raising his cup.

"Hear, hear!" came a chorus of rousing replies. As glasses and cups were raised and wine and ale sloshed freely onto the table, Richard laughed out loud, his headache quite forgotten. He ignored for the moment the sacrilege of Buckingham's muddled simile and the growing strain between them. He forgot for a time the shame of their shared guilt. Instead he thought only of the warm, effusive host who had hovered over him, anticipating his lightest whim as if the kingdom itself depended on it. And he thought of the loyal friend who had stood beside him in the troubled days as well as the triumphant ones.

His gaze shifted around the table to stolid, dependable Howard, whose ready smile split his homely face, and then to Stanley, who was a trifle uncomfortable perhaps among his new friends but smiling too, his cup raised as high as any in the room. And then there were his own handpicked knights, the men who had served him on his northern council, his *crème de la crème*. Regretfully, Richard Ratcliff was once more absent in the north, attending to some of his lord's less pleasant business, but the others were here: Lovell, Percy, Assheton, Tyrell, Tom Lynom (who had managed to tear himself away from Jane Shore's side in honor of the event), Robert Brackenbury (newly appointed constable of the Tower), and Will Catesby (forgetful for once of his disloyalty to Hastings, thinking now only of this newfound loyalty).

Richard bathed in the lambent glow of their goodwill and, despite his earlier misgivings, was glad, very glad, that he had been persuaded to come. Then his gaze rested on one face less familiar than the others, one seamed down the left cheek by a long jagged scar. Until that moment, he had not even been aware of William Percival's presence. He sat near the end of the table in utter silence and sobriety, his pale yellow-green eyes looking full into Richard's without embarrassment or apology. His plum-colored sleeve remained firmly on the table; his fingers toyed absently with the stem of his goblet.

"What's this, Percival?" Rob Percy bawled down the table. "Won't you drink to your king? Or must I mend your manners for you?"

"I was not aware that the title had been given," Percival said evenly. "You must forgive my . . . tardiness." Slowly, with high effect, he lifted the glass to his lips. His insolent eyes never left Richard's face.

Recalling the incident as he entered his own courtyard, Richard felt a chill at the base of his spine and the knowledge of something so sinister he could put no name to it. Percy, on the other hand, had talked of little else except "that churlish swine" and "that impudent spawn of the devil" all the way home. Brackenbury, in whom the milk of human kindness flowed almost too freely, had defended Percival. "No doubt he felt like a stranger in our midst," he told Percy, "surrounded as he was by the protector's men."

"He's no stranger to my lord of Buckingham by all accounts," Percy replied hotly. Assheton shot him a warning glance that Richard intercepted but chose to ignore. His men were worse than fishwives on a market day when it came to idle gossip. He had long since learned to disregard it.

Much to his surprise, the courtyard of Crosby Place was brimming with activity as he entered it. Beside the fountain, which sparkled invitingly in the sunlight, rested an elaborate but old-fashioned horse litter, its mulberry leather curtains flapping in the light breeze. Four men-at-arms in blue-and-murrey livery stamped with the blue-boar badge slumped over dice on the flagstones while a pair of pages in the same livery splashed barefoot in the fountain. Although the Dowager Duchess of York did not normally allow her servants such diversions on the Holy Sabbath, there could be no doubt that these were attached to her household.

Anne met him halfway up the steps. "Dickon, your mother is here!" she cried, running toward him. He was not so startled by this unannounced visit from his reclusive dam that he failed to notice what the excitement did for Anne. Her cheeks were flushed a soft pink that almost exactly matched the sprigs of rosebuds in her muslin gown, and her hair, escaping from its cauls, hung loose and red-lighted about her face.

"So I gathered," he replied.

"She's been waiting for hours—since noon—and it's past nones now."

"I trust you kept her entertained, Nan," Richard said, putting a hand on her waist and guiding her up the marble stair.

"No, Dickon, though I tried. I offered her meat and drink and Renard to strum the lute for her, but she would have none of it. To tell you the truth," she added, her voice dropping, "I think she's in some kind of fit. Her face is screwed up like a persimmon, and she wouldn't tell me anything of why she came. She's been waiting all this while in the solar. I've turned the glass three times."

"No doubt the wait has not improved her disposition?"

"I daresay, Dickon. What do you think?"

What infraction am I guilty of this time? he wondered as he made for the solar. *Which invisible rule have I broken?* He had been careful to inform his mother of all his plans, had even done her the honor of seeking her counsel. For her part, the duchess, who had long known of her eldest son's marital irregularities, had offered only token resistance to the change in government. What then could be bothering her now?

Anne reached out to give his hand a reassuring squeeze before disappearing in a whisper of muslin into her own chambers. Richard walked on. With a heavy hand, he pushed open the solar door.

"Well, madam?" he said formally. "This is an unexpected pleasure."

The recluse of Baynard's Castle and Syon Abbey regarded him with icy-dark eyes. She sat rigid and erect on a simple straight-backed oak chair, ignoring the cushioned benches and chairs of scarlet damask Richard had only recently purchased. She ignored as well his filial kiss on her cheek.

"Unexpected? I can well imagine. But a pleasure? I hardly think so." Despite the coolness of her voice, Richard felt her seethe with inner agitation. A bright spot of color burned high on each cheekbone.

He dropped down onto the scarlet damask. "I must confess that I'm at a loss to know how I have offended you."

"Are you really, Dickon? By the rood, don't come to me pretending to be the dutiful son when, on your behalf, my name is slandered from half the pulpits of London."

Richard's jaw dropped in astonishment. "On my behalf, you are slandered? I don't know what you're talking about."

Swiftly, she spilled out the tale, biting off the ends of her words as if she would spit them out. Although she had as usual heard mass in her private chapel that morning, one of her tiring women had gone with her betrothed to the service at St. Martin's-in-the-Field, where the priest had chosen a most unusual sermon topic. It concerned no less a matter than the dynastic difficulties of the House of York. In particular, it asserted that the late King Edward had not been the son of the Duke of York. Rather, he had been unlawfully begotten on his duchess by an archer named Blaybourne, a man of great height who had served in the duke's train at Rouen.

"Oh, it's not the first time I've heard that story," Cecily went on. "It's old gossip by now and stale as last week's bread, but I had thought it was dead. I certainly hadn't expected you to make use of it to further your own ends."

"Are you sure your woman heard correctly? Might she not have been more interested in her lover than in the sermon?"

"She was interested enough to come home in tears," Cecily countered. "Elise is very loyal to me, and I've no doubt she heard correctly. Besides," she added, regarding him with renewed hostility, "I've made inquiries. It was not the only such sermon preached today. What I want to know is why that old lie of the devil was resurrected in your name to be cried from the best pulpits in London."

Richard could not answer that question though an awful suspicion was beginning to grow in his mind. He stood and walked to the window, where he could look down on the garden below, on the riot of musk roses, full blown now, in fragrant ripening clusters of pink and yellow and white, and on the luxuriant brush of honeysuckle climbing a wall of cream-colored stone.

He remembered without wishing to the jarring portion of Friar Shaw's own sermon the reference to himself as the rightful and undoubted son of his father York. The very spit and image of his father—wasn't that what the friar had said? In a family where the legitimacy of some of the offspring was in doubt, how many times was it that the son with the closest physical resemblance to his sire was named the heir?

And he remembered something else as well: the dissection of Edward's amours, the poking and prodding among the very scum on York. He had thought at the time this came from Friar Ralph's own excessive rectitude, but now he was not so sure.

"Well, Dickon? I'm waiting for your answer," Cecily said.

He turned a face to her that surprised her with its sudden anguish. "I don't know," he said, and his voice came out with unusual harshness. "By the sacred head of my father, do you think that I would ever do such a thing?"

"If not you, then who? Who would dare?"

"I . . . I will find out. He—they will be severely reprimanded. You may be sure of that."

Cecily was somewhat mollified now, the mother's concern beginning to assert itself over the injured woman's indignation. She unclasped the large hands that had been held stiffly in her lap and smoothed the lavender-scented folds of her gown.

"If I were you, my son, I would exercise a little more discretion in my choice of counselors. He who brands your father a cuckold and your mother a whore is no friend to York nor to you."

"Yes, of course. You are right. I will see to it."

"You have already told me that." She rose and came to him, placing a large blue-veined hand on his arm. "You must forgive my asking this, but are you feeling well? I didn't think my wrath would distress you so."

"I'm quite well, lady," he replied, but his face was parchment white, and a tiny muscle jumped in his cheek. "In fact," he added almost bitterly, "I've never felt better. Won't this very week bring me the fruition of all my hopes?"

"Will it, Dickon?" she asked softly. "Did you ever hope for this, I wonder? The little lad I reared at Fotheringhay seemed content enough to march in the shadow of his older brothers."

"Aye, but there comes a time when a man must find his own way. And in any case, there are no older brothers left to me now, are there?"

A spasm of pain crossed Cecily's face. Here he stood, the last of her four sons, as valiant as Edward or as Edmund, dead in his teens at

Wakefield, and surely more gifted with sense than ill-fated Clarence. Of all that remarkable golden brood of boys she had born to her lord of York, only this dark changeling, the runt of the litter, remained. Yet the preachers had been right about one thing. There was more of his father in this one than in all of the others put together.

"You will do well, my son," she said as she bent her cheek for his farewell kiss. "You will do very well indeed. I am certain of it."

Laughter and music drifted from the slightly opened door of Anne's apartments. He had come here after his mother's departure, scarcely thinking where he was going, drawn for solace to his wife's warmth and quiet understanding. Now he stood frozen on the threshold, feeling himself an unwelcome intruder. All around him, except for this one bright bubble of gaiety, the house was as quiet as an empty church. Curious, he pushed the door open an inch further and stood there, unacknowledged, in watchful silence.

Renard, the French minstrel, was strumming his lute and regaling his audience with a bawdy little lay, but his pet monkey, newly acquired from a Neapolitan trader, was the real source of attention. The Duchess of Gloucester and Lady Percy sat on the floor like schoolgirls, skirts spread around them, feeding the beast candied orange slices, which it took between its tiny paws and devoured greedily. Anne laughed with delight at its screwed-up face.

"Oh, look, Francois," she said to Lovell, who squatted on the floor beside her. "Isn't he the prettiest little creature in the world?"

"Indeed, my lady." Lovell pretended to stop and consider the question. "He is quite pretty, yet I know of at least one other creature in this room who is prettier by far."

Anne blushed at this gallantry, her eyes on the monkey, who had climbed onto the low table beside her in search of the sweetmeats. However, Lovell's eyes were on Anne, on the warm curve of her neck and the swelling whiteness of shoulder and breast where the low-necked gown had slid down her arm.

"*Non, ma petite!*" Anne chided the beast, gathering it in her arms though its grasping tail still clung to the table leg. "You stay here on the floor, and I will feed you, like so."

"Ah, what I wouldn't give, my lady, for such devoted attention," said Lovell wistfully.

Whey-faced Anna Lovell, who sat in a nearby chair, embroidering a cambric shirt for her son, pursed her lips together in prim disapproval. She had learned to suffer silently her husband's flirtations, both playful and serious. Richard could not be quite so passive. Lovell, of all people, showing attentions to Anne! But then, even in childhood, they had both vied for her affections. Strange how he kept forgetting that.

"You make entirely too much noise, Francis," Percy said, his thatched red head resting comfortably in his lady's ample lap. "How is a fellow supposed to get his hard-earned rest? What a day it's been! First the preaching, then the feasting, then that Percival lout . . ."

"Poor Rob," Anne said, bending over to give him an affectionate shove. "Is my husband such a hard taskmaster then?"

"The hardest," Percy replied, trapping her hand in his. He opened one blue eye to stare up at her. "But his service does have its compensations."

Anne's warm laughter rippled again. "You shall both spoil me outrageously if you keep this up."

"Then high time, Nan, that somebody did," said Lovell.

Richard cleared his throat and thrust the door fully open. The lute and laughter died together. "Well, if this isn't a cozy little domestic scene! Entertainments for a Sabbath afternoon, I take it. Strange that no one saw fit to invite the master of the household."

Anne stood up, truly coloring now, but she looked him straight in the eye. "Dickon! Has your lady mother left then?"

"Yes, she is gone. I regret that she failed to keep me occupied as long as you might have wished."

"What do you mean by that?"

"Anything I have to say to you, madam, I'll say when your guests have departed. In the meantime, cover yourself. I'll not have my duchess displaying her charms like a brazen street strumpet for my henchmen and chief musician to see."

Anne fumbled at the flimsy stuff of her gown while Lovell took issue. "Now see here, Dickon, I don't know what you're thinking, but there's nothing wrong here. Indeed we are doubly chaperoned. My wife, here, and Rob's—"

"Sweet blood of Jesus!" Percy bellowed. "What do you take us for?"

"That isn't the question of the moment," Richard said. "Nor can I see that your presence here is required further."

"B-but—"

"Out!" Richard cried, pointing to the door. "All of you, out! And take that mangy, flea-bitten beast with you."

When they had trooped silently out, the monkey dangling forlornly from the musician's arm, Anne wheeled on him in a frenzy. "What right have you to come bursting in here like a wild animal and shame me in front of my friends?"

"I have every right, lady. I am your husband as you may perhaps in a calmer moment recall. And as for your friends, are you certain that is all they are?"

"Yes, that is all they are! And frankly, I am glad of them. I don't know what I would do without them."

"Or their pretty gallantries?"

"Very well, yes," she nodded. "Once in a while, it's good to have such attention. It has been sadly lacking of late from . . . other sources."

"Oh, I see." Richard laughed grimly. "I have only just come from an interview where I was berated for being an unnatural son. Now, if I'm not mistaken, you're about to add to my stripes by naming me a neglectful husband."

Anne absently rearranged some damask roses that stood in a vase of Venetian cut glass. She picked one out and sniffed the fragrant heart of its blossom. "If the shoe fits . . ."

"And what would you have me do, Nan? Give up the thing I seek?"

"If the price of it is so great, yes."

"You didn't shrink from a crown when your father wanted to make you queen. Mighty Warwick's daughter you were then in truth."

Anne wrenched her head away then so that her face was hidden by the copper-dark masses of her hair. He had broken the tacit agreement they had kept over the years never to speak of those old hurts, of her father's treason, and of her own brief, ill-starred marriage to the Lancastrian Prince of Wales, slain at Tewkesbury.

"I was a child then," she said softly, "or little more. I didn't know. But very well, Dickon, if you would have it out, let's have it out. Shall I show you all I have left of my father and my erstwhile husband?" She swept past him into the adjoining bedchamber, and at the foot of her curtained bed with the arms of Neville and Plantagenet quartered on the counterpane, she knelt before her linenfold dower chest. Mole-like, she dug deep among the pale silks and yellowed linens until she found a scrap of fabric that looked as though it didn't belong there. Unfolding it, she revealed the bear and ragged staff banner of the Earl of Warwick, torn and dirtied with dark-brown smudges that could have been either mud or long-dried bloodstains.

"My father's banner picked up from the gory mire of Barnet field. Won't you look at it, Dickon? And here, this spur, souvenir of a young knight's first battle—fine gold—but look how it's bent where Edward of Lancaster's horse fell on it at Tewkesbury. It's of no further use now, but no matter, that. Its owner will require it no more. Grim reminders, you say? These men perished while seeking the very same thing you do now. Do you hope to fare any better than they did?"

He was shaken more than he cared to admit, but he could not take his eyes from her face, warmly colored by the intensity of her emotion. "It is mine by right," was the only answer he could give. For him, it was irrefutable in its logic.

"I don't dispute that," Anne said, "and never shall. I only dispute that you should wish it. What value is it, of what consequence, if you lose everything worth having in the gaining of it? Why, it's only a golden bauble, a toy for men to play with who should have put away such childish things long ago. I don't know how you have offended your lady mother. Perhaps I don't want to know. But before God, I know how you have offended me. How long has it been since you've sought my bed? Not since my first night in London before you learned Bishop Stillington's foul knowledge. Since then, in a fortnight, you are changed. I hardly know you now. Buckingham is more wife to you than I am. Why, it's always Buckingham's company you seek. He's forever on your arm or at your elbow, fawning, flattering, insinuating . . ."

She stopped suddenly, biting her tongue as she caught the fierceness in his eyes. "Leave Buckingham out of this," he said, his voice dangerously low. "He has nothing to do with it."

"Ah, but you're wrong there, Dickon. He has everything in the world to do with it."

"No, most merciful God, no!" he cried, seizing her by the shoulders. "I won't have you speak of him, I won't!"

She looked up at him, silent but unblinking. Fear struggled with the taunting knowledge in her wide, dark eyes. Her breath came in sharp, panting gasps. He could feel the blood pulsing through her resilient skin beneath his fingers, turning cool ivory to warm flame, the same soft skin she had so carelessly displayed to Lovell and Percy. Her infidelity and his own tormented him.

His mouth came down on hers, bruising hard, then traveled downward to the smooth curve of her neck and lower still to the flesh that swelled over the top of her bodice. He felt her body stiffen as she tried to push him away.

"No, Dickon, not like this. Not in anger."

He pinned her firmly in his arms. "Yea, lady," he murmured against her naked breast where he had roughly pushed away the soft stuff of her gown. "Haven't you just complained to me of neglect? If you would play the wanton, you shall play it with me."

Sweeping her up featherlight in his arms, he deposited her none too gently on the bed. He did not even bother to remove her dress, only pushed its skirts up around her waist and took her as if she were a tavern slut. He hardly heard the strangled little bleats of protest that came from her. He cared only for the coal-velvet blackness of oblivion and for relief from a hurt too great to be borne.

Later, Anne lay still beneath his weight, the rose-sprigged dress a twisted, sweat-sodden ruin beneath her. Her body ached from the unaccustomed invasion. Never before had he treated her like this. Always he had handled her as if she were the most delicate porcelain and would shatter at a touch. But she was tougher than he knew, and as she stroked his damp hair, she felt a strange content. She was far from understanding what had just happened, far from explaining the violent fit that had taken him, but one thing she did know. For the first time in nine years, she held like a vessel the seed of his body within her, the sacred Plantagenet seed to flower into new life. She would pray to her own St. Anne, mother of the Blessed Virgin, that it might be so.

Richard stirred against her. "Forgive me, Nan," he murmured. "I've behaved like a boar in truth."

She shook her head, and though he could not see it, she smiled. "There's nothing to forgive, my love."

"Ah, but there is," came the distant protest. "You don't know . . ."

"I know everything that needs to be known, and I still say there is nothing to forgive. Hush now and rest."

But he was already asleep, or at least he said no more. Like a milk-full babe, he lay with one hand cupping her breast in drowsy content.

$\mathfrak{C}$hapter 29

RICHARD WAS KING. Proclaimed by an act of Parliament, sealed by the will of his people, he had that day assumed the marble chair at Westminster.

Richard was king. That night, the hall of Baynard's Castle gleamed with the light of one thousand wax tapers, and there was feasting and drinking and rejoicing such as even that venerable vault had seldom witnessed. Rhenish and malmsey flowed like water; stewards scurried about, carrying huge platters of roast swan and oxen, saddles of hare, legs of lamb, lark pies, and the crowning achievement of the chef's art, an exotic cockyntryce, borne in from the kitchens and set before Richard with a flourish of justifiable pride. The cockyntryce was a strange beast and one quite unknown in nature. The front quarters of a pig and the hind quarters of a capon had been stitched together with surgical skill; stuffed with eggs, bread, and suet; roasted on a spit; then glazed with eggs and ginger, saffron and parsley.

"Royal meat indeed!" cheered Buckingham, raising his hanap.

Richard was flushed with wine and victory. His eyes glowed in the candle shine, the light catching the golden flecks against their darker blue. Gratefully, he returned the salute before attacking some of the exotic fantasy his carver set before him on the board. On his opposite side, next to Duchess Cecily, John Howard looked quite content also. Buckingham wondered, not for the first time, why he had been honored with a place at the high table when the other barons, including Stanley, sat at their own board below. Whatever the reason, Howard seemed well pleased with himself. He smiled a great deal and occasionally burst forth in rich, rollicking laughter, most uncommon in him, over some remark of the sharp-witted duchess.

Dame Cecily had not deigned to favor Buckingham with more than a icy glance, for all that he had apologized most profusely over the excesses of the preachers. And he found little Anne, who sat between him and Richard, a dull dinner companion. Small and shy as a field lark, despite her elevation in rank, she pushed the food around on her gilded plate as a child might, and the head that was so soon to wear a crown kept downcast eyes. In all that merry company, she alone seemed sad. God take these women who did not know when they were well-off!

Buckingham was left in comparative solitude with his own thoughts, and these made far from pleasant company. The past few days, filled with triumph as they had been, had also been fraught with near disaster. Richard's sudden coolness had hurt and perplexed him, and Buckingham considered that he had been positively unreasonable over the matter of the preachers. As if he, Henry Stafford, had manufactured that old scandal! Most decidedly, he had not; he had simply made use of it in a way that could only redound to Richard's benefit.

Reluctantly, he lived again through those moments of chagrin and discomfiture when, after a victorious session at Guildhall two days before, where he had expounded eloquently on the protector's rights and merits, he had been attacked by a grimly outspoken Richard. Perhaps he should have guessed something was amiss from the moment he had entered Crosby Place. Sumpter mules and wagons stood loaded in the courtyard; a press of porters filled the halls. Even Richard's great bed, carved on its headboard with scenes of the Holy Sepulcher, had been dismantled and was being carried down the steps. Buckingham felt very much like a salmon swimming against the current as he made his way to Richard's apartments. If he had any thought save for his own glowing report, he might have pondered this turn of events before he went further. Why should

Richard be leaving Crosby Place? Was he already planning a move to Westminster Palace?

Richard's reply had been clipped and brief. It was not Westminster he went to but Baynard's.

"Baynard's? That drafty old pile? But why?"

"Because I must seek to dissociate myself from those who would slander my mother's honor."

His pointed glance left little doubt of whom he spoke. For once at a loss for words, Buckingham stammered out an explanation. Richard would have none of it. He turned away to supervise the packing of his jewel chest. Buckingham had been left alone with Howard and Assheton who, a chessboard between them, had witnessed the scene. Howard's lips lifted in an involuntary smirk, while Assheton stroked his long chin and watched him rather intently. Both men, it seemed, were not at all unhappy to see him stumble.

Swallowing his pride, he had run after Richard, mumbling apologies, but Richard had cut him off. "You may apologize to York's duchess. She is the one you have offended."

Buckingham had left then without even mentioning the glorious triumph at Guildhall. Like a chastened schoolboy, he had pouted all the way back to his own mansion and might have remained there for days, sulking behind its walls, had not Percival pointed out the folly of crossing Richard further.

"He rides a swelling wave to the throne, a wave that you yourself have set in motion. Do you think you can leap so easily from its crest without being swamped beneath it? Think again. Later perhaps you may allow yourself the luxury of disaffection, but not now. Not yet."

He had been forced to admit the accuracy of Percival's assessment and, bitter tonic that it was, had gone before Parliament the very next day to extol Richard's virtues and hymn his praises. He had held them all in his sway from Bishop Russell, perched on his lord chancellor's woolsack, to the lowliest London apprentice who had managed to worm his way into the abbey chapter house that day. He began to wonder then if he could exercise such power on behalf of another, and one for whom at that moment his feelings were clearly ambivalent, what could he not do for himself?

He indulged such speculations because Richard was proving less and less tractable to his guidance. Henry Stafford had conceived of their climb to the crown as a joint venture, jointly undertaken and jointly shared. He had naturally expected to be consulted on all decisions. Imagine his utter astonishment that very day when Richard's first act upon assuming the marble throne of King's Bench at Westminster was to pardon Sir John Fogge, a Woodville cousin. Fogge had been languishing in prison since the night the queen's party fell from power. Richard had ordered him brought into the hall, a pale and wary figure who had every reason to expect he would be condemned for treason then and there. But no. Instead, Richard takes him by the hand, pardons him, and names him justice of the peace for Kent!

"I'd sooner appoint a fox to guard the hen house," protested the stunned Buckingham later.

The new king had shaken his head. "No, cousin. If I behave generously toward him, he will be loyal to me. Today I have ordered the executions of Rivers and his cohorts, but I would have their minor adherents reconciled to me. It's only a beginning, but you must understand that I am no longer the leader of a faction but the king of all England, including the Woodvilles."

Buckingham had not understood it then; he did not understand it now. An enemy was an enemy. Pardoning him and giving him a fancy title did not change that. The spoils of victory should be distributed among those of proven worth, such as himself and his men, not tossed before swine like John Fogge. Why, it was no more than a hopeful bribe to buy the man's allegiance—allegiance that would probably not be forthcoming anyway while Edward V and his brother still lived.

He shook his head in disbelief even now as a page offered him a bowl of scented water for dipping his fingers. The banquet was over. Butlers and sewers were clearing away plates from the high table while below other servants were dismantling the trestles. He had done small justice to the feast, but that hardly mattered. He had not been hungry anyway.

There were the usual entertainments that, in his present mood, appealed to him little more than had the food. Renard, Richard's minstrel, came in dressed like a troubadour, and after him followed a troop of jugglers and acrobats and a dancing bear, just as easily ignored. Then came the clowns. He was prepared to yawn through these as well. They began conventionally enough. One with a pig's bladder went about knighting with mock ceremony some who already boasted their golden spurs and a few who didn't, while another, a dwarf and horribly deformed, attempted to run off with their ladies. It was all mildly amusing but certainly not mind riveting, and Buckingham slumped back further still in his chair.

Suddenly, he sat bolt upright. One of the fools entered dressed in exact imitation of Richard and wearing a brown wig that curled about his shoulders. The physical resemblance was staggering. As he strutted about, he even held one shoulder higher than the other in recognition of the defect that had plagued Richard from boyhood. Just as staggering was his mimicry of Richard's behavior. All around the hall he went, toying with his paste rings and wooden dagger for all the world as if he had studied the new king's every movement, adopted his every mannerism. There was an uneasy murmur among the guests. How would Richard react to this imposter?

The other fools bore him a tinsel crown on a satin pillow and, with a great deal of exaggerated gesticulating, tried to prevail upon him to accept it. It was only too obvious that the fool-Richard's fingers itched toward the crown, that his whole being was drawn to it like iron filings to a magnet, but at the last moment, he backed away, suddenly coy, bashful as a courted maid.

The real Richard, high flown with wine and good humor, let out a hearty laugh, seeing only too clearly a mirror to the day's events. He had indeed refused the crown when it was first offered, like a bishop at his consecration must twice deny that he would be a bishop even though he has already paid lavishly for the papal bulls. He did not want to appear to be too eager to supplant his nephew, but no one had been misled. And now, at the sound of his merriment, there were titters and guffaws from the whole company. Buckingham's rich laughter rolled as freely as any. The fool was a wonder, after all, and Richard should not take this good-natured mockery amiss. Applause mingled with laughter as the fool-Richard once again was offered the crown and once more managed an even more reluctant refusal. Finally, after one more covert inspection of the object, he gingerly laid a hand on it and with increasing relish grasped it and set it on his brow. Well pleased with himself now, he admired his own reflection in a hand mirror as he capered around the hall, coming at last to the real Richard and bowing low with more thunderous applause in his ears.

Richard rose to his feet as did the entire company, but it seemed that the entertainment was not over. Into the hall trooped other mummers decked out in animal masks. With some regret, Buckingham was forced back into his seat. What was this then? He recognized a cat, a dog, a bewhiskered rat, an eagle with a fierce beak and blazing eyes, and no less than two lions—one in blue and the other in silver. The fool-king had donned a white boar mask and stood in the center of the group. So they represented Richard and his lords and knights then. The cat was Catesby and the rat Ratcliffe—that was obvious. And the dog, who but Lovell with his wolf dog badge and his spaniel eyes? The eagle would be Stanley, whose cognizance was the eagle displayed, and the blue and silver lions would represent Percy and Howard, respectively, fierce beasts in the service of the boar.

A very pretty display, Buckingham thought, yet his eye roved restlessly over the fools seeking for one he could tie to himself. Surely they could not have forgotten him. He was greater than all the rest put together. From the title of his dukedom, he could expect to be portrayed as a buck, a noble animal and an altogether fitting one to represent him. But though he searched for an antler mask, there was none to be seen. Then he heard a ripple of laughter from the far end of the hall, growing swiftly into a great wave of mirth as people stretched and craned their necks to see. It swept through the assembly like wind through a wheat field and laid it almost flat with laughter.

One of the fools came arrayed like a peacock in gaudy blue and green and gold, complete with a long train sewn all over with sequins and feathers like a tail. Their iridescence caught the candlelight, and they glowed like gems, sapphire, emerald, amber. Prinking, prancing, preening, the apparition strutted to the high table, swishing its tail for effect, stumbling at times over the outrageously long points of its slippers. Finding its way to the duke, it bowed low, its feathered crown bobbing above a grotesquely painted face, its train spread daintily around it like a fan. For a moment, it stood there, leering at Buckingham in solitary splendor. All its fellows, feigning fear or intense dislike as it passed, had dived for cover behind the ladies' skirts.

Buckingham felt his cheeks crimson as he managed a dry chuckle. "My lord," he muttered to Richard as the thing retreated, "this is an outrage! They are mocking you and all your nobles. Surely they go too far."

Richard shook his head. He was enjoying himself immensely and had in fact almost split a seam in his new cloth-of-gold doublet laughing at the antics of the peacock. "No, Harry, it's only sport and rare sport at that. You yourself were laughing earlier. Don't deny it. In their way, they honor us, these fools. Have another cup of wine, and you'll be laughing again soon enough."

The troop had at last finished their performance and stood with hands linked before the dais, ready to take their final bows. Richard motioned to the one who had played himself. "Tell me, sirrah, do you have anywhere in your menagerie a ducal coronet for your silver lion?"

The quick-witted knave blinked in surprise but hesitated only a moment before removing his tinsel crown and placing it on the head of the kneeling lion. There was a collective gasp of astonishment from the guests then loud applause as Richard stood, his arm about the shoulder of John Howard, his new duke.

Norfolk, Buckingham thought, *it has to be Norfolk that Richard is giving away.* Howard was kin to the Mowbrays, hereditary dukes of Norfolk, on his mother's side. *Distant kin,* a voice in his mind reiterated, *and by no stretch of the imagination in line for the duchy.* And now he, Henry Stafford, descendant in the direct male line from Edward III, would be forced to treat this East Anglian upstart as an equal. Like the gross prancing of the peacock, it smacked of intolerable insult.

He had no idea how long he sat there in stunned silence, but he came to at last at the touch of a familiar hand on his shoulder. Turning, he met Richard's gently inquisitive gaze. "Come, Harry, join me in my privy chamber for a while. I'm not quite ready for bed and would be glad of your company."

Buckingham nodded assent. "Your Grace knows that I am yours to command." If there was an edge to his voice, Richard chose to ignore it.

Indeed the king was almost apologetic when they reached his apartments. As if by prearrangement, they were left alone except for the single page who attended Richard, slipping off the cloth-of-gold doublet heavily encrusted with jewels and replacing it with a dressing gown of violet tissue silk.

"By the rood, what a relief!" Richard breathed once rid of the magnificent costume. "It's too tight and a trifle overstiff. I felt like a wax doll inside it."

The page retired, and they were quite alone. There was not yet the ceremony that attended the disrobing and bedding of a king, the chamberlains and knights and squires of the body, the gentlemen ushers and yeomen of the bedchamber, each with his own function to perform. Soon Richard would be quite removed from him, hidden behind a veil of ceremony and protocol. Intimate moments like this would cease altogether.

The casement was open to the summer night. Below he heard the sounds of barges being pushed away from the docks as the banquet goers made for their own dwellings. Laughter and parting cries and boatmen's shouts came to him on warm air bearing the salty scent of the incoming tide. He listened to the steady plop of oars dipping in the current and in the near dark watched lanterns bobbing on bow and stern of the departing vessels. And then it was quite dark, quite still. There was only the gentle slap of the Thames against the castle moorings.

"Would you like an almond cake?" Richard asked. "I noticed you ate precious little at dinner. Was the food not to your liking?"

"I had no appetite for it," Buckingham replied truthfully. And then, wearily, he added, "What do you want of me, Your Grace?"

"'Want,' Harry? A strange choice of words. Must a man want something to seek the company of his friend?"

"Privacy is a dearly bought commodity for a king, yet we two have it aplenty. Don't be devious with me, Dickon. It doesn't become you."

"Very well then. I believe I owe you an explanation if not an apology for some of this day's events."

Buckingham shrugged, struggling to make his voice light. "You are the king. It has always been my understanding that a king may do as he pleases."

Richard nodded. "Precisely so, or at least so I saw it. I would have taken your advice on these matters as I have on everything else, and yet I must learn to follow my own counsel."

"The royal prerogative," Buckingham replied, accepting a goblet of sweet sack from Richard's hand while ignoring the almond cakes. Richard was sobering slightly, losing the pink flush that had suffused his sallow cheeks while keeping intact the good humor engendered by wine and triumph. He was obviously feeling somewhat contrite, and Buckingham regarded him with new interest. Perhaps some of Richard's regret could be turned to Harry Stafford's advantage. This could be the time to raise the two issues that were most important to him, including the one that was nearest to his heart.

"I hope the fools didn't offend you too much," Richard was saying. "Now that I think about it, they may have gone too far."

Buckingham said, "I was only concerned for Your Grace. Some of their mimicry of you and your closest adherents seemed to be in questionable taste. That's all."

"'All,' Harry?" Richard replied with a teasing smile. "Strange that you uttered no protest until you yourself came under attack, if such it was. These fools exaggerate everything to suit their ends. You know that. But let it pass. It is Howard and the duchy of Norfolk I particularly wish to discuss with you. As you know, he has served me well, and I've long wished to reward him in like measure. Yet, I didn't mean to blurt it out as I did before the entire company without telling you first. I'm afraid it was the wine and the emotion of the evening that spoke."

Buckingham did not respond, so Richard continued, "It's a pity that the flower of our nobility has been so badly crushed by these wars between York and Lancaster. For years now, we've been at each other's throats like dogs who would tear one another to pieces. How well we have succeeded! You and my brother-in-law of Suffolk are the only dukes left in the realm. And Norfolk's rich duchy was going begging. Howard didn't ask me for it, not outright, but I knew he judged it a not-inappropriate grant. And I thought myself well served to reward him. Surely you can understand that."

"I understand, sire. The gift is rich, and no doubt . . . no doubt John Howard has earned . . . some recompense."

"Some, but not all. Eh, Harry?"

"He is of low birth."

"His mother was a cousin of the Mowbrays."

"And his father?"

"Of good stock."

"But scarcely noble."

They bantered back and forth, feinting at each other like two boxers. At last, Richard conceded. "No, not noble, but he is a man I can trust, a man I myself have lifted up. These are the men I would have around me, men who owe to me their rank and status and who will therefore be true to me, my men entire. I would not be betrayed by . . . by another overmighty Hastings."

"And I, Dickon? What of me?"

Richard laughed a little nervously in his throat then grew solemn, considering. "Well, I can hardly make you a duke when you are one already. Nor can I reward you as you deserve for all your service to me. I fear I am in your debt and not the other way round. What would you have me do? Empty the royal coffers to heap honors on you? The debt I owe you can never be repaid."

"The service itself is payment," Buckingham said, tracing the rim of his cup with one forefinger, "and the love of a prince is treasure beyond rubies."

Richard smiled uncertainly as if the word *love* had evoked memories he considered best forgotten. A night breeze stirred the curtain of the casement and fanned his cheek. He shifted in his chair and looked at Buckingham. "Nonetheless, there should be something I can do. Come, Harry, I'm in a generous mood tonight, and I see you are brooding. It's a sight that grieves me deeply. Come, name what you will, anything you wish, and I will try to grant it."

"There is nothing . . ."

"Nothing? Ah, I know you better than that."

"Why then since you ask me, I have a fancy of sorts to possess the de Bohun lands. I am, as you recall, in possession of half of them through my mother, but the other half . . . the other half was held by poor, mad Harry VI and reverted to the crown under his attainder."

"And you would have the whole?"

"If you see fit."

"They are not altogether mine to grant," Richard replied. "Parliament attainted old Henry and all his heirs. Parliament must dispose of the lands."

"But you have some influence?"

"Influence? Yes, of course. Or so I should think, though I must say that it amuses me a little that your claim rests on your family ties to Lancaster."

Buckingham would have protested this observation when Richard held up his hand in surrender. "Ah, but let it be. The better shall those lands serve the cause of York. Granted, Harry, so far as it lies in my power. I'll have Kendall draw up the letters patent in the morning."

Buckingham murmured his gratitude, but his voice trailed off, a tenuous thread in the semidarkness.

"Is there something else?" Richard asked, indulgent.

"There is . . . ah . . . one more thing, sire, though it isn't riches or titles or lands . . . or anything of that sort. Call it, if you will, a pledge of our friendship, a joining of our blood in the strongest, most intimate of ties."

Richard faltered in the act of raising his hanap. He held it poised in midair, suspended as he was himself. "Harry . . ."

"No, Dickon, don't refuse me until you've heard me out. You have a son and I a daughter of like age."

Richard's shoulders sagged in such obvious relief that for a moment Buckingham thought he would grant the boon, any boon, as long as it was not the one thing he most feared. "And you would have them trothplight?"

"Yes," Buckingham replied, leaning forward in anticipation. "What could be better? Anne is a likely enough child—oh, aye, a little bashful now, but she'll be a beauty someday. And her dowry won't shame her either. All the de Bohun lands go with her and more besides, all into your hands. A fitting bride for any prince. Come, what do you say?"

Richard could hear from the tremor in the duke's voice how much this request meant to him. He looked up into Buckingham's eager face and slowly, very slowly—because he did not wish to refuse—shook his head.

"A fitting bride for any prince? Holy Jesu, I'm sure of that. And if I were not the king, if Ned were not my only heir, nothing would give me greater pleasure."

"If you were not . . . if he were not . . . you're speaking in riddles. Are you trying to tell me that my daughter isn't worthy to be Queen of England? Many less worthy have sat in that seat, believe me."

The anger was building swift and sure, but Richard held fast. "It's hardly a question of worth nor even of personal preference. The marriage of a prince, of the heir to the throne, is a delicate matter dictated by necessity and vouchsafed by treaties. It isn't families who are joined here but nations. I . . . I had thought to marry Ned to a princess of France."

"But you have an English queen," Buckingham protested. "Don't tell me that Anne Neville is a hindrance to you or that you sought to join nations by your match."

"Splendor of God, Harry!" cried Richard, exasperated. "You're playing the very mule for obstinacy. My situation was not the same, and you know it. When I married Anne, I had no expectation of becoming king and therefore no reason to behave like one. Now everything is changed. If this had not happened, I would gladly have wed my son to your daughter and counted the match most fortunate. But then," he added, his voice dropping, "I wonder if you would have asked."

Buckingham lowered his gaze in the face of this quiet accusation. He had lost, and he knew it. It was gone, the secret dream he had nourished in his heart through all the past weeks. The natural and logical consummation of all his hopes, it had seemed to him once, and adequate compensation for his lost access to Richard's bed. His daughter, Princess of Wales and, eventually, Queen of England. In due course, his grandson and Richard's, King of England. Fled now, perished on the breath of the night breeze. Such was the gratitude of princes.

Far away, upriver, the bells of the Clochard at Westminster chimed the hour. Closer to them, Bow Bell tolled its deep reply. Its dying echo faded into the night. Buckingham saw that the candles had burned down to their nub ends and were guttering in their sconces.

"Midnight," Richard said. "It's gotten late, and I must be up at dawn."

"And I as well," Buckingham said with forced lightness. "There is so much to be done in the next ten days—a coronation to prepare, a king to crown."

"You don't hold it against me that I have refused you?" Richard questioned, taking the duke's hand in both of his own. "I would hate to think—"

"Hold it against you?" Buckingham echoed, incredulous. "How could I ever do that?" He flashed Richard a radiant smile then took his leave, stepping past the watchful men-at-arms and the mastiffs that guarded the king's door, striding down the dim corridors of the silent castle where torches flared in their niches and only the sentries stirred. They let him pass without a word, down the river steps to dockside where his knights and his barge awaited him, flying its emblem of the burning wheel. He took his cushioned seat in the vessel's stern, but as the oars dipped into the dark current, he spoke to no one, and no one spoke to him. He was not smiling anymore.

Chapter 30

IT HAD BEEN raining all morning—not a driving, torrential rain (there might have been some relief in that), but a melancholy sort of mizzling, enough to keep Morton a prisoner in his room in Buckingham's mansion. He had paced the oak floor of that room a hundred times at least, restless as an old caged lion, pausing at the end of each round to look down on the garden that the rain had forbidden to him. On sunny days, his imprisonment was at least bearable. He could sit on the stone bench under the great willow and listen to the city noises just beyond the garden wall. The rattling of a cart on the cobbles, the cry of a hawker, the lowered voices of men deep in conversation: these were music to his straining ears. As a free man, he had dearly loved to bustle about London busy with this matter and that always in the thick of activity. It was the harshest restriction of his confinement that he could no longer do so; he could only listen to other men more fortunate than he, and on rainy days, he could not do even that.

Not that the terms of his imprisonment were particularly harsh. The room provided to him was a vast improvement over the small, dank Tower cell of his early incarceration. The duke's servants who attended him were unfailingly courteous though not overly informative, and even Buckingham himself treated him with a polite, deferential indifference.

Buckingham. Now there was food for thought. After a fortnight in the duke's household, Morton confessed that he was puzzled. At meals in the hall, he marked his host's downcast moods and long brooding silences, strange indeed in one who had scored such a great triumph. Although Morton seldom saw him at other times and then never alone, this change in Buckingham's demeanor occupied much of his thought. He had expected to find a gloating braggart as gorged with honors as a glutton with meat, but he had encountered instead a sulking adolescent, chafing under injuries unknown and as yet unguessed at. Very well, if there was trouble between the boar and his closest adherent, it could only play into Morton's own hands eventually.

The sound of footsteps in the corridor outside brought him back to reality. Quickly, he made for the room's one comfortable chair, picked up the open breviary he had hitherto ignored and composed his face into a pious mask.

He hardly needed to have bothered. Behind the shoulder of the page who opened the door was the welcome, familiar face of Lady Stanley.

"Margaret, my dear!" he cried, jumping up and catching both of her hands in his. "How good of you to come and cheer my prison house!"

She watched as the door clicked shut behind the retreating page. "I thought it possible that you might have need of cheering. This can't be easy for you."

He shrugged with more indifference than he felt. "Yes, but what of it? I have known reversals before and lived to tell the tale. In any case, I always welcome your company, Meg, as well you know, but isn't it a little dangerous for you to seek mine?"

She made an impatient gesture with her hands. "Perhaps . . . no, I think not. My lord stands high now in Richard's favor. He scarcely ever leaves his side. He is to carry the constable's mace at the coronation, while I"—she danced a little mincing step—"I am to bear the queen's train. Did you know that?"

Morton looked at her with unconcealed amusement. As always, she was plainly, even severely dressed in the dark-gray wool that declared the ascetic in her, but the lines of her long, narrow face were not far from breaking into open laughter, a luxury she seldom allowed herself.

"So they've made a good Yorkist out of you at last?"

She grimaced. "No, not that. Hardly that. It's just an honor I haven't the means to refuse. After all, Richard is king."

Morton was thoughtful for a long moment, and when he spoke the words came out slowly as if he were measuring each one. "Yes . . . Richard is king, though I think that fact needn't alarm either of us unnecessarily."

Margaret's eyebrows arched her surprise. "I find it strange for you to say so, John, when your own imprisonment here is a direct result of your efforts to keep him from the throne."

"Misguided efforts as I see it now. I should rather have let him use my back as a footstool to climb to it."

She shook her head. "I don't understand you. Have *you* turned to York in your dotage?"

"I do what I can where I can, Meg, you know that. But the heart that beats in this bosom is as true to the red rose of Lancaster as any heart ever was. Only listen," he added, leaning closer and dropping his voice to a whisper. "When the boar seized the throne from his nephew, it was the first breach in years in the front of York. Not since Warwick's defection has opportunity beckoned so clearly to us."

The light of sudden understanding dawned in Margaret's eyes. "But of course! Was I so blinded by his honors? How dense of me not to see it."

"I didn't see it either, not till this moment. We have become lax of late, Meg. We have grown almost accustomed to the dominion of York. Yet I think it's not too late. The boar is not secure on his throne. There are many elements of dissatisfaction in the land that cry for a leader, many who find Bishop Stillington's tale a bit too pat, a little too contrived to fit the circumstances."

"Parliament believed it," Margaret reminded him. "When they drafted *Titulus Regis*, they swallowed it whole."

"And Parliament will be only too glad to revoke it when the time comes."

"But how are we to go about it? How do we bring together all those discords and press them into a single mold? That won't be easy, I warrant you."

"No, my dear, but it can be done. I don't know how yet, but I believe we shall both live to see your son King of England."

Margaret clapped her hands in delight. "Do you really think so? Oh, I pray you're right. My poor Harry is growing weary of his exile. It's high time he came home to his rightful inheritance."

Morton found her enthusiasm infectious. He returned her smile readily. "And that he shall, lady, I promise you. That he shall."

Chapter 31

THE DAY BEFORE the coronation dawned sultry and hot. It was the fifth day of July and high summer, normally a time when any who could afford it left the stinking, sweltering, plague-infested capital for manors in the green countryside. This year, no one had done so.

Circumstance had decreed that Richard be crowned at this particularly inappropriate time, and Richard had bowed to circumstance. Since he had come to the crown by the postern gate, he could not long delay in taking it to himself. Anointed and crowned monarchs were not so easily set aside as those who had not yet received that unction. It was a fact he had used to his own advantage in the deposition of Edward V, but it was a two-edged sword that another might also use against him, hence the unrelenting—some would say indecent—haste with which the coronation was proceeding. He had been declared King of England and of France and Lord of Ireland only ten days before.

The heat of summer was stifling in the royal bedchamber of the Tower. He was sweating profusely as Piers Curteys, master of the Royal Wardrobe, and Francis Lovell, his new lord chamberlain, dressed him in royal finery for the procession through London to Westminster, where he would spend the night. This progress was almost as vital a part of the coronation ritual as the crowning itself and demanded little less in the way of magnificence: hose and shirt, coat and surcoat, mantle and hood, all of heavy crimson satin; doublet and stomacher of blue cloth-of-gold wrought with nets and pineapples; a tabard of white sarcenet, a coif of lawn; shoes covered with crimson cloth-of-gold; a hat of estate with beak in front and rolled brim behind; and over all, a robe of crimson velvet embroidered with gold and furred with miniver.

"Splendor of God!" Richard exclaimed as they placed the robe around his shoulders. "This would all be well enough if it were December and snow was flying in the yard, but surely we might dispense with some of it today."

Piers Curteys rose from the floor, where he had adjusted the train. Beneath his reddened eyes, there were deep, dark circles. Richard instantly regretted the criticism, for he knew that the master of the Royal Wardrobe had slept hardly at all in the past two weeks. "I would apologize for the heat, sire, if it were in my power to control it. Since it is not, I still would not have you less regally arrayed than any of your predecessors."

"Yes, of course," Richard acknowledged, "though I wonder if any of my predecessors have toppled in a royal faint. I should hate to be the first."

Curteys managed a smile as he arranged a tassel on Richard's shoulder.

Lovell said, "I've known you a long time, sire, and have never known you to faint. You must bear your heavy finery somehow. It is the custom."

It is the custom. Richard had heard those words too often of late, always resounding to his immediate discomfort. Strange how he had never before realized how much the life of a king was bound and circumscribed by convention. He was almost a prisoner in his own palace, hedged in by the hundreds of servants who attended him as much as by the masonry of the palace walls. Nor could he fail to observe every jot and iota of the custom when he had yet to prove himself its rightful heir.

At last, they were finished with him and Curteys stood back to admire his handiwork. "I have never seen anyone look more regal," he declared, "even your late brother in his day." Richard thought this was outrageous flattery until he stood before the glass and noted how the peaked cap and the long unbroken line of the robe added inches to his height and concealed the defects of his bearing.

"In truth, every inch of him a king."

He had not heard Buckingham enter, yet somehow he was there in the same room with them, and the words too well remembered had tripped easily from his lips.

"And you, noble cousin, look little less than a king yourself." Richard turned to greet the duke and to acknowledge his low bow. Buckingham wore blue velvet, doublet and coat, surcoat and robe, embroidered all over in gold thread with flaming cartwheels. He looked splendid. In his right hand, he clasped the white wand of the lord high steward.

"Everything is ready below, sire," Buckingham said, lifting the wand lightly, "whenever you give the signal to depart."

Richard could hear the sounds of shouting and laughter from the great hall below, where the nobles and knights who would ride with him in the procession were gathered. Like Buckingham, they awaited the royal pleasure. Everyone was waiting for him. Suddenly, Richard felt himself the victim of all this pomp rather than its focus. It was Buckingham who was the architect, the genius of the coronation, as he had been of Richard's ascension. And no one, not even the king himself, would dare wrest from him the shining moment of his triumph.

Howard had tried. He had claimed the hereditary right to the lord high stewardship that the Mowbrays as Dukes of Norfolk had long enjoyed and, with it, the privilege of being the first officer of the coronation. Buckingham had balked. He might not have been able to prevent the ducal coronet that graced Howard's brow or the silver belt that girdled his eldest son's waist as Earl of Surrey, but he would not yield the white wand nor relinquish his jurisdiction over the ceremonies. Though Howard might become lord high steward after it was all over, he must content himself with being mere Earl Marshall for the present and with bearing the crown in tomorrow's walking procession to Westminster Abbey. High enough honors, Buckingham had implied, for the son of an East Anglian squire.

Richard had finally acquiesced to Buckingham's demands and had attempted to placate his new Duke of Norfolk as best he could. It troubled him, this rift between his two most powerful adherents. Such stubbornness he had come to expect from Buckingham, but Howard had shown a streak of obstinacy that was at least its equal. Now the two men scarcely spoke to each other. Richard wondered where it would end.

"Come, sire," Buckingham beckoned to him from the window. "Come, look below. It's quite a sight to behold. The heralds and the horses, the lord mayor and his aldermen, all the banners flying—" Suddenly, he stopped, his handsome face contorted with shock and displeasure. "What deviltry is this? How dare they?" His voice shook with fury.

Richard did not need to ask what caused the duke such distress. He knew. Heavily, beneath the weight of the regalia and his own sinking heart, he moved to the window and looked down on two youths clad in simple white linen tunics. They stood in sharp contrast to the bright magnificence a few feet away from them, and seemingly oblivious to it, they shot at the butt on the Tower Green.

Richard had initiated no contact with his nephews since he had entered the Tower several days before. He had, of course, ordered their removal from the royal apartments prior to his arrival, and they were now quite comfortably installed—yes, he had made certain of that—in the Garden Tower, so called because it fronted on the constable's garden. He had hoped they would make use of it for their recreation, but persistently, doggedly, Edward had chosen the vast green in full view of the royal apartments.

"They come here every day," Richard explained, "to use the butt . . ."

"But today of all days, they should have been kept indoors," Buckingham sputtered. "Someone will be flogged for this. I'll have the bastards hauled away and locked up safely till this is over."

Richard laid a gloved hand, stiff with seed pearls, on his sleeve. "Wait, cousin. This is their home now, after all, while I'm only a temporary and most unwelcome intruder. If I could have avoided this stay here . . ."

"Nonsense," Buckingham snapped. "Kings must lodge here before they are crowned. It's the custom. And as for those two interlopers . . ." He began to draw the curtain, but Richard stayed his hand.

"No. I must be able to bear the watching."

"Nor are you the only one who watches. Look how the people take them in! Why, the older one seems almost to exhibit himself. Every movement of his body cries out for pity from heaven and earth and proclaims you a tyrant and usurper."

Richard flinched, but he could not doubt the accuracy of that assessment. Edward moved listlessly, seldom bothering even to aim his arrows, yet every line of his body was stamped with purposeful intent. Never had he performed before a larger audience. Pressed against the portcullis were the faces of a multitude of people, most of whom had been drawn by preparations for the procession but whose attention was now riveted on the slight, plainly dressed figures of Edward's two dispossessed heirs. Abruptly, Richard drew the curtain.

"They are dangerous, sire, the way they attract the rabble."

"They are only boys and secure enough here. They can do no harm."

Buckingham shook his head. "There is power in them yet."

"What do you suggest I do with them then? Restrict their freedom even more? Not allow them even their small games on the green?"

The duke's face was bland, impenetrable. "I suggest nothing, sire. I simply made an observation."

"I could have them removed to the north," Richard said slowly. "To Pontefract or Sheriff Hutton."

"Yes, . . . or dispose of them in some other fashion."

"I don't like the sound of that!" Richard bellowed so loudly that, across the room, Piers Curteys dropped a bolt of scarlet cloth he was carrying. "No harm shall come to them," Richard added, much lower. "I swore it on my brother's grave."

"Then they may harm you."

"I shall have to take that chance," Richard said, pointedly turning away and ignoring Buckingham's cluck of disapproval as he made for the door and the yard below. "Come, Harry. Let's get this over with."

In the dim transept crossing of Westminster Abbey, light filtered down from the two giant rose windows in subtle, jewel-like shafts. On the dais, magnificent in alb and stola, mitre and chasuble, Thomas Bourchier, archbishop of Canterbury, stood, flanked by the bishop of London and the abbot of Westminster, and prayed that neither his fellow prelates nor the mighty congregation in the nave would know how much his heart misgave him. Soon, very soon, he would crown a King of England even though he himself was not convinced that the man who would shortly be presented for that consecration was the one who was rightly entitled to it. Bourchier had held long debate within himself and had spent painful hours on arthritic knees in his private chapel in Lambeth Palace, agonizing over whether he should be here at all. To refuse would be akin to treason. To refuse might well mean he could end his long years of service incarcerated in the Tower dungeon or worse. On the other hand, to accept might be a sin in the sight of God.

Sadly, there were many churchmen who cared more for political expediency than divine guidance, but Thomas Bourchier was not one of them. For all the power and panoply of his position, he had about him an ascetic streak, clearly engraved in the leanness of his face and in the thin, high-bridged nose. But though he had prayed ceaselessly on the matter before him, no answer had come. He was forced to revert instead to what he knew of Richard as a boy and as a man. There had never been deceit in the boy; could the man then be trusted? Or had ambition eaten him up inside as it had others of his house? Stillington, a fellow cleric, had been swift to corroborate Richard's claim, but Stillington lacked a certain strength of character. He was mild, almost timid. Perhaps his words had been twisted until they bore little resemblance to the facts. Bourchier shook his head slightly, still uncertain. The moment of truth drew nearer.

The procession was entering the abbey now; the organ bellowed a loud crescendo as the monks voices in the choir soared in a great "Te Deum." They came to the altar on a narrow ribbon of red satin—

the heralds and the bishops, the knights and the nobles handpicked by the new king for this moment's honor. The hawk-like Earl of Northumberland, Richard's rival for power in the north, came first, carrying the pointless sword of mercy. Bourchier thought it was a rather unlikely choice and more hopeful than prophetic. Then came Lord Stanley with the mace of lord high constable, though he did not possess the office.

Behind him were the others, old friends and relatives of Richard whose presence was more to be expected: the Earl of Kent and Viscount Lovell with the pointed swords of justice; Richard's brother-in-law, the Duke of Suffolk, with the scepter; and his nephew the Earl of Lincoln with the orb. Then came the newly installed Earl of Surrey bearing the sword of state, held upright in its scabbard, while the earl's father, the Duke of Norfolk, came last, balancing the heavy weight of St. Edward's crown on a purple cushion.

There was a pause before Richard entered the abbey. From a distance, he seemed even smaller than he was, dwarfed by the grandeur that had preceded and attended him. He walked beneath a canopy supported by the wardens of the Cinque Ports, large men all. On either side of him was a bishop: Durham on the right and, appropriately, Bath and Wells on the left. Behind him, clutching the ermine robe of state as if he would never let it go, came the Duke of Buckingham.

Bourchier's tongue caught between his teeth, his throat thickened. Here was the moment come upon him when he must either accept or reject the royal charge. Unashamedly, his eyes sought Richard's face. He knew now that if he found there the faintest hint of triumph or smug satisfaction, he would divest himself of his archbishop's regalia and flee the abbey. They could bring out Rotherham to do the job. Thoroughly chastened and eager to ingratiate himself with the new sovereign, he would not refuse.

Richard's eyes were lowered as he approached the dais, but he raised them to take in Bourchier's frankly appraising stare. Behind the archbishop, something else caught his eye: the oak coronation chair with its painted back and gilded arms and, beneath it, oddly humble in the center of the coronation panoply, the Stone of Scone, reputed to be the rock where Jacob had rested his head when he dreamed of angels. Suddenly, Richard was filled with awe at both the enormity of the occasion and his own unworthiness. He moved as if he feared the thing he sought, as if he were drawn to this divine unction almost against his will.

And so, if Bourchier's voice faltered as he took Richard to the four corners of the dais and presented him to the congregation, if he halted and stumbled as he mouthed the words of the formula, it was perhaps not so much from doubt of the words he spoke as from the emotion of the moment.

"Here present is Richard, rightful and undoubted inheritor—" his voice broke, he swallowed and went on, "by the laws of God and man, to the crown and royal dignity of this realm of England, France, and Ireland. Will you serve him at this time and give your wills and assent to the same unction and coronation?"

"Yea, yea," came the ringing affirmation. "So be it. King Richard, King Richard!" It remained for him, Thomas Bourchier, servant of God and of man, to set the crown on his head.

Finally, it was over. Richard had been disrobed from the waist up; anointed on forehead, breast and shoulder, back and elbow with holy oil from the eagle-shaped ampulla; dressed once more in even finer raiment; presented with gloves and spurs, orb and scepter; had been crowned; then had received the homage of his lords temporal and spiritual as he sat in the coronation chair. Afterward, he had heard a lengthy mass. And now, fully five hours after entering the abbey, he sank exhausted onto a bench in the royal apartments of the palace and tried not to think of the hours of banqueting and merry-making that lay ahead of him in Westminster Hall.

"Well, it's done," he said to Anne.

"Yes," she replied wearily. "Thank God for that. The crown is heavy." She removed the glittering circlet from her dark hair and set it before her on the table. They were alone, sharing the only moment of privacy they were likely to enjoy in that busy, emotion-charged day.

Richard looked at her as if seeing her for the first time. Her eyes looked unnaturally dark, fiery dark, in her white face.

"Are you ill, Nan?"

She gave him a dry chuckle. "Would it matter if I were? It wouldn't do, I think, for the queen to miss the coronation banquet." Then to his look of concern, she added, "Oh, I'm all right. You mustn't worry. The abbey was hot, the ceremony long. I hadn't realized. I have a small headache, that's all."

Richard was not convinced. He had insisted that she share almost as an equal in the ceremony. With him, she had been anointed, with him presented her own objects of the royal regalia, with him she had been crowned. Now he wondered if he had not used her selfishly as a bulwark against the loneliness and isolation that came with his new status. Worse, it seemed he had pushed her meager stamina to its limits. She had grown thinner and more frail in the past month; her face had a blurred, ethereal look as if she were melting away before his eyes.

He crossed the floor and drew her gently to him. "I don't think London agrees with you, Nan. I confess, I too find it a little overwhelming, but we can leave it soon, I think."

Her eyes searched his face. "Where would we go? To Windsor?"

"Further than that. I was thinking of a royal progress. We should show ourselves to our subjects, you know, and they are not all in London. There are in fact a considerable number in the north."

Her eyes shone now with excitement. "Oh, Dickon! Do you mean Middleham?"

"Where else, lady?" he asked laughing. "Where else? Don't you know that I miss the treasure of Middleham almost as much as you do?" He was referring, of course, to their son, Ned, who had not been strong enough to make the journey to London. He stroked her cheek and bent to kiss her lightly on the lips.

Suddenly, she drew back. "Oh, blessed St. Mary!" she cried, clapping a hand to her mouth. "I've almost forgotten!"

"Forgotten what?" he asked uncertainly.

"I have a gift for you," she said. "A coronation gift." She was like a small bird with her quick, darting motions. Running to the wardrobe, she brought it out, a wealth of maroon velvet and white damask spilling over her small arms. Richard saw white roses and the triple sons of York.

"It is . . . magnificent!" he exclaimed, holding up the robe. "But where, how did you have it made?"

"I prevailed upon Piers Curteys to make it for me."

"Then you are a wizard, lady," Richard said as he examined the fine stitchery. "Or he is, for I don't know where he found the time."

"He dared not refuse his queen," said Anne with mock hauteur. "Oh, do put it on, Dickon. I'm most anxious to see how it fits."

He needed little prompting. It fit perfectly, sloping gently over the shoulders, hem barely brushing the floor. He still wore his crown, not the heavy state crown of St. Edward that had been placed on his head in the abbey, but a lighter, smaller one centered with the huge uncut stone known as the Black Prince's Ruby. It glowed back at him from the mirror, and the shade of the robe almost exactly matched it.

"Now at last," he said lightly, "I shall be a match for Buckingham."

Anne did not share his laughter. She bit her lip, and her face, so animated a moment ago, fell. "I wouldn't care to rival him," she said coldly.

"But, Anne—"

"No, let me speak. I fear the man, fear him for your sake even if you do not. When you were crowned today, he wrenched his head away as if he couldn't bear the sight. By the mass, Dickon, I saw him. Others did too. There will be talk of it in London tonight, and it will be true."

Richard sighed. Perhaps he had been lax in rewarding the duke. Perhaps he had chided him too heavily for his various misdemeanors. Perhaps he had offended him by raising Howard so high and by refusing to assent to the marriage of their children. Buckingham sought the office of lord high constable. Very well, he could have it, the highest military post in the realm. And something else he must have too, some mark of favor so high, some gift so rare he would be bound to Richard forever.

Anne was watching him, waiting for his answer, but there was none to give her. "Come along," he said wearily. "I'm afraid you must don your coronet once more, and we must be off to the banquet."

Two puppets commanded to perform under the supervision of hundreds of prying eyes, he thought, but he did not tell her that.

While she dutifully set the diadem back on her head, Richard removed his new robe and replaced it with the other, the one in which he had left the abbey. He noticed the sudden, quickly veiled hurt in her eyes that he had not chosen to wear her gift instead, but he could not tell her the reason. How could he explain the way her words had cut him, all the more so because he knew them to be true? The robe was a reminder of a fact he could not face unless and until he was driven to it.

Chapter 32

John Morton sat in his favorite spot in Buckingham's garden. The dinner hour had just passed, and he was well sated. Leaning back against the trunk of an ancient willow, his hands clasped lightly across his belly, he appeared to doze without actually doing so.

It was a peaceful spot, and he was not blind to its charms. The distant murmur of the city came to him faint and far away from beyond the high garden wall. More loudly in his ears sounded the noontime quiet: the whir of a locust, the chirp of a nearby cricket, the bottle-blue hum of a dragonfly suspended. Beyond the swaying fronds of the willow lay a small pond that floated between reed-fringed banks like a brilliant sun-washed gem. He watched it now lazily from beneath half-lowered lids: the glide of a white swan rippling the mirror surface, the pink cups of water lilies floating like dreams and, close to shore, a speckled, rainbow-hued carp that looked at him balefully with one cold eye from the shadow of a lily pad. He watched its fat, sleek, undulating body as he had for days now, wondering if he ought to return to the house for a hook and line then thought better of it when a frog plopped into the water nearby and the fish turned tail and vanished.

Beyond the tiny lake, well-clipped lawns stretched away to the yew and boxwood hedges that bordered the extensive rose gardens. Until quite recently, those lawns had been the special domain of a magnificent flock of peafowl. They had kept him amused for hours with their raucous cries, their battles, their matings, and with the shimmering iridescence of their spreading tails. Then suddenly they had vanished from the gardens, only to reappear the next day on the dinner table, delectably seasoned perhaps but not quite to Morton's taste. Surely the duke's purse was not in such a sorry state that he was reduced to killing off his household pets for food! Perhaps that extravagant gesture, the taking on of Hastings's retainers, had proven to be too much, even for him. But no. Further observation had convinced Morton that there was nothing whatever wrong with Buckingham's finances. If anything, he seemed to be growing steadily more wealthy or at least more conspicuous with his wealth.

The whole affair remained an unsolved mystery, one of the many that drew Morton's interest. Since Margaret Stanley's visit, his life had taken on meaning and purpose once more. Far from resenting his imprisonment, he now saw it as a most fortuitous opportunity. Beneath the facade of the sleepy, laconic dreamer, the wheels of his mind were turning with well-oiled precision. Already he had observed much and made note of it for future reference.

He saw that the carp had returned to its spot beneath the lily pad. "We are alike, old fish, are we not?" he whispered. "Even when we appear to slumber, we are still wary. But I'll catch you yet if I can."

Then a shadow passed over the pond edge, and once more Morton watched his quarry shiver away to deeper water. He sighed. Perhaps tomorrow.

He looked up to see what had created this latest disturbance. "Well, Margaret," he chuckled, rising to help her to the stone bench. "So you haven't forgotten me after all."

"Forgotten you?" she asked. "And how, pray, might I do that?"

He shrugged. "Well, it's been two weeks since the coronation. I was afraid your new respectability would keep you away from an old reprobate like me."

Margaret sniffed in mock displeasure. "Another word about my 'new respectability,' and you'll find your too-forward tongue will keep me away in earnest."

They fell into the easy laughter of old friends, friends who have known each other for years and understand one another implicitly.

"At any rate," she continued, "I felt it only fitting that I should bid you farewell, 'old reprobate' that you are. I hear you're bound for Brecon."

"Unfortunately, yes."

"Isn't it strange that His Grace of Buckingham doesn't plan to accompany King Richard on his progress?" Margaret's voice was light, almost innocent. Her eyes were on the graceful curved neck of the swan.

Morton paused before replying, a long pause pregnant in its silence. "I don't think everything is well between them," he said at last.

Her quick eyes darted to his face. "You know that for a fact?"

"As well as I know my own name . . . or that today is Tuesday . . . or that it rained last night. Richard is at Windsor, preparing to embark on a progress. Henry Stafford is here, preparing to leave for Wales. Their ways will take them as far apart as their minds are now."

Margaret was not overly surprised by this revelation. After all, she had an unimpeachable source of information in her own husband, who was now with the king at Windsor.

"Richard has given Buckingham more lands and the constableship as well," she said. "Why shouldn't he be content?"

"Richard has also given more manors to Norfolk and made him lord high admiral. And even Northumberland, Henry Percy, Richard's old rival, has received provisional grants from him. Obviously, the king does not intend for Buckingham to be preeminent in the realm. In Wales, yes, in the west of England perhaps, but in the rest of England, he must share his greatness. Sour wine indeed to one with his ambitions."

"He . . . he has spoken to you of this?"

"No, not yet," Morton admitted, "though at times he has looked at me as if he were about to speak. Other times I have surprised him staring at me with a sort of scheming look in his eye. It's a look I know well enough."

"As well you should. You are wearing it yourself at this very moment."

"Why, Meg, when you think about it, why else would he have taken me into his custody if he didn't mean to make use of me? He hardly needs another household priest, not that he overtaxes the ones he has already. I happen to have a reputation of which I am justly proud. And there are ways we can make use of him, I daresay."

She nodded agreement. "There are . . . other stirrings in the realm which might prove beneficial to us as well. Rumor has it that the Woodvilles are hatching a plot to restore Edward V."

"Indeed?" Morton asked. "Though that shouldn't come as any surprise really. The queen dowager—or . . . ah . . . excuse me, Dame Gray—won't be content to sit behind sanctuary walls indefinitely. Rumors, you say. Anything specific?"

"Very little. The movement is based in the southern and western counties, they tell me. A well-tuned ear might well hear more, and I intend to listen."

They lapsed into a comfortable, companionable silence. The whole garden breathed its noontime quiet like a benediction, for the street noises were muffled and far away. The drone of the locust, the soft ripple of water in the swan's wake were all that could be heard.

Then Margaret sat up sharply, suddenly alert. "Where are the duke's peacocks? I knew something was missing the moment I stepped into the garden. It's too quiet without them."

"And likely to remain so, I'm afraid. I myself have wondered why, but rest assured they are gone. A part of them is here," he added, affectionately patting the bulge of his stomach.

"Killed and eaten?"

"Yes."

Margaret chuckled. "I might have guessed it. For our vainglorious popinjay, they no doubt acquired unpleasant associations." She told him then of the banquet on the night of Richard's ascension and of the mummers' performance.

"So the duke was annoyed?" Morton asked.

"He was livid. I thought he would suffer an apoplexy on the spot. His face was so red."

"And Richard?"

"Laughed as loudly as any."

Morton smiled as he pictured it. "Being mewed up here does have its drawbacks," he said. "I'd give five years off my life to have seen it, and now that I think about it, the comparison is only too apt. I think the duke has probably spread his tail feathers for Richard many times. Perhaps that's what went wrong between them," he added thoughtfully, grasping at this new revelation. "Perhaps Richard did not respond as fully as he might have hoped."

Margaret gave him a swift, sharp look. "Are you implying more than you're willing to say?"

"I live in this house, Meg, and I have . . . seen things. I know now why Henry Stafford has such little regard for women, why his own wife was kept at Brecknock during the coronation."

"She is a Woodville. She might not have wished to participate."

Morton shrugged. "Maybe. But I rather think she was not invited. The duke's fancies run . . . in other directions. He doted on Richard and Richard on him, though probably not as much as Buckingham had wished."

"It was like that between them then?"

"Possibly, and what of it? The king's bed is an ancient and almost honorable means to power. Dame Woodville Grey could tell you that."

"But this time it was not so successful."

"Apparently not. I've never seen a man better play the spurned lover than our noble duke."

Margaret's hands absently flattened the folds of her dark skirt. "I wonder how we might employ this duke and, for that matter, the Woodvilles if it comes to that. Surely our cause is not their cause."

"No," Morton admitted, "but we do have one important goal in common, and that the most difficult of all. We must unseat Richard. After that . . . well, they can be managed, I think."

Margaret was skeptical. "I hope so, and yet Buckingham is so powerful. Can he be as easily led as that?"

"My word on it, Meg," he assured her, reaching over to press her hand. "Buckingham can be played upon like a finely tuned viol. His vices and ambitions leave him open to it. And the tune that is played shall be one of our choosing."

Margaret looked up and gave a small start of surprise. Standing a little way off, beyond the pond rushes and, she hoped, out of earshot was Sir William Percival. The white scar pulsed slightly on his cheek, his pale eyes focused on them with unabashed curiosity. Quickly, she froze her face into a mask of contempt. Lady Margaret Stanley, Countess of Richmond and mother of the true King of England, was not to be shaken by a man who was in reality only a highly placed servant.

Morton's hand shot up in a friendly wave. "Ah, Percival! Good day to you. We were about to send for some refreshments. Won't you join us? You are, of course, acquainted with the Lady Stanley?"

"I have had that honor," Percival replied with an ironic bow. "Though I'm afraid I must refuse your offer of refreshments. I have other matters to attend to." As suddenly and as noiselessly as he had appeared, he was gone.

"What an utterly unpleasant man!" Margaret said, visibly relaxing as he walked away. "Do you think he heard us?"

"No, I doubt it. I've grown accustomed to the comings and goings of Sir William. I was even aware of his coming upon us now, but though he was too far away to hear us, he would have noticed instantly any abrupt change in our conversation. I don't mean to minimize his importance. There is no one nearer the duke, and he will be much more difficult to win."

"I don't care to win the likes of him."

"Don't be too sure of that," Morton admonished, wagging a finger at her. "He can be useful to us, very useful."

"I shudder to think how," she said. Drawing her skirts around her, she rose, forgetting completely Morton's offer of refreshments.

"Are you going then?" he asked.

"Yes."

"But you won't forget me?" His eyes sparkled with mischief. He knew that she could not and would not forget.

"Have no fear of that. When you need me, you have only to send me word. My man Bray well knows the way to Wales, and he would find you even if you were removed to the very ends of the earth."

After she was gone, Morton resumed once more his sleepy pose in case Percival should still be lurking nearby. The fat carp, frightened no doubt by the murmur of their voices, still had not returned to his accustomed place beneath the lily pad, but Morton felt certain that he would very soon. And when he did, the bishop would be ready.

Smiling to himself, he trotted back to the house for a line and hook.

Chapter 33

WINDSOR CASTLE SHIMMERED in the heat of a July haze. On the Round Tower, across the inner ward from the royal apartments, Russell could see the banner bearing the king's standard trailing limply down the flagstaff. There was no hint of a breeze to stir it. Beyond the keep, the battlemented roof of St. George's Chapel, the towers of the outer bailey, as well as the palisades and parks beyond them danced like gypsies in sunstruck incandescence. He shut his eyes against the window's cruel light as he wiped a much-used kerchief across his damp forehead.

"I had thought the countryside would be cool," he said. "It's as hot as London."

"Indeed, my good bishop," Stanley replied airily from across the table. "If you could only convince mass breakers that hell is this hot, the churches would overflow with congregants."

"A good point, my lord, and one which you yourself might do well to heed."

Stanley reddened a little since, unlike his wife, he was not known to be particularly devout. "As a matter of fact, it should be noted that I partook of the body and blood this very morning in the king's private chapel."

"It was hoped that His Grace would influence you to some good purpose," Russell said. He added, his voice dropping, "Does he always hear mass in the small chapel then?"

Stanley nodded, glancing furtively across the room to where Richard stood with Lovell and Kendall before a large map of England. Since coming to Windsor, he had ignored the elaborate new Chapel of St. George, begun in a fit of piety by his brother Edward, in favor of the much smaller, much plainer one erected by Henry III two hundred years before. Although only the choir of St. George's was completed, it was still worthy of the king's attention with its carved oak stalls, glorious fan vaulting, and magnificent stained-glass windows. But there as well was the tomb of his brother Edward and, next to it, the decapitated corpse of William Lord Hastings.

"I wonder if he'll ever be able to forgive himself," Russell remarked sadly.

Stanley's fingers absently traced the ugly red welt that still creased his scalp at the hairline. It was fading now but would surely leave a scar. "For which?" he drawled. "For Hastings or the other?"

Russell's pink face, beaded with drops of sweat, took on more color. "Richard III," he said stiffly, "is king by the grace of God and the will of the English people. He who thinks otherwise betrays his own weakness. Edward's line was bastardized."

"Of course, bishop. You don't need to convince me. I carried the constable's mace at Richard's coronation, remember?"

Russell shrugged. He had never been sure of Stanley and was even less so now despite the fact that he had stuck to Richard's side like a burr since his reinstatement. He noted the hooded wariness in the hazel eyes as Stanley glanced over at the white samite-clad figure who was King of England. Then Russell sighed and tugged forth the damp handkerchief once more. It was too miserably hot to contemplate conspiracy, let alone to plan one. He looked forward to the cooling barge trip down the Thames that afternoon when his business at Windsor was concluded. A pity the castle stood so high above the river on its chalk bluff, too high to catch any grudging breezes the Thames might have bestowed. But then it had been built long ago in less secure times by builders who obviously placed the monarch's safety above his comfort.

"Russell, Stanley, your opinions, if you please." Richard beckoned them with the hand that wore the heavy coronation ring.

Despite the heat, he appeared animated as he motioned to the map though two large half-moons of sweat soaked the armholes of his white tunic. "Francis here has suggested that I should begin my progress by sweeping to the south here through Kent and Surrey. I, on the other hand, had planned to head for the west, to Oxford and Gloucester, then work my way north to York. What do you think?"

"A difficult question, sire," said Stanley, eying the map with the same furtive caution with which he looked at the king.

"To be sure," Russell said, "but a valid one, I believe." He took in the tanned and handsome face of Viscount Francis Lovell, the expressive mouth and the sensitive eyes, too quick to show pain or hurt. Not for nothing did he dispute with his lord. "Your friend tells you the truth, sire. Though it grieves me to say it, your hold on the southern counties is not as strong as it is in the north. You would do well to show yourself there. God forbid that there should be trouble so early in your reign, but if the Woodvilles intend to stir it up, that is where they'll begin."

Out of deference to the king, he did not mention one of his greatest concerns—Sir John Fogge, newly appointed justice of the peace for Kent, elevated by Richard's too-great generosity. What mischief he might create there in the tender ministrations of his office, Russell did not care to consider.

Richard chewed his lower lip and stared hard at the map as if willing it to shorten the distance between Kent and Yorkshire. He twirled round his thumb the coronation ring, which, having been sized for his brother's hand, was somewhat loose on his. "If only it weren't so far," he mused. "July is almost over. Soon it will be August then September and, after that, the autumn gales. If I were to go to Kent here"—he poked a finger at the bottom right of the map—"if I'm to make a decent showing, there won't be time to go to York and return to London while the weather holds."

"But Your Grace is already well known in York," Lovell argued, "and reverenced for Your Good Lordship. It's the south that's likely to prove treacherous."

Richard frowned, and a deep furrow cut between his eyebrows. "Do you really believe the situation is so desperate that treason will flourish like rank weeds in a garden the moment I turn my back?"

"I don't know, Dickon," said Lovell, lapsing back into the easy familiarity of their boyhood. "But the south and west have always been hotbeds of rebellion."

"Well, I don't need to worry about the west at any rate," Richard said, relief smoothing his face. "Buckingham will be here at Brecknock, a most effective guard."

Russell shot him a look of surprise. "Then the duke won't be accompanying you on your progress?"

Richard looked up from the map. A mist seemed to veil his eyes. "Regretfully, no. He begs leave to attend to his estates in Wales from which he has long been absent, and we have assented to his request. Norfolk too shall remain in London for a time, and he has graciously consented to see to the remodeling of Crosby Place in our absence. He and his son Surrey and you, my Lord Chancellor, will have to keep an eye on the southern counties for me. I can't spare the time to visit them now."

The decision made, Russell and Lovell could do little more than bow their heads in agreement, but Russell saw that the younger man looked hurt as well as concerned. Stanley, on the other hand, was quick to concur with a shrug of his green-padded shoulders. "If you wish to go to York, sire, that is your royal prerogative. Surely a few short weeks can't matter so much. And if the winter proves mild . . ." His voice trailed off, leaving the tantalizing suggestion that a later journey to the nearby south might not prove too difficult.

"Very good!" Richard exclaimed, clapping his hands together. "Now that that's settled, let's plan our route."

However, they had not gone very far in that particular exercise when a page announced the arrival of Master Thomas Woode. Richard looked up with sudden pleasure as the goldsmith appeared, beaming self-importance and carrying a large latten jewel casket exultantly before him. Richard turned apologetically to the others.

"I'm most sorry, my lords, but I must ask you to excuse us for a few minutes." There was a thud as the casket was laid on the table where the map was spread.

"What the devil?" Stanley muttered to Russell as they went out.

"Who knows?" Russell replied, losing interest. "Perhaps some trinket for the queen . . ." But privately he thought that whatever was inside the casket seemed far too heavy to adorn the frail body of Anne Neville.

No more than twenty-four hours later, Richard paced outside the closed door of Anne's bedchamber. He had been waiting for what seemed an interminable length of time. Behind it, the queen was sick, perhaps dying, and neither of the two royal physicians, Master Hobbes and Master Wilde, seemed to be able to tell him the reason.

"Poison!" Anna Lovell had said with grim certainty as Anne had clutched her abdomen at the dinner table and swooned in a dead faint. "Poison, sire," she repeated. "I've seen it before."

For a moment, Richard had been taken aback. He had watched helplessly as Anne had slumped to one side and the pearl diadem fell from her head and rolled noisily into a corner. And he had heard the shocked echo "Poison!" from the tables below. Then he had sprung up and caught her in his arms. She was still breathing though her skin was very white and her lips bluish. When he lifted her, she groaned in pain. She was still alive then, but only barely—and for how long?

Now as he waited, he disagreed with Lady Lovell's quick diagnosis. This was not the first indication that all was not well with Anne though he had managed to ignore earlier signs. Unless someone was plotting her death by inches, a few grains of arsenic in her food each day, it could not be poison. Some disease no less virulent perhaps but one inflicted by God, not man. How could he have been so blind not to see it?

Self-reproach came easily to Richard, and he allowed it full rein in those anxious moments. If only he had not insisted on the hunt yesterday! Yet it had seemed such a good idea at the time. Russell and Woode had both returned to London in the early afternoon, marking a reprieve from official and semiofficial duties. The copse at Windsor Park, newly stocked with red deer, beckoned like a cool green cave mouth. All very well, as he saw it now, but he should not have insisted that Anne accompany him.

Truth to tell, he had almost forgotten her in the thrill of the chase. The huntsmen had quickly found game, a proud buck with thick-branched antlers who had come down to drink from a stream in the afternoon heat. It led them a merry romp through field and forest, grove and thicket, the hounds baying after it and the men and horses in close pursuit.

Anne had been someplace behind when they finally reached the clearing where the dogs held the stag at bay, barking and jumping and showing the whites of their fangs. He had raised his bow, inserted an arrow and was about to shoot when he heard her cry.

"No, Dickon! Spare him please!"

He had turned on her almost in anger and caught a blurred image of dark eyes large in her face then had shaken his head vigorously. The buck would make a magnificent trophy, and he had a hunger for fresh venison.

His arrow had caught the beast's throat, tearing it rudely open. Almost with a sigh, the huge body settled to earth. He watched with satisfaction as blood gushed down the glossy brown coat, streaking it bright red where sweat had already streaked it dark, and watched too as the proud, bewildered eyes glazed over in death.

He had dismounted and, with his knife, dug the arrow from the stag's neck, spattering himself with gore. His men gathered round to applaud as if he had performed some marvelous feat. They reminded him of the hounds that still circled the kill, whining and whimpering but not touching it. Well trained dogs—they left the meat for him.

"My lord, the queen!" Anna Lovell's cry had caught his attention away to where Anne lay on the ground, half-supported by Margaret Percy, vomiting onto the mossy stones.

He could not understand it. She had never been squeamish. She had always enjoyed the hawking and the hunting almost as much as he. This time though she had begged him not to shoot, and now she had robbed him outright of his joy in the kill. *How exasperating women are*, he had thought even as he had gone to her side.

Hobbes had assured him yesterday that her malady was only a passing humor and had prescribed a posset of capers in warmed honey. Today, he had scratched his head in bewilderment and muttered something about the heat.

Perhaps after all he was right. Perhaps she had grown too accustomed to the cooler north, where clean, cutting winds swept down Wensleydale and could no longer endure the oppressive heat of the south. The air hung about him, heavy, stagnant, still. The sky, no longer blue but milky white, glared down as if in anger. Far below, the Thames lay low and sluggish between muddy banks. There was no wind, no breeze anywhere, only an ominous, deafening stillness that seemed to grip the castle in a sleeping spell. There was no sound either from behind the closed door that barred his admittance to Anne's chamber. Was she dying there? Was she already dead? And was there nothing he could do?

There was one thing. Almost without conscious thought, he sought the little chapel of Henry III across the courtyard. He moved down the twisted stair, crossed the North Terrace blessedly shaded from the sun, and strode through the Canon's Cloister and the Dean's Cloister. The chapel doors with their ornate scrollwork were covered with scarlet gesso that smote heat back into his face, but there was welcome relief within, beneath the narthex arches, between the six stately pillars of Purbeck marble. There the only lights were the ruby tongues of flame that burned on the altar and emitted the holy perfume of incense. They lit with soft, rosy radiance the silver-gilt statue of the Virgin.

With no more thought than a child with a simple boon to seek, he dropped to his knees before her. "Ave Maria . . . Hail Mary, full of grace. Blessed art thou among women."

He returned to consciousness sometime later, still on his knees, his hands folded before him. Behind him, he felt another presence, a human presence. Swiftly he rose and turned.

"Master Wilde!"

The physician stood there unmoving, his face shadowed by one of the pillars. Only the hands, clenched into fists at his sides, revealed his strain.

Richard reached out a hand toward him. "Please . . . tell me. How is she?"

"The queen has miscarried of a child."

For a moment, Richard was dumbstruck. "A child? But she wasn't breeding. How could she be? How did . . . ?" Then guilt and fearful knowledge choked off his words and flung them back in his face. He clutched at the pillar with one shaking hand.

"How did it happen?" Wilde parroted his unfinished thought. "Why, in the usual manner, I believe. A man lies with his wife and gets her with child. Immaculate Conception is rare in our day." He glanced at the statue, silver and serene in its niche above the altar. Richard saw in the ruby light how all the muscles in his face seemed bunched together, how the corded tendons protruded from his neck. Wilde was devoted to Anne. He had tended her from babyhood.

"You knew she was frail," came the accusing voice, "you knew she could bear you no more children, that another pregnancy might well cost her her life. Yet you got her with child anyway. Why? Why?"

Why indeed? No doubt Wilde would accuse him of risking his wife's health to secure his feeble dynasty. What did it matter if she died? There were other women, foreign princesses with wide hips for childbearing who would not scruple to share his bed. Richard could read the unspoken indictment in Wilde's stormy eyes. Well, let him think what he wished since Richard could give him no better explanation.

"How is she?" he asked again.

"If God is gracious, she may live. She has lost a great deal of blood. Hobbes is with her now."

"May . . . may I see her?"

"Yes, I see no harm in that. And she has asked for you." His anger seemed to have spent itself. Wilde looked only very weary.

"Asked for me?" Richard repeated. "Why didn't you say so, foolish man?" He pushed past the leech and out into the cloister where the brightness was no longer as intense as it had been earlier. Maybe after all, there would be rain.

Anne's bedchamber was dim with only a pair of ambergris pannikins burning on either side of the bed. There was a stench in the room of something dying or perhaps already dead. Hobbes was bent over his patient, and he greeted Richard with none of the recriminations that Wilde had heaped upon him. "A great pity, sire. I would have saved the child if I could."

Richard shook his head. "No, leech. Better that you save the queen."

Hobbes looked doubtful. "We've done all we can for now. I think she may recover, but I can promise nothing."

On the other side of the bed, Richard glimpsed Anna Lovell's delicate patrician profile. She clutched one of the queen's hands and wept a little, noiselessly, the tears sliding unchecked down her cheeks. Next to her, Margaret Percy looked at him with eyes round and black as raisins in a suet pudding. With a wave of his hand, he dismissed them both. Gathering up his instruments and potions, Hobbes also took his leave. Richard was alone with his wife.

Anne looked as though she slept, but the ordeal she had suffered was stamped in every line of her face, in the sunken purple hollows beneath eye and cheekbone, in the pale transparency of her skin, even in the heavy, dark, sweat-matted hair. Lying on the ornate canopied bed with the royal arms above her and a gold-embossed crown on the coverlet, the Queen of England looked like a wraith. The rise and fall of her small breasts was painfully shallow, and Richard had to turn his eyes away from the reproach of her slender hips too narrow for childbearing.

"Anne!" The cry was torn from him by some force greater than his will.

Slowly, she opened her eyes. "Dickon," she whispered, so low he had to bend over to hear her. "Ah, Dickon, I . . . I wanted to give you a son." Tears stuck on her lashes, drying them into points.

Tentatively, he stroked the damp hair back from her forehead. "I want no more sons from you, Nan, not if they take you away from me."

"But . . . a king needs sons."

"We have a son."

"Ned," she murmured, her voice flat. "But Ned . . . is like me, I'm afraid—frail, delicate. Oh, Dickon, I was so happy when the time passed for my menses. I had hoped . . . but I've lost it now, the babe. Can you ever forgive me for that?"

He shook his head. "It's I who should be asking for forgiveness. Can you forgive me for putting you in this peril?"

Her lips made a grimace as if she tried to smile but could not. "I told you once there's nothing to forgive. Nothing." Sighing deeply, she closed her eyes in sleep.

For a long time, he sat beside her, motionless. Servants came and went unobtrusively, bearing away the bloody linens that contained all that was left of the latest hope of York. From time to time, the physicians would come in, check Anne's pulse or breathing, bob a bow in Richard's direction, and go out once more. And still Richard sat, holding one of her limp hands in both his own as if willing her to return from the edge of some vast, dark void. He loved her; he needed her. He could not go on without her. It wasn't fair that she should be snatched away from him like this.

Then inevitably his thoughts strayed back to the conception of this ill-fated seed, and he realized with a sudden shock that it was both fair and eminently just that he should lose her in exactly this way. He had taken her in anger, forced her against her will, used her to slake the guilt and frustration of another lust too painful to be borne.

"Anne, what of her?" The other voice, wheedling, pleading, even taunting echoed in his brain. "Would I be taking anything from her that is hers? She has a son from you, hasn't she?" And "Men are the superior creatures. Women are mere vessels for the habitation of our children, dross to our gold."

Anne's hand was wet, glistening with tears he suddenly realized were his own. He lifted it to his lips, tasting the salt. "There is much to forgive, Nan. You don't know how much. I pray you never know."

Toward nightfall, recognizable only as a deeper dusk in the already darkened room, she awoke. It had begun to rain about an hour before, a hard, slashing rain that drove against the windows. Now there was lightning and the rumble of thunder in the distance.

"Thirsty," she said, moistening chapped lips with her tongue. "Water . . . please."

"Water!" Richard bellowed, rising so fast that he knocked over his chair. "Water for the queen!"

Doctors and servants rushed to the bedside, bearing water in anything that would carry it: basins, ewers, pitchers. Anne looked up and smiled, this time a true smile of amusement. "I asked for a drink. I didn't expect the whole River Thames."

After the drink, she managed some broth and a little gruel, and even Wilde had to concede that she seemed to be growing stronger moment by moment. Hobbes by this time was more concerned for Richard, who refused to leave her side and was beginning to show signs of the strain. At last, he convinced him to accept a cup of mulled wine blended with a little poppy juice. "To help you sleep, sire."

"Sleep!" Richard snapped with unusual bitterness. "I wonder if I deserve ever to sleep again." But he took the cup and drained it at a gulp, leaving Hobbes to shake his head in wonder. The queen, it appeared, would recover. But now, what ailed the king?

Chapter 34

RICHARD STOOD ON a high bluff at the western edge of the Cotswolds and looked out over the broad plain of the Severn that stretched away beneath him, fading in the distance into the purple-smudged mountains of Wales. On his right hand, the river ran like a silver ripple through meadow and wood and farmland out of neighboring Worcestershire; on his left, it opened into a wide, shining estuary, dotted here and there with white sails bound for Bristol. A little to the north of the estuary lay the market town of Gloucester, his current destination. It was a town of some importance, as proclaimed both by its thick walls, though from here they looked no mightier than a child's toy fortress, and by the proud tower of the Benedictine Abbey of St. Peter.

Buckingham was to meet him in Gloucester—Buckingham, whom he had not seen in more than three weeks. The duke's messenger had caught up with him at Burford two days ago. It was not impossible that Henry Stafford, traveling from London with greater haste and a much smaller retinue, was already in Gloucester waiting for him. At that thought, Richard's heart began to drum in quick, pounding strokes, but he could not have told if it was anticipation or dread that caused his agitation.

"If we don't press on, sire, we'll never make Gloucester by noon," Lovell reminded him.

Richard did not need the reminder. No doubt the good citizens of Gloucester, like those of the smaller towns they had passed through along their route, had an elaborate reception planned for the king and his entourage. It would hardly do to keep them waiting. He lifted his hand in the signal to move on, and slowly the cumbersome, mile-long train came to life behind him, twisting like a snake down the hillside. Barons and knights on geldings and stallions, bishops and justices on palfreys and in litters, servants and retainers on mules and donkeys, and finally, the heavy and inevitable baggage wagons that were needed to support such a company.

Thus far, the progress had been most successful, even enjoyable. Anne had been unable to accompany him, of course, but she had been strong enough to come down to the Lower Ward at Windsor Castle to see him off and offer him the stirrup cup. And she had promised to join him later in his progress, perhaps at Warwick, but certainly before York. Richard smiled as he thought of that: the treasure at Middleham would draw her on despite illness, fire, or flood.

He had been surprised and gratified by the warmth and enthusiasm of the welcome accorded him along the way. If there were doubts about the justice of his ascension and if there was, as some had suggested, unrest in his kingdom, it certainly had not been evident in the Thames Valley or the Cotswold villages he had visited to date. Of course, he had done everything in his power to create a favorable climate, everything from impressing the dons of many-towered Oxford with his own considerable learning to restoring to the citizens of Woodstock the forest lands of Wychwood that had been unjustly appropriated some years before by his brother Edward. His justices of the King's Bench had heard complaints from any man who dared speak them and had passed judgment without regard to rank, wealth, or influence.

But perhaps the one thing that had most endeared him to his people was his refusal to accept the purses crammed with golden coins that had been offered to him in almost every town and village. To a people long oppressed by taxes and benevolences, this was a wonder indeed. They gaped in open astonishment as Richard shook his head and explained, "It isn't your gold but your hearts I seek."

At Gloucester, there was more of the same sort of welcome he had grown accustomed to, though perhaps the throng of citizens was larger, the cheers somewhat louder, the banners and flags even more numerous and colorful than they had been elsewhere on his route. Certainly the obligatory silk purse was heavier and the mayor's speech in the market square, making much of the king's previous title Duke of Gloucester, more long-winded than any he had heard lately.

Afterward, there was a little time to see what news the courier had brought from London before the midday meal was served in the abbot's palace. Along with the official correspondence from Lord Chancellor Russell and a report from Howard on the renovations at Crosby Place, there was a small ivory oblong, neatly folded and lettered in Tom Lynom's elaborate hand. Richard frowned as he picked it up and wondered why it bore not the seal of the solicitor general, which Lynom was now entitled to use, but only his small private one.

There was no time for learning the answer to this riddle, for a sentry announced the arrival of His Grace, the Duke of Buckingham. Richard thrust Lynom's letter into an inner pocket of his doublet, unopened and for the moment forgotten.

The duke had lost none of his sense of the dramatic. He moved confidently, even a little arrogantly, through the servants and retainers that jammed the hall, his eyes on Richard all the while. And Richard, trying to return his ready smile, was only aware that where his hand gripped the arms of his chair, the skin over his knuckles had turned white. With effort, he managed to extend a hand to Buckingham's kiss of greeting, but he found speech difficult.

"I . . . we . . . hope you are well, cousin. We have . . . ah . . . much missed your presence in our train." How stumbling and inane the words sounded, even to his own ears.

"Is that so, Your Grace?" Buckingham asked smoothly, turning his head slightly to survey the crowded hall. "I would have thought my absence scarcely to be noted among so great a company. Certainly it did not diminish the magnitude of your welcome. All the way from London, I've heard naught but songs in your praise."

"It has gone . . . er . . . rather well," Richard admitted. "We consider ourselves fortunate that our people appear to love us—a fact that should perhaps be no less gratifying to you than it is to us."

"Of course," Buckingham nodded and looked as if he were about to say more when Richard abruptly cut him off.

"The steward has just given us the signal that the noon meal will be served in a few minutes. You and your party will no doubt wish to wash off the dust of the road beforehand. Here, boy," he shouted to a page, "would you show my lord duke to his chambers?"

For one quick moment, there was a glimmer of hurt in Buckingham's eyes at this abrupt dismissal before politic courtesy clamped down over them like a steel visor. Without another word, he allowed himself to be led away with the same self-assurance as when he had entered.

The meal was awkward. With Buckingham at his right hand, Richard could do little more than pick at the baked, stuffed Wye trout, the eel pasties, and the roast saddle of lamb, which he found to be dry and a little tough. In contrast, the duke ate heartily, drank immoderately, and talked expansively. Most of it was small talk as if he were trying to put Richard at his ease. But then as his dagger stabbed a morsel of lamb left on his plate, his gaze grew suddenly calculating.

"Ah, yes, sire, you did well to leave London in these summer months. The heat is dangerous. I swear it addles a man's wits. Now you take poor Tom Lynom . . ."

"Tom?" Richard questioned, suddenly aware of the scratch of the unopened letter next to his chest.

"Why, yes, surely you've heard . . ." Then to the slow shake of Richard's head, he flushed uncomfortably. "Sweet blood of our Lord. I didn't want to be the one to tell you." He toyed with the stem of his wine goblet, unwilling to meet Richard's eyes, and at last, reluctantly he spoke. "It seems he is about to take a wife."

Richard smiled in relief. "But that's wonderful news! And here I've been worried because he seemed so entranced with Jane Shore. Just what Tom needs, a proper wife. Did he make a good match, or is he still letting his heart rule his head?"

"The latter, I'm afraid," Buckingham said with a small groan. "In fact, as I hear it, he wishes to wed the Mistress Shore."

"Wed her!" Richard gasped. "Wed her?" he repeated to a chorus of shocked disbelief. Only Morton, on the other side of Buckingham, and Percival, at the lower end of the table, were silent, presumably because they already knew. "But there must be some mistake. Men don't marry their harlots. And I have always assumed the . . . ah . . . lady already had a husband somewhere."

"Jane had her marriage to Will Shore annulled several years ago," Buckingham informed him, wiping his mouth with a napkin, "on the grounds that he was impotent. That prevented her from her stated desire to bear children."

Richard could not quite control a smirk at this bit of gossip. "Nonetheless, it's unthinkable. Absolutely out of the question."

"I most heartily agree."

"A proven whore and a traitoress as well. What is he thinking of? When I made him solicitor general, I expected him to exercise good sense, good judgment."

"Of course," came Buckingham's soothing murmur. "And to learn of it like this, from nowhere, so to speak. He might have had the decency to inform you himself."

"Well, ah, as to that, Harry, I think he tried." He pulled out the crumpled letter and broke the seal. "This reached me today. I haven't had the time to read it." He read it now, hurriedly. It was short, obviously well rehearsed, and to the point. But despite that, Tom's natural charm flowed through somehow to his flourishing script, reminding Richard, even in the heat of his anger, how much he had always liked him. Damn the boy anyway!

Also, the sense of the letter was a little different from Buckingham's description of the situation. Tom realized quite well the absurdity of his request, but "being deeply in love with her and she with me," dared to brave Richard's wrath to ask permission to marry her. "I have no reason to believe this boon will be granted"— that much he acknowledged anyway—"and swear to Your Grace by all that's holy that if it is not, I will turn from her and not attempt to see her again. Yet that would be a pity for us both, for I think even you would find her much changed from what she was . . ."

Thoughtfully, Richard refolded the letter and stuck it back in his doublet.

"So now you see for yourself, sire. Isn't it just as I told you?" Buckingham asked.

"More or less," Richard hedged, "more or less."

"Surely you can't be weakening. Why, the woman is notorious! Your solicitor will make himself a laughingstock."

"That's for him to decide. I don't know . . ."

"You don't know?" Now it was Buckingham's turn for disbelief. "Morton, you have some experience with the woman in question. What do you have to say about all this?"

The bishop of Ely had remained unusually reticent throughout the meal, all deference and decorum in his seat next to the duke. Thoughtfully now, he considered the question as he sugared his wine. "Not being fully aware of the situation," he intoned at last, "I am hardly qualified to judge. Yet I have full confidence that our gracious sovereign, knowing both of the principals in this matter, will make the proper decision. His moral rectitude is a byword in our land."

A skillful evasion, Richard thought and wondered if there might be a hidden irony in those last words, bland as they were. But no, Morton did not know of his lapse from "moral rectitude." How could he possibly know? And Buckingham's squeals of outrage were silenced, temporarily at least. He could hardly object to anything that the bishop had said.

Looking now from Morton to Stanley, who sat at the same table, Richard realized that he himself could offer only weak objections to the match. He had restored Stanley, while Buckingham had obviously raised Morton, who was nominally his prisoner, to a place of some importance in his household. Even old Rotherham had been given his seat on the council once more. Of all the survivors of the Hastings conspiracy, only Jane Shore was still in prison and in disgrace. Of course, he still did not approve of Tom's marrying her, and he meant to ask Russell to intervene with him, but frankly, he doubted that he would have much success. If the chancellor could not persuade him to change his mind, then Tom could have her, for all the good it would do him. Richard would not stand in his way.

He did not see Buckingham again until nightfall. He had spent the afternoon with his justices, hearing cases in the chapter house, and since the number of petitioners was great, he had been busy far into the evening. Now he dropped wearily into a chair in the abbot's bedroom, allocated to him during his stay in Gloucester, and watched as a black-robed monk lit the cressets against the deepening gloom. Suddenly, unannounced, Buckingham's face materialized out of the shadows. Richard drew himself up, startled.

"Harry!"

"My lord, forgive me. I didn't mean to alarm you."

"No? Then what do you want?"

"I've come to ask if I might have your permission to take my leave in the morning."

Richard gestured to the monk to retreat, leaving the large room still in semidarkness. "So soon, Harry? But you've only just arrived. We haven't had much opportunity to speak together yet."

Buckingham shrugged. "Your duties seem to prevent that, sire. And I have my own affairs to attend to. I would like to be in Brecon for the collection of any overdue Lamas Day rents."

"Ah, yes, I had forgotten. You still must play the lord of the manor." Even Richard heard the edge that had crept into his voice.

"You have your kingdom, sire, and I, my own small acreage. Both must be attended to."

Richard regarded him sharply in the gathering dusk. The words had come as from a disembodied shadow. "Do I detect a note of bitterness, Harry? You're not still smarting over the Lynom affair, I hope?"

"Of course not!" Buckingham replied with a dry, mirthless chuckle. "Having been informed by the bishop of Ely that the whole thing is none of my business, I bow to Your Grace's will. Your 'moral rectitude' will aid you in deciding the case rightly, I'm sure."

This time, there could be no doubt of the irony. Richard could only shake his head. "Harry . . . ah, Harry, please! What's gone wrong between us? Why is it we can't even talk together anymore without . . . without fencing with verbal swords. This is me, Dickon, your cousin and the friend who loves you."

"If only I could believe that."

Richard heard the painful intake of his own breath. "Please, let's not open that Pandora's box again. I want it sealed forever."

"*Le roi le voit,*" Buckingham said with a mock bow. "As the king wishes." But his voice was cold.

"You don't understand," Richard objected. He had not meant to bring Anne into their discussions, yet suddenly he found himself grasping for reasons, for explanations. "It . . . it hasn't been as easy for me as you might think. Anne, the queen, has miscarried of a child and almost died herself. I . . . I did it to her through carelessness, made her conceive when the doctors told me she hadn't the strength. All these years, I had been . . . most careful. I was . . . not myself when I did it."

Buckingham remained impassive, his body dark against the candle shine. "My condolences to Your Grace. I hope the queen mends."

"She is doing well now. Christ, Harry! It wasn't to receive your condolences that I told you about this."

"Why then?" Buckingham demanded with sudden fury. "Do you wish me to believe that in some perverse way, your love for me resulted in your getting your wife with child and that, guilt stricken, you must now renounce me? Well, renounce me then! Renounce me and have done with it. Or do you merely seek to arouse my sympathies? As if you needed them! You, who know the ultimate joy of wearing the crown of England. Compared to that, what's the loss of a small bit of tissue from your wife's womb? Or even of your wife? Or for that matter," he added, his voice dropping, "of one who loved you more than life itself?"

Richard stood astounded at this outburst, and even Buckingham seemed rooted to the floor in amazement at his own daring. Slowly, the duke composed himself. "Your Grace, forgive me. Neither have I been myself of late."

"So I see," Richard said softly. "I did not know. I begin to understand."

"Then may I have your leave to depart?"

"If that's what you wish. I won't try to hold you against your will."

"I'll come to court again, of course," Buckingham said lightly. "Perhaps for the Christmas revels."

"Yes, of course," Richard murmured as the duke bowed and backed away. "I didn't mean to suggest that you should not."

Only after Buckingham was gone did Richard remember the gift. It lay forgotten in the latten casket on the table beside him. Unfortunately, it was too late now to run after him. Perhaps it might have done something to heal the breach between them, to suture the open, festering wound.

Outside, a few swallows twittered around the abbey belfry before taking to their nests inside it. The tower itself was still darkly silhouetted against the evening sky. There would be time in the morning to present the gift, he decided, although without many of the fair words and praises he had thought to bestow with it earlier.

When Richard at last drew the thing from its casket next morning in the abbey close, it drew a startled chorus of oohs and ahs from the admiring crowd. Not even he, as King of England, had so magnificent a jewel. The familiar heraldic collar of York, with its white roses and triple suns, had been wrought with unparalleled beauty and richness. Richard had specified to Master Woode that it be so: made of the purest gold; intricately worked into petals and leaves, rays, and overlapping circles; encrusted with diamonds and pearls, emeralds and topazes, some as big as a man's thumbnail. From it hung a white boar carved of ivory, with golden tusks and ruby eyes. In the early morning sun, shafting into the close, the collar shimmered with a life of its own.

Buckingham could not take his eyes off it. Even as Richard did him the honor of slipping it around his neck, his gaze fell downward toward the amassed richness on his breast. He seemed speechless.

"I had intended to give this to you last night," Richard told him, "but other matters prevented me. Take it now and wear it proudly, for you are the foremost servant of your king and of York." He spoke those last words loudly for he wanted them to be heard, not least of all by Morton, who watched the two men with a wondering eye.

"I . . . I am humbled by this honor," Buckingham stammered. Recovering quickly, he added, "I shall always treasure it even as I treasure the one who gives it to me."

They embraced then, heartily and spontaneously, and for a moment, it seemed as though there had never been a rift between them and never would be again. Then Buckingham sprang into Saladin's saddle and, with a quick salute of his gloved hand, turned the horse's head toward St. Mary's Street. His retinue, led by Percival and Morton, spurred their horses after him.

Richard stood alone, watching only Buckingham and the bright flash of the jewels until they became blurred, wavering orbs of color. Then with the final wink of a diamond, the duke was gone, turning the corner into Westgate Street, which led to the Severn and to Wales. And still Richard stood there on the green, looking after him for a ridiculously long time until even the echoes of the horses' hooves on the cobbles were no more than a memory.

BOOK IV

𝕿𝖍𝖊 𝕮𝖔𝖑𝖑𝖆𝖗

August 4 to November 2, 1483

Chapter 35

THE ROAD FROM Gloucester to Brecon was not long. That was the one consolation Morton would admit as they stepped off the Severn Ferry and took to their saddles once more. He found riding horseback a purgatory scarcely to be tolerated under any other circumstances. A chariot perhaps or, at the very least, a litter—those were the conveyances he might have chosen for himself. They would have been slower, no doubt, but infinitely more comfortable. He could have reclined on satin pillows instead of feeling his rump jostled roughly over every rut in the road.

Of course, he had not dared to suggest such an alternative to Buckingham. Although his relationship with that eminent had been progressing remarkably well, Morton had no desire to challenge the duke's rough looks or harsh laughter. There was a black humor on him the bishop thought it best to respect, and so he made what peace he could with the beast between his legs, a gentle enough palfrey but a horse nonetheless.

He tried to show a proper appreciation for the Herefordshire countryside through which they passed, but the monotony of apple orchards and hop gardens, one following fast upon the other, and of white-faced red cattle grazing contentedly on low hills, failed to enchant him.

There was in fact only one thought that proved sufficiently riveting to distract him from the pain in his buttocks, and that was of Buckingham. Henry Stafford rode on toward Brecon like a man possessed, saying nothing to anyone and ignoring completely the brief showers the heavens splashed down upon them. His face was grim and determined, and Morton could only speculate with increasing interest at what was going on in the mind behind it.

Around the duke's neck, Richard's collar sparkled in the fitful sun. *How heavy it must be*, thought Morton, *in both weight and portent!* Oh, it was magnificent, no doubt of that, the most magnificent piece of jewelry that Morton had ever seen. Still, it was no less heavy than the iron collar worn by a serf, proclaiming to all and sundry that the proud Duke of Buckingham was no more than a vassal to the king and wore his cognizance. It was in fact only a golden chain forged to bind Henry Stafford more tightly to Richard. But perhaps it might also provide the means of severing him. Morton's fertile mind toyed with that thought as the road unwound its weary way through Herefordshire then pushed it aside as they skirted the Black Mountains of Wales, where he found it necessary to give more attention to his horsemanship.

The country had grown wild and uncivilized. All signs of human habitation vanished. No cot, no farm, no village greeted his eye. Through deep chasms cut by foaming streams, past rocky crags loose with falling stones, the horse picked its way. On either hand, the mountains rose, a vast impenetrable wall. So this harsh and hostile land was Wales. He thought almost longingly of the flat fen country around Ely, which was so easily dominated by the towers of his cathedral church. Above the flooded marsh, it often appeared like a ship in full sail. Yet if one were to drop Ely Cathedral into this glen, it would be utterly lost.

He thought with even greater longing of London—that busy, bustling city on the gentle Thames, the center of his universe, the home of all his hopes—and he knew a moment's keen desolation at the thought of how far he had come into this wild hinterland and how far he had yet to go. Perhaps there was some consolation in Holy Writ. "He who would find his life must lose it." Yes, of course, he must think of the larger scheme, the greater plan, which rendered this pilgrimage not only necessary but desirable. His eyes slid speculatively for the hundredth time that day to the duke who rode far ahead of him down the narrow defile.

They came out of the cleft into the Usk Valley and to the town of Abergavenny, where they were to spend the night. Morton's spirits rose a little, for the valley was green and fertile and dotted here and there with cots and farms. Lush meadows were bordered with plum trees hung with hard gobbets of green fruit already turning a pale pink. The River Usk flowed clear and limpid between banks lined with willow and alder and slipped with scarcely a murmur between the stone piers of an ancient bridge. Even the town of Abergavenny, while hardly a metropolis, was sizeable enough to give promise of comfortable accommodations.

Unfortunately, it was a promise that was not to be kept. Morton wondered at the cool reluctance, bordering on surliness, with which the innkeeper greeted the duke. The service was poorer than he would have believed possible. When pressed, the landlord managed to bring out a particularly stringy piece of cold mutton, telling them his wife had been ill that day and the oven had not been lit. The bread was stale (Morton judged it to be no less than a week old), the cheese green with mold, and the lukewarm ale, thin and sour.

Morton watched the duke to see if he would fly into one of his rages, but Buckingham seemed curiously stoic as if he had expected no more. He gave the bishop a sardonic smile.

"I fear, Morton, that you're receiving a rather poor impression of the power and influence of the king's legate in Wales."

Morton waved his hand in a deprecating gesture. "We are far into the country," he replied, "and can hardly expect to be feted as if we were in London. Fortunately, I am a simple man of simple tastes and find the fare to be passable if not grand. Then too the man's wife is ill. Surely that explains any lapse in hospitality."

Buckingham laughed at that. "Most surely, my good bishop, it does not. The fact is that reverence for the king's grace and for his emissaries does not extend across the marches."

"Therefore," Morton said unctuously, "the king's grace has most wisely chosen a man of proven strength and ability to govern this most difficult of domains on his behalf. He is truly blessed to have such a one at his disposal."

Buckingham took a swallow of ale, made a grotesque face, and spat it out onto the rushes. "Bah! Of course, I might yet string that impudent baggage of a landlord up by his thumbs. I have the power."

"As none would dispute," Morton agreed. "But you also have the wisdom to know that would not be the best way to keep the king's peace in Wales. Perhaps Richard will make us a king after all . . . if he keeps such men about him."

Buckingham gave him a questioning look. "You are resigned to him then?"

"My lord, I haven't the means anymore to be otherwise, and I suppose I'm becoming accustomed to changes in my fortune. I served poor Harry VI till he was laid in the grave, and though I had wished to see his blood inherit, I gave my support to Edward of York. Again, I would have preferred to see Edward's son on the throne after him, but God, in his infinite wisdom, has been pleased to grant us Richard of Gloucester, and with his will, I must be content—even though," he added slowly, "concerning King Richard . . ."

"Yes?" Buckingham asked, leaning closer to him. Morton could feel the duke's hot breath on his cheek.

"No," Morton replied, pushing back his chair. "I've said enough. God forgive my impertinence if I should meddle any further in worldly affairs. Henceforth, I shall devote all my attention to my beads and my breviary. With your kind permission, I'll seek my chamber."

Buckingham sighed his exasperation. "Oh, very well. I grant it to you. But I would talk with you further on this matter."

"I am Your Grace's humble servant," Morton said, bending slightly at the waist. "And I don't doubt that there will be much opportunity for . . . talk." He turned slowly and climbed the stairs to his chamber.

The bed was no better than the supper had been. Morton slept badly on a mattress of lumpy straw. From the expression on

Buckingham's face as they made their early departure, it appeared that he had fared no better.

In the yard, Morton settled himself carefully into the saddle, mindful as always of his bruised posterior. He gave a silent "Te Deum" that this would be the last time he would have to submit himself to such torture—at least for the foreseeable future. Tonight he would be blessedly stationary at Brecknock, an end that lured him like the very hope of heaven. He already knew what hell would be.

They made their way up the Usk Valley, climbing slowly but steadily along a grassy track. Soon the river frothed and bubbled beneath them, constrained in a steep, narrow gorge. The pastoral peace of Abergavenny, it seemed, had been an illusion. They climbed more sharply upward as the hills threw jagged spurs across their way. The road became an endless series of jouncing ruts, recalled all too clearly from the day before, leading upward, ever upward.

Then suddenly it stopped altogether or seemed to. Buckingham gave a signal, and his whole troop came to a halt. The river below them that had raced, roaring, over a series of cascades soothed to a murmur and flowed broad and placid once more. Far in the distance, they could see it winding in great, shining loops that caught the midday sun. They stood on the crest of a ridge, but below them, the slope was gentle, merging almost imperceptibly with a vast expanse of green moorland, etched with small trees where the river wound its way and fading to purple hills in the northwest.

But the sight that caught the eye and held it was that of three tall peaks thrust up without preliminary or warning as if from the very bowels of the earth itself. These were no hills, no gentle undulation of the land. These were mountains higher than any they had passed by far, sharp and steep-sided with gashes of red stone showing on their flanks. With ease, they commanded all the countryside. Morton gasped in genuine astonishment.

Beside him, Buckingham smiled. "The Brecon Beacons," he said, indicating them with a quite unnecessary sweep of his hand. "All that you see now belongs to me. Over there is Brecknock. Let's go on."

The rest of the journey was mercifully brief. Their way took them through pastures dotted with sheep and fattening cattle and past strips of cultivated fields where tenant farmers and iron-collared serfs attended the crops. The men tugged at their forelocks as the duke's party passed, but their sunburnt faces showed little welcome. There were no smiles of greeting for their liege lord.

They were granted a more cordial reception in the town of Brecon, where the scarlet-robed mayor and his aldermen turned out to greet them. Brecon itself, picturesquely situated on the north bank of the Usk, surprised Morton with its size and apparent importance. It was not London, certainly, but then it was no mere country village either. As they passed through the gate in its red sandstone walls and wound their way through the narrow tangle of its streets, Morton noted with approval the numerous shop signs for tailors, glovers, and cobblers. Whatever deprivations he might be called upon to suffer in his exile, being poorly clad should not be one of them.

His bishop's eye also lighted on two fine churches: the parish Church of St. Mary and, larger and more impressive, the Benedictine Priory of St. John the Evangelist with its low, square Norman tower. Of course, neither could compare with his own cathedral at Ely—he was suddenly very proud of Ely—but they assured him that he also would not suffer from spiritual deprivation at Brecon.

He was in fact beginning to feel rather complacent about the whole adventure when suddenly, at the western edge of the town, a swift-flowing stream barred their way. He looked up to see beyond it the battlemented ramparts of a mighty castle-fortress.

This he had not expected. In London, the duke kept a household replete with every imaginable comfort and luxury. The Manor of the Rose was as lovely as its name, built in the modern style with large windows and pleasant gardens and many lofty private chambers. This castle, on the other hand, looked like a throwback to the Conqueror's day. Though obviously in good repair, it was old, very old. The windows in the curtain wall were little more than arrow slits, and the twin octagonal towers that guarded the gate had no windows at all, only a few squint holes in the masonry. Beyond them, he could make out the top of a great Norman keep that appeared from this distance scarcely more habitable.

"Brecknock Castle?" he asked the duke, fervently praying for a denial.

"Yes," Buckingham replied. "My humble seat."

"It looks . . . most formidable," Morton said, struggling for a word to do it justice.

"So it appears . . . from the outside. And so it would be if some-one tried to attack." Suddenly, Buckingham tossed back his head and laughed heartily. "Ah, Morton," he said finally, "I see what you're afraid of. 'A simple man of simple tastes' indeed! Well, don't concern yourself unnecessarily. Brecknock Castle is not as forbidding within as she is from without. An English ruler in Wales must make such a show. But I am hardly a simple man of simple tastes, my dear bishop, nor do I make any pretense of being one. I am fond of the amenities of life and would not do without them in a place where I must of necessity spend so much time."

"I am most grateful for that," Morton said sincerely.

From one of the towers came the call of a trumpet followed by the creaking of ropes and pulleys as the drawbridge was lowered over the stream, which served the castle as part of its moat. Slowly the iron-barred portcullis rose before the great gate, and a dozen servants scurried to push open the heavy lead-bound doors. With a stance worthy of a returning conqueror, Buckingham spurred Saladin over the drawbridge of Brecknock Castle.

A flurry of activity greeted their arrival. Porters streamed like ants from the castle keep to unload their baggage, grooms appeared from nowhere to lead their horses to stable, stewards came to attend the lord's every wish. The retinue was carefully but surreptitiously scrutinized. Morton felt himself the object of intense curiosity, the only stranger in a place where strangers were probably rare. But Buckingham's splendid new collar was an even greater source of awe. Even in this far corner of the realm, removed though it was from the events of recent months, people could hardly fail to have heard of Richard's ascension and of Buckingham's prominent role in it nor of his increased power in Wales. The collar, with its white boar appended, was a visible symbol of his new status and obviously a source of wonderment to them all.

All but one. She stood a little apart from the bustle in the court-yard as if she were uncertain or perhaps unwilling to assert herself further. But her head was high, her bearing proud, and there was no uncertainty in her eyes. Even if he had not remembered her from her younger days when she had briefly illumined Edward's court, Morton would have known her now for the resemblance she bore her royal sister. For this was Katherine Woodville, Duchess of Buckingham.

Her husband had to go to her, of course. It would have been most unseemly if he had not. But there was no eagerness in his step as he approached the place where she stood, holding their two older children by the hand.

"You are most welcome to Brecknock, my lord," she said. Her voice was low and rich but strangely cold.

"It's good to be home," he murmured as if mouthing a formula. She lifted her cheek, and he brushed it perfunctorily with his lips. Then briefly he turned to each of the children. The boy, a handsome lad of about twelve, gazed up at his father in obvious adoration, but his sister, two or three years younger, drew back in a spasm of shyness. Her reply to her father's greeting was little more than a stammer.

Katherine of Buckingham quickly turned her attention to Morton, and this time, her smile contained genuine warmth. "My lord bishop, you are also most welcome here. It isn't often that we receive such a distinguished guest." Dropping gracefully, she knelt to kiss his episcopal ring while Morton marveled that Buckingham could remain unmoved by her.

For she was beautiful—not perhaps with the flawless, porce-lain perfection of her sister, which had in any case always seemed to Morton to be unusually cold, but with the vibrant, warm appeal of a living woman. She shared Elizabeth Woodville's features, though here they were not so finely cut, and her hair, like the former queen's, was blonde though not of the same pale gilt. Katherine's was instead of a bronze luster, streaked here and there to a golden sheen by the sun. Apparently, the duchess spent a great deal of time in the sun. Her face and neck were tanned to a shade of warm honey, and a tiny web of lines around her eyes marked many hours squinting into its light. The hand she extended to him was calloused and rimed beneath the nails with half-moons of dirt, as if she had just been digging in a garden.

Morton looked into her eyes as she rose, trying to fathom her. Ah yes, her eyes spoke volumes even when she smiled. Here again were her sister's eyes, deep blue shading into violet and fringed with dark-gold lashes, but they told more of pain and sorrow than Elizabeth's ever could. There was a lingering shadow that her smile, warm as it was, could not banish. Morton looked from her to her husband and surprised himself with a swift stab of sympathy for Katherine Woodville. How difficult it must be to be married to such a man, a man who had never forgiven her for their forced union, a man who had only just returned from destroying the rights of her family, a man who, if rumor spoke true, almost hated her.

Unfortunately, Morton's own schemes were hardly calculated to bring her any more happiness than she already knew, so he forced down the unfamiliar wave of empathy. Still, he vowed, if there was ever a way in which he might improve her lot, somehow he would do it.

With that thought, he allowed her to show him to his chamber. Buckingham had been right about that at any rate; Brecknock Castle revealed a far more cheerful aspect from within that it had from the outside. The great hall was still in the Norman keep, but the family living quarters were a recent addition of lavish proportions.

Morton found little to criticize in his own accommodations, which occupied the top-most floor of one of the turrets, an airy circular chamber with leaded diamond-paned windows looking out on the moors. The walls, wainscoted below and lightly plastered above, were covered with tapestries that echoed the jewel tones of wine, gold, and blue in the Turkey carpet. The furnishings were few but tastefully rich: an oak chest bound with bronze, a carved box chair, a prie-dieu with ivory crucifix, and a large tester bed with blue silk coverlet furred with marten and intricately worked with Stafford knots. On a pedestal next to the bed, there was a vase of freshly picked marguerites mixed with late roses, bright red.

Morton paused for a moment to admire them, wondering as he did so if Buckingham's duchess had consciously selected two of the foremost symbols of Lancaster out of consideration for his old allegiance. He felt pleasure at the thought but instinctively curbed it. It would not be wise to acknowledge Lancaster now.

"As your husband's prisoner, I did not expect such luxury," he said when he had completed his inspection. "Thank you, my lady . . . my most gracious lady."

Katherine flushed and smiled, the soft smile that did not quite touch her eyes. "My husband ordered that you were to have the best that Brecknock has to offer. And even if he hadn't, I would have seen to it myself in return for the good service you have done my sister the queen."

"My service was not good enough, I'm afraid. It failed to stop the boar."

She gave a little involuntary grimace. "Yes, I know. My husband—" She broke off abruptly, biting her lip at the disloyal thought. "But your attempt was a valiant one, and for that, I salute you." The small moment of confidentiality was past. When she spoke again, it was as the mistress of a great house. "You must be tired and dusty from your travels. I will have a page bring you refreshments and warm water so you can bathe."

With that, she was gone. But even while he could still hear the jingle of keys slapping at her waist as she moved down the stairs, Morton was wondering what part she might play in the coming conspiracy.

Chapter 36

Rain was slashing down by the time Morton received the summons for supper. Like everything else about that wild country, the rain came hard and driving, blown by a wind that whistled around the castle parapets and threatened to breach the very masonry itself.

It had grown chilly as well, and Morton was glad of the two wide hearths, one at either end of the hall, blazing with great fires despite the fact that it was only early August. In fact, the hall seemed altogether warm, cozy, and almost intimate given the wild storm outside. An old Norman construction, it occupied the first two floors of the original keep, but it too had been much modified for comfort and beauty. Most of the round double arches remained, but the furnishings were modern and rich. Colorful tapestries hung from the gallery, and the floor appeared to have been recently tiled. Morton surveyed the room with approval, noting especially the banners of the House of Stafford hanging proudly from the double–hammer beam ceiling as he warmed himself before one of the fires. There was an occasional hiss as a flurry of rain found its way down the chimney. Outside he could hear a rumble of thunder as the storm lashed its fury against the Beacons.

At supper, he shared the high table with the duke and duchess. The fare left nothing to be desired, even to his discerning palate. It was both abundant and elaborately prepared. One dish followed another as plum-liveried servers flocked to the dais in great numbers, each bearing his heaped platter. Eel tarts, blandissory, wine soup, baked pork in a coffin of pastry surrounded by raisins, dates, and hard-boiled eggs, a flock of roast pheasants superbly dressed. Morton partook heartily of each offering and drank more of the sweet Rhenish and malmsey than he had intended. He had long been guilty of the sin of gluttony as the girth of his belly betrayed, but he would still have to do penance for this night's work.

Both Buckingham and his lady expressed concern over the dishes. "Was the blandissory prepared to my lord bishop's liking?" "Do they serve such eels at Holburn?" "Would my lord care for a drop more wine?" The duke was particularly solicitous, especially when one considered that Morton had been dining at his table, though not the high table, for more than six weeks and he had never been consulted before. Through a brain fogged by excessive wine, Morton perceived that the whole banquet was somehow extraordinary and that Buckingham was actively wooing him. To what end, he could perhaps guess.

Between the duke and duchess, there seemed a tenuous truce, but whether out of honor for his visit or from long habit, he did not know. Once or twice, he caught Katherine's eyes fastened on Richard's collar with an expression of almost-naked pain.

"What, Kate?" asked Buckingham. "You don't fancy my newest bauble?"

She reddened and looked quickly away. "My lord, I said nothing."

"No, but you thought much, I daresay. It's most rare. Worth a king's ransom, wouldn't you guess? A token of Richard's love and thanks for the service I've done him, for I've done him good service, Kate, very good service indeed." His face too was flushed, perhaps with wine, for he had consumed a considerable quantity. Drunken laughter rumbled in his throat like thunder among the Beacons.

Kate did not reply. Beneath the gold of her suntanned face, it seemed that every drop of blood had left her.

At last, the dessert was brought in, a huge fruit tart rich with clotted cream in a thick golden crust, and after that figs and nuts and cheeses to be washed down with yet more Rhenish. Finally, Morton pushed back his chair and belched contentedly into his napkin.

"Come, Morton," cried Buckingham, bounding up with as much energy as if he had just sat down to supper. "I want you to meet my son and heir."

"Will you excuse us, my lady?" Morton asked Kate. It was a civility the duke had omitted.

"Yes, my lords," she replied. "Tell the children that I'll be up soon to hear their prayers."

The nursery was the province of the English governess, a thin-lipped maypole of a woman who wore a perpetual scowl. The duke's younger children were already in bed, but the older boy and girl were there to greet their father and his guest.

"Morton, I give you my son Harry, someday to be the third Duke of Buckingham."

The youth extended a solemn hand to the bishop. He was a sturdy-looking lad and quite old enough to be a page in some noble household. The duke rumpled the boy's hair with a playful gesture, and the young Harry, pleased at this attention, beamed up at his father with the same unabashed adoration Morton had seen that afternoon.

"And this little lady, who might she be?"

She was half-hidden behind the skirts of the governess, using them for a refuge as she had used her mother's earlier. From that vantage point, she looked out at the world through wide, pale-lashed eyes. However, the governess was not one to tolerate such poor manners in her charge. Rudely, she thrust the lass forward.

"Her?" Buckingham asked absently. "Oh, this is Anne . . . my daughter."

"Do you forget yourself, gir-rl?" the governess questioned. "Haven't I spent long hours teaching you the art of a proper curtsy?"

The commanded curtsy was a clumsy affair that stopped just short of a stumble. Buckingham's sigh declared that he had expected little more. A pity really. Were it not for her painful shyness, she would have been quite a beauty with her nimbus of red-gold curls and white unfreckled skin.

"They're lovely children," Morton said politely as the nursery door shut behind them.

"The boy will do, particularly when you consider he had the misfortune of being born half a Woodville. The girl . . . well, as you have seen, a timid, puling little thing, and more than half Woodville from the look of her. I don't see any Stafford in her getting. Richard did well not to take her."

Morton guessed at the import of this last remark but chose not to press it. Instead he said softly, "The Woodvilles gave us a queen."

"No! They only gave the king a whore."

Morton shrugged. "All proclaimed her queen. She was anointed, crowned. How can a few words from an old man's mouth change that?"

The duke did not reply. He appeared to have other matters on his mind than the irregularity of Edward's marriage. He led Morton to his own privy chamber, where a great, roaring peat fire blazed on the hearth. Two cushioned chairs had been set before it, and between them was a low table with a decanter of ruby Venetian glass glowing in gold filigree, two matching hanaps, and a plate of cakes. Morton's nose caught the pungent odor of clove and cinnamon and ginger.

"Come," the duke beckoned him, "won't you share a sip of hippocras with me?"

The words were on Morton's lips to refuse. He needed no more to drink and particularly not the heavy, thickly spiced wine. However, it occurred to him that this cozy little scene had been carefully arranged for his benefit. Tonight at last they would have their tête-à-tête. He settled himself into the chair while Buckingham poured the wine.

"I must confess, I am rather proud of my son," he said casually, handing Morton a goblet. "I realize that I'm flouting custom by not farming him out to get an education under a stranger's roof, but I can't bring myself to do it. It seems that all the education needful for the third Duke of Buckingham can be obtained right here at Brecknock."

"I'm sure you're right about that," Morton agreed, "though if I may say so, the lad has many years yet for the gaining of worldly experience before he is called to that dignity. Your Grace has hardly reached your prime. The day of your son's dukedom is a long way off—unless of course . . ."

Buckingham lifted his head, suddenly alert. The jewels in his collar winked green and orange with the movement. "Unless? Unless what?"

Morton frowned as if he had said too much and was afraid to continue. "I . . . I merely thought that if Your Grace were to attain . . . a higher title, that would leave your present estate open for your son."

"There is only one higher title."

"Yes, of course. An idle thought."

Buckingham did not immediately reply. He only sat and thrust the poker restlessly at the innards of the fire. Morton thought the heat was almost suffocating as it was. Why so hot a fire in August, even on a cool stormy evening? He relaxed in his chair and pretended drowsiness, but his half-closed eyes were fixed on his host, who appeared to be in a state of great agitation. Beads of sweat glistened on his forehead and upper lip as the poker went again and again into the heart of the fire. Morton knew that he himself presented a complete contrast: the country parson about to drift off to sleep after an unaccustomed feast—warm, satiated, complacent, content.

"Dammit, Morton!" Buckingham spat. "You wily old fox!" The bishop's eyes flew open with a start. "You have the most maddening habit of starting to speak then breaking off in midsentence or of implying more than you're willing to come out with. But still it hangs there. You always leave it dangling. Like a man on a gallows, you can hardly ignore it."

Morton gave him a look of feigned contrition. "I am most sorry, my lord, if my ways give you offense. Perhaps I'm too accustomed to being alone, where I speak only with myself or with God. Both of us know what I'm thinking even if I don't speak it aloud."

"Yes, I know that story. You with your book and your beads and your cloistered walls. I've heard it all before but never believed it. You scheming devil, the cloister's not for you."

This last was said not without a certain affection, and Morton smiled a little to himself. "If Your Grace specifically desires my opinion on any subject, you have only to ask. I shall try not to . . . er . . . evade the issue."

"Good!" Buckingham refilled his own empty goblet and sugared his wine with a heavy hand. "Last night in Abergavenny, we were speaking of Richard. You were about to say something concerning him then shut your mouth like a steel trap."

"I would speak no ill of the king."

"Yet you thought it, or so you would have me believe. Will you or will you not be open with me?"

Morton's eyes fastened on a glowing coal. He wondered how far he dared provoke Buckingham. "But, my lord, you are Richard's chief supporter. He is nothing except what you have made him, and to speak to you of such matters is much the same as speaking to the king himself. Even now, you wear his badge, the mark of his affection. How then, for my own safety's sake, would I presume to speak ill of him to you?"

"So this is what troubles you then?" Buckingham asked. Morton watched, incredulous, as he lifted the collar from his neck and held it in his hands for a moment as if weighing it. Then he dashed it into the fire's maw, pushing and banging at it with the poker as if it were a living evil that might at any moment arise from the flames and attack him. The white-hot coals swallowed it with a sigh. "There now," Buckingham said, sitting back with an air of satisfaction. "The boar is gone from between us. You may speak frankly."

But Morton was temporarily speechless. The magnitude of the act overwhelmed him. How the duke must hate Richard, but why? Surely only a fool or a madman would deliberately destroy an article which, if sold, would keep Brecknock fed through many a long winter. The bishop cleared his throat, but when at last he opened his mouth, his voice still wavered. "Regarding . . . ah . . . regarding King Richard, I would, of course, take nothing away from his virtues. But," he added, raising a hand to forestall the duke's inevitable bleats of protest, "I have often wished that God might have endowed him with some of the qualities in which Your Grace excels."

"Is that all?" Buckingham demanded. "I destroy a priceless object in order to pry your mouth open, and that's all you have to say?"

"All?" Morton replied, affronted. "I have just stated outright that you have the qualities to make us a . . . ah . . . better king than the one we have. What higher praise can I give you? What more can I say than that?"

"Yes, yes. But I would *be* king. I won't play second to any man, Morton. I cannot abide it, and I will not. Yes, perhaps I am close to Richard as you imply. Perhaps I am second to him in the realm. Yet I only see how far I am from being a king, how great a gulf there is between a king and a duke, even the first duke in all the land. Why should it be? The very same stuff flows through my veins as flows through Richard's. At first, I thought it would be grand to be a king-maker, to set on the throne one of my own choosing. Yes, I thought to reign with him, to share everything with him." His voice cracked a bit; he sighed and went on. "But it didn't turn out that way. Richard has the throne, and I have nothing. Nothing! I won't wear another man's yoke, no matter how thickly encrusted with gold and jewels. Do you understand me, Morton? I will not!"

"Perhaps . . . you shall not always have to," Morton said softly.

"What did you say? Speak out, man!"

"Please, Your Grace, you must give me time to think, time to plan. I can't wrap it all up and give it to you here tonight. By the five wounds of our Lord, these things take some doing. There are means to remedy your situation. I cannot speak of them yet, but they are there."

Buckingham was obviously impatient to hear more, but the firmness in Morton's voice cut him off short. "And now," the bishop said, rising, "if you will excuse an old man who has just completed a long journey, who slept badly last night, and who has partaken of an overabundance of food and drink tonight, I'll seek my bed."

"Yes, I'll excuse you, you old scoundrel," Buckingham said, lifting his glass in a farewell salute. "Until tomorrow. Sleep well, for I have great need of your clear head on the morrow and in the days to come."

Chapter 37

EARLY THE NEXT morning, Kate went riding. After the rain, the air was sweet and fresh as newly washed linen. She gulped in great breaths of it as she walked to the stables.

Clean, she thought sadly. *Will I ever feel clean again?*

The groom gave her a sullen, disapproving look as he saddled Doucette, her spirited sorrel mare.

Riding out alone again? his eyes seemed to say. *And dressed like a man in a tunic and hose! And with the master not home yet twenty-four hours by the clock. Disgraceful—that's what it is.*

More tongue clicking as she mounted, throwing a shapely leg over the mare's back. No lady of breeding rode astride like a man. It was more graceful, more dignified to use the sidesaddle, the fashion that Anne of Bohemia, queen of Richard II, had introduced to Britain a hundred years before. More graceful and dignified, Kate would have admitted, but hardly as comfortable and seldom as secure. The rider should be one with her mount, not perched on top of it like a marchpane bride on a wedding cake.

The portcullis creaked open as she approached, the drawbridge was lowered. Though it was still early—from the position of the rising sun, she judged it was only a little past prime—the castle was already stirring. The night watch was coming away from the gate tower; the household servants, seeking their posts. From the kitchens came the heady aroma of baking bread.

She was almost certain that one at least still slept in the castle, but why then did she feel that strange prickling on her arms, that uneasiness between her shoulder blades as if she were being watched? When she turned in the saddle to look, there was only Morton, dressed in his nightshirt and waving to her from the window of his room. Over the duke's windows, the curtains were still tightly drawn.

She did not plan her route; indeed, there was no need to. Through the beech grove that stretched north from St. John's Priory and up the valley of the Honddu, she rode. The gray-skinned trees trembled as if a light breath stirred them. Doucette's hoof falls were muffled by a carpet of beech mast scored by long patterns of sun and shadow. They splashed across a narrow stream swollen with rain and left the beeches behind them. Ahead lay the steadily rising moors.

All this Kate passed without seeing, for her thoughts were elsewhere that morning, and they were far from pleasant. They seldom were when he was at home. Three months and more he had been gone from Brecon this time—three eventful months in her own life, whatever had been happening in the far-off world of London, three months of unaccustomed luxury, of spring and early summer when her laughter had come as often as the birds' songs and her heart had danced for sheer delight on the breeze. Three months, and her little quota of freedom was spent. He had returned with a heavy, oppressive hand to slap her down as though from heaven, to bend her as always to his will and his way.

She had hoped that he would leave her alone last night, that his appetites would have been sated by the numerous pleasures of London. Crawling into bed, she had breathed a frenzied prayer that he would not disturb her rest. Sometime later, she awakened to the rustling of bed curtains and the rasp of drunken breathing. She smelled faintly the sour reek of wine.

She had allowed it as she would have allowed a rapist who held a knife to her throat. The act itself was a brutal humiliation. There had never been any love between them and, for many years, not even a residue of tenderness. Yet there were times, and last night had been one, when he took a perverse pleasure in coaxing a response from her unwilling body. Then he had drawn away from her without ceremony and gloated over her.

"Well then, fair Kate, what a pity you can't convince your cunt to share your low opinion of me." He laid a proprietary hand on the mound of her belly, and a wave of revulsion, stronger than languor, overcame her. Sharply, she pushed him away.

"What fire, my pretty! But then I always did admire your spirit except perhaps when it interferes with my rights in the conjugal bed."

"Oh, go find Percival!" Kate had snapped. "He's certainly more to your taste than I'll ever be."

Undaunted, Buckingham had chuckled. "Why, that's exactly what I intend to do, although my tastes, as you call them, are considerably more varied than that. And since I've been away for so long, I thought you might have need of a lusty young buck between your sheets."

"That I do not!" she replied, turning on her side so she could not see him, the satin sliding beneath her naked skin as she drew up her knees for solace and protection.

His laughter rippled over her, cold as the winter wind that blew off the Mynnd Epjynt, the low range of hills across the moors. "Such ingratitude, lady, ill becomes you."

She had felt rather than seen him leave, felt the bed suddenly empty of his weight, heard him groping for his hose in the dark. Then the door had clicked shut behind him, leaving her to her unquiet dreams.

Those dreams had not faded yet, even though by now she was far from Brecknock. The bracken and gorse of the moor had given way to bare, hummocky hills, notched here and there by deep wooded glens. Up one of these, she rode almost by instinct, through a forest where birch and pine and a few scarlet maples mingled with the smooth boles of the beech. Beside her, the merry splashing of a stream as it tumbled over a series of falls and the cries of the birds overhead, made a mockery of her melancholy. Her heart began to beat very fast. And then there it was at the edge of the clearing, a sheepherder's hut, stone walled and sod roofed. It gave no sign of human habitation.

"Kate! What the devil? I didn't expect you today."

He stepped out, stooping through the low doorframe, but nothing about him proclaimed that he belonged there. To be sure, he was dressed simply enough: an open-collared shirt of lawn, leather jupon and boots, plain tawny hose. Yet he possessed a lean native elegance that defied the humbleness of his surroundings.

"Oh, Robin," she cried. "Thank God you're here. For a moment I was afraid you weren't."

"Lucky for you, *cariad,* that I am," he said with mock sternness, "particularly since we had no appointment to meet."

"Doucette brought me here. You may blame her."

"Incorrigible horse! For that, you shall have a sugar lump." The wet nostrils nuzzled for a moment at the palm of his hand. The outrageous luxury of the sugar lump was consumed with one toss of the head.

"So you encourage her bad habits!" Kate teased him.

"Ah, yes," he said, smiling his mock-stern smile. "I can readily see that this is all Doucette's doing. You only follow where she leads."

"Not entirely," she confessed. "Should I not have my reward as well?"

He stood, head slightly cocked, regarding her with the slaty blue eyes that could at times be as hard as the rock of his native hills. There was a majesty about him that never ceased to awe her. At twenty-six, Robin Vaughan was a true son of the *uchelwyr,* the Welsh chieftains who had once ruled here. His hair, pure black and smooth as a raven's wing, attested to his Celtic ancestry. He had inherited something else from those ancestors as well: an innate and formidable power that seemed to rise from the land itself. She trembled now under his stern gaze, fearing the whim of rejection. Then his eyes softened.

"Yes," he said gently, lifting a hand to stroke her cheek. "Yes, you shall have your reward." Taking her hand in his, he helped her dismount and led her into the cot.

It was the most primitive place she had ever known, bare of all except the most necessary furnishings and smelling of animal flesh. Their bed was a pile of straw hastily covered with an old cloak. She would not have traded it for a queen's couch. In the windowless dark, their bodies glowed translucent, two pale candle flames intertwined. She was safe and at peace. Gone was the initial fear that he would not want her, gone too the memories of her husband's unwelcome caresses. Both were consumed by the flame of their love. Cleansed, purified, she lay in his arms, innocent as a babe. She ran her fingers lightly over the matting of hair on his chest while he pulled her nearer and murmured an endearment in his musical Welsh tongue: "*Dwi'n dy garu di.*" The words were strange to her, the language a barrier between them, for it reminded her as always of the two irreconcilable worlds in which they lived their separate lives and which yielded them up to each other only for a little while.

Against her thigh, she felt him stiffen, and that she understood well enough. Soon they would make love again, more gently this time. The first had been wild, tumultuous, full of desperate, longing passion. The next was infinite sweetness, calling forth the very soul from her body to stand beside his. For one shining, piercing moment, they were one. And then once again, they were two though still love-locked.

His voice came to her from far away. "So he didn't come home then?"

"Yesterday," she replied, heavy with love and sleep. "In the afternoon."

She felt the sharp intake of his breath, the sudden rise of his chest where her head was pillowed. "And still you came?"

"I had to. You don't know what it's like, how awful it is." Involuntarily, she shuddered. "Please, Robin, don't be cross with me."

"No, *'nghariad i*, that I could never be. But I thought we had agreed. It's too risky for you to come here while he is at Brecknock. I don't fear for myself, though I'm sure he'd like to get his hands on me. But you . . . do you have any idea what he might do to you?"

"He hurts me merely by being alive. Can't you see that? His hatred withers me. It's now that I need you most—now, when he is here."

He sighed and, in answer, kissed her forehead. They lay in silence for a time, lost in their own thoughts.

"And he's come back loaded with honors, I suppose," Vaughan said at last.

"Oh, yes. To hear him tell it, Richard has given him all of Wales."

"Such a gift can never be given!" he cried fiercely. "No, nor taken either. Wales is not for the likes of him."

Kate felt a trembling fear. She would never fully understand this passion for his native land nor the bitterness he felt toward its English rulers. It clutched at him always, like a jealous mistress, and she prayed he would never be forced to choose between this other love and herself.

"There . . . there was someone else with him," she said, hoping to change the subject. "The bishop of Ely is our prisoner or our guest. I don't know which."

"Ah, the wily John Morton."

"You know him then?"

"Know of him. Who doesn't?"

"But why do you call him wily? I don't understand. He seemed most courteous to me and perhaps a trifle careworn."

"It's his reputation. Some of my people would say he has the 'sight.' He seems to read men's minds and acts on what he finds there. I believe he is only extraordinarily clever and dangerous too perhaps."

"He looks harmless enough. And he has been a good and loyal friend to my sister the queen."

"So therefore he must be a good man," he said teasingly. She saw the curve of his smile in the semidarkness and took no offense. "But you will see, Kate, that loyalty is not as simple a thing as you might think. What you perceive as loyalty may be mere expediency once you scratch its surface. You are wise in many ways, but your isolation here has kept you naive as a child in others, for which perhaps God be thanked." He tipped her chin back with his finger so that her lips met his own, and so ended all discussion for the time.

Later, too much later, she was awakened by his hand on her shoulder. He was already dressed and now stooped by the bed. "Wake up, *cariad*. I think you'd better be going."

She yawned awake. "Is it late?"

"If you hurry, you may be back at Brecknock for the midday meal."

There was no time for dallying. She rose and dressed quickly and, in her usual fashion, haphazardly. She had never cared much for clothes. However, when it came to the parting, she was reluctant to leave, for she never knew when, or even if, she would see him again. She clung to him in wordless despair, and it was he who finally detached her hands from his neck and set her in the saddle. She was close to tears as he urged the horse away, but she did not look back. The sun caught her flying hair and flamed it like a beacon. She could feel his eyes upon her until the forest swallowed her.

Her absence had gone unnoticed at Brecknock, or at least uncommented. She was informed that the duke had gone out riding with the bishop of Ely and was not expected back until later in the afternoon. She thanked God for that brief respite and also for the fact that their paths had not crossed. Robin was right. It had been dangerous for her to seek him out when her husband might stumble on them at any moment. If he should find her in the arms of his sworn enemy, the consequences would be too awful even to contemplate.

She took a solitary luncheon in her apartment, but had not even finished it when she heard a knock on the door. She opened it to one of the maids, a Welsh girl named Morgan, a rather pretty young woman of seventeen with tightly coiled auburn hair and a fey look in her normally downcast eyes. Today, however, those eyes were wide with fear as she stood in the anteroom, clutching a dirty, crudely wrapped bundle.

"Why, Morgan! What is it, child?"

"Oh, milady, I . . . I've found something most . . . most 'orrible."

"Horrible? Let me see it. I'm sure it can't be as bad as all that."

Silently the girl handed over her burden, and when Kate had undone the linen wrappings, she too gasped.

"Where did you find this?" she demanded.

"In . . . in the master's rooms when I was cleaning the hearth. Oh please, my lady, you must believe me. I didn't do it."

"No one is accusing you of that. But who then? Who would dare?"

"I . . . I don't know, milady, to be sure. I was sweeping out the grate in the m-master's privy chamber, and I saw somethin' a-shinin' like down in the ashes. I bent to p-pick it up, and there it was. It . . . it must 'a been witches that done it."

"No, not witches, child," Kate said thoughtfully. "I don't believe it was witches." And she added as the girl's forehead puckered in a frown, "You say you didn't do it, and I believe you. It's quite all right. Run along now."

For a long time, Kate stood alone and wondered how it had happened, this wanton destruction of the duke's proud new collar. She could not believe that any of the servants, even the most fervent of the Welsh, would dare lay a finger on the king's gift. Even though she herself bore Richard no love, she could not have done such a thing. It had been beautiful, after all, in a garish way, the metal filigree of leaves and twisted branches exquisitely worked, the gems large and flawless. It was exactly the sort of ornament Buckingham favored: rich, costly, ostentatious. Richard had read him well. How angry would he be with her, with the entire household, to find it in such a state, the delicate filigree melted and blurred, sockets that once held gems gaping like blackened holes, emeralds and topazes cracked by heat in their settings. And the boar, that great pendant of rare ivory, burned and dented to a lump of charred ash.

She slipped it back into its wrappings, for the sight of such wanton destruction sickened her. But the question still tormented her. Who? Who would dare? And then suddenly the answer came. Who but Buckingham himself? She still did not know why; she could scarcely conceive of any *why* great enough, but she did know there was no other possibility. The collar had not been dropped into the fire by accident. Buckingham was never that careless with anything so fine. No, from the look of it, it had been thrust deliberately into the hottest part of the flames then smashed hard and quite willfully with the poker.

The idea was so stunning that she had to sit down quickly on the bed to steady herself. After the first wave of shock had passed, she was surprised to feel a twinge of sympathy for her family's old enemy, Richard of Gloucester. She still bore him no love but recognized a dawning pity in her heart because her husband, the chief of his supporters, was about to play him false.

With a certain solemnity, she laid the mangled collar in the very bottom of her dower chest, sure in the knowledge that Buckingham would never seek to know its fate. Robin had been right. Loyalty was not always what it appeared to be. And to pretend a loyalty where none existed, that was the greatest wrong of all.

Chapter 38

JOHN MORTON WOULD have been glad never to see the back of another horse. He had not yet quieted the nagging complaint in his posterior whenever he sat for any length of time. On the other hand, Buckingham was already restless on his first full day back in Brecon, and Buckingham wanted the bishop by his side. If the duke wished to go abroad, Morton must attend him.

He played the lord of the manor that morning, inspecting his estates, collecting some overdue Lamas Day rents and tithes, seeing to the progress of his crops in the fields, his sheep and cattle in the pastures. His estates were vast, much more extensive than Morton had imagined. Obviously, the duke meant to impress his guest with the extent of his wealth. Morton was impressed by something else as well. Everywhere the duke was received with the cool politeness that veils strong resentment. He would never make a king. Once the impressiveness of his face and bearing had been probed, he was like a dumb-show king, without substance. Nevertheless, he would prove entirely satisfactory for Morton's purposes. Morton had never intended to make him king.

At midday, they rode up into the high hills that bordered the Beacons. Here, in one of the cliff-edged *cwms*, a cool stream flowed out of a forest. It was one of the few real forests on the Beacon flanks, shadowed deep green and cool, protected by the mountain's steep sides. It was also the duke's hunting preserve. Morton noted that the other members of their party, including Percival, remained well out of earshot on the lower slopes. They had spotted a wild boar and taken up the chase. Even now, far away, he could hear their excited shouts.

Meanwhile, the duke and bishop sat on silken cushions by the banks of the stream, the sun bright overhead, the grass and tufted lady ferns a fresh-washed green around them. From the nearby wood came the occasional chirp of a bird and the snapping of a twig or scraping in the underbrush that marked the course of some small animal. The murmur of the stream in its stony bed was the only other sound.

They had brought an excellent luncheon: spicy sausages fragrant with herbs, fresh bread with creamy cheese, and a pale light wine that they cooled in the stream. Morton ate heartily. Buckingham only nibbled at it and seemed preoccupied.

"Have you thought any more about the matter we discussed last night?" the duke asked.

"Indeed, I have . . . somewhat," Morton replied with his usual maddening hesitancy. He was engrossed in the slow journey of a great scarab beetle, polished to a red-brown lacquer like a living cabochon, on a twig he had picked up from the ground. "Look how the poor creature walks from one end to the other, trying to find an exit. He labors all the way up, but when he reaches the top, I turn the stick over, and he must begin again."

"Most fascinating," Buckingham said acidly.

"But most purposeful. You will note that he never stops to rest. Such will deserves to be rewarded." He laid the twig gently on the ground and watched the beetle amble away awkwardly through the grass.

"Morton! Did you or did you not hear my question?"

"Yes, my lord, I heard it. And I told you I had given the matter some thought."

"Well then?"

"We must turn the people against Richard."

"Is that all?" The duke laughed in derision. "A two-year-old child could have told me as much."

Morton assumed an injured air. "And could he also have told you how?"

Buckingham sobered. "No, that isn't so simple."

"Well then," Morton replied, leaning back against his cushion. "At least we agree on that. As you know, Richard is quite popular. He has set out to win the people's hearts and gives every indication of succeeding. If we allow him to enjoy the fruits of his usurpation much longer, he may become too firmly seated for us to remove him, and that would be a pity."

"We must act soon then."

"Yes, soon." Morton's eyes shone with purpose. "The act must be a sudden one and also particularly repugnant. And it must, without question, be laid to Richard's door. Not by the merest breath of suspicion should it touch us, though we shall be standing by to reap its benefits."

"And what might this act be?"

"We must slay the princes."

The sun was very hot. Morton could feel its burning touch on his nose and high-domed forehead. Beside him an army of black ants attacked the remains of his lunch.

"Aye, I've thought about that," Buckingham replied at last with none of the surprise and shock that Morton had expected. "I thought Richard should have disposed of them long ago for his own safety when I—when his safety still mattered to me. But he would have none of it."

"In that, he acted most wisely."

"How can you say so?"

"Because the slaughter of those two innocent babes is the surest way I know to turn the people against him, to turn love into hate. It would make him the most despised man in the kingdom, and he knows it."

"I don't think he thought of it like that," said Buckingham, a distant look in his eyes.

"Quiet, man!" Morton said sharply. "Are you forever going to play the romantic fool?"

Buckingham hung his head. Like an animal revealing a vulnerable underside, he hastened to protect himself. "Well, I urged him to do it at any rate. I thought the Woodvilles would try to restore their brats as long as one of them was alive."

"So they would. So in Kent and Sussex and the southern counties, they are trying to do even now. Even as I would have done . . . had not a better opportunity presented itself."

"You're a strange one, Morton," the duke said, stretching his body full length on the grass and plucking at a delicate lady fern. He regarded the bishop with a mixture of suspicion and awe. "A most strange man. All those years you served Edward IV then risked your very neck to keep his son on the throne. Yet now you speak blithely of his murder."

"Nothing less than murder, as you call it, will do," Morton replied vehemently, "though I prefer to think of it as a sacrifice. Do you think I enjoy the prospect of killing young children, that I delight in it? Nay, I shudder at it. My heart quakes within me. It's a vile and loathsome necessity to obtain a greater good. Otherwise, you'll have the Woodvilles waging battle on one hand and Richard on the other fighting to contain them. And what do you do then, man? Do you pop up between them like a jack out of the box and say, 'I'd like a crack at this thing too'? At best, they would spit in your face. More probably, one or the other of them would skewer you on the point of a lance. No, you must come up on one side or the other, and your best move right now is to align yourself with the Woodville cause."

"The Woodville cause?" Buckingham sputtered with laughter. "You must be joking, bishop."

"You announce—very privately, of course—that you have had a change of heart and now repent of your aid to the usurper. You wish to restore the boy Edward."

"But who would believe me? I've always hated the whole tribe and made no secret of it."

"You have also had the benefit of my . . . ah . . . influence these past weeks to point out the error of your ways. And your wife—"

"Kate?"

"—is a Woodville. You are strongly connected by marriage. She could mediate between you and Elizabeth. If you can manage to convince her, she'll convince the rest of them. They can hardly afford to spurn your aid. Their cause is still in its fledgling state. You can guide it, give it direction."

Buckingham was listening now with rapt attention. "And when they learn that Edward and his brother are dead?"

"They will have you to turn to. And you, full of righteous wrath and indignation at the magnitude of the boar's crimes, will have an army at your back, ready to sweep the fiend into the dustbin. The rest of the people, even setting aside the Woodvilles and their supporters, will turn to you too when they see you are prepared to lead them. Who else will they have? Who else of the blood royal is of an age to govern? Despite your previous, unfortunate alliance with an unscrupulous murderer—whom you will, of course, openly and vigorously repudiate—they will have to accept you. There will be no one else."

"There is Henry Tudor."

Morton coughed sharply, bringing a flood of bright crimson to his face. He sometimes forgot that, for all of the duke's vaunting ambition, he was not a stupid man. "Yes, so there is," he said when he had recovered himself. "But I don't think he needs to concern us too much. A penniless exile in a foreign court. He is not near the scene as you are, nor does he have your popularity with the people. Sometimes I think even the old blood of Lancaster has forgotten him."

"Do you really? And you such a good friend of his mother, the Lady Margaret? You haven't forgotten him at any rate, that I'll warrant."

For once, Morton had nothing to say. He sat still on his cushion, his eyes riveted on the rainbow of bubbles made by a tiny waterfall. A school of minnows fluttered black against the stony bottom. He dipped his finger into the pool, and they fled, lightning quick.

Sometimes, he reflected, *it is better to remain silent.*

"Oh well," Buckingham said presently, "I suppose you're right. Certainly he doesn't appear like much of a threat now. I've heard that he's by no means fair to look upon. Rather sharp and narrow, they say, like his mother. Quite unimpressive. Not the stuff in him to make us a proper king."

"Yes, so they say." The big popinjay! So he thought that looks were all of it, did he? He, who had them in such abundance! So he thought that being chosen king was much like courting a maid. Well, just let him think it. Let him aspire to what he considered his rightful destiny. At the proper moment, Morton would have to relieve him of his illusions, but not now. Not yet. Let him get himself in deeper first, like a fly in treacle, then bang! The trap would spring, and this fine and noble duke, this big popinjay, would be well and truly caught.

Buckingham rose, brushing crumbs and grass from his hose as he did so. Even in less formal attire than he wore in London, he was still well turned out. He dressed the part he yearned to play; there was no mistaking that.

"Come, Morton, we'd best get back to Brecknock. Unless I misconstrue the look of those clouds, we're apt to get another shower before evening."

Morton was glad to oblige despite the prospect of mounting his palfrey, docile old nag that she was. Their conversation had gone far enough for one day, too far indeed for his own comfort.

Buckingham found Kate in the garden on the second morning after his return. She was much surprised though she did not show it. The garden was her preserve; he never entered it. She had planted it, nurtured it as it sprouted, and watered it in the dry seasons. She had pulled out the choking weeds and nettles with her own fingers and with her hands dug deep into the soil. It had never been elaborate: a few bushes blooming now with late roses making a scarlet splash in the sun; fragrant lavender, germander, and mint geranium; white-starred marguerites. The kitchen herbs grew in profusion in their neatly marked beds: marjoram and thyme; sage, parsley, and rosemary; rue, vervain, and valerian. There were also two apple trees and a plum hung with hard green fruit.

He sat down on a stone bench, one she often used for her own contemplations, and watched as she knelt on the flagstone walk, her fingers busy plucking out the weeds that had sprung up since the rain. She felt the keen disapproval in his gaze.

"Why you find it necessary to use yourself like a cotter's wife, Kate, I'll never understand." His voice had the nagging whine she so hated. "Look at your face and arms, brown as a villein's. And your hands, black with dirt and calloused as a scullery maid's." She drew back sharply the hand he had taken for his scrutiny. "And you, such a great lady, my duchess! Why, in all the land, you should give place only to the queen."

It's only a title, she thought though she did not say it aloud. *An empty, meaningless title. I would be happier married to a cotter with my own patch of earth free to the sky than with this little walled garden in the shadow of a castle I cannot call my home.* Aloud she said, "I enjoy my garden. It occupies my time."

"As you enjoy your riding?"

She gave him a quick, searching look, trying to keep the working rhythm of her hands steady so that they would not betray her. The expression in his eyes was impenetrable.

"Yes," she replied, grasping a handful of nettles, "as I enjoy my riding. But surely, my lord, you didn't come out here merely to reproach me for my various shortcomings. Do you have some business to discuss?" She stood, brushing her hands on her apron and giving him her full attention.

"Ah, Kate, you're right," he said, slumping on the bench. "I didn't mean to carp at you. Just the opposite as a matter of fact. I know I've treated you shamefully over the years because of . . . the unfortunate accident of your low birth and because I felt you had been foisted off on me against my will. Now I see it's I who have been the churl and you the lady. I am . . . most sorry for it."

She stood stone-still, unable to believe the words of apology and regret she had never expected to hear from his lips.

"I have been blind," he went on, "blind and mistaken about many things. I . . . I have helped a usurper to the throne of England. Because of my unreasoning, insensitive hatred toward your family, I have supplanted your blood. I have raged with a boy's bitterness and false pride. I only hope that a man's strength and courage will help me put things to right."

"What are you saying? What are you trying to tell me?"

"I mean to restore Edward V to the throne."

In the sun-washed square of the garden, time itself stopped. She heard the trickle of water in the fountain, a fat bee buzzing in the roses. Everything else almost seemed to have ceased being.

"And Richard?"

He spat at the name. "I hate him! He has most marvelously misled me."

She could not quarrel with his assertion of hatred. She had proof of it, wrapped in dirty linen and stowed in her bride's chest.

"What do you want me to do?"

"Write to your sister the queen. Tell her . . . tell her of my change of heart. It must be done with the utmost secrecy, of course. I'm still high in Richard's favor, and it's best for our cause that I remain there for some time longer."

Kate continued to stare at him, disbelief warring with her desire to take what was offered—the highest noble in the land, the chief prop to Richard's throne. Without him, Richard surely must fall. Yet why did he hate the king so much? What could have happened to throw Henry Stafford so abruptly into the arms of his old enemies?

"Ah, Kate, fair Kate," he murmured. Seizing the hand that a moment before he had held up in derision, he began to kiss her dirt-rimmed fingers. "I've been a sorry bargain as a husband, I'm afraid. But if you will do this one thing for me, it will be better after this, I promise. You'll come to London with me, Kate, and take a place of high honor—wife of the first duke of the realm, aunt of the king. Perhaps we shall find time there to rediscover each other. When we were younger, there were a few times . . . I almost fancied myself in love with you despite everything. Perhaps—"

She pulled back her hand and absently wiped off the moist print of his lips on her apron. "You don't have to offer such enticements, my lord. I'll write your letter."

He broke into an engaging smile, a smile he seldom turned on her. "You've made me a happy man, Kate, the most happy of men. You are providing the means for my salvation." Quickly, too quickly, he sprang to his feet. "I'm going to the chapel now to confess my sins and pray for the success of our venture. Won't you come with me?"

"No, my lord," she replied tartly. "I have no sins to confess."

"And the letter?"

"I'll write it today."

"Good. We must get it off."

"You're not afraid that Richard's guards might seize it?"

"My dear," he intoned patiently as if she were a backward child, "the sanctuary guards are my handpicked men. They will hardly stop one of their own."

Kate noted that even if her husband despised Richard, he did not yet despise the power that Richard's favor gave him. But then Buckingham would never despise power from whatever source it came.

She did not immediately follow him in. With her heart pounding loudly in her ears, she stayed behind to tidy up the garden plot, to prune the roses, to gather a bit of aromatic thyme and sage for the evening's roast duckling. Yet her mind was far removed from these tasks. She could hardly conceive that the duke did not have some motive of his own in this, unseen and unknown to her. Still, he had spoken almost reverently of her sister as the queen, whereas before she had been, mockingly, "Dame Grey, the king's whore." Something had changed him then, but what?

Slowly she turned back toward the castle. Again she felt eyes on her, and looking up, she caught the face of Morton latticed behind the diamond panes of an oriel window. How long had he been standing there, staring down at her with his tiny watchful eyes? He gave her a friendly smile as she looked up, a smile wreathed by the jowls of his chin. Involuntarily, she returned the greeting with a smile of her own.

But of course! It must have been Morton who had wrought this change in her husband. Who else could it have been? Robin's words echoed with new meaning: *wily, clever, dangerous*. Was he right? But if such a one took up your own cause, couldn't he be invaluable? Still wondering, she passed through the arched entry of the keep into the castle.

Elizabeth Woodville let the letter drop from her long jeweled fingers. "It is most fortunate that this letter comes in my sister's hand. I could hardly credit it otherwise." The skepticism in her violet eyes revealed that even so some doubt remained.

Percival regarded her without expression, his eyes very pale, the long white scar on his cheek even paler against the darker skin. "You may trust His Grace on this, madam. He has utterly renounced the usurper."

"Privately, of course."

"Of course. How else could he be of service to Your Grace?"

She sighed. "I would like to believe it, but you must admit his past history gives me little cause. Was it Kate? Has she somehow managed this . . . this transformation?"

"I believe the Lady Katherine had some influence, yes. And the bishop of Ely—"

"Morton? I should have guessed it."

From the abbey choir of Westminster, the interminable chant of the plainsong rose and fell and rose again. She walked over to the window and gazed out at the free, nonmonastic world where a fine mist of rain dripped from leaden skies. Two black-habited monks pulled their cowls over their heads as they made for the monastery's postern gate. Oh, to be free at last of those monks and this abbey! To be safely installed once more in the palace on the riverbank!

Aid from an unlikely source. The Tarot cards, her companions in exile, had told her to expect it; they had also warned her to be wary of it. Yet she recalled the day that Jane Shore had come to her with an offer of aid almost as improbable. Hastings had proven himself genuine with his life. Now, her own sister vouchsafed a change of heart in the man who, next to the boar himself, had been her worst enemy and at a time when her partisans were laying the groundwork for a plot to restore her son to the throne. What couldn't they do with the mighty Duke of Buckingham at their head?

Finally, she turned back to Percival. He had not moved during all those long moments. The eyes that watched her were wintry cold with none of the admiration she was accustomed to seeing in men's eyes. Something else was there instead, something deeply shadowed and even sinister. Contempt? A chill shook her to the marrow of her bones, to be as quickly dismissed. What had she, rightful Queen of England, to fear from a mere courier?

"You may tell your master and Bishop Morton that we accept with gratitude their offer of assistance. We shall be in contact with our son Dorset and our brother Salisbury and tell them to accept aid from whatever quarter it comes. You may take back with you our fondest greetings to our dear sister Katherine, your duchess, and to your lord, her husband."

Percival bowed with every mark of respect. "Your Grace," he murmured as he backed away from her toward the door.

A small trace of a smile lit Elizabeth Woodville's lips as the momentary tremor of fear was replaced by elation. She had never in her entire life expected to see such reverence from Buckingham or any of his adherents. It seemed that victory was within her reach at last.

Chapter 39

BUCKINGHAM DID NOT know when it was in the midst of his own high hopes and expectations that he first noticed the change in Morton. When had they begun—these downcast expressions, the long inexplicable silences, the deep sighs welling up from some dark void? Surely there was no outward explanation for the bishop's melancholy. The duke had kept his guest royally entertained. During the mellow days of late summer, there were hunting and hawking expeditions, though Buckingham had begun to suspect that Morton endured these more for the sake of courtesy than he actually enjoyed them. In the evenings, there were lute singers and jugglers and masques after the duke's ample kitchens had yielded up the best their variety and ingenuity could offer.

Still, Morton remained strangely despondent, and Buckingham, attributing his depression to homesickness, was quite beside himself, trying to concoct new entertainments and diversions. Like Richard before him, Morton had become the focal point of his world, the lodestar that guided him and all his bright prospects.

Nothing seemed to help. Even Percival's triumphant return from London with the news that the queen dowager had accepted their services was greeted only with a disconsolate "Good then" and a muffled sigh before the bishop turned away from Buckingham's enthusiastic embrace.

Not until the unexpected arrival of Reginald Bray did the duke begin to piece together the pattern of Morton's odd behavior.

Margaret Stanley's most trusted man of affairs was a slight figure, well into middle age, and reputed to be scholarly. The eyes that peered at Buckingham were red rimmed and nearsighted, perhaps from long hours of reading manuscripts. He was hardly the sort to cause alarm, the duke reflected as he watched this latest arrival being ushered away to Morton's chamber. Yet he had come in such obvious haste that his livery was still dusty from the road; he had not even taken the time to brush it. Uneasily, Buckingham recalled that Margaret herself had visited Morton while they were still in London. Percival had come upon them in the garden, heads bent together like conspirators. He had dismissed the report with a wave of his hand then. Now he remembered and was worried.

"Now see here, Morton! What the devil's going on?" He barged into Morton's room without knocking as soon as Bray had quit it and found the bishop kneeling like a penitent before the prie-dieu, his plump white hands folded before him, his eyes fixed unwaveringly on the agony of the cross.

Heavily, Morton rose from the faldstool, crossing himself as he did so. His look was one of the utmost dejection.

"What is Reginald Bray doing at Brecon?" Buckingham pressed. "Since he seems to have become my guest, I think I have the right to know."

"He has been sent, I suppose, to keep my feet on the true path."

"Henry Tudor!" Buckingham spat. "I should have guessed it, you contemptible old fox!"

"Please, Your Grace," Morton said, "don't be angry. I have . . . the question has tormented me for days. No one in England has a better claim to the throne than you do—no one! Your lineage is impeccable. I myself freely admit that the Tudor and Beaufort lines are both . . . well, rather in doubt, crossed with the bend sinister, one might say. But Henry Tudor is the acknowledged Lancastrian heir. He will have all their support, and it is not . . . unformidable. Also, he will be free to wed the Princess Elizabeth. Once the princes are disposed of, she will be York's true heiress. It is too perfect. It cannot fail."

Buckingham's mouth gaped open in amazement and out-rage. "God's nails, Morton, you've tricked me. You lying devil!" he screamed. "You have tricked me!"

Morton held up a restraining hand. "Pray, my lord, do calm yourself. Do you want the whole world to hear? I mean you no harm. This is simply a better plan. It gives greater promise of success."

"Where are all those you said would rally to me? I would have the support of the entire kingdom. Weren't those your words?"

"I . . . I believe I may have said . . . something to that effect, yes. But suppose for a moment that Henry Tudor decides to avail himself of the same opportunities. Take the Woodvilles. How long do you think you could keep their support with Elizabeth espoused to the Tudor?"

"Ah, but you've forgotten one thing, you wily old bastard, one very important detail. What's to stop me from going to Richard and telling him everything I know?"

Morton blinked in surprise. "What's to stop you? But perhaps Your Grace has forgotten. You are one with us now. The queen dow-ager has your letter, proof of your complicity. Bray knows, I know, your duchess knows. Surely you can't rid yourself of all of us. Then there is . . . ah . . . the matter of Richard's collar. A magnificent gift, that, a pearl of great price, a token of the bond between you. It would be most . . . inconvenient, would it not, if Richard asked you to produce it? And undoubtedly he would wonder at its absence. A pity that it is scarcely in a state to be seen . . . even if you knew where to find it."

He had him. The trap was sprung. Buckingham's anger had spent itself, drowned in a great, dark pit while Morton, watching him keenly from heavy-lidded eyes, lost for the first time in days all traces of despondency.

"You won't be any less valuable to us now simply because the focus of our small movement has . . . ah . . . shifted," Morton's voice oozed on. "You are mighty in this land, and we have need of your power and authority. Your cooperation is critical to us. Who else can open the doors and accomplish the deeds that are necessary to our end? And when King Henry comes into his own, you shall not go unrewarded."

The duke gave him a bitter laugh. "So I'm to play kingmaker again, am I?"

"And what's wrong with that?" Morton wanted to know. "To make a king and break him. To set another in his place. Who will be your equal? None! Word will go out that as Henry Stafford ordains it, so shall it be. He who can put even kings through their paces."

"It wasn't so with Richard."

"That was Richard. Henry is of a different mettle. He knows how to express . . . gratitude."

"I . . . I must think about this."

"Then think. But don't be too long about it. We must act soon. I'm sure that after you've thought, you will decide there is but one conclusion, one choice left Your Grace."

One choice. Yes, Morton had made certain of that. How artfully he had contrived it; how skillfully the trap had been set! Tears misted Buckingham's eyes as he fled the room. Richard had never used him thus—playing on his fondest hopes, only to betray him. And Richard had amply rewarded him. He could see that now. He had been greedy, wanting more than Richard had been able to give. Morton had dangled an alternative before him with glittering promises, and he had grasped at it. There could be no retreat for him now, no going back. He could not crawl into Richard's bosom and be safe. He had already started on the long, dark path that led to an end he could not guess.

And yet wasn't there a chance that affairs would turn out differently than even Morton planned? After Richard was deposed, before the Tudor had taken his seat, the throne would be empty for a short but very crucial time. He would watch and take his chances, using Morton as Morton had used him. He would never allow himself to be a footstool for Henry Tudor or for the bishop of Ely either.

Kate often went out riding during those last days of August. With the return of Percival and, shortly thereafter, the arrival of the man called Bray, a change had come to Brecknock. The air was as charged with tension as the sky before a storm. There were many meetings behind closed doors: Morton and Bray, Morton and Buckingham, the three of them together. Sometimes Percival was included in these conferences; at other times, he and his lord met alone.

What strategies were being hatched in these sessions, Kate did not know. After the first day in the garden, she had received no more confidences. She had served her purpose and been cast aside, though that in itself hardly dismayed her. She only wondered what they were about, these men. And who was Bray? Was he her sister's man? Odd then that Elizabeth had never mentioned him in her correspondence. Odd too that he had not come forward to pay his respects to her as might have been expected.

Then too Buckingham had changed. Deep lines puckered his forehead, and his full lips were tightly set. He went about his business with a joyless determination so different from his high good humor of a few days before.

Left to her own devices, Kate rode out every day, far and wide across the sweep of mountain and moorland purpling with heather. On occasion, she dared go to the sheepherder's hut on the far side of the valley, but she found it deserted. The ashes were cold in the grate, and it had obviously not been used for some time. Robin's absences did not disturb her; they had been frequent and unexplained ever since the day almost four months ago when he had found her seeking shelter from a sudden storm in this very place. He had known her then for the wife of his enemy and had loved her despite that.

She could not go there often. Although her husband appeared to be preoccupied with other matters, she knew he could have her followed if he wished. She must be careful at all costs. Instead, her horse picked its way up the steep slopes of Pen-y-fan, highest of the Beacons, with the broad expanse of moor rolling away beneath it and, far to the southwest, the shining sea of the Bristol Channel. Then she rode up Pen-y-crug to Brecon Gaer. Not as high as the Beacons but better situated, Pen-y-crug commanded the focal point of several valleys that radiated out from it like the spokes of a cartwheel. Here the early Britons, ancestors of the Vaughans, had built a hill fort. It lay in ruins now, its stones a jumble. But even here she felt a nearness to Robin and his ancient lineage.

Then one morning she saw it, the sight she had been hoping for—a plume of blue smoke lifting gently down the valley. She ran back to the place where she had tethered Doucette, stumbling over rocks and hummocks and bracken roots, her heart pounding a sweet music in her ears. The mare almost flew down steep-sided Pen-y-crug and was lathered with sweat by the time they reached the hut. He came out to greet her, the warm light of welcome in his eyes.

"So you've come," he said simply. "I had hoped that you would." He caught her in his arms as she half-leapt, half-fell from the horse. "Easy, *cariad*, easy. It would hardly do to break any of those pretty bones and particularly not here."

Inside the hut, there was the comfort of the fire to take the edge from the morning's chill, and there were his hands, tender and experienced, to pull off her worn man's garments and reveal the soft woman's flesh beneath.

"You are beautiful, Kate," he murmured, "and where the sun doesn't reach, your skin is still white as mountain snow."

However, now it was washed pink by the firelight. She felt the warm urgency of his lips upon her, the exploratory longing of his fingers, and she gave herself up to him in joyful surrender.

Later they sat naked before the fire, sipping a cup of ale together in the afterglow of love. "Have you been back long?" she asked, suddenly afraid that she might have missed him earlier.

"No, only since last night. I'll admit that the fire was a bit of a ploy to bring you here. Against my own advice, I might add. I hoped you would see it from the high places."

"I'm glad you lit it," she said, burrowing beneath the crook of his raised arm. "You stayed away so long, Robin. Too long. Where were you?"

"Hush, Kate," he said, shaking his head. "That's not something you should know for your own safety as well as mine."

The rebuke chilled her even though it was gently given. Once more she was aware of how small a part she shared of his life.

"Nor for that matter, should you even be here, though I will take part of the blame for that."

"Please don't tell me that, Robin. I have to come here. I must escape. The tension at Brecknock is horrible. Something is afoot there, and though I hope that good will come from it in the end, it is almost unbearable now." Before she was even aware of it, she had spilled out the whole story: the jeweled collar pulled from the ashes, Buckingham's rejection of King Richard, his decision to throw in his lot with the Woodvilles, and the appearance on the scene of Bray, the stranger whose role in all this she could not guess.

He listened with more than cursory interest to all that she told him, and when she had finished, he looked thoughtful. "I'm not sure you should have told me this, though I'm grateful that you did."

"Does it mean something to you?" she asked in surprise.

The firelight glinted in his eyes. "It may. It may indeed."

"What then?"

"There isn't much I can say. I will only tell you for your own knowledge that if war comes, we may fight for King Richard."

The words hit her like a hammer blow. Had it finally happened as she had always feared it would? Were they facing each other from the opposite sides of a gulf? "King Richard? But why? I thought you hated all things English."

"Not *all* things, English, Kate, as you surely should know by now." He reached out a tentative finger and traced the curve of her breast. "We hate the English rule, true enough, but if we must be ruled by one who is not our own, you will at least allow us to have a say in his choosing. Yes, I know, your nephew would be king if your husband's maneuverings succeed. It is that you are hoping for, isn't it? But for the country at large, for England and for Wales, Richard is clearly the better choice. He is fair and just and means to do right by us, I think, even despite his grants to Buckingham. The error of that gesture he will see soon enough.

"Richard was governor of the marches once when I was little more than a youth, but my father has often said he ruled well, as well as any Englishman could. Da' had his knighthood from Richard and considered it no shame. In fact, I think that only if a Welshman aimed at the crown would we desert Richard's cause. Your nephew Edward, if you'll forgive me, Kate, is still a babe who needs his mother to wipe his nose. As for your husband . . . well, I mistrust his motives altogether. Surely you don't mean to defend him to me, do you?"

"N-no," she said, on the verge of tears.

"My words may have sounded harsh. I didn't mean for them to be, but you must understand why you can no longer tell me freely of all the doings at Brecknock. Although I would listen greedily, for it is information we need, I can't allow you to so hurt your own cause. You are linked to it by ties of blood and marriage—strong ties that cannot be broken, even for a love like ours."

She wept at that soundlessly. Only the shaking of her shoulders revealed her to him. "Kate," he said huskily and reached out a hand to touch her. Quickly, he drew it back. He no longer had that right.

"No, Robin, please no. I . . . I must go." She stood slowly. Even in her sorrow, there was a dignity in her nakedness. She dressed the same way, without haste, scarcely seeming to know what she did. He said nothing, only watched her from the depths of his own despair.

"Good-bye, Robin. I wish you well. I . . . I only wish—" but her teeth bit back the words, and she could say no more. She walked from the hut in a trance, leading Doucette by the reins. Later, she would feel grateful that he had not tried to use her. She would see a measure of love in that. But for the time, she felt nothing. There was nothing left in her that was capable of feeling.

Quite on her own, Doucette found the way back to Brecknock. Left to herself, Kate might have wandered the moors forever. So it had ended. She told herself with the regularity of a refrain that she had always known it would end. Why then did it come as such a terrible shock? Why did she feel so helpless, so lost?

Then suddenly, surprisingly, the towers of the castle, the thick gray walls of her prison, reared above her. She drew her reins in sharply as two men clattered across the drawbridge and passed her without notice in the street. Percival and Bray. On through the town, they rode in great haste. Later, she was informed that they had taken the high road to London on the duke's business. What that business might be, no one would say, nor was she at that moment particularly inclined to care.

Chapter 40

THE OARS OF their small skiff dipped noiselessly into the Thames's dark current. Percival and Bray had passed the terraced gardens of the Strand, the mansions behind them dousing their lights one by one. Behind them too were the gray hulk of Baynard's Castle, rising sheer from the water's edge and the great cranes of the Steelyard, black skeletons against the night sky. Under an arch of London Bridge, they had slipped, silent as a moth, at low tide. Now they drew even with the piers of commerce that were by day the very heartbeat of London. At night, they were deserted, and the huge carracks of Venice and Genoa swung and creaked uneasily at their moorings.

Beyond the ships' masts, the Tower rose, its walls glowing a faint chalky white in the light of a haloed full moon. Beneath their oars, they felt the unmistakable tug of a rising tide.

Percival cast an anxious look upward and scowled. "A curse on that moon," he muttered. "On any other night, it would have been black as a witch's cunt, maybe even a little rain if it had not been wanted. Now the very tide goes against us, God rot it."

"I don't think we can expect God to work for us tonight," Bray said, trying to keep the heaviness he was feeling from sounding in his voice. "What matter the moon anyway since our filthy task is to be done indoors?"

"Aye, but we must leave afterward, or haven't you considered that?"

Bray had not. In fact, he had considered nothing beyond the deed itself. Once it was accomplished, he expected the retribution of heaven to be both swift and violent. He wiped a sweating palm nervously on his hose.

"Oh, I suppose it will go well enough," said Percival, favoring Bray with a lopsided smile. The scar was a livid white slash in the moonlight. "Well enough indeed with what I carry in my pocket." He patted the place over his chest where he had stowed both the duke's official order and a vial of white powder.

Bray did not like to think about that vial nor about how it had been obtained—coaxed from a very reluctant Margaret Stanley only the day before. Her eyes had mirrored shock and disbelief.

"Has Morton taken leave of his senses?" she demanded. "Even to suggest such a thing!"

"I don't like it any better than you do, my lady," Bray had admitted, "but there does seem to be no other way."

"Couldn't the boys—oh, I don't know—be taken away somewhere to a place where Richard won't find them, where no one will be able to prove for certain whether they are dead or alive?"

"We've discussed that possibility," Bray explained with more patience than he felt, "but what would happen later if they were found after Lord Henry was on the throne? Surely, it would prove . . . most inconvenient, particularly if his title rests in part on the claim of his wife in right of her brothers."

The gray eyes had blazed at that. "Are you suggesting that my son's claim is not sufficient in itself? That he must depend on a Yorkist doxy if he hopes to take what is his by right?"

The debate had gone on much longer with Margaret more than usually obstinate. Bray was growing weary of the fight when Percival, who until that point had remained silent, intervened.

"Madam, you should know that we mean to accomplish this deed with your aid or without it. If you grant us your assistance, their deaths will be easy and painless. I'm told that your apothecary is very skilled in the use of certain . . . ah . . . potions. A bit of monk's bane in their milk instead of a struggle and screaming and knife wounds and blood—the choice is yours."

"Stop!" she had cried, clapping her hands over her ears. "Please stop. I'll do anything you say, anything. Only, never mention it to me again."

Bray had no intention of disobeying her. Indeed, the act was growing so repugnant in his own mind that he could no longer recall why he had urged her to it. Now that they were at the Tower, the dread in him was strong enough to be almost palpable. He tried to concentrate on the task at hand, the difficult one of pulling against the current to bring the skiff beneath the arched water gate of the Tower. In a rush of dark water, they were in. Percival, nimble as a cat, leapt ashore to secure the boat to its moorings.

"Halt! Who goes there?" The challenge, though not unexpected, caused Bray to start. He slipped on the slime of the lower step and, catching himself, looked up through iron bars and flaring torchlight into the face of a Tower guard.

"We come on urgent business with your constable," Percival replied, "from the lord high constable of England." The flame dipped nearer as the guard inspected the burning wheel badge on Percival's sleeve, the eagle displayed on Bray's.

"Begging your pardons, sirs, but one can't be too careful these days, what with all the unrest to the south. A pretty peck o' trouble there'd be if some I could name got within these walls."

"Indeed." Bray heard the squeak of his own voice as the massive gates swung open to admit them. Percival was already striding ahead as if he owned the Tower, purpose in his step. Bray followed behind with the air of a small boy tagging along after an elder. There were a few resin torches smoking in sconces along the walls and an occasional streak of moonlight where an unglazed window slit opened. But for the most part, darkness and dampness seemed to permeate the very stones. Sweat trickled in rivulets down their rough-hewn surfaces.

The constable's apartments along the inner southwest wall were more congenial. A servant let them into a comfortable, well-furnished room where a small fire still crackled on the hearth. Before it was a long, cushioned settle and an old mastiff stretched and twitching in sleep. The constable, Sir Robert Brackenbury, had apparently retired for the evening, for when he stepped from an inner chamber, he was tying a deep-blue silk dressing gown around his ample waist, and his eyes were heavy lidded from sleep.

"Well, gentlemen," he said, running a hand over his thinning, tousled hair, "this is a surprise. What brings you to London, Percival? I thought you were at Brecknock with the duke, taming all those wild Welshmen."

Percival managed a smile that was almost cordial. "Wild Welshmen must wait their turn, Brackenbury, when my master has other duties to perform for our sovereign lord."

Brackenbury moved to the hearth, bestowing a cursory pat on the dog's head as he went, and removed a kettle from the hob. "If we are properly to discuss your business, might I first offer you some tea?"

Over the rim of his cup, as he sipped the hot and bitter liquid, Bray took the measure of the Tower constable. Of middle years and long a supporter of Richard in the north, Brackenbury had come to his important post not by shrewdness—he had none—nor even by exceptional ambition. He was a simple, easy-going fellow, the kind the king liked around him. And he was loyal to Richard, loyal as the midsummer's day was long. He would fight to the death for him if need be, though just now that prospect must have seemed remote. The warrior in Brackenbury had given place to the gentleman of leisure. The easy affluence of his position told in the slack line of his jaw, the thickened girth of his waistline, and the rustle of French silks about his body.

Percival drew Buckingham's letter from his pocket and gave it to the constable. Carefully, Brackenbury broke the seal, the flamboyant scarlet seal of the lord high constable, and held a candle close to read it. The first flicker of doubt showed in his brown eyes as he raised them to Percival's.

"So Richard favors removing the lords bastard to Brecknock," he said, rubbing one big hand over the stubble on his jaw. "Odd that he hasn't sent me some word."

"There wasn't time," Bray ventured, but his voice was a squeak, and the words came out all in a rush. He took another swig from his cup and prayed that Percival would carry it from there. And Percival, cup in hand, booted legs crossed languidly before him, showed no reluctance.

"You are aware, of course, that the king's grace and my lord duke have often discussed the removal of Edward's sons from London but have never been able to decide on an appropriate place, one that would offer security yet would not be . . . ah . . . unpleasant for them."

Brackenbury nodded. Whether or not he was privy to such discussions, he certainly could not disclaim knowledge.

"I needn't remind you," Percival went on, "how highly the king regards both of his brother's bastards. Nor need I tell you how deeply he would regret the discomfort caused by establishing them in some strange and unfamiliar place."

The constable leaned forward, nodding eagerly. "How well I know it! Though I'll not hide the fact that it gladdens my ears to hear someone else say it. There are rumors in London, unspeakable rumors, that Dickon means the lads harm. Can you believe it?"

"Bones of the saints, no!" Bray croaked.

"Why, every time I hear it, I feel like taking my fists to him that says it and teaching him a thing or two about his king, if he'll learn it no other way." Shaking himself like a ruffled turkey cock, Brackenbury sat back on his bench.

Percival shook his head. "Unfortunately, that would accomplish little, my good constable. What you're hearing are Woodville slanders started by those who wish Londoners to believe the boys are in danger. They hope for a storm of sympathy to break down the Tower gates. You yourself know how absurd such gossip is. The boys are in your keeping, and you look like a man who would scarcely harm a flea."

Brackenbury shifted uneasily in his seat as if wondering whether to take offense at this remark while Percival pressed smoothly on.

"Of course, the Woodvilles would delight to get their hands on Edward's sons if they could. There is no doubt what would happen then. Though the bastards are obviously removed from the succession, an attempt to restore them might cause Richard some inconvenience. Don't you agree?"

"Oh yes, to be sure."

"Tell me, Brackenbury, have rumors reached you yet concerning the unrest in Kent?"

"Why, yes, only yesterday. John Fogge and St. Leger, the king's own brother-in-law, mind you." He clucked his tongue in harsh disapproval. "Francis, that would be Lord Lovell, of course, argued that Dickon should make a progress through the southern counties, but he's stubborn, Dickon, like an old mule—meaning no disrespect to the king, of course—and sometimes . . ."

"Sometimes he doesn't seem to know what's best for him . . . or else he learns it too late. That's the case now. He should have tended to his nephews before he left London, but he lingered. Now he is at York, and they are still here. Like a magnet, they draw all the disaffected to them. Wouldn't it be better if they were removed to a place of safety and comfort? Wales is a fine land for boys to grow up in, far removed from the filth of the city. And at Brecknock, they would have the care of their own aunt, my lady duchess, who, though a Woodville by birth, has been influenced to her betterment by my lord duke's devotion to King Richard. There too they would have for companions their young cousins, who are of an age with them."

"Aye," Brackenbury agreed, his eyes clouding. "Too often have I watched them, poor motherless urchins, shooting at butts or playing at bowls on the green, and I've pitied them in my heart that they are so alone here, that they seem sometimes . . . well, almost like prisoners."

"Their graces mean to remedy that," Bray said.

Still the constable hesitated. He was not a stupid man, but Percival, playing sweetly on his most cherished loyalties and sensibilities, could not have failed to woo him away from the dictates of his own common sense. Now however, he looked up once more from examining the leaves at the bottom of his cup and gave them an appraising look devoid of sentiment. "I must admit I'd feel more . . . ah . . . comfortable about this if I had the king's own word. It's all very well that the duke—"

"And when, sir," Percival barked, "have you seen one act without the counsel of the other?"

Brackenbury lowered his gaze. He watched as the dog twisted and whined in sleep then lay still. "Nay, never . . . not of late."

"Then you may be sure that King Richard will commend you heartily if you act swiftly in this. We leave for Brecon tonight."

"Yes, of course."

Percival rose to his feet, and Bray somehow managed to stagger to his own as his companion droned on. "Time is essential in this as, of course, is secrecy. We will leave by the water gate. The success of our venture, perhaps even the security of Richard's throne, demand that we not be observed by anyone, not even by the jackanapes of a guard you have on duty down there. Do you understand?"

Brackenbury bridled a little. "Are you suggesting I withdraw my guards?"

"Do you have any whose loyalty you would stake with your life? It could very well come to that, I assure you."

Brackenbury hesitated momentarily, but fear burned in his eyes. Life was a commodity too precious to chance. "I will withdraw them."

"And the duke's letter? It wouldn't be seemly if some page were to pick it up."

"No, of course not." He took the candle and held the paper to its flame, watching as the edges blackened and crumbled into ash, as the red wax of the seal melted and dripped into a tiny puddle at his feet. Then he cast it into the dying fire.

"You will take us to them?"

"I go for my keys."

When Brackenbury returned a short time later, he was dressed for going out. He walked before them down the narrow passage, a lighted cresset held aloft and a great bulging key ring tucked into his girdle. The Garden Tower was not far from the constable's own apartments. Soon, too soon, he lifted a hand to halt them.

"Best to wait here," he whispered, "while I tend to the guards."

Percival smiled and nodded. Bray could hardly believe how willingly Brackenbury was playing into their hands. Mild, easy-going, eager-to-please Brackenbury.

A few seconds later, they heard his voice raised in consternation. "*Nom de Dieu!* What's this I see? Dicing again, by the mass! I don't doubt Lady Grey herself could come and steal her bastards from under your very noses and all you'd see would be spots on the dice. You're a disgrace to the guard, both of you. I'll have your liveries for this night's work. Just see if I don't. Now get out of here. I'll guard the lads myself."

They heard the guards' mumbled denials, pleadings, and apologies then the shuffle of retreating footsteps. A moment later, Brackenbury beckoned to them from around a corner.

"Hated to do it to 'em," he said, selecting a heavy key and slipping it into the lock. "They're good lads, both of them, and the nights are uncommon long here. Still, gaming on duty is against the rules, though I'm like as not to wink at it."

"It made a convenient pretext for their dismissal tonight," Percival said, smiling his faint half smile.

"Yes, yes, of course," Brackenbury replied as the lead-bound door swung open. "I'll let them off tomorrow with a fine."

Inside, the constable dipped his cresset to a rush light, and the chamber glowed into shadowy life. They stood in the lower room of the Garden Tower, which served Edward's sons as hall and parlor. It was small but rather fine, with a high-vaulted ceiling and a broad mantle over the hearth. Arras tapestries hung on the stone walls, perhaps to blot out the damp, while fresh rushes covered the floor. By day there would be a view of the flowers and the fountain of the constable's garden through the small arched windows. Now the silvery sheen of moonlight touched it with a ghostly radiance.

A large table of polished oak dominated the room, and on it were several books bound with leather. Bray recalled that Edward was said to be scholarly. He too fancied himself a scholar, and books were enough of a rarity to capture his attention even at such a time as this. Or perhaps, he thought wryly, at such a time as this, any distraction would have sufficed.

Lovingly, he ran his hand over one of the leather-tooled bindings. Percival was asking Brackenbury for bread and cheese to serve as a wayfaring meal for the boys. "Aye, and a pitcher of milk to wash it down. We must travel far tonight, and it'll be a long time till breakfast."

Long indeed, Bray thought. *Jesu, the whole sweet sleep of eternity.*

The pages were smoothest vellum, the language was Latin, but the author was English enough. It was the Lord Rivers's *Dictes of the Philosophers* that flowed beneath Bray's fingers. That would be the boys' uncle—no, their late uncle, whose head had been struck from his shoulders at Pontefract, slain by the tyrant Richard. Slain. Gooseflesh prickled the back of the hand resting on the vellum page.

On the frontispiece was a print of the boy Edward standing with his parents while Rivers, kneeling before them, presented his book. Well drawn, it was. The artist had caught their likenesses; they seemed about to move or speak. On the flyleaf, neatly if self-consciously inscribed, was the legend "Edwardus Quintus Rex." Abruptly, Bray snapped the cover shut and looked up to meet Percival's contemptuous stare.

"If I had known that you preferred reading to the duties we must perform tonight, I would have left you at Westminster by the Red Pale so you could inspect Master Caxton's works at your leisure."

"I-I'm sorry. I suppose we should . . . er . . . get on with it?"

"If you're quite ready." Percival gave him a mock bow. "They are up there," he said, pointing to the upper chamber. "They must be awakened."

"And you want me to . . . ?"

"Do you see anyone else? God's teeth, man, are you going to stand around all night like a lazy wantwit and leave all the work to me?"

Reluctantly, Bray climbed the narrow, twisted stair. At the top was a second room, lower but otherwise almost identical to the one below. Edward slept in a large tester bed, his brother in a smaller trundle next to it. Bray could barely make out their shapes in the flickering light of his candle.

"Who is it?" Edward asked suddenly, propping himself up on one elbow. "Who's there?"

"Don't be afraid, my lord. It's Reginald Bray, Lord Stanley's man."

"Stanley?" Edward's nose wrinkled in the dim light as he apparently considered what he knew of Stanley. "But what are you doing here?"

"We've come on the king's orders . . . to take you on a journey."

"A journey? Now? But it's the dead of night."

"Bow bell has just tolled twelve."

"An odd hour to begin a journey, Master . . . ah . . . Bray, is it not?"

"Be that as it may, Edward, you had best get up and be quick about it, and wake your brother as well. There's no time to waste." The speaker was Percival. Bray turned, startled. He had not heard his companion's catlike tread on the stair.

"Ah, Percival," Edward said. "So it's you. I might have known."

"At your service." Another mock bow.

"You may address me as 'my lord,'" Edward said haughtily. "Or has it been so long you've forgotten?"

"As you will . . . my lord." Percival tossed back the bedcovers, leaving Edward lying there in his nightshirt. The boy looked warily from one to the other.

"And where do you propose to take me?"

"To Brecknock," Percival replied, "in Wales."

"Aye, my lord," Bray nodded. "A fair green country much more wholesome for growing boys than this sweating pile of stones."

"I am familiar with Wales, Bray. Lest you forget, I once had the honor of being its prince. But how do you happen to know so much about it? I understood that Lord Stanley's estates were mainly in Lancashire. Although his lady . . . I know she has some connection to Wales."

Bray cleared his throat awkwardly. "There are times, my lord, when I needs must travel."

"As you must," Percival added to Edward. "Enough of this prattle. We must be going, so be quick about it."

Still obviously puzzled, Edward swung his long legs over the side of the bed. He could hardly regret the necessity for leaving the Tower. After all, what was there for him here? With no visible reluctance, he knelt by his brother's bed and gently shook him awake. As he watched, Bray felt an ineffable sadness consume him. What fine lads they were! True Plantagenets. The downy golden hair of the sleeping youth made a glowing aureole, like a saint's, on the pillow. Bray tried to recall Henry Tudor's image to mind and failed. There was little Plantagenet in him by anyone's reckoning, yet to him, Bray's fealty had long ago been pledged.

In the meantime, Richard, one-time Duke of York, looked from Bray to Percival with lower lip extended and a fist rubbing one sleepy eye as Edward told him of the journey.

"Come on, lads," Percival said. "You must get dressed."

"Dressed?" Dickon asked, looking about him doubtfully. "But where are our squires?"

"You're old enough to dress yourself, boy," Percival said. "Others younger than you do it every day. " The stinging harshness of the rebuke brought tears to the younger boy's eyes.

"Come, Your Grace," Bray said kindly. "I'll be your squire. Best to dress warmly. There's a ring around the moon tonight, and we're like to have rain before morning."

He rummaged through the wardrobe chest, discarding as he went items of apparel that were too flimsy or too impractical for the journey. With a start, he realized that he had almost come to believe the fiction they had created. Percival gave him a swiftly guarded look of contempt as he pulled breeches and cambric shirts and sturdy woolen cloaks from the chest and tossed them on the bed.

"There," he said gruffly. "That should do it."

The boys dressed slowly in the dim candlelight, their hands fumbling at the unaccustomed buckles and laces. Edward let out a long sigh as Percival started down the steps.

"I wish we weren't going to Brecknock," he confided to Bray. "I'm afraid that devil will become my keeper again."

"I . . . I don't think your Uncle Buckingham intends to keep you under guard," Bray replied. He was helping little York fasten the buckles of his shoes.

Edward shook his head. "I never know what my Uncle Buckingham intends. There are places I would rather go than Brecknock. I had hoped perhaps Sheriff Hutton with my cousins Warwick and Lincoln . . ."

"Perhaps later," Bray offered.

Edward was quiet for a time. He had finished dressing and stood at the window, watching the moonlight silver the garden below and twinkle on the drops of the fountain. "Yes, later."

Brackenbury had returned. They could hear the booming of his voice in the room below and Percival's low interspersed replies. He had brought oatcakes, honey, new cheese, and a flitch of bacon. He apologized that there was very little milk, scarcely half a pitcher, but there would be no more until morning.

Percival muttered an oath under his breath, but when he turned to Brackenbury, his tone was pleasant enough. "It will do, I think. Thank you for your trouble. His Grace will be most pleased." Dismissal was implicit in his voice.

However, Brackenbury made for the stairs. Bray could hear the creaking of his boots, the jangle of keys as he came up. Then he stood in the doorframe, a big bear of a man suddenly overcome by emotion.

"I . . . I wish you safe journey and Godspeed, gentlemen. And you, my lords, my most dear lords."

Young Dickon ran to him and threw his arms about the constable's waist. "I'll miss you, Sir Robert. I wish you were coming with us."

"Nay, lad," Brackenbury replied, rumpling his hair. "I have too much to attend to here, though I'll do it with a heavier heart."

Edward was more restrained in his leave-taking. For him, a manly handclasp sufficed though it was plain that he too had grown fond of the Tower constable.

Percival came up behind him and stood in the doorway, breathing his impatience. At last, Brackenbury took the hint. Percival ushered him down the stair, and there was the click of the closing door. Meanwhile, Bray supervised the packing of the few small treasures the boys wished to take with them and tried not to vision the scene downstairs as Percival laid out the little repast. He did not want to think about the leather pouch and the glass vial filled with white powder that Percival would be opening now, the powder slipped into the meager portion of milk.

"Ah, the *Dictes!*" Edward exclaimed. "I certainly don't want to forget that." Before Bray was well aware, Edward had one foot on the top step.

Bray felt his face go white as ashes. "You . . . ah . . . can get that later, Your Grace. Are you . . . ah . . . quite certain you have everything you need up here?"

Edward turned to Bray with a curious look. He was certainly no imbecile, and perhaps the months of captivity, the inevitable fears for his safety, had sharpened his senses. He was about to take issue when Percival reappeared on the top stair.

"Your supper is served, milords."

"Supper?" Dickon wailed. "But we supped before bed. I don't want anything to eat. I want to go back to sleep."

"A few miles down the road, and you'll be glad you ate now," Bray told him. "It'll be a long time until breakfast."

The meal was simply laid out. On each plate was an oatcake dabbed with honey, a chunk of cheese, and a rasher of bacon. Beside each plate was a cup of milk, half-full. The boys sat down and began to nibble, leaving the cups untouched. Percival busied himself stashing their gear by the door. And Bray watched almost against his will, fascinated at the scene before him that was charged with grotesque unreality.

"You may have my milk, Dickon," Edward said, pushing his mug across the table. "I don't drink it anymore."

"There's enough for you both," said Percival too sharply. "You both should have some."

"Milk's for babes and sucklings," replied Edward tauntingly. "I'm at least past the suckling age even though I'm apparently not yet old enough to be treated as a man."

"Me too," Dickon agreed solemnly, pushing his own cup away.

"Master Brackenbury went to a lot of trouble to find some for you," Percival said. "Is this how you repay him?"

Shamed by that thought, Dickon reached a tentative paw toward his mug while Edward gazed at Percival with wary eyes. "You make much over the milk, sirrah. Could it be you have reasons of your own for wanting us to drink it?"

Sweat popped out on Bray's forehead; he pulled out a kerchief to wipe it away. Percival though merely shrugged. "Reasons of my own? Yes, I daresay I have. A dry meal gives rise later to great thirst. And I refuse to stop at every wellhole between here and Brecon to appease it, nor will I listen with good grace to your pleadings. Therefore, you may suit yourselves, but do not trouble me later."

Edward considered this as Percival turned away, deliberately uncaring, to fasten leather straps around the baggage. He raised the cup to his lips, took the tiniest of sips, then quickly spat it out. "By Our Lady, it tastes strange."

"Most likely, it's the morning's milk. Has it started to turn?" Bray asked.

Edward shook his head. "No, it's not sour. Rather the opposite, in fact, as if there were honey in it."

"Sir Robert may have added a drop or two," Percival said. "What of it? Come, drink up! It's getting late."

Edward gave him another swift, canny look. "Is there something else in the milk, Percival? A potion of some sort? A sleeping draught? Or perhaps . . . another draught for a long, long sleep?"

"I don't know what you're talking about. Would you prefer to go to Bedlam instead of Brecon? You're babbling like a lunatic."

"No," Edward said softly. "I think not. If this is to be my last moment on earth, let me at least perceive it to the full. I don't want to be ignorant as a lamb led to the slaughter."

"What's wrong, Ned?" his brother wailed. "What are you talking about?"

Edward did not reply. He might not even have heard. He looked from Percival to Bray and back again with a kind of wonder. "I wish my uncle had been content to rob me only of my crown. I wish he had not seen fit to take my life as well. Even so, I'll drink to him to the last." He lifted the mug. "To my right noble uncle Richard III, by the grace of God and his own treachery, King of England and of France and Lord of Ireland. May his soul burn in hell for this night's work." Tossing back his head, he drained the cup.

Later, Bray could not have said how long they stayed there, waiting for Edward to die. Even the child watched, eyes riveted on his brother's face in the flickering rushlight as it went slowly, slowly waxen white as if the blood were being drained away from beneath his skin drop by scarlet drop. His eyes were closed as if he were praying. Suddenly, belatedly, Bray regretted the lack of a priest. Edward deserved shriving, for the taint of a suicide was on him now. Unhinged perhaps by madness, he had taken his own life in the end with full awareness and full knowledge.

Edward waited for death, hands folded before him, lips moving soundlessly. "*In manus tuas, Domine* . . ." Then without a moan, without a cry, with only the lightest of sighs, his life winked out like a guttering candle. Edward V of England was dead.

"An easy end, Bray," Percival said, almost as if he were congratulating him. "Your lady knows her poisons well."

Dickon rushed to his brother's side. "Ned!" he cried. "Oh, Ned, wake up. Please wake up." He touched him then shook him. The body tumbled over onto the floor. "Why are you sleeping now?"

"No, Dickon," Percival said. "Your brother does not sleep—at least not a sleep from which he will ever awake."

"Is he dead then? Have you killed him?"

Bray would have gone to him if he dared. "Let's say he is now at peace with Christ and all the angels winging his soul to paradise."

"Ah, yes, let's say that then," said Percival, mocking. "It makes a pretty enough tale at any rate. And you, my lad, could be with him. You can see him again any time you wish." He held out the remaining cup. "Won't you follow his lead?"

The boy's face grew suddenly sly. He accepted the cup as if he meant to drink it then upended it so that all the precious white liquid trickled away into the rushes. "I don't want to die," he declared, clenching his fists at his sides as he turned to give battle. "I will not!"

"You'll live to regret that rash act, my boy," Percival sneered. His face was as purple as his livery. "You've just deprived yourself of your only means of salvation. That way would have been much easier."

"Why should I make it easy for you to kill me? You won't have me as readily as you had Ned."

Percival blocked the one sure means of escape, the door that led outside and to help. The only other exit led to the bedchamber, and to that he ran, clambering easily up the twisted stair. It was a futile protest at best; even the child must have known that. But Bray was forced to admire the infant cunning, the sheer force of his will to survive. There were no tears, no pleading for mercy, not even any mourning for his dead brother. The body had been abandoned as soon as he realized that it was lifeless.

Now standing behind Edward's bed, he faced both of them and fought like a Saracen for his life. He flung the pillows at them and the bedcovers, trying to blind them. In the dim bedchamber, with only a pale shaft of moonlight for illumination, he achieved some success.

"The rush lamp, Bray!" Percival croaked. "Sweet tits of Mary, get me a light!"

Bray stumbled down to the parlor, but his hands were trembling so violently that the lamp slipped from his grasp, spilling a stream of hot oil over his naked skin.

"Holy Jesu!" he cried. For an instant, he feared that the lamp would fall to the floor. If its flame had touched the dry rushes, they would all be cooked like oxen on a spit. By what miracle he caught it, he did not know.

"Bray! What the devil's keeping you?"

When he returned to the bedchamber, the boy was dodging back and forth just beyond Percival's reach, twisting on his toes like a madly spinning top. He cried for help now, weird animal sounds that began low in his throat and ended on a high, piercing wail.

"The noise!" Bray objected.

"The walls are over a foot thick. They won't be able to hear him. No one can help him now. Hold the light aloft so I can see."

For a long moment, the shadows danced on the wall like giant hobgoblins, then Percival made a great lunge across the bed. "Got him!" he cried as he pulled the boy up by his ankles. They collapsed onto the bed as Percival fumbled for his knife.

"No, not that way!" Bray objected again. "The blood!"

Percival's hand fell away. "Aye, you're right for once." He looked around for some less telltale means of execution. The beds had been stripped to their feather mattresses; bedclothing and pillows were tumbled in a pile on the floor some feet away.

"Hand me that pillow."

Dickon had gone quiet. He lay pinned beneath Percival's weight, panting hard, the breath escaping from his mouth in hard, wheezing gasps. He fixed his eyes on Bray but did not speak a word.

Bray shook his head. "I . . . I can't."

"As I feared! Have you gone soft on me? Would you leave this one alive to babble like a brook of his fellow downstairs? Come, man, the pillow! Even if you have an urge to hang, I do not."

Still Bray hesitated. The boy was struggling again, taking advantage of Percival's distraction to wriggle about beneath him like a snake. He was almost free when his tormentor stunned him with a sudden blow to the temple. He fell back on the bed. With one hand, Percival held him there while his other groped along the floor for a pillow. Had he been quick enough, Bray would have kicked it out of his way, but he stood there and did nothing. The scene blurred before his eyes as if it was playing out before him on a stage, and he had neither the will nor the means to stop it.

The pillow went over the boy's face and was pressed down with savage strength. He heard the muffled cries, the choking for breath, saw the last convulsive shuddering of the small body. Then it lay still, and there was only silence in the room.

"Well, that's done." Percival stood and wiped a hand across his sweating forehead. "Though no thanks to you, I must say. Why didn't you help me when I asked for it?"

"I . . . I could not. So young, so very young, and wanting so much to live. How could I have thought I could do it? How could I have thought it needed to be done?"

"You argued quite well for it once."

"It . . . it didn't seem the same in concept as it did here in this room."

"You're a fool, Bray, a hopeless, good-for-nothing fool. One of your fine scholars, no doubt, who lives his life by books. Well, this is life—hard, brutal, ugly. Take a good look at it, why don't you? Engrave it on your memory along with the writings of the philosophers. This is what it all comes down to in the end, and you must soil your hands in it whether you wish to or no."

Bray hung his head. There was nothing he could say.

"Well, I suppose we ought to tidy up a bit, eh?"

"Tidy up?"

"Unless you would leave our housekeeping chores to Sir Robert and his men, which you must admit would have certain unpleasant consequences for us both. If you could persuade your too-tender conscience to lend me some assistance now, I would be most humbly grateful."

Bray had given no thought to this part. Suddenly, the two small bodies seemed huge. Where in all of London could they be hidden? However, Percival showed no sign of distress. With scarcely a moment's hesitation, he opened the heavy wardrobe chest from which Bray, an eternity before, had pulled out the boys' traveling gear. But it was Bray who placed first Edward and then Dickon inside with a gentleness he knew Percival would be incapable of showing.

Edward's face was beautiful in death. The querulous lines around his mouth were smoothed away, and his skin was as clear and translucent as alabaster save where some peach fuzz, the beginnings of a manly beard that would never be, bloomed on his chin and upper lip. He looked as if he slept. Little York, though, showed all too plainly the terror of his last struggle. The small features were contorted into a horrible death mask, the skin purple red, the open mouth congealing into a rictus of pain. The eyes, which had half-popped out of the skull, were glazed now but still wildly staring. Reverently, Bray reached out a forefinger and lowered the lids over that desperate, accusing gaze.

"You're happy now," he whispered, "that I'll warrant, in a heaven I no longer hope to know."

Percival's step never faltered through all that dark, winding labyrinth.

"But where?" Bray had asked when, after the chamber had been restored to order, Percival had motioned him to lift one end of the wardrobe chest.

"There are some kitchen pits not far from here that are no longer in use."

"How did you know that?"

"I have studied the Tower well. Perhaps you did not know that I was once Edward's chief guard?"

Bray shook his head dumbly. Between them, the cumbersome trunk with the dead bodies inside was very heavy. This was another issue he had not considered before. The wood scraped his burned hand raw, and his feet felt like lead weights. When the load grew too heavy to carry, the two men pushed, pulled, and dragged it along behind them through half-forgotten ways where rats and spiders held sway, past high-barred doors that led down to the dungeons. The only sounds were the ones they made, the scrape of the chest, the shuffle of their footfalls on the paving stones.

An eternity later, they reached the pits. Without ceremony, Percival slid the trunk through a netting of cobwebs into the void. They heard it thud as it struck the bottom several long seconds later. The echoes reverberated from rock and wall.

"Jesu . . . someone will hear."

"No one will hear, Bray. The Tower sleeps. And no one has been this way for centuries."

"I thought I heard something."

"You heard nothing, unless it was the cowardly beating of your own heart. Even in my ears, it sounds like a drum. Still we had best get out of here. I do not entirely trust Brackenbury."

Bray stood and wiped his burning hand on his thigh. His back ached from the unaccustomed strain. Before him, the pit yawned, deep and dark and secret. His body tensed.

Percival caught his sleeve. "That way lies madness and does no one any good—not your lady, not her Tudor spawn, not even the bodies we have just committed to earth. It will not make them rise up again."

Bray shook his head. The impulse to jump was strong and seemed the only possible way for him to forget the horrors he had witnessed. If it were not for the sure and certain judgment of God that awaited him after death, he might have ended his life then and there.

Percival shrugged. "Suit yourself, but if you do plan to stay on this earth, I don't want to leave you here wandering about the Tower and raving like a lunatic. Come, and be quick about it."

Numbly, Bray fell into step behind Percival. They passed down more corridors, damp and narrow, until they stood at last on the unguarded steps of the water gate and the cool night air blew in their faces. High overhead, the moon rode, making a shining ripple on the Thames.

"The moon did not hinder us after all," Bray said wonderingly. "Our guilt lies in the dark and hidden places where neither sun nor moon ever shines."

"And our victory lies before us," Percival said as he unwound the coil of rope that had held the skiff. "You shall have your lady's thanks and I my lord's, and it will be worth it all."

Bray was not so sure. As he mechanically dipped his oar into the black river, he did not turn to look back at the Tower, ghostly white within its walls, but he could feel the chill that emanated from it to his very bones.

Chapter 41

"MOTHER, WHAT'S WRONG?"

Kate heard Anne's question through a mist that seemed as real as the one that wrapped the castle walls. Following her daughter's stare, she looked down and saw that the garland of ivy she was twining for Michaelmas had slid from her lap and lay, disregarded, in a heap on the floor.

"It's nothing, child, nothing," she replied, bending to pick it up. In the process, several of the leaves became dislodged. Her hands plucked another from the basket, and she fumbled awkwardly, trying to work it in. It was a tedious labor, and the number of garlands required to festoon the great hall for the feast day seemed suddenly immense.

"I hope you aren't going to be sad again," Anne said as if she were the mother and Kate the child. "It's a time to be happy, don't you think? The ivy is so green this year, and the geese are so fat. Cook says I can help baste our goose. Just think how the fat will hiss in the fire! It'll be a beautiful feast, won't it, with the apple tart and the jugglers and the dancing. Oh, please, Maman, mayn't I stay up for all of it? Harry did last year."

"I suppose so," Kate said absently. At another time, she might have been gratified by Anne's excitement and warmed by the unaccustomed blush of color in her daughter's cheeks. Today, however, she could only look out the solar window and sigh. There was little to be seen because of the fog, but that somehow made it worse. She imagined the hut as it would look now with the oaks above it turning russet and the stream making a stony murmur in its bed. Robin would be wearing a woolen cloak against the chill now . . . if he were even there.

The ring of an anvil from the inner ward, which had lately been turned into a forge, startled both Kate and Anne. The girl dropped her garland with a pained expression. "Not again!" she moaned. "Oh please, Maman, can't you do something? I'm so sick of the noise." The steady pounding continued, swallowing up some of her words. "And at night, the flames light up my room so I can hardly sleep."

"I know, I know." Kate nodded, recalling the awful red glare that seemed like the mouth of hell. "But there's nothing to be done about it. Anyway, it will soon be over once your father has enough weapons for his army. It will all be worth it once your cousin Edward is restored to the throne."

Anne's lower lip trembled in a sulk, and she twisted a fat red curl around her finger. "Yes, that's what he says, but then he laughs like it's all a fine joke. And I don't understand why he's trying to help Edward now when before . . ."

"He has repented, that's all," said Kate. "He was wrong, and he has admitted it."

Anne shook her head. "All I know is that I'll be glad when it's over. Nothing's the same anymore. That dreadful noise, and all those strange men who keep coming here—like them. Who are they, Mother?"

Kate recognized the oddly assorted trio who had just entered the solar. She knew their names and something of their backgrounds: John Rush, a pompous and apparently successful London merchant; Sir William Knyvet, an aging, battle-scarred knight; and strangest of the three, Thomas Nandick, an astrologer who affected a vacant, dreamy-eyed expression and long blue robes worked with mystic symbols. What they were doing at Brecknock remained something of a mystery.

Knyvet bowed as he spotted her. "Begging Your Grace's pardon," he said courteously. "We did not mean to intrude. We heard there was a bit of a fire in here, and as the day has turned cold . . ."

"Oh, Her Ladyship won't mind sharing her fire with us," Rush interjected. "We'll not steal her coals." He took for himself the cushioned box chair nearest the blaze and held out his hands to it. "Cold weather for September," he muttered to Knyvet. "Should ha' stayed in London. Be comfortable there, I don't doubt."

"It's those clouds I mistrust the most," said Knyvet who remained standing, looking out a window. "Armies can fight in cold, but in rain . . . ?"

"Aye and the Tudor needs fair weather to land. If the wind's from the west . . ." The hammering began again, swallowing up the rest of his words.

Nandick's high, shrill voice soared above the noise outside. "It's at Milford Haven Henry Tudor's going to land. I've seen enough to know that."

"Milford Haven?" Rush scoffed. "So far to the west? Bah! He'll be lucky enough to make it across the channel at all when the autumn gales start to blow. It's Kent, man, or Sussex—that's where he'll land. We're ready for him there."

"Milford Haven!" Nandick repeated, undaunted. "The stars cannot lie. At Milford Haven he'll land, and he'll march through Wales to victory. I've seen it as plain as I see you right now."

"After how many cups of wine?" Rush asked, taunting. Nandick drew his robes around him as if to preserve his injured dignity and ignored the question.

They seemed to have forgotten Kate's presence, and she was careful not to remind them. After they had moved on to another subject, Anne tugged on her sleeve. "But who is Henry Tudor, Maman?" she whispered. "I don't understand."

"Nor do I," Kate replied. "But I have every intention of finding out."

That evening, she went to her husband's apartments, the first time in years she had done so willingly. Only by the arch of one eyebrow did he show his surprise. Though his face was otherwise expressionless, she could see that he had already been drinking heavily.

"Well, fair Kate, what may I ask brings you to this forbidden country? Surely, I cannot hope that you've come to desire my company."

She shook her head. "No, my lord, it's not that."

The room was warm, almost cozy. Logs blazed brightly beneath the wide arch of the hearth while rain washed down the tiny-paned windows, creating a bubble of false intimacy. She glanced around the room that had become so alien to her, luxurious with its furs and velvets, its jeweled hangings and deep-piled Turkish carpets. The Plantagenet arms were a gold sprawl on the curtained bed. Then she turned back to the man who was almost equally unfamiliar.

He had changed of late. There was a redness in his eyes and a puffiness around his jowls that had never been there before. He had been drinking too much ever since his return from London. Even now his hands shook a little as he poured out the last dregs of wine from a crystal decanter. She watched the play of candlelight and firelight on silk as his arms moved, the way the neck of his maroon dressing gown gaped for an instant over the broad V of his chest. The look in his eyes was oddly hopeful as he held out the goblet to her. She shook her head, and his face hardened as he set down the cup.

"Well, Kate, I am waiting. You must have some purpose."

Now that the moment had come, she resisted it. She did not want to know the truth, not really. But she found herself asking anyway, her voice a wobbly treble. "What part is Henry Tudor to play in your schemes?"

He did not answer her directly. He picked up the goblet he had poured for her and downed it at a gulp. "Henry Tudor? And where might you have heard that name?"

"Let's just say that certain of your . . . uh . . . associates have used it rather freely in my presence."

He swore an oath under his breath. "My trio of would-be advisors, I'll be damned. I told Morton they weren't to be trusted." He turned his back to her, his arms stretched along the mantelpiece, his eyes staring down into the fire.

"What does it matter where I heard it? The fact is that I did hear it, and I want to know what it means."

"Henry Tudor, my dear, happens to be the focal point of our little endeavor."

"And Edward, my nephew Edward? What of him? It was for him you were to fight. You told me . . ."

"There has been a wind change, I'm afraid. It blows now from France."

"So that's it! Edward has been used and is now to be discarded. How much of your support do you think to discard with him? What will you do when Elizabeth finds out?"

His voice was barely a murmur. "Elizabeth already knows."

"But if she knows, I don't see how . . ."

"We continue to enjoy her unquestioned support. In fact, if anything, it's been redoubled. Her daughter Bess is to wed the Tudor."

"You're lying. She would never give permission for such a scheme, not while Edward is still alive."

"Ah, but that's it, don't you see? He is no longer alive. Edward and little York are both quite . . . dead."

"Dead?" She sank heavily into a chair. "Dead?" she repeated. "But how? Why?"

"You must know enough history, Kate, to realize that the life expectancy of deposed kings—and aye, of their heirs—is not overlong."

"But children?"

"Dangerous children." His voice was almost a caress. "Dangerous, not for what they might do, I grant you that, but for what others might seek to do on their behalf."

"You knew this and didn't tell me? Or was I not important enough to know?"

The maroon silk shimmered as he lifted his shoulders in a shrug. "I saw no need to upset you. Knowing of your devotion to your sister and her family . . ."

"No need to upset me! By St. Agnes, how long has it been since you cared that much?"

"Kate . . ."

She pushed away his hand. "No, don't offer me your pity. I don't want it. Only tell me—was it Richard?"

His eyes took on a wild, uncertain look, shifting away from hers for the minutest fraction of a second. When he spoke again, his mouth had a peculiar twist to it like a sneer. "Yes," he snapped, "of course, it was Richard. Who else could it have been?"

"You," she said softly, hardly aware that she had uttered the word aloud. "It could have been you. You had the access, the means . . ."

"As did others," he said, not bothering to deny her implied accusation. "What difference does it make who killed them or why? The only thing that matters now is that they are gone and will play no role in future events except, of course, as motivation for overthrowing the tyrant. Ah yes, they will be most useful there."

She began to weep, silently but steadily, and though he did not try to touch her, he gave her a look that was almost sympathetic. "You'll get over it," he said. "You must learn to be practical, like your sister. Thwarted by fate in one direction, she finds another—and a means to vengeance. She is cunning, resourceful—qualities to be admired."

"Yes, of course," she murmured. "I daresay you're right." She dried her eyes on her sleeve and rose with effort. "I beg pardon for taking so much of your time."

"You may come here whenever you wish," he said. His eyes roamed her body with a gaze that was more proprietary than lustful. "You're still my wife. Remember that."

"I would to God I could forget. Good night, my lord."

Elizabeth's two boys had been much younger when she had last seen them, but now they filled completely the eye of her mind: the elder pensive and serious as befits a future monarch; the younger with his rosy cheeks and huge bright eyes always on the verge of open laughter. She had become pregnant with her own Harry while Elizabeth was carrying Edward, the long-hoped-for male heir. They were almost of an age, these cousins, and now one of them was dead.

What had Elizabeth thought, what had she felt, when she heard the terrible news? How could she have borne it? Yet apparently she had borne it if Buckingham spoke the truth. She had borne it and was ready to fight back with the only weapon left at her disposal.

Only one thing was wrong: Elizabeth did not know the real enemy. She would strike at Richard, but Kate knew with a sudden, staggering conviction that the fiend was not Richard. The real enemy lay much closer to her than Richard, literally at times in her own bed. And she had helped him in his devious betrayal. The memory of that fact chilled her. She had told Elizabeth to trust him. She was as much to blame as anyone for the terrible thing that had happened.

With new clarity, Kate recalled the morning a few weeks before when she had seen William Percival and Reginald Bray clattering over the drawbridge of Brecknock Castle and making hell-bent for London. If anyone were capable of such a heinous act as the slaying of two innocent children, Percival certainly was. And if, as she had since learned, Bray was employed by Henry Tudor's mother, the murder of the princes was in some sense understandable. With his own claim to the throne weak at best, the Tudor would need to ally himself to the late King Edward's surviving heir, his eldest daughter, and for that scheme to work, her younger brothers would have to be out of the way. She still did not understand why or how her own husband had been drawn into this unseemly plot, but that scarcely mattered at this point. He was in it now as deep as he could be.

At that moment, she vowed the duke would never reap the fruits of his labors. She would watch and listen and learn his exact plans, where he would strike and when. She would take advantage of Morton's obvious regard for her, though she must be careful there. Safer and more profitable veins of knowledge might be mined from Rush, Knyvet, and Nandick as they squabbled among themselves. Even Buckingham, who had so wantonly misled her, might prove useful. He had always been susceptible to flattery and cajolery. Even an occasional connubial visit—her flesh shuddered at the thought—might be risked if it yielded up a piece of valuable information.

And then when she knew all there was to know, when she could lay out her facts and march them like an army, she knew where she could go for help. She knew one who could blunt the edge of her husband's attack and leave him stranded and forlorn in the mountain fastness of Wales.

Early in October, she returned to the hut. It was not a good day for riding. Thick mists blanketed the moors, and in the beech groves, moisture dripped ceaselessly from yellowing trees. Carefully she picked her way across the soggy carpet of fallen leaves and beech mast. The branches clutched at her from out of the fog then disappeared back into its shroud as she passed. The stillness was absolute. No bird sang; no small animal skittered through the underbrush.

The moor was worse, blank and featureless except for the occasional splash of hawthorn berries or rowan leaves, eerie crimson against the all-pervasive gray. With her knees, Kate urged Doucette on, eager to reach the hut, suddenly afraid of the dead silence that engulfed her. But the mare seemed strangely reluctant, tossing back her head and blowing wetly down her nostrils as if to ask why her mistress had chosen this particular day for an outing. Once or twice, she stopped short and pricked back her ears as if listening for some sound Kate could not catch.

Impatiently, Kate slapped at the horse's rump with her riding crop. She was not afraid of pursuit. How could anyone follow her in the enveloping mists? Not until much later did she remember the dainty prints Doucette's newly shod hooves made in the damp earth and in the mud beside the stream bed.

She came to the clearing at last and gave a strangled cry of relief. A thin trail of blue smoke poured up from the hole in the roof and blended with the fog. Her greatest fear was gone. Robin was here. She dismounted with more dignity than usual. Though her brain was singing wildly and her pulse racing, she strove for control. Deliberately, she tethered Doucette to the rough trunk of an oak then drew herself up and breathed deeply. Behind her, the sound of the horse's gentle cropping steadied her.

She entered without knocking and stood in the doorframe, throwing back her hood and shaking water droplets from the bronze strands that clung around her face. He was sitting cross-legged before the fire, his eyes bright with its shine. His fingers strummed a melancholy lay on a lute.

"Robin!" He looked up then. The lute gave one last swelling wail as his startled fingers let it fall. Joy leapt into his eyes as he jumped up to receive her. His arms were warm and comforting, for she was wet through and shivering.

"Ah, Kate, dearest Kate, you've come back. I knew you would come back," he said, nuzzling her hair.

The joy in his eyes changed to bewilderment as she drew away from his embrace. His hands were fumbling at the lacings of her cloak. Resolutely, she stilled them. "Yes, Robin, I've come back, but not for that, not this time. I'm afraid there is no softness left in me to give a man pleasure."

"No softness?" he asked with a look of tender amusement. His finger brushed her breast, very lightly. "This doesn't feel like stone to me."

"Nevertheless . . ." she began and stopped as he buried his lips against her neck. "Robin, listen to me!" She was close to tears. "Please, you must listen. You are the only one who can help me, and by God, I need your help desperately. There is evil loose in the world, Robin, such evil you will hardly be able to conceive it."

He stopped then and was silent, drawing her down beside him on the bed. When she had her breath back, he said, "Very well, *cariad.* Tell me all about it."

The tale took long in the telling, far longer than she had expected. The fire had burned down to ashes by the time she finished. Through it all, he had not spoken, had scarcely even grunted, and the glowing coals of the fire, which threw red lights and darks across his face, had left his eyes strangely veiled. It unnerved her that she could read no expression there, neither hatred nor shock nor outrage.

"You have some . . . some proof of this?" he asked finally.

"Proof? Why do you need proof? Isn't it enough that I tell you so?"

A hint, just a hint, of the old tender amusement was in his voice. "For me, yes. For my father and brothers, something more may be required if you mean for us to fight."

She was already drawing the scorched collar from the folds of her cloak. She had brought it with her almost as an afterthought. A small tremulous doubt disturbed her even as she gave it to him. "If I mean for you to fight? But of course, you must fight. You must right this terrible wrong."

Very slowly, he shook his head. "How clearly you see things, Kate. Your vision is like a child's. Right and wrong, good and evil, they exist for you. The right untainted by wrong, the good untouched by evil. And yet . . ."

"And yet, what Robin? I don't see . . . You told me you were for Richard. Now you have the means to fight for him. Take this to him. Show him. He will reward you, and he will slay my . . . my husband for the foul traitor, the murderer that he is. It is simple, so simple."

"No, *'nghariad i*, it is not. For if what you are telling me is true, Buckingham has allied himself with Henry Tudor, and the Tudor is Welsh."

Her heart stopped beating. There it was again, the wall between them she had thought was torn down, forever destroyed. Why was it there now when she needed him most? If he never again held her in his arms, never touched her, if she never again even looked on his face, she would count it well worth the cost if he performed for her, for their love, this last great act. She was a woman twice betrayed—first by her husband, now by her lover.

"Kate . . ."

"Don't touch me!" she spat. "I am not Welsh, nor would I wish to be if to harbor infanticides is considered a virtue by the Welsh."

He rose and heaped more logs on the fire. She watched the straight, determined motions of his back with eyes that were beginning to brim. The edges of darkness receded a little; a blurred orb of light held them both as well as the blackened thing between them, which was now not only repulsive but useless as well. For a time, he studied it, tracing the once-fine craftsmanship with his long fingers.

"He must be mad, quite mad indeed," Vaughan said slowly. "What must the Tudor be thinking to ally himself with a madman? Surely, he cannot know."

"Ah, but the Tudor is Welsh," Kate said acidly, "so what does it matter if he rakes the lunatic asylums of France, England, and Wales for his henchmen? I have no doubt that you and my lord husband will fight side by side in the thickest of the fray, hacking and hewing about like butchers for the greater glory of Henry Tudor." She stood, stiffening her back like a cat facing an enemy. She wanted nothing more now than to flee him, flee the hut, poignant with so many memories sweeter than this.

"Stay a while, Kate. We haven't finished talking yet."

"I can think of nothing more we have to say to each other."

"Sit down!" he commanded, and she sat.

"I did not say that we would of a certainty declare for the Tudor. That decision is not mine to make. My father, my brothers, my cousins, and I will make that decision together, and I will voice my opinion. You may be sure of that. I should warn you, however, that my father's bard preaches the Tudor a second Arthur, the fulfillment of Merlin's prophecies of a savior for Wales. You know the tale? Then you must see that your opposition is . . . formidable."

"Then what use . . . ?"

"Hear me out, Kate. I, for one, happen to give no more than lip service to these tales. You see, I knew Henry Tudor as a boy. We are the same age, he and I, and I once served at Pembroke Castle as a page under his guardian, Lord William Herbert. For a time, we shared the same schoolroom, tilted at the same quintain, slept in the same dorter, cut our master's meat at the same board."

"You told me nothing of this."

"There is much I haven't told you, Kate, much I cannot."

"A friend of your boyhood," she murmured bleakly.

"I did not say he was a friend."

She lifted her eyes to his. The fire caught their leap of sudden hope.

"Nay, nor foe either. Shall I tell you how I remember Henry Tudor? Not surely as a son of great Arthur. Oh, I'll grant you, he was wily and crafty enough even then, with sly, sliding eyes that took in everything in his path and much outside it for that matter as if he were in constant danger from some unknown source. On the lists and at the quintain where we sported and trained as boys, he always hung back as if he was afraid to damage his sacred skin.

"And, ah, this part I had almost forgotten, but it will perhaps tell you more of him than anything else I might say. I came upon him once digging in the ground of the outer ward. Of course, I wondered what he was doing. Imagine my amazement when he told me he was burying a groat Lord William had given him to spend at a fair in the town. Meanwhile, my own groat was burning a hole in my pocket.

"He looked up at me with those expressionless eyes of his. I remember he even smiled a little. 'Ah, but when the fair is over,' he said, 'you will have a belly gripe from eating too much or a headache from drinking too much. Mayhap you'll even get the pox from sleeping with a whore. Whatever happens, your groat will be gone. I will suffer none of those afflictions, and my groat will be here still.'

"And doubtless, Kate, it is there still. He must have left behind a veritable treasure hoard when his Uncle Jasper came and spirited him off to France. So there you have him, *cariad*. Henry Tudor. A miser and a coward. Fine stuff to make into a king, don't you think?"

Despite herself, Kate laughed aloud at the image he had painted for her. He saw her merriment and again grew serious. "But I don't know how it will go at home, what my father and brothers will say—and of course, the bard. Old Rhys will have his word in the debate, you may be sure of that. I can promise you nothing, it seems, except that I will argue your case as best I can. If it were up to me, I have seen Richard, and he is worth a thousand Buckinghams with five hundred Tudors thrown in for good measure. He is a man I might have served, and gladly, if the land lay differently between us. Then too . . . your lord has greatly wronged you. I'd remedy that if I could." His voice grew husky with tenderness, and she did not protest when he drew her against him.

"Will it ever be the same between us as it once was," he asked, "when this is all over?"

She shook her head. "I don't know. I wish I could give you a fair answer."

"Darling Katherine," he said in mock seriousness, "if I can have no fair answer from your sweet lips, then a sweet kiss must content me."

She gave him that in full and generous measure. For a time, she sat there, savoring the nearness of him, the musty animal smell of the hut, the pine-scented warmth of the fire, but when he tried to draw her down on the cot, she pushed him gently away.

"No, Robin. I've stayed too long as it is. I must go now. Doucette is still outside, a signal flag if there are any eyes to see."

Reluctantly, he loosed her. It seemed to her then that every muscle of his body strained toward her, yet he let her go. He walked to the doorway with her and fastened the ribbands of her hood beneath her chin. She reached up and gave him a last parting kiss then stepped out into the cold, winter-turning world. How bleak and somber it all seemed! The mists still hung heavy on the treetops; the leaf-strewn ground was sodden beneath her feet. The mare greeted her with a welcoming neigh that seemed to echo through the forest and down the glen.

"Hush, my beauty," Kate cautioned, suddenly afraid. The forest seemed empty of all life except for the two of them, yet at that moment, the danger was so near that she could feel its chill breath on the back of her neck. Her fingers shook as she untied the reins; a cobweb brushed her cheek, and she stifled a scream. Only a cobweb after all! The trunks of the ancient oaks were as gnarled and knotted as the faces of old men. They stared at her almost contemptuously, mocking her. The stream made a song like a hollow gurgle as she led Doucette over its mossy slippery rocks. Once across, she would mount her and fly home like the wind. She had a sudden, unreasoning desire to be home, to be safe.

At last, she stepped up onto the bank. She had only to lift her foot into the stirrup now, swing her leg across the horse's back. One light, easy movement, then she would fly from the unknown, the nameless danger. She did not hear him approach, nor, intent on mounting Doucette, did she see him. Yet suddenly, he was there before her, blocking her way. He doffed his cap in greeting. His manner was casual, deliberately so, but the question he asked was not.

"And how does my lady's leman?"

"What are you doing here, Percival? I cannot believe you found me by chance."

The yellow eyes stared at her with grim amusement; his thin lips twisted into a truncated smile. "No, not by chance. I saw you ride out this morning. To say the least, it seemed an odd day to choose for such an excursion, particularly when you have neglected your riding of late."

"So you followed to see that I didn't lose my way in the fog or meet with outlaws perhaps," she said coldly. "Your concern is commendable."

"Now I see that you had no need of my protection. It seems my lady has found another protector."

"I am not your lady," she snapped, ignoring the rest of it.

"Ah, but you are my lord's lady—and therefore mine."

He mounted his own horse, which had come at his whistle from a nearby thicket, and took Doucette's reins with a proprietary hand. It would be useless to protest, she realized, useless and dangerous. He would have no qualms about killing her where she stood, and then Robin . . . Robin! What would become of him? They had been discovered, but at that moment, Percival seemed to be concerned only with her. Let it be then. Let it remain so. She would gladly follow him along the dripping eaves of the forest all the way back to Brecknock and whatever fate awaited her there as long as Robin was safe.

Her resolution failed her somewhat by the time they reached the castle. She was painfully aware of the gateward's long stare, for Percival continued his firm grasp on her reins. She was brought in like a wayward child or a prisoner. Only the manacles were lacking. When they dismounted, his grip on her upper arm was like a vise as if even now she might turn and run. He took her straight to the great hall, where Buckingham and the household were finishing the midday meal. Percival, it appeared, was bent on publicly humiliating her. He half-led, half-dragged her to the dais. She found it impossible to match his long strides, nor did she care to try. A profound hush settled over the hall as they passed. Necks were craned everywhere as everyone from the lowest scullery maid to Rush, Nandick, and Knyvet at the high table jockeyed for a glimpse of the oddly paired couple. Only Morton, sitting at Buckingham's right hand, flashed her a look of sympathy as if, without knowing, he knew already. The duke himself leaned forward in amazement.

"I have found this out on the moor, my lord," said Percival, flinging her forward. In the hush, his shrill voice carried to every corner of the room.

"What, Kate," said the duke, still uncomprehending, "were you lost in the fog?"

She remained silent.

"Where were you, Kate?" he asked, his voice rising. "I have asked you a question."

"My lord, I found this, Your Grace's property, in the humble hut of a shepherd. There was also a man, a young man, with her."

Buckingham's face darkened ominously. Behind her, Kate heard a great collective gasp from the spectators. "What do you have to say to this charge?" the duke asked. "Do you have a lover?"

"Yes," she whispered. Then feeling her strength gathering within, she cried out. "Yes, I have a lover. Do you think I could survive here if I did not?"

"How dare you!" he bellowed, his voice shaking with rage. "How dare you put antlers on me! You will learn—I shall teach you—that no one can do this to Harry Buckingham!"

"But haven't you done it to me? In various ways and with various . . . people?"

Somewhere there was a titter of laughter quickly muffled. Buckingham ignored it. "That's not the same thing, and you know it. Slut! Witch! Whore! You shall be beaten, Kate. I shall have you stripped naked and whipped right here in this very hall for all the household to see. I shall give all my churls leave to enjoy your favors. Ah, you should enjoy that, you lecherous wench. And then I shall have you cast into the lowest dungeon where the rats and fleas and vermin will have their enjoyment of you for all eternity—you, who dare to spurn me and seek the arms of . . . of a sheep herd!"

She stood her ground before the onslaught. She did not cringe or tremble or plead for mercy. She did not offer to leave his roof and seek a convent. She only waited for his anger to spend itself as she knew by its very prodigality it must.

Morton reached over and laid a hand on the duke's arm. "Her offense is very great, my lord," he said in a voice that conveyed precisely the proper amount of outrage mingled with sweet reason. "No one could dispute your righteous anger. Yet if you do as you suggest, will you not heap more dishonor on yourself and on your children?"

"She should be punished."

"Yes, of course. I would not suggest otherwise. But perhaps a more reasonable punishment than the one you propose. Think for a moment how our Woodville allies would react if they learned you had publicly disgraced and humiliated the queen's sister."

"But she has richly earned it."

"So she has. But we should not allow that to interfere with our cause when it is so near its blossoming. Let's not lose all for the sake of one faithless woman. Lock her in her room, if you wish, and go out and find her lover. You may safely vent your spleen on him, I think, and punish her in the process."

Buckingham considered this, flicking his tongue over his full lips as if in anticipation. "Why, yes, Morton, of course! He should be the one to make an example of. God's blood, none will dare trifle with me again. Do you hear me, Kate? Shall I tell you what I will do to him?"

"Come, come, man!" Morton said, the merest suggestion of impatience creeping into his voice. "You must catch him first."

"You're right, my dear bishop, as always. Percival, do you think you could lead us back to the place where you found this loathsome creature?"

"Yes, my lord," he replied. "With the greatest of pleasure."

"Morton is no friend of mine," Kate repeated to herself later that afternoon, locked in the prison cell of her room. Perhaps he had meant well, diverting the tide of the duke's wrath away from her, but she could conceive of no worse torment than seeing Robin in chains, dragged back to Brecknock, herself forced to watch him made the foul sport of Percival and her husband: tortured, sodomized, castrated, disemboweled, and at last, at long grateful last, killed.

All through that long, dreary afternoon, when the castle around her was hushed as a tomb, she knelt before her prie-dieu and prayed to the Virgin and her own St. Catherine that they would not find him or that they would kill him outright, anything so long as he did not suffer. Then she remembered the mission she had entrusted to him, and she prayed desperately—selfishly—for the success of that as well. "Oh, Lord, Blessed St. Mary, please . . . please!"

It was dusk when they returned. She heard the commotion in the courtyard below and wondered if, even after all the hours of waiting, she dared to look. Crossing herself, she stood and moved stiffly to the fogged, diamond-paned casement. She wiped a little path of moisture clear with her hand.

At least the weather had held. If anything, the fog was thicker than it had been earlier. Dampness trickled in tiny rivulets down the castle walls. Though it was not yet dark, a swarm of torchbearers greeted the small army of men who dismounted. Buckingham, it seemed, had pressed every able-bodied man into the search. She noted in passing that the duke was not riding Saladin; no, that great black beast seemed to have thrown a shoe and was led away, limping, by a groom. Was it that mishap that made the duke's face so livid in the torchlight? Or was it something else? Her eyes darted over the men below, and as they did, a rising tide of joy swept through her. He was not there among the duke's men either in chains or in a box. Robin had escaped!

By the time Morgan brought her supper, her hopes had risen to new heights. Robin would be successful; he would warn Richard of Buckingham's treachery. The duke would be slain and his informer rewarded with the hand of his widow in marriage. Suddenly, it all seemed possible now: a life together for her and Robin with her husband's remains stowed safely away in the priory crypt.

The thought lent added relish to her supper tray. Though Buckingham had ordered strict rations of bread and water for her, Morgan had managed to smuggle a browned hare pasty, roast leg of capon, spiced apple conserve, and hot mulled ale beneath her skirts. The mingled odors of the hot food and drink almost made her swoon.

"Stay a while, Morgan," Kate said as she sat down on her dower chest and attacked the feast. She had a ravenous appetite; she had not eaten anything since breakfast. Her teeth sank into the capon leg. "I have need of company," she said as the girl's eyes strayed to the door.

Morgan looked uncomfortable. She would not meet Kate's eyes. "It is forbidden, ma'am. I might only bring the tray."

Kate took a bit of the pasty and smiled. "But as you can see, my lord has quite forgotten me. He didn't find the one he sought, did he? Is he very angry?"

"Angry? Oh yes, milady. Most wondrous wroth! He vows he'll tear down the mountains stone by stone before he gives up the search."

"Let him do it then," Kate said smugly. "It will do him no good."

Morgan gave her mistress a fey look from beneath her sooty lashes. Her voice came, hesitant. "As to that, ma'am, I don't know, for they did see him."

Alarm prickled the flesh on Kate's arms. "They saw him? And let him escape?"

"Garth—he being my intended, ye ken—he told me that when they neared the cot, a man took to his horse as if to flee. They could scarce make it out in the mist. Sir Percival it was who loosed an arrow, though Garth swore as it twanged the bowstring that if it hit true in that fog, the di'el himself must have guided it."

"Ah, small wonder," Kate said with a sinking heart, "since the devil himself loosed it. Did it . . . does Garth know . . . if it hit him?"

Morgan's fingers played nervously with the silk tassel of the bed curtains. The pointed toe of her slipper sketched a circle on the parquet floor. "Well, milady, they didn't find his body, if that's what you fear, but . . . there was blood. There was a deal of blood."

Kate's hands were a cold knot of fear; her stomach dropped within her. "So he was injured then," she said at last, her voice barely audible.

"Aye, it gave them a trail to follow, but they didn't find him. Milord duke, he would have kept up the search all night, for all that his horse had been lamed by a rock. But the bishop now . . . he ordered a halt, said they were bound to lose themselves in the fog and the mountains and be none the better for it. The sheep herd—begging pardon, milady—the sheep herd was a dead man anyway, said the bishop. None could bleed so free and live.

"The master, he yielded at last, though sulky about it as could be. He ordered torches set to the hut, saying—beggin' your pardon again, milady—that his wife would no more whore herself there with any shepherd, if shepherd he be . . ."

At that moment, the door to the bedchamber burst open, and Kate whirled around to see Percival standing in the doorframe, looking suspiciously from Morgan to Kate. The flaming wheel badge blazed on his shoulder.

Kate swallowed a wave of pure panic. "Haven't you been taught to knock before entering a lady's bedchamber?" she asked.

"If in truth it is a *lady's* bedchamber, yes," he replied scornfully, "but we all know how you have abused the title today. You have earned other titles much less seemly."

Kate stood erect and faced him. "Fortunately, that is not for you to judge. Have you come from my husband? Has he sent for me?"

"He?" Percival spat on the floor. "Nay, not he. The priest has vented him of his spleen. You may be grateful to whatever gods there be that you have that one for a friend. Though more's the pity. You would have made fine sport . . ." His yellow eyes stripped her naked before focusing their attention on Morgan. "No, it's for this wench I have come. She stays too long in my lady's chamber, and I see as well that, despite all orders to the contrary, she has been overgenerous with her master's larder."

"It was only a cold pasty left over from the servant's mess yesterday and fit for naught but the garbage pail."

"Then it was still far too good for the likes of her. Come along now. You've stayed too long already, and the duke's orders are strict on that subject as well. No visitors. I'll wager that means a beating for you who have no grand bishop to defend you."

Morgan winced as he grasped her wrist and dragged her from the room. He did not even acknowledge Kate's cries of protest. However, he did give her a one-sided smile from the open doorway. "God grant Your Grace sweet and restful dreams . . . even though there are no more sweet young lovers to fulfill them."

The door slammed shut behind him, and seconds later, Kate heard a bolt fall into place across it.

Chapter 42

RICHARD WOULD REMEMBER that golden summer for the rest of his life. It was during that summer that he realized how glorious it was to be a king. There were no problems that could not be solved, no situation that a flick of his pen on parchment and the pressure of his seal in hot wax, could not change. Everywhere he saw pride and reverence on the faces of his subjects. How they loved him, and how he loved them!

He was in the north. Rumors of unrest in the south reached him like the sound of distant thunder, but he paid them little heed. He was loved in the north; he would be loved in the south as well. He established commissions of oyer and terminer to discover the source of the unrest, but beyond that, he had complete faith in his council in London and in his two chief lieutenants, Buckingham and Norfolk, to handle whatever troubles arose. He heard regularly and at some length from Norfolk in London; from Brecon, the letters, though dutifully penned, were much briefer and scarcer in number. Richard chuckled at that. He had hardly expected Buckingham to be a dedicated correspondent.

From Gloucester, he had ridden up the valley of the Severn to Tewkesbury—site of the last and, he hoped, the final confrontation between York and Lancaster twelve years before. The battlefield was much changed. Where he had half-expected to find bleached bones whitened by the sun and weapons rusting in the grass, there were only marguerites and anemones starring the greensward with yellow and white.

Inside the Norman abbey church, he had knelt before the tomb that bore the remains of George, Duke of Clarence. Here he had known a moment's unease. Clarence had paid with his life for possessing the very knowledge that had lifted Richard up so high. Between traitor and king then, there was a very small gap, only a few years. If Clarence had been more patient . . . But Richard did not like to think about that. He had risen abruptly from his knees and assuaged the naggings of his conscience with a lavish donation to the abbey so that masses might be said for the soul of his less-fortunate brother. He declined to examine too closely the guilt that had prompted this generosity.

When he had reached Warwick Castle on its bluff overlooking the River Avon, Anne was waiting for him. Although she was still pale and a trifle too thin, she seemed to have fully recovered from her miscarriage. He greeted her with genuine pleasure, sweeping her up in his arms, almost oblivious to the astonished look on the face of the Spanish envoy Anne had brought with her from Windsor.

The highlight of the progress had come at Pontefract Castle, south of the city of York, for there they were joined by their son. Anne's joy was unbounded. She had quickly masked any disappointment that Ned was not well enough to ride his pony and, running down the steps, had engulfed him in her arms even before he had alighted from his chariot. Richard had been close behind her.

Several days later, they had entered York together. Escorted by the mayor and two sheriffs of the city and by the chief citizens in brilliant scarlet, Richard, Anne, and Ned had passed through Micklegate Bar, the royal gate. The northern capital was swollen with pride and triumph. Throngs of citizens lined the narrow street and cheered his name. The sound was a joyful, deafening acclamation in his ears. Banners of the House of York were everywhere along with garlands of late-summer flowers. Replicas of the king and queen, clad in their coronation regalia, adorned shop windows. There were lavish entertainments—acrobats, musicians, pageants. It all bore not a little resemblance to the coronation procession through the streets of

London, yet it was infinitely sweeter. This was York. Many of the faces that lined the route were familiar; many of the participants were his friends. Then, too, Ned was with him, riding beside him on a sorrel pony and plainly enchanted with everything he saw.

At the River Ouse, a dancing bear had delighted the boy, and he turned to Richard with shining eyes. "It must be wonderful to be king, Father. I had not thought before there would be so much . . . ." Richard followed his son's hand as it pointed out the crowds of people lining the bridge and the riverbank, the boats crammed to sinking with still more. Each neck craned for a glimpse of the sovereign. Each voice added to the tumult of welcome. The boy turned back to him. "Will I ever be king?"

A shadow crossed over Richard's face as he looked at his son, at the thin cheeks flushed by excitement to a semblance of health, at the dark eyes too large for the small face. The unnamable doubt haunted him as he answered, "Yes, after me, when I die, you will be king. You will be crowned at Westminster."

Ned gave the tiniest sigh. "As you were? How I wish I could have been there."

Of course, he should have been there. The Prince of Wales and heir to the throne should have had a place of high honor in the ceremony if persistent ill health had not kept him in the north.

"Yes," Richard agreed, "I wish you could have been there too, and yet I think the Prince of Wales deserves a coronation of his own."

It was then that he hit upon it, the investiture of Edward as Prince of Wales at York Minster. It was at once a gesture of gratitude to the city of York and a justifiable indulgence of a much-loved son. Predictably, Anne had fretted a little over the ceremony, fearing it would strain the boy's stamina. The fine line between her brows grew more pronounced, but she made little protest. Perhaps the joint excitement of husband and son silenced her. Richard sent to the Royal Wardrobe in London that very day for the coronation regalia. One week later, on the eighth day of September, he and Anne, with Ned between them and the royal crowns of England flashing fire from their brows, had walked to York Minster through streets that rang anew with acclamation.

Inside, Ned had been almost dwarfed by the color and grandeur of the mighty cathedral. The morning sun, shafting through the vast expanse of the great east window, gilded his small figure more than all the silks and jewels so hastily brought from London. When Richard at last set the plain gold coronet on the boy's head, Edward had looked up at him through a haze of joy and wonder. It seemed to Richard then that the moment was well worth whatever risks he had taken. It was a shining hour, the most glorious of his life.

However, later that night as he tossed on his bed in the guest-house of St. Mary's Abbey, his thoughts were far from tranquil. The news that had come north with the coronation regalia had not been good. Despite the commissions of oyer and terminer he had appointed in August, grumblings and moanings of dissension were still heard in Kent and Surrey. There was nothing specific—there was never anything specific—but rumor had it that several noble and powerful men wished to see Edward V restored to the throne. Even more mysterious were the reports of some Westminster sanctuary guards that they had seen prominent Lancastrians, among them Margaret Stanley herself, slipping past them in disguise into Dame Woodville Grey's chambers. Once again, the reports were unsubstantiated. None of the presumed offenders had actually been caught, and Richard, who couldn't conceive of even a tenuous link between Woodville and Lancaster, was tempted to dismiss them as groundless. Yet their very existence was disquieting. Perhaps he had been away from his capital too long.

Still, he did not immediately take the southern road. He lingered in York a fortnight more, lulled into a sense of peace and security by the glowing autumn days, the companionship of old friends, the nearness of his wife and son. It would be difficult to leave them. He would be leaving Anne behind as well as Ned, for she had decided to return to Middleham and would not come to London again until Christmas, three long months away. He lingered as long as he dared, trusting still that his capable lieutenants could deal with whatever troubles arose.

The day he picked to resume his journey was a fine one, as bright and mild a September morning as a man could hope for in the variable north country. Though it was near Michaelmas, a soft breeze sprung off the dales and gently fluttered the royal banners on the heralds' staffs. The sky was a deep-blue vault dotted with puffs of cloud, like sky-borne sheep. It was a fine morning indeed and a sanguine one, a good omen for the days ahead.

Only Anne was sad, a sorrow that seemed deeper than their temporary parting. He caught the look in her eyes as she handed him the stirrup cup, a pleading look almost as if she were asking him to abdicate his kingship and return with her to Middleham. He could not do that, surely. It would be unthinkable.

Of course, he would have preferred to have both wife and son accompany him. It was a pity the boy was so delicate, the Neville strain so weak. Too much inbreeding, the crofters said. It wasn't good for stock or for folk either. Anne's father, Warwick, had been Richard's first cousin. Perhaps their blood was too close; perhaps he should have married outside the family. But he had loved her. Swounds! Watching the sun glint copper lights from her unbound hair, he loved her still. A moment's indiscretion did not change that.

For an instant, brief and tantalizing, the thought of Buckingham came back to him unbidden. Powerfully, he recalled the duke on his knees before him and the awful knowledge of that first touch. And then with sudden force, he pushed it all from his mind, swept it away like so many dirty rushes. He would not think about it now. Better never to think of it again! He bent from the saddle and gave Anne a more fervent farewell kiss than the one he had intended.

His southern pace was leisurely. With his now much shrunken retinue—many of the nobles, knights and bishops who had attended him earlier in his progress had departed for their own estates—he stopped at several towns along the way to listen to citizens' complaints and to dispense justice. He allowed no sense of urgency. It was well into October before he crossed the River Witham and entered the city of Lincoln. Here he was given one of the warmest welcomes of his progress. No doubt Bishop Russell was partially responsible for that. Although the lord chancellor was ailing and had been forced to remain in London, he had carefully instructed the cathedral dean and chapter to give the king a most cordial reception and to make certain that nothing marred his stay in Lincoln.

It hardly seemed a necessary precaution. Richard had always been fond of the town perched on its steep hill above the river, and he particularly admired the triple-spired cathedral. He was looking forward to his stay here. Nothing told him as he rode into the sun-washed courtyard of Lincoln Castle on that mild October morning that he would never again know another moment of lasting peace.

William Catesby paced back and forth in the anteroom to the royal apartments. Since their arrival in Lincoln earlier that morning, Richard had been closeted with John Kendall, attending to the thick pile of documents and correspondence that had awaited him.

Catesby spared only a glance at the courier, clad in the deep-blue livery and silver-lion badge of Norfolk, who sprawled now on a nearby bench. The man was near exhaustion, having ridden all the way from London almost without stopping, but Catesby had forgotten about him after reading the parchment the man had brought. It lay now on the oaken table, covered with a hasty ink-blotted scrawl. Next to it was a sizable bundle clumsily wrapped in stained linen as well as a second smaller letter.

That he should once again have to tell Richard such terrible news! For the third time in twice as many months, why should it fall to him to deliver the blow, recite the loss and suffer the anger of the royal frown? Yet there was no help for it. The thing had to be done. Once again, the task had fallen peculiarly to him.

Norfolk had written the letter in his own hand. Catesby considered letting Richard read it as it was, without preamble or explanation, but Norfolk was a blunt man and unfailingly honest. He had made no attempt to gloss the truth or to administer it in small easily palatable doses. Catesby wondered if John Howard had found the necessity for such a letter entirely abhorrent. But then, John Howard did not have to stand by Richard as he read it.

Richard looked up from the papers strewn across the writing table, a trace of agitation tugging at the corners of his mouth. Beside him, Master Kendall's pen still scratched over a document.

"Well, Catesby?" Richard asked. "I thought I told you I wasn't to be disturbed."

Catesby's eyes looked beyond Richard, beyond the open window, and focused briefly on the broad front of the cathedral shining golden pale in the afternoon sun. With effort, he wrenched his eyes back to the king. "Your Grace . . . may I have a word with you alone?"

Richard started to deny the necessity of this request, shrugged, and turned to his secretary. "Will you excuse us for a moment, John?"

Swiftly, as if he were used to such intrusions, Kendall shook sand over the pages that bore his tall, spidery script and gathered them up in his long fingers. The door closed softly behind him.

"Well, what is it Catesby? Bad news? I can see that by the look of you."

Catesby gulped and swallowed. "There's a messenger outside, sire, from the Duke of Norfolk. He . . . he reports some men of Kent have risen in rebellion."

Richard expelled a long breath. "Well, I must say it doesn't take me completely by surprise. Still, it is a damned nuisance when I had been looking forward to spending a few days in Lincoln." His fingers toyed with the silver-gilt sand shaker. "How bad is it? Did he say?"

"I . . . well, no."

"A few disgruntled peasants perhaps? Easily enough remedied."

Catesby twisted the letter in his hands. "No, sire, I think not. The rebels claim to have many supporters throughout the south and west. These apparently have risen before their appointed date, but they say in a week's time there will be more such uprisings."

"The Woodvilles are behind all this, of course?"

"Yes. They have . . . a hand in it."

"'A hand? Only a hand? What do you mean by that?" Richard's eyes narrowed suspiciously, and Catesby could feel the sweat popping out on his own brow.

"Only this. The Woodvilles seem to have . . . ah . . . allied themselves with Lancaster. They have declared for Henry Tudor."

"Henry Tudor!" Richard dropped the shaker. A pile of fine sand sifted onto the table unnoticed. "But what of their precious Edward? What of the lords bastard?"

"Dead, Your Grace, or so they give out."

"Dead? Dead? But how so?"

"That no one knows or is willing to say."

"Of course," Richard said with a grim smile. "They hope to lay it to my door. Do they take me for such a simpleton as to think that I won't produce my nephews and expose their falsehood for what it is?"

"If they are . . . capable of being produced."

Richard gave him a long, questioning look. For the first time, Catesby saw that he was afraid. "And you, Will, my evil angel, do you have reason to believe they are not?"

The broad cathedral front swam before Catesby's eyes. His hands gripped tightly the linen parcel and Howard's letter with its dangling seal. His voice was a whisper that he himself scarcely heard. "Yes. The Kentish rebels have named their leader, the leader of all this mischief, I'm afraid. Sire, I regret, it is none other than the Duke of Buckingham."

He did not believe it, of course. How could he believe it? He looked at Catesby and laughed out loud. "Buckingham, guilty of treason? Whose cock-and-bull story is this? Which of his enemies?"

Catesby looked down at the bundle he carried in his shaking hands. "I . . . I didn't think you would believe me. There is . . . ah . . . more substantial evidence against him."

"Evidence?"

"Aye. This was sent by the Vaughans in Breconshire along with a letter to Your Grace. You will perhaps remember them?"

"Of course, I remember them!" Richard snapped. "Bring it here."

Richard ignored the letter momentarily and turned his attention to the package. He was puzzled and a trifle wary as he unfolded the dirty, blood-stained wrappings, but by no means was he prepared for what he saw there.

He gave a cry that strangled in his throat. "What mischief is this?" he questioned. "By our Holy Lady, what has he done?" He held up the once-beautiful collar and stared at it with lurid fascination.

"It has been thrust into the fire, or s-so it would appear."

"I can see that! How did the Vaughans come by it?"

Catesby chafed at his hands as if he were trying to warm them. "The l-letter may explain that. H-Howard says only that Robin, old Sir Roger's youngest son, was mortally wounded in the getting of it. It was apparently his death at the hands of Buckingham's men that has allied the Vaughans to your cause in preference to the Tudor."

Richard's mind flashed back briefly to the young Welshman who had been so instrumental in giving him custody of Edward at Stony Stratford. He felt a pang of sorrow at the loss which was not quite overshadowed by his shock and outrage over Buckingham's apparent defection. He turned again to the collar. "They might have stolen it and then destroyed it in an attempt to discredit Buckingham. There is much bad blood between them."

Catesby shrugged, but his eyes looked doubtful.

"No," Richard admitted finally. "I can see you don't believe that any more than I do. Even as I gave it to him, I knew . . . I knew he was slipping away from me. I only hoped its richness would bind him to me once more. How miserably I've failed, Catesby. He hates me so much he could not even keep the thing for its intrinsic worth. He had to destroy it. And Henry Tudor—why on earth would Buckingham throw in his lot with the Tudor? Does he expect that a new king will reward him more than I have done?"

There was in truth no answer to that question. Catesby shifted his weight from one foot to the other. He was growing increasingly uneasy in the room's close, fetid atmosphere. The wanton destruction of the collar sickened him, and the privileged glimpse of Richard's anguish was an intimacy he no longer wished to share.

"Well, Catesby, my evil angel, I see you are anxious to go."

"N-no, sire."

"Are you not? Then why do you stand there shivering? Do you fear that as the bearer of such ill tidings, you shall suffer the brunt of my wrath?"

"N-no."

Richard shook his head knowingly. "I think, Catesby, that you have a yellow liver in you. I wonder how you'd stand if it came to a battle."

"Sire, I would stand by you to the death," he protested, but his eyes were on the rushes at his feet.

"Would you indeed? I wonder. Let's hope you won't have to be so sorely tested. Now leave me. I wish to be alone for a while."

Like a small boy released by the schoolmaster, Catesby bowed quickly and backed away toward the door, almost knocking over a chair in his eagerness to be free.

At last, Richard opened his eyes. Whether minutes had passed or hours, he did not know. He was vaguely surprised that ripe October sunlight still slanted through the tall casement window. In the tunnels of his mind, it had been blackest night.

Somewhere within him, there had been ripped open a raw, gaping wound. Such wounds he had seen in the bodies sprawled on the fields of Barnet and Tewkesbury, the skin torn and frayed around the edges, muscles and ligaments and organs exposed, the life's blood oozing away over the ground. Somewhere within him, there was such a hurt, viscous and deadly.

To the day he succumbed to it at last, to the day they laid his body in the earth, he would be crying out with the wounded man's pain and confusion. Why? Why had Buckingham betrayed him? He knew even then that he would probably never know the answer. He suspected that it dwelt in paths too perilous, too twisted to explore. He had no will left even to attempt it, though he knew that fragments of memory would grasp at him in idle moments as twigs trip an unwary traveler. The answer, he knew, lay somewhere in the unclean thing between them. He had been blind to too many of the duke's excesses because of it.

He sighed and stood up. There was much to be done and little time for brooding. Perhaps it was best. In their letter to him, the Vaughans promised their support and provided him with something of a timetable for the duke's rebellion. It was information that would prove invaluable in the coming days. If he briefly wondered how they had obtained both the collar and the information, his curiosity was quickly swallowed up by the immensity of the task before him.

He must send to London and obtain the great seal from Chancellor Russell. An army must be raised. Proclamations must be issued, denouncing the rebels and calling on all his good subjects to manifest their loyalty. And he must question Stanley. Howard's letter had left no doubt that Lady Margaret was deeply involved in these intrigues. Could her husband, who had been riveted to Richard's side all summer, be entirely innocent?

Somehow as well, he must delve into the unknown fate of Edward's sons. Brackenbury would be summoned and questioned. The boys had been left in his care. Surely, he too had not betrayed Richard. Surely, this last and greatest nightmare, the shedding of innocent blood, would be spared him.

There was no reluctance in his fingers as he picked up the brass bell on his desk and rang it with all his might. Let them come to him. Let them all come to him: his secretary, his nobles, his knights and squires and yeomen, his men-at-arms. He needed every mother's son of them by him now.

One week later, he was in Leicester for the muster of his army. The weather had turned foul in the intervening days. Great clouds had rolled in from the west. *From Wales,* he thought grimly. *Another pestilence from Wales.* It rained, though not enough to be a hindrance, only enough to be a nuisance.

Richard scarcely had an eye for the mist-hung country-side through which he passed. The woods were ablaze with color. Sherwood Forest had oaks that were a deep burnished rust, maples like scarlet flames, beeches a tawny gold—a veritable jewel box of color even beneath the somber skies. Everywhere he looked, his country groaned with the weight of a rich harvest. Wheat, oats, and barley had been gathered to the barns, hops to the oast houses. The fields were brown stubble now behind their hedgerows. Fat cattle grazed unwitting of the slaughter soon to come at Martinmas. From the roofs and chimneys of hut and cot and manor house, wisps of blue smoke rose to join the gray overcast. It would be good weather to be home, safe within doors and to know that all was well.

On the surface, events were moving better than might have been expected. The news from London was heartening. Norfolk had acquitted himself honorably. He had cut off completely those precipitous rebels of Kent and Surrey, stopping their march to London at Gravesend on the mouth of the Thames. Lady Margaret Stanley was in custody, awaiting the king's pleasure. The capital was secure.

Lady Margaret's husband still rode beside Richard, not in custody but in a place of close watchfulness. It had been a pale and obviously shaken Tom Stanley who had been ushered none too gently into Richard's presence that afternoon in Lincoln. In fact, so stunned and frightened had he appeared that Richard was inclined to believe his denials of complicity in the plot. However, he had not been sufficiently convinced to allow Tom Stanley to return to his estates in Lancashire for the purpose of raising an army. No, he preferred to keep him close at hand.

The seal had reached Richard on his march at Grantham, and there without delay he had signed the death warrant of the Duke of Buckingham. With that gesture, he wiped his once great and mighty friend from his consciousness, or thought he did. The matter was finished. The duke had only to be caught, convicted, and executed.

There remained only Brackenbury and the increasingly troublesome question of Edward's sons.

"Your Grace, I don't know," said the Tower constable. "I just don't know what became of them." He stood before Richard in the king's tent, dressed for the muster in full armor, his sallet tucked under his arm. He had changed a great deal in the weeks since Richard had last seen him. His face was grim where once he had been quick to laugh; his eyes were puffy from lack of sleep. Even his armor seemed to hang loosely on his frame.

"You don't know?" Richard repeated, incredulous. "But they were left in your care. Surely you must have some idea . . ."

"An idea, yes, but little more than that. They were removed from the Tower early in September by Sir William Percival and Reginald Bray."

Richard's eyes widened. "Removed? By whose order did you release them?"

"The Duke of Buckingham's, sire."

There was no surprise there, not anymore, but Richard's spleen rose again to think how long and how craftily the duke had plotted his ruin. "Buckingham!" he exploded. "Sweet blood of Jesus, was he the king that you should have obeyed him?"

Brackenbury's eyes met his master's with unflinching honesty. "So he was, sire, almost."

It was Richard who lowered his gaze. Brackenbury did not need to remind him who had invested the duke with his vice-regal powers.

"Yes," Richard agreed at last. "So he was, much to my undoing." He rose from his chair and walked to the raised tent flap. Darkness had fallen, and the light of a thousand campfires seemed to wink back at him through a light drizzle.

"You must remember," Brackenbury was saying, "that neither of us knew he was false then. You had no reason to suspect him, and I no reason to disobey him. Of course, I feel my own guilt heavily now. If I had only been stronger, held out against them—"

"You feel guilt!" Richard snapped. "What do you think I feel?" The red light of the brazier flickered over his face like the very flames of hell. "My brother's sons, and I have allowed them to be given over to—" He stopped, remembering he still did not know. He poured himself some wine from a flagon and drank deeply. "Do you think that they are dead?"

The big man shrugged. "I don't know. They told me they were removing them to Brecknock, but . . ."

"But?"

"It's very strange. I wondered at the time. Edward's book, the *Dictes* . . . well, it was still there the next day, and I doubt he would have left it behind at any cost. It was given to him by his Uncle Rivers, you know."

"Yes, yes, I know. Go on."

"The book was still there, yet the wardrobe chest was missing. It seemed odd to me that two men in a boat or on horseback would have bothered with such a hindrance. How they got out, I don't know. No one saw them leave the Tower."

"No one saw them leave?" Richard asked, incredulous. "With two boys and a large trunk, no one saw them leave? Where were your guards?"

"I had . . . er . . . removed the guards. Their orders."

Richard sighed. "Yes, of course. Have you conducted a search to see if in fact the boys were taken?"

"Yes, I have searched as much as I could. It was only in the past two weeks that I began to suspect them—with the news of Buckingham's treachery, you understand."

"And?"

"I found nothing. If they are still alive, they are not in the Tower."

"And if they are dead, there are a thousand places where their bodies might be buried. We could tear the Tower apart, stone by stone, and be left with only a pile of rubble."

"Nonetheless, sire, I will continue the search if you wish it."

Richard shook his head. "If they are at Brecknock, we shall know soon enough. And if they are not . . . there will be no resurrection for them until the Day of Judgment." He passed a hand over his face. "God's bones, Brackenbury, I would not have had them killed. Little Dickon, my godchild! So full of life and spirit."

"Yes, my liege. I also came to love them. Both of them."

Richard bridled at this implied reproach, then his face softened. "Poor Edward. To be a king, then not a king. I took him away from everything he loved, yet I could not love him. Oh yes, there were excuses—the need for security, the boy's hostility, and eventually the bastardy that made him an outcast. But there is nothing that excuses this. I made him vulnerable when I removed him from the throne, then sealed his fate when I made Buckingham lord high constable. The fault is mine." Then he added wearily, "It's getting late, Brackenbury, and we must march at dawn. Send in my body squires on your way out. I'm for my bed."

Yet even as he spoke, he knew that sleep would be a stranger to him that night and for many nights to come. He had sinned. There was no sleep deep enough, except perhaps that of death itself, that would ever allow him to forget it.

Chapter 43

IT RAINED THAT October as it had never before rained in the memory of living men. Day after day and night after night, a solid sheet of water washed down the panes of the castle windows. It was seldom possible to see beyond them.

Welshmen spoke of the necromancy of Owen Glendower who, eighty years before, had created a similar storm and put his English foes to rout. *If that were true,* Morton wondered, *why had the fickle Welsh climate now turned against the allies of the Welsh savior, Henry Tudor?* It made no sense. When asked to explain the apparent inconsistency, Nandik the astrologer only shrugged his shoulders and muttered some nonsense about the peregrinations of the stars, none of which was very enlightening. But then Nandik was London born and bred.

There were other things that made no sense as well. Take the poor excuse for an army Buckingham had managed to muster at Brecknock. Viewed from the castle wall during a momentary slackening in the rain, tents of the bivouac sprang up like mushrooms from the damp earth. There were probably a thousand of them clustered around the fortress, but Morton could see that there were not enough. There were not nearly enough.

Buckingham had promised ten thousand men, but as that fateful Saturday, the eighteenth day of October, approached, it was obvious that figure would prove an empty boast. Those who had come were mainly the duke's own tenants and retainers with a smattering of such Welshmen as he could enlist by cajoling and coercion. Where were the legions of valiant archers who would flock to the red dragon of Cadwallader? Where were the stalwart lads weaned on tales of King Arthur? Where were the rebellious Welsh? Plainly, they were not bivouacked beneath the walls of Brecknock Castle.

Those who had come were a reluctant, unhappy lot; the noise of their discontent sounded loudly in Morton's ears as he passed through the camp with Buckingham. Already their bread was moldy, their bedrolls saturated. Sudden wind gusts snapped tent poles like twigs. Rain trickled down the necks of their hauberks, rusted their chainmail, and soaked through their quilted linen jerkins. Huddled in mutual misery around smoking cook fires, they would look up at Buckingham and Morton with sullen, resentful stares. Once or twice, the duke had ordered a man flogged for outright insolence. The sight of such punishments did little to lessen the ill will in the camp, though it might have inspired more discretion about expressing it.

Nor was this all that had gone wrong with their great scheme. More troublesome yet were the unexplained raids on Brecknock lands. Barns that stored the recently harvested grain were set ablaze; the smoke smell was acrid in the rainy wind. Cattle and sheep intended to provide sustenance for the army were found dead in the pastures with arrows protruding from their sides. Their stinking carcasses rotted quickly in the damp and were soon picked clean by vultures. The duke's men who rode north and west into Wales to gather recruits returned bearing the bodies of slain comrades across their saddles. Even the army itself was not immune to such attacks. One morning, four of the duke's henchmen were found dead in their tent, their throats slit.

"Who is doing these things, my lord?" Morton asked as they emerged from the tent. "Who would dare to harass you in this way?"

"I think I know the answer to that," the duke said bitterly. "A tribe called the Vaughans. If it weren't for our urgency and this wretched weather, I'd make short work of them, believe me!" He shook his fist toward the northwest where a range of distant hills was cloaked in clouds.

"But . . . I don't understand," said Morton, for once truly perplexed. "Aren't they Welsh? Shouldn't they be for us rather than against us?"

Buckingham gave him a grim laugh. "Never ask what a Welshman is for nor what he wants. Never ask the reason for his madness, for you won't find it. The most treacherous pack of thieves and murderers on God's earth—may he rot the lot of 'em!"

To Morton, perhaps the most disquieting of all the troubles of those last weeks was the change in Buckingham. He was like a man driven almost against his will to an end in which he no longer believed. He poured all his formidable energy into the building of an army, yet it was as if he already knew himself defeated and was merely going through the motions of acting out a grim fate. On one point, he seemed to have taken leave of his senses entirely. He wished to take his young son with them on the march.

"But surely, my lord," Morton protested, "that would be most unwise. Body and blood, he's little more than a child."

"High time then that he learned to be a man, to live and fight in a man's world. He has excelled at the quintain and with the sword. And he wants to go, don't you, Harry?"

"Oh yes, Father. Yes!" the lad replied with his shining eyes.

"B-but the weather," Morton had persisted, "the rain. Surely it can't be healthy for a youngster and your eldest son and heir."

"It will be more healthy for him to be with me than here in the charge of that vile strumpet that mothered him. My daughter, if you could call her that, I've lost already, and good riddance. A skittish, simpering child. But my son . . . my son is mine with nothing of his mother in him. He'll go where I go."

Morton marked the paternal arm heavy on the boy's shoulder and young Harry's rapt, upturned gaze, and he turned away in disgust. He thought about Kate, in disgrace and under guard in her chambers, and wondered what she would have to say about her son's going off to war. He had seen her but seldom since the day two weeks before when Percival had burst into the great hall, dragging her behind him. He wondered too whether the duke's humor might have improved if they had apprehended her lover out on the moors instead of watching him make a distant escape, obviously wounded but uncaptured. Any hope Buckingham may have had to wreak vengeance upon him and salvage what was left of his own tarnished honor had vanished with the young shepherd into the shadows of the Mynydd Epynt.

So it was that on a soggy morning in mid-October, without his mother's blessing or even her presence, twelve-year-old Henry Stafford, someday to be the third Duke of Buckingham, was with them at the head of the line, riding a pony and wearing a small suit of armor newly fashioned for him. Banners were unfurled to hostile skies: the red dragon of Wales in the van and, close behind it, Buckingham's flaming wheel. Slowly the procession began to move to the east and toward the confrontation with Richard. They rode for a time beside the swollen Honddu, made dark red by the mud that washed into it from red sandstone hills upstream. It was an evil omen, that river, running bloody red when no lance had yet been lifted and no bow strung.

Morton, who rode next to the duke in the vanguard, was unusually quiet. Already his agile mind was leapfrogging over the days ahead, making contingency plans if this venture should fail. He had little hope now that it could succeed. Despite the ease and comfort he had known of late, he was a veteran of too many battles, a devotee of too many lost causes not to recognize the stench of defeat when it assaulted his senses. Even as the ranks of the duke's army—mounted knights and lancers, archers and pikemen, weapons wagons and heavy cannon—ground slowly forward toward the valley of the Wye and the Severn crossing, he was calculating how and when he would make his escape.

The march was a nightmare greater even than Morton could have imagined. The roadways, where they had not been washed away altogether, were thick with muddy ooze in which horses sank to their pasterns and men to their boot tops. Sometimes the heavy wagons containing their gear became mired to their wheel hubs and had to be abandoned. In that way, they lost many weapons and cannon. More were lost to the raging water courses, mere trickles in most seasons, that swept down from the mountains and proved to be major obstacles as well to horses and men in armor. In many places, bridges and fords had either been washed away or purposely destroyed by their enemies.

Long before they reached Bronllys, where the road descended to the Wye Valley, the red dragon dangled limp and wet from his staff, his army depleted, the morale of his leaders in a shambles. They had watched helplessly as men and horses and weapons were swept downstream by fierce torrents. They had listened to grumbling from the men who made it across grow louder and more ominous with each plodding step. In places where beech and alder thickets came down close to the road, they had seen their force dwindle as men slipped away beneath the cover of the welcoming trees.

Through it all, the rain drummed down from a leaden sky. And then a deadlier rain began. Morton saw the first arrow as it caught a pikeman in the thigh.

"Arrows!" Buckingham exclaimed. "What new deviltry is this?"

Morton wondered also. Even he knew a driving rain ruined bowstrings for shooting, but it didn't seem to deter these archers. Whenever they passed beneath a rocky outcropping, the arrows fell upon them, thick as heaven's rain. Their tormenters remained unseen. The most Morton could detect when he looked up were the shadows of men and longbows melting into the darkness of the oaks that crowned the cliffs. There was no question of pursuit. Clad in cumbersome armor, they could hardly scramble up mud banks or climb over slippery rocks. So they marched on, listening to the cries of panic and misery that came from the unarmored men in the rear.

However, it was not the reluctant Welsh soldiers who were the targets of this deadly attack, though some of them fell to be sure. No, it was Buckingham's chief henchmen, his best knights, the very cream of his army who dropped lifeless in the mud or who nursed grievous hurts. They were English almost to a man. Percival was one of the first to fall, pierced by an arrow through the throat.

Buckingham's grief was terrible to see. He dismounted at once, bringing the whole unwieldy train behind him to a grinding halt, and rushed to the side of his fallen favorite. The arrow had been well aimed. Percival, heedless to the last, had been wearing neither sallet nor gorget and had taken the stroke directly in his jugular. Although a veritable cascade of blood spurted from the wound, the duke was on his knees beside him, distractedly calling his name over and over again as if by its very repetition, Percival must answer.

Morton went to him in a rare frenzy of fear. What was he thinking? They had no time to dally here, motionless targets for more mischief. He was even more appalled when Buckingham shook his mailed fist at the empty cliff above them.

"I'm going up after them," he announced. "They aren't getting away with this, not while I still live and breathe. I'm going up!"

"What, and land like a turtle on your back?" Morton asked hotly. "Do you see anything up there? Whom do you hope to catch?"

"But Percival—"

"He's dead. Can't you see that? You can't help him now. And we must get away from here before they fall on us in earnest."

As if in answer, a second arrow whizzed past, close to the duke's ear. Morton handed him his helmet. "My lord, I think you should put this on at once."

Buckingham took it but did not immediately obey. He dropped to his knees once more beside Percival, and his forefinger gently traced the outline of the scar on the dead man's cheek. "It was in defense of me that he got this. A highwayman tried to rob me once, and he paid most dearly for it. He was always . . . loyal was Percival. My heart's true companion, though I sometimes wronged him. I will not wrong him now. If I cannot avenge him, then at least let me bury him."

"There isn't time," Morton argued.

"B-but I can't leave him here to the kites and buzzards," Buckingham pleaded, "like . . . like so much useless baggage."

"But you must, Father. There is no other way."

Morton had almost forgotten young Harry. Standing now at his father's side, his hand on the duke's shoulder, the boy seemed to exert a calming influence that Morton himself could not. Buckingham rose from the mud and allowed his son to lead him back to Saladin, allowed him to hold the stirrup as he mounted. Once in the saddle, he gave the signal to march and went forward without another look back, but he spoke to no one for several long hours. Morton found himself marveling at the attachment that had bound the two men. No one could argue that they had not been well matched.

They made a miserable camp that evening on the soggy floor of the Wye Valley. Beside their tents, the normally placid river foamed and churned in its banks. They could not hope to cross it unless somewhere a bridge remained standing. How, then, the mighty Severn? Morton took the measure of the river and of the man he served. Buckingham's face sagged as a squire removed his sallet; the full mouth drooped. Beneath the hauberk, his jerkin was soaked through, and still the rain slashed down, pounding on the canvas tent, wicking through in little puddles at his feet.

"Perhaps tomorrow will bring a break in the weather," Morton offered, at great pains not to reveal the extent of his own hopelessness.

"Aye, perhaps," Buckingham grunted sardonically. "And perhaps the angels of heaven will come down and dispose themselves to do battle for us. Isn't that the only thing that will save us?"

Morton only shrugged. He lifted the tent flap and stepped outside. Oddly enough, the rain did seem to have let up a little. Here and there, a torch-light flickered in the darkness. There were, of course, no cook fires, no singing, no rowdiness. Men spoke in low, disgruntled whispers. Cold rations and an early bed, damp pallets for the duke's army tonight. The tents stretched away like a pale forest in the dark, ominous quiet. Only the muted roar of the river and the pelting of the rain broke the stillness.

"I wonder whose house that is," said a voice behind him. Morton turned, somewhat startled. He had not heard the duke come out. Now he followed Buckingham's finger up a tributary of the Wye where a large manor house stood on a slight rise. Lights glowed down the valley from its upper story windows.

"I don't know," Morton replied, "though I guess we must be nearing Weobley."

"Lord Ferrers's manor perhaps?" Buckingham gave the bishop a speculative glance. "An old acquaintance of yours, isn't he? You weren't thinking, I hope, that a bed in that mansion would be more comfortable than a soggy bedroll in my tent?"

Morton reddened, thankful for the covering dark. In fact, he had been in the midst of formulating just such an opinion. "I can scarcely deny the truth of that," he replied with the proper degree of wounded innocence. "But I take it ill that you think I'd turn tail and run just as our plans are nearing glorious fruition."

"Glorious fruition!" Buckingham spat. "Mother of God, do you take me for such a fool?"

Morton's voice was low, consoling. "My lord, you are distraught. You have suffered a great loss today, and I'm afraid you're not yourself. The night is black, but everything will seem different in the morning. Trust me."

Buckingham shook his head doubtfully, but he did permit the bishop to lead him back into the tent and put him to bed beside his son, who slumbered fitfully on his own pallet. Morton himself slept very little and shivered in the midnight cold long after Buckingham's snores resounded through the tent.

Morning did not bring the promised renewal of hope. Instead it brought more rain and the news that a sizeable portion of the army had melted away in the night, leaving several of the duke's hand-picked sentries dead in the mud.

"God blast the cowardly Welsh!" Buckingham muttered. "I should have known their mettle at Stony Stratford when they gave up King Edward to Richard with nary a moment's fight. Give me one good Englishman with a sword in his hand. Give me a Percival, and you may keep all your demented Welsh!" He would have torn down the dragon standard before his tent, but Morton prevented him.

"The Tudor's part Welsh, it's true, but there's as much of England in him as of Wales. Remember that."

Buckingham gave Morton a grim look while a squire buckled his chain mail over the padded doublet and slipped the hauberk over that. It went on stiffly for the joints had begun to rust and the squires' most diligent polishing had failed to restore their smoothness. Morton was already clad in his ill-fitting brigandine and anxious to get on with the day's march. Nandik babbled about triumph and victory and successful crossings of both the Wye and Severn. Morton seized on these prophecies like a spinster on a suitor. Between them, they seemed to rejuvenate the flagging duke. His eyes shone bright with purpose between the slits of his sallet.

God help him, for he really is a fool, Morton thought as they rode out from their watery camp.

At first, it seemed they had indeed left some misfortune behind them. The deadly, insidious rain of arrows ceased as soon as they entered the marches. At Hereford, they found a bridge that still straddled the Wye, though the swollen river crested just beneath its arches and swept furiously around its piers. They made it safely across and set out on the high road to Worcester and the mighty Severn, the last major obstacle in their course.

Here their luck deserted them. Standing on the Severn bank, they could easily look across into England, gaze at Worcester with its many tall chimneys and church steeples and the proud tower of its cathedral. They could stand and look as long as they wished, but they would never make it across. The door to England was slammed shut in their faces.

The Severn bridge had been destroyed. Not by floodwaters, although the Severn made the Wye look like a millstream, but by a mischief so great that Buckingham at first refused to believe it. The great middle arch of the bridge was a blackened ruin, shattered by an explosion of gunpowder. On the opposite bank of the river, laughing at him even as England laughed, stood his cousin Sir Humphrey Stafford and his men. Buckingham had expected them to join his army at Worcester to swell its depleted ranks. Now he saw that this had been not only an idle hope but also an outright miscalculation. Humphrey remained loyal to Richard.

Utterly defeated, the duke threw himself on the ground, pounding on it with his fists and screaming in an agony of frustration. Once again, Morton feared for his sanity. When he came to himself again, the bishop feebly suggested that they march up the Severn to Bridgnorth, where there might still be a bridge left standing. Buckingham did not even honor that proposal with a reply.

Desertions, the storm, and the unseen enemy had taken their toll on his army. They had only a small remnant remaining, at most a few hundred men, not nearly enough to do battle. And even those were so wracked by fever and dysentery they were like walking corpses.

Also, Percival's death had been only the beginning of a series of personal misfortunes for the duke. Saladin, his mighty destrier, had lamed his leg on the march and had to be destroyed. Buckingham now rode a much inferior mount. Young Harry had been seized by an attack of sneezing and coughing so violent that Morton feared pneumonia, and even the duke was forced to admit that his son's health had suffered from the incredible rigors of the journey.

It was this last concern that caused Buckingham to seek the reluctant hospitality of Walter Devereux, Lord Ferrers, at Weobley. The baron greeted their small band with a notable lack of enthusiasm. Had it not been for the ailing child, it was doubtful that he would have taken them in at all. He relented from his icy stare only a moment as he watched young Harry, wrapped in blankets, sip a cup of mutton broth before the fire, but his gaze hardened as it turned on Buckingham.

"You can't stay here," he warned, wagging a finger in the duke's face. "I won't have you at Weobley. Only until you've rested, and then you must be gone."

"And where would you have me go, my good fellow?" Buckingham questioned.

"That," Ferrers replied tartly, "is hardly any concern of mine. All I know is that you've got a price on your head now, and I'll not be responsible for harboring a felon." This said, he sat down by the fireside and watched from the settle as they finished their supper.

Morton at least had no intention of imposing upon the baron's hospitality any longer than absolutely necessary. He meant to be on his way long before dawn broke over the Wye Valley. It was a great distance to the fen country around Ely, but once he reached it, he knew the monks at Croyland would give him sanctuary for a time. From there, he could secure passage over the Narrow Sea to Flanders or France—and to Henry Tudor. Buckingham's abortive rebellion was finished, but he, John Morton, would live to do battle another day. He only prayed that somehow the Tudor had gotten wind of this failure and had not set sail for England as he had planned.

Morton had some gold sovereigns left in his purse and had used one of them that afternoon to purchase an old donkey from a servant of Lord Ferrers. It was hardly a lordly beast, he conceded that night in the stable, and it had been grossly overpriced, but it was sturdy enough and would serve his purpose far better than the noble animal Buckingham had provided for him. Such a magnificent mount would have attracted unwanted attention. With his loose woolen cloak and cowled hood, his plump legs dangling over the donkey's sides almost to the ground, who would question that he was anything other than he appeared, a simple monk on his way back to the cloister? In one sense, that was true enough, Morton thought, and he chuckled to himself.

The night had turned cold. A chill wind rattled the leaves in the stable yard. There might be frost before morning, but at least there would be no more rain. High above him, between the tattered rag tails of the clouds, shone the clear-cut crystal of a single bright star. Perhaps she would soon be accompanied by some of her sisters. The new moon, thin as a fingernail paring, had set shortly after the sun. He said a small prayer that the stars would provide him with some light to see by but not enough for unfriendly eyes to see him.

In the manor of Weobley, both unwilling host and weary guests slept. Morton drew the folds of coarse wool more tightly about him to ward off the chill. The donkey brayed a soft protest as he settled his bulk carefully on her back, but a short kick in her sides ended resistance. Slowly, she lumbered forward, down the poplar-lined avenue, and out to the road. Morton did not spare a backward glance or, for that matter, a backward thought for the hapless fool of a duke left behind in deep and ignorant slumber.

Chapter 44

Buckingham awoke the next morning in a warm, dry bed, but almost at once he had a vague sensation that something was not quite right. There were noises in the house, unusual noises for such an early hour—shouts and running feet, doors opening and slamming shut. Through the bed curtains, he could see that the sky was clear, a welcome sight after a fortnight of rain. Beside him, his son still slept, his breathing heavy but regular.

Suddenly, the door to his bedchamber burst open, and the strange trio of Rush, Knyvet, and Nandik entered unbidden. He thrust back the bed curtains, about to reprimand them, then stopped in midsentence.

"Where's Morton?" he asked, suddenly afraid.

"Gone, Your Grace," Rush replied. "Or so it seems. His bed has not been slept in."

"Gone?" Buckingham parroted, dropping his legs over the edge of the bed. "But where?"

"As to that, we don't know," said Rush. Buckingham could see he trembled at the news as did his two companions, who huddled together behind him. "One of the servants says the bishop bought a sumpter from him yesterday. We may assume that he is on it."

The duke was aghast. While Morton had remained with him, in a peculiar way, hope had remained also. He was clever enough to pull it out of the fire yet even after the near disaster of the past days.

He could raise new armies, gather new weapons. There was nothing he could not do.

"It can't be!" Buckingham cried, leaping from the bed. "Surely there must be some other explanation. Even now he may be out rousing the countryside to our cause. Look! The sun is shining. The storm is over. We can begin all over again. Morton will return and bring an army with him."

Rush shook his head. Behind him, Sir William Knyvet cleared his throat. "No, Your Grace, I think not. Wouldn't he have told us if that were his plan?"

"But you, Thomas," Buckingham argued, turning on Nandik, the astrologer. "Didn't you foresee success for our venture? Didn't you foretell the fall of the boar?"

"So I did, Your Grace," the soothsayer replied, smoothing his blue, star-painted robes. "And he will fall. There's no doubt of that. I only fear that . . . my timing was amiss. The stars cannot lie, of course, but they may mislead. It seems that is what has happened."

"That for your stars!" Buckingham spat, making an obscene gesture with his fingers. "Tell me, what am I to do now? You are my advisors, you brought me here. Now where am I supposed to go?"

The three whispered together, trying to decide, while Buckingham was interrupted by a cry from the bed. "Father, what's wrong? What's all the fuss about? Do we have to leave here?"

"Yes, Harry, I'm afraid so. But we'll find another place, never fear."

"Can't we . . . can't we just go home?" It was the wail of a much younger child, sick, homesick, and afraid.

"No, we can't. Home is the first place they'll look for us and is therefore the last place we can go."

The boy's face puckered as if he were about to cry.

"Now, none of that," Buckingham said sternly. "You must learn to be a man, Harry, and your first lesson is that the world doesn't always go along with a man's wishes. Now get up and get dressed. We must be gone as soon as we can."

He gave the boy a playful slap across the buttocks as he scurried for the chair where his clothes were piled. Despite his brave words,

Buckingham himself had small stomach for the day's journey. In reality, it would be no journey at all but a headlong, reckless flight of two mice scampering from the claws of a cat. There would be no hot food or soft bed waiting at their destination. Indeed, there was not even a destination.

"There's a price on my head," he said, turning back to his erstwhile advisors. "How much is it?"

"A thousand pounds," Rush replied, "or lands worth a hundred pounds a year."

Buckingham let out a low whistle. "It seems I'm still valuable to the king's grace in one way or another. It makes me laugh to think how much Richard would cherish my dead carcass."

Young Harry's eyes glazed with fear. "You won't let him catch you, will you?"

"No, of course not. It's I who shall catch him, even yet. You'll see, my son. Your sire has charms to soothe the raging boar or, if not, a knife to gut him." He threw back his head and laughed in unrestrained amusement at a joke no one else could share. Rush, Nandik, Knyvet, and even young Harry all stared at him in wonder.

"Well, why do you stand there gaping at me?" Buckingham questioned the three men. "Shouldn't you be out procuring the means of my departure? Or do you, my worthy counselors, think I should wait until tomorrow or maybe two weeks from Sunday? 'Hap the stars will look on me with more favor then." He turned his withering gaze on Nandik then clapped his hands together. "Get out of here, you lazy wantwits, out of here, I say! Out, out, out!"

They fled the room, crowding at the door in unison, afraid he might attack them physically at any moment. In the haste, Knyvet tripped on the hem of Nandik's gown, leaving a large tear in the fabric, but the unfortunate astrologer did not pause to assess the damage.

There was no difficulty in finding means for the duke to quit Weobley. There was no one at Weobley, including the remnant of his own men, who was not glad to see the back of him. He knew he was abandoning what was left of his army, but he no longer cared. The men could find their own way home, and they at least did not have a price on their heads. He hoped that Richard would be merciful to them, but there was nothing he could do to enforce that. He who had once been so mighty in the land now had no power left to him.

Lord Ferrers robbed his stable to provide a fast, reliable bay gelding, and a squire and a page gladly agreed to an exchange of clothing with Buckingham and his son. The roughness of the coarse homespun next to his skin was both unfamiliar and unwelcome, but he knew there was no alternative. He was aware now that new discomforts and inconveniences would greet him at every turn, but he didn't care. The only thing that mattered was that he escape with his life.

They rode all that day and far into the night. Buckingham surmised Richard was moving toward the south; therefore, he made for the north. At first, his track led over the rugged hill country of the marches, through dense forests, and up the gorge of the River Teme. Settlements were few in the turbulent border area, and he skirted such towns as there were, Leominster, Brimfield, Ludlow. He could not risk going near them. When horses' hooves sounded in the road ahead, he turned his own gelding off into the forests or ravines or hid behind rocks until they passed. Overwhelming loneliness rode with him. Except for Harry, he was cut off from all humanity, isolated from everything he had known. He, who had been England's mightiest lord, did not dare stop and ask a farmer's wife for a cup of water from her well, did not dare seek a night's lodging at the most humble country inn, did not even dare a "Good day" or a "God be with you" from a fellow traveler on the road.

He thought it all over that night as he settled down in the forest on a pile of wet leaves. Harry, wrapped in their only blanket, slept the sleep of exhaustion, but Buckingham was plagued by a thousand questions. How could this humiliation be happening to him? Why was it happening? What had he done to deserve this horrible fate?

The answer to his questions came suddenly clear. It was Morton—Morton who had tricked him, Morton who had misled him, Morton who had deserted him. Hadn't Richard warned him that the bishop was a clever devil and a master of deceit? Yes, it had been Morton, playing on his own very natural ambitions, who had led him astray. Surely, Richard would pardon him for that, wouldn't he? Richard understood human frailty. Richard knew what inordinate ambition could do to a man. And most importantly of all, Richard loved him. He could not have been mistaken about that.

He fell asleep then, oddly comforted, lulled by the distant murmur of a stream. The cold of the night, the strange sounds of the forest, the hardness of the ground, even the hoarseness of Harry's breathing—these were all temporary misfortunes soon to be overcome. The next morning, he awoke late when a shaft of sunlight touched his face. He devoured the remaining bread and cheese they had brought from Weobley. Harry, pale and still listless, only nibbled at his share before declaring a lack of appetite.

"Never mind," said Buckingham, rumpling the boy's hair. "We'll find better fare by nightfall."

They rode that day along the ridge known as the Long Mynd and crossed the Severn at Shrewsbury with almost ridiculous ease. Suddenly, he knew where they were bound. He had an estate north of Wem, which had come to him through his mother. It was a minor holding of little consequence with an unpretentious manor house and a few tenants. One of these, he recalled from his childhood with a certain fondness, was a Ralph . . . what was his surname? Borrister? Barrister? Oh yes, Bannister, that was it: Ralph Bannister. As a boy, the duke had taken refuge there with his mother during one of the many reversals in the fortunes of Lancaster after the death of his father. He had not seen it since or, for that matter, had he given it much thought. It had been only a name on the tally rolls, one of the less significant integers in the massing of his wealth. Now its very obscurity proved a godsend. He would have time to plot his next move, a chance to think about how he would approach Richard.

At that thought, a slight shiver passed through him. Suppose Richard would not forgive him? Suppose he proved to be unreasonable over the matter of the princes? But then Richard should be grateful to him for that. Hadn't they been a stumbling block to him as well? If he had been wise, he would have removed them himself. Perhaps he might even see fit to reward Buckingham in some way for ridding him of the problem.

They reached Wem long after nightfall. The way had been dark with no moon to guide them or light their way. The manor had never been fortified, but the gates should have been locked at sunset. They creaked open at a touch. Beyond, the avenue was deserted. There had once been a stately border of elms. They were gone now, and grass grew between the paving stones. Dead leaves rattled across his path. The whole place had a derelict air as if it had died in another time.

The house stood at the end of the walk, a two-story edifice of red sandstone with tall chimneys at either end. It was dark, of course, with no lights in the windows and no one to greet him, though that could be remedied. Odd, though, how those black patches marred the walls. He did not recall that ivy had ever grown there. Then as he drew closer, he could see more clearly in the fitful starlight and gasped in dismay. Wem Manor had been on fire. The house was completely gutted. Only the walls still stood.

There was no time to think what he must do. Harry awoke to a fit of coughing and sneezing. "Are we there yet, Father?"

"Not yet, my son."

"How much longer?"

"Soon, very soon."

The cottage that had once belonged to Ralph Bannister was not far away. At first, he feared that it too was deserted. The outbuildings were in disrepair, the roof needed thatch, and it appeared that some stones were missing from the wall itself.

Yet as he slid from the saddle, his foot touched something soft and slippery: animal droppings. The whole yard reeked of them. Hard upon his natural revulsion came relief. Where animals flocked in such numbers, there must also be people. He walked to the cottage door and beat loudly on it. Silence. He knocked again, louder. Someone stirred inside; he heard footsteps on an earthen floor accompanied by a low undertone of muttering. Then the door was opened, and a lighted lantern pushed in his face.

"Cock's muddy bones! What's the meaning of this?" asked a gruff voice. "Can't a man take a well-earned rest in his own home?"

"Ralph—Ralph Bannister!" Buckingham cried, relief flooding his voice with warmth. "Don't you remember me?"

The man raised a hand to his forehead and scratched it thoughtfully. "Nay . . . can't say as I do."

"It's been a long time, too long I fear. Don't you recall a small lad who used to follow you around this yard?"

"My lord Harry? Can it be? After all these years?"

The lantern was lowered now, and Buckingham could see the other man's face clearly for the first time. It had grown older, thinner, and more wizened but was still blessedly familiar. Bannister's smile of welcome, however, was tinged with anxiety.

"I beg pardon, m'lord, for the house. It got a-fire two summers ago, struck by lightnin', I think. I . . . I didn't expect Your Lordship, and I . . . I've had no time nor the means to repair it. And now, well . . . uh . . . I don't rightly know where to put you up."

"If it wouldn't be too much trouble, perhaps I could share the shelter of your roof tonight. I've brought my son, and he's ailing. We need only a bed and some food. If you would be so kind . . ." He hated the thought that it had come to this, begging for favors from his own servant, pleading where he should command.

Bannister held the lantern aloft, shining its light into the yard, as if searching for the henchmen and retainers who could be expected to swell the progress of a duke. Puzzled, he took in the one horse, the lone boy, but he asked no questions.

"Your Grace is most welcome," he said, "and the young lord with you."

Ralph quickly got a fire going in the grate then set ale and the remains of a cold hare pasty on the table before them. Harry nibbled only a little at the tart; obviously, he had passed beyond hunger hours ago. Buckingham, on the other hand, devoured it greedily and wished for more. It was hardly the fare he was used to, yet he had never tasted anything so delicious.

Throughout the meal, he was aware of two black eyes fixed relentlessly on him. These belonged to Emma, Ralph's shrunken old crone of a wife and far and away the ugliest woman Buckingham had ever seen. Her eyes, small and hard as tiny beads of jet in their deep sockets, smote him with hostility as he ate.

Ralph did not appear to notice his wife's displeasure. He had introduced her proudly enough and had ignored, as if from long habit, her sour reply.

"So a royal dook turns up on me doorstep in the dead o' night," she had said, and the black bristles on her chin had quivered with indignation. "Am I expected to drop Ye'r Grace a curtsy?"

"There's no need," Buckingham had replied rather grandly.

"Faugh!" she had answered as if in complete agreement.

Now, under her hard gaze, the duke wondered if he had done something to anger her. Could he perhaps have devoured the supper she had planned for the next night? Unlikely thought. There had not been enough there to appease the hunger of one, let alone two. And they would, of course, be well recompensed for their hospitality. He had no money with him. Stupidly, he had forgotten to bring any when he had fled Weobley. Under normal circumstances, he would not have to bother with such trifles. That he should find himself alone and pressed was a joke of the most laughable strangeness. It would amuse him later when all was made right again. He must remember to tell Richard.

Young Harry's head drooped on his neck like a dandelion wilting on its stalk. "I warrant the lad wants his bed more than he wants his victuals," Ralph said kindly. He drew the boy to him and led him from the table.

"And where might ye be takin' him, Ralph Bannister?" asked a voice sharp as old cheese.

"Why, to the bed, woman. Where else?"

"We've naught but one bed in this house. Have ye forgot that?"

"Nay, I've not forgot. But we also have new hay in the loft."

"Let them sleep there then. I'll not be put out of me own bed."

"Aye, woman." The husband's voice managed a flicker of authority. "That ye will be. This," he said, gesturing to the bed, "is scarce fit to be offered to the duke, and for sure, 'twill not be the loft for him."

"Faugh!" she said, and Buckingham heard all the resentment her eyes had darted at him in the curt dismissal. He might have intervened. Actually, the straw pallet with its one blanket looked little more comfortable than the hay would have been. However, Bannister was right. It was fitting that they remember his station despite the abruptness with which he had burst upon them, despite his somewhat straitened circumstances. It was only proper that they treat him with the deference that was his due—within their humble capacity, of course. He granted them their limitations.

Bannister wasn't a bad sort, surely. His face was as brown and seamed as a walnut, but his eyes still crinkled with good humor. Emma, now, was another matter entirely. She would have to watch herself if she hoped to share in the reward he would give to her husband. He wouldn't tolerate her insolence for long. However, tonight he was too tired to give her more than a lordly frown as he made his way to the bed that Ralph Bannister had won for him.

Emma was as furious as Ralph had ever seen her.

"Come now, lass," he said winningly when they were settled beneath their quilt. "There's naught to get so wrought up about, is there now? I'm not so far gone in years that I don't recall we used to have a pretty good tumble now and again in the hay mound."

"You've grown addled in the wits, Ralph Bannister, and that's the fact of it," came the tart reply.

"But, honeypot," he protested, "what was I to do? He's the master of Wem and second to the king in all the land as I hear tell."

"Master of Wem!" she snorted. "I daresay, and a fine master he's made us over the years. We might ha' starved for all the help he's given us. And as for being second to the king . . ." she added, her voice dropping, "how many dooks come creepin' round at midnight like filthy footpads in clothes no yeoman would wear? Tell me that, Ralph Bannister."

Ralph was silent. He had no answer. Emma's voice croaked on. "There's trouble in the south, rebellion 'gainst King Richard. Aye, I've heard it. Like as not, his high and mighty grace of Buckingham has gone and got hisself in the thick o' it and flees for his life."

"'Tis but rumor, my good wife. Ye know no more than I what goes on in t'south."

"Rumor, is it then? Ye'll not think so when 'tis ourselves that gets in trouble for the keepin' of him."

"But I can't toss him out in the cold. I knew him as a lad. A bright, golden-haired lad he was, like to his own bairn."

"Aye, and wi' yer fool's heart, ye loved him, no doubt. What has he done in return for that love? I ask you, what has he done?"

The last barb struck home. In the dim starlight that slanted through the broken boards of the barn, she lay rigid and still.

So that's it, he thought. She had nursed her grudge against the duke all these years when no favor had come from high places, when the duke had forgotten his old manor of Wem and the boyhood friend who had once sheltered him from York. How could he answer her? Hadn't the resentment clawed at him too in the bitter years, the drought-stricken years, the years when the biddies in the coop had stopped laying and when the ewes had dropped their lambs dead? Hadn't he, through all those years, been a loyal and dutiful steward, tilling the lord's lands and returning their bounty to the lord's bailiff? How did one answer that neglect? How explain it?

"Hush, woman," he said at last. "You shouldn't be speaking so of your betters. He'll reward us for what we've done for him tonight, just see if he doesn't. Rich as kings we'll be by Christmas, the devil take me if we aren't. Now go to sleep. Dawn comes too soon."

Amazingly, she obeyed him. Perhaps it was the promise of reward that quieted her objections. Money had always sounded in Emma Bannister's ears like tones of sweetest dulcet. Presently, she sighed and moved against him, and her deep breathing told him that she slept. He put a hand on one withered pap. He could remember when her breasts had been as white as new-skimmed cream and as plump as partridges. Long years ago, it seemed now. Her life had been far from easy.

He himself could not sleep. The questions she had asked, the doubts he felt but could not express kept him wakeful till gray light crept between the broken boards.

They lived together for almost a week in a state of uneasy truce. Too soon, however, the strain began to tell on all of them. Emma Bannister's face grew each day longer and more sullen. The presence of her unwelcome guests underfoot in the tiny one-room cot did little to improve her disposition.

""'Tis staring at me he is, all the day long," she told Ralph in exasperation. "I can't make a move, but 'e's there where I want to step. It's too much for a body to bear. The young'un' now," she added, her voice softening a trifle, "he's not so much of a hardship. A right comely lad . . .""

With this, Bannister agreed. How many pleasant memories were roused in his heart just by the sight of that golden cherub tagging along as he went about his chores! The duke himself was another matter altogether. He could not be persuaded to leave the cot unless it was to use the privy and only then when Emma began to mutter about the number of times she had to empty the chamber pot.

Oh, Buckingham was courteous enough when he spoke, though in truth he said very little. His mind seemed to have gone wandering—wool gathering, Emma called it. Sometimes he wore a desperate, frightened look like a bear in a trap; other times he seemed about to break into secret laughter. He never said a word about leaving and made no move to go.

That he must go and soon was becoming increasingly apparent to Ralph as he inspected his dwindling stores of food. Both the duke and his son could easily put away more provisions in a day than the two Bannisters normally consumed in a week. To make matters worse, Ralph felt compelled to serve fare his guests would consider more palatable than the black bread, onions, and cheese that were the mainstays of his own diet. A litter of piglets had been the first casualty. Next, the chickens had begun to disappear from the coop and reappear, swimming in thin broth, on the dinner table. Emma had squawked as if she herself were one of the endangered fowl, for the eggs those chickens laid were one of their chief sources of livelihood. Finally, the calf that Bannister had hoped to nurse through the winter and raise into a steer had fallen victim to his axe.

"Cotsbody!" he groaned to Emma that night. "Will it not have an end? If they are not gone soon, I don't know what we ourselves shall be eating next week."

Emma was oddly quiet. She had said surprisingly little over the past two days, but Ralph had caught the scheming, almost crafty look in her eyes. "They'll be gone soon," she said with childlike assurance. "Aye, they'll be gone."

"How can ye say so, woman?" Ralph questioned. "How can ye be so sure?"

But she only shrugged and grinned and rolled over in the hay to fall soundly asleep.

The next day, in a gray dawn that snapped with frost, she rode to Shrewsbury market in the dilapidated old trap that Ralph kept working only through great diligence. It was very seldom that either of them ventured so far. The ten-mile journey was long and sometimes hazardous, but these considerations did not deter Emma now.

She returned that night with a triumphant gleam in her eye. Throughout dinner, she deferred to Buckingham with unusual courtesy, but Ralph sensed that her whole body was strung taut with excitement. There had been news then in Shrewsbury.

"Well, husband," she said later, climbing into the loft beside him, "you were right when ye said there was money to be made from this duke."

"Money?" he repeated dumbly.

"Aye, a reward, what else? 'E's in the thick o' the rebellion along w' the Woodville queen's kin. King Richard hisself'll make ye a rich man, Ralph Bannister."

"So there's a bounty on his head," he said slowly. He had known it for days though he hadn't wanted to admit it, not even to Emma. Especially not to Emma.

"Aye, a bounty. Are ye such a sluggard ye canna take me meanin'?"

"No, I take it well enough. But to turn him in . . . it's a Judas trick. I want no part of it. Besides, he might reward us yet, he himself."

"When 'e's given us naught in the past? Don't be a simpleton! Only listen to me. 'Tis a thousand pounds the king offers for him. A thousand pounds! Twice as much as for the marquis," she added, almost proudly.

"A thousand pounds!" Bannister repeated, rolling the words around on his tongue. It was a fortune.

"Or lands worth a hundred a year," she added as an afterthought.

Plainly the hard currency was what appealed most to Emma, though Ralph considered the second alternative even more attractive. No longer would he have to wrest a living from this grim plot, no longer serve another's interests before his own. In the light of the lantern, Emma's thin face was lit with the excitement that transformed it. Color glowed in cheeks that had been bereft of color for many a year, and her black eyes sparkled. Breathless as a young girl, she awaited her husband's verdict. Her face mirrored shock, surprise, and anger as he slowly shook his head.

"Nay, 'twould still be wrong. I canna do it."

"And is it right to let a rebel and a traitor walk free?"

"Ralph Bannister never profited yet from another wight's misfortune. I'll not start now."

"Faugh! Misfortune you calls it. Dark treachery says I. Me cousin Maud, she saw Richard last Lammastide at Warwick. A right goodly man, says she, our anointed king. And this duke, who ye'll not turn in, has taken arms against him, has turned traitor and for no good cause. Very well then keep him 'ere an' ye must. But what will ye feed 'im, I wonder, after the calf is gone? Will ye kill the cow as well?"

Perhaps it was her last remark that convinced him. Left to himself, Buckingham might stay on indefinitely. That he could not be permitted to do so was becoming increasingly obvious.

"But the lad," he protested weakly. "What's to become of him?"

Emma shrugged. "'E'll go home to his mother, what else? No harm'll come to him. Do ye go then for the sheriff?"

He could find no answer in himself to her eagerness. Fortunately, Master Mitton, the sheriff, did not live far. He could be there and back, on the duke's gelding, before morning.

"Aye," he nodded heavily. "Aye, I'll go." And slipping like a shadow down the ladder, he was lost among the shadows of the night.

Salisbury was ringed by fire on All Hallow's Eve. On the heights surrounding the city, huge bonfires kept at bay witches and goblins and ghosts of the dead who walked forth that night. On the vast plain to the north, more but smaller fires blazed, the campfires of Richard's army. It was assembled there in full strength though no battle had yet been fought.

"Aye, and there needed none," Buckingham heard the sheriff tell one of his men, "with the rebel leader here trapped like a pig in a poke. Soon as the rebels heard about that, the whole conspiracy fell apart like a puffball in t'wind. They fled, aye, how they fled, those treasonous swine. Some to their holes, some to sanctuary, some even to France. They'll not trouble the king again, God save His Grace."

Buckingham heard these words, the epitaph to his great scheme, through the same drifting fog that had surrounded him ever since Master Mitton had come pounding on the door of Ralph Bannister's cot two—or was it three?—nights before. To be sure, there had been a moment of wild panic when the torchlight glared in his face, when the manacles had been slapped on his wrists. It had been an unprecedented violation of his noble person, and he had longed to lash out, to run away, but there had been no place to go. A dozen pikes had barred his escape.

And so he had stood there, numb and compliant in the crowded cot, while his mind raced ahead to Salisbury, they said, and to Richard. He had been only dimly aware of the Bannisters, of Ralph's shamefaced look that would not meet his own, of Emma's mocking, triumphant smirk.

The more fools they, he thought. They had betrayed him for a paltry thousand pounds. He would have rewarded them three times as amply. They would not have found Harry Buckingham ungrateful. Well, perhaps they had done him a service at that. He was fast tiring of his cramped, humble lodgings. He had been wishing for a change in status.

For his son, the tears sliding unchecked down the boy's smooth cheeks, he could feel some compassion, even though the sheriff assured him the lad would be returned safely to Brecknock.

"God go with you, Harry," he had murmured with unusual gentleness. He was seized with a desperate desire to protect the youth from this collapse of all their dreams, yet he could do nothing. He reached out and attempted an embrace made awkward both by the chains and lack of practice. "Don't be afraid, my son," he told him. "All will yet be well. Richard loves me, and when I see him, when I explain to him, no harm will come to me—you'll see."

"I'd not be so sure of that if I was you," the sheriff warned. "Richard's in a powerful fury, so I've heard. But come, man, enough of this nonsense. You've had your leave-taking, and I have my orders, which are to bear you to Salisbury. That being no mean distance, I intend to begin immediately . . . if Your Grace be willing."

Buckingham only raised his chin to a more haughty angle. He found the sheriff to be an officious man, large, overbearing, and bristling with self-importance. He had a keen eye to duty and, no doubt, to his own purse. Obviously, the duke was a greater fish than he had ever hoped to catch in his net. The strange mixture of awe at his good fortune and contempt for his prisoner had marked Mitton's behavior during the days and nights of their long journey from Shropshire.

The duke had ignored him with unspoken scorn of his own. He made it plain to Master Mitten that his thoughts were elsewhere and that even if he were a prisoner, he was also the first duke of the realm. He was not to be so easily disposed of. Even Richard could not dispose of him as easily as that.

Chapter 45

RICHARD WAS RESTLESS. In the upper-story parlor of the White Hart Inn, where he was lodging in Salisbury, the air was hot with blazing candles and thick with tension. No one spoke. Earlier, the king's favorite fool had been brought in for his amusement but had been dismissed just as abruptly. Later, three musicians who had hoped to soothe his black humor had fled in terror of their lives when he cried out, "Enough! I'll have no more of your grating on my ears." Lastly, Ralph Assheton had attempted to engage him in a game of chess, normally one of Richard's favorite pastimes. However, after a few desultory moves, the king had lost interest. He lacked the concentration for chess.

It seemed that he lacked the concentration for almost any activity that night. For hours, he stalked the floor of the brilliantly lit chamber, the furred hem of his gold Flemish gown slapping against his thighs with maddening rhythm, the light of the tapers glancing off him in swift shards of ruby, topaz, and amethyst. Richard was as tense and unsettled as one of the caged black leopards in the Tower zoo, and there seemed to be nothing anyone could do to help him.

If only our enemies had given battle, Assheton thought, watching his lord and king burn in the fires of inner torment. *If only they had turned and attacked instead of running into hiding like so many scurrying rats.*

It was battle that Richard Plantagenet needed, White Surrey between his legs, the heft of a sword in his hands, clank of metal on metal, consummation of steel driving through flesh. These things might has eased him and left him the glory of victory—not this hollow triumph, empty of all he had hoped to win except the winning itself and deluded of the chief prize who still walked free somewhere in English air.

The atmosphere was suffocating in the upper room, where the candle flames devoured the air and the night outside pushed at the futile but defiant light within. For the first time, Assheton almost regretted the recent promotion to high office that had placed him within the intimate circle of the king's advisors. Together with Ratcliffe, Lovell, and Catesby, he was forced to share his lord's agonies, to view the restless pain that burned in his eyes. Vice constable of England—it was a grand title, particularly since the lord high constable lurked a fugitive, none knew where. It was a title to be grateful for were not the king perhaps a little mad.

Faithful Lord Francis, Viscount Lovell, mixed Richard a potion of hellebore leaves, the plant some called the bear's claw and was said could cure melancholy. He ground them up fine with mortar and pestle so that their stink filled the room, and mixed them with claret in a crystal goblet.

"It will help you sleep, sire," he said as he offered it to Richard.

"Does it taste as evil as it smells?" the king asked, wrinkling his nose in distaste.

"For a good night's slumber," said Catesby, "it might be worth it."

Richard nodded. "I suppose I must take the remedy, however foul." He tossed back his head, downing it at a gulp.

From the large bow window that overlooked the courtyard, Ratcliffe gave an excited cry. "Look, sire! Maybe there's a better remedy here. Unless I am much mistaken . . ."

Gagging a little on the brew, Richard set the goblet down hard on a table and moved quickly to the window. The others followed close behind. Through the tiny leaded panes, the view below was curiously fragmented, like so many pieces of a puzzle. There were a number of torches reflected in wavering light from puddles of water that stood in the yard. And there were many men, most of them on horseback. The one that Ratcliffe pointed to was partly swathed in shadow beyond the range of the torches, but there was a heart-stopping familiarity in the set of his broad shoulders and the proud way he sat his horse. As they watched, he moved a little, shaking off his hood, and the flickering torchlight caught the sheen of gold ringlets, the flash of metal on fettered wrists.

Richard's hands clutched the miniver revers of his gown. "Holy Jesu!" he breathed. "They have found him."

A chorus of excited congratulations echoed in the room, but Richard did not seem to hear them. His eyes, indeed his whole being, were riveted on the scene below. And then Buckingham, as if he sensed he was being watched, looked up and stared hard at the bow window. Groaning, Richard backed sharply away, his hands covering his face.

"Sire, what is it?" asked Lovell.

"I will not see him. Do you understand? I must not see him."

"But of course, there's no need to see him tonight. It's quite late. Tomorrow—"

"No, you don't understand. I won't see him. Not tonight. Not tomorrow. Not ever."

There was a knock on the door. Ratcliffe opened it to a wide-eyed page while the king called Assheton to him.

"Master Vice Constable, you have a prisoner below. I charge him into your hands."

"I'll see to him, sire," Assheton assured him, "right quickly."

Richard went on, ignoring him. "I would have a trial—the form of a trial—tomorrow. I don't want him so swiftly dispatched as poor Hastings. That was a mistake. I won't have more blood on my conscience, even blood as foul as his." He shuddered a little, then added, "You know him guilty, as do I."

Assheton bowed deeply. "It shall be as you command, sire."

"Very good," Richard said, smiling for the first time that evening. "I think I shall sleep better tonight. Perhaps your medicine, Francis, has worked after all. Or perhaps another medicine has surpassed it." He nodded toward the window. "I charge you, Sir Ralph, on pain of your life, to get from him the answer to the . . . uh . . .

riddle that has plagued us through these past weeks. Knowing that, maybe I'll be able to rest easily once more."

Edward's sons, Assheton thought as Lovell and Catesby led Richard to the bedchamber, where his own bed had been assembled, the great oak bed with scenes of the holy sepulcher carved on the headboard. He vowed it was the only bed in which he could sleep, and he had ordered it brought down from London. Assheton knew too well, as all knew who kept that unquiet watch, that even in that bed Richard was wakeful, and all knew the reason. The fate of his nephews tormented him like a brand. Would the fugitive who waited below in chains provide the answer that might ease him?

The night air was brisk with the sharpness of the coming winter in it. Assheton shivered in his budge-lined cloak. Overhead a sky of frosty stars and a waxing gibbous moon paled in the smoky torch-light. Yes, it was Buckingham, all right, no doubt about that, though a Buckingham much changed. He was both older and thinner than Assheton remembered him, garbed in rough hemp like a beggar, with a stubble of beard and a smear of dirt down one cheek.

However, his blue eyes were alert, quickly taking in the consta-ble's mace that dangled from Assheton's belt.

"The constable, I believe," Buckingham intoned, "the lord high constable of England, if I'm not mistaken. Here, bailiff, you may release your prize."

"Not on your say-so," snapped the sheriff, a fat huffing chimney of a man. Assheton silenced him with a curt nod and turned back to the prisoner.

"You have risen to high estate, Sir Ralph," Buckingham said. His voice could still drip honey at need. "I offer my congratulations."

"No need of that. I'm only the vice constable. The higher post is still held by another."

"Indeed?" The duke's brows arched slightly, and there was no mistaking the flare of hope in his eyes.

"For a while. Only for a while." Not for the first time, Assheton wondered why Richard had not removed Buckingham from the office well before this.

"Here, sir," the sheriff broke in, obviously impatient at being ignored. "I've ridden hard all the way from Shropshire to bring this traitorous felon to the king. Surely some sort of consideration is warranted."

"You are assured of His Grace's deepest gratitude," Assheton said blandly.

"I had hoped for . . ."

"For more material recompense?"

The fat face reddened. "Why, yes . . ."

"The king's steward will see to that in the morning. I'm sure you'll find Richard generous. There is also the matter of the reward, the thousand pounds. Do you claim that also?"

"Why . . . ah . . . yes, of course. We heard he was seen . . . er . . . fleeing north from Shrewsbury. I took my men out and hunted him night and day—"

The rumble of Buckingham's rich laughter exploded between them. "Richard is as poorly served as I am myself," the duke said finally. "And this one claims more than his due. It wasn't this scoundrel but my own servant, Ralph Bannister of Wem, who turned me in. Filthy turncoat." He spat on the flagged court. "No doubt he would have sold his own soul for a mess of porridge, but I won't have him cheated of his due. He shall know Harry Buckingham a generous master to the end."

"He has done good service to a higher master."

"Or to his own purse."

Assheton ignored this. The night was turning colder. Above the inn roof, Orion's belt glittered like icy diamonds. "Come along now," he said to Buckingham. "It's getting late, and we must find a place for you."

"I . . . I had expected . . . to see His Grace." Buckingham's voice was low, but Assheton felt the muscles of his arm tighten beneath the rough hemp.

"He has retired for the evening."

Buckingham's full lower lip quivered. "But I saw him—there in that window!" He pointed to the darkened parlor. "And surely he saw me. I know he did. He and I have much to discuss. Could it be he didn't recognize me? That's it, isn't it? It was dark. He couldn't see me clearly, and to be honest, I've never looked like this before. Tell him, Sir Ralph. Go tell him I'm here."

Assheton hesitated, wondering why he didn't just blurt out the unkind truth. "His Grace has retired for the evening," he repeated. "He left orders not to be disturbed."

"Ha! Does he have a wench with him tonight that he guards his privacy so jealously? I wouldn't have believed it of him."

"Nor need you believe it now," Assheton replied, annoyed. "My only concern is to find a place to stash you."

"He'll see me in the morning," Buckingham said, confidence restored. "He'll not rest once he learns I'm here. I know him even better than you do, Sir Ralph. He loves me, Dickon, loves me well."

Finding a place to dispose of the prisoner when Salisbury jails already groaned with Woodville adherents was no small matter. Finally, they took him to the cathedral deanery within the walled close, where the dean, roused from sleep, stumbled over his own feet in his eagerness to provide the necessary accommodation. Perhaps he wished to dissociate himself from the treasonous activities of Salisbury's bishop, Lionel Woodville. The bishop himself had long since fled.

The dean led them down a twisted stair to the cellar below, a dank, evil-smelling place with water from the nearby Avon puddling the floor. Past barrels of salted pork and casks of wine and ale, he took them to a small front chamber with a heavy bolted door and a high barred window. Evidently, it had served the office of a prison in days past. A red-eyed rat scurried from their torches.

"This should do the job, I think," the dean said. "He'll be secure enough here."

"Yes, I quite agree," Assheton nodded, giving the cell a cursory inspection. "In you go, Your Grace," he said to Buckingham, who showed some hesitation before the guards gave him a shove.

He stumbled then caught his balance. He turned to Assheton with a smile of almost melting sweetness. "Everything will be all right tomorrow, Sir Ralph. Dickon won't be angry with you for long because you treat me so unkindly."

"Tomorrow?" Assheton repeated. "Tomorrow, you are to be brought to trial before me and a commission of my choosing."

The duke shook his head. "Certainly there's no need for that. They were lies, all lies that you heard about me. I was misused, ill led, betrayed. I know Richard would understand if I could only explain. Such a bother over . . . over a misunderstanding between two friends! You must let me see Dickon."

Assheton's words dropped between them like cold stones. "On that matter, the king's grace has given most specific instructions. He will not see you nor have anything to do with you ever again."

He spun quickly on his heel beyond the reach of the clutching hand, but not before he saw the look of anguished astonishment that leapt like a demon in the duke's eyes.

The bell that tolled from the campanile for All Soul's Day was muffled by the stone bulk of the mighty cathedral and fell only dimly, like an echo, into the octagonal chapter house. Nonetheless, it permeated the room like the pale November sunlight falling gray green through the luminous walls of grisaille glass.

Still anxious to be of service, the dean had only that morning agreed to the use of the chapter house for Buckingham's trial. Assheton found himself smiling at the irony that Lionel Woodville's episcopal seat was proving so useful in the condemnation of his noble brother-in-law and fellow traitor. Assheton sat in front of the dean's seat behind a long table with Ratcliffe on one side of him and Catesby on the other. Master Kendall was at one end, his pen poised, ready to record the duke's words.

The prisoner who came toward them wore an entirely different face from the one Assheton had seen the night before. Abject, defeated, his face gray in the swimming light, he appeared to have spent the past night in hell. He walked slowly and uncertainly across the tiled floor. One of the guards had to prod him with a pikestaff to speed him along. When at last he stood before them, he refused to meet Assheton's eyes.

"Henry Stafford, otherwise known as the second Duke of Buckingham, you stand accused of inciting rebellion and most heinous treason against King Richard and of conspiring to put another on the throne in his place. Have you anything to say in your defense?"

"Please!" Assheton had to strain to catch the duke's hoarse whisper. "I beg you for pity's sake. I have a great deal to say, but it is for the king's ears only."

Assheton exchanged glances with Ratcliffe. The duke's plea was not unexpected in view of his insistence of the previous night, but the vice constable shook his head as he turned back to the prisoner. "As I have told you, His Grace does not wish to be disturbed. He has appointed us as his deputies to hear your case and pronounce judgment." He spoke slowly and carefully as he might have spoken to a confused child.

"I know much . . . much that I would tell His Grace concerning his true enemies. Other matters as well. I know much."

"Then I suggest you tell us here, everything, just as you would tell Richard." To Buckingham's still doubtful look, he held out a crumb of hope. "If you cooperate fully, I will do what I can to obtain an audience for you with the king. That's all I can promise."

Incredibly, it worked, that crumb of hope. The words poured from Buckingham's slack lips like water falling from a wellspring. He spared nothing, least of all the state of his own mind as he now conceived it to have been. There was a great deal in this spate of words that was extraneous to guilt or innocence, much that might well have been of interest to Richard himself but left his deputies mystified. Why had Buckingham turned so sharply against the king? In all that confused torrent of resentment, frustration, and ambition, motivation was still oddly lacking. And why did he now throw himself on Richard's mercy with, it appeared, every expectation of pardon? In one sentence, he declared his forthright devotion to the king; in the next and by the ringing testimony of his deeds, he seemed to hate him.

Interwoven in the monologue were names of others who had taken part in the conspiracy. Morton's name kept recurring over and over again until it became almost a refrain in the duke's litany: Morton, who had misled the guileless duke by a kind of witchcraft; Morton, who had shamefully used him for the glory of a Henry Tudor he had not seen since boyhood and, moreover, had not liked even then; Morton, who at other times had been employed by Buckingham, unsuccessfully as it turned out, for his own undefined ends. There were other names: Margaret Stanley and her man Bray, who seemed to have been a key link between London and Brecon; the Woodvilles (Dorset, Sir Edward, the priestly Lionel, and of course, Elizabeth herself); Richard Guildford, responsible for the hasty and abortive rebellion in Kent and Surrey; Sir John Fogge, whose pardon had been Richard's first royal edict; Sir Thomas St. Leger of Exeter, husband to Anne, Richard's eldest sister.

When at last the patter of names ceased and their echoes died in the vast room, Assheton gave a little sigh of exasperation. It was an impressive array of names and facts to be sure but not a new one in the entire rambling diatribe. There was nothing here that Richard did not know already as well as, if not better than, the duke himself. On the central point, the nature of the weld between these disparate and ill-united factions, there had been utter silence. For the first time, Assheton was forced to address a direct question to the prisoner.

"And Edward's sons—their . . . uh . . . disposal was so essential for the unity of Woodville and Lancaster—what became of them?"

Buckingham's eyes were fixed on the frieze carved on the chapter house wall that depicted Old Testament stories. "What of them?" he asked. "Am I supposed to know?"

"We have reason to believe you do," said Assheton. "We are aware that your man Percival, along with Reginald Bray, removed them from the Tower."

"Percival." The word dropped heavily from Buckingham's lips, and tears filled his eyes. "He's dead now, you know. An arrow in the jugular. There was blood, a great deal of blood. The river ran red with it."

"The prisoner will please address himself to the question," said Catesby.

"The question?"

"Edward's sons, the princes!"

"They weren't princes," Buckingham said in disgust. "They were bastards, no more than bastards."

"Be that as it may," said Assheton, striving to maintain his composure, "where are they? What happened to them? You have publicly declared they are dead."

"Why, then they must be dead." A look of almost childlike innocence crossed his face.

"Would you tell their fate to King Richard?" Ratcliffe asked. "You seem unwilling to tell this tribunal, but would you tell Richard to his face?"

Buckingham puzzled over this question for a moment then broke into a grin. "Why, of course, I'll tell Richard. I'll tell him everything, everything he wants to know. Didn't I say that already? When may I see him?"

"That remains to be seen," Assheton replied. "Nevertheless, I'll go to him and see what I can do. Master Kendall, will you accompany me please?"

Richard greeted them with barely concealed eagerness. "How goes the trial, Sir Ralph?"

"Well enough, sire," said Assheton, "as you may hear for yourself." Kendall read the duke's testimony in his deep, sonorous voice while Richard listened expressionless, staring out of the bow window.

"He's certainly convicted himself," Richard said when the secretary was finished.

'Yes," Assheton agreed. "He deserves to die a thousand times over."

"And he will die," said Richard, "at sunrise tomorrow."

"Tomorrow, sire?" Assheton asked in surprise. "B-but . . . Your Grace has perhaps forgotten that tomorrow is the Sabbath."

"I know very well what day of the week it is," Richard snapped. "Can you think of a better day to rid the world of this unholy varlet?"

"No, sire. It shall be as you wish." He swallowed further protest, thinking of more practical matters. How would he be able to erect a scaffold and hire an executioner in so short a time?

"Did he . . . say anything about my nephews?"

"I'm afraid not. In fact, that's why we're here. He won't say a word concerning them, except to you alone."

Richard's thin lips twitched into a smile. "You know that is impossible."

"Sire, if I might make a suggestion. We could put him to the torture. He's so weak. I'm sure a few twists of the rack will break him."

Richard brought his fist down hard upon the sill. "No!" he cried. His eyes were tightly shut as if he were trying to blot from them an image of torn muscles, broken bones, bleeding flesh.

Assheton was amazed. Moments ago, Richard had spoken almost cheerfully of the duke's execution; now he shrank from the use of a little torture. It made no sense whatsoever. "But, sire—" he protested.

"No! If that's the only way we can wrench his filthy secret from him, he can take it to the grave. I don't care. I will not do it."

Even if it means being tormented by nagging uncertainty for the rest of your life? Assheton wondered, but he did not say it aloud. Richard was king; one did not contradict a king. He bobbed a bow in Richard's direction and left to return to his prisoner.

Buckingham's reaction to Richard's refusal was even more amazing. He fell to the floor, tore at his hair, beat his breast. He screamed, kicked, and cried. He cursed Richard, God, and fate. When he finally grew quiet, the tumult spent, Assheton looked at him almost with pity. He thought of Richard, alone in his chamber at the White Hart, unable to put Henry Stafford to much-deserved torture, and he looked at the man cringing before him like a wounded animal. He realized then how tightly they were linked, bound by a tie that neither man could sever completely though both had tried. It was a mystery too great for him to puzzle out, so he dismissed it from his mind almost at once.

Clutching the constable's mace on the table before him, he sentenced the first duke of the realm, the lord high constable of England, to death by beheading for high treason.

The walk back to the cell in the deanery basement was mercifully brief through the arched and vaulted cloisters, past the garth with its magnificent cedars, across the cathedral close. Buckingham had managed to regain some composure since his collapse in the chapter house. His mind had lapsed into a comforting numbness. None of this was real; it could not be happening to him. It was a dream, a terrible nightmare from which he must soon awake.

The axe carried before him with its blade turned toward him to signify his death sentence, the armed guards that surrounded him on all sides, the curious townspeople who lined his path, the small boys from the choristers' school who darted in and out of the crowd and flung horse dung in his direction—all seemed as insubstantial as ghosts. He did not even blink when one of the missiles hit home. It was not real. It could not touch him.

But later, when he was alone in his prison cell once more, when he did not awaken safe in his curtained bed at Brecknock, he had to admit that something was very wrong. What was that infernal banging that drummed through to his brain when nothing else could? What was that buzzing and rapping and sawing that burst though the lone window? It was too high for him to see out, but by straining, he could grab hold of the bars and pull himself up. What he saw startled him back to full consciousness. A scaffold was being erected on the cathedral green. He even caught snatches of words the workmen shouted to one another.

"Richard's in a powerful haste to rid himself of this duke!" And the answer: "Can you blame him?"

After that, he lapsed again into semiconsciousness on the damp, putrid straw that was his bed. A rat scrambled across his belly, and he did not move. His jailor opened the door and left him a bowl of gruel; he did not touch it. How long he lay there, how many hours passed or days, he had no inkling. Then he heard a sound that made him leap up in wonder. There was the blast of a trumpet, followed by a herald's call, "Way, way, for the king. Make way for King Richard."

This was it, the summons he had been waiting for, the end of his nightmare. Richard was coming to him. He had had his punishment. Now would come pardon. Richard had frightened him to within an inch of his life, had toyed with him as a cat toys with a mouse, but all of that was over now. He could not, would not let him die.

Once again, he pulled himself up to the window, grasped the iron bars, and hung suspended until his arms ached. A small crowd was gathering along the street. At first, he could see nothing between the tangle of long skirts and hosed calves. Then he saw Richard. Riding White Surrey he was, tall and proud down the West Walk. He was dressed in a velvet cloak lined with squirrel, for the late afternoon air was chill. Buckingham could see his own breath puffing through the bars.

Behind the king rode a host of courtiers, men he knew and would no doubt have recognized if he had taken the time to look. His eyes were fixed on Richard. He could see his face now quite clearly. It seemed that if he stretched out his hand, he might even have touched him. He was astounded, even awed, by the change in him. The king's face was gaunt, ravaged. He looked older by ten years than he had last summer. Beneath the familiar eyes, the compassionate deep blue eyes he remembered so well, there were sunken hollows, purple filled.

Richard looked straight ahead. He turned neither to the right nor to the left. He did not acknowledge the swelling acclamation of the crowd, nor did he as much as glance at the deanery. He made no move to halt the procession.

"Dickon, Dickon!" Buckingham cried. "Please, Dickon, here I am! Here!"

Still Richard did not turn. If he heard, he gave no sign. Buckingham's knuckles turned white where they clenched the bars, his body strained to stay aloft even as he felt himself sliding down the rough, damp stones. Richard must see him. He must.

But Richard rode on. Buckingham watched helplessly as he turned White Surrey toward the cathedral. He was only going to vespers after all. He had not come to free Henry Stafford.

Buckingham lay half-dazed on the straw where he had fallen, whimpering a little. His hands were raw and bleeding where they had scraped down the wall, but no matter. The royal procession had passed; the workmen had finished their grim task, packed up their tools, and gone home to supper. The small square window was dark.

Richard had not come. Richard had not heard. Or if he had heard, he had not heeded. Henry Stafford, Duke of Buckingham, would die in the morning. Yet he had his victory, his vengeance, joyless though it might be. He had left his mark on Richard. His triumph was written in the hard and bitter lines of the king's face.

Richard accepted without expression Assheton's declaration that the duke was dead. Standing alone at the bow window of his parlor in the White Hart, he had heard both the tolling of the passing bell and the great collective shout from the crowd gathered on the cathedral green. It was over, and he had triumphed. On the morrow, he would leave for Exeter to clear away the last remnants of the rebel band. They had failed, and their chief had paid with his life for that failure.

Henry Tudor, canny and clever beyond his years, had not been caught in the same trap. Several days earlier, he had attempted a landing at Plymouth, and though Richard's men had tried to lure him in, shouting that they were agents of Buckingham and that the day was theirs, the ruse had not worked. The Tudor had been too well conditioned by duplicity in his young life not to grow suspicious over the enthusiasm of his reception. He had set his sails for return to Brittany and slipped from the net. Richard knew that he would live to plague him another day, a constant, unrelenting threat.

Still, he knew what to expect from the Tudor, a man he had never met but whom an accident of birth had made his avowed enemy. He was exactly what he appeared to be, and lately, Richard had come to value that as a virtue, especially in an enemy. It was the others who did the damage, the Hastings and the Buckinghams of the world who proclaimed their loyalty and love even as they maneuvered secretly to destroy him. They were the deadly ones.

He looked at the circle of intimate advisors who ringed him in: Catesby and Lovell, Assheton and Ratcliffe, Percy and Tyrell (who only yesterday had returned from their mission in the west country), and Stanley. He knew each of them well; most of them had been with him for years. But the thought troubled him now: whoever truly knew the inner workings of another man's mind? Wrapped in that circle, he had never felt more alone. Perhaps in the end, only God could help him.

"Come," he said at last. "It's Sunday morning, and I wish to hear mass."

The men looked at him and at one another, and he could read their shocked expressions. No matter his justification, he had bloodied the Holy Sabbath, and he had not yet made confession or asked forgiveness. Already, he could hear the condemnations of the monkish chroniclers. How then did he presume to partake of the body and blood of Christ?

"I have not sinned!" he cried suddenly. "Buckingham begged for his fate. He richly deserved to die."

"Yes, sire," came the immediate and unanimous response as seven heads bobbed in unison. Had he expected dissent? There was not a man among them who would dare.

"You give me your yeas," he said with a faint unhappy smile. "I only wish I could know your hearts. But that's not possible, is it?" He was thinking once more of Buckingham and of Hastings before him. He would never know why they had betrayed him. He was quite certain it had not been out of sheer perversity. Perhaps they had thought their reasons just and good. The blade of an axe had ended such rationale for both of them. He had won, but he felt no triumph and doubted that he ever would again. He allowed himself a little mirthless chuckle, a sound so unusual that it startled his counselors.

"Your Grace?"

He shook his head to their anxious looks. "Nothing," he said. "It's nothing." He might have told them of his loneliness, raised to a pinnacle no one else could share, where no man was truly his friend and every man a potential enemy. But they would not have understood. They would have protested their love and loyalty with all the vehemence of wounded innocence, even as the traitors had done before them. Somehow, on this particular morning, he did not wish to hear it.

In the silence that followed, the peal of a bell came sweetly from the cathedral campanile. "To mass!" he cried, rising.

Dutifully, to a man, they followed in his wake.

EPILOGUE

THIS IS A work of fiction, and as with most fiction, certain liberties have been taken with the characters and the story. In fact, at the time I wrote this book, the players seemed to take over the story and plot lines, and I was only a scribe writing down what they thought, felt, and did. It was a most strange sensation. Some of the characters—William Percival and Robin Vaughan among them—are entirely fictional, but they all play an important role in the narrative that unfolded. As for the other players, here is a short summation of what happened to their real-life counterparts.

The rest of the short but eventful life of Richard III is perhaps a story for another time. Before his death at the Battle of Bosworth Field, less than two years after Buckingham's execution, he would lose both his son and his queen. He would also become involved in a most unusual—some would say unsavory—relationship with his niece Elizabeth of York (Bess in my story). What exactly transpired between them is one of history's riddles. It has been suggested that Richard planned to take her, his blood niece, for his second wife after the death of Queen Anne. Both Catesby and Ratcliffe are given credit for dissuading him from this possibly calamitous course of action.

Richard did not die alone at Bosworth. John Howard, Richard Ratcliffe, and Robert Brackenbury also succumbed to the Tudors' forces there. William Catesby survived the battle only to be executed by the new king three days later. Possibly, this was an act of vengeance for Catesby's abortive attempt to convince the French king, Henry Tudor's then sponsor, to turn the Lancastrian pretender over to Richard.

At the time of the battle, James Tyrell was in France and so played no role at Bosworth. Later he was pardoned by Henry, who evidently found his talents useful. Much later, in 1502, he was convicted of treason for supporting the Yorkist heir, Edmund de la Pole, the son of Richard's niece Margaret. Henry evidently found it convenient at that time also to rid himself of the swirling rumors that one of the "princes in the Tower" was still alive and in hiding somewhere. Under torture, Tyrell confessed to the murders of both boys at the behest of Richard III, although he was unable to say where the bodies were buried. He was executed several days later.

Francis Lovell also met a dubious end. He survived Bosworth but continued to support the Yorkist claimants to the throne. After the Battle of Stoke in 1487, he disappeared from view. The discovery two hundred years later of a man's skeleton in Minster Lovell gave rise to the romantic legend that he had shut himself away in a secret room and died of starvation when the servant who was supposed to attend him either died or abandoned him.

Tom Lynom and Jane Shore had a happier ending. They did indeed marry in 1483, with the approval and presumably in the presence of King Richard, and had a daughter. Tom continued his service as Richard's solicitor general until Bosworth. Henry deprived him of the title but allowed him to serve in a lesser capacity in the Tudor bureaucracy. Jane Shore lived a long life, dying around the age of eighty-two. Thomas More, who saw her when she was an old woman, stated that he could still detect signs of her former beauty.

It should come as no surprise that those who had favored the Tudor cause fared much better than Richard's supporters in the aftermath of Bosworth. Thomas Stanley remained neutral during the battle though his brother Sir William threw in his lot with the Tudor's forces and possibly swung the tide of victory to Henry. Thomas had reason not to commit himself. His eldest son, Lord Strange, was being held by Richard as a hostage for his father's support, although Tom was heard to say that he had "other sons." At the end of the battle, Thomas was there to place the crown, which had fallen from the dead king's helmet and rolled into a thornbush, on the head of his victorious stepson.

It has been said that the man who found the crown in the thornbush was none other than Reginald Bray. Of course, Bray's role in the murder of the princes is my own invention, but it is certainly possible that one of Henry's adherents was either responsible for or collaborated in their deaths. Bray became Henry's chief of staff and so fared very well at the hands of the new king.

Stanley also prospered by being named Earl of Derby. Margaret Stanley, who had been in disgrace and under house arrest after Buckingham's rebellion, thus became a countess once again. Even more importantly, she became known as "my lady, the king's mother," a position that seems to have been equal to—or at times superior to—that of the queen herself. She sought and was granted the right to divorce Stanley—or at least to be responsible for her own fortune and no longer be beholden to her husband. Theirs would seem to define the term "marriage of convenience," and both of them profited exceptionally from it.

John Morton also did extremely well under the new king. He was granted the lord chancellor position he had been denied under Richard (at least in my telling of the story). When Thomas Bourchier, archbishop of Canterbury, died a year or so after Henry came to the throne, Morton succeeded him in that position and was eventually named a cardinal by the church. I must confess that I probably took more liberties with Morton than with any other "real" character in the book, yet I think it is entirely probable he is guilty as charged of most of the activities I have laid to his door. I found myself quite entranced with his guile and subtlety. I wanted to hate him for the harm he had brought to Richard, and yet I could not. I was surprised to learn that Morton was sixty-three during the year of this story, a very ripe age for the time. His shrewdness and cleverness would seem to come from a much younger man.

True to his word, Henry VII did marry Elizabeth of York, though in his own good time. Interestingly, he had himself declared king by conquest, thus obviating the weakness of his bloodline and disregarding the far purer one of his espoused wife. In all appearances, it seems that their marriage was a happy one. She gave birth to the baby who would grow to be Henry VIII and thus became the grandmother of Elizabeth I, her namesake and one of England's greatest monarchs. All future monarchs of England, down to the present day, are descended from Elizabeth of York. Sadly, the matriarch of the Tudors passed away prematurely on her thirty-seventh birthday while giving birth to her last child. The grief of her husband was wondrous to behold, and the sometimes miserly Henry spared no expense on her funeral.

Even before Henry married Elizabeth, his uncle Jasper Tudor, the new Duke of Bedford, wed Katherine Woodville, the Dowager Duchess of Buckingham, making her a duchess once again. We can only hope that this marriage was a happier one for her though the great difference in their ages might have augured against that. At least, this husband did not feel slighted by her base blood! After he died in 1495, she married for a third time one of Henry's courtiers, Richard Wingfield, a man near her own age, and he outlived her. In my story, of course, she has an affair with Robin Vaughan, the fictional scion of an old Welsh family. I can only say that the character Kate, one of my favorite people in this story, led me to this. I had to give her something to compensate for the bleak life she otherwise was forced to endure. If there wasn't a Robin Vaughan in her life, perhaps there should have been. Although Robin Vaughan is a fictional character, his presence in the story does help to explain why the real Vaughan family supported Richard rather than the half-Welsh pretender Henry Tudor during Buckingham's rebellion.

Katherine's sister Elizabeth, the former queen, was restored to court life by an arrangement with Richard in the spring of 1484. It has been said by Richard's supporters that it is unlikely she would have left sanctuary and accepted the king's offer of protection for herself and her daughters if she thought he was guilty of the murder of her sons. Although I do not believe Richard culpable for this crime, I have difficulty with this line of reasoning. He had already executed both her second son, Lord Richard Grey, as well as her brother Anthony, the Earl Rivers. She surely could not have had warm feelings toward the king and may only have been very fatigued after almost a year in the self-imposed prison of sanctuary. Her fate under Henry VII was mixed. As the mother of the new queen, she should have enjoyed a high place at court, and at times, she did. However, she seems to have been banished at some point—perhaps for supporting one of the pretenders claiming to be her younger son—and ended her days in a nunnery. Hers is perhaps one of the sadder stories to emerge from this episode.

Of course, the saddest story of all is that of her two boys. Without their bodies to view, it is impossible to tell how or even if they died in the Tower. Certainly, after Henry was on the throne, there were a number of young men who claimed to be the Duke of York, the younger of the two princes. If Henry knew their fate, he certainly did not reveal it and appeared to have been genuinely threatened by some of the imposters.

In 1674, workmen dug up a wooden box in the Tower containing two small human skeletons. The bones were widely accepted at the time to be those of the two princes although this was never proven. Charles II had them reinterred in Westminster Abbey, where they remain to this day. It seems that in a time of DNA analysis, which confirmed the discovery of Richard III's remains, perhaps those bones could now be subjected to the same testing. That could confirm once and for all the fate of the two boys, although not who killed them, or it could leave the question of their disappearance open to history.

Kathleen M. Kelley
Ann Arbor, Michigan
Kathleenkelley48108@gmail.com

ABOUT THE AUTHOR

KATHLEEN M. KELLEY is an inveterate Anglophile who sometimes suspects she was born on the wrong side of the Atlantic. From as early as she can remember, she has been fascinated by English history, literature, and architecture, especially by the kings and queens of England.

As an English major and a dedicated enthusiast of Shakespeare, she always accepted without question his portrait of Richard III as a misshapen villain, usurper, and murderer. It wasn't until she read Thomas B. Costain's very different account in *The Last Plantagenets* that a new image of the fifteenth-century king emerged, a revelation that was to lead her down her own path of discovery. Based on what she learned, she sought redemption for Richard with this novel that seemed at times almost to write itself.

Although she took a master's degree in English, Ms. Kelley ended up with a career in accounting, a field that was rewarding in its own way. Over the years, she has been fortunate to be able to visit the British Isles on several occasions and explore some of the places mentioned in this novel. Since retirement, she has also pursued an interest in art and is an accomplished colored-pencil artist specializing in drawings based on her travels. When she isn't indulging her passion for travel, she lives with her husband in Ann Arbor, Michigan.

CPSIA information can be obtained
at www.ICGtesting.com
Printed in the USA
FSOW01n1546190717
36348FS